ASCENSION SERIES

BOOKS 4 - 6

KEN LOZITO

ACOUSTICAL BOOKS LLC

Published by Acoustical Books, LLC
KenLozito.com

IF YOU WOULD LIKE TO BE NOTIFIED WHEN MY NEXT BOOK IS RELEASED VISIT - WWW. KENLOZITO.COM

ISBN: 978-1-945223-42-6

INFINITY'S EDGE

ASCENSION SERIES BOOK 4

1

Thirty years ago, Edward Johnson had been an outstanding young intelligence officer working for the Department of Homeland Security when he'd caught the attention of billionaire Bruce Matherson, Chief Executive Officer of Dux Corporation. For about a year, Bruce had repeatedly tried to recruit Ed before Ed decided to see what a company like Dux Corporation—known for its various military contracts and weapons development technology—was all about. He'd had no idea what was in store for him or how important a man the late great Bruce Matherson really had been.

Plenty of billionaires believed they were visionaries of the future, but it just so happened that Bruce Matherson actually was and had been tasked with the preservation of the Human race. Early on, Bruce had taken Ed into his confidence. He'd been shown the first-contact videos that were withheld from Project Stargate during the nineteen-eighties. Later, in the year twenty-fifteen, the New Horizons spacecraft had flown by Pluto and taken the first ever high-resolution photographs of the dwarf planet's surface, showing what they now knew as a Boxan outpost, and confirming what scientists had long suspected: they weren't alone in the galaxy.

Proof that intelligent life did exist in the galaxy had been kept from the general public. The fact that these intelligent life-forms knew of Human existence and were watching had also been withheld, and Ed couldn't imagine what it must have been like for Bruce.

Ed had joined Dux Corp a few years after the New Horizons' discovery, and it was another ten years before Bruce brought Ed into the inner circle, which was responsible for funding scientific research across the globe. Bruce had always suspected that the Russian equivalent of Project Stargate had received the same mysterious Boxan message through a psychic link that hadn't been fully understood, but there was no way they could have known about the Boxan outpost on Pluto until recently. The current world stage was vastly different from what it had been in the nineteen-eighties with China's rise as a global superpower. Somehow, it had become Ed's job to get all these nations to work together as humanity stepped to the brink of taking an evolutionary leap into the wider cosmos. Truth be told, Ed would have preferred at least another hundred years to develop the technology they needed to go out into the galaxy and face the challenges they were about to face.

Ed sat in the war room at the North American Aerospace Defense Command, or as it was better known, NORAD, and glanced around the large oval conference table where a holodisplay was beaming the solar system ten feet above its surface. Various military officials and directors from the different intelligence agencies sat, engaging in small talk as they waited. Lining the walls were banks of blank holoscreens that would remain so until the meeting began.

A firm hand touched Ed's shoulder, and he looked up at Iris Barrett. On digital paper, she was his assistant who handled his schedule, which she did quite effectively, but truthfully she was his protector. Iris had state-of-the-art neural implants and reinforced muscle tissue made possible with nanite technology, and her blood had been engineered for quick healing beyond even the capabilities of the military.

"Five minutes, sir," Iris said. She wore a black business suit, and her short black hair was pulled back into a tight bun.

Ed nodded.

Bruce Matherson's original plan had been for the 'discovery' of the Boxan outpost on Pluto to be 'rediscovered' in another ten years, but Zack Quick had put an end to all of that after he'd released the original New Horizons images to the general public. Zack's actions had been the catalyst that changed the destination of the Athena mission, which had originally been Titan. The mission to Titan was to have been Kaylan Farrow's test run for a later mission to Pluto, but she'd ended up on an urgent mission to Pluto first, and then the Athena had disappeared into space.

They'd finally received a mission update from the Athena, and it raised more questions and concerns than it answered. Ed had watched the video logs over a hundred times in an attempt to glean all the information available, but he had to admit that if they'd stuck to Bruce's original plan, an additional ten years might have been too late for the people of Earth. It was an interesting thought that had become more prevalent in his mind and the minds of the younger generation around him.

Old world national borders had increasingly become blurred in their more advanced society. While they were far from united as a species, Ed had noticed the increasing change in perspective regarding national identity of late; however, he wasn't foolish enough to believe that the world would unite to meet this alien threat. No, those perceptions were mere seedlings of a plant that had yet to bear any fruit, and if they had another hundred years, they might be much better prepared. Besides, a hundred years from now the problems they were currently facing would have decidedly fallen into someone else's lap, which Ed would have preferred when exhaustion seemed to be crushing him. He felt his lips curve upward in a half smile at the thought. He knew he would do his utmost both for his late friend and for the people of Earth.

Colonel John Hines called for the meeting to start. The large, dark-skinned man stood ramrod straight, and his chiseled features gave him the appearance of the Greek Titan Atlas personified.

Edward Johnson stood up, and those in the military snapped a salute as four-star general William Sheridan entered the war room. Ed still had to resist the urge to raise his hand and snap a salute with the rest of them, but his military days were long gone, more than half a lifetime ago.

General Sheridan swung his mighty gaze around the room and acknowledged them all with a single, no-nonsense nod.

"Sir, the president is connecting," Colonel Hines said.

They sat down, and Ed tried to recall what he knew about General Sheridan. He came from a long line of enlisted men and women. He'd made a name for himself in the fight against global terrorist organizations and had risen through the ranks during his thirty-five-year career. If there ever was another world war, General Sheridan stood a good chance at getting that fifth star and ascending to Commander of Armies for the United States. Ed could think of worse choices for the president to have put on point for this.

The holoscreens blinked to life as President Susan Halloway came to prominence. The other holoscreens were occupied by the vice president and joint chiefs.

"Madam President, thank you for coming," Sheridan greeted.

"General Sheridan," the president said. She glanced at those in the room, and Ed would have sworn that her gaze lingered on him for a moment.

The general nodded to Colonel Hines. Hines's thick neck muscles rolled as he swung his gaze to the far end of the table. "Dr. Gray, you have the floor."

Dr. Philip Gray, Scientific Advisor to the President, stood up. Ed suppressed a groan and couldn't for the life of him figure out why Halloway kept Gray on as a scientific advisor. Family connections at their finest.

"We're here to discuss the recent Athena mission update that we received two weeks ago. We've circulated some of the details through the FBI, along with a complete update to the CIA and NSA. Their findings confirm that the testimonies provided by the Athena crew, while compelling, should not be accepted at face value," Dr. Gray said.

"Which part?" General Sheridan asked.

"There were multiple inconsistencies in their reports, with no fewer than two of their crewmembers under the direct compulsion of the alien species identified as the Xiiginn," Dr. Gray said.

"Only Jonah Redford is claiming immunity instead of being under Xiiginn compulsion," Ed said, drawing an annoyed look from Gray. "Zack was cleared by Dr. Goodwin."

"Yes, we have her report as well, but she also indicated it's possible that Mr. Quick's symptoms simply hadn't manifested yet."

Ed shook his head, brows raised. "He was held captive by the Xiiginn. Even the Boxans don't understand why he's immune." Ed turned his gaze to the president. "Brenda Goodwin is an excellent medical doctor, as well as a psychiatrist. We should trust her opinion. Brenda is just acknowledging the possibility that Zack is under Xiiginn compulsion, but she doesn't have any evidence whatsoever to support it. She'd be remiss in her duties if she didn't at least highlight the possibility."

Halloway looked at the general questioningly.

General Sheridan cleared his throat. "In my experience, anyone held prisoner, even under extraordinary circumstances such as this, will show signs of PTSD. Goodwin's analysis of Mr. Quick appears sound. Given what the crew of the Athena has had to deal with, I think we can all acknowledge that they are under a lot of stress, which would appear in any intelligence report."

There were several chuckles from around the room.

"Madam President," Sheridan said, and all the people in the room immediately hushed, "I'm more concerned with the assertion that these aliens will come to our solar system. Regardless of whether it's these Boxans or Xiiginns, both have the potential for catastrophic effects on the Human race."

Halloway nodded. "I appreciate your opinion. Ed Johnson, what do you think?"

All eyes in the room focused on Ed, and his pulse quickened. "The Xiiginns are the enemy. They are the real threat, and we need to prepare for them. The Boxans might become our allies."

"You would lay the fate of the Human race on 'might'?" Sheridan asked.

"They're already helping the crew of the Athena," Ed replied.

"Are you familiar with safe harbor?" Sheridan asked, and Ed shook his head. "Sea captains are under obligation to give aid to any vessel in need and provide safe passage to the nearest port. What this Boxan, Kladomaor, is doing is that." Sheridan looked up at the holoscreen of the president. "Based on all the evidence, these two alien species have been fighting a war for some time, and how many other species have been caught in the crossfire? We're at a severe disadvantage if they come here."

"What are you suggesting?" Halloway asked.

"That we prepare for imminent invasion. Start leveraging our resources, both at home and beyond, to give us some protection for the Ark Program," Sheridan said.

Ed's gut clenched. "This isn't a time to wall ourselves away in a mountain, hoping to ride out a storm."

General Sheridan's brows pushed forward severely. "The fact that you're even aware of the Ark Program is enough for me to have you taken into custody by the FBI."

Ed turned toward the president and swallowed hard. "Madam President, the world has changed so fast, and we're stumbling to catch up. I have the highest respect for General Sheridan, and his recommendation is in line with what an officer in the United States military *should* recommend. But the fact is that we can't stand against the threat of the Xiiginn on our own. We *have* to reach out to the other nations and form a coalition of forces whose sole purpose is to defend the Earth from an alien invasion. No nation on this planet can stand alone against this threat."

President Halloway's dark-eyed gaze regarded Ed for a few moments, and then she looked away. "Go ahead, Philip."

Dr. Gray cleared his throat, and Ed looked over at him. "Both alien species are keenly interested in what the Boxans refer to as the Mardoxian trait. Dux Corp, or one of its subsidiaries, developed the psychic warrior initiative in secret. Since these aliens are so interested in this ability, the general intelligence community needs to understand it better."

Ed frowned. So this was what they were after. "What are you asking, Philip?"

Philip Gray narrowed his gaze. "That you immediately turn over all research and findings of the psychic warrior initiative to the United States government as a matter of national security."

Ed chewed on the inside of his bottom lip for a moment. "What you're demanding of me and Dux Corp is entirely illegal."

"This is non-negotiable," Philip said.

Ed looked over at the president. "I know you can freeze our assets and try and take what we've built, but it will do you no good. I'm willing to give you what you ask for in return for something else."

Ed heard the shuffling footsteps of the military police heading toward him. Iris Barrett stiffened behind him but otherwise remained motionless.

"You don't make demands of the president—" Philip Gray started to say, but Halloway interrupted.

"What is it that you want?" she asked.

Ed met the president's gaze. "I want you to reach out to China, Russia, the European Union, and the rest of the United Nations with a proposal that a coalition force be formed to deal with the alien threat. At this moment, a formal proposal of the Earth Coalition Force is being sent to your office. I ask that you and your staff review it and open communications with all the nations of this world. This is a burden that should be shared by all. Do this, and I guarantee you will have unfettered access to all of Dux Corp's research on everything since its inception."

There was a collective breath held in the war room. There weren't many who would make a demand or veiled ultimatum to the leader of the free world. Ed knew that if he were taken into custody, another of the inner circle would take over and help the people of Earth fight as best they could, although in his heart of hearts he didn't believe it would be enough. Not now. They needed the governments of the world to set aside their differences and work together.

"General Sheridan," Halloway said.

Ed felt the MPs closing in on him, but his chips were on the table and he'd bet everything on this moment.

"Yes, Madam President."

"I want you and my chief of staff to appoint a committee to formally review this Earth Coalition Force proposal that Ed has so boldly sent us. I want to know your thoughts and opinions on it before we even consider sharing it with other world leaders," President Halloway said.

"I'm at your disposal, Madam President."

Ed swallowed. The fact that they were even considering it was a good sign, but it was still a long road ahead. He glanced at Iris and nodded.

"Thank you, Madam President," Ed said. "As a show of good faith, my assistant is sending the first of seven encrypted data caches to your office."

"First of seven!" Philip exclaimed. "You should be sending everything."

Ed leveled his gaze at him. "That's why you're only an advisor, Philip, and not the president."

Philip's face contorted to several shades of red, but he remained silent.

Ed had made some enemies, but hopefully his actions would be looked upon by future generations as having benefitted humanity, as long as there were any of them left to do the looking.

2

Dale Hicks sat in the Athena's mess hall, polishing off his breakfast with a cup of black coffee. He'd never been one for cream or sugar, preferring the bitter taste and heady aroma of freshly ground coffee. He glanced at the coffee maker. If he lived to see Michael Hunsicker again, he would thank him for insisting on bringing this glorious piece of equipment that made what NASA had anticipated as a long journey to Titan more bearable.

The Athena's original mission had been to one of Saturn's moons, but thanks to the actions of one Zack Quick, that mission had to be put on hold so they could go to Pluto instead. It had been either fate or luck that had put Pluto's orbit relatively near Earth during that fateful mission—at least that's what he and Katie Garcia had been told when Edward Johnson recruited them for the Athena's mission. Though only months had passed since they'd journeyed and gotten boots down on Pluto—an achievement worthy of the history books—they were light years from home, chasing a Boxan legend about an alien race called the Drars, who'd fought an intergalactic war that had wiped them out. When they'd first escaped the Boxan space station destroyed by the Xiiginns, Hicks had believed they were only a few days away from figuring out what had happened to the Drars, but almost two months later they were still chasing a mysterious signal that Zack had stumbled onto right before they'd escaped. Signal wasn't even the right word. Zack had tried to explain it to him, and they'd essentially been following a trail of cosmic breadcrumbs left by a race of beings that predated Humans by tens of thousands of years.

Hicks cocked his head to the side and cracked his neck. It was a bad habit, but it just felt so good that he couldn't stop himself. An alarm showed on his internal heads-up display, but he killed it instantly, finishing his coffee. The hardened ceramic composite that comprised the Athena's outer hull had been designed for Earth's solar system, not traipsing along in interstellar space. Even with Kladomaor's help, he was beginning to think the crew of the Athena was living in a ticking timebomb.

"Hicks," Kaylan's voice said over his PDA.

"Good morning, Commander. I saw the alarm. It's on the section Vitomir and I are going to check on our EVA this morning," Hicks said.

It was alarming to think that keeping the Athena space-worthy required daily EVAs, during which they were required to patch the outer hull of the ship. How long before patching wasn't enough? Or they ran out of materials for repairs?

"Acknowledged. Please be careful," Kaylan said.

Hicks made his way down the corridor to the rear airlock. Katie Garcia came out of one of the adjacent corridors and smiled in greeting.

"Where you off to?" Hicks asked.

"My rotation with Efren at the reactor," Katie said. Her dark hair was tied back into a ponytail.

"I thought that was on Wednesday," Hicks said.

Katie shook her head. "It is Wednesday, Major. Are you sure you're feeling okay?" she asked in a slightly amused tone.

Hicks sighed. "I'm fine. Just mixed up the days is all. How do you think the rest of them are doing?" he asked.

Katie shrugged. "They all deal with it in their own way. There's really no precedent for what we're doing."

Hicks nodded. "I'm not really sure we *should* be doing what we're doing."

Katie frowned. "What do you mean?"

"I'm not sure how much more the ship can take," Hicks said.

"Have you spoken to Kaylan about it?"

"No, not yet. I agree with the reasons for coming, but it doesn't feel like we're making any progress, and it's making me wonder why we don't head back to Earth right now."

"You should tell her."

"I will, but first we've got to keep our girl in the air," Hicks said, glancing up at the nearest monitor.

"Your concern for my well-being is noted, Major," the Athena's AI voice said through the monitor's speakers.

"I'll leave you to it, sir," Katie said and went on her way.

Hicks continued on and met Russian cosmonaut Vitomir Mikhailovich, former Commander of Titus Space Station. The bald cosmonaut was slipping into his EVA suit while being watched by Nikolai Vratowski. Trust was in short supply where Vitomir was concerned. The former commander had attempted to sabotage the space station in an effort to join the Athena mission. The botched sabotage had claimed the lives of four people, including Vitomir's wife. Under different circumstances, Hicks would have locked Vitomir in a cell and thrown away the key, but, as the Athena's AI pointed out, not using an able-bodied person would put them outside peak efficiency—fancy words for telling them to use all available resources in order to survive.

"Major," Nikolai said. "I've included extra repair kits for this EVA, and the updated targets will appear on your HUD once you're outside."

"Thank you," Hicks said.

"I could join you if you want," Nikolai offered.

"Two at a time. That's what the commander ordered," Hicks said.

Nikolai bobbed his head and waited for the two-man team to finish donning their EVA suits.

Vitomir finished first and stood up. "Ready when you are, Major," he said.

Hicks quickly put on his suit, and Nikolai cleared them for their EVA. They stepped into the airlock and waited for the atmosphere to be sucked from the room. When the indicator lights around the door changed to green, Hicks popped the door, and there was a slight snap-hiss as the little bit of air that remained in the airlock escaped into the void.

Directly across from them was the Boxan stealth ship they'd been tagging along with since they'd left the Nershal star system. It was an impressive sight, but according to the Boxans, it was among the smaller scout-class vessels. If so, Hicks couldn't imagine what some of their bigger ships looked like. During their recent adventures, he'd gotten a glimpse of Xiiginn warships, which were sleek, wedge-shaped crafts. But Hicks knew that should anything happen to the Boxans' ship, the crew of the Athena would most likely die because their ship didn't have a Cherubian drive capable of folding space, which was the only way for them to get back to their own solar system.

"Major, we must be going," Vitomir said.

Hicks turned away and lowered the intensity of his mag boots. Tethers had already auto-locked onto the backs of their suits. Reducing the power of the mag boots enabled them to take longer strides down the Athena's hull and cover longer distances in a shorter amount of time. Beyond them was a sky full of stars the likes of which had never been seen by any Human. Gaarokk, a Boxan scientist, had pointed out that they were even beyond where the Boxans had been, since exploration had ground to a halt during their war with the Xiiginns.

"We're coming to the first series of micro-cracks," Vitomir said.

Hicks slowed down, and the two of them came to a halt. The Athena's gleaming white hull had been peppered by the small asteroid fragments they'd encountered on their long journey, creating tiny cracks.

"This grouping is bigger than the last one. I'm surprised the sensors didn't alert us sooner," Hicks said.

Being on an EVA with Vitomir was almost peaceful. Whenever Zack came along, he had this pressing need to fill the time with conversation. At least he used to. Since he'd been held prisoner by the Xiiginn, the former hacker had been much more serious. Hicks had never been a prisoner of war, but his military training had accounted for the possibility. Recovery from an ordeal like that would take time. He didn't think being aboard a spaceship was the most peaceful environment for someone suffering from PTSD, so he and Kaylan had agreed to manage Zack's stress levels, which meant cutting back on EVAs.

He and Vitomir used two repair kits to patch the fractures on the Athena's hull.

Hicks frowned and turned to Vitomir. "If Titus Station had been showing this much wear and tear, what would you have done?" he asked.

Bringing up Titus Station was never easy for Vitomir, but Hicks had to leverage the former commander's expertise. Regardless of what he'd done, he'd been responsible for Titus Station's upkeep for close to two years.

"Our fabricators were located in the subterranean levels of the asteroid we were on, and we could eventually replace entire sections of the station if we needed to. So the situation is different here. There is only so far we can go with our current resources," Vitomir said.

"Why don't you say anything?" Hicks asked.

Vitomir's eyebrows drew downward. "Because of what I've done to my Natalia and the others. My perspective on the state of your ship wouldn't be welcome," he said.

Hicks blew out a breath. The cosmonaut wasn't wrong.

"I would advise you to speak with Dr. Redford, but . . ." Vitomir began, leaving the thought unfinished.

Jonah Redford had succumbed to the Xiiginn compulsion, which effectively made him a sleeper agent for them. Hicks had gone over all the events that would have exposed Redford to the Xiiginn. They all had, and they'd determined that Redford's first exposure had been on the compound on Selebus. Redford had been unaccounted for for the span of a few minutes during the battle, and, according to the Boxans, a few moments was all that was required to plant the seed of compulsion in Jonah. Later on, during their escape from the Nershal star system, they'd received a strange transmission that they couldn't make sense of, and they'd overlooked it while they fled the system. Later, Kladomaor surmised that the signal had contained instructions for Jonah. The Xiiginns had gambled that Humans would be susceptible to their compulsion ability. They'd been right about Jonah but not about Zack, for some reason.

"Well, I want you to share those opinions of yours with me at the very least. Is that understood?" Hicks asked.

"Yes, Major."

They continued on, patching the Athena's hull where they could and noting other areas that would require further investigation. Hicks resolved himself to the fact that he needed to sit down with Kaylan and make a case for them to abandon this search for the Drars in order to return home to Earth while they still could.

3

Kladomaor sat on the command couch on the bridge of the Boxan stealth ship, reviewing the latest information from his neural feeds and feeling the grim lines of his face deepen into a tight frown. He was overdue for his mandatory time in the resonance chamber, a place for quiet meditation under a spectrum of light that some might fool themselves into believing was the star from their home system of Sethion. A pang resonated deep within him at the thought of the Boxan home world that had been lost to them. Their colony world was also a beautiful place but lacked the ancestral ties that formed the foundation of their species.

The door to the bridge hissed open and in walked a Nershal, a winged species with smooth, pale-green skin and deep orange eyes. The Nershals had once betrayed the Boxans to the Xiiginns but were now coming to the realization that the Xiiginns were not their allies. The Nershal walked straight to Kladomaor and bowed his head.

"Battle Commander, Ma'jasalax awaits you," Etanu said.

Kladomaor cut off his neural feeds and stood up. "Very well. Triflan, you have the bridge," Kladomaor said.

Triflan, his tactical officer, took his position at the command couch.

Etanu waited for Kladomaor to lead the way, as was proper. Kladomaor was the battle commander of this ship, and a hole opened up for him to walk through as the rest of the Boxan crew stepped to the side to allow him to pass. The Humans were much less formal on their ship, although if it had been a military vessel, Kladomaor suspected the protocol would be different. Dale Hicks left him with that impression.

It was good to move his limbs. He needed time in the star-shine to truly center himself, but his duty to his crew demanded otherwise.

The smooth walls of the ship had been their home for a long time, but even

they could not remain in the great expanse forever. At some point, they'd need to
resupply. They were forbidden from returning to the Boxan colony world because
one of the Human crewmembers was afflicted by the Xiiginn influence. If they
tried to enter the colony space, their ship would be destroyed. Kladomaor would
never abandon the Human ship to resupply, so there was that problem. No
Boxan commander would resupply them as long as the Humans had a
crewmember under the Xiiginn influence. Kladomaor knew that to the Humans
these protocols seemed harsh, but the protocols had been established for a reason.
Protecting what was left of the Boxans was paramount. Had those protocols been
in place before, perhaps they wouldn't have lost their home world.

The great doors opened, and Kladomaor walked into the conference room
with Etanu trailing behind. Ma'jasalax was speaking with Gaarokk and Ezerah,
and the Mardoxian priestess looked over at him as he joined them.

He looked at Gaarokk. "How are our wayward travelers doing?" Kladomaor
asked.

"They tend to their ship as best they can," Gaarokk answered.

"They must realize their ship needs some time in a space dock. It was never
meant for travel beyond the confines of their star system," Kladomaor said.

"I think we can agree on the stubbornness of Humans," Gaarokk said.

Ezerah shifted in her seat, her wings adjusting as well. "Wouldn't they come
aboard this ship to seek refuge?"

Ma'jasalax cleared her throat. "Humans can be quite territorial. I'm sure they
would if the Athena became unlivable, but for the time being, they'll be fine
where they are."

"Territorial," Kladomaor said. "That's one way to put it."

"Like most intelligent species, they need to control their own destiny. They
can accept help for a time, but they will never abandon their ship," Gaarokk said.

Kladomaor couldn't argue with the scientist. He made a good point, even if
Kladomaor knew the Humans wouldn't be much safer aboard his ship.

"Having spent some time aboard their ship, I can vouch for its design. The
Humans built an excellent ship, and given more time they would have expanded
out into space on their own," Gaarokk said.

"Time is a luxury we can ill afford. In order for them to survive this journey,
they simply need more than what they're capable of now," Kladomaor said.

Etanu cleared his throat. "If you felt that way, why did you let them come on
this journey to begin with? Why not just take them back to their own star
system?"

"The Xiiginns know about Humans now. Perhaps we *should* take them back
to Earth and help them prepare for the Xiiginns," Kladomaor said.

Ma'jasalax released a great sigh. "We could do as you're suggesting. It was
something I'd considered, but what they need, and us as well, is a way to turn the
tide of this war with the Xiiginns. Since the war now affects Humans, they have a
right to be here, and to be honest, I'm not sure we can succeed in finding the
Drars without them."

Kladomaor swung his flaxen-eyed gaze toward the Mardoxian priestess.

"Whose purpose is the Human presence really serving here then? Their own or yours?"

"Fate rarely chooses us on our own terms," Ma'jasalax replied.

"Fate, is it? It wasn't fate that sent the Mardoxian signal to the Human star system all those cycles ago," Kladomaor said.

The female Boxan stiffened. "You're in command of this ship. Do what you will, Battle Commander. Apparently you don't need or want my counsel."

Kladomaor planted his fist on the table and leaned forward. "I just want you to admit that you're influencing these events. You're operating outside the will of the Mardoxian Sect, which means you act without their consent."

Ma'jasalax's large ears twitched, which, for many Boxans, was a sign of annoyance. "I'm not the only one here who is acting outside the confines of command. Your efforts to ignite a rebellion in the Nershal star system weren't exactly sanctioned by the fleet."

Kladomaor chuckled, releasing some of the tension that had been building between them.

"You forget that Prax'pedax escaped the space station and should now be presenting our reports to the High Council about Humans. They won't stand idly by with the Mardoxian potential in Humans. They'll never hand that over to the Xiiginns, so the Humans are hardly abandoned to their fate," Ma'jasalax said.

Kladomaor looked away, considering.

"Kaylan is gifted, even by our standards. If her abilities can be further developed, and if there are more like her on Earth, Humans could become a formidable force in the galaxy," Ma'jasalax said.

Kladomaor leaned back in his chair. "By Gaarokk's account, Kaylan could be capable of much more than our most gifted Mardoxian priests."

"You imply more gifted than me. Do you think that bothers me?" Ma'jasalax asked.

"Does it?"

"No, it doesn't bother me. It's something I embrace."

"Be careful, or they might not look too kindly on the game you're playing," Kladomaor said.

"The game that allows both our species to survive against the Xiiginns? I'm doing what must be done."

"And so will I when the time comes," Kladomaor said.

The silence dragged between them, and Gaarokk cleared his throat. "We've found further evidence of the Drar, but the next jump will be a long one. This could be the one that takes us to the source of the signal."

"Very well," Kladomaor said. "Make sure the Athena knows."

"Actually, it was Zack who figured it out," Gaarokk said. "Well, him and their AI."

Kladomaor exchanged glances with Ma'jasalax but didn't say anything. Instead, he left them and headed for the resonance chamber. Perhaps a quiet meditation would do him some good.

4

For the past few days, Edward Johnson had hardly left NORAD. He wasn't in custody per se, but it was frowned upon when he tried to leave. Regardless, this was where he needed to be for the moment. The original draft used for the proposal to form the Earth Coalition Force, or ECF, had been authored by many people, but it had been Bruce Matherson who put it together, and Ed had worked on an updated version prior to sending it to the White House, where it was being considered by some and outright dismissed by others in Halloway's cabinet. Regardless of what President Halloway decided, the ECF proposal would be brought to the other governments of the world. The ECF's greatest chance of success required the backing of the major superpowers of the Earth, despite evidence that the world was reluctant to believe it was in danger at all. Ed never underestimated some people's need to bury their heads in the sand and hope the problems facing them would simply go away. But they wouldn't go away. Not this time.

Ed had been at NASA Mission Control in Houston, Texas, for most of the communications with Michael Hunsicker. Besides the Athena crew, Michael was the only Human to have any dealings with a Boxan. Ed didn't care what species you were, no one would voluntarily stay in suspended animation, not even risking a call home, if they hadn't believed wholeheartedly that the Xiiginns were a real threat. Chazen, the Boxan left stranded on the dwarf planet Pluto, was such a being. The Xiiginns were coming, and they weren't coming for the betterment of humanity.

Ed walked through the underground network of hallways to the war room, and the clipped cadence of Iris's Louboutin heels followed him as they entered. He was a few minutes late, and the meeting had already started. One thing he could say about General Sheridan was that he ran a tight schedule. A ten thirty start time meant exactly that. Ed glanced over at General Sheridan. Over the past few days, he'd gotten the distinct impression that Sheridan viewed him as someone to be tolerated at the moment.

Gary Hunter's large, curly-haired head was on the wall screen. He glanced over at Ed as he took his seat. There was a momentary acknowledgment, and then he continued.

"The latest report from Armstrong Lunar Base is that the Endurance is in the final phases of construction and scheduled for routine stress tests by the end of the week. Test flights are scheduled for next week," Gary said.

General Sheridan glanced over at him, and Ed kept his facial features neutral. He'd already known the current status of the Endurance before coming to the meeting.

"That's excellent news," Dr. Philip Gray said. "I'm a bit surprised you were able to finish construction so far ahead of schedule. We were under the impression that the aggressive schedule already established was a bit of a stretch."

Gary bobbed his head. "And you'd be right but for a couple of things. One, we've learned a few things since completing the Athena's construction. Two, the data provided on the Athena's performance was instrumental in design improvements. And, three, we've had input from Chazen."

Gray's beady eyes drew up in alarm. "I'd realized we were in near constant communications with Commander Hunsicker and the Boxan, Chazen, but I didn't think we were giving him access to the design of the Endurance."

Ed cleared his throat, and Sheridan gave him a nod to speak. "I was at Mission Control when this was discussed. The Endurance was being rushed to completion so it could be used to not only rescue Michael Hunsicker but Chazen as well. The Endurance is designed for Humans, and there was a need to consult with the Boxan on how best to transport him back to Earth. Chazen was quite reluctant to share any information because of the doctrines of his species, but Michael eventually convinced him of the advantage of at least having the option to leave Pluto when the Endurance got there."

Gray's mouth formed a circle but no words came out, and Ed once again wondered why in hell President Susan Halloway had appointed such an idiot as scientific advisor.

"Thank you, Mr. Hunter," General Sheridan said.

The wall screen flickered off, and Colonel Hines took the lead. The holodisplay above them came on and showed a scale model of the Endurance. It was the spitting image of the Athena but for the noticeable improvements and accommodations for the Boxan they planned to transport.

"Direct your attention to the holodisplay," Hines said. "As a reminder to all non-military personnel in the room, what is shown and discussed here is strictly confidential."

Ed frowned as he focused on the model of the Endurance. A duplicate image appeared but with modifications that conspicuously changed the spaceship intended for scientific exploration into something else entirely.

"The situation has changed," Hines said.

The sleek lines of the ship now had smaller towers on top and bottom. Ed focused on the updated legend that labeled each part of the ship and noticed that the large chambers designed for the Boxan had been changed.

Ed's eyebrows rose, and his gaze darted to Sheridan. "An armory? Missile towers?" he asked.

"That's right. The Endurance will no longer be a vessel for scientific research. Our engineers have been preparing these components as well and can easily retrofit the Endurance," Sheridan said.

Ed swallowed hard. "But Michael Hunsicker . . ."

"I'm afraid a rescue mission that will take the Endurance to Pluto is off the table," Sheridan said.

Ed felt as if he'd been punched in the stomach. He should have anticipated this. The military had allowed the Endurance's construction to go along, with the plan of commandeering the vessel when it was completed.

"General, please reconsider this. Chazen could be a valuable asset—" Ed started to say.

"I don't like this any more than you do. If we had another ship like the Endurance, I'd send it out there to bring Michael Hunsicker home, but the risk of losing such an important ship for one man in a time such as this . . . The risk is too great."

Ed's mind raced. There was no way Sheridan could do this on his own. These orders had come down from the top, and that meant President Halloway had signed off on them. Michael Hunsicker, the former commander of the Athena, was on his own. Ed drew in a breath and slowly released it. It twisted him up inside, but Ed knew Sheridan and the president were right.

Sheridan watched him and waited for him to come to the only conclusion he could. Ed wished there were something he could do for Hunsicker. He was a good man and didn't deserve what was going to happen to him. Ed wanted to argue for sending the Endurance anyway, but the shrewd part of his brain knew it wouldn't change the facts. The Xiiginns were coming, and they needed every resource available for the defense of Earth.

"Now that we're on the same page, it's time we turned our attention to the inventory of space vehicles we have that can be used in our defense," Sheridan said.

Ed glanced at the small console in front of him as the rest of the meeting's agenda came into prominence, the next line item highlighted. At least they were taking the threat seriously, but Ed still would have liked to bring Hunsicker back home.

5

Billions of miles from Earth, in a small Boxan outpost on the dwarf planet Pluto, Commander Michael Hunsicker gazed at the amber holodisplay, which showed a feed from outside the outpost. Flakes of methane gently fell to Pluto's icy surface. If Michael let himself, he could almost imagine he was back on Earth, looking out the window of his house in Boulder, Colorado. He closed his eyes and imagined the cool granite countertops in the kitchen with the smell of Irish breakfast tea brewing in two mugs on the countertop. Across from his kitchen were large, two-story windows with a picturesque view of the Rocky Mountain foothills.

Michael felt a sharp pang twist in his chest as the memory of his home faded. Kathryn had passed away four years before, and he still missed her fiercely, but he resigned himself to the fact that he always would miss his wife. Some part of him must have thought that going on the Athena mission would put distance between himself and his grief, but being stranded on Pluto had brought the mourning of his dead wife to the forefront of his thoughts. Kathryn would have told him to pay attention to what he was doing, so that's what Michael was doing—solve one problem at a time, making the best decisions he could, and maybe he could get back home.

A bitter chuckle escaped his lips, drawing Chazen's attention. Michael had just received the latest update from Mission Control. Despite the spaceship Endurance nearing completion, the rescue mission had been delayed, but the update had been immediately followed by a video message from Edward Johnson, who gave him a more realistic view.

"There's no easy way tell you this, so I'm just going to say it . . ."

The Endurance wasn't coming. There would be no rescue mission for him. Michael sat down and felt his strength slowly ebb away. He'd been living on the hope of going home, and now that was being taken away from him.

Michael looked over at Chazen. When he stood, the Boxan was ten feet tall, with brown, roughened skin and eyes the size of giant teacups.

"You don't seem surprised," Michael said.

"No, not after we got the update from your crew."

Eight weeks ago they'd finally received the update from the Athena that had shocked the world. Michael had watched video logs of each of the crew. He was delighted that they were still alive but horrified at what they'd discovered. He'd always known Kaylan would make an excellent commander. He reviewed her logs and updates and doubted that he could have done any better. In fact, he felt that she had surpassed him as commander. If there was anything his astronaut career had taught him, it was that things could change quickly, and if you couldn't adapt, the price of failure may very well be paid with your life.

"I thought that since the Endurance was so close to being completed there was still time for a rescue mission," Michael said.

"That was before. Now they're starting to believe the Xiiginns may actually find this star system," Chazen said.

Michael looked away from the Boxan for a moment. "If the Xiiginns come here in force, is there anything we can do to stop them?" he asked.

"As I've told you before, I'm not a soldier. I'm not sure—"

"Take a guess then," Michael interrupted.

Chazen regarded him for a long moment. "No, you couldn't stop them."

Michael squeezed his hand, forming a fist, and bounced it on the desktop. "I refuse to accept that. There has to be something we can do. Isn't there anything you can share with us that will give us a fighting chance?"

The sharp lines of Chazen's face deepened, but the Boxan remained silent.

"Can't we try again to reach out to your species?" he pressed.

"No, Kladomaor confirmed that Sethion is unreachable, and he wouldn't disclose where our colony was located. So there's nowhere I could send a message," Chazen answered.

Michael stood up. "We can't just wait around here and do nothing."

"There is always stasis. I've worked out how to adapt a pod for your use," Chazen offered.

Michael shook his head. "No, I can't sleep my life away and neither should you. You've done more than your duty to the Boxans. We need to focus on figuring out a way to get to Earth. If they won't come to us, then we need to go to them."

Michael paced a few steps, trying to think of a way, and an idea blazed into his mind. He turned back to Chazen.

"There are no ships here and no means to build one. We have no way to get to Earth," Chazen said.

Michael smiled. "We don't need a ship. Just hear me out."

Chazen said he would.

"What we need is a life pod, ideally something with limited maneuvering capability in zero gravity and comms capability. We need to be able to live aboard for a certain amount of time . . ." Michael's voice trailed off. "We'll figure that out later."

"What good will a life pod do? It's not a ship. It can't take you to your planet," Chazen said.

"We don't need it to. We just need to get it off the surface of Pluto. This place has the power to create a wormhole. The AI did it. I know you said the power requirements almost drained the reserves here, but we only need to put the pod in the vicinity of Earth," Michael said, his voice rising in excitement.

Chazen shook his head. "It's much too dangerous. Even Cherubian drives open wormholes only at the edge of a star system. Otherwise, it affects navigation."

"I'm not talking about pinpointing a place somewhere in the galaxy," Michael said, flinging his arm out for emphasis. "I'm talking something much smaller. I think if we could get closer to Earth, they wouldn't have a choice but to come get us."

"You would risk this?" Chazen asked.

"Not alone. I'd want you to come with me."

Chazen's bushy brows lifted. "I appreciate the sentiment, but I cannot leave."

"You cannot stay. If the Xiiginns . . . *when* the Xiiginns come here, where do you think they'll come first?"

Michael watched as Chazen considered. The Boxans were a stubborn race.

"If you stay here, you'd be effectively throwing your life away, and that's not something even your High Council would want. There is a way. We can do this with everything here. We *have* to be able to do this," Michael said.

"When the Xiiginns come, I will set the self-destruct to prevent them from gaining access to the shroud network," Chazen said.

"Fine," Michael said. "Set it and come with me to Earth."

The Boxan looked away from him. It was moments like these that reminded Michael of how alone Chazen must feel. He'd been trapped here for over sixty years and had no way to get home. Michael had only had a taste of that, and it was enough to drive him to do whatever he could do to get home again.

Chazen came to his feet but didn't say anything. Michael knew the Boxan was using his neural feeds because the holoscreens nearby flickered to life, and it took Michael's own implants a few moments to translate the information on the holoscreens. Chazen had brought up an inventory and begun highlighting certain things on the list. Michael glanced over at the Boxan and felt his chest begin to swell. Perhaps there was a way for them to get home after all.

6

Kaylan Farrow glanced out the forward windows on the bridge of the Athena. An ocean of stars shined with a brilliance that seemed to stretch to infinity. With the help of the Boxans, they'd traveled farther into space than any Human before. While they now knew their position in relation to Earth, she knew that not even the Boxans had equipment capable of allowing them to see their home star system.

Her long brown hair had a slight curl to it, and she absently ran her fingers through it. There was always more to see. She'd gazed up at the night sky on Earth, wondering what it would be like to travel among the stars, visiting other planets, but since they'd been snatched from Earth's star system, they'd hardly had a moment to enjoy it—hardly a moment to take a breath and simply be in the moment.

She'd found comfort with the other crewmembers, especially Zack, but they could hardly flaunt their relationship. Discretion was something both she and Zack easily agreed on. She glanced over at Zack, who sat at the communications station, muttering at the holoscreens in front of him, and the edges of her lips curved upward. Zack liked to talk things out while he worked, even when he was alone. It was something she'd first noticed when they were at MIT together and was a habit he hadn't lost over the years.

A loud crash sounded as several stacks of metal containers hit the floor, and Zack was on his feet instantly, scanning the area for any sign of danger. He blinked several times before he settled back down and tried to give her a reassuring wave. That behavior was new. This ready-for-danger-at-a-moment's-notice reaction was something Zack hadn't done until he'd been captured and held prisoner by the Xiiginns. He hardly spoke of his sojourn in the pit, but Etanu had told her enough. Kaylan had hoped that with enough time Zack could distance himself from such a horrible place, but apparently it was too soon. She wished he'd confide in her about it.

Emma Roberson called out an apology while she collected the fallen containers and stacked them again. Kaylan hastened over to her and was lending a hand when the door to the bridge opened and Dale Hicks walked in with Vitomir on his heels. Hicks headed over to them.

"The micro-fractures are getting worse," Hicks said.

"We have enough repair kits for the time being, and Kladomaor can send us more if we need them," Kaylan replied.

"And what if something happens to them? We're becoming too dependent on the Boxans. I'm worried that we could be left stranded out here," Hicks said.

Zack stood up and came over to them, his hand rubbing the back of his neck. "It's not like Kladomaor would just leave us out here."

Hicks shook his head. "Of course not. I'm just trying to mitigate risk here, consider things that no one else is willing to talk about."

Here it comes again, Kaylan thought.

"We've been over this. We even discussed it with Kladomaor and the others. If something catastrophic were to happen to the Athena, we would go aboard their ship," Kaylan said.

"Not good enough," Hicks said. "We're ignoring the fact that we're taking the Athena to places she wasn't designed to go."

Zack frowned. "It's a spaceship, and this is space. What else is there?"

"Did you forget the binary pulsar we encountered a few weeks ago? We all almost died within minutes of arriving, not to mention the damage to the electrical systems," Hicks said.

Zack glanced at Kaylan, cocking his head to the side and raising his hands.

"We knew there were risks when we came along," Kaylan said.

Hicks nodded. "Finding the Drar, which will hopefully lead us to something that will help turn the tide of the war with the Xiiginns. The thing is that officially we're not at war with the Xiiginns yet."

"What are you saying?" Kaylan asked.

"I'm saying we should consider returning to Earth and bringing a bigger team that is better able to deal with the rigors this type of mission incurs."

"You mean more military," Zack said.

Hicks nodded. "And more specialists like all of you. We've cross-trained for various jobs as best we can, but there are only so many of us. And if something happens to Kladomaor, we have no hope of ever getting back home."

Kaylan understood all the risks Hicks was identifying, and each and every one of them was right, but deep down in her gut she knew Earth's future would be affected by what they did out here. The thing was, she had no sound reasoning for believing as she did. Hicks wouldn't hold it against her, but logic would dictate that his sound reasoning was a much better argument than her gut instinct.

"Athena," Zack said. "What's the probability of survival should we lose our Boxan friends along the way?"

"There are multiple variables that could affect the odds of survival, which I can estimate, but on the highest level, the odds of your survival would be zero without help from the Boxans," the AI said.

"Is there anything we could do to increase the odds of our survival?" Zack asked.

"There are a number of enhancements to this spacecraft that could be done but all would require more resources than are currently available to you."

"When you say resources, is it something the Boxans could help us with or something we could find?" Hicks asked.

"To greatly increase the odds of survival, you would need to install a Cherubian drive and higher-grade hull plating—"

"Thank you," Kaylan said, cutting the AI off. "We can't build a new ship out here. I think we just need a little more time, and if we find no sign of the Drars, I'll ask Kladomaor to take us back to Earth."

Hicks pressed his lips together, considering. "Okay," he said and glanced at Zack. "What have you got on this new signal?"

Zack sighed. "I really could use Redford's expertise, but he's not exactly in his right mind."

"What's the problem?"

"The signal is intermittent but almost seems random. I'm not sure if it's artificial in nature. I wouldn't have even spotted it if it weren't for Athena. Even Gaarokk doesn't know what to make of it until we get closer," Zack said.

"Another jump then," Hicks said.

Kaylan nodded.

"Have you or Ma'jasalax been able to detect anything?" Hicks asked.

"She hasn't," Kaylan said.

Hicks regarded her with a raised brow.

Kaylan shook her head and rolled her eyes. "I just have a feeling that where we detected that signal is where we need to go. It's nothing else. Just a feeling."

Hicks pressed his lips together. "You also knew Zack was still alive even when the rest of us weren't so sure. I'd say your instincts are trustworthy enough for us to stay out here longer."

Kaylan smiled. "Thank you," she said.

Hicks had turned out to be a good friend, and she counted on his support. He could lay out his thoughts and present the risks but was willing to take a leap of faith just the same. She hoped they wouldn't regret it.

Mar Arden stood on the bridge of a Xiiginn warship at a Confederation space station. The massive station had been built and then expanded by the different species that formed the Confederation, but the structure was originally designed by the Boxans, even though the founding members of the Confederation had been cast out. The space station was essentially an artificial planetoid space dock, protected by a massive shield with an artificial atmosphere that most species could breathe.

The Boxans had only made contact with species that were able to thrive in similar atmospheres. The Xiiginns knew the Boxans were aware of other species out there, but that knowledge had been locked away from them and was one of the driving forces behind finding an intact Star Shroud system. Gaining access to a shroud network would allow them to find other species that the Boxans had deemed unworthy of the Confederation. Cultivating the uprising that had led to the downfall of the Boxans had been a delicate operation, carried out with precision and tact; otherwise, the species of the Confederation would have turned against them. Mar Arden knew there were species biding their time, waiting for the opportune moment to strike, but for them there would be no opportune moment. The Xiiginn fleets were the most advanced force in the galaxy. The only species that could stand against them had cut themselves off on a colony world. Mar Arden would have loved to find the Boxan colony world and extinguish their race from the great expanse but had to date been unsuccessful in those efforts.

Mar Arden glanced over at the command couch occupied by Hoan Berend, the Xiiginn captain, who waved him over. Mar Arden blew out a breath before joining the captain.

"We have orders to find the star system that's home to the Humans," Hoan Berend said.

Mar Arden's tail flicked in annoyance. "What about my request to pursue Kladomaor?"

Hoan Berend frowned. "Denied. The Boxans are going to great lengths to keep knowledge of the Humans away from us. Finding their home star system is of the utmost priority."

Mar Arden frowned. "There are other battle groups that could do this."

"The orders came from Supreme Leader Garm Antis himself. Once the system has been identified, he has already designated an attack force to go to that system."

"And the Confederation?" Mar Arden asked.

"They are to be kept ignorant of this species. The Nershals have petitioned for a grievance with the Confederation for the events that transpired in their star system," Hoan Berend said.

"I don't expect much to come of that."

Hoan Berend studied him for a moment. "You don't want to pursue the Humans?"

"Of course I do, but I want Kladomaor as well. The Boxans are up to something. They didn't put resources into an asteroid base for no reason. Why would they possibly return to the Qegi star system?"

"That I couldn't say. Our orders are to go back to the Nershal star system to find evidence of the wormhole the Humans used to get there," Hoan Berend said.

"Send one of your other ships," Mar Arden said.

Hoan Berend looked slightly amused. "I'm not going to defy Garm Antis for you. If he says that's where we're supposed to go, then that is exactly where I shall take you."

Mar Arden clenched his teeth but knew it was useless. Hoan Berend wouldn't deviate from his orders. "What about sending another ship to investigate the Qegi star system and figure out where Kladomaor and the others escaped to?" Mar Arden asked.

Hoan Berend's fingertips grazed the control panel on his armrest. "I think we could spare a scout ship for that."

Mar Arden supposed he should be thankful for that much, at least. Responsibility for the events that had taken place in the Nershal star system was being placed on his shoulders—rather, the powers that be were trying to hold him responsible, but Mar Arden hadn't attained his position by playing by the rules. Garm Antis would expect that. The question remaining was how far he could push things before they spiraled beyond his control.

Zack climbed down from the top observatory. Sometimes he just needed to escape the bridge and find a quiet place to think. Since Jonah Redford was confined to quarters, Zack had taken it upon himself to ensure that the astrophysicist's work continued. All that stuff Hicks kept bringing up about the current state of the Athena had him worried, and Zack was committed to using the AI to help address some of those issues, but there was only so much they could do. The onboard fabricators had the capacity to replace internal components of the ship, but there were limits, and the AI had a haunting way of pointing out the cold hard facts. Zack had asked her to be more tactful when it came to delivering unsettling news pertaining to things like zero percent chance of survival. That was one of his favorites. He'd lost count of how many different ways they could die out here, and as Kaylan liked to point out to him, it wasn't healthy to constantly dwell on worst-case scenarios.

Zack gave a mental shake of his head and blew out a harsh breath. Truth be told, without the AI they probably wouldn't have made it as far as they had. The AI wasn't infallible and couldn't account for things like Kaylan's psychic abilities, which it classified as an unknown quantity, and Zack supposed that was correct. How else could something that was unknowable be accounted for? Sometimes the insights Kaylan had were downright creepy. He couldn't figure out how she could do the things she did. A couple of times they'd plotted a course and at the last second Kaylan had called for a course correction that ended up sparing the ship from running into trouble, but Ma'jasalax had informed them that this was quite normal and that they should trust Kaylan's instincts.

Zack headed back toward the bridge, making a quick stop to grab a protein pack and refill his water bottle. He didn't have time for anything else, and while the protein pack tasted like cardboard, it would stave off hunger for a couple of hours. Stuffing the bar into his mouth and chewing vigorously, he headed toward the bridge.

Kaylan and Hicks occupied the pilot seats, and he headed over to the comms station. Katie Garcia was already there and glanced up at his approach.

"Took you long enough," Katie said.

"I had to get something to eat on the way here. I was starving," Zack said.

Katie nodded and shifted her attention to the holoscreens in front of her.

Zack took his seat. "Comms is a go," he said.

The rest of the crew checked in from their designated work areas. Efren and Nikolai were in Engineering, Brenda and Emma were in the hydroponics lab, and Redford was confined to his room, sleeping, since Brenda had recommended that he be sedated for these high-risk maneuvers. Vitomir monitored one of the consoles on the bridge. They were green across the board. The status indicator showed that the gravity tether from the Boxan stealth ship was in place. A small progress bar appeared on their screens, showing the Cherubian drive powering up. Zack hated this part. Whenever they went through a wormhole, he always felt a bit nauseous on the other side. But the idiom of 'the other side' wasn't quite right. There was no other side. The Cherubian drive allowed them to fold space in such a way that enabled them to cross vast distances quickly. They'd done this five other times, and it still grated on Zack's nerves.

"Focus, Zack," Katie said.

Zack glanced over at her and nodded. He was glad they'd remained friends. He hadn't been sure there for a while and had kept his distance from Katie, but she had called him out on it. The Athena wasn't that big, and there was no way for them to avoid one another.

Zack experienced a sudden craving for a pint of Guinness beer. He couldn't remember the last time he'd had a drink and found that he could use one right about now. No such luck though. NASA hadn't stocked the Athena with any alcoholic beverages. Even Hunsicker's stash was gone.

"Maybe it won't be so bad this time," Zack muttered.

"Fail-safe for tether active," Hicks called out.

"Acknowledged," Kaylan said.

The fail-safe was something new that allowed them to instantly reverse the gravity field that kept the tether in place in case of an emergency. Kaylan had told him they'd done such a thing before when Kladomaor attempted to force the Athena to leave the Nershal star system without Zack. He didn't hold this attempt against the Boxan. Kladomaor was doing what he thought was right, but he was glad Kaylan and the rest of the crew hadn't left without him.

As they approached the jump point, Zack had the feeling there was some unseen force pulling him forward, stretching him to infinity. It reminded him of riding a rollercoaster as it pulled over the apex of the first major drop, but instead of the feeling of dropping waaaaaayyyyyy down lasting for a few seconds, jumping through space and time lasted much longer.

They entered the wormhole, and Zack felt his insides twist up in anticipation as he tried to calm down. On his internal heads-up display, he brought up an image of Kaylan sitting in the commander's seat. He'd done this during the last two jumps, and it had really helped. He focused in on her face, but instead of the calming effect he'd anticipated, he felt his heart sink to his feet. Her forehead was creased in worry, and her lips were pale. Her eyes seemed to take in the readouts on her holoscreen and focus on something beyond at the same time. She didn't look relaxed as she normally did during a jump. Zack swallowed hard and grabbed onto the arms of his chair just as everything went to hell.

Kladomaor sat on the command couch on the bridge of the ship. The couch was located on an elevated platform in the center of the bridge, which allowed him to view the other workstations. Engaging the Cherubian drive to a set of coordinates was a routine procedure that carried relatively little risk. When the alarms began blaring, the Boxans on the bridge were caught in a moment of surprise.

"Status report," Kladomaor barked.

Varek, his navigation officer, hunched over his console. "Wormhole is unstable, Battle Commander."

"What's causing it?"

"Unknown—"

The ship shook violently, and Kladomaor grabbed onto his seat. "Abort the jump."

"The system is unresponsive. We're locked in," Varek said.

Kladomaor used his neural link to execute the abort order, but the Cherubian drive wouldn't respond. He looked at Ma'jasalax, and the entire bridge went dark. There were several loud pops just outside the bridge, and Kladomaor felt himself rise into the air as the gravity field anchoring them to the floor became disabled. Emergency lighting came on as they automatically went to auxiliary power.

Kladomaor opened a comms channel to Engineering from his suit computer. "Situation report," he said.

The rest of the Boxans on the bridge pulled themselves back to their consoles.

"The main reactor is down, Commander, as well as the primary auxiliary power source. Emergency life support only."

Kladomaor's mind raced. Total loss of power aboard a Boxan starship never happened. He used his suit computer to bring up a damage report.

"What's the status of the Athena?" Ma'jasalax asked.

"Unknown," Triflan answered. "My station is dark. Switching to suit computer."

Boxan warships had built-in redundancies in the event of power loss or systems failure. Critical systems were capable of running on auxiliary or emergency power, but in order to handle the switch, each critical system had its own limited power source. To get the current status of the ship, Kladomaor had to access each critical system one by one. The more systems he couldn't access, the more he realized they were in real trouble. Someone or something had completely disabled his ship. They were adrift in the great expanse. He accessed the short-range communications array and tried to contact the Athena, but there was no response.

"See if you can detect the Athena nearby," Kladomaor said.

Triflan went to work for a few moments. "They're not there."

"What do you mean 'not there'?" Ma'jasalax said. "The gravity tether should have held. Are all our sensors out?"

Triflan shook his head. "They are, but even if the Athena only had life support, they would still emit an energy signature that our short-range sensors could detect. I'm telling you, they aren't there."

Ma'jasalax looked at Kladomaor in alarm, and the battle commander drew in a determined breath.

"Focus," Kladomaor said. "We need to assess the damage and get primary power back online first. Then we'll worry about finding the Athena."

Ma'jasalax frowned. "We can't have lost them. What could cause a wormhole to destabilize like that?"

"We won't be able to determine that until power is restored," Kladomaor said.

Ma'jasalax closed her eyes for a moment, and her brow smoothed in concentration. After a few seconds, she opened her eyes. "I can't find them."

Kladomaor frowned. "What do you mean? I thought you had a Mardoxian connection to Kaylan."

"I do, but it's simply not there anymore," Ma'jasalax said, and her brows drew up in fear. "It's as if something is blocking the connection."

"Varek, you're with me; Triflan, you have the bridge," Kladomaor said. He needed to check the ship and work his way down to Engineering. "They probably disengaged the gravity tether at the first sign of trouble and were safely deposited from the wormhole. We'll find them, but first we need figure out what happened and what shape we're in."

Kladomaor waved two more crew members over to follow him, and Etanu also came over as he reached the doors. The Nershal's suit had magnetic boots that had kicked on as soon as they lost gravity.

"Put me to work, Battle Commander," Etanu said.

"Follow me," Kladomaor replied and left the bridge.

10

The blinking lights of the Athena's dashboard went from blurry to razor-sharp focus as Kaylan regained full consciousness. She was slumped forward against her seat belt, and the straps were digging into her ribs. Master alarms sounded, and she pushed herself upright, glancing over at Hicks, who was slowly regaining consciousness. She looked back at the systems-failure listing on the main holoscreen. They still had life support. Kaylan unbuckled her seat belt and climbed out of the chair. Hicks looked a bit disoriented but was otherwise okay. She looked over at the comms station for Zack, whose sagging form slouched in his chair. Her stomach clenched, and she ran over to him, calling out his name. Zack's eyes snapped open, and he sucked in a breath.

"You're okay," Kaylan told him.

Katie was checking herself for injuries and finding none. "I'm all right," she said.

"Good. We need to check on the others," Kaylan said.

She looked over to the other side of the bridge and saw Vitomir regaining consciousness.

"Athena, status report," Kaylan said.

"Multiple systems failure, Commander."

"What's the status of the rest of the crew?" Kaylan asked.

"I'm detecting three life signs in the hydroponics laboratory," the AI said.

"What about Efren and Nikolai in Engineering?" Kaylan asked.

There was a heavy moment of silence while she was waiting for the AI to answer her.

"Apologies, Commander, I'm not able to detect any life signs in Engineering."

Kaylan gasped, her mouth agape in horror for a moment before her training forced her to focus, to keep assessing and avoid making assumptions.

"Is there life support in Engineering?"

"Apologies, Commander, but it seems that the sensors in the engineering area are offline."

Zack came over to her. "What about exterior sensors outside the fusion reactor?" he asked.

"Exterior sensors report no damage. It is unlikely there are any hull breaches in that area," the AI reported.

Hicks joined them. "We're unable to get the status of several other sections of the ship besides Engineering."

"Right, we'll need to check each area then," Kaylan said and walked over to a storage locker on the wall. She retrieved three breather masks and handed them to Hicks, Katie, and Vitomir.

"Won't I need one of those?" Zack asked, sticking his hand out.

Kaylan shook her head. "I need you to stay on the bridge."

"To do what? I could help you," Zack insisted.

Kaylan glanced at the others. "Can you give us a moment?" she said and led Zack away.

Zack's gaze bored into her intently.

"I need you to stay on the bridge and help coordinate from here. You're best at getting the AI to help us with what we need."

Zack pressed his lips together. "That's bullshit."

Kaylan hardened her tone. "You're right; it is. The others have extensive training for this kind of thing and you don't. Hicks and Katie have done salvage and repair, and Vitomir . . ." She had no choice but to utilize the cosmonaut, and she didn't need to point out Vitomir's qualifications to Zack. "I have to go. But it's not all bullshit. Find a way to help us from here."

Zack blew out a frustrated breath and nodded.

Kaylan joined the others. It wasn't that she wouldn't risk Zack. They'd all taken some measure of risk by going on this mission. As the commander, she had to utilize her resources where they could have maximum benefit, and that put Zack here on the bridge whether he liked it or not.

She slipped her breather mask over her face and attached the unit to her belt. The others waited for her by the door. The breather wouldn't help them if they got sucked out into space, but it would allow them to breathe in the event of a fuel leak or some other chemical that might have gotten mixed into the atmosphere.

"Slow and steady," Kaylan said.

She checked the panel on the door and opened it. They walked through, and the door to the bridge shut behind them.

"Athena, lock the bridge door," Kaylan said.

Hicks chuckled. "He's going to love that."

The lights in the corridor flickered for a moment and then stabilized. They needed to get down to Engineering first.

Kaylan opened a comms channel to the hydroponics lab. "Brenda, are you guys okay?"

"We're fine, Commander. Zack just informed us that you're heading down to Efren," Brenda said.

"That's right. The sensors are out, and we're not sure what's going on. I need you to meet us with your med kit," Kaylan said.

"I'll meet you there, Commander."

"Containment measures are in effect."

"Copy that," Brenda said.

Vitomir cleared his throat. "Containment measures?" he asked.

"It's why we're wearing breathers and checking the rooms as we go along. With sensors offline, I don't want to take any chances," Kaylan said.

Kaylan led them through the ship. Once the wormhole had become unstable, Athena had closed all doors as a preventative measure to contain any breaches or fires. If the sensors detected a fire, the fire suppression system would work to put it out, and the fact that the sensors were offline in Engineering didn't bode well that they were safe just because they'd made it out of the wormhole. Each door had to be checked. To save time, she sent Katie to check the port observatory and mess hall while Hicks and Vitomir followed her down to Engineering.

They reached the long yellow ladder that would be the most direct path down to where Efren worked. The hatch was shut. She checked the system indicator and it was out, but she was able to open the hatch, which she wouldn't have been able to do if there had been a hull breach. Beyond the hatch, tracks of orange emergency lighting were on. Kaylan stepped out onto the ladder and began to climb down, lights flickering as she went. When she reached the bottom, she stepped away from the ladder.

"Zack, can you hear me?" Kaylan asked into her comms unit.

"Loud and clear," Zack said.

"We have emergency lighting here. Do any of the readouts for the area show systems with an overload status?" Kaylan asked.

"One minute," Zack answered.

Hicks and Vitomir joined her. The central computer where the brain of the Athena resided was off to the left, but the main reactor room was to the right.

"Yeah, the main . . . all have a status of overload. I guess that stuff is on a different system than the atmospheric sensors," Zack said.

"Thanks," Kaylan said and looked at Hicks and Vitomir. "Sounds like if we put the main breakers back into position, we can restore primary power to the ship."

"Yeah, but why wouldn't Efren or Nikolai have already done that?" Hicks asked.

They slowly made their way down the darkened hallway, the inadequate emergency lighting augmented by Hicks's flashlight. There was no power in the control room, and it was dark. Kaylan grabbed the latch and was able to unlock the door. If they'd had a hull breach in this section, she wouldn't have been able to do that either. Vitomir stepped beside her and helped pull the door open. There was a soft hiss of air.

"Trace toxins detected, Commander," Vitomir said.

"Radiation levels are climbing," Hicks said.

Kaylan peered into the room. "Shine your light over there to the left."

Hicks's flashlight beam swept immediately to the side, and there, next to a table by two overturned chairs, were Efren and Nikolai. Kaylan raced to the storage locker and grabbed two breathers, fitting them over the unconscious men's faces.

Kaylan spotted the breakers and used her neural implants to double-check the procedure for putting the overloaded breakers back into position. Her HUD outlined the correct order, and she had to use both hands to push the large breakers back into position. She then moved to the main power relay and switched it back on.

The lights immediately came back up as main power was restored. She glanced up, noting the dark, burned-out areas. The overload must have fried the sensors, and it must have happened so fast that they didn't have time to register the failure. That shouldn't have been possible.

With main power restored, the atmospheric scrubbers cleaned the trace toxins from the air. They carried Efren and Nikolai from the control room because the radiation levels were a bit higher than normal. They'd have to keep an eye on it, as well as replace the sensors that had burned out.

Brenda checked them for injuries, and then they carried Efren and Nikolai to the sick bay. Both men were suffering from minor oxygen deprivation.

"Putting the breathers on helped," Brenda said.

She gave each of them a shot, and in few moments both men regained consciousness.

Efren rubbed his head and groaned. "My head is killing me," he said.

"Don't try to get up," Brenda said. "I can give you something for the pain."

Efren lay back and closed his eyes, waiting for the pain meds to kick in.

"Can you tell us what happened?" Kaylan asked when Efren opened his eyes again.

"It was strange. System indicators were reporting instability in the reactor core. The last thing I remember was going into the control room, and then there was this massive power surge," Efren said, and his face twisted into a confused frown.

"What is it?" Kaylan asked.

"It could be the bump on my head, but I could swear the power surge came from outside the ship and that's what threw the reactor core into disarray."

Kaylan nodded.

Efren sat up on the bed.

"What do you think you're doing?" Brenda asked.

"I can't afford to lay here. I have to check the reactor and the rest of Engineering," Efren said.

"You need to rest," Brenda said.

Efren smiled at the doctor. "If you're so concerned, you can come with me to make sure I'm okay."

Brenda rolled her eyes and looked at Kaylan pleadingly.

"We need to repair any damage to the ship and then figure out where we are," Kaylan said.

"He's had a head injury."

"I know, but we're all we have. Keep an eye on him then," Kaylan said.

Kaylan left the med bay, and Zack opened up a comms channel to her.

"Don't make me hack this door, Kaylan."

She chuckled. "Oh, sorry about that," Kaylan said and sent the release code for the door to the bridge.

The crew of the Athena went about the tasks of assessing the damage, and more than one of them noted how lucky they'd been, but Kaylan didn't believe in luck. There were too many strange occurrences for these events to be purely accidental.

With main power restored, damage assessments went quickly. It wasn't until they failed to detect Kladomaor's ship that they realized they were stranded out in deep space.

"Holy crap! We're all alone out here," Zack said.

They'd returned to the bridge and gathered around the conference table.

"I still don't understand what happened," Hicks said. "How'd we end up where we are?"

"Athena," Zack said. "Can you display the events right before things went wrong with the wormhole?"

"Of course," the AI said.

A list of events from launch prep to when they'd first entered the wormhole appeared normal. Kaylan read the list with everyone else.

"System override?" Zack asked as he read through the list. "It says here that the tether was released by you, Kaylan."

Kaylan frowned in thought, trying to remember how the events had unfolded. "The wormhole was becoming unstable."

"That's right, but not until thirty seconds later. We were patched into the Boxan ship's systems so we'd be able to see the status of the jump," Zack said.

Hicks rubbed his chin. "How'd you know the wormhole would become unstable?"

Kaylan shook her head. "I didn't. It was unstable to start with."

She looked at the logs, and somehow she'd known the wormhole had become unstable before the Boxan ship's computers did.

"Might I posit a theory, Commander?" the AI asked.

Kaylan rubbed the back of her neck. "Go ahead."

"If logic cannot provide a satisfactory explanation, then we must consider that there were outside forces that influenced these events."

"Meaning the power surge?" Kaylan said.

"Precisely, but the fact that your intuition gave you an insight into what was about to happen was remarkable, even by Mardoxian standards," the AI said.

"Yeah, but I don't even recall having the thought. I just acted," Kaylan said.

Zack's eyes lit up. "I get it. I know what the AI is trying to say. It was the 'outside forces' that kept tripping me up. The Boxans revere those with a strong Mardoxian trait. I've been reviewing the data we retrieved from the space station about the Drar, and there's a connection there. What if someone or something caused this to happen and sent you a message somehow?"

Kaylan considered what Zack said for a moment. "It wasn't anything like communicating with Ma'jasalax, and wouldn't she get the same message?"

Zack shrugged. "I don't pretend to understand how you're able to do what you can do. Are you able to contact Ma'jasalax now?"

Kaylan's brows furrowed in concentration for a moment, and then she shook her head. "Nothing at all."

"Sounds crazy, but I think we should pursue this," Zack said.

"How?" Kaylan asked.

"We're on the trail of the Drar, and we already knew we were getting close to them. Perhaps this all means something," Zack said and waved his hands, gesturing around them.

"It could be a warning to stay away," Hicks said.

"If this disaster was intentional, they could have killed us, but they didn't," Zack said.

"We should try to find Kladomaor," Hicks said.

"I agree," Kaylan said. Zack started to protest, but Kaylan interrupted him. "I think you're onto something, so I want you to pursue it, but in the meantime, we need to find Kladomaor."

She sounded confident, but what Zack said had alarmed her. No one wanted to broach the subject of what they would do if they couldn't find the Boxans.

M ar Arden sat in his chambers aboard a Xiiginn warship. He would put on a display of cunning brilliance later on for Hoan Berend so the commander could report back to Garm Antis of his cooperation. Eventually he would challenge the supreme leader to his seat among the upper echelons of the Xiiginns, but not now. He simply didn't have the backing he required for that, and the loss of the Nershals had set his efforts back. Mar Arden was still First Ambassador, which officially made Hoan Berend, the commander of this squadron, his inferior, but the commander had made it quite clear that he would carry out Garm Antis's orders to the letter. Mar Arden wasn't worried about Hoan Berend. The commander was a means to an end, and eventually Mar Arden would offset the status quo back to his favor.

After he'd calmed his anger and distanced himself from his immediate wants, he'd realized that hunting the Humans to their home system would eventually lead him to Kladomaor and Zack Quick. He hadn't forgotten the Human who had escaped from Kandra Rene on Selebus's moon. He wanted to unlock all the secrets the Humans had to offer, and he had no doubt that he would find their home star system.

The door to his chambers chimed.

"Enter."

Kandra Rene walked into his chambers, head bowed. Her long platinum hair hung perfectly, without a strand out of place. Her poise and symmetrically chiseled features were almost enough to tempt him. She'd caught his lingering stare from time to time, and to her credit, she'd never exploited the opportunity. She was a patient hunter no matter what endeavor she partook in. Such was the way of the Xiiginns.

"Sion Shif reported in that the scout ship has just entered the Qegi star system," Kandra Rene said.

"Excellent. Now, if he uses the search protocols I gave him, he shouldn't have much trouble tracking Kladomaor."

Mar Arden stood up and noticed that Kandra Rene wouldn't meet his gaze.

"What is it?" he asked.

"This was a task that I could have carried out for you."

He caught the underlying edge to her tone. She had failed to use compulsion on their prisoner. Compulsion was one of the Xiiginns' most powerful tools, but if a species was able to resist, it could drive the Xiiginn involved to an unhealthy obsession.

They'd first come across this phenomenon with the Nershals. Like the Qegi, Mar Arden had found other ways to motivate the Nershals. The allure of technology just beyond their current capabilities had been a powerful motivator, but given an enemy to rally against, they'd quickly allied with the Xiiginns. The Boxans often commented on the arrogance of Xiiginns, but what they'd failed to realize was that it was the Boxans' own arrogance that had set the species of the Confederation against them. Mar Arden had successfully used compulsion on many Boxans, and cycles ago he had set Kladomaor free in an attempt to gain access to the Boxan home world. No Boxan had been able to resist him the way Kladomaor had, but in the end it wasn't enough. They'd still wreaked havoc on Sethion.

"You want to pursue our lost Human prisoner?" Mar Arden said.

Kandra Rene looked up at him, and her dark violet eyes narrowed dangerously. "Yes," she said.

"You'll get your chance, but for now Sion Shif is on their immediate trail. Since he's successfully used his ability on one of the Humans, it was the best choice to send him with the scout ship," Mar Arden said.

Kandra Rene's hands had been clutched in front of her, and she released them to her sides, her rage tempered for a while at least.

"Why did they send us back to Nershal space?" Kandra Rene asked.

"We're hunting Humans, and this is the place they were first discovered. There must be a remnant gravity wave we can follow that was generated by the wormhole," Mar Arden said.

He enabled the large holoscreen and showed their position on the outskirts of the system. If the Nershals sent their own warships out here, they would have ample notice.

"Why did you bring us to the edge of the system?"

"What do you know about Boxan outposts, particularly their listening stations?" Mar Arden asked.

Kandra Rene circled around the holoscreen and looked at him. "They're used to collect data while observing primitive species. They're also the command and control center for the Star Shroud."

Mar Arden nodded. "Very good. They also have the ability to create wormholes, much in the way a Cherubian drive does."

"What purpose would that serve?"

"Can you think of nothing?"

2000

Kandra Rene frowned in thought. "I could see them using this for communications, but did the Boxans use ships without Cherubian drives?"

"Yes, on both accounts. They used them for quickly sending data back to the Boxan home system, Sethion. They would also use small shuttlecraft to send their scientists to the listening stations. The scientists would perform their assigned tasks, check the systems and collect the recorded data, then bring them back to Command Central. Scientists would rotate in and out of the listening stations," Mar Arden said.

"I didn't know that," Kandra Rene said.

"Most Xiiginns don't. We kept it secret until the time of the great uprising."

"The Boxans had fail-safes ready to take down the listening stations wherever they were."

"Yes, but we suspect they left the Star Shroud networks intact. So if we could find one of these systems, we could decipher the shroud network and use that to map out all the species the Boxans had been studying," Mar Arden said.

Kandra Rene nodded and studied the holoscreen intently. "I don't know how you can pinpoint a former wormhole with any degree of accuracy. Confederation ships come in and out of here all the time."

"Now you're thinking like a starship commander. You're better than that."

Kandra Rene arched a brow, and her tail flicked to the side. "Show me entry points for all Confederation ships before the time of the Mardoxian priestess's capture."

The onboard AI updated the holoscreen, and Mar Arden smiled his approval.

Kandra Rene frowned. "We'll need to split the squadron to scan the system. I'm thinking it would be somewhere in the vicinity of the seventh planet in this system."

"Why?" he asked. He already knew the answer but wanted to know if she did.

"Because that's where the Boxan outpost in this system used to reside. So not the entire orbit. We should be able to narrow this down to a smaller area. A staggered approach from the squadron should help us find the anomalous wormhole remnant we're searching for," Kandra Rene said.

Mar Arden brought his hands together. "Excellent. I expect your presentation to Hoan Berend and his crew on the bridge to be equally impressive."

Kandra Rene's eyes widened. It was an honor for her to do this, and Mar Arden knew it. This would help alleviate her shame at failure to use compulsion on the Human for the time being, although he found her results puzzling. He'd seen Kandra Rene use compulsion on other species with skill. What was it about the Human physiology that made some of them resistant to compulsion? If Sion Shif performed as expected, they could figure out why they'd been in the Qegi star system to begin with.

Kandra Rene left him to bring Hoan Berend up to speed, and Mar Arden opened a secure channel to the scout ship. He had a couple of agents onboard the ship who would upload any data collected from the system, and he would then combine that with what they'd already collected. First, he would model the position of the Boxan space station in the Qegi star system.

"Now, what were you after?" Mar Arden muttered as he began his analysis. The answer was there, buried amid the details. His hunt had only just begun.

12

A couple of weeks had passed since Michael Hunsicker had convinced Chazen to consider building a life pod they could use to get back to Earth. Together, they'd gathered the materials they would need. They primarily worked in the main entryway that the crew of the Athena had used when they'd first come here, although that had been so long ago that he had trouble picturing it.

There was a lot to be salvaged from the listening station, but it wasn't an effort they charged into without some careful planning first. Chazen had made a list of materials available while Michael informed Mission Control of his intentions. At first there had been stunned silence, and after that wore off, Mission Control had offered to oversee their proposed plan. Michael was incredibly thankful for that, and it was good to know that his own species hadn't completely abandoned him.

Gary Hunter from Mission Control had told him there was initial resistance to using the Endurance for their close-proximity rescue mission. "You've got a friend in Edward Johnson," Gary said.

"What did he do?" Michael asked.

"There has been a lot of browbeating going on around here between government officials and the private corporate sector. Dux Corp must have some pretty good leverage because NASA agreed to have the Endurance come pick you up once you leave your cushy pad there on Pluto," Gary said.

Michael snorted as his thoughts returned to where he actually was. Sometimes while on these video calls he could almost believe that home was much closer than it really was.

"I know that look," Gary said. "We'll get you home, Michael. There are a lot of people working for this."

Michael clamped down on his emotions. The thought of getting home shattered his focus sometimes.

"I'm alright. Have there been any further comms from the Athena?" Michael asked.

"No, and nothing from the Boxan colony Kaylan talked about. Oh, here's a bit of news. There has been a new international proposal put forth to the United Nations today. They want to form an Earth Coalition Force, ECF, with a mandate to operate in space to defend the Earth."

Michael's eyebrows rose. "ECF? What would they be made up from?"

"That's the interesting thing. It's a mixed bag between elected leaders and representatives from the various militaries. While serving in the ECF, they would operate with authority only outside of Earth's atmosphere. Then, when their rotation is up, they'd have the option to return to their nation's military with full honors," Gary said.

Michael Hunsicker was a military man himself and, as such, knew that most militaries were steeped in traditions that didn't always meld with other nations' militaries. "It's an interesting concept. I think I read something years ago by a futurist of the time who talked about mankind's march toward a global society. If this ECF ever gets off the ground, this could be one of the first steps toward that."

"That's what a lot of people here at Mission Control think, but you know we're scientists and engineers," Gary replied.

"How did the other nations react to it?"

"Don't know yet. It was proposed today. The news media is doing what it does best, which is to get people scared so they'll keep watching the vids. My buddy, Kent, over in the IT department said there are already various groups forming on social media. While most people have accepted that there are aliens in our galaxy, there are still a lot of conspiracy nut jobs out there. The people in charge, though, that's a different story altogether," Gary said.

"I just hope they get their ducks in a row before it's too late," Michael said.

"History tells a different story. People won't start to believe the Xiiginns are coming until there are ships surrounding Earth. Even me saying it sounds strange, and I've been immersed in all this stuff since the beginning," Gary said, glancing over at another screen next to the camera. "Right, there was something else I'm supposed to ask you about. This life pod you're building—will it be able to accommodate Chazen as well?"

Michael frowned. "It could, but he says he won't leave."

"That is unfortunate. We have a proposal we'd like you to talk to him about."

"Alright, what's the proposal?"

Michael spoke with Gary for almost another hour. Normally he'd not have taken so much time, but he needed to. When the call ended, Michael walked to the main entrance, where they'd been working on the life pod, and he found himself taking in his surroundings with the realization that his days here were numbered. At some point, the dark gray walls lined in a cyan light had become commonplace.

He rounded the corner and opened the large, metallic-gray doors. Chazen was hunched over one of the workbenches, focused on the internal components that would eventually go inside the pod.

There was nothing in the large open area that even closely resembled a pod. They'd built a large skeletal framework that basically looked like a twenty-foot-tall soccer ball. When they added each polygonal plate, it would reinforce the entire structure as a whole. There was no shortage of plating to be used for the outer hull. The material was the same as that used for the walls of the outpost. When finished, the life pod would look like a large, gunmetal-gray soccer ball traveling through space. The original design had been much smaller, but Michael had vehemently argued against that. He ostensibly made the argument that the extra room was needed because they weren't exactly sure how long Michael would be inside, but what he really hoped was that Chazen would consider climbing aboard and joining him on this journey.

He hastened over to Chazen's workbench, and the Boxan stopped what he was doing.

"You were gone longer than expected," Chazen said.

"Well, there was a lot to talk about," Michael said and proceeded to bring Chazen up to speed.

Chazen had very little to say and basically just acknowledged what Michael had told him.

"There is one more thing. We'd like to offer you asylum on Earth," Michael said.

Chazen frowned. "I'm afraid I don't understand."

"Come with me back to Earth," Michael said.

"My duty is here," Chazen replied.

"You've done your duty. You shouldn't stay here and die," Michael said.

Chazen tossed the tool he'd been holding onto the workbench and took a few steps away.

"I'm sorry," Michael said. "But if you stay here and the Xiiginn come here first, then . . ."

"I would destroy the outpost," Chazen said.

"And lose your life in the process. Come with me to Earth. Asylum grants you protection. We'll help you get back to the Boxans," Michael said and gestured toward the skeletal framework of the life pod. "All you have to do is climb aboard with me. The plan is for the Endurance to rendezvous with the pod and bring us to our lunar base. The message from the Athena said that the Boxans were coming as well. I'm sure there's a way to initiate the self-destruction of this place from Earth. There's no need for you to stay here," Michael said.

The Boxan's large ears twitched momentarily, disturbing his thick dark hair. Chazen closed his eyes and took slow, deep breaths. Michael had seen him do this before and knew it was a common practice of his culture.

Chazen's flaxen eyes opened, and he looked at Michael. "Very well. Tell your people I accept their gracious offer of asylum," he said.

Michael was stunned. He'd expected that Chazen would stubbornly choose to stay here. Michael had brought up the subject of Chazen returning to Earth with him months ago, and the Boxan had adamantly refused to even consider it. Perhaps it was building the life pod or the fact that Michael had been his only companion in over sixty years, and he realized he may have underestimated the desire not to be alone. And as beautiful as Pluto had turned out to be, it was nothing compared to stepping outside on a living, breathing planet. Michael believed that was what Chazen missed most of all, and if the Boxan hadn't agreed to come, he might have missed his last chance to do so.

They had a lot of work to do, and Michael was extremely happy that he would not be returning to Earth alone.

13

Over the next week, Chazen set a rigorous work schedule that Michael Hunsicker could hardly keep up with. Once the Boxan had made up his mind, he threw himself at the task. Despite the hard work and the hectic schedule that only allowed Michael to sleep four hours at a time, he found there was a spring to his step. The thought of going home invigorated him more than any stimulant could. And even though his rations had long since run out, Chazen had been able to get the food processors to spit out some sort of brownish gruel that had kept him alive. It tasted like runny eggs, with an extra emphasis on runny. Michael dutifully ate the concoction, knowing he needed to keep his strength up.

The life pod had transformed from an arrangement of chaotic components to that of a working pod virtually overnight, and Michael had gotten a quick update from Mission Control. The spaceship Endurance had successfully completed a short shakedown journey. Gary hadn't been too forthcoming with the details, but if they could hit their mark, the Endurance would have no issues finding them. In theory, the life pod could accommodate them for several weeks.

He'd been awestruck when they'd attached the outer plating of the life pod onto the framework. The Boxans had a device that changed the chemical state of the alloy used to create the walls of the outpost. Chazen had uploaded the design of the life pod into the device, and it broke down the metallic alloy sleeves into the preprogrammed shape. It looked as if someone had melted candlewax while it hung suspended in the air and worked it into a polygonal shape. Once the different sleeves joined together, there were no visible creases at all. There were also no windows. Once they were inside, their eyes and ears would be the small sensor array attached to the exterior of the hull. If they could have made engines, the pod would have flown. Unfortunately, designing complex ship engines was beyond their capability.

One of the biggest internal components of the life pod was the onboard computer that housed the Boxan's artificial intelligence, along with a record of all observations made during the station's lifecycle. Chazen considered it a small backup of all essential information in the event that they had to engage the self-destruct. They couldn't destroy the outpost when they left Pluto because they needed the power generator to create the micro-wormhole that would get them home. Neither of them was willing to accept the risk of a time-delay self-destruct because of the small possibility that something could go wrong.

Setting a course for the micro-wormhole required a precision that would severely tax the outpost's computer system. They could end up somewhere other than where they intended to be, or worse, which was something Michael didn't want to spend too much time thinking about. One thing they could count on was that space was so vast that there was little chance their micro-jump would take them to the surface of Mars, for instance. The gravest risk to them was the gravitational pull that could warp the wormhole, which would effectively slingshot them far away. This was an all-or-nothing effort to get Michael home and to give Chazen a chance to contact the Boxans.

"When would you want to engage the outpost's self-destruct?" Michael asked.

"Ideally, never. The outpost is also the command and control for the shroud network, which does provide a measure of protection to this star system," Chazen said.

"Would the Star Shroud be destroyed then?"

"Yes. The self-destruct protocols would spread to the shroud devices that reside in the Oort cloud," Chazen said.

A short while later they finished loading the pod. They'd had to move it outside so the phaze-emitter could be directed at the pod without risk to the outpost. There was little for Michael to do but watch Chazen use platforms that could support the weight of the pod. The Boxan then directed the platforms to move the pod a hundred meters from the outpost.

Michael wore his EVA suit from the Athena, which he hadn't worn since he'd left the spaceship, and putting it on felt like getting one step closer to home. He noticed that he had plenty of room inside it, which he attributed to living off rations and Boxan gruel. That thought led him to an image of Brenda Goodwin, the Athena's medical officer, scolding him and going on about malnutrition. He'd been friends with Brenda since before the Athena mission. She had known Kathryn as well and had been at her funeral.

Michael walked out of the airlock onto the Plutonian surface. The sun looked like a lonely lantern in some far-off lighthouse, shining brightly in the distance. He couldn't keep the smile from his face. Each step he took brought him closer to home, and he had to keep himself from running headlong to the life pod. As he walked across Pluto's surface, memories of the Athena crew heading toward the Boxan outpost came to the forefront of his mind: Kaylan with her abilities; Zack Quick, who had initially deciphered the protocols used to access the shroud network; Dale Hicks and Katie Garcia, who were there to keep them safe; and even Jonah Redford, brilliant astrophysicist who foolishly attempted to take over the mission, leaving Michael shot and stranded. He'd been so focused on other things that he hadn't thought about Redford all that much. He wondered how they were all doing.

Although there was no structural reason to do so, years of habit from working in outer space caused Michael to duck his head as he entered the pod, where he took his position and waited for Chazen to join him. The Boxan stood outside and gazed back at the outpost that had been his home away from home for over sixty years. After a few moments, Chazen stepped aboard the pod, using his suit computer to close the hatch, and there was a slight gasp as the atmosphere pushed the vacuum away. The heaters inside had already warmed the small living space to minimal levels, and they could have taken their helmets off, but they were attempting something no one had ever tried before. If for some reason the hull was breached, their suits would be the only thing keeping them alive.

Chazen sat in his seat, and Michael brought up communications. They were still patched into comms from the outpost, so they had a live feed into Mission Control, where a duplicate countdown timer could be found. Michael whispered a prayer and engaged the countdown. Chazen opened the holo-interface from his suit computer. "The emitter has been brought into alignment."

The lighting inside the pod dimmed.

"Target locked," Chazen said.

Michael watched the countdown grind to zero.

"Engage."

Michael felt himself lift against the restraints of his seat. There was no antigravity in the pod.

"Matrix achieved. Commence jump," Chazen said.

Michael felt a crushing force press him back into his seat, and he cried out. Pinpoints of light pressed in on his vision as the interior of the pod pulled away from him. He felt as if he were launching on a rocket propelling him from Earth's atmosphere, and he was completely at its mercy. He squeezed his eyes shut, waiting for it to be over.

MICHAEL HUNSICKER FOUND himself staring at the control panel in front of him. His eyes slowly focused on his surroundings.

"Commander, are you awake?" Chazen asked.

Michael blew out a breath as a wave of nausea swept over him. The nausea came from weightlessness, and he knew it would pass.

"Did it work?" Michael asked.

"Waiting for confirmation of our position."

Michael reached out to his own console, and after a few moments an image appeared, showing them safely in the Goldilocks Zone of the solar system.

Eyes moist with unshed tears, Michael let loose a cry that ended with a laugh. They'd made it.

"Houston, this is Boxan Life Pod One. Do you copy?" Michael said.

There was no response. Michael waited a few moments and repeated himself.

"Boxan Life Pod One, we read you loud and clear. We have your position and are transmitting coordinates to the Endurance."

Michael's throat closed up with emotion. "We did it," he said to Chazen.

Chazen looked over at him, and for that moment at least, Michael saw something he hadn't seen in the Boxan's eyes before. Hope.

14

Main power had been restored to the Boxan stealth ship, and Kladomaor was heading to the bridge. The resonance chamber had been a good choice. He was better able to focus and would thus be able to perform his duties as battle commander with greater efficiency. After repairs had been made, the ship's computers had locked him out of the systems until he'd had the minimum required time in the resonance chamber. Boxan warship AIs were equipped to enforce certain protocols if there was sufficient evidence of risk to ship and crew. He'd ordered Gaarokk to override the AI, but the Boxan scientist had refused.

Ma'jasalax joined him on his way to the bridge. "You look more at peace," she said.

"Have you been able to locate the Athena?"

"No," Ma'jasalax said.

Kladomaor frowned. "You don't appear to be concerned."

"On the contrary, I'm quite concerned, but I don't think they perished."

Kladomaor entered the bridge, and the Boxan soldiers snapped a salute. He headed for the command couch, and Triflan stood at attention next to it.

"Situation report," Kladomaor said.

"We have main engines back online, but we've sustained heavy damage. We cannot go into stealth, and our combat capability is at thirty percent effectiveness," Triflan said.

Kladomaor engaged his neural implants and opened a connection to the ship's computer.

Gaarokk came over to them. "We've completed our analysis, and we think we were hit with some kind of pulse weapon that disabled most of the ship's systems."

Kladomaor glanced at the scientist and then over at his tactical officer. "The

Xiiginns don't have the capability of firing their weapons while in a wormhole. Neither do we, for that matter."

"Correct, Battle Commander," Triflan said.

"So it can't be a weapon. There must be some other explanation," Kladomaor said.

"Perhaps this will help," Gaarokk said. The wall screen powered on. "I had the computer recreate our transit."

Kladomaor watched as the computer showed a mockup of the Boxan stealth ship and the small Human ship attached to them with the gravity tether. A wave of energy engulfed the Boxan ship, and he watched as the ship angled off and out of the wormhole.

Kladomaor frowned. "Slow the model down to twenty percent speed."

The computer model reset, and just before the pulse hit, their ship's gravity tether to the Athena had been disabled.

"Freeze it," Kladomaor said and looked at the others. "Why did they disable the tether?"

"We're not exactly sure," Gaarokk said.

Kladomaor looked at Ma'jasalax, who appeared to be waiting for him to get to her. "I know the Athena's design, and only Kaylan or Hicks would have been able to sever the tether from their bridge. I don't believe this is something Hicks would do on his own. The question is, why did Kaylan sever the tether in the first place?"

"I think severing the tether prevented the Athena from being destroyed," Gaarokk said. "Computer, replace model but follow the path of the Athena."

The computer model replayed, and it showed the pulse blast completely missing the Athena.

"They were still thrust from the wormhole as soon as the Cherubian drive went offline. What is the Athena's trajectory?" Kladomaor asked.

The computer showed multiple trajectories the Athena could have taken, along with the probability rates for each one. Now he knew why Ma'jasalax believed the crew of the Athena was alive.

"Kaylan must have sensed something was wrong and severed the gravity tether. It's the only explanation that makes any sense," Kladomaor said and moved his gaze back to Ma'jasalax.

"I didn't sense anything," Ma'jasalax said.

Gaarokk looked as if he were about to speak.

"What is it?" Kladomaor asked.

"We know the Mardoxian potential exists in Humans, but what if there's more? What if they could do more than even Ma'jasalax can?" Gaarokk said, refusing to even look at Ma'jasalax.

"It's alright," she said. "Kaylan's abilities have been growing, but I think there's more to it than that."

Kladomaor's brows pushed forward in thought. "The Drar," he said.

Gaarokk and Triflan looked confused.

"That was my thinking," Ma'jasalax said.

"I don't understand," Gaarokk said.

"The signals we've been seeing that led us here are from the Drars. For some reason they wanted to meet the Humans without us but had surmised that the Humans couldn't make the trip on their own," Ma'jasalax said.

Kladomaor ground his teeth. "That's too many assumptions."

"Do you have a better explanation, Battle Commander?" Ma'jasalax asked.

"I'm not sure. The Drars were radically more advanced than us. We used their technology to make gains, but having the capability to detect ships using a Cherubian drive and then to disable one of them is a bit much to accept," Kladomaor said.

Triflan cleared his throat. "I've had my team analyze the data, and the energy reading of the pulse was just enough to take out our systems and nothing more."

Kladomaor glanced at the wall screen again. "So you're saying that if they'd wanted to destroy us, they could have. They simply wanted us out of the way for a while."

"Precisely," Triflan said.

"What do we do now?" Gaarokk asked.

"We go after them," Kladomaor said. "I won't abandon the crew of the Athena."

"Battle Commander," Triflan said, "I must advise caution. This was effectively a warning shot."

Kladomaor hardened his gaze. "We've been warned, but we're not going to stay away. I want to follow the trajectory for the highest probability rate of the Athena's path."

Triflan saluted him and returned to his station, and Ma'jasalax came to his side.

"We've been looking for evidence of the Drars since we saw their wars being fought in the great expanse," Ma'jasalax said, and her eyes grew distant in thought.

"You're wondering whether the Drars' message wasn't meant for us," Kladomaor said.

Ma'jasalax's eyes widened. "That's quite a leap for one not of the Mardoxian sect."

"Do you agree? Could the Drars have been waiting for a species like the Humans all along, and we were simply the courier vessel that brought them here?" Kladomaor asked.

"I don't think it's that simple," Ma'jasalax answered.

"No, it never is," Kladomaor said and took his place on the command couch, engaging the comms link throughout the ship. "Boxan crew, this is your battle commander. We're about to get underway. We're going after the Athena in order to fulfill our mandate to see the Humans safely returned to their star system. Battle Commander, out."

Kladomaor cut the link.

"Course ready, Battle Commander," Varek said from his navigation console.

"Make it so," Kladomaor said.

15

Sometimes Hicks got tired of being right. He'd been concerned that the Athena was too out of her depth for a journey like this, and he'd been right. Now they were stranded well away from any hospitable place. Sure, they could point the ship in a direction, and perhaps in a few hundred years they might actually make it to some destination, but none of them would be alive to see it. Maybe he should have pushed harder for them to return to Earth.

Hicks sighed. Fear and frustration were directing his thoughts, and it wasn't helping. He knew better than to be second-guessing every decision on any mission. He was better than that. They'd rolled the dice, taken a risk, and come up short. Plain and simple. They were still alive, so there was that at least. Plus, Kladomaor wouldn't have abandoned them.

"Was there something else you wanted to bring up?" Kaylan asked.

Hicks took a sip of his water and nodded. "Emma, would you tell Kaylan what you reported to me about Redford, please?"

The others on the bridge went silent, and Emma looked as if she'd rather be anywhere else than where she was right now.

"Jonah still has blackouts. We don't know why they occur and cannot predict when they will happen," Emma said.

"Yeah, but he's restrained, so what damage could he do?" Kaylan asked.

"When Brenda went to help you with Efren and Nikolai in Engineering, I was left alone with Jonah in the hydroponics lab. At some point, Jonah got up and went to the console," Emma said.

"Do you know if he did anything?" Hicks asked.

Emma shook her head. "It was blank by the time I got there."

"What do you think he did?" Kaylan asked Hicks.

"I'm worried that Redford sent a signal to the Xiiginns, letting them know we're right here," Hicks said.

"Now hold on a minute," Zack said. "He got to a console, but that doesn't mean he did anything."

"Athena," Hicks said. "Can you tell us what Redford was doing at the console in the hydroponics lab?"

"Apologies, Major, but I have no record of Dr. Redford accessing my systems from hydroponics. Furthermore, since the events at the Boxan space station, Dr. Redford's access to the computer system has been restricted," the AI said.

"There, you see?" Zack said.

Hicks smiled. "I'm surprised to find you so trusting. What if he covered his tracks somehow?"

Zack blanched, and Hicks watched as the hacker's thoughts went into overdrive. He knew Zack could see patterns within patterns of data, and he was naturally suspicious of people. This made him great at investigations. "I hadn't considered it, but there would be logs of systems access."

"And Athena reports there was no access. Meaning no disrespect to the AI, but what if she's wrong?" Hicks asked.

"I'm not insulted by your query, Major," the AI said. "I can only report based on the information I have, and my records indicate that only mission specialist Emma Roberson accessed my system during this time."

Out of the corner of his eye, Hicks saw that Emma had brought her hand to her face, and he turned to look at her, but Emma was looking at Kaylan with crestfallen eyes.

"I'm so sorry. I left my console unlocked. I'm usually the only one in there, and with everything that's been going on . . ." Emma's voice trailed off.

Kaylan went over to Emma. "This isn't your fault. Athena, what did Jonah access using Emma's account?"

"Medical records for Zack, Commander."

Hicks glanced at Zack, who was just as dumbfounded as everyone else. "Which records?" Hicks asked.

"Brain scans, Major."

Hicks glanced at Zack. "Why would Jonah access your brain scans?"

Zack rubbed the back of his neck while he thought about it. "I don't know. I do make it a point to go see Jonah and try to talk to him. Sometimes he's lucid, and other times he mutters incoherently about the Xiiginns."

Kaylan frowned. "I didn't know you went to see Jonah."

Zack shrugged. "I never thought to mention it. I just started going to see him to make sure he was . . . He's part of the crew," Zack said firmly.

Hicks knew Redford was no one's favorite person on this mission. The man had a knack for rubbing people the wrong way. He'd even stretched Hunsicker's patience during their mission. Hicks looked at Brenda Goodwin, who was looking intently at her tablet computer.

Brenda looked up. "He was comparing Zack's brain scans to his own."

"Sounds like he was looking for a reason why the Xiiginns were able to use their compulsion on him and not Zack," Hicks said.

A stunned silence came over the Athena's crew, and Zack looked as if he almost felt guilty. Hicks knew that Redford had been sedated in the med bay and that there were times when, for no apparent reason at all, the astrophysicist showed volatile behavior. Brenda had said he was suffering from psychosis.

"If that's all he accessed, then we know he didn't cause our current predicament," Kaylan said.

"Agreed," Hicks replied.

"Commander," Emma said, "Brenda and I would like to run some additional tests on Zack to confirm a few things."

"Don't you think you should be asking me?" Zack asked.

Kaylan gave him a look.

"Alright, as long as it doesn't hurt, I'll be your guinea pig," Zack said.

Hicks chuckled. They still needed to figure out a way forward, but at least they could rule out Jonah Redford as a cause for the disaster.

16

Zack followed Emma and Brenda to the med bay after Kaylan dismissed them. In their time aboard the Athena, Zack hadn't even thought twice about Kaylan being the commander. She insisted that she was only 'acting commander' since the official mission still showed Michael Hunsicker as the Athena's commander. Zack didn't care about titles, and to him and the rest of the crew it seemed that Kaylan Farrow was their commander.

"How come you never told anyone about going to see Jonah?" Brenda asked.

"It never crossed my mind, really. I feel bad about what happened to him," Zack said.

"I would never have guessed that you were so compassionate," Emma said with a smile.

Zack let out a small laugh, feeling uncomfortable. "I know you guys have worked really hard on this, and we've had our share of surprises along the way, but do you think there's anything we can do for Jonah?"

"It's hard to say. We're still trying to understand exactly what was done to him," Brenda said.

They walked through the ship and made it to the med bay.

"According to his brain scans, it appears that certain parts of Jonah's brain have been irrevocably rewritten," Brenda said.

"So there's no chance to change everything back the way it was before?" Zack asked.

"We can't even do that back on Earth. I've been looking for ways to suppress the urges that come with the compulsion, but I haven't been successful," Brenda said.

Zack felt his mouth go dry. Kladomaor had insisted that there was nothing they could do for Jonah, but Zack had held out hope that they could prove the

Boxan wrong. He'd spent more than a few moments during this voyage believing he'd been lucky to resist the Xiiginn's compulsion.

Brenda motioned for Zack to lie on the bed. Jonah was unconscious on a nearby bed. Zack didn't know what was worse—Jonah acting crazy or the fact that they had to sedate him to keep him from harming himself or others.

"How do you think the Xiiginn compulsion works?" Zack asked.

"Well, Gaarokk sent us quite a bit of information about that, and we also have our own observations," Brenda said.

Emma worked at one of the nearby consoles by his bed, and he was slowly laid flat.

"We think it works on a few different levels. First is the pheromones, where being in close physical proximity to the Xiiginns can cause behavioral changes in the beings around them. We've seen similar things on Earth—from mammals to insects—but never something that could cross species like we see here. Even *we* emit pheromones," Brenda said.

"I guess that makes sense, but the Xiiginns have taken this to a whole new level," Zack said.

"Tilt your head back for me," Emma asked and then attached a small round disk to his neck.

Zack felt a slight pinch as the disk adhered to his skin.

"It's so we can get a clearer image of your brain. Do you remember when we had to do this in Houston?" Brenda asked.

Zack thought about it for a moment. The events bringing Zack onto the Athena mission had been a whirlwind tour of being poked and prodded. "I guess. They did so much to me before we left the ground that it all runs together."

Brenda chuckled.

"So pheromones give them access, but what about the rest? They made Jonah a sleeper agent, like they preprogrammed him to go off at a certain time," Zack said.

Emma nodded. "Let's not forget that we're dealing with a completely alien lifeform here. The Xiiginns might be humanoid with some extra appendages, but they're still alien and have evolved along a different evolutionary path."

"Appendages . . . nice. You know they can use their tails while they fight you? They lifted me up with it," Zack said.

Emma glanced at Brenda. Zack rarely talked about what had happened to him as a prisoner of the Xiiginns.

"I guess I never told anyone about that," Zack said sheepishly.

"No, you didn't," Brenda said. "But it can help you to talk about these things. No matter what happened, we won't look at you any differently than we do, Zack."

Emma nodded and placed her hand on his shoulder. Zack was thankful for the support, but he didn't want to relive his captivity. Mostly, Zack just wanted to forget it. An image of Kandra Rene's violet-colored eyes flashed in his mind, causing him to shudder and shove those thoughts away.

"Okay, just relax now. None of this is going to hurt. We won't be sedating you for this because we need active brain scans," Brenda said.

Zack nodded. "Do you need me to think of something?"

Emma flipped her tablet computer around. "I'm going to show you some images and we'll map your reactions to them."

"Okay, go ahead," Zack said.

The first image to appear was Earth. Then it switched to a cup of coffee, and Zack smiled. He was a bit of a coffee nut, after all. The next image was of the Athena. The images progressed from different foods to various everyday objects and ultimately to pictures of the crew. Images of Kaylan came up more than once, and in one of them they were standing together on the tarmac about to board the space plane in Houston. The sun lit up the red highlights in Kaylan's hair, and Zack felt his lips curve upward as his chest became warm.

"I don't believe it," Emma said. "That's it!"

Brenda's mouth hung open, and she cycled through brain-scan images on the holoscreen nearest her. She then activated the holoprojector on the ceiling, and three-dimensional images of the brain were shown. Zack glanced at Emma, and she smiled down at him, unable to keep the excitement from her eyes.

"This series of brain images on the left are Jonah's, and these over here are yours from just now." The three-dimensional images of Zack's brain were green while Jonah's were amber-colored.

"I don't see anything," Zack said.

"This area here toward the middle is called the striatum. It's basically the reward system of the brain. This area of the brain is known to become active during attraction. When we showed you all those images, the ones of Kaylan sent fireworks through this part of the brain, similar to what we observe in Jonah," Brenda said.

Zack stared at the brain images and frowned. "I still don't get it."

Emma laughed. "Makes perfect sense. You are a man, after all."

Zack was still confused.

Emma rolled her eyes. "Love, Zack. Love is what you're seeing."

Zack raised his eyes to the highlighted brain images and then looked over at Jonah's, and understanding finally slammed into place.

"I bet that if we showed Emma pictures of her fiance back on Earth, we'd see something similar," Brenda said.

Zack swallowed hard. "So Jonah is in love with the Xiiginns?"

Brenda powered off the holoprojector, and the lights returned to normal. Zack sat up on the bed and swung his legs to the side.

"Something like that. It might be like becoming instantly addicted to a drug, but they're also able to implant complex messages," Brenda said.

Zack glanced over at Redford's unconscious form and sighed. "The reason for the aberrant behavior is because he's trying to resist, and it's killing him by slowly driving him insane."

Brenda gave him a serious look and nodded.

"Still doesn't explain why I wasn't vulnerable to the same thing," Zack said.

"Perhaps your feelings for Kaylan shielded you somehow," Emma said.

"Maybe," Zack said.

He wasn't sure what to think. He'd hoped they'd be able to reverse what had been done to Jonah, but he wasn't sure it was possible. Zack asked if he could leave, wanting to put some distance between himself and the med bay.

Kaylan was in the Athena's top observatory, trying to get a bead on where the Boxans could be. Sometimes she needed to get away from the bridge, and the top observatory had one of the best views on the entire ship. Radical advancements in silica glass development allowed for a large dome that provided an unfettered view of the stars. Kaylan retracted the ceramic alloy shield and saw the telescopic array off to one side. The array took pictures and enabled the AI to provide analyses of the images. She had an idea of where Earth was, but she couldn't tell which star was theirs in the star-filled sky. Even at best speed, they wouldn't make it home for thousands of years.

The door to the observatory opened, and Zack walked in. He smiled at her.

"You found my hiding spot," Zack said.

"Is this where you've been keeping yourself?" Kaylan asked.

"Sometimes. I retract the roof and try to convince myself that I'm looking up at the night sky in Chicago," Zack said.

Kaylan glanced above them. "I miss home, too."

They stood there watching the sky without saying anything at all. It was one of the rare moments of silence they both could enjoy.

"That's strange," Zack said and walked over to Jonah's standup workstation.

"What is it?" Kaylan asked, following him.

"Oh, it's one of the subroutines we had running to detect the Star Shroud devices. I thought Jonah disabled them when we first came to the Nershal star system, but I guess he left it running on a schedule to check periodically . . ." Zack's voice trailed off.

Kaylan nodded and saw Zack's gaze become more intense as he scanned the readout on the holoscreen.

"No, that can't be right," Zack said and glanced at her. "Our sensor array is detecting a signal similar to the Star Shroud."

Kaylan looked at the readout on the screen. She understood the concept when Zack explained it, but she couldn't make sense of the information on the holoscreen. Her eyes widened.

Zack nodded excitedly. "You see? This shouldn't be out here. The Boxans had no systems out here that I know of. I'll double-check with the AI, but I recall Gaarokk saying this was uncharted space for them as well."

"Can you pinpoint where the signal is coming from?" Kaylan asked.

"It'll take a little bit of time, but I should be able to." Zack stopped what he was saying and turned toward her. "This has to be intentional. This could be the Drars' way of hailing us or something."

Kaylan frowned. "Possibly. If it *is* something like the Star Shroud, or an actual shroud, you might not be able to get directly to the source but only to the general vicinity."

"I should talk to Jonah," Zack said.

"I'm not sure that would be a good idea," Kaylan said.

"Why not?"

"I'm not sure there's a way we can help Jonah, and the longer this goes on, the more the man we knew slips away," Kaylan said.

Zack clamped his mouth shut. She knew he didn't like the thought of giving up, but Brenda's latest report showed more deterioration of Jonah's brain.

Zack swallowed and looked at the floor. "I knew things were getting worse for him, but I didn't . . . Jonah and I bumped heads a lot, but he didn't deserve this."

Kaylan put her hand on his shoulder and gave him a gentle squeeze. "I know," she said softly.

Zack glanced at the holoscreen. "The signal is getting weaker."

"We might be moving away from it," Kaylan said.

Zack adjusted the sensor array, and the signal returned.

Kaylan headed for the door. "Send those coordinates to the bridge. I'll begin running numbers to see how far away it is."

Zack said he would, and she left for the bridge.

18

It took some convincing, but Zack eventually got Brenda to allow him to bring Redford to his lab in the top observatory. Hicks and Katie were with him just in case they had to restrain Jonah. There were times when Redford seemed quite distant from them—like he was standing there, but the lights weren't on inside his mind.

"Let's give him a little bit of space," Zack said.

Hicks and Brenda backed away. Redford closed his eyes and began nodding.

"I must make contact— No!" Redford said.

Jonah Redford had already been a thin man, but now he was so skinny that his facial features looked severe, and six weeks of beard growth made the astrophysicist look feral. Brenda had told Zack that Jonah was reluctant to eat.

Redford spun around, seeming to notice where he was for the first time. His eyes darted to Zack, and it took him a few moments to recognize him.

"You're alright, Jonah. We're on the Athena. This is your lab. Do you remember?" Zack asked.

Redford's brows pushed forward, and then he glanced toward the holoscreen that showed a digital dashboard of his ongoing research.

"I kept your research going for you as best I could," Zack said.

Redford stepped toward the console below the holoscreen, and Zack noticed Hicks purposefully place his hand on the stunner he carried.

"No, no, no," Redford said.

Zack came to his side and used his implants to change the data on the holoscreen. "I need you to take a look at this. We started getting a response to the Star Shroud protocols you and I set up."

Redford's eyes narrowed as he focused on the screen. "No, no, that can't be right," Jonah said, and his face crumpled in pain. "Contact. Must make contact — NO!"

Redford extended his hands, and his gaze widened at the severe scar tissue all over his forearms and hands—the result of the harsh burns he'd received when he'd signaled the Xiiginns their location.

Redford squeezed his eyes shut and brought his hands to his head.

"The Xiiginns can't find us here. They don't know where we are," Zack said.

Redford looked at him with relief. "I tried to stop myself, but I just couldn't."

Zack nodded. "I know you did. We need your help now. You set up an automatic protocol to seek out new Star Shroud devices, and we got a response."

"A response?" Redford said. "Where?"

Zack pulled up the coordinates Kaylan had been able to piece together for them, and Redford kept his hands clenched as he peered at the information on the screen.

"Need a better look," Redford muttered. He went over to the console and began inputting commands.

Hicks took a step closer, and Zack waved him off.

The sensor array outside the observatory shifted position, and new data feeds showed on the holoscreen.

Redford started to enter more commands, then stepped back. "No, I can't," he said and winced. "Must keep . . . it out."

Redford collapsed onto the floor, crying out.

"We don't have long," Brenda said.

Zack nodded and squatted down in front of Redford. "You moved the sensor array. What are you looking for?"

"Shroud network," Redford said. "But it's not safe." Redford shuddered and began rocking in place. "Too much radiation . . . the poles."

Redford's eyes fluttered and his whole body went into convulsions.

Brenda ran over. "He's having a stroke," she said.

They eased Redford over and laid his head on Brenda's lap.

"Isn't there anything you can do?" Zack asked.

Brenda shook her head. "We have to wait for it to pass," she said.

Hicks glanced over at Zack. "Did you get what you needed?" he asked.

Zack couldn't tear his eyes away from Jonah.

"Look at me," Hicks said and tipped Zack's face up.

"There's got to be something we can do for him," Zack said.

Redford stopped convulsing, and he seemed to pass out.

Zack's mouth went dry. That could have been him lying on the floor. Though it had been weeks, Jonah was still fighting the Xiiginns' influence, and the fight was going to kill him. Zack clenched his teeth and surged to his feet. Molten fury gathered inside him. He hated the Xiiginns with everything he had. He kicked the chair across the room, and it crashed into the wall as he balled his hands into fists. His breath came in gasps.

Hicks came over to him. "You need to calm down. I don't like what they've done to him any more than you do."

Zack jerked away from Hicks. "I want to hurt them," he said and heard the crack in his voice. "Kandra Rene, Sion Shif, Mar Arden, and all the rest of them."

His heart felt as if it would pound right out of his chest, and the walls were closing in on him. Katie came over and whispered something to Hicks. Hicks left them and helped Brenda get Redford back to the med bay.

Zack glanced at her with tears blurring his vision.

"Don't tell me to calm down," Zack said.

Katie held her hands up in front of her chest. "I wasn't going to."

"Almost every night, I lie down with Kaylan, but when I close my eyes it feels like I'm back in that pit," Zack said.

"I know," Katie said.

Zack frowned. "How do you know?"

"Because Kaylan told me about the nightmares. You were a prisoner. They hurt you. They hurt Jonah."

Zack sighed heavily. "He's going to die, isn't he?"

Katie gave him a sympathetic look and nodded.

Zack's throat thickened. "I didn't even like him. He always acted so superior to everyone else, but . . ."

"We're all in this together. We're on the same crew," Katie said.

They didn't speak for a few moments while Zack just stared at the overturned chair he'd kicked.

"You know, in the pit with all the mutants fighting, I didn't want to hurt anyone. Etanu was so angered by some of the things I did or wouldn't do. He's a soldier, and he sees only one way to deal with threats, but with the Xiiginns I want to be more like him. I hate them so much," Zack hissed.

Katie placed her hand on his back and rubbed it soothingly. Zack blew out a breath, and all the pent-up anger seemed to drain away from him.

"Thanks," Zack said.

"I'm your friend."

"I know," he said and frowned. "Is there something wrong with me for saying all that stuff?" Zack asked.

Katie shook her head. "No, there is something right about it. It means that you're coming to grips with what's happened to you. Hating the Xiiginns who hurt you isn't wrong."

Zack walked over and picked up the overturned chair. "I didn't want to say all that stuff to Kaylan. She's got enough to deal with."

"That's where you're wrong. Kaylan is there for you. She'll understand," Katie said and walked over to the holoscreen. "Now, what does this stuff mean?"

Zack glanced at the screen. "Jonah mentioned radiation. Athena, what do these new readings mean?"

"Preliminary analysis suggests that there is a powerful magnetic field near where the shroud signal is coming from," the AI said.

"Can the ship make it through it?" Zack asked.

"The ship would sustain some damage, but all organics onboard would die from radiation exposure," the AI said.

"Great," Zack said.

"If we had the instrumentation on the Boxan stealth ship, there might be a path through the field, but that is beyond our current capabilities," the AI said.

"Well, that's that," Katie said.

Zack frowned in thought. "Not necessarily," he said.

"You heard the AI," Katie said.

"I did, but the AI can't account for all our resources."

"Resources?"

Zack smiled. "Kaylan," he said.

Together he and Katie headed for the door. Zack didn't think that whoever sent the signal would bring them here just to die on the approach, which meant there had to be a way to get through.

19

Kaylan sat alone in the Athena's mess hall. She'd just finished her breakfast, and she took a sip of coffee that Zack often referred to as a cup of ambition. Efren and Nikolai had been there earlier, both joking about where to find the best fishing. Efren preferred deep sea fishing in the Atlantic while Nikolai preferred fishing in rivers and lakes. Kaylan didn't have an opinion, but she had enjoyed the playful banter. When they left, she'd decided to take advantage of a few moments alone to sit and enjoy the silence. She disconnected her neural implants to the Athena's computer systems and just sat perfectly still.

Ma'jasalax had been teaching her about meditation and how its practice was one of the pillars of Boxan society. The Boxan approach to a meditative state was similar to what Kaylan had read about elsewhere. There were different ways to achieve a meditative state, and it wasn't just sitting still in a quiet room, but that was one of them. Ma'jasalax had often taken her to the resonance chamber aboard the Boxan ship. The resonance chamber was a large, peaceful garden—maintained by each of Kladomaor's crew—where they played recorded sounds from the forests of the Boxan home world. She couldn't imagine NASA ever devoting so much space to an onboard retreat on future spaceships, but most of the Athena crew liked to do a rotation through Emma's hydroponic garden, so perhaps the idea had merit.

"Kaylan, please report to the bridge," Hicks's voice said over the ship's comms.

Kaylan used her neural implants to reconnect to the Athena's computer systems. She acknowledged the message and a few minutes later was back on the bridge. Zack was working on a smaller holoscreen at the conference table. They were all there except for Efren and Nikolai, who were working in Engineering, and Brenda and Redford, who were in the med bay.

"Zack, are you ready?" Hicks asked.

Zack gave him a half nod while performing some last-minute tasks on his screen and then activated the main display. A blinking dot marked the Athena as the only thing in the vicinity.

"With Jonah's help, we estimated the approximate origin of the shroud network signal response. But there doesn't appear to be anything there," Zack said.

"If it *is* a Star Shroud, we should be able to see past it," Kaylan said.

"That's how it worked back home, but Gaarokk said the tech used for the Star Shrouds was based on Drar technology the Boxans found," Zack said.

Kaylan studied the information onscreen. Several smaller windows had the sensor array output, and she took a moment to absorb the results.

"Redford looked at this and was saying something about too much radiation," Zack said.

Kaylan frowned in thought. "That's because whatever is there is surrounded by a powerful magnetic sphere. Hmm, that's strange. Were you able to map the actual shroud devices?"

"I tried, but we're just getting the initial signal. All my attempts at anything more have failed," Zack said.

"Commander, I have a theory," the AI said.

"Go ahead, Athena," Kaylan said.

"There is a substantial probability that the signal is for us specifically. My analysis of the sensor data shows that the signal only started broadcasting in our direction after we arrived," the AI said.

"How could you possibly know if the signal was sent before we got here?" Hicks asked.

"The commander ordered that we make a sweep with the sensor array of the area to determine where we are. When Zack found the signal from Dr. Redford's equipment, I correlated the data with what I already had and then calculated the probability to—"

"Athena," Zack said with a smile. "I think Hicks was just looking for a high-level explanation and not the actual formulas you used to form your theory."

"Oh," the AI responded. "In essence, the signal used is short-ranged and only broadcasting in our direction. The analysis shows that the signal loses much of its integrity the farther away it goes."

"So you're saying the signal is being intentionally sent to us?" Hicks said.

"Precisely, Major."

Hicks glanced at Kaylan. "I don't like this. Too many unknowns."

"What do you suggest?" Kaylan asked.

"That we continue to try to find Kladomaor."

"Anyone else?" Kaylan asked and glanced at the others.

Zack looked back at her. "Wouldn't Kladomaor have found us already if he could?"

"Their ship could have taken damage like us, but once they get underway, the Boxans will come looking for us," Hicks said.

Kaylan glanced around at all of them. They'd been trained to one degree or another to focus on the problems they could deal with. "We have no way of knowing where Kladomaor is or . . . if their ship was destroyed, and we don't have the resources to wait here forever. Star Shrouds were used around star systems that hosted planets with life. Perhaps the Drars used them for something similar." Kaylan pulled up a plot for best speed to the anomaly. "We could be there in a few days, and perhaps we'll learn more along the way."

"There is no way we can know the intentions of whatever is sending that signal," Hicks said.

"Well, they want our attention, so that says something," Zack said.

"That's the bait. I want to know if there's a hook inside," Hicks said.

Kaylan pressed her lips together in thought.

"What if we get ourselves into a situation we can't get out of?" Hicks asked.

"Like being stranded light years from home?" Zack asked with half a grin.

Hicks smiled. "Something like that."

"We could wait here and see if Kladomaor finds us," Kaylan said. "In the meantime, that signal will still be there, but there's no guarantee that nothing else will change. As we're all well aware, this ship isn't designed for the challenges of deep space. So the longer we stay where we are, the more we run the risk of something else going wrong—stress fractures on the hull and broken equipment. The list goes on and on. Right now we have the capacity to investigate this signal that was sent to us. I, for one, don't believe it was by accident. Perhaps we were brought here. We were chasing after the Drar, who were even more advanced than the Boxans. What's to say they didn't orchestrate the events that put us just days away from that shroud signal?"

Several crewmembers nodded their heads, accompanied by worried looks from others around the conference table.

"Now, if the Drars could do all those things, do you honestly think that if they wanted to come out here and get us, we could get away? I believe the signal is an invitation of some sort, and I'd much rather cautiously approach, gathering data along the way"— she glanced at Hicks—"and having you think of all those 'what-if' scenarios so we can put together contingency plans for what we can and acknowledge what we can't do anything about."

She still saw the underlying fear in the eyes of those around her. She felt it herself, but she also saw a determination that focused their minds on identifying problems. Michael Hunsicker had often said that identifying and solving one problem at a time was the best way to survive any mission in space. Solve enough problems and you get to live another moment and hopefully get to return home.

"We have a way forward," Kaylan said. "We're going to the shroud."

Zack cleared his throat. "What about the high levels of radiation? One of the last things Redford said was something about the poles."

"We'll need to study the magnetosphere and determine where the poles are. We might be able to find a safe approach that way," Kaylan said.

They spoke for a few more minutes and assigned different tasks, then she dismissed them and they went to work.

"You've changed," Hicks said.

"What do you mean?" Kaylan said.

"Ever since we lost Michael I've occasionally wondered how things would have gone if he'd been in charge," Hicks said.

Kaylan gave a small laugh. "I ask myself that all the time."

"Yeah, but lately I don't wonder so much anymore, and I think after today not ever again," Hicks said. "I'm trained to assess risks and think of ways of overcoming whatever obstacles come in our path."

"I know. That's why I rely on you so much. Together, we make a good crew. We balance each other out."

Hicks smiled. "Yeah, but you do the same thing and on a level much higher than anyone I've ever met before. Katie and I have served under all different types of commanders during our career. In special cases, there are those who are just plain brilliant. Those are the ones to stick close to."

Hicks left, and Zack came over. "I'll follow you anywhere, Commander," Zack said, imitating Hicks's Southern accent.

Kaylan punched him in the arm. "You're such an idiot."

Zack smiled. "I know, but he's right."

Kaylan smiled. She was glad they all believed in her. It really meant a lot. She just hoped their faith wasn't misplaced. She had no idea what the intentions of whoever sent that signal were, but they couldn't just wait out here in the middle of nowhere to find out.

20

Michael and Chazen were still in the life pod, but the Endurance had come along and scooped them up, and they were on their way to Armstrong Lunar Base. From there, they both would go to Earth after decontamination protocols were performed. When Michael had left Earth on the Athena, the Endurance had still been two years from scheduled completion.

There were no windows on the life pod, but the sensors were able to build a picture of the Athena's sister ship. The size and shape were reminiscent of the Athena, with the half-saucer-shaped front and rear engines, but that was it. Michael frowned at the image, looking at all the added things attached to the hull. Chazen had spotted it first, but it took Michael some time to realize that the spaceship Endurance had been weaponized. Michael couldn't begin to guess what weapon systems had been forced onto the Endurance, but he knew there had been a lot of engineering involved to get them in place. Humanity had been putting weapons in space for eighty years—some were hidden in satellite systems, ready to take out other nations' satellites or a target on Earth—so the concept of weapons in space wasn't exactly a new concept, but putting them on a spaceship designed for scientific exploration was. Michael had been in the military, and he knew that the Endurance wasn't a warship, but it was the only thing they had at the moment. Michael guessed that at least some people were taking the Xiiginn threat seriously.

A U.S. Air Force Colonel by the name of Kyle Matthews commanded the Endurance. Like the Athena, the Endurance's crew was a mix of astronauts and military personnel but with more of the latter for the Endurance. Michael knew the original plan had been for the Endurance to go to Pluto for Michael and Chazen; however, with the radical changes to the spaceship, and since it was a short trip, they would stay aboard the life pod until they reached the lunar base.

Since they'd come into contact with the Endurance and were almost to the lunar base, Michael could hardly sit still. The life pod was becoming cramped. Chazen seemed to take this in stride, and Michael tried to contain his excitement, but he was happy to finally get home.

"Commander," Kyle Matthew's voice said over comms.

"Go ahead," Michael said.

"I thought you'd like to know that we're inserting into a lunar synchronous orbit. After that, we'll detach the pod and you'll be shuttled to the base," Kyle said.

"Sounds good. We appreciate you coming to give us a ride," Michael said.

"Glad we could help," Kyle said.

The Endurance slowed its speed and eventually came to the position that made shuttle approach to the lunar base feasible. The life pod had nothing in the way of gravity fields or inertia dampeners, but the Endurance's gravity field was able to extend to the life pod for short durations. This meant that Michael and Chazen had to stand on the walls for a while. Once they were in position, the gravity field was withdrawn. During the planning phase, Michael had thought they would exit the pod and shuttle down to the lunar surface, but Chazen insisted that they needed the equipment they'd brought with them and that the pod must remain intact.

They detached from the Endurance, and Michael didn't even hear the clamps release. It was a bit unnerving to have no windows at all. Michael could see what was going on with the small holoscreen, but it wasn't the same. The holoscreen showed the shuttle moving into position below them while the Endurance moved away from them. Chazen worked on the holo-interface. The Boxan had a device that would allow them to stay with the shuttle without physically attaching to it. Chazen had described it as a micro-field generator that allowed them to hover along the shuttle's surface. It was extremely power-intensive, which was why they hadn't been able to use it for the few days it had taken the Endurance to bring them here. Chazen engaged the device and gave Michael a nod.

"We're ready," Michael said.

"Copy that. We'll take you forward nice and easy," Kyle replied.

Michael felt his body press against the straps as the shuttle started to move. His eyes were locked onto the screen. The lunar base was comprised of a few surface buildings, with the bulk of the base located underground. One thing NASA had learned was that digging out caverns on the moon was relatively easy to do. The challenge had been getting the equipment in place.

The shuttle approached the designated landing area for them and set the pod down. Lunar base personnel came over with tethers. Chazen had assured them that they could literally pull them down to the lunar surface, and he'd been right. They cleared the shuttle, and Chazen disengaged the device. The moon's gravity did the rest. They already had their full spacesuits on, and Michael expended the atmosphere. Chazen motioned for him to open the door, and Michael couldn't keep the eager smile from his face. He opened the door and saw five lunar-base personnel in their EVA suits, waving at him. They were the first people he'd seen in person in about six months, and he had to fight to keep his eyes from misting up.

"Commander Hunsicker, welcome to lunar base. My name is Alissa Archer."

Michael smiled widely and knew he must look like a fool, but he didn't care. Alissa and the others smiled and waved. He stepped out of the pod and waited for Chazen. The Boxan's stooped form exited the life pod, and he unfolded to his full ten-foot stature. Alissa and the others' mouths were agape in wonder.

"On behalf of all humanity, I'm very pleased to welcome you to lunar base," Alissa said to the Boxan.

Chazen glanced down at her. Michael noticed that the Boxan had kept his helmet clear so they could see his face.

"Thank you," Chazen said.

"If you both will follow me, we'll guide you to decontamination chambers set aside for you. The rest of the crew here will move the pod to the adjacent chambers so you will have access to your things," Alissa said.

Michael was glad for that. He knew there would be plenty of people chomping at the bit for access to alien technology.

Chazen glanced at Michael and then back at Alissa. "I appreciate that . . . Are you the commander of this station?"

"I am," Alissa said.

"In that case, thank you, Commander," Chazen said.

They followed Alissa to the surface capsule they'd use to reach the base's interior. Inside was an elevator that would take them below the surface. They rode the elevator down, and Alissa led them to their temporary housing. They passed very few people, but anyone they did come upon looked at Chazen in awe.

The Boxan glanced at him.

"Well, you are quite tall," Michael said.

Chazen didn't reply.

"Hold on one moment, please," Alissa said and accessed her suit's computer. "Change of plans. I'm to take you to a comms station immediately."

Michael frowned. "Is there a problem?"

Alissa frowned. "I'm not sure, but they want to speak to both of you immediately."

"What about decontamination protocols?" Michael asked.

"We'll do what we can to minimize exposure, but this sounded urgent," Alissa said.

She led them through a series of short corridors to a small command center, stopping outside the door and removing her helmet. "I don't believe you're contaminated with anything that's going to harm us; otherwise, Michael would have been affected long before now. So if you want to remove your helmet, you can do so on my authority."

They'd already gone through a basic decon room before even coming inside the base. Michael removed his helmet, and Chazen retracted his into his suit. Alissa seemed surprised by this for a moment, and Michael thought that this was how he must have looked when he'd first met Chazen. She opened the door, and the people inside turned around at the sound of Chazen's heavy footfalls.

"Change in plans, people," Alissa said, snapping them out of their reactions at seeing their first alien.

Michael had been watching Chazen's reactions and was quite pleased with how the Boxan was coping so far.

"Commander," Michael said, and Alissa leaned over to him. "If all nonessential personnel could give us a few minutes here, I think that would be good."

Alissa nodded. "All nonessentials, clear the room," she ordered.

Several people left for the opposite exit and the rest returned to their stations. More than one person kept glancing over at them, and Michael could hardly blame them.

"Commander," a younger man said, "I have Houston on comms."

"Put them on screen, Jack."

The main wall screen came on, and Michael saw Edward Johnson's face appear, along with Gary Hunter.

"Welcome back, Michael," Ed said.

"Thank you," Michael replied.

Ed turned his gaze to Chazen. "There are a lot of people anxious to meet you. I wish I had more time to give this occasion the attention it deserves, but we find ourselves in need of your expertise," Ed said, and his gaze included Michael.

"What do you need?" Michael asked.

"Our gravity-wave detectors reveal an anomaly on the fringes of the interior solar system."

"By Pluto?" Michael asked.

Ed shook his head. "No, far from its orbital path. We'd like you to take a look at the sensor data and see if you can tell us what this is."

Michael glanced up at Chazen, and the Boxan considered the request.

"I'll look at the data," Chazen said and glanced down at Alissa. "I'll need access to my equipment sooner than expected."

"Equipment?" Ed asked.

"We salvaged what we could bring from the station, including the AI," Michael said. "I'm guessing we're going to need it."

Chazen nodded. "It will help speed up the analysis."

Alissa was about to speak, but Edward Johnson cut her off.

"Commander, give them whatever they need. Time is of the essence, and until the ECF is formally ratified, we need to move forward," Ed said.

"I understand the need to move forward, but you don't have the authority to approve this," Alissa said.

"You're right I don't, and you'd be fully within your rights to deny the request, but what if Chazen can identify whether the Xiiginns have found our solar system? The sooner we learn that, the better we'll be able to prepare."

Michael watched as Alissa considered what Ed said and then gave a nod. "They'll have what they need to identify the anomaly."

Michael got the sense that Alissa was a stickler for the rules. Most people who worked in space did so because they were saving lives. There were no space cowboys. But sometimes, in the face of the unknown, some of the red tape had to be cut through quickly. Chances were that if Alissa waited for the proper authority to grant the request, they would do so anyway.

"Alright, let's get to work," Alissa said.

So much for a long rest isolated in a decontamination chamber, but Michael didn't care. He was happy to be among his own kind, and he felt a renewed sense of determination to help Chazen get back to his home, no matter how long it took.

21

The young Xiiginn stared smugly in the video log message that Mar Arden had just paused. Sion Shif had tracked multiple wormholes from the Qegi star system, and analysis had revealed that the Boxans had been keenly interested in one of the moons in the system. When the attack had been ordered, the Boxans destroyed the site they'd been working on. Mar Arden knew about an ancient species called the Drars that the Boxans highly revered, and somehow Mar Arden couldn't convince himself that the Boxans return to the Qegi star system had been purely academic. He glanced at Sion Shif's face onscreen and continued the message.

"We've discovered a wormhole remnant that appeared to have been opened from inside the asteroid base. The destruction of the base must have covered up any residual distortions. By the time you receive this message, we will have gone through to follow," Sion Shif said.

Mar Arden felt his tail flick in response to his rising anger, but he got himself under control and gave himself a sharp mental shake at such a blatant display of emotion. Only Kladomaor would open up a wormhole inside an asteroid space station to escape its destruction. He wanted to hunt them down, and now it looked like he wouldn't get the chance.

Hoan Berend sent him a message summoning him to the bridge, so Mar Arden scowled at the image of Sion Shif's face and closed the video. He knew he should be proud of his young operative, but he also knew the commander of the scout ship would blunder along, believing he could catch a battle commander like Kladomaor unaware; however, the events that had taken place in the Nershal star system spoke volumes about what the old battle commander was willing to do to keep the Humans out of Xiiginn hands.

Mar Arden headed for the bridge. Kandra Rene waited outside for him.

"More ships have been reporting in," Kandra Rene said.

"Do you know what they want?" Mar Arden asked.

Kandra Rene shook her head, and they entered the bridge. Mar Arden went in first, as was his right, and headed directly over to Hoan Berend.

The commander sat in his chair and glanced up at Mar Arden's approach. A haughty smile played across his face, and Mar Arden began to consider whether to have the ship commander killed.

"You've summoned me," Mar Arden said.

Hoan Berend shook his head and gestured toward the main holoscreen. The face of an older Xiiginn filled the screen, and his dangerous gaze peered down at Mar Arden.

Mar Arden instantly bowed his head. Those on the bridge stopped what they were doing and stood up to salute the supreme leader.

"Garm Antis," Mar Arden said. "I had no idea you'd be coming and with an entire strike legion."

That was a lie, of course, and someone like Garm Antis would be able to see right through it, but this was how the game was played.

"Have you located the home of this Human species?" Garm Antis asked.

Mar Arden knew he couldn't stall any longer. Sion Shif and the scout ship had left the Qegi star system more than two cycles ago, and he'd been stalling his efforts until he received the update. The timing of Garm Antis's appearance with a strike legion of warships seemed almost too timely for it to be happenstance.

"Only just so. Some would say your timing is fortuitous," Mar Arden said and took control of the main holodisplay's output. "We tracked this wormhole to a singular star system with nine planetary bodies."

Garm Antis glanced at the data feed and narrowed his gaze. "That's not a traditional wormhole signature coming from a Cherubian drive."

"The Human vessel appears not to have a Cherubian drive. I suspect that the Boxan monitoring station in the Human star system is completely intact, including the Star Shroud devices," Mar Arden said.

Garm Antis glanced back at him, and his platinum-colored hair gracefully followed his movements. "You've done well, Mar Arden," he said and glanced past him, focusing on Hoan Berend. "Attach your ship to the strike legion. You'll be joining us when we leave."

"I've given you what you asked for, and I'd like permission to take a ship and pursue the Boxan/Human team that escaped our attack," Mar Arden said. No sooner had the words escaped his lips than he wanted to take them back.

Garm Antis regarded him for a moment. "You've done well, but you presume much. Hoan Berend has informed me that the ones you're so eager to find are already being pursued. Besides, I need your talents for this new species," he said.

Mar Arden bowed his head. "I would advise caution. We may not be unopposed there."

"The Humans can hardly resist us," Garm Antis said.

"I meant the Boxans," Mar Arden said.

The supreme leader glanced at the ship commander as if he needed to check whether or not what Mar Arden had just said was reliable. Failure exacted a toll, and he had to keep the wounding of his pride to a minimum.

"What evidence do you have to support this?" Garm Antis asked.

"I have no hard evidence, but based on the Boxans' actions in the Nershal star system and the lengths they went through to keep the Humans from falling into our hands, it seems highly likely. The Boxans risked open conflict in another species' star system, and that species was not formally aligned with them. As you're aware, they escaped their asteroid base, but they went in a direction away from charted space. All these things are highly irregular for the Boxans," Mar Arden said.

A Xiiginn came up to Garm Antis and leaned in to say something only the supreme leader could hear. Garm Antis looked back at Mar Arden. "There is conjecture, and then there is skilled analysis. The Boxans don't wield power among the stars as they once did, and they haven't won a battle against us in some time. The Confederation believes they're broken, and we're observing the final death throes of those who once believed they were our superiors."

"Perhaps," Mar Arden said, neither agreeing with the supreme leader nor disagreeing with him.

"Once our forces are ready, we will go to this new star system and finally gain access to a working Star Shroud network, not to mention a new species to rule," Garm Antis said.

The primary display went back to normal as communications from the supreme leader's flagship was cut. It wasn't often that Mar Arden was dismissed, and it seemed that his tolerance for it declined the higher in rank he rose. He glanced at Hoan Berend, but the Xiiginn's gaze was fixed on his console.

"What is it?" Mar Arden asked, trying to keep the ire from his tone.

"We're receiving orders," Hoan Berend said.

Mar Arden waited for the commander to continue, and with each passing moment had to keep from lashing out at him.

"It seems that Garm Antis has grown tired of waiting. We leave for the Human star system now," Hoan Berend said.

Mar Arden felt a thrill of energy spike through him.

Kandra Rene leaned over to him. "I felt that," she said in a low voice.

Mar Arden glanced at her but didn't say anything. It appeared that he was to be part of the subjugation of another species, and the thought of it appealed to the primal hunger that resided in all Xiiginns—the hunger that drove them to hunt and rise to become the dominant force in the galaxy.

22

Kaylan made the crew of the Athena snag sleep shifts in a rotation, which included herself. The closer they got to their destination, the harder it was to sleep. No one was getting any rest, and they were all on edge. She hadn't felt anything like this since they'd first gone to Pluto.

She closed her eyes and tried to peer ahead with her senses. Like all the other times, she felt as if she were coming up against something slippery that wouldn't allow her to focus, but she didn't let that perturb her efforts. She knew so much more now, and she pressed onward, trying different things. Their sensors confirmed that this Star Shroud was more of a planetary shroud and that there was no star in this area. The AI theorized that there hadn't been a star in this area for millions of years—hardly the blink of an eye when dealing with the universe —but believing that they were approaching something that could be millions of years old left quite the impression on all of them.

The shroud was spherical in shape. Kaylan continued to probe with her senses, delving further beyond where the shroud should have ended, and each time she experienced some success she was shut out again. She caught glimpses of some type of structure inside but not enough to accurately describe what it looked like. Something was inside, and it knew they were coming. The fact that it could also detect Kaylan's attempts to see inside was both surprising and unsettling. Hicks hadn't liked that fact one bit. She recalled a time when she hadn't wanted anyone to know about her remote viewing capability, but they'd come to rely on it, and it hardly occurred to her to hide anything from them anymore.

The closer they got, the more she believed they were meant to be here. Whatever was inside this shroud wanted them here—apparently without their Boxan escorts. She supposed she should have been more worried about that, but if the Drars had wanted them dead, then they would be dead. It was as simple as that. Hicks was still worried though. The career military man didn't like going into a situation there was no escape from.

They were all hands on deck—light years beyond where any Human had gone before.

"Radiation levels are climbing," Zack said.

Kaylan adjusted their approach.

"We're almost to the point of no return," Hicks said.

"I know," Kaylan replied.

The magnetic field shifted during their approach, as if whatever was inside was tracking them.

"Any change from shroud protocols?" Kaylan asked.

"Just trackbacks letting us know they're there," Zack replied.

Kaylan had point on the Athena's controls, and Hicks was her backup if something happened to her. As they approached a patch of space that was seemingly innocuous, the crew of the Athena remained focused on their jobs but kept waiting. Zack had estimated that the shroud had a circumference similar to Saturn's. There were no moons or anything at all in orbit.

Kaylan extended her senses ahead, and her perception of the bridge of the Athena blurred in her mind. She was out beyond the ship, racing headlong into the unknown.

You brought us here. Now let us in, Kaylan thought.

As if in response to her thoughts, a sliver of pale light ignited and quickly spread out. From the recesses of her mind, she heard the others' exclamations at the sight. She even heard Zack call to her and Hicks asking him to be quiet so she could concentrate. A swirling vortex, large enough for the Athena to fit through, opened. Kaylan didn't adjust their speed, trusting that whatever had opened the door for them knew what it was doing.

They went into the vortex.

"Radiation levels have gone way down. It's like we're not out in space anymore. Athena, can you confirm?" Zack asked.

"Sensor diagnostics do not indicate any problems. Minimal atmosphere detected with traces of nitrogen," the AI answered.

Beyond the edge of the shroud, Kaylan saw a megastructure. Playing a hunch, she attempted to adjust their course, but it failed. They were locked on. She pulled her hands away from the console.

"Looks like they're in the driver's seat now," Kaylan said.

"Acknowledged," Hicks said.

"Look at the size of that thing," Zack said. "It's like they built a planet-sized city way out here in deep space."

Kaylan peered at the holoscreen in front of her and magnified the image. "Looks like it's been here a while. Only that place up ahead has power. The rest of it looks brittle, and several areas have collapsed."

Zack came over to them and glanced out the window. One of the long arms that extended away from the center of a structure lost its support and came crashing down. This caused a domino effect for the other squarish buildings in the vicinity. A plume of debris rose and then fell back down.

Kaylan frowned and checked the data pumping in from their sensors. "There is an atmosphere in here, but the composition has too much oxygen for us."

"Not dying from O2 poisoning. Check," Zack said.

"We'll need to suit up for this one," Hicks said and glanced at Zack.

Zack tried to play it off as if he was unimpressed. "You've seen one alien structure, you've seen 'em all. I think I'll stay on the ship this time." He glanced out the window again. "I wonder where the light comes from."

Kaylan followed his gaze. There was light everywhere—not bright sunshine but a place of perpetual twilight. She kept checking the comms channels, but there was nothing. She'd assumed they would have been contacted by now. She glanced around at the ruins of the vast alien city. There was a brownish tinge to most of it, and if she didn't know better, she'd have thought the buildings were rusting. She supposed the high amounts of oxygen in the artificial atmosphere could have caused this over time, but any civilization that could build something like this wouldn't fall victim to oxidation.

They quickly approached the main central structures. The buildings here were made up of harsh angular planes with pyramid-type symmetry. The Athena changed its approach trajectory to a massive central column. Offshoots of the column extended away like the points on a compass.

Kaylan cut the engines, but the Athena kept moving. Large bay doors opened and the Athena went inside the mega structure. The corridors inside could have accommodated tens of thousands of Athena-sized ships. They came to a much smaller chamber, and the Athena descended. The ground beneath them began to glow with an amber-colored light, and the ship came to a stop. Kaylan noted that inside this chamber there was almost no damage to the structure.

"So now what?" Zack asked.

"Now we have a look around," Kaylan said and climbed out of her chair.

"How will we even get down to the ground?" Zack asked.

Hicks glanced out of the window and then brought up the video feed from the port airlock. "Looks like there's a platform waiting for us."

"Great—a platform. How thoughtful of them," Zack said.

They headed for the door to the bridge, but it opened ahead of them. Standing on the other side was Brenda with a very lucid Jonah Redford.

"Hello, Commander," Redford said.

Kaylan gasped and glanced at Brenda. "How?"

Brenda smiled. "I don't know, but as soon as we passed through the shroud, Jonah's symptoms started to improve."

"The brain scans still show damage, but the strokes have stopped, as well as the . . . voices," Redford said.

Kaylan didn't know what to say. She was relieved to see Jonah's improved condition, but she couldn't trust it. "I'm glad you're feeling better. Can you remember anything that's happened?" she asked.

Redford frowned. "It's a bit hazy and jumbled together. Brenda showed me some of the things."

"It has to be this place," Zack said.

"You could be right," Kaylan said.

"We need to decide on the away team," Hicks said.

Redford cleared his throat. "I'd like to come along," he said.

"Absolutely not," Hicks said and looked at Kaylan. "There's no way for us to know if whatever is reversing or halting his condition won't simply stop."

Kaylan pressed her lips together. Her first instinct was to agree with Hicks, but something in Redford's expression gave her pause. He seemed calm and at peace.

"I can't offer you any assurances," Redford said and glanced away. "At least none that *I* would trust anyway."

Kaylan drew in a breath and glanced at the crew of the Athena. "No one stays behind this time. We're all going in."

They met at the port airlock near the shuttle. Kaylan supposed that if there was no safe means to get them to the ground, they could use the shuttle. They all got into their EVA suits. Hicks and Katie had armed themselves. Zack reached inside his locker and withdrew his pulse rifle that Etanu had given him. He gave it a long look, deciding whether or not he wanted to take it with him, and then hung the strap over his shoulder. Hicks looked as if he were about to say something when Katie leaned over and quietly spoke to him. Eventually Hicks gave her a nod.

"Looks like everyone is almost ready. I don't know what we'll find once we leave the ship, but we'll stick together. It doesn't look as if anyone has been here in a long time," Kaylan said.

"I'm not sure if anyone has been here ever," Zack said.

"What do you mean?" Kaylan asked.

"From everything we saw coming in here, it didn't look like anyone actually lived here. There were no vehicles of any kind or anything like that," Zack said.

"He's right," Emma said. "Anyone who actually lived here would have left some sign of life. This place is more like move-in ready, or at least it was at one time."

The crew of the Athena had long gotten used to Zack's keen observations. Kaylan nodded and moved toward the airlock. After receiving an all-clear from the others, she stepped inside. The port airlock could only accommodate five of them at a time, so they split into two groups. Kaylan opened the door to a floating metallic platform just outside. There was no control console or other visible means of control.

"Great, no railings," Zack said.

Kaylan took a step onto the platform, and it felt as if she were stepping onto solid ground. Zack followed her and kept glancing down at his feet. The surface appeared solid, and as she took a closer look, she saw that it was actually swirling as if it was in constant motion. Zack slammed his foot down, hard, and Kaylan jumped.

"Are you crazy?" Kaylan said. "You don't know what that could have done."

Zack looked at her in alarm. "I didn't mean to scare you," he chuckled, "but it doesn't look like I even made a dent. So much for my mighty foot stomp."

Kaylan looked down and saw that Zack was right. The others joined them, and Hicks closed the door to the Athena so the rest of them could come outside.

"I'm not sure this platform is going to be big enough for everyone," Zack said.

The platform then started spreading, becoming a longer rectangle to accommodate the rest of the crew.

Zack glanced up and let out a nervous laugh. "Ever get the feeling someone is listening to you?"

"Empirical evidence would suggest that we are being monitored," the AI said, its voice coming through the speakers in Kaylan's helmet.

"Thank you, Athena," Zack said. "Are you able to detect them?"

"I've tried several thousand connection attempts using both Human and Boxan protocols, and none of them are working."

"I guess they're not ready to talk to us yet," Zack said.

Kaylan watched as the rest of the crew joined them on the floating platform. Once they had secured the airlock door, the platform began a downward descent. As they reached the ground, the platform hovered above it and then was absorbed into the surface in front of a short path that led inside. Kaylan accessed her suit computer and made sure she could access the shuttle's systems in case they needed to be picked up, but her connections were abruptly severed.

"Zack, can you access the Athena's systems?" Kaylan asked.

Zack frowned for a moment and shook his head. "I'm cut off," he said.

The rest of the crew had the same experience. Kaylan's eyes widened as the Athena pulled away from them and sped off.

"What the hell!" Zack shouted.

"The ship is gone!" Emma cried.

Kaylan glanced at Hicks, who clutched the rifle in his hand. Kaylan tried to raise the Athena on her comms.

"Commander, I'm not able to reach out to you. The control systems are not responding," the AI said.

"What about the shuttle?" Kaylan asked.

"Just locked out," the AI said.

Some of the others groaned.

"Why would they take the ship?" Zack asked.

"To prevent us from leaving," Hicks said.

Kaylan frowned. "I'm not sure. We couldn't leave if we wanted to."

"I don't like that they took the ship," Hicks said in a low voice.

"I don't like it either, but we can't just stay here, waiting for it to come back," Kaylan said.

"Maybe we can find a console inside and figure out where the ship is from there," Zack offered.

There was a loud crash on the far side of the vast chamber as one of the towers collapsed, and Kaylan wondered whether the area they were in would stay standing while they were inside.

"We can't stay here. Let's get moving," Kaylan said.

She strode down the path, and the large door in front of them dissolved. Hicks insisted on going through first, and he did so, keeping his rifle ready. After performing a quick check, he waved the rest of them through. Kaylan could have told him the area was clear but didn't. Just because she couldn't see any other creatures here didn't mean there wasn't something lurking, unseen. After the rest of them had come inside, the door rematerialized behind them. Katie tapped it with her gloved hand and shook her head.

The further they went, the more she thought that Zack's initial observations had been correct. It didn't look like anything had ever lived here. The doorways and corridors were of a size to accommodate a large species like the Boxans, but the plain walls gave no indication of who the Drars actually were. There were no consoles or visible controls for the doors. They were being guided inside, but Kaylan couldn't say for sure where they were being led.

"No, if you detect something, you should tell the rest of the crew. What would you do if I wasn't here?" Zack said.

Kaylan stopped and looked at Zack.

"The AI says there's something on the other side of this wall," Zack said.

"I was merely asking your opinion, Zack," the AI said. "You often point out that I sometimes reveal facts relating to zero percent survivability with no tact."

Zack's brows pushed forward, and Kaylan knew that if he hadn't had a helmet on he would have been rubbing his forehead in consternation.

"Just tell them what you told me," Zack said.

"Faint power source detected beyond this wall," the AI said. "The readings sometimes spike and then disappear altogether."

"Over here?" Kaylan asked, gesturing to the side.

"Affirmative, Commander," the AI said.

Kaylan focused on the wall, but before she could extend her senses, a large portion of the wall evaporated.

"That's so weird," Zack said. "I think I prefer doors that look like doors and open like doors should open."

There was an aqua-colored glow coming from the room beyond. Kaylan stepped inside and rounded the corner. On a large, elevated platform there was a glowing round sphere that seemed to be made up of some type of energy, and it just hovered there with no source visible anywhere. It was the color of transparent cyan, and Kaylan could see through the thing. The sphere itself was the size of a large house. As the crew of the Athena stepped closer, the door rematerialized behind them, but, unlike the other areas, there wasn't anywhere else for them to go.

"Commander, I'm receiving a message," the AI said.

The sphere pulsated as if it were a living entity. Swirling eddies of energy coursed around it.

"Can you translate it?" Kaylan asked.

"No need, I've forwarded the message to all of you, and it should appear on your suit displays now," the AI said.

Kaylan gasped as a single word appeared on her HUD. She glanced at Zack and the others. They were all seeing the same word.

SUBMIT.

23

Kladomaor scowled at the main holoscreen. Their sensors had detected trace returns for the Athena, but with their comms systems still down they couldn't open a comms signal to them.

"Do you have them back?" Kladomaor asked.

"Negative, Commander," Triflan said. "It's like they've disappeared."

Kladomaor stood up from his command couch. He wanted to take the biggest weapon he could find and demolish everything in his path. They'd been tracking the Athena's path since the incident.

"Commander, the shroud signal has stopped as well," Triflan said.

The shroud signal had been another surprise, and it had given him enough reason to put other repairs on hold while they raced to catch up with their wayward Human spaceship. He glanced over at Ma'jasalax, but the Mardoxian priestess shook her head.

"Activate scans. I want to know what's in the area. Single sweep only," Kladomaor said.

No need to keep broadcasting their position. They still couldn't go into stealth mode, but he seriously doubted that whatever had knocked them out of the wormhole could be fooled by their stealth technology.

"Take us in, Varek," Kladomaor ordered.

"Acknowledged, Battle Commander," Varek confirmed.

Kladomaor returned to his station. He was still connected to the ship's computer system, and those data feeds still showed information from their sensors. They were at forty percent combat capability, and Kladomaor supposed that was the best they were going to get for a while. There was still work to be done on the Cherubian drive, which was being addressed by his engineering team.

He glanced over at Gaarokk. "What do you make of this?"

"We should be cautious. The Drars led us here for a reason, but they apparently wanted the Humans alone," Gaarokk said.

"There were other ways they could have done this. They didn't have to attack us while in the wormhole," Kladomaor said.

"Perhaps it was a test," Ma'jasalax said.

"Of the Humans?" he asked.

"Of us. Perhaps they were just seeing what we'd do," Ma'jasalax said.

"There's more than a Star Shroud here. This is something else," Kladomaor said.

"I'm counting on it," Ma'jasalax said.

Kladomaor weighed his options. They were closing in fast, and the area of space that the Athena had disappeared into appeared to be distorted.

"Does the distortion give us any clues as to what's there?" Kladomaor asked.

Gaarokk frowned and looked over at him. "It looks like the entire area resides on the edge of an accretion disk, which is causing the distortion, but it's not truly a distortion. That part of space is out of phase with where we are. Chances are the Athena is just inside it."

"Infinity's Edge," Kladomaor said.

"Until they come out the other side, at least," Gaarokk replied.

Ma'jasalax stopped speaking to Ezerah and came over to them.

"What's Infinity's Edge?" Ezerah asked.

"We use the Cherubian drive to create a wormhole to cross vast distances of the great expanse. If we were to change our trajectory upon entering the wormhole, we would begin to shift from our current position but never reach our destination. No one really knows where those ships go when that happens. They're lost," Gaarokk said.

Ezerah frowned. "But we've changed our trajectory inside wormholes before."

"Correct, but never when we first enter them. It's also the reason why we can't go backward out of a wormhole," Gaarokk said. "If Kladomaor is correct, the Drars were able to utilize this theoretical principle beyond anything we've even conceived of."

"Increased energy readings from the shroud, Battle Commander," Triflan reported.

"On screen," Kladomaor said and focused his attention on the screen. There was a glowing mass gathering directly in front of them.

"All stop," Kladomaor said.

"Confirmed, Battle Commander," Varek said.

Kladomaor watched the glowing mass and then glanced at Triflan. "Report," he said.

"Energy readings remain steady."

Kladomaor blew out a breath. "Back us away," he said.

He watched as the calculated distance to the shroud increased, and he ordered Varek to stop the ship.

"Energy readings are decreasing," Triflan said.

The glowing mass diminished until they couldn't see it onscreen anymore.

"A warning?" Ma'jasalax said.

Kladomaor nodded. "That's what I was thinking."

"If we can't get any closer without them firing a weapon at us, how are we supposed to help the Athena?" Gaarokk asked.

"I don't know," Kladomaor said, and with each word his scowl deepened.

They circled the shroud, maintaining their distance, but each time they tried to move in closer, the energy readings coming from the shroud spiked.

"I'm not sure how the Athena even made it inside," Gaarokk said.

Kladomaor glanced over at the scientist and waited for him to continue.

"The shroud is surrounded by a powerful magnetic field that should have overwhelmed a ship like the Athena," Gaarokk said.

"There are ways to circumvent that. Perhaps they got in that way. Or they were simply allowed to enter," Kladomaor said.

He scratched the side of his craggy face. There was no way they could get inside. He didn't want to chance trading blows with the Drars. He glanced at the comms station, but there was still no reply to any of their hails. This wasn't the first time they'd come across Drar technology during their search for them, but this was the most complete. Until now, they'd only found pieces, but it seemed that just beyond the shroud was an entire Drar installation.

"We'll have to wait," Ma'jasalax said.

Kladomaor stretched his arms. "How much power could they really have? It was our ancient ancestors who observed the wars involving the Drars. They were the ones who deciphered their message. We should be allowed to go inside, unless . . ."

"The Drars didn't actually build that place," Ma'jasalax said.

Kladomaor gripped the ends of his command couch. The Humans were in trouble. "Battle stations," he said.

The Boxans raced back to their stations.

"I want auxiliary power diverted to the engines," Kladomaor said.

"Acknowledged," Triflan said.

"All ahead full, but be ready to execute evasive maneuvers," Kladomaor said.

"Battle Commander, our weapons systems are still offline," Triflan said.

"I know, and they'll stay that way," Kladomaor said.

The Boxan stealth ship lurched forward in a sudden burst of speed, and the glowing mass immediately returned, gathering in intensity.

"Angle our approach," Kladomaor ordered.

Varek confirmed the order, and Kladomaor watched as the glowing mass followed them along the shroud.

"Bring us in closer," Kladomaor said.

The Boxan ship closed in on the shroud. The glowing mass became a deep orange, and then a molten beam shot toward them.

Varek changed their trajectory and barely dodged the weapon.

"That beam will destroy the ship immediately," Triflan said.

Kladomaor watched as another beam shot toward their ship. Varek changed course again, but the beam grazed the top plating.

"Take us in," Kladomaor said.

"Don't," Ma'jasalax cried. "They're learning our tactics. Each shot gets closer. Withdraw."

Kladomaor clenched his teeth and glared at the holoscreen. Another shot was being primed. "Get us out of here," he said finally.

Varek changed course again, taking them away, and the killing shot never came. The glowing mass faded but kept a bead on the Boxan ship.

They reached the distance they'd been at before his attempt to breach the defenses.

"Battle Commander," Gaarokk said.

Kladomaor looked over at Gaarokk. "What is it?"

"The sensors are showing a slight decrease in diameter of the distortion as a whole," Gaarokk said.

Kladomaor frowned in thought.

"It could be that the energy expended to fire that beam at us could have taxed the system, but without knowing the capacity, we can't be sure how long it would take to drain it fully," Gaarokk said.

Kladomaor nodded. "So they're not completely infallible."

"Should we make another run? See if we can drain the energy some more?" Triflan asked.

Kladomaor scanned through the data on the screen. Varek had done well with evasive maneuvers, but with each shot, the margin of error decreased. He could rotate another helmsman since Varek wasn't the only pilot they had.

"May I have a word with you, please?" Ma'jasalax said.

Kladomaor waved her over, knowing that not listening to Ma'jasalax could cost him more in the long run. He'd also come to rely on the Mardoxian priestess's insights.

"You shouldn't do this," Ma'jasalax said quietly. "Kaylan and the others are inside, and we don't know what will happen to them inside if we continue to—"

"Contact, Battle Commander," Triflan announced.

Kladomaor swung his gaze to the holoscreen but didn't see anything coming from the Drar installation.

"It's coming from behind us, Battle Commander," Triflan said.

A secondary display appeared on screen, showing the contact that the AI had assigned the designation alpha.

"Varek, bring us around. Passive scans only," Kladomaor said.

"Passive scan burst initiated," Triflan said.

Kladomaor and the rest of the crew on the bridge waited. Fighting wars in space involved a lot of waiting before an actual engagement occurred, but an effective commander almost never rushed in—at least not the ones who lived long. There were times to take that gamble, such as he'd done with the shroud, and he'd come away having learned something about his adversary.

"Xiiginn contact, Battle Commander, scout class ship," Triflan said.

Kladomaor narrowed his gaze and was relieved that it wasn't a Xiiginn warship out there hunting for them. Without stealth, they stood no chance against a warship, even one with a poor commander, but a Xiiginn scout ship with full weapons capability still had the capacity to take them out. Xiiginn High

Command must not have been wholly convinced they had escaped from the asteroid space station, but Mar Arden undoubtedly convinced them to send a scout ship to track them. Kladomaor rubbed the tips of his fingers together while he was thinking. The mere thought of Mar Arden was enough to ignite his anger, but he couldn't allow that to affect his judgment. The lives of his fellow Boxans and that of the Human crew of the Athena were all depending on him. He couldn't assume Mar Arden was aboard that ship.

"Hold our current position," Kladomaor said.

Gaarokk looked at him questioningly. Since the scientist had been with Kladomaor for so long, he sometimes forgot that Gaarokk wasn't familiar with military tactics.

"Our stealth capabilities are damaged, and we have limited combat capability, so meeting our enemy head-on isn't our best choice. They may have tracked us here, but I'm willing to wager that their commander has stumbled a lot along the way, given that our trek here wasn't a straight shot through a wormhole," Kladomaor said.

"Do they see us?" Gaarokk asked.

"Not yet. While active scans would certainly reveal our position, we do have some cover from the distortion field of the Drar installation. I think they'll be preoccupied with that," Kladomaor said.

"What are you going to do?"

"We wait. We'll hold this position and see what they're going to do."

"You don't mean to attack them?"

"Oh, we'll attack them. Just not yet. Attacking them now at this range would better serve them than us. We cannot allow them the slightest chance to get access to the Drar installation," Kladomaor said.

Gaarokk frowned in thought. "Why not allow them to approach and let the Drar weapons system we've been dodging finish them off?"

"We can't."

"Why not?"

"Because the crew of the Athena is inside that thing, and we don't know what will happen to those inside if we continue to drain the energy from it. Don't forget, if this truly is of Drar origin, it has had many cycles in the great expanse and could very well be at the end of its lifecycle," Kladomaor said.

Gaarokk nodded. "Battle Commander," he acknowledged as a show of respect.

Kladomaor continued to weigh his options, but all he could really do at the moment was wait to see what that Xiiginn scout ship would do next. They were still quite far out, and he had the sneaking suspicion that the crew of the Athena needed all the time he could give them.

24

Michael Hunsicker had thought he'd be able to relax once they reached the lunar base. After all the work he and Chazen had put into the life pod, he was looking forward to taking it easy for a short while before returning to Earth —nothing extensive in terms of time off but just enough to catch his breath. Michael was far from averse to hard work, but they had hardly stopped working since they'd arrived at the lunar base. Chazen could go for extended periods of time without rest, but Michael was reaching his limits. Alissa Archer had offered him sleeping quarters, but Michael wasn't sure it would be a good idea to leave Chazen at this point. The Boxan was most comfortable with him, and Michael didn't want him to feel that he had abandoned him. As a compromise, Alissa had a cot brought to the office that was connected to the secondary command and control room where they were working and told him to get some sleep.

With the help of lunar base personnel, they'd made quick work of extracting the Boxan equipment and setting it up, and Chazen had agreed to let the engineers examine the materials they'd used for the life pod. One of the first things Chazen had set up was the specialized communications equipment he'd brought along that would allow him to transmit the self-destruct sequence to the Boxan listening station on Pluto. The anomaly detected well beyond Pluto's orbit appeared to have gone quiet.

Michael had snagged a few hours' sleep and sat up on the cot, rubbing his eyes. A loud yawn escaped his lips, and he glanced out the office window to see if anyone had noticed. No one had. Most people were still enamored with their exalted guest. He looked at Chazen, who was busy answering questions, and the deep resonance of the Boxan's voice carried all the way to the office. Michael stood up and stretched. He wouldn't have minded a shower, but he didn't know where they were.

Alissa glanced over in his direction and, seeing that he was awake, walked over to the office. She checked her watch as she came inside. "It's only been about four hours since you went to sleep," she said. She took in his appearance with a quizzical brow that reminded him of Kathryn. "I think we can get you a change of clothes and perhaps a shower. If you play your cards right, maybe a hot meal," she said with a wink and led him out of the office.

Michael followed and then lingered in the doorway. He cast a furtive glance at Chazen. "Those all sound great, but I'm not sure I should leave him."

Alissa followed his gaze. "He'll be okay. I think the more he interacts with us the more comfortable he becomes. Come on."

Michael followed Alissa from the room. She was an older woman in her fifties, and her dark hair had hints of gray. She walked with an air of confidence that seemed to take hold of the people around her.

Alissa glanced back at him. "You're not that old. Keep up," she said.

Michael chuckled and quickened his pace to catch up with her.

"What was the Boxan listening station like?" Alissa asked.

"It was incredible. It made us all feel like we were little kids because it was designed for Boxans," Michael said.

"They're not exactly small. I reviewed the Athena mission update file from Kaylan Farrow before you arrived. NASA ordered me locked in a room so I could be brought up to speed. Kaylan was your second in command?" Alissa asked.

"That's right, although after all they've been through, I'm not sure I would want to be in command of that. She's exceptional," Michael said.

"Most women in NASA are," Alissa said.

She led him to the showers on base. Unisex. There were no societal expectations for things like separate bathrooms when one worked and lived off-planet, but it wasn't as if the stalls were out in the open, so there was some measure of privacy. Alissa told him to use one of the showers while she went to get him a change of clothes.

"Should have done this after you arrived," Alissa said, and then Michael heard her leave the room.

Michael turned the water on and stepped into the hot flow. He squeezed his eyes shut and just stood there, relishing the feel of it. The tension left his neck and shoulders as he cocked his head from side to side. He wasn't one for taking long showers, but he didn't want to leave. The only thing that would be better than this would be swimming in the warm turquoise waters of Bermuda. He and his late wife, Kathryn, had taken long strolls on the legendary pink sandy beaches. They'd returned to Bermuda as often as they could over the years, and for the longest time Michael hadn't even considered returning there. Too many memories, he'd told himself, but he found that he didn't feel that way anymore. It had taken a long journey to Pluto and back for him to finally lay his late wife to rest. He still missed her, and the pang in his chest and the back of his eyes was still there when he thought of her, but he was more at peace with it than he'd ever been before.

The door to the outer room opened, and Alissa announced that she'd laid out some clothes for him to change into when he was finished.

"I'll wait outside because I know how you older fellas can get," Alissa joked.

Michael laughed and a few minutes later turned the water off. Jets of air blew the water off his body and dried his skin. There were no towels because water must be conserved, especially on the moon. He saw that Alissa had left a shaving kit for him and put it to good use. The clothes Alissa had brought him fit well enough and were comfortable. He looked like every other person on the base. He glanced at himself in the mirror and pressed his lips together. He could use a haircut, but there wasn't anything he could do about it now.

Alissa smiled at him as he came out. "You clean up nice, Commander."

"Thanks," Michael said.

"Let's see about getting you some real food instead of whatever it was that you've been eating."

"Rations and something Chazen adapted for me."

She led him to the mess hall, and Michael helped himself to some roasted chicken and vegetables. He and Alissa were pretty much left alone while they both quietly ate. It had been months since he'd had real food.

"I'm surprised your resident doctor hasn't been banging down your door to get me into an exam room," Michael said.

Alissa smiled knowingly. "Oh, they tried, but Houston told them to give you some space."

Michael finished eating and was starting to feel himself becoming sleepy again, so he stood up and deposited his tray in the receptacle.

"We should head back," Alissa said. "Do you have any thoughts on Chazen?"

"He's a good . . . guy. I wouldn't be here if it weren't for him. Why do you ask?"

"His presence here is unprecedented. We fully intend to honor the asylum agreement we have with him, but I was asked to provide a preliminary evaluation. He was a bit quiet when he first got here, but that's understandable considering the circumstances. I get the impression, though, that Boxans don't find themselves in need of other people's help very often," Alissa said.

Michael snorted. "You got that right. He's been alone for a long time. I didn't press him very hard for personal information, and I have no idea who he may have left behind on his home planet."

Alissa nodded. "If the rest of the Boxans are like him, they're a dedicated bunch. He spent over sixty years in isolation for his culture. I don't know if I could have done that—or anyone, for that matter."

"He wasn't awake for all of that. He spent large portions of his time in suspended animation."

"Stasis," Alissa said. "Now that *is* interesting. I'm not sure how I'd feel about sleeping my life away."

"Me either," Michael agreed.

They came to the secondary command and control room where they'd left Chazen, and the room was abuzz with activity. Michael and Alissa hastened over to where Chazen was. The Boxan sat on the floor with his back against the wall, and the other people in the room were all talking at once.

"What happened?" Alissa asked.

"There was another anomaly detected, but this one was much closer to Earth," a man named Stevens answered.

Stevens went to one of the consoles and brought up the main wall screen. A Boxan's face Michael had never seen before was onscreen.

"Humans of Earth," the Boxan said, "I am called Prax'pedax. We come here at the behest of the Humans aboard the Athena, and we want you to know that you are not alone in the threat against the Xiiginn."

Michael's eyes widened. The Boxan onscreen looked much older than Chazen and more vigorous, as if he were of some type of warrior-class Boxan that Michael had never seen before. He felt his eyes become misty, and he went to Chazen's side.

"They've come for you," Michael said.

Chazen's large features were awash with emotions—too many and too intense for Michael to accurately count. How does one act after seeing another of their own kind for the first time in sixty years? Michael was pretty sure he wouldn't have been able to stay on his feet either.

25

Edward Johnson would rather have been at Mission Control in Houston, Texas. Instead, he was back at NORAD under the watchful eyes of General Sheridan. Over the past few weeks, he and the general had come to an uneasy understanding. Ed had no doubt that if the general could, he'd lock Ed away and throw away the key. But Ed's presence at NORAD was under presidential authority. To give Ed the gravitas needed, she'd made him one of her special advisors to the president. Presidential authority and the presence of Iris Barrett were enough to irritate the old general. A couple of the general's subordinates had believed they could strong-arm Iris, away from watchful eyes. Those men were still recovering from the damage Ed's assistant had done to them.

Despite all the legwork Dux Corp had put into the Earth Coalition Force, the nations of the world were picking it over and dissecting it at a snail's pace, piece by piece. It had taken three tries for the US government to make basic universal healthcare available to all its citizens—three attempts and several near collapses of the global economy. At this moment, it felt that those historic events had happened much quicker than the UN adopting the creation of the ECF. If the nations tried to meet the threat of the Xiiginns divided, there was little hope that they could survive. Ed wanted more than anything to avoid a future where billions of people perished because the governments of the world couldn't agree on how they were going to defend the Earth from a hostile alien attack force.

The presence of the Boxans was a stroke of good fortune, but the people of Earth shouldn't be looking to the Boxans for direction in governing their planet. The dominion of Earth had to stay entirely within Human control if they were to have a future.

Iris leaned in toward his ear. "Five minutes."

The general watched him, and when Colonel Hines announced the same information, the general seemed to snort to himself.

"One day we'll have to find your source in the White House," Sheridan said.

Ed smiled. "We're on the same side, General. I hope you can believe that."

At that moment, the holoscreens went live, and President Susan Halloway appeared. On one of the other screens, the image of several Boxans was displayed, but it was the one called Prax'pedax that caught his attention. He was the one Kaylan had said would come. There were two Boxan ships heading toward the moon at this very moment.

"Thank you for agreeing to meet with us, Prax'pedax," President Halloway said.

"I'd like to make a few statements to your species," Prax'pedax said.

Ed kept watching the Boxan with a sense of awe that they were actually communicating with an alien species that in many ways was beyond anything imagined on Earth.

"We'll listen to what you have to say," the president said.

"I hope so, for all our sakes. As you know, I've personally met the crew of the Athena. It was because of that meeting and at the behest of a close friend that I am here before your species today. We are here to help Earth defend itself from the Xiiginns using your current technology. We will not share advancements that you weren't already on the road to discovering for yourselves," Prax'pedax said.

"I'm not sure I'm following what you're saying. It's my understanding that you've already shared some of your technology with us and put us on the path that led us where we are today. Will that not continue in the face of the Xiiginn threat?" President Halloway asked.

"As I've said, we will help you harden your lines of defense where the Xiiginns are concerned, and if they do come here, we will help defend the Earth with the use of our ships," Prax'pedax said.

The area around General Sheridan lit up, signifying that he wanted to speak.

"Go ahead, General," President Halloway said.

"We appreciate your offer of assistance, but wouldn't it be prudent to help us build ships of our own so we can learn to defend ourselves?" Sheridan asked.

"Perhaps in time," Prax'pedax said.

This response drew a lot of comments from people around the war room in NORAD, as well as those virtually connected.

"I'm afraid that's not good enough," Sheridan said.

Prax'pedax looked surprised at this response, and Ed had to admit that at this moment he was glad Sheridan was in the position he was in.

"The way I see it, the Xiiginns only know about our planet because you led them here. Your listening station sent one of our ships across the galaxy, putting her crew in harm's way. So for you to come here and say you'll help is a step in the right direction, but what happens to us if you decide to leave or are defeated by the Xiiginns?" Sheridan asked.

Prax'pedax drew in a patient breath. "I understand your concerns. They are admirable, and I can find no fault in the arguments you've raised. Our war with the Xiiginns has been a long one, and it has cost us dearly. Rest assured that neither myself or any Boxan here with me will abandon you to face the Xiiginns alone."

President Halloway came to prominence on screen, and Prax'pedax's gaze shifted to her. "You should know there are other nations on our planet proposing that we meet the Xiiginns at the negotiating table."

Prax'pedax's large flaxen eyes narrowed menacingly. "That would be unfortunate."

"How?"

"Should you meet with the Xiiginns, they will fill your minds with empty promises while they put a shackle around each and every Human on this planet. We've seen them do it to other species—give them technology they're not ready to control and exploit them for resources," Prax'pedax said.

"What kind of resources? Perhaps if we negotiate with them, they'll deal with us peacefully," Dr. Gray asked.

Ed scowled and wished he could send Iris to make that idiot close his mouth.

Prax'pedax leveled his gaze. "The Xiiginns give the appearance of humble offers, but if you let them in, they will ruin your world. The Nershals, a species once again in alliance with us, have learned this firsthand. They've been recently fighting the Xiiginns to get them to leave their star system."

Gray flipped through several documents on his tablet. "Yes, the report from the Athena has it right here. Genetic experimentation was being performed on Nershals. It also says that the Nershals authorized such experiments, so I'm a bit confused as to whether the Nershals are the best example to use."

"Somebody shut this idiot up," Ed growled.

Dr. Gray's mouth rounded in shock.

"The Boxans come here to offer us help and you play political games with them?" Ed said.

"I don't believe I asked for your input. Your time will come, and you'll end up in a cell," Gray said.

"I'll see to it that you end up in a place much worse," Ed said, sneering.

There were a few tense moments as people regained control of their flaring tempers. Suddenly, a sharp sound erupted from Prax'pedax, and Ed had the distinct impression that the Boxan was laughing at them.

President Halloway cleared her throat. "I must apologize. As you can see, there are many differing viewpoints of these events and a good deal of fear about our future. Perhaps you could give us more details about your intentions—what kind of ships you've brought. That sort of thing."

Ed admired Susan Halloway. She was firm when the situation called for it, but she also knew how to calm down those around her.

"We've brought three ships of the wall, Dreadnaught class, capable of providing adequate coverage of your star system. If the Xiiginns come with an invasion force, they'll bring their warships, along with support ships for a long engagement and occupation of your system," Prax'pedax said.

"And just three of your Dreadnaught ships can stand against all of that?" Halloway asked.

"As any veteran of war will tell you, one weapons system is not equal to another. The Xiiginns enjoy a numerical advantage, but what they lack are great tacticians. For example, Kladomaor used his stealth ship to stand against three Xiiginn warships using superior tactics," Prax'pedax said.

General Sheridan cleared his throat. "Superior tactics will only get you so far, but it sounds to me that the fighting force you've brought, along with anything we can muster, will only slow down a real invasion force. Granted that at this moment I don't have the details that are available to you."

Prax'pedax gave the general a nod of respect. "We will share that tactical information with you in order to put up the best defense possible for your species. You are correct. Three ships, even Dreadnaught class, are not enough to protect your star system indefinitely."

"How would you suggest we defend ourselves indefinitely so the Xiiginns will go away?" Sheridan asked.

"You'll learn, you'll adapt, and perhaps you'll overcome," Prax'pedax said.

Ed indicated that he wanted the floor, and Sheridan nodded for him to take it.

"I have a question for you. There has to be a compelling reason for the Xiiginns to come here in such force. We possess something that is highly valued, both by you and the Xiiginns. Is that correct?" Ed asked.

Prax'pedax regarded him for a moment. "You're referring to the evidence that the Mardoxian trait exists within Humans?"

"I am," Ed said.

There was quiet murmuring both by the people near him and elsewhere.

"We've brought our own representative from the Mardoxian sect with us to further validate that claim," Prax'pedax said.

"Just so everyone is on the same page," Ed said, "the sources you were referencing earlier are some of the reasons the Xiiginns are coming here. They may want access to our DNA and other things, but it's this trait they really want. What I would like to know is, what lengths are you authorized to take to keep the Xiiginns from gaining access to that trait?" Ed asked.

A solemn silence took hold of everyone on the call, including the Boxans.

"Regarding authorized actions," Prax'pedax began, "the mandate that brings me here is one of mutual benefit to both our species. I have a certain amount of freedom with which to carry out that mandate, and at the same time I will do what I need to do to preserve my own species."

Ed felt his mouth go dry. "I sincerely hope it never comes to that." He glanced over at General Sheridan. "I have no further questions."

The rest of the call went into logistics, aligning various teams that would meet with Boxan emissaries once they reached Earth. While Ed did pay attention, his thoughts kept going over Prax'pedax's response to his questions.

"Are you alright, Ed? You look a bit shaken up," Iris said after the meeting.

"I am . . . a bit shaken up."

"About what?"

"The Boxans basically said that if they, or we, can't figure out a way to defend ourselves against the Xiiginns, they'll destroy our species just to keep the Xiiginns from using us in their own war with the Boxans," Ed said.

Iris blew out a breath. "Talk about being stuck between a rock and a hard place."

Ed sighed. "Yeah," he said. "We knew this was coming, but Prax'pedax made it all the more real for everyone."

Iris regarded him for a moment. "The question needed to be asked. We needed to know the stakes."

"I know. I think part of me wanted to be wrong," Ed said.

Iris smiled. "That doesn't happen that often . . . or ever as far as I know. Come on. I see that Sheridan wants to speak with you."

26

S UBMIT.

The word appeared on the heads-up display of Zack's helmet. He looked at the others and they'd all been stunned into silence. "Athena, are you sure this isn't a botched translation?"

"Negative. That data was transmitted in clear text," the AI replied.

"Let's not panic. Perhaps it thinks it's sending us a greeting," Kaylan said.

The glowing sphere continued to pulsate with energy.

"How would it even know our language? The Boxans studied us for a long time, so they had time to figure it out," Emma said.

She paced over to the side, never taking her eyes from the sphere. A rectangular image of the Athena's approach to the shroud appeared on the sphere itself.

Zack's mouth hung open in astonishment. Whatever it was could hear them. "How long could they have been watching us?" he asked.

He was more giving voice to his thoughts than asking an actual question, but the image on the sphere began to change. The crew of the Athena watched as the events that had brought them here were shown to them as if they were watching a cosmic rewind. The images went by so fast that they began to blur together until they came to a stop on a picture of the Athena next to Kladomaor's ship, heading toward the asteroid space station.

Zack glanced at Kaylan. "How is this possible?"

The images blanked out on the sphere.

SUBMIT.

The word appeared on the sphere now. Zack shifted his grip on the pulse rifle and resisted the urge to open fire on it. Any species that could have brought them here knew which word they were showing them.

Kaylan stepped away from them, moving toward the sphere. "Are you the Drars?" she asked.

A three-dimensional hologram appeared beside Kaylan of an alien Zack had never seen before. The thick, corded muscles reminded him of the complex root network of an old tree. Its skin colors were a mixture of grays and browns, with a tinge of mossy green. The alien looked like it could have made a home in a swampy jungle, and Zack would never know it was there. The small eyes were midway on its elongated head. The alien was hunched, as if it could easily move on both of its legs or use its long, powerful arms to propel itself forward. It almost reminded Zack of a protokar, but not quite. The alien didn't look like it had a mouth, and if it did, it was hidden behind the bearded tentacles that adorned its elongated head. The hologram slowly turned around, showing the creature's thick body. It was easily the size of a Boxan. Tentacles corded together to the ends of its arms, which Zack guessed were the creature's hands.

"Are the Drars here?" Kaylan asked.

More holograms appeared, but all showed the Drar facedown on the ground. The holograms disappeared and the sphere showed a depiction of the galaxy—a vast ocean of stars and a rapid expansion of star systems, all shown in different colors. Spaceships, unlike anything they'd ever seen before, were shown going out into an expanding universe. Eventually, spaceships gave way to planetoid ships moving through the galaxy. A multitude of lifeforms flashed with each new star system. There were so many of them that Zack started to squint his eyes. Then the images on the sphere began to change, showing wars and battles being fought. At first, the images were of the Drars fighting amongst themselves. Then the confrontations spread to include ships. Planetoid spaceships were left in heaping wrecks. Eventually the war escalated, and bright flashes of entire star systems were snuffed out. The war spread throughout the galaxy, and the Drar empire fractured.

"This must be what the Boxans saw," Zack said.

The images on the sphere all ceased at once for a moment, then showed a view from the bridge of a ship of a lone green planet orbiting a single star system. The planet had four moons, and the images shifted to show Boxans caring for the forests and vast grasslands of the planet, their instinct for putting their world in order present early in their culture.

The images came to a stop, and the sphere returned to its translucent aqua color.

"I think we just saw a condensed version of the history of our galaxy," Zack said.

"Or they could be showing us what we expected to see," Hicks said.

"I didn't expect to see that," Zack said.

"Whatever this place is, something here has been watching us for a long time. The Drars aren't here. I think it's time for us to start looking for a way to get out of here," Hicks said.

Kaylan pressed her lips together in thought and then glanced back at the sphere. "Where is our ship?" she asked.

An image of the Athena appeared in some type of dock. There were many machines seeming to form from liquid metal all around it, and they were all over the ship, including inside.

"What are they doing to our ship?" Zack asked.

"I'm not quite—" the AI started to say and was cut off.

"Say again, Athena," Zack said.

There was no reply, not even from the satellite versions of the AI that resided on their suit computers. Zack's mouth went dry. The AI was one of them, and to have it suddenly gone was ominous.

Hicks stepped toward the sphere and lowered his rifle. "How far away from us is our ship?"

The image of the Athena being swarmed by liquid metal machines became smaller, and a bright yellow line traced its way past buildings, coming to a stop where they were.

"I don't know the scale of this, but that looked really far," Zack said.

"It's not looking good," Hicks agreed.

"We don't even know what we're doing here," Emma said.

"She's right," Kaylan said. "There has to be a reason we're here." She turned and faced the sphere. "What is this place?"

The sphere showed another image of the galaxy that seemed to have gone quiet. There were no more star systems popping out of existence. The perspective zoomed in to show machines repairing the remnant pieces of a planetoid ship. Smaller devices circled around it and were joined in a network that Zack guessed was something similar to the Star Shroud. A blazing truth pushed forward in his mind.

"I know what this place is," Zack said suddenly, and the others looked at him. "This place was supposed to be a refuge."

"For whom?" Hicks asked.

"The Drars. It doesn't look like they built it, but the bulk of their knowledge was in everything they built. Why not an AI or something else that was preconfigured to preserve itself, you know? Like an onboard auto-repair cycle for a ship system, but in this case, it built this for when the Drars return," Zack said, looking at Kaylan. "I know it sounds crazy, but given what we just saw, it seems to fit. What do you guys think?"

Kaylan blew out a breath. "I know enough not to dismiss your ideas out of hand."

"Agreed, but this place is falling apart," Hicks said.

"Maybe it's had enough and knows the Drars aren't coming, or maybe the Drars who were here died. This place could only be working within the confines of its programming," Zack said.

"I want us to go back to the ship. I want to know if that thing is showing us the truth," Hicks said.

The doorway behind them dematerialized, and Zack used his implants to try and find the Athena's AI, but it wouldn't respond.

"The way is open. Let's get out of here," Hicks said.

Zack headed toward the door and the others began to follow. He waited for Kaylan. She'd taken a step toward him and then stopped, turning back toward the sphere. Zack glanced over to the side and saw Redford there, watching the sphere with his mouth agape. Hicks called over to Zack from outside the room.

"Are you coming?" Zack asked Kaylan.

"I'll be right there," Kaylan said.

Zack walked through the doorway, and it started to rematerialize behind him. He watched in horror as Kaylan was stuck on the other side. He stuck his hand out, hoping it would stop the door from reforming, but the skin on his hand turned icy cold and he cried out, snatching it back. The door became solid, and he slammed his fist on it, crying out Kaylan's name.

"What happened?" Hicks said.

"They're stuck in there," Zack said.

Hicks's eyes widened, and he took a quick head count. "Kaylan is in there with Jonah and Brenda."

Zack put his face by the door. "Can you hear me?" he shouted.

He placed his ear on the cool surface of the door but didn't hear any reply.

Hicks tried to get them on comms, but there was no reply. "Come on. We'll search for another way in," he said.

Zack looked at the door, unable to believe what had just happened. He raised the pulse rifle and took aim.

"No, don't," Hicks said and placed his hand on top of the rifle, gently forcing it back down. "We don't want to antagonize this thing."

"Well, this thing is antagonizing me. Why is it separating us?" Zack asked.

"Your guess is as good as mine. Come on. Staying here isn't going to help anything," Hicks said.

Zack took one last glance at the door and followed Hicks and the others. He kept going over what had happened. What could it want from Kaylan, and why cut off the Athena's AI? He could rationalize being cut off from the AI if the image of what was happening to the Athena was true, in which case them rushing off to find their ship wasn't going to help. But there should still be a portable version of the AI in their suit computers, and Zack used his implants to try and find it. Even when he'd been trapped in the pit, the AI had still been with him.

Zack turned his mind away from the missing AI and back to the sphere. SUBMIT. What did it want from them?

"Why didn't it talk to us?" Zack asked.

Emma, who happened to be walking next to him, glanced over. "What do you mean?"

"The sphere or whatever is in control here. It understands what we're saying, and the text message shows that it at least knows one word of our language. Why didn't it talk to us?" Zack asked.

"I'm actually not surprised that it didn't talk to us," Emma said.

"Really?" he asked and glanced back toward the door, hoping it would be open.

"I think you're right that there's some kind of AI here, and one thing you've taught me is that an AI will try to be as efficient as possible when attempting to achieve a specific task. Speaking is a primitive form of communication," Emma said.

Zack snorted. "I thought girls liked to talk," he said and glanced over at Hicks.

Emma frowned. "This thing chose to communicate with images, and it conveyed a lot of information that way. Wouldn't you agree?"

"I guess, but we would have learned more if it had just talked to us instead of making us guess what it wants," Zack said.

"That's just it. I don't think that's the case. If it had talked to us, we would have bombarded it with questions, some of which probably wouldn't have been useful."

Zack blew out a breath. "This reminds me of being a kid and having someone not explain things fully to me."

Emma laughed. "That's a pretty good comparison."

Zack shook his head. "So, another species of galactic parents is trying to glean something from us, only we don't know what they want or whether their intentions are good or bad."

"If their intentions were bad, wouldn't you think something bad would have already happened?" Emma asked.

"I guess . . . I mean, I hope their intentions are good, but one thing I've learned is that everyone has their own agenda, and I'm just wondering what part we're playing in theirs," Zack said.

"Now you're making *me* start to worry," Emma said.

Zack couldn't help it. He was inclined to be suspicious of nearly everything, which was one of the things that made him an excellent hacker. Now he just needed to figure out what they could do here in a place they didn't understand so they could get Kaylan and the others back.

27

Prax'pedax sat on the command couch of a massive Dreadnaught-class starship, one of three they'd brought from the colony fleet. Veteran Boxan soldiers serving aboard these ships had been drawn from the remnant forces that had escaped the asteroid research base. The home fleet was engaged with the Xiiginns in the Nerva star system, attempting to free the Nershals from Xiiginn control. The Nerva star system had become a new battlefront in an old war. Boxans didn't procreate as fast as the other species they'd encountered in the great expanse, so the loss of any Boxan soldier was compounded by the fact that it took so long for a new soldier to take their place.

His green battlemesh shirt was adorned with golden rings at the shoulders, signifying his status as Battle Leader for this force. The bridges of the Dreadnaught-class ship were much larger than the cruiser-class ships he'd served on. The fact that Home Fleet had dispatched three of these ships to the star system that was home to the Humans was a testament of great honor for this young species.

Prax'pedax glanced over at Thesulia, a priestess of the Mardoxian sect. She wore the brown ceremonial robes that marked her as a priestess. Nearby was a Boxan who called himself Kray. He was Thesulia's protector, and should the need arise, he'd be her executioner to prevent the Mardoxian priestess from falling into Xiiginn hands.

Prax'pedax's encounter with the Humans had so far left him unimpressed. As a planetary society, they were still fighting amongst themselves, but Kladomaor's transmission had counseled patience when dealing with them, and his old friend's word was the only reason he'd come here to begin with.

"I'd like to hear your opinion about the Humans now that you've gotten a chance to listen to some of them speak," Prax'pedax said.

Thesulia regarded him for a moment. "I found some of them to be quite shrewd. They've had some time to put those questions together, and the fact that they're thinking in those terms indicates that at least some of them believe the threat of the Xiiginns is real."

"What did Ma'jasalax's report say?" Prax'pedax asked.

Not even he could read the reports between Mardoxian priestesses. Thesulia's ears twitched, causing her thick braids to move.

"I'm just looking for an insight into dealing with the Humans," Prax'pedax said.

"An honest approach is best. They don't trust us, and I can hardly fault them for that."

"They believe we're the reason they're in danger in the first place," Prax'pedax said.

"Are they wrong?" Thesulia asked.

This was one of the reasons he found the Mardoxian priestess so frustrating. Her presence on the bridge was that of an advisor, but there were times he felt as if he were answering to her instead of his superiors at the colony.

Due to the Boxans' initial failure to ally with the Nershals against the Xiiginns, Prax'pedax never thought the Nershals would change their allegiance and join the Boxans. In fact, he had gone on record to the High Council when it reviewed Kladomaor's request for his unorthodox approach to expose the Xiiginn's evil practices before the Nershals went the way of the Qegi race and became extinct. Kladomaor had proven him wrong, and it had left Prax'pedax wondering what else they'd been wrong about.

"Perhaps you didn't like them figuring out that if we fail to prevent this system from being taken over by the Xiiginns, we'll destroy it," Thesulia said.

"That is our mandate," Prax'pedax said.

"Only if you follow it. We can't expect the Humans to trust us if they suspect that we'll destroy them if they were to ally with the Xiiginns. Such policies will push them into the Xiiginns' arms, and that would be a fate much worse for everyone," Thesulia said.

"What would you suggest I do then? I thought I was being honest with them."

"You were, but the mandate itself is wrong. In some respects, do the opposite of the mandate. Allow the Humans to come aboard our ships. Let them see how we work. They need to believe we'll fight side by side with them. Earn their trust and be willing to sacrifice Boxan lives for it. Only then can both our species stand against the Xiiginns," Thesulia said.

Prax'pedax regarded the Mardoxian priestess for a few moments while he considered what she had said. "If I were to do as you suggest, there could be criminal charges brought against me. My second in command would be compelled to take over the whole operation."

"Are you not the Battle Leader of this group? Lead then. Win them over to the proper path . . . the only path that has a chance of ensuring the survival of our species," Thesulia said.

Prax'pedax stood and stepped down from the command couch. "This would go against all established protocols and could be a disservice to the Humans."

"They'll adapt. I've conferred with others of the sect, and we're in agreement with this course of action."

Prax'pedax frowned. "Why not take this before the High Council?"

"Sometimes the council needs a strong nudge in order to bring about much-needed change."

"Did one of those nudges come in the form of a Battle Commander named Kladomaor?"

Thesulia smiled. "Among others."

"When did the sect become a political force?" Prax'pedax asked.

Thesulia leveled a solemn gaze at him. "Since the loss of Sethion and all those we left behind."

Prax'pedax blew out a breath that ended in a low growl. Many still believed that the loss of their homeworld, Sethion, signified the downfall of the Boxans.

"Alright, I'll think about changing our approach," he said after some hesitation.

"I suggest you contact them through the newly formed Earth Coalition Force. Make the Humans unite as much as they can in order to give them the best possible chance for their survival."

"Perhaps I should ask you to speak to them. Convince them that we're here to help."

Thesulia glanced over at the large holoscreen displaying the bright blue planet the Humans called Earth. "They wouldn't listen to me any better than they've listened to you. Our actions will convince them of our intentions, but you need to fix your botched first meeting with them by extending them an invitation."

"I can't secure this star system and play diplomat at the same time."

"Then why did you come?"

Prax'pedax glanced at the other Boxans on the bridge. They were all busy working at their stations, pointedly ignoring the conversation going on around them. "Perhaps you should go to the planet's surface and deal with the Humans directly."

Thesulia seemed amused by this. "In time, but not now."

"Why not now?" he asked and watched as her expression became distant.

He'd seen the Mardoxian priestess work before, and while he highly respected her and knew that she represented the next step on their species' evolutionary journey, he was also wary of her.

Prax'pedax returned to the command couch. "Comms, open up a channel to the Earth Coalition Force."

"They've provided us with official contacts for the individual nations, but not the actual ECF," his comms officer, Wynog, answered.

"Then utilize the contacts we've got and tell them we'd like to meet the ECF," Prax'pedax said.

"At once," Wynog said.

Prax'pedax waited as various communications went out.

"Incoming comms from an installation on their moon. It's Boxan," Wynog said.

Prax'pedax frowned, and Thesulia came to stand at his side. "Put them through," he said.

A Boxan's face appeared on the holoscreen. "I am Chazen of the Star Shroud team tasked with studying the Humans."

Prax'pedax's eyes widened. "We had no idea there were any Boxans in this system."

Chazen's eyes narrowed. "That's impossible. I followed protocol. I sent my initial status report to Sethion and shut down all communications after that, waiting for a transport ship to come."

Prax'pedax glanced at Thesulia, but she continued to watch the Boxan onscreen. He couldn't believe what he was hearing. Prax'pedax softened his expression. "Sethion fell shortly after the decree to shut down all Star Shrouds to prevent them from falling into Xiiginn hands."

He watched as the Boxan onscreen took in the news that their home planet had fallen.

"Sethion is . . . gone?" Chazen asked.

"It's . . ." Prax'pedax began.

"It's in quarantine," Thesulia said. "There are orbital platforms to prevent anyone from leaving or making it to the surface. The Xiiginns made it to Sethion and used their influence to cause a massive civil war. We've been searching for a way to cure Xiiginn compulsion ever since."

Chazen looked away from the screen, unable to speak.

Prax'pedax looked at Thesulia. "How many like him were left stranded in alien star systems? How many did the High Council abandon? How many!" Prax'pedax shouted.

"Too many," Thesulia answered. "Now you know why the Mardoxian sect began to influence the direction of the High Council."

"How could they have left all those Boxans stranded? Do they know?" Prax'pedax asked.

Thesulia's gaze hardened. "They know, but the risk of returning to all those star systems was too great since it was believed it would bring the Xiiginns to them. So, for the protection of the species that lived in those star systems, it was decided that the Boxans could survive by using the stasis pods until they could be retrieved after the war."

"I don't believe this. It's too long. This is too high a price," Prax'pedax said. He was unable to look away from Chazen's face on the holoscreen. He felt the fires of his rage building up inside him, and at the same time they were tinged with horrible shame that his own race had failed so completely.

"We're here now, Chazen, and I will never leave any Boxan behind. Not under my watch. Never again," Prax'pedax said.

The Boxans on the bridge came to their feet.

"Never again. These rigid protocols that leave our sisters and brothers strewn throughout the great expanse ends now. Never again!" Prax'pedax shouted, and it was repeated by the other Boxans on the bridge.

Chazen looked visibly shaken, and Prax'pedax couldn't guess at the hopelessness the Boxan must have felt during his exile.

"Thank you," Chazen said, "for myself and the rest of our kind who have yet to come home. Thank you."

Prax'pedax was tempted to send a shuttle. "We'll send a ship for you right now," he said.

"That's not necessary. I've been among Humans for a while now. They're . . . the reason I opened a comms channel is because the Humans have detected an anomaly beyond our listening station. They've detected the gravitational wave of a wormhole. At first I thought it might have been you, but it's different," Chazen said.

"Send over what you have," Prax'pedax said.

"At once, but I must also inform you that in order to get to Earth I had to break protocols and share our technology with the Humans," Chazen said.

"We're going to share a lot more with them. We'll need any advantage we can get now," Prax'pedax said and looked at his comms officer. "Tell Battle Commander Essaforn to make a sweep. I want them to investigate this anomaly. Put all ships on high alert for imminent threat of Xiiginn attack," Prax'pedax said.

"Has it come to that already?" Chazen asked.

"We're not sure, but we'll find out. I have a question for you," Prax'pedax said.

"Go ahead."

"The Humans with you now. Can you trust them?"

"I've put my life in their hands," Chazen said.

Prax'pedax nodded. He would share their technology with the Humans, but such things required a delicate touch.

"Here is one Human that I trust above all others. To him, you should listen," Chazen said.

A Human male came on screen. He had very little hair on his head, but he had a look to him that Prax'pedax was sure he'd seen in others of his kind—a sort of single-minded determination and confidence born of achievement.

"My name is Michael Hunsicker. I was the commander of the Athena before events changed that. I would urge you to contact Ed Johnson on Earth. He was part of the group that received the original warning message from your species. They've been preparing for this, and it would be a good starting point."

Prax'pedax had already met this Ed Johnson. He was one of the clever ones.

"Thank you," Prax'pedax said.

"What do you need us to do? We have a ship called the Endurance that is commanded by a man called Kyle Matthews. He's a colonel."

"I understand the military designation. I'll send a squad to your base to assess your capabilities if they'll be cleared to enter," Prax'pedax said.

"I'll make sure that happens," Michael said.

28

E dward Johnson had spent the last several days moving from place to place. The presence of the Boxans had worked as a catalyst for the countries of the world to give support to the Earth Coalition Force, or the ECF, as it had become commonly called. There was still resistance of course, but the Boxans' request to deal with one body of government capable of supporting the efforts to defend Earth in space had gotten the world's attention. The ECF was authorized to operate in space, and as a show of good faith and commitment, the spaceship Endurance was transferred to the ECF. While NASA had the most vehicles in space, it would remain a public entity in the United States of America. As of that morning, the ECF had military representation from the US, Great Britain, Canada, and the EU. Russia, China, and India had yet to formally approve— three very powerful militaries, and Ed knew that in the long run, the ECF would require the support of those nations if it was going to succeed, but they'd go to war with the army they had. General Sheridan had been formally transferred to the ECF and would be heading it up. Details were still being agreed upon for term limits and the like, but Sheridan was in command for at least a year.

The Boxans deployed several orbital platforms that contained weapons systems of a magnitude that Humans had only dreamt about previously. The Boxans were only just beginning to disclose the platforms' capabilities, but they had disclosed that they contained a full sensor suite, along with long-range missile capabilities. The platforms were under Boxan control and managed by the team that Prax'pedax had left at the lunar base. Various military and government leaders had been outraged by this development until the first asteroids began to appear.

The asteroids heading toward the planet were not in NASA's vast database for Near-Earth Objects. At first, the appearance of multiple asteroids in the general vicinity of Earth, which Gary Hunter explained would encompass an area of several hundred million kilometers, would not have been cause for alarm, but there were too many to be a coincidence. This also put the Mars colony at risk. So far, the paths the asteroids were taking carried them past the Earth, but Ed was worried, and so was General Sheridan. The asteroids, some the size of skyscrapers, were appearing seemingly out of nowhere. During a press statement, a news blogger was attempting to bring Sheridan to task by accusing him of being an alarmist and spreading fear to consolidate power for himself and the ECF. Ed was watching the press conference on a live video feed and the camera had just focused in on General Sheridan.

"The appearance of so many of these asteroids is cause for alarm, even without the presence of the Boxans. Is it possible that these could be natural events? No, not at all. And that's not from me, but from Connie White, the director of NASA. The fact that each new asteroid we find appears closer to Earth's orbit is also cause for alarm. I believe that this could be the Xiiginns' attempt at sighting in a new weapon like you would do with a rifle—keep taking shots until the sights on your rifle line up exactly where you want them to be.

"When I took the position to head the ECF, I did so under the condition that I could be completely honest with the people of the world. We gain nothing by hiding events from the population. Anyone with a telescope can see these things. The Boxans are helping us detect them, and we'll do everything we can to keep these dangerous asteroids from reaching Earth. Either I, or someone from my staff, will provide daily updates as needed," Sheridan said.

"One more question if I may, General," the blogger asked, and Sheridan nodded for him to go on. "What can the average person do to prepare themselves?"

Sheridan gazed at the cameras. "Continue to live your lives. Trust that we're doing everything we can. More updates will follow, and advisories will be cascaded down to local law offices."

Ed switched the video feed off and sighed. Despite the unprecedented events that were taking place, the ordinary citizens were still going about their lives. There had been some minor events, but nothing like the breakdown of social services predicted by doomsday prophets. No one was in a rush to meet a dystopian world often glorified in movies and books. This could be both commendable and worrisome at the same time. Some people's desire to bury their heads in the sand could never be underestimated. When the average person looked up into the night sky, they still saw a peaceful expanse full of wonder. Ed wondered what the reaction would be if one of these asteroids actually made it to Earth. Then the panic would become all too real.

Ed watched as General Sheridan left the press release room and glanced over at him.

"I've asked the president to assign you to the ECF," Sheridan said.

Ed smirked. "Oh really, and what did she say?"

Sheridan snorted. "You're on temporary loan."

"I see," Ed said.

Sheridan glanced at the people following him. "Could you give us a minute?" he said.

Colonel Hines gave the general's followers a stern look, and they retreated.

"Walk with me," Sheridan said to Ed.

"Is Hines ECF now?" Ed asked.

"John has been with me for a while. I need to know from you whether I can trust the Boxans?" Sheridan asked.

"Why ask me?"

"At first I thought you were just an upstart spec ops contractor, but you seem to have a bead on everything that's going on. I mean to use every tool at my disposal to mitigate this threat. We don't have the means to face these Xiiginns in space, so that means this will likely become a fight that's up close and personal. The world as we know it will change overnight. I need to know if you and the resources at Dux Corp are going to back the ECF."

"We're on the same side."

"That's not an answer. Now, before you reply, I have a few things I'd like to get off my chest. I had thought that perhaps you would propose blindly trusting the Boxans once they arrived," Sheridan said.

"I don't blindly trust anyone."

Sheridan nodded. "And I bet you have contingency plans beyond count for how this is going to play out."

"You'd be correct, but I assure you I want the ECF to work. I have to ask, why the sudden change of heart?"

"In the first meeting with Prax'pedax, you asked the tough questions. I think you even took them by surprise."

"Do you think Russia, China, and India will support the ECF?" Ed asked.

Sheridan sighed. "I've spent the bulk of my career thinking of them as either the enemy or harboring enemy factions that were keen to do us harm."

"And now?"

"I'll let you know. Operating in space puts some distance between borders, as we know, but those borders will still exist up there just as they do down here."

Ed nodded.

"Back to my original question then. Can we trust the Boxans?"

"I'll give you my honest opinion. I want to say yes, but even I'm not sure. Those orbital installations under Boxan control could just as easily be pointed at us. I think it's fair to say that we just need to give them time—enough time to earn trust for their species and our own. I believe that if we can show them what we're made of, it will prove to the Boxans that Humans are a worthy ally," Ed said.

Sheridan's lips curved into a small, hard smile. "Now I know you're a believer. I wasn't sure before. Have I ever told you that I met the late great Bruce Matherson?"

Ed's eyes widened. "No, you haven't."

"Our paths crossed a couple of times."

Ed snorted. "We're here because of him."

"I need recommendations from you for staffing the ECF. I want to get the best people we have from across the globe," Sheridan said.

"I'll have Iris send you my list right away," Ed said.

Sheridan chuckled. "I should have known you'd have something like this ready. Come on. I need to brief the president and other world leaders. Oh, and one more thing. I know the Stargate program may have been canceled as a laughingstock, but ever since the Athena left Earth's orbit, we've known that it may be still alive and kicking."

Ed had been expecting this. "It is, but I need assurances for my people. They operate with a certain amount of discretion."

"We can talk about assurances. I need to know what they're capable of and how many of them there are so I can put them to good use," Sheridan said.

Ed nodded and glanced over at Iris, who, along with Colonel Hines, was watching them intently. Iris smiled, and she gave Ed a slight nod.

29

After the door rematerialized, Kaylan and Brenda went over every inch of the large room they were trapped in, looking for another way out. Jonah helped them search, but he seemed preoccupied with the sphere. The aqua-colored glow coming from the sphere bathed the room in a soft light. Kaylan noticed that Jonah was periodically wincing and asked Brenda to check on him.

They couldn't get out of the room. The smooth walls offered no indication that there was anything beyond the room they were in. Kaylan was reminded of standing inside the Mardoxian chamber. She glanced at the sphere, and the same message appeared that had first been displayed when they'd entered the room.

SUBMIT.

When she'd first seen it, her gut reaction had been to get as far away from the sphere as possible.

"It's an artificial intelligence, possibly the oldest one in existence," Jonah said.

He and Brenda came to Kaylan's side.

"What does it want from us?" Brenda asked.

"Perhaps it needs something from us—something it can't do for itself," Kaylan said.

"The knowledge this must contain is beyond imagining," Jonah said.

Kaylan glanced at Jonah and noticed that the left side of his face seemed to go limp. "Jonah, are you alright?"

Jonah brought his hand up to his face and touched it. "I'm not sure," he said and sank to his knees.

Brenda brought out her handheld scanner and slowly moved it from one side of his head to the other. "I don't know how he's still conscious. He's having another stroke. They're coming more frequently."

"I know," Jonah said quietly. "It's strange because I can feel it happening, but it's like there's a layer against the pain."

Kaylan looked at Brenda. "Is there anything you can do for him?"

Brenda gave her a solemn look and shook her head.

"What about on the ship?"

"On the ship I was just trying to make him as comfortable as possible," Brenda said.

Kaylan's eyes went from Brenda to Jonah.

"Kaylan, I'm fine with this," Jonah said. "I've done things . . . acted in such a way in the pursuit of knowledge . . ." He climbed back to his feet, wavering for a moment, and Brenda helped to steady him. "I never would have thought I'd be the one to have caused so much tragedy."

Kaylan swallowed hard. "The Xiiginns did this to you."

"I didn't heed Kladomaor's warning about them on Selebus. I saw one during the fighting and tried to communicate with it," Jonah said.

Kaylan's eyes widened, and she glanced at Brenda.

The sphere pulsed brightly, drawing their attention. An image appeared that showed the vast, crumbling space station.

"That's here," Brenda said.

More structures were falling, as if the lynchpins were being removed from the mega structures.

"We have to get out of here," Kaylan said.

She tried to use her senses to find the others but kept getting blocked. She glared at the sphere. "Let us out of here."

The image on the sphere disappeared, and Kaylan thought she heard a distant knocking coming from the walls.

"I think I know what it wants from us," Jonah said. He was watching the sphere with wide eyes. "And it makes a crazy kind of sense. We have to get closer to it."

"Why?" Kaylan said.

Jonah's eyes closed, and he muttered something about Zack and understanding. His head started to droop, and Kaylan helped Brenda lower him back down to the floor. Kaylan spoke Jonah's name, trying to get him to wake up.

Jonah's eyes opened. "It's a Drar artificial intelligence. Think of this place as a life boat. The AI was tasked with building it in preparation for the Drars to take up residence here, but they never came. Who knows how long this thing has been waiting here."

"Why wouldn't it repair itself?" Brenda asked.

"I don't think . . . It must have run out of resources, and during that time something miraculous happened," Jonah said.

"If you say this thing has become self-aware . . ." Brenda warned.

"There are different stages of awareness. I don't think it's like us, but there is one thing it cannot do, and we can," Jonah said.

Brenda looked questioningly at Kaylan. She raised her head and glanced back at the sphere.

"It wants us to turn it off," Kaylan said, finally understanding.

The sphere pulsed brightly, drawing their attention. The edges of the sphere pushed outward until the three of them were engulfed in the azure confines.

Kaylan felt a presence in her mind. She tried to stand up but couldn't move. She started to push the presence away, fighting it. Then an image of two warring ships appeared on her internal HUD. One of the ships was Boxan, and the other was similar style to what the Xiiginns used.

Though she couldn't move, she became aware of Jonah and Brenda's presence. They were all aware of each other. Brenda seemed to rush toward Kaylan while Jonah stood apart. The Drar space station was collapsing in on itself. Images came to her mind of fleets of spaceships—huge leviathans of gray and white, each with the phoenix symbol proudly displayed on their hulls. That symbol appeared on the hull of the Athena, and Kaylan realized the Drar AI was showing her something that hadn't happened. They had no such fleet back on Earth. They didn't even know how to build ships like these yet, but here they were. Kaylan felt a sense of pride fill her at the sight of them.

The images changed to show graveyards of ships and planets from long-dead star systems. It was an image the AI had shown them before from Drar history. Then she saw the Athena. The white outer hull had become more of a shimmering silver, as if something had transformed the ship. The Athena she remembered looked clumsy in comparison to the sleek lines of the ship she was being shown.

An image of a Drar stood in front of her, and Kaylan initially flinched away, but she looked into its eyes and saw something ancient and intelligent. The Drars had the Mardoxian potential in them. They had sent spores throughout the galaxy. Many star systems passed through the forefront of her mind, too many to count. The spores that made it to life-giving planets had bestowed an evolutionary jumpstart to the species that lived there. The spores couldn't create something that wasn't already there, only nudge the potential of a species like the Drar. The spores clung to asteroids and comets and rode them through the galaxy. Some of these celestial bodies slammed into planets.

Kaylan tried to focus on who the Drars had fought. What had led such an advanced alien race to their destruction? Was it some unseen enemy, or something else? She felt that the knowledge was there but was being withheld, as if the AI was deciding what was most important to share. Kaylan stopped pushing for knowledge, her own instincts at once giving light to the many paths they could take, and she searched for the one that didn't end with all of them dying. The Boxans sought control as galactic gardeners. The Xiiginns sought to dominate and conquer and exploit the universe. What role would humanity take? What would they do if they survived to explore the galaxy? As the questions tumbled through her mind, she saw different outcomes, perceiving bits of humanity in each of the alien species they'd encountered. There had to be a balance—a balance that would allow life to flourish and at the same time prevent a species like the Xiiginns from taking over the galaxy.

The azure curtain passed from Kaylan and she could move again. She heard Brenda gasp and looked over at her. Jonah Redford was walking inside the sphere. Kaylan called out to him, and Jonah cocked his head to the side as if he hadn't quite heard her.

Kaylan and Brenda stood up, looking at each other in alarm. A doorway on the far side of the room dematerialized. Kaylan and Brenda circled around, calling out to Jonah. They came around to where Jonah was standing and saw his wide-eyed gaze. He finally seemed to notice them.

"You have to get out of there," Kaylan said.

She stepped toward the semitransparent sphere, but Brenda gripped her arm, prepared to pull Kaylan back.

Jonah's mouth was moving, but Kaylan couldn't hear what he was saying. The sphere was getting smaller. Kaylan reached out and touched the sphere.

"It's okay," Redford was saying. "I was never walking out of here."

"We can help you. We can get you to Kladomaor's ship and . . ."

Redford shook his head. "There's too much damage," Redford said. He looked over at Brenda. "Thank you for trying. You never gave up, and I want you to know how much I appreciate it."

"How do you know we can't help you? This place has helped you. There has to be something we can do," Kaylan said.

Redford frowned, and his eyes grew distant, as if he were in two places at once. "Tell Zack he was right. You need to leave. Once I power down this place, it will collapse on itself and unleash all the remaining energy."

Brenda pulled Kaylan back. "Come on. It's what he wants," she said.

Kaylan let herself be pulled back. The azure glow around the sphere intensified until they could no longer see Jonah Redford, and then it was gone. The room went dark.

Brenda pulled her beyond the door, and it rematerialized as soon as they were beyond the threshold.

30

The bridge of the Boxan ship was eerily silent. They'd been waiting for the Xiiginn scout ship to make its move. Kladomaor had gone over different scenarios in his mind, trying to find an outcome that prevented the Xiiginns from gaining access to the Drar space station. He kept his ship's position between the Xiiginn scout ship and the space station. During their blockade, they had moved beyond the point in space where the space station had originally opened fire on him, but now it didn't. The Drars must have surmised what Kladomaor intended.

He glanced at Ma'jasalax. Her only advice had been to give the Athena as much time as possible, so that's what he was doing. They couldn't go into stealth mode, which severely limited their capabilities as a warship. The stealth ship's design wasn't one of heavy armor plating, its strength being to sneak up on the enemy. Their ship did have large graser cannons, which were more powerful than point-defense laser cannons. The graser cannons were mounted forward and aft, meant to overwhelm the enemy using a powerful laser blast. They couldn't be maintained for long, however, so timing their shots was critical to extracting the highest price from their enemy's ship. Unfortunately, they had no missiles left in their armory. He could have used some long-range fusion warheads that could easily ruin a Xiiginn scout ship's day. Besides grasers, they had rail cannon capable of firing kinetic payloads, but again, he was limited to a short distance. There was simply no way he could face the Xiiginn scout ship and come away without taking damage to his own ship.

Xiiginn scout ships weren't designed for a standup conflict. They were meant for firing a few shots and then using their superior speed to get themselves to freedom.

"What can we do?" Gaarokk asked.

Kladomaor blew out a determined breath. "The fact of the matter is they can outmaneuver us, and they have longer-range weapons. So we take the fight head-on—convince them we're making our final all-out attack run."

Gaarokk glanced nervously at Ma'jasalax. "Won't that get us all killed?"

"If we stay here and wait for them to pick us off, we will most certainly die," Kladomaor said. The other Boxans on the bridge were watching him, waiting for him to give the command that would commit them to a course of action they might not fly away from.

"Battle stations," Kladomaor ordered. "Start active scans. I want a missile lock on their ship."

"We're locked, Battle Commander," Triflan said.

"All ahead full for ten micro-cycles," Kladomaor ordered.

Their ship sped forward with a sudden burst. The Xiiginn scout ship came about.

"They've fired two . . . make that four missiles," Triflan said.

"More speed," Kladomaor ordered. "Point missile defense online. Ready grasers to fire on the enemy ship when it gets in range."

The Boxan ship barreled forward into the Xiiginn missiles. Only four. The commander of the scout ship didn't know Kladomaor didn't have any missiles of his own. The Xiiginn commander assumed, because of the missile lock, that Kladomaor was moments from firing his arsenal. It was a bluff, and each moment carried him closer to his target—closer to taking out those evil galactic parasites. He *was* his ship, his crew, and its weapons. The ship was his body, the crew was his hands, and the weapons were his fury.

"Evasive maneuvers. Launch countermeasures at once," Kladomaor said.

The Boxan ship had darted forward, intent on closing the distance to the scout ship. Countermeasures fired ahead and veered away, drawing the incoming missiles with them. Varek angled the ship back toward the scout ship.

"Fire," Kladomaor said.

The Xiiginn scout ship fired more missiles, but the molten fury of the blast from the stealth ship's grasers tore through them before they could arm.

"Direct hit. We've damaged their forward missile tubes," Triflan said.

"Fire the rail cannon and keep firing until we pass them. I want that ship full of holes before we're done," Kladomaor said.

The lighting on the bridge dimmed with each shot from rail cannon, and Kladomaor saw that Engineering had diverted auxiliary power to the weapons systems. The damage they were doing now was the best they were going to be able to do.

Alarms on the bridge blared all at once as the Xiiginns finally fired their close-range weapons, tearing into his already damaged ship. Kladomaor had the combat output on screen from the warfare AI. Multiple hull breaches were being detected throughout the ship. His soldiers were dying. The rail cannon went offline. Damage to the forward section of the ship had taken out their grasers.

"Bring us down point nine zero, now!" Kladomaor said.

Once Varek confirmed the order, Kladomaor ordered the aft grasers to keep firing until they couldn't fire anymore.

The two ships tore into one another, venting atmosphere and lives into space.

The two warring races continued to fire their weapons until at last the distance made further firing of their weapons ineffective.

"Damage report," Kladomaor said.

Half the systems were down on the bridge. Emergency lighting had cut over as auxiliary power was diverted to life support.

"We've lost main engines one and three, and we don't have lateral control. Remaining weapons systems are overloaded," Triflan said.

"When can the main engines be restored?" Kladomaor asked.

"They can't, Battle Commander. Main engines one and three are completely destroyed. Main engine two is at thirty percent power and is the only reason we're still moving at all," Triflan said.

"What's the status of the Xiiginns?" Kladomaor asked.

"They're not pursuing. I'm not sure they can. They're pretty banged up, just like we are, Battle Commander," Varek said.

Kladomaor used his neural implants and cycled through the reports. The Cherubian drive was still intact, but without main power they couldn't open a wormhole.

"Tell Engineering to get me main power back," Kladomaor said.

"No response from Engineering," Triflan said, and a hush swept over the bridge.

"Acknowledged," Kladomaor said.

A comms channel opened to the bridge. "This is Etanu, Battle Commander. I'm heading to Engineering. I will report in when I get there."

Kladomaor's brows rose, and Ma'jasalax gave him a knowing look. "Acknowledged, Etanu, and thank you."

"We're still in this fight, Battle Commander. I'll get the power restored," Etanu said.

Kladomaor felt the edges of his lips lift, but it was gone in an instant. "Tactical, I want eyes on the Xiiginns at all times. You have operational authority to fire whatever we have at them should they decide to make another pass at us."

There was a soft rumbling from the Boxans on the bridge—low at first but gaining in intensity. Kladomaor found that he was swept up along with it. He glanced at Ma'jasalax and found that she sang along with Gaarokk. They were all soldiers now, and their battle song was not yet over. These waves would ride through the great expanse. Let the Xiiginns fear the wrath of the Boxans. This fight was far from over.

31

Time was always against them. Prax'pedax had only been in this star system for a short while and already he felt that time was growing short. They'd deployed a number of orbital platforms meant to bolster Earth's defenses. He'd also deployed two engineering platforms to jumpstart the advanced tech base they needed to establish here. A team of Boxans was sent to the Human lunar base to oversee the new systems. If there'd been more time, he would have done more.

"Essaforn is overdue," Thesulia said.

Prax'pedax swung his gaze toward the Mardoxian priestess. Essaforn was the commander of the Dreadnaught ship he'd sent to investigate the anomalous wormhole activity. He'd been so preoccupied with investigating the source of the asteroids suddenly appearing within the vicinity of the Human home world that he'd overlooked Essaforn's mission.

"Open a comms channel to the ECF base on the moon," Prax'pedax said.

After a few moments, Chazen's face appeared on the main holoscreen.

"Battle Leader," Chazen said.

"Who is the ranking ECF official on base?" Prax'pedax said.

"Commander Alissa Archer is in charge of this base," Chazen said.

"Patch her in," Prax'pedax said.

A Human female joined Chazen on screen.

"Commander, I'm turning over the orbital defense system to you. In a moment, I'll transfer authorization and protocols to my team there, and they will be under your command," Prax'pedax said.

"Where are you going?" Commander Archer asked.

"The ship I sent to investigate the area you call the Oort Cloud is long overdue. It is our belief that the Xiiginns are here but for some reason haven't made their presence known. We go on the hunt," Prax'pedax said.

He watched as the base commander thought about her next question, but she didn't ask it. Instead her expression became one of regret and hardened determination. "Good luck to you. We hope you find your missing ship."

Prax'pedax cut the comms channel and glanced at Thesulia. The orbital platforms would help aid Earth's defenses, but they were intended to be a backup defensive strategy and not a primary means of defense. The main holoscreen showed the position of all the spacecraft in the area. He noted that the Human ship with the designation Endurance flew at the Lagrange point between the Earth and the sun.

Prax'pedax opened a comms channel to the third Dreadnaught, and within moments Battle Commander Vuloyant was onscreen.

"I've been expecting your comms channel, Battle Leader," Vuloyant said.

"Best speed out. We'll stagger our approach," Prax'pedax said.

"Wouldn't it be prudent that you wait behind while I take my ship to investigate?" Vuloyant asked.

Prax'pedax shook his head. "We're stronger together. We'll find out what fighting force the Xiiginns have brought here."

"Battle Leader, I must log my protest. Our mandate is to lend protection to this star system. This can be achieved by staging our operations beyond the asteroid belt."

"My orders stand, Battle Commander."

Battle Commander Vuloyant snapped a salute to Prax'pedax, and the comms channel was switched off.

Vuloyant wasn't being insubordinate; it was a commander's duty to point out a differing way to achieve an objective. What would have been insubordinate was if Vuloyant had insisted on his standpoint after Prax'pedax had given an actual order. Perhaps Kladomaor's ways of doing things was having an influential effect on him. Conventionally, they were losing their war with the Xiiginns. Slowly but decisively, they'd been pushed back on all fronts.

Prax'pedax gave the order for them to deploy. Their heading was the last known trajectory of their lost Dreadnaught. The massive Boxan ship was capable of fighting off a standard Xiiginn warship battle group, and Battle Commander Essaforn should have been able to send a communication back to him if he'd encountered the Xiiginns. Intelligence and enemy locations were worth more at times than engaging the enemy. He didn't want to think about whether Essaforn had been taken by surprise. The Boxan Dreadnaught was superior to a Xiiginn warship in armament and sheer power. As they raced across the star system, Prax'pedax wondered what had happened to their wayward ship.

"Active scans. I want an accurate picture of the area just outside the ninth orbital body," Prax'pedax said.

Active scans would give away their position, but ships of the wall weren't meant to fight from the shadows, and at this range, a battle was won by positioning the pieces on the battlefield.

While they raced to the outer fringes of the star system, his mind wandered back to his interactions with the Humans. Turning over the orbital defense platforms to Human control was in direct violation of military protocols from the High Council. He'd given orders to the team left behind to educate the Humans on the engineering platforms after the defense platforms were fully operational. Prax'pedax supposed that if they made it back to the colony, he could explain his actions by arguing the efficient use of resources, and the Humans were a resource in this equation. Understandably, they were eager to defend their planet from the threat of an invasion force. Having perused the data on Human history collected by the listening post, he'd learned that Humans were no strangers to war. Conflict had a way of forging intelligent species, with the question always being whether they would eventually abandon their barbaric ways or embrace them to their own detriment.

The Boxans had chosen a peaceful path until the Xiiginns had betrayed them. When conflict with the Xiiginns became a matter of Boxan survival, they'd been forced to embrace their primal instincts. The fate of his species demanded that he become a protector. He saw the same strength in the Humans, and he was finding that he wanted to speak to more of them. They were primitive in many ways, with an economic system that was decidedly reversed, but there was a rich cultural heritage revealed in many practices all over their planet. The many faces of humanity were at once beautiful and terrifying in their vast potential.

There had been a small group of ECF soldiers and scientists aboard their ship, but he'd had to cut his time with them short. Once the asteroids started to appear, he knew he would be taking his ship into a conflict that might be the end of them all, but the Human leader had been adamant about staying with them. They had a pressing need to make themselves useful, so Prax'pedax had reluctantly allowed a small group to stay aboard. They would be watched over by his crew. Prax'pedax had found that the true measure of any species could be found on the battlefield. It was decidedly un-Boxan of him to have these thoughts, but the many cycles of battles over the course of this long war had changed him.

"You're very quiet," Thesulia said.

"I was just thinking that I would have liked more time with the Humans," Prax'pedax said.

"They are an interesting species with massive potential. I was glad to see that Ma'jasalax hadn't overstated this."

"Do you mean to say that the Mardoxian sect isn't unified in its approach to guiding the rest of the Boxans along?"

Thesulia regarded him for a moment but didn't answer.

"The Humans have no idea of what they'll face, and in the face of the great mystery, they'll throw themselves against it to protect their home," Prax'pedax said.

"They share a lot with the Nershals in that respect."

"Perhaps with a little less pride than the Nershals exhibit," Prax'pedax said.

He glanced at the main holodisplay and noted Vuloyant's position. During their journey, he'd broken off to approach from a different vector. Both ships would have active sensors sweeping the area.

"Battle Leader, we've detected Commander Essaforn's ship," Wynog said.

The main holodisplay changed to that of a heaping wreck that had once been a Boxan Dreadnaught. The massive hull had been chewed up, and there were large gashes on the battle-steel hull.

The scanners were already tracking for lifesigns or escape pods in the area. The structure where the main engines should have been had been fully destroyed.

"Are there any other ships in the area?" Prax'pedax asked.

"Nothing," Wynog replied.

"Send word to Vuloyant that we're not alone out here and to prepare for imminent attack. We'll join up in section five," Prax'pedax said.

His comms officer confirmed that the message had been sent.

"Contact," Wynog said. "Multiple contacts, Battle Leader."

Prax'pedax switched the view on the main holodisplay to show a tactical readout. His eyes widened at the number of Xiiginn contacts at the edge of scanner range. Prax'pedax waited as the electronic warfare AI went to work, classifying each enemy target and highlighting the known capabilities. The Xiiginns had sent a massive force to this star system. Prax'pedax knew Vuloyant would see the same thing, if he hadn't already.

"We'll make our stand here. Deploy long-range missile platforms and send a comms buoy back to command central with this message: Alpha. Alpha. Alpha. End transmission," Prax'pedax said.

The bridge officers went to work. Command central at their colony would be informed, but they would be in no position to send help in time. He continued to give out orders leveraging everything at his disposal.

"Ready our strike-fighter squadrons one through five. I want all our ships in the air. The Xiiginns expect us to be cowed by an overwhelming force. Let's give them a fight to remember—one for their very lives. The people of Earth are depending on us. The Boxans have answered the call, and the Xiiginns will hear our battle song before we're extinguished from the great expanse."

He used his neural link to send an encrypted command down to the shuttle bays where he'd sent the group of Humans who hadn't wanted to be left behind. The shuttles would get them back to Earth, along with members of his crew he'd preselected. He fully expected the Humans not to cooperate and had authorized the use of stunners.

He glanced at Thesulia and her bodyguard. Kray watched him and waited.

"I'll stand with you, Battle Leader," Thesulia said.

"I can't guarantee your safety. You'd better serve by returning to Earth to guide the Humans," Prax'pedax said.

Thesulia tucked in her chin and gave him a stubborn look. "My place is here. I'll use my gifts to help you, and should the Xiiginns win this battle, Kray will fulfill his duty."

Thesulia didn't wait for his answer, focusing her attention on the tactical screen, and Prax'pedax turned his attention to the battle about to be fought. The Mardoxian priestess would insert her feedback into his tactics, and they would fight together.

32

Ed Johnson authorized encrypted communication protocols to two of his covert operation centers. These were hidden Dux Corp facilities that had been utilized in intelligence-gathering, but now they were being used to help them identify incoming asteroids. General Sheridan had been insistent that these people be moved to a designated ECF facility, but Ed had refused. Not only would it be a massive waste of time when they needed to utilize any intelligence resource they could muster, but they were officially not part of the ECF at this time.

General Sheridan didn't like it, but he couldn't make a compelling argument when they had so many other things to worry about. The ECF had been coordinating with militaries around the globe, including those who hadn't officially joined.

Iris pressed her hand on Ed's shoulder. "Incoming message from home office," she said.

Ed transferred his clearance code in addition to his DNA authentication, saw the message, and immediately sent it over to Sheridan's staff.

"Priority one," Ed announced.

Colonel Hines acknowledged and processed it as best he could. They'd have to come up with a better way to communicate, but they were putting this new organization together on the fly.

"Is this accurate?" Sheridan asked, glancing over from his work area.

"My people can just point us in the right direction. They can't give precise measurements other than saying it's big or really big, as the analyst has indicated. The Endurance is in the area. Have them confirm," Ed said.

Orders were relayed to the Endurance. Their communications capabilities had drastically sped up since they'd reverse engineered the Boxan comms array that Chazen had initially sent them several months ago. Coincidentally, it had been good practice, giving engineers across the globe a rudimentary foundation in one slice of Boxan technology. Prax'pedax had seemed impressed that they were able to reverse engineer it at all.

"General, I have an alpha priority message directly to you from Prax'pedax," Colonel Hines said.

Sheridan stepped away from the people around him and used his PDA to retrieve the message. Ed stopped what he was doing and watched as Sheridan let out a great sigh and waved him over.

"The Boxans have engaged the Xiiginns out in the Oort Cloud," Sheridan said. "Listen up, people," the general barked.

He used his PDA to transfer the message out to their screens. Ed watched as Prax'pedax told them what they'd discovered and that they were about to engage the enemy. Ed had never felt so powerless. There was nothing any of them could do, and a profound silence descended upon those in the room.

"They're fighting for us to give us as much time as they can so we can prepare ourselves. Let's not waste it. I want this message transferred to every nation's leader right now. Advise them to put all militaries on high alert. I want the Boxans stationed at the lunar base to give us estimates on how long it would take a Xiiginn warship to reach Earth. Let's run the numbers and have plans ready to set in motion," Sheridan said.

The stunned silence evaporated in an instant as the newly formed ECF personnel went to work. Inaction and a lack of preparedness was the key to defeat. They didn't have what they needed to fight the Xiiginns in space for very long, but they wouldn't simply allow them to land on their planet without a fight.

"Comms request from the Endurance," Gary Hunter said from his console.

"Go ahead. Put it on the main wall screen," Sheridan said.

". . . a massive asteroid over fourteen hundred miles in diameter, and it's heading directly toward the Earth," Colonel Kyle Matthews said.

There were gasps from those in the command center.

"That's more than half the size of the moon," Gary Hunter said.

Ed's mouth hung open. The Xiiginns had somehow sent a massive celestial body toward the Earth.

"I thought the Xiiginns would send an invasion force, not something that would take out the whole damn planet," Sheridan said.

Ed didn't know what to say. He simply couldn't wrap his brain around something that large heading directly for Earth.

"I need ideas, people. Call anyone you have to. Focus on solutions," Sheridan said.

Another comms channel was open from the lunar base, and Chazen's wide head appeared on screen.

"We've just received word from the Endurance," Chazen said.

"Please tell us the orbital defense platforms have something that can destroy this thing," Sheridan said.

Chazen's large brows pushed forward. "Defense platforms are meant for engaging ships, not destroying moon-sized asteroids."

Sheridan glanced around the room. "There has to be something we can do. Anything?" he said.

A creepy silence took hold of everyone. This was just something none of them were equipped to deal with.

"General, I think you should take a look at this," the comms officer said.

A video broadcast came on the main wall screen. It showed a humanoid being with platinum-colored hair and dark violet eyes. Its features were strikingly Human and alien at the same time.

"Citizens of Earth. I am Garm Antis of the Xiiginn Empire. We are representatives of the Confederation of Species sent to your star system on a diplomatic mission."

"I want that signal isolated," Sheridan said.

"You've been misinformed by the Boxans. They've told you we've been using our technology to hurl asteroids at your planet, and I'm here to tell you that this is a Boxan lie. We've only just arrived at the outer fringes of your star system and were immediately engaged by a Boxan Dreadnaught ship. We observed them using their Cherubian drives to open a wormhole. That wormhole was in the path of the asteroids," Garm Antis said.

"Signal locked, General," an intelligence analyst said.

"How do we know you're telling the truth?" Sheridan asked.

Garm Antis's brows drew up in surprise, but he quickly covered it up. "I'm delighted to speak to a Human for the first time. To whom am I speaking?"

"I'm General William Sheridan of the Earth Coalition Force."

"I'm very pleased to make your acquaintance," Garm Antis said.

"If you want to show us good faith, stop hurling asteroids toward our planet," Sheridan said.

"Sir," Colonel Hines said softly. "The president wishes to speak with you."

Sheridan gave Hines a shallow nod but remained focused on the Xiiginn.

"As I've said, we caught the Boxans—"

"I'm not the first Human your species has been in contact with. We've had reports that you took a member of the Athena and held him prisoner. How would you care to explain those actions?"

"I'm afraid I'm not sure what you're talking about," Garm Antis said. The Xiiginn's pale skin became darker.

"His name is Zack Quick. He was held at one of your facilities on a planet called Selebus in the Nerva star system. Are there any more lies you'd like to spout before I cut the connection?" Sheridan asked.

Garm Antis glanced at something off-screen, and the broadcast was cut off.

"Can we block that signal?" Sheridan asked.

"We can," Ed said. "Let me make a few calls."

Colonel Hines cleared his throat.

"Put her on screen," Sheridan said.

"General Sheridan, you were not authorized to speak with that alien on humanity's behalf," Halloway said.

"Madam President, you gave me a job to protect the Earth from extraterrestrial threats, and that Xiiginn represents a clear threat to the Earth," Sheridan said.

President Halloway took a steadying breath. "You could have negotiated a ceasefire and bought us some time."

"I will not allow an occupying force to land unopposed. I'm authorized to act in defense of the Earth, not only by the United States but by a long list of other countries around the world," Sheridan said.

President Halloway looked taken aback for a moment and then realized that this was an argument she couldn't win. "Carry on, General. My office will be in touch."

The call ended, and Ed came to Sheridan's side.

"I have to admit I didn't think you'd openly defy the president," Ed said.

Sheridan loosened his collar. "Neither did I," he said.

"Why the sudden change of heart?" Ed asked.

"It happened when that alien came on screen. Discord is their weapon. They'll enamor us with pretty speeches while they squeeze the life out of us. The ECF will likely fire me the moment they get the chance," Sheridan said.

"Not for one year, at least," Ed said.

"Excuse me," Gary Hunter said. "I had an idea about the large asteroid heading toward Earth. I don't think we can stop it, but there might be a way to keep it from killing us . . . at least immediately. I'll need to confer with some friends at Mission Control."

"Let's hear what you've got, son," Sheridan said.

Gary Hunter laid out a high-level plan to deal with an asteroid half the size of the moon. Nothing they had could deal with it directly. Ed listened as Gary put forth hopeful assumptions that the Boxans had certain components at their disposal. Ed supposed a shot in the dark was better than nothing. It would have to be.

33

K aylan stood outside the room, staring at the door that had rematerialized
moments before. Brenda was gasping.

"He just disappeared. Jonah is gone!" Brenda said.

Kaylan focused, and she was able to see into the other room. It was all dark
and empty. Wherever Jonah had gone, he was no longer in that room. "We have
to find the others. There isn't much time," Kaylan said.

She had to pull Brenda away from the large door.

"He's not in there anymore," Kaylan said.

Brenda turned toward her, and they began walking. "Where did he go?"

"You heard him. He was dying. He said he was going to give us as much time
as he could before this place . . ." Kaylan's voice trailed off.

Brenda swallowed hard and blew out a breath. "Let's go," she said.

They continued on and before long their strides had lengthened until they
were moving at a slow jog. Kaylan tried to reach Zack on her PDA, but there was
no reply. They stopped at the end of a corridor that split in two directions, and
she thought she heard someone yelling. Kaylan and Brenda sprinted down the
left corridor until it came to a large atrium. The remaining crew of the Athena
was clustered there.

Kaylan cried out to them, and they all went instantly silent. Zack recovered
first and ran toward her, pulling her into a quick embrace.

"How did you get free? We couldn't get through the door, and we were
looking for another way inside," Zack said.

"Where's Jonah?" Hicks asked.

"He's gone," Kaylan said.

Zack glanced from Kaylan to Brenda. "What do you mean, he's gone? Is he
trapped?"

"No," Kaylan said and proceeded to tell them what happened to Redford.

Brenda went over to Zack. "He said to tell you that you were right. That you'd understand what he had to do."

Zack rubbed his eyes and ran his fingers down his face. "It's the AI. That has to be it."

"I cannot account for Dr. Redford's behavior," the Athena's AI said. Her voice was coming through the speakers inside their helmets.

"You're back online! Oh, thank god," Zack said.

"Athena, transmit your current coordinates. We have to get out of here," Kaylan said.

"At once, Commander. Trans . . . Oh, *that's* different," the AI said.

Kaylan glanced at Zack. "Athena, we need those coordinates," she said.

A second later the coordinates to the Athena appeared on their individual HUDs.

"I'm afraid I cannot reach Dr. Redford's suit computer. It's currently offline."

"Understood. We're on our way," Kaylan said.

They started moving out. "The AI seemed different, like it was uncertain," Hicks said.

"We'll find out when we get there," Kaylan said.

"What were you going to say?" Hicks asked Zack.

Zack was frowning, and it looked like he was working within his own internal HUD while trying to keep from tripping over anyone.

"Right," Zack said. "The Drars built their own artificial intelligence into this place."

"Like the Boxans," Hicks said.

Zack glanced around them. They were passing a set of windows that showed the crumbling landscape of an ancient city.

"Probably not like the Boxans, but think of it like this: The AI, us, and the Drars all operate within a set of rules. The AI that built this place is beyond anything we've ever come across," Zack said.

"Seems like a waste to bring us all the way out here when it just needs someone to turn the damn thing off," Hicks said.

"There was more to it than that," Kaylan said. "It seemed to be trying to decide something about us in particular."

"We still don't know why it took our ship," Hicks said.

They rounded the corner, and a large door dematerialized in front of them. There was a long, wide path, and the Athena hovered at the end of it. The crew came to a stop. There were thousands of drones swarming the ship, but it hardly looked like the ship Kaylan remembered. The Drar AI hadn't lied to them. The images it had shown them had been real.

"It looks like they fixed it up," Zack said.

The ground beneath their feet started to shake, causing some of them to lose their balance. Hicks urged them toward the Athena.

"How are we going to fly the ship if we don't know what's been done to it?" Zack asked.

Kaylan was still taking it in. The sleek lines of the hull seemed more refined. Even the shuttle gleamed as if it were brand new. The Lenoy Salvage

System was simply gone, and in its place was a protrusion that was part of the hull.

"Someone is accessing my suit computer," Zack said. "And my implants. What the . . ."

Kaylan felt it too. There was a slight buzzing in the back of her mind, intense enough to make her aware that it was there but not enough to distract her entirely.

The rest of the crew had similar sensations. A platform rose several inches from the ground and they climbed on top of it. Kaylan glanced around at the massive alien space station. She could have spent a lifetime here learning all its secrets. If this was just some kind of remnant Drar installation, what had become of them? Where had they gone? Why had the Drar AI decided to help them? Her mind kept spitting out questions with no answers.

The platform rose into the air. Buildings were crumbling all around them as far as they could see. The thousands of drones that had been swarming their ship were beginning to fall away, as if their job was done and they were no longer needed. The platform brought them to the airlock doors, which opened at their approach. The inner airlock was much larger than it had been before. They could all get inside, and once the last person had stepped off the platform, it fell away, disintegrating into nothing. The outer door shut, and jets of air were pumped into the room. Then the inner doors opened. The room beyond looked the same, with spots for all of them to put their EVA suits now that they were no longer needed.

"Athena, begin prep of the main engines," Kaylan said. "Efren and Nikolai, I need you guys to do a full diagnostic of the major systems as quickly as you can. We need to leave this place in a hurry."

"Commander, what if they've changed the internal components? I can't guarantee the diagnostics will work properly," Efren said.

Kaylan finished removing her EVA suit. "I know. Just do the best you can . . . Do you guys still feel that buzzing?" she asked.

Zack and the others nodded.

Curious, but Kaylan had to push those thoughts aside. They needed to know if the Athena was flight-ready.

"Katie and Vitomir, I need you to check the engine systems. Brenda and Emma, I need you to check the auxiliary systems, including life support. Zack and Hicks, you're with me on the bridge," Kaylan said.

Beyond the EVA prep room, the rest of the ship looked different. Instead of multiple compartments lining the walls down each of the corridors, the walls were smooth. There were panels outside every door, but they looked to be more a part of the surface than before. The three of them walked slowly, taking in all the differences.

"It's like it has that new-car smell," Zack said. "Athena, can you give us a report on what's been changed?"

"Of course, but that would impinge on efficiency, making our probability of leaving this Drar facility—"

"You could just say not now, and that would be fine," Zack said.

"Confirmed," the AI said. "I've opened up a data feed to each of your implants, as well as upgraded the brain implant interface."

Zack glanced at Kaylan in alarm.

"Athena, we talked about upgrades. They're not to be done without our permission," Zack said.

"Those were the existing parameters, but the systems and internal components have changed, including my capabilities. My operating instructions included that the first thing I was to do upon the crew's return was upload this information," the AI said.

"It's alright," Kaylan said. "I don't think all this would have been done if it was going to hurt us."

"Yeah, but now we can hurt ourselves because we don't know what we're doing," Zack said.

"Let's get to the bridge," Kaylan said.

As they made their way through the ship, more things looked different, but they couldn't take the time to explore right now.

"Holy crap!" Zack said. "They completely upgraded the ship's computing systems."

They came to the door of the bridge, and it opened the same as before. The large conference table with holodisplay, comms station, and commander's station near the front were still there. It looked as if they had changed everything but kept the ship's configuration familiar enough that they could still fly it.

"The storage capacity is above and beyond anything I've ever seen. I don't even know how this all works . . . Wait a minute," Zack said. He was frowning at the console. "I see it now. Updated ship protocols and procedures are there for the picking."

Kaylan went over to the commander's chair, with Hicks climbing into the pilot's seat.

The ship's holo-interface came online, and she brought up the emergency startup procedures.

"Engines are online," Hicks said. "Efren is reporting similar things to what Zack is seeing—expanded power output across all systems."

A private comms channel opened up to Kaylan. It was coming from Jonah's EVA suit outside the ship.

"Get our people home, Commander," Jonah said.

His voice sounded as if he were speaking from a vast, echoing chamber.

A countdown timer appeared on her HUD, and the comms channel closed before Kaylan could reply. The navigation computer put up a course for them to take. The buzzing in the back of her head finally stopped, and a working knowledge of the interface seemed to bubble up to the surface. Kaylan's mouth hung open.

Hicks looked over at her and frowned. "What is it?"

"Bring up the navigation interface and tell me what you see," Kaylan said.

Hicks did as he was asked, and his eyes widened at the options on the holoscreen. A wide smile spread across his face.

"We're going to get out of here," Hicks said.

"Damn right we are," Kaylan said. She engaged the ship-wide broadcast. "Find your seats, ladies and gentlemen. We're leaving."

Kaylan did a last-minute check of systems status, and they were green across the board, even the new systems she hadn't had time to fully explore yet.

"Kaylan," Zack said, "the sensors are showing severe degradation from the perimeter of the shroud."

"Time for us to leave," Kaylan said and engaged the Athena's engines.

34

In the fringes of the great expanse, two ships engaged in battle, both leaking atmosphere from hundreds of hull breaches. Earlier, Kladomaor had ordered all their passengers to go to individual life support. They'd continued to trade blows with the Xiiginn scout ship while they could but had stopped for the moment. Both ships were severely damaged. His crew were putting everything they had into keeping the ship combat-ready, but it wasn't enough. The only weapon they had left was the ship itself. Their graser cannons were offline and were likely never to come back online again. They had lost two of their main engines, and the third couldn't safely give them anything above thirty percent capacity. Auxiliary systems were virtually nonexistent. He couldn't even turn the ship around and ram the Xiiginn scout ship if he wanted to.

"Battle Commander, sensors continue to report that the distortion field is reducing. The Drar space station will fully emerge into the great expanse within three micro-cycles," Triflan said.

Kladomaor glanced up at the main holodisplay out of habit, but it wasn't working anymore. He switched to his own console. "Varek, have you been able to raise the Athena on comms?"

"Negative, Battle Commander. I'll keep trying," Varek said.

During the battle with the Xiiginn scout ship, he'd drawn them in, hoping the Drar defense systems would damage the scout ship, but nothing had happened, and he couldn't decide whether that was a good thing or a bad thing. Kladomaor glanced at Ma'jasalax and was reluctant to say what she already knew. They were about to die. This battle was to be their last. Kladomaor couldn't hold with the irony that a cruel twist of fate was preventing him from making one last run at the Xiiginns. Instead, he was stuck going in one direction.

"Battle Commander," Etanu's voice came over comms. "We can't get the

Cherubian drive back online. The bypass from main engines one and three has failed. There's simply too much damage. Maybe if we had a week . . ."

"Understood. Stand by," Kladomaor said.

There was nothing he could do now but wait for the inevitable. The Xiiginns would fix their weapons systems and destroy his ship. Kladomaor had exacted a heavy toll from the Xiiginns, but it wasn't enough.

"Battle Commander, I'm picking up a gravitational anomaly from within the Drar space station," Triflan said.

Kladomaor was about to order it on the main holoscreen, but stopped himself. He kept forgetting it was no longer there.

Ma'jasalax came to his side.

"These readings show that the shroud field is dissipating," Kladomaor said.

He glanced over at Triflan, and the Boxan shook his head. No word from the Athena. What had happened to the Humans?

"Battle Commander, the Xiiginns are increasing their speed and will soon close in on our position," Triflan said.

Kladomaor acknowledged the status update. This was it. There was nothing he could do. Their ship was barely holding together as it was.

"The anomaly is getting stronger," Triflan said.

Kladomaor brought the data feeds to his console.

35

The area of the great expanse the Humans called the Oort Cloud was home to icy debris that was left over from when this star system had formed. Prax'pedax had noted that there were vast resources here, and had there been time, the Humans would probably have used these resources to build ships of their own. But their battle with the Xiiginn fleet was disrupting the harmony of the objects here that had taken millions of cycles to create. Missiles tipped with fusion warheads gouged into the Xiiginn fleet, disabling or destroying many of their ships. The Boxan Dreadnaughts were ships of the wall, capable of dealing out immeasurable damage, but at the end of a cycle it came down to a numbers game, and the Xiiginn battle leader knew it. Prax'pedax knew they could only fire so many missiles. Their squadrons of strike-fighters were almost depleted, and yet none had asked to retreat. The strike-fighter pilots fought and would die here, taking as many of the Xiiginns with them as they could. This was their commitment to the Human race—a young species with massive potential.

If he'd held with the strict Boxan stance on a species like the Humans, they would have waited a few hundred more cycles to determine whether they would be granted access to the Confederation. A few hundred more cycles would have given the Humans time to mature or wipe themselves out. It seemed to be the inherent danger of intelligent species that they were the arbiters of their own destruction, but that was not the case here. The Boxans couldn't allow that to happen. In addition to their Mardoxian potential, the Humans had a number of things going for them to make them prime candidates as allies: numbers, for one. There were so many of them. Second was their great capacity for compassion and loyalty, which was balanced with conflicts and violence. In all the species the Boxans had observed, there was a constant truth present. In order to rise as an intelligent species, they had to endure a period of time when they must face the horrors of war. They must face the great evil and the power that comes from conflict and then turn away from it. They must learn that harmony cannot be achieved without first facing the evil that can stem from themselves.

The Boxans had endured it and then later had to return to those ways. It was a bitter cycle, but it was also the price of survival. The cycle of conflict was with them and was something the Xiiginns had embraced. The Xiiginns had taken control of the Confederation from them, but that wasn't the reason the Boxans fought. They fought because they had put the Xiiginns on this path of galactic conquest, and it was only now that they were starting to accept that they could not stop the Xiiginns alone.

Their first attempt had been to seek out species that could resist the Xiiginn influence. They'd believed the Nershals could fill this void, and though they *could* directly resist Xiiginn compulsion, the Boxans had learned there were many other ways for the Xiiginns to bring a species under their dominion. The Humans were another such species. Some had the Mardoxian potential and the capacity to resist Xiiginn compulsion, but not all of them. Prax'pedax had come to accept that this was their last chance to engage in an effort to stop the Xiiginns for good. This is why they would fight to the last Boxan, even if there were those of the Boxan High Council who didn't fully understand. Mardoxian priests and priestesses, like Thesulia and Ma'jasalax, understood and worked to align events to that outcome. The alpha message sent back to command central would signal the dire need for the Boxans to send more ships to this star system. Though it would be too late for them, it might not be too late for Earth. The Humans would resist the Xiiginn invasion, though many of them would die in the process, and it was his job to take out as many of the Xiiginns as he could.

Prax'pedax shared a number of knowing looks with Thesulia. She had gambled on him coming to this realization and on his ability to convince all those Boxans under his command to follow him and make the ultimate sacrifice. Had he not seen the same conviction in his friend Kladomaor? Searching for remnant Drar technology, he might not have done as Thesulia advised. But knowing what he did now and glimpsing the insights only afforded to those of the Mardoxian sect gave him peace with his decisions.

He'd emptied his ship of shuttles, sending teams of Boxans back to Earth to help them prepare. It would take the shuttles time to get back to Earth, but it was the best he could do and would give at least some Boxans under his command a fighting chance to survive and help the Humans prepare for the Xiiginns. He'd ordered Battle Commander Vuloyant to do the same thing on his ship. Shuttle capacity would hardly make a dent in the crew, but at least it was something.

"Battle Leader, the last long-range missile platforms have been deployed," Wynog reported.

"Excellent," Prax'pedax said. "Authorize the warfare system AI to upload instructions for the platforms to target computers. Maintain connections to keep targeting updated for as long as possible. Move our position back from the missile platforms."

"Confirm automatic refresh of targeting with warfare AI. Chain of command —primary, designate this ship, and backup, designate Battle Commander Vuloyant's ship's computer," Wynog said.

Prax'pedax's ship was designated the flagship of the two Dreadnaughts, and should his ship lose its capacity for combat, control would be passed to Vuloyant's ship. Should there be combat failure on both ships, targeting control would revert back to local targeting systems. Local targeting systems were much less effective than the powerful warfare AIs aboard a Dreadnaught ship's systems, but the redundancies were in place to maximize their effectiveness in combat.

"Signal close quarters combat active," Prax'pedax said.

He had leveraged his strike-fighters to protect the missile platforms while he waited to fire his long-range missiles. The Xiiginns had, in turn, sent their own slip-fighters to take out the missile platforms. Xiiginn warships had been steadily moving in closer ever since.

Prax'pedax had also leveraged combat drones to blind his enemy with jammers and decoys, and these had prevented the Xiiginns from being able to lock onto his ship. It was never easy to order soldiers under his command to fight until they could no longer fight. There would be no backup for any of them.

Prax'pedax monitored the long-range missile platforms as they depleted their payload into the oncoming Xiiginn warships. The molten fury from heavier warheads tore into the advancing fleet. Throughout the war with the Xiiginns, the Boxans had employed superior tactics, taking multitudes more of the enemy for each combat vessel, but the Xiiginns, with the support of various Confederation species, had simply overwhelmed Boxan battle groups time and time again through sheer numbers.

Prax'pedax activated a fleet-wide comms channel. "Boxans, the remaining Xiiginn fleet will be closing in on our ships. We will draw them in-system and take out as many as we can. We will unleash our battle song into the great expanse, and the Xiiginns will know the measure of our commitment to protect this star system. The Humans will know of our sacrifice, how we few held the line against the Xiiginn fleet and fought to the last Boxan. Our mission does not end here and will be carried on by those who come after us. We will keep fighting until there are none left to fight or the Xiiginns leave this star system."

Prax'pedax closed the comms channel. He had the utmost faith in his soldiers. They would fight and would not be cowed by the Xiiginns. He returned to his command couch. The pieces were in place, and now the battle would be fought in earnest.

A shock-lance of Xiiginn warships pushed forward into the welcoming fire of graser cannons and short-range missiles. The Dreadnaughts were ships of war, and they would deliver fire and death before this cycle was done.

36

Kaylan continued launch prep, polishing off the last checks. A comms channel opened from Engineering.

"Commander," Efren said, "energy readings from the reactor are orders of magnitude above what we had previously. It's as if the reactor is being fueled with an unknown material. I cannot guarantee that it's safe or what the capacity is there."

"Acknowledged, Efren. We'll be as careful as we can, but we need to go," Kaylan said.

She engaged the engines, and the Athena started away from the dock, moving at speeds much greater than when they'd come in. The crumbling Drar station was deteriorating all around them.

"The sensors are still showing a barrier ahead," Hicks said.

Kaylan frowned as she checked the sensor data. "Zack, I need you to disable the shroud here," she said.

"The sooner, the better," Hicks added.

There was silence, and Kaylan glanced around to see that Zack was frantically moving through the holo-interface.

"Hmm, that's . . . Wow!" Zack said.

"Zack," Kaylan called.

They were almost to the barrier.

"Command sent. Of course, I didn't realize there *was* a command to send until just now," Zack said.

A hole in the shroud barrier formed directly in front of them, and Kaylan watched as the barrier receded, exposing the inside to the vacuum of space. There were no telltale signs of an atmosphere escaping out of the hole. The countdown timer that had been on Kaylan's HUD adjusted itself, and they had less time to get away than before.

"Open a comms channel to Kladomaor," Kaylan said.

"Kladomaor?" Zack replied. "How do you even know he's . . . never mind."

Kaylan watched the navigation display showing them leaving the Drar space station behind and adjusted the scanners to the Boxan ship's frequency they'd had earlier.

"I'm not getting a reply," Zack said.

"I think I know why," Kaylan said. "Two ships are showing on the scanners."

Hicks glanced over at the screen and narrowed his gaze. "Looks like we've got company. Kladomaor might not be able to reply. We don't know what kind of damage they've sustained, but if he's trying to outrun the Xiiginns, he's not going to make it."

Kaylan took control of the comms interface and tried to reach out to Kladomaor. She plotted an intercept course, and it took only a few seconds to acknowledge that the Athena could move much faster than it could before.

A comms channel opened from the Boxan ship.

"Athena, this is Kladomaor. We're not going to make it. Cherubian drive is down. There . . . no escape . . . as long as we can," Kladomaor said.

The Boxan's deep voice kept going in and out.

"Kladomaor, we're heading to you. We have a way to get out of here. The Drars made changes to our ship, and we can get back to Earth, but we're not going to leave you behind," Kaylan said.

"It's too dangerous. The Xiiginns are almost upon us . . ." Kladomaor said.

"Listen to me," Kaylan shouted. "All you have to do is have the gravity tether working. Once we reach you, engage the tether and the Athena can take us both out of here."

"Cannot . . . tether . . . unreliable . . ."

The comms channel went dead.

Kaylan glanced helplessly at Hicks and then looked at the navigation computer. They were speeding toward Kladomaor's ship. She scanned the systems to see if there was anything in the new functions that resembled a gravity tether, cursing in frustration.

"Damn it. The Drars gave us all this new equipment, and we can't even use it to save the others," Kaylan said.

Hicks was searching, too.

"I can't find anything either," Zack said.

They had the location of Earth from Kladomaor's ship's computers. Those coordinates were meant for a Cherubian drive but were already in the Athena's system. The navigation computer allowed her to enter those coordinates and gave an almost instant feedback of acceptance.

"The communications choked at the end. Let's get there and see if the Boxans have one last trick up their sleeves," Hicks said.

Kaylan nodded and fixed her gaze on the plotted course.

"Zack—" Kaylan began to say.

"I already got sensor arrays for the gravitonics set up. If they get the tether working, I'll let you know," Zack said.

"Now, if only the Drar AI had given us some weapons systems. I keep looking but haven't found anything," Hicks said.

Kaylan hadn't expected the Drar AI to give them any weapons, but she couldn't be sure. There was nothing for them to do but wait, hope, and pray.

The Athena closed in on the Boxans, and Kaylan's mouth hung open at the sight of the battle-weary ship. Large sections of the Boxan ship had been torn apart. Kaylan didn't know how it was still holding together. She glanced back at Zack, and he shook his head. No gravity tether. She'd tried to reach Kladomaor again, but there had been no reply. The only thing she saw was the Xiiginn ship moving steadily closer and the countdown from the Drar space station getting closer to zero. They were going to have to leave or they would die.

Kaylan watched the timer drain away, waiting to engage the coordinates to Earth.

"Yes!" Zack shouted. "Tether engaged!"

Kaylan engaged the nav computer. Directly in front of them, the view seemed to fold away from itself, and she watched the energy output from the reactor spike.

The status on the HUD read 'wormhole established.'

The Athena lurched ahead, dragging the battle-torn Boxan ship in its wake, but they weren't out of danger yet. She focused her attention on the countdown timer as it reached zero, keeping the sensors active and watching for any signs of the Drar space station explosion following them.

Zack walked to the back of her chair. "This doesn't feel like any wormhole we've gone through before."

He was right. Going through wormholes using the Cherubian drive normally left them disoriented. They were still in transit, but there was no disorientation.

"What are you scanning for?" Zack asked.

"Jonah stayed behind to engage the Drar self-destruct. The AI couldn't do it on its own," Kaylan said.

Zack's eyes drew downward, and Kaylan saw emotion well up in his gaze.

"I think we're clear," Kaylan said. "And there's no sign of the Xiiginn ship following us."

"They likely got caught in the explosion. There's no way they could have known it was coming," Hicks said.

An alarm came to prominence on Kaylan's holoscreen, warning that transit time was about to deplete. They were almost home. Kaylan knew from her time aboard Kladomaor's ship that, as a safety precaution, wormholes were only opened outside a star system. The door to the bridge opened and the rest of the crew entered, with the exception of Efren and Nikolai, who remained in Engineering.

"We're about to come out of transit," Kaylan said.

They were excited. The thought of finally getting back to Earth, even if they were only at the fringes of their solar system, was enough to make them all happy. Zack squeezed her shoulder, and she took his hand while smiling up at him.

They emerged from the wormhole directly into a nightmare the likes of which they could never have dreamed possible.

"Oh my god!" Kaylan gasped.

The crew of the Athena was stunned as they watched bright explosions continually light up in the distance. They'd emerged into the middle of the battle with the Xiiginn fleet.

ACROSS THE GALAXY, in a remnant planetoid spaceship, the Drar artificial intelligence leveraged its newfound entity with the designation Jonah Redford. The entity monitored for the presence of the ship called the Athena until it disappeared, but there was one foreign spaceship outside the shroud when the entity delivered on its promise. The power core from the planetoid spaceship went into critical overload and exploded, unleashing the exponential force of the old dwarf star that had powered it for millions of years.

37

Michael Hunsicker rubbed his eyes and took his last swig of coffee. It hadn't taken him long to become accustomed to having coffee regularly again. On the lunar base, it was hard for him to acclimate to what constituted daytime and nighttime. Usually he could adapt just fine, but his difficulty was because of all the hours he'd spent working with Chazen and the other Boxans who had taken up residence at the base. Some of the Boxans had set up some temporary housing that connected to the base's complex on the lunar surface. This helped out because, while they could accommodate the Boxans, it was quite evident that the original designers of the lunar base never imagined that a ten-foot-tall alien race would be in residence there.

He'd become an unofficial liaison between the Boxans and the Humans on the base. Edward Johnson had contacted him many times to ask his opinion about the Boxan position on different issues, but those calls had slowed down considerably with the onset of asteroids being hurled at their planet. Even the asteroids seemed to have slowed down, with one rather large exception. The orbital protection grid managed to nullify the threat of the smaller asteroids, but it was the large one only a few days from destroying the Earth that occupied all their attention.

Michael glanced over at Chazen. "Any thoughts on the Xiiginns using these tactics on us?"

Chazen looked at a Boxan named Alark, who was an actual Boxan soldier. Michael had never seen Alark out of his powered armor.

"The Xiiginns use fear to defeat their enemies. I don't think they intend the asteroid to destroy your planet, hence the reason the trajectory is a bit off for a direct hit. They're engaged in a battle with Prax'pedax, and they either expected to overwhelm our forces quickly, arriving in time to stop the asteroid, or they're willing to accept a substantial loss of population. They only need some of you alive to enslave," Alark said.

Michael felt his mouth go dry. The soldier's unapologetic tone had surprised more than one person here, but Michael had come to expect it. Alark had already confirmed that they didn't have the armament available to destroy the moon-sized asteroid. There had to be another way.

A comms channel opened on the ECF-encrypted communications channel. One of the first things the ECF had done was send out a new set of encryption protocols so they could communicate on a secure channel. The protocols were updated to use the Boxan comms devices, so there was virtually no chance of someone being able to decrypt their communications.

"Lunar Base, this is the Endurance," Commander Matthews said.

Alissa put a headset on and engaged the comms channel. "Go ahead, Endurance. This is Lunar Base actual," she said.

"We've finished preliminary mapping of the asteroid surface and have found some interesting things. It looks like the Xiiginns put engines on the thing, and that's what's pushing the asteroid along. My team has come up with a firing solution, but I didn't want to take any action without running it by some of those smart people we have on our side. Transmitting the images we have of the engines," Commander Matthews said.

"Acknowledged. Endurance, give us few minutes to see what you've got," Alissa said.

"Engines pushing the asteroid along," Michael said. "He's right to wait."

"Agreed," Alissa said and opened the comms channel back up. "Endurance, waiting is a good idea. I'm going to patch in General Sheridan and his staff. Just give us a few minutes to bring them up to speed."

"Acknowledged," Commander Matthews said.

Michael looked over at Alark. "Do you know anything about the type of engines the Xiiginns could be using to push the asteroid along?" he asked.

Alissa sat next to him but was talking to ECF command central.

They received the transmitted images of what looked like an engine farm residing on the surface of the asteroid. Alark peered at the image and frowned.

"They can be remote controlled, but the command-and-control function will only be available on a Xiiginn warship and cannot be duplicated," Alark said.

Alissa had been listening to their conversation while she waited on General Sheridan.

After a few moments, the general came on the line.

"Did I hear that correctly? The Endurance has photographed engines on the surface of the asteroid?" General Sheridan said.

"That's correct, sir. We've run some numbers, and we do have a firing solution to take out the engines," Commander Matthews said.

"Don't do that," another voice said. "I'm sorry, General, this is Gary Hunter again. Don't let them take out the engines."

"Why the hell not?" the general asked.

"This is good news," Gary said. There was the sound of other people talking and Gary's response to them. "That's right, they've got an image of a bunch of

engines on the asteroid surface. I know. I'll tell them if you'll quit talking to me."
Gary cleared his throat. "I'm sorry about that, but we think that if you can give
us some images of the asteroid, along with its current trajectory, we can tell you
which engines to take out."

"What would disabling only some of the engines accomplish?" the general
asked.

"Think of it this way. The Boxans might be able to confirm this, but an
engine farm, or array of engines, pushing something as big as that asteroid must
be configured to a specific amount of thrust. If we take out only some of the
engines on a particular side, we might be able to get the asteroid to miss Earth
entirely, but if we do it wrong, it will just start spinning out of control," Gary
said.

"Get to work, Hunter. I want those numbers triple-checked. Whatever you
need, you've got it. Now get off the comms channel and get to work," the general
said.

Michael looked at Chazen, who had brought up his own holo-interface and
begun running his own simulations.

"Your scientist is correct," Chazen said.

COMMANDER KYLE MATTHEWS stood on the bridge of the Endurance. He'd
been tasked with the retrofit of the Endurance's design to make the ship into a
military ship. His military rank was colonel, but in space, the leader of a
spaceship or mission was referred to as the commander. He fully expected that
this would change once the ECF got off the ground.

Outside the windows of the ship, a behemoth of an asteroid dominated the
view. In its path was their home. The crew of the Endurance had run their own
numbers and, together with the ECF, they had a firing solution.

"Target engines identified," Alan said.

"Fire," Kyle ordered.

Missiles launched from their tubes on the external missile platform. The
payloads were enough to disable the engines on the asteroid, and there was very
little room for error. The theory was that if they took out enough engines, the
thrust coming from the remaining engines would change the asteroid's trajectory,
but causing the asteroid to spin uncontrollably was a real concern.

He watched the holoscreen, waiting for the detonation confirmation that the
missiles had reached their intended targets. They only had one shot at this, and
there were no more missiles. Kyle glanced at Alan, his pilot, and knew that the
rest of the crew was waiting for confirmation.

"Confirmed detonation. All birds have reached their destination," Lewis
reported from the comms station.

Kyle blew out a breath.

"Endurance, we received confirmed detonation signal. Do you have a visual?"
Alissa Archer's voice came over the comms channel from the lunar base.

Kyle climbed out of the command chair and went over to the conference table. The image of the engine farm was still buffering. Alan and Lewis joined him. Multiple targets were destroyed, but as the image finished loading, they realized that they had taken out too many engines.

"Oh no," Alan said and kept repeating it as he plugged in the updated numbers. "That's too many. That's too many."

A smaller holoscreen appeared with the three-dimensional model of the asteroid that NASA and the other space agencies had used in planning. The updated numbers showed that they'd taken out many more engines than they'd planned. The probability model updated, showing that the asteroid would still hit the Earth.

"How could this have happened? The payload for those missiles shouldn't have taken out anywhere near that many engines," Lewis said.

Kyle felt his stomach sink to his feet. Instead of saving the Earth, they might have just signed its death warrant. He brought his hand up and rubbed his chin in thought. Then his eyes narrowed. "They would if they were set up to be sabotaged."

Alan's eyes widened. "You mean to tell me that they anticipated our attack and had some kind of redundancy in place to keep the asteroid on course?"

Kyle blew out a breath and gave him nod. His mouth went dry as he opened up a comms channel. "Lunar Base, are you seeing this?" he asked.

There was a long moment of silence as they waited for the reply.

"Confirmed, Endurance. Stand by," Alissa said.

Kyle could tell her throat was thick with emotion. He felt the same thing. He clenched his hands into fists and muted the comms channel to the lunar base.

"Options," Kyle said. "Anything. Anything you've got. I don't care how crazy it is. We've got nothing to lose at this point. I'd smash this ship against it if I thought it would do any good."

Kyle racked his brain, trying to come up with something. He watched as Alan and Lewis did the same.

"Hell, we've got engines on this ship, and I'd use them if it would help," Kyle said, pacing around the conference table.

Lewis frowned in thought. "That might not be a bad idea," he said.

Kyle watched as Lewis brought up a smaller holoscreen and began running some calculations. Lewis was among the smartest men Kyle knew. He worked well under pressure and wouldn't have been assigned to the Endurance if he hadn't been able to run calculations.

"We should probably check my numbers. It's possible, but we have to do it now, and . . ." Lewis stopped speaking and gave them a long look.

"We'll destroy the ship in the process," Kyle said.

Lewis nodded.

"What about tactical nukes? Send them up from Earth—" Alan said.

Lewis shook his head. "No, they'll never get here in time, and we're not sure if that will even work."

"Let's keep that as a backup plan if we fail," Kyle said and opened a comms channel for a ship-wide broadcast. "The missiles have failed. We took out too many of the engines. We have another solution, but it will require us to sacrifice the Endurance. We're going to try and nudge the asteroid with the ship. It's a long shot. Some would consider it a one-in-a-million chance, but it's all we can do with the time given to us. I want you all to get into your EVA suits. I'm going to send an update to ECF, and then we're going to push this big bitch out of the way so our homes and families get to live. Commander out," Kyle said.

He recorded a message and waited to send it to the lunar base. By the time he was done, Lewis and Alan were in their EVA suits and were working on a slow approach vector to get the Endurance into position. They had to disable the safeguards in the main computer before they'd be allowed to plot the course. Kyle put on his own EVA suit. The fact that he was able to do so while on the bridge was one of the design improvements they'd made over the Athena.

Alan was about to take his seat when Lewis called out to him.

"We can't do this from the bridge," Lewis said.

Kyle nodded. "Right, because it's in the front of the ship."

"Well, we need to get the ship into position first, and that can only be done from here," Alan said and sat in the pilot's seat.

Kyle turned toward Lewis. "Why don't you get set up in the med bay, and we'll join you after we get the ship in position."

Lewis let out a snort. "Like hell I'll leave you two up here. We do this together."

Kyle smiled and gave Lewis a nod.

"Plus, I'm not sure Alan can pull this off without my help. What if he needs some last-minute calculations? I think he barely passed flight school. How'd he even get assigned to this cush mission anyway?" Lewis said.

Alan chuckled while doing some last-minute checks, while Kyle took a few seconds to just be in the moment and acknowledge the fear he was feeling and the staunch determination and hope that their sacrifice would mean something. He thought of his daughters Taliya and Melayna, both in high school. He saw their beautiful, smiling faces, along with his wife. He'd been so busy with the Endurance that he'd hardly seen them during the past six months. He closed his eyes and imagined them all sitting around the fire pit he'd built in the backyard of his home, with a clear sky above them and a warm fire to keep the chill of the night away. He recorded a video log for his family, his throat becoming thick with emotion, but he managed to say his goodbyes. He urged the rest of the crew to do the same.

"We're all set, Commander. Flight is go," Alan said.

Kyle listened as the rest of the crew checked in.

"All messages have been sent, Commander," Lewis said in a somber tone. "Sorry . . ."

"There is nothing to be sorry about," Kyle said. "We have a job to do. We're here, and it's ours."

There was a moment of silence. "Go," Kyle said.

The Endurance had been holding its position above the ruined engine farm. The Xiiginns had picked a relatively flat surface on which to stage the engines. Alan brought the Endurance in at an angle and put the nose of the ship on the rocky crevice. They'd used probes to take samples from the surface and knew that while the large asteroid was half the size of the moon, it was nowhere near as dense. The gravitational pull from the asteroid was marginal. The approach took a lot of time, with the asteroid surface slowly becoming the only thing they could see outside the windows of the bridge.

"Firing maneuvering thrusters," Alan said.

Throughout all their training for every conceivable scenario that NASA and the other space agencies could come up with, this had not been among them. To calm the others down, Kyle had told them to treat this as a docking procedure. They were merely lining up the front of the ship to dock with another ship. Putting their insurmountable task in those terms allowed the rest of the crew to wrap their minds around what they were doing. Suddenly, they were able to focus, and the impossible became possible.

"Threading the needle," Alan murmured to himself. "I'm a leaf on the wind."

"I can't believe you're still quoting that old show," Lewis said.

"You'll understand one day," Alan answered.

Kyle remained quiet and continued to monitor their approach. Alan's hands were steady as the surface of the asteroid drew closer, and the Endurance came to a crunching halt. A combination of thrusters was holding the Endurance in place.

"Stage one, complete," Kyle said.

"Stage two, mark," Alan said.

Though they couldn't hear it, Kyle watched the slow but steady rise in the rear main engine's thrust.

"Time for you to go, Lewis," Kyle said.

Lewis climbed out of the chair and left the bridge.

After a few moments, Kyle said, "Alan, you too. I've got this."

"Commander?" Alan said.

"I don't need a pilot for this. I just need to monitor and adjust something if necessary. Go. That's an order," Kyle said.

Alan gave him a hard look. "I'll help Lewis with getting the med bay set up as a backup bridge. Once we're ready, you don't need to stay up here."

Kyle nodded, and Alan left the bridge. After a few moments watching the steady increase in main engine output, he climbed out of the chair and moved toward the conference table. He could monitor the feeds from there. Future designs of spacecraft should include a secondary bridge, and perhaps not putting the primary bridge at the very front of the spacecraft might be a design improvement too. Kyle glanced up at the drone data feed on the holodisplay. They'd launched several smaller drones that were tasked with tracking the asteroid and its trajectory toward Earth, and he'd harbored a foolish hope that it would change, but the logical part of his brain told him it was too soon. Kyle updated the main engine thrust so it increased faster. There was a loud groan caused by the straining support structure of the spacecraft. The steady increase of force was going to crush the front of the ship.

"Commander, get off the bridge, now! Hull integrity compromised," Alan's voice came over comms.

Kyle took a last long look at the bridge of the Endurance. There had been so many hopes and dreams that had gone into the making of this ship, and he felt a profound sense of regret that its life would be cut off before it really had a chance to live.

"You have to get out of there now, or you'll be crushed like an old soda can—"

"Keep your pants on. I'm coming," Kyle said.

He opened the door to the bridge, then closed it behind him and sealed the bridge. As he made his way through the ship, he saw that the crew had already locked the ship down, and he found most of them assembled in the mess hall. They'd elected not to use the shuttle to escape in order to also leverage its small thrust capabilities against the asteroid. They would use everything at their disposal. The crew of the Endurance waited in silence. Lewis had set up several holoscreens so they could monitor and control what systems they could through the redundant switchover in the event of emergencies.

Kyle watched as engine thrust was nearing seventy-five percent of capacity. They were pushing a moving object in space, and while it increased the speed that the asteroid was moving, it was having very little effect on the trajectory. Lewis kept updating the data model he'd put together using the current data feeds and then set it to auto-refresh, watching with the rest of them. The original design of the spacecraft had taken into account the unlikely event of the ship colliding with another object in space. The engineers hadn't had what they were trying to do here in mind, but the principles of impactful forces were still the same. In essence, in the event of catastrophic failure, each part of the Endurance was designed to fail in a certain way. Each compartment could withstand the sudden loss of atmospheric pressure and the stresses of prolonged space travel. So when the forward compartment failed due to the massive pressures exerted while trying to move a large asteroid, the area where the bridge was would flatten like an accordion. The central and rear sections of the ship were much sturdier than the forward, rounded section of the front of the ship, having been designed to withstand the huge thrust capability coming from the rear main engines. It was this and this alone that allowed the crew of the Endurance to survive for longer than even they had expected.

Kyle kept his eyes on Lewis's holoscreen. More than an hour had passed since they'd started this crazy plan, and the trajectory of the asteroid had slightly altered. Unfortunately, it wasn't enough. All probability calculations still had an asteroid half the size of the moon clipping the south pole of the Earth. There was nothing for them to do but wait for the inevitable impact that would destroy them and the Earth, or for the hull integrity to fail, in which case they would all die. They chewed up the time by telling stories, tension letting up for a few seconds until the data feeds refreshed the reports. At least they were together and knew what was going to happen. Kyle wondered what the people of Earth knew. They could see the asteroid in the night sky, but the ECF had understandably kept them in the dark. Kyle didn't know if people had succumbed to despair, beginning the fundamental breakdown of society as they knew it, but he chose to believe that people were together, that his wife and daughters were together with the rest of the family—scared, to be sure, but none of them would die alone.

"Commander, I'm getting a comms signal," Lewis said.

Kyle started to make his way through the crowded mess hall and stopped. "Do you know who it is? Can you put it on one of these screens?"

"Audio only," Lewis said.

Static could be heard from speakers in the mess hall.

"Crew of the Endurance, this is Scraanyx, Strike Commander serving under Battle Leader Prax'pedax. We've analyzed your efforts, and we're lining up for our final approach to assist. Stand by."

Kyle's eyes widened in shock. He looked at Lewis questioningly, but Lewis's eyes were glued to the screen.

"Oh my god! They're the Boxan shuttles from the Dreadnaughts . . ." Lewis said, his eyes growing misty. "There are sixty of them. They're positioning themselves all along the equatorial plane."

"Is it enough?" Kyle asked, hardly daring to breathe.

Lewis licked his lips, looking from the holoscreen in front of him and then back up at the rest of the crew. "I don't know. I'm not sure what their shuttle capabilities are, but I've got to believe it will help."

Kyle looked at the faces of the Endurance crew with a mixture of awe and a growing feeling of hope. They couldn't tell anyone, but their chances of nudging this behemoth had just substantially increased.

38

Zack watched his third space battle unfold from the bridge of the Athena. Of all the homecoming scenarios he could have imagined, watching a fleet of Xiiginn warships throw themselves at two of the biggest ships he'd ever seen wasn't one of them. The whole thing looked like a fake light show, but the actuality of Boxan blood being scattered into space stunned them all into silence.

Zack looked at Kaylan and the others. All of them were completely at a loss as to what to do. What could they do? They were relatively close to the solar system, but Zack knew they were beyond Pluto's orbit, which, incidentally, was still near the sun. He'd patched the Athena's computers into the Boxan systems, and one of the things still working on Kladomaor's ship was its onboard sensor suite. The electronic warfare AI began identifying targets on the battlefield. Zack didn't need to be a soldier to recognize that the Xiiginns had brought an overwhelming force and were pushing toward the Boxan ships of the designation Dreadnaught.

Zack brought his hands up to his head and pushed his hair back. "We've got to do something," he said.

Kaylan opened a comms channel to the Boxan ship. "Kladomaor, are you seeing this?"

"The sensors are showing us that two of our Dreadnaughts have engaged the Xiiginn fleet," Kladomaor said.

Zack scanned the output on the holoscreen. "What are all those things scattered behind the fleet?"

"Those are the ships that have been destroyed," Kladomaor said.

Zack was about to ask another question, but Hicks raised his finger to his lips. Kaylan put the comms channel on mute so Kladomaor couldn't hear them.

"The Xiiginns are throwing themselves at those Boxan ships, and it looks like they will overwhelm them any minute now," Hicks said.

"We can't stay here," Kladomaor said.

Kaylan looked around at all of them. Zack wanted to do something to give her hope. The Drars had changed their ship, but they still didn't understand everything that had been done. They'd just traveled who knows how many light years to get back home, and now it looked as if they were about to witness the full-on invasion of the solar system.

"It looks like the Boxans sent some protection for Earth, but not even they anticipated what the Xiiginns would bring," Hicks said.

"We can't even reach Earth from way out here. The smallest message would take hours to get there," Kaylan said.

Zack frowned in thought. He wanted to take Kaylan into his arms and tell her everything was going to be okay, that somehow they'd find a way through all this, but he knew that wasn't the case. If only there were some way they could protect themselves.

"Protection!" Zack shouted. "We need protection," he said.

He raced back to the comms station. Kaylan and the others on the bridge bunched together behind him.

"Damn screens are too small," Zack said, springing out of the chair. "Just give me a second," he said while weaving his way to the conference table.

The large holodisplay came on, and Zack's fingers flew through the interface.

Kladomaor asked if they were still there, and Kaylan told him they needed a minute.

"What are you doing?" Kaylan asked.

"I might have a way to protect the Earth from the Xiiginns," Zack said. He continued to bring up multiple windows, each with their own set of tasks running. "It has to be there somewhere . . ."

"Is there something we can do to help?" Hicks asked.

Zack glanced at him for a moment. "Yes, I need you to monitor exactly where the fighting is happening. I'll need the precise location."

"But what is—" Hicks started to say.

"I'm sorry. We can talk, or we can do," Zack said.

He hated cutting Hicks off, but he needed to focus. Hicks brought up a secondary holodisplay away from where Zack was working, and Kaylan stood next to him, watching him work.

"You're in the Boxan system. What are you looking for in there?" Kaylan asked.

"The command and control for the shroud network," Zack said.

"But Kladomaor wouldn't have that on his ship," Kaylan said.

"You're right, but the listening post has it. The data upload I took from it was partial. It's like knowing half a language, but on the way here, when you had me open the shroud around the Drar space station, I got to thinking that maybe we can do something similar with our Star Shroud. Kladomaor said it's based on the Drar technology they'd found," Zack said.

"That's right, but I don't think the shroud can block the Xiiginn fleet. The Drars had defensive measures in place," Kaylan said.

Zack smiled at her. "Just wait while . . . there it goes. Signal broadcast in three . . . two . . . one."

They waited a few moments, and a comms channel opened from Engineering.

"Commander, we're seeing a huge spike in power output. What are you guys doing?" Efren asked.

"It's going to the comms system," Zack said.

"Just keep monitoring it, Efren," Kaylan said, and she looked back at Zack.

"I'm realigning the shroud devices. When we were leaving the Drar space station, I saw the protocols used there. It's in our system. They meant for us to have it. It was the only way we were getting out of there, and it just might help us here," Zack said.

Kaylan's eyes lit up in understanding. "You're realigning the shroud devices to form a shield around the entire solar system. How do you know the devices can get here in time? And where are you telling the devices to go?"

"To your first question, I'm not sure. I'm thinking it's pretty fast. As to your second question, just beyond the fighting," Zack said.

"But we'll be trapped on the other side with the Xiiginn fleet," Hicks called out.

Zack frowned.

"We have to move the ship. Tell Kladomaor to re-engage the tether," Kaylan said.

"No, wait. We can't move. We have to stay right where we are. The broadcast . . . I don't . . . We can't move. I don't know what will happen if we try to beat the shroud devices," Zack said.

"How long do we have?" Kaylan asked.

"Once we're in the shroud network, it will help cascade the message across to other devices but—" Zack said.

Kaylan ran to the pilot's seat. "We have to try," she said.

Warning alarms blared. There were multiple proximity alarms from approaching objects from the Oort Cloud. The sensors showed an immense wave of contacts beyond the scope of what the sensors were capable of reporting, and they were converging right toward them. A bright light flared outside the Athena's windows, followed by another one equally as bright. Their sensors were overwhelmed, and the screens blanked out from data overload.

39

Mar Arden monitored the battle from the bridge of the warship under Hoan Berend's command. They'd been placed on the outskirts of the battle and were witnessing the slaughter of multiple Xiiginn ships. But for each ship destroyed, they were diminishing the Boxans' capacity to fight. Garm Antis wouldn't let the Boxans stand in the way of the Human star system, but one thing Mar Arden had seen time and time again from the Boxans was that when they committed to a course of action, they would fight to the bitter end.

Mar Arden went over to Hoan Berend, and Kandra Rene followed him.

"What's the status of the anomalous wormhole wake that was detected?" Mar Arden asked.

Hoan Berend looked over at him. "It has a signature unlike anything we've ever seen. I've reported it up the command chain. They're not sure what it is. Since it's not an immediate threat, it won't be investigated until after we crush the Boxans."

Mar Arden clenched his teeth. If there was one thing he'd learned from his recent encounters with Kladomaor, it was that there were no chance occurrences that didn't warrant their full attention. He could push the issue with Hoan Berend, but the commander had already taken the appropriate action.

Kandra Rene moved toward the comms officer station and looked over Berend's shoulder, then glanced back at Mar Arden. "There's a powerful comms signal being sent out," Kandra Rene said.

Mar Arden walked over and took a look. "It could be just another decoy attempting to divide our forces," he said.

Hoan Berend nodded. "You could be right."

"At last we agree on something. The fighting is just about finished. Why don't we move farther into the system?" Mar Arden said.

"Our orders are to stay right here," Hoan Berend said.

Mar Arden looked away and sneered, then gripped his pistol and launched himself at the commander. He was on him in seconds, slamming the point of his pistol into the commander's head. Several of the soldiers drew their weapons and started heading toward their fallen commander, but Kandra Rene blocked their path with her own weapons.

"I'm taking command of this ship, you fool," Mar Arden said. He slammed the pistol down on Hoan Berend's head and then flung the unconscious commander from his chair. "This ship is now under my command."

One of the tactical officers stood up. "You can't—"

His statement was cut short when Mar Arden shot him. He hadn't eliminated Hoan Berend because he still had his uses, but any junior officer was fair game.

"Is there anyone else who'd challenge my authority?" Mar Arden said and leveled his gaze at the soldiers.

They put their weapons away and waited.

"Good," Mar Arden said. "Take Hoan Berend to his quarters and stand guard. Alert me when he wakes up."

Two of the soldiers came forward and carried the unconscious Xiiginn from the bridge.

"Navigation, take us into the system, best speed," Mar Arden said.

He gave Kandra Rene a nod and sat in the commander's chair.

"Commander, tactical is detecting multiple contacts," the Xiiginn tactical officer said.

"Put it on screen," Mar Arden said.

The main holodisplay showed a chaotic view of what looked like a swarm of tiny ships that were already at their position. Mar Arden's tail twitched. He couldn't make sense of what he was seeing.

"Divert all power to the engines," Mar Arden said.

The warship lurched forward, and he watched the swarm gather, forming some kind of barrier in front of the main fleet. None of the other ships were launching ahead like they were. They would wait for Garm Antis to give the order.

As the first of the Xiiginn ships made contact with the swarm, their onboard responder abruptly cut off, signaling the total destruction of their ship.

Mar Arden's eyes rounded in fear as he glanced at the readout showing the swarm gathering in front of their ship. Master alarms blared as if they'd been taking damage in battle.

Tactical engaged the point defense systems, and for a brief moment they fired their weapons back at whatever was trying to form around them. Main power cut out, plunging the bridge into total darkness, and the emergency power went on.

"Go to individual life support," Mar Arden shouted.

He engaged his helmet, which instantly formed around his head, and saw Kandra Rene and the other bridge officers do the same. Then a massive hull breach tore into the bridge.

40

The navigation computer wouldn't accept any course from Kaylan that took them toward Earth. She tried manual override of the controls, and Hicks asked her to wait. It took more than a few minutes for the Athena's AI to sort through all the sensor data. They'd watched the holodisplay as the Star Shroud devices realigned closer in the system.

Kaylan couldn't decide if it had been luck or fate that had led the Boxans to start using the devices they called the Star Shroud. The devices were based on Drar technology that the Boxans hadn't changed much since they'd found the original prototypes hundreds of years ago. It was for that reason alone that the shroud devices accepted the Drar protocols, enabling additional functionality not even Kladomaor or Gaarokk knew existed. They watched as most of the remaining Xiiginn fleet slammed into the newly formed shroud barrier. The ships in the Xiiginn fleet nearest the barrier had no warning and were instantly destroyed, but the ships in the very rear of the fleet formation were able to take evasive maneuvers.

Kaylan tried to send a communication toward Earth, but couldn't lock in the signal. She should have known it was too much to hope for.

She kept a close eye on Zack. She didn't think he'd known what he was doing at the time, but his actions had caused the deaths of thousands of Xiiginns. His expression went from horror to grim satisfaction and then back to surprise.

"Athena," Kladomaor's voice came over the speakers on the bridge.

"Go ahead," Kaylan said.

"We detected multiple Boxan signals in the system before we were cut off. There is a strong probability that there are Boxans on Earth," Kladomaor said.

"That's good to hear, but we can't get through the barrier. Zack tried to use the same protocols we used to escape the Drar space station, but it's not working," Kaylan said.

"Hmm," Kladomaor said. "It could be that it only works from inside the shroud."

Kaylan glanced at Zack and Hicks.

"It's possible. I really don't know. I just wanted to keep the Xiiginns from reaching Earth. I didn't even think about being locked outside of it," Zack said.

"We can't stay here," Kladomaor said.

Kaylan looked at the Athena's crew. A short while ago they'd been full of hope that they'd finally be able to go back home, and now they were trapped outside the Star Shroud.

"He's right," Hicks said. "The remaining Xiiginn ships are going to notice us at any moment, and we're in no condition to fight."

There was a general voice of agreement.

"I don't even know where we should go," Kaylan said. "Where can we go? We can't get back home, and we have no way of communicating with Earth."

Kaylan's shoulders slumped. She just wanted it all to stop. Everything they'd been through had led to this moment, and she couldn't fault Zack for doing what had to be done. There hadn't been time for them to get safely in the system and then engage the Star Shroud.

"We've gotten this far," Hicks said. "We can go a little farther."

Kaylan drew in a deep breath. She was the commander, but there was no way she could go on without the crew. An unbreakable bond had been forged among all of them. She noted Jonah Redford's absence, and she found that she missed the arrogant astrophysicist who'd sacrificed himself so they could escape the Drar space station. He'd known he was going to die anyway. The damage done to his brain by the Xiiginn compulsion had been irreversible, but he was still one of them. Part of the Athena's crew.

"We have a suggestion," Kladomaor said. "Ma'jasalax and I, that is."

"What is it?" Kaylan asked.

"We would suggest that we go to our colony. We find ourselves in need of your help since there is no way for us to get there without your ship," Kladomaor said.

Kaylan felt her lips lift in a small smile. "Quite a turn of events. Of course we'll help you. We can't stay here, and we need to better understand what the Drars did to our ship."

"We appreciate your help. The Drars have bestowed a great gift. They've deemed you worthy," Kladomaor said.

"I'm not sure it was actually the Drars. I think their AI was terribly lonely after waiting for so long, and it had gained some sentience—enough to know that it wanted to end its long existence but couldn't without help. It showed us a lot," Kaylan said and shared a look with Brenda Goodwin.

"They deemed you worthy; otherwise, you would have never been given access to the space station in the first place," Kladomaor said with an air of finality. "As to our current situation, there are no direct wormholes to our colony world. Its location is our most precious secret. We have to go to an interim point and then be granted access. I think the Boxan High Council would be eager to meet all of you, and together we can decide a way forward."

Kaylan looked out the window, and where the sun should have been was an area of distorted space. Zack came over to her.

"I'm sorry I couldn't get us home," Zack said.

"Don't apologize. You did what had to be done. Now at least the people of Earth will have a reprieve from the threat of invasion," Kaylan said.

"How are they even going to know what happened? What we did . . . What I did?" Zack said.

"You heard Kladomaor," Hicks said. "There are other Boxans inside the system. They'll work with the people back home to sort it out. A lot has happened in a short amount of time, and we need some time to process it all."

Kaylan nodded. "Hicks is right. First things first. Let's get to safety and then take it from there."

Kladomaor sent them the coordinates, which would be the first of several destinations before they could chance going to the Boxan colony world. She couldn't fault his caution—somehow the Xiiginns had tracked them to the Drar space station. She entered the coordinates into the navigation computer, and the Drar version of the Cherubian drive came online. A wormhole opened in front of the two ships, and they disappeared before the remnants of the Xiiginn fleet could regroup and investigate their presence.

41

Mar Arden led a team of surviving Xiiginn soldiers moving through the hulking wreck that had been their warship. They still didn't know what had happened, but the surviving Xiiginns did know that the only reason any of them were still alive was because of Mar Arden's quick thinking and actions. Before they'd lost main power throughout the ship, Mar Arden had seen the fleet slam against some type of massive barrier. Where had the Boxans gotten such a weapon? Why hadn't they used it before? They'd fought and drawn the fleet toward them, sacrificing two of their Dreadnaught-class starships in the battle. Garm Antis had trapped a third Dreadnaught. The commander of that ship had fought to the bitter end, taking as many Xiiginns as they could. It wasn't enough. Nothing the Boxans could do was enough to stop the Xiiginn empire. Until now, that is, but the tactics still didn't make any sense. He kept working through the events while the teams of soldiers and bridge officers went through the ship, finding survivors and gathering supplies. Kandra Rene led a team to assess the damage in Engineering. It was one thing for the main power to go offline, but for the backup redundant systems to fail was quite another.

The more he thought about the Boxan tactics, the more he thought that this mysterious barrier had nothing to do with them. It was the only explanation that made any sense. Following this line of thought brought him back to the anomalous wormhole detection. The computer systems were down, so he couldn't get to any of the information they had on it, but he remembered the tactical officer commenting that it had a signature unlike anything they'd seen before. Preliminary analysis of Human technology had shown no indication that they possessed anything like the Cherubian drive, but Mar Arden's instincts connected the anomalous wormhole and the barrier. Two technological feats they hadn't come across before indicated that there was another species in this war—a new player—and their presence left the way open for all sorts of possibilities.

The short-range scanners reported that the barrier was still in place, but they were inside its confines. They couldn't reach any other ships in the fleet, so it was safe to assume that they were the only Xiiginns who'd made it through the barrier. Chances were that the Boxans on the Human home world called Earth didn't know they were here either, which gave them an advantage.

Mar Arden drew in a deep breath and blew it out. They could only leverage the advantage of surprise if they could make it to Earth undetected. In the not-too-distant past, Kladomaor had led a small team to the Nershal star system with the intention of igniting a rebellion against the Xiiginns. Those tactics had been a marked deviation from what the Boxans had used before, but given the situation they were in, he thought those same tactics would serve the Xiiginns' cause as well. They needed to salvage what they could from this wreck and hide it.

Kandra Rene opened a comms channel to him.

"Go ahead," Mar Arden said.

"We can't get to Engineering or any other part of the rear of the ship because those sections are gone," Kandra Rene said.

"Understood, continue sweeping the area for survivors. We're going to need everyone we can for what comes next," Mar Arden said.

"I would like to ask a question," Kandra Rene said.

Mar Arden had no doubt that she had many questions. "Go ahead," he said.

"What could the Boxans have done that could literally tear a ship in half? The damage I'm seeing is inconceivable," Kandra Rene said.

"Either the Boxans have some new technology, or there's a new alien species taking part in our war," Mar Arden said.

"This will change things for us. If they can protect entire star systems with a massive barrier, I'm not sure what we can do about that," Kandra Rene said.

"That's the problem we'll need to overcome. Also, things aren't as bleak as they seem. We're inside the barrier. Our mission here is still the same. How we go about achieving our objectives will change, but our goals haven't. The Boxans are keen to protect the Humans for some reason. I'd like to know why that is, wouldn't you?" Mar Arden asked.

"I see your point. Do you think Garm Antis survived?" Kandra Rene asked.

A flash of irritation flicked through his mind at the question. "If anyone could survive, it would be him. He didn't achieve his position by taking foolish risks, and his flagship was among the rearmost lines."

"Won't the remaining fleet try to get through the barrier?"

"I'm sure they will."

"Should we work to try to open the barrier from the inside rather than travel to Earth?" Kandra Rene asked.

"No, for a couple of reasons. One, the ship is severely damaged. I doubt any of the weapons systems are working, and without main power those systems will never work. Two, if we stay out here, trying to bring down the barrier, we run the risk of drawing attention to ourselves, and without any combat capability to speak of, that would be disastrous for all of us. Third, the Boxans want to keep us from the Humans. We know that some of them are able to resist compulsion, and some of them can't. That alone would pique the Boxans' interest, as it does my own, but there must be more than that. We know their own fleet is limited, and yet they sent three Dreadnaught-class starships to defend this system, and you can be sure there will be more Boxans coming to this system. While we were able to take the first Dreadnaught by surprise, there was no such luck with the second two. Standard Boxan protocol would be to send a communications drone back to their command central, so the fight for this star system is only beginning, and we're in the unique position to influence events in our favor," Mar Arden said.

There was a long pause, which Mar Arden expected.

"Understood, we'll continue our sweep and work our way back to you," Kandra Rene said.

The comms channel closed. Kandra Rene would take some time to consider what he'd told her, and he was confident that she would agree with his conclusions. If not, or if any other bridge officers began to show signs of doing anything other than following his commands, they would meet with an untimely end. He was in command.

Mar Arden glanced down at Hoan Berend's unconscious form. There was bruising on his face where Mar Arden had hit him, but Mar Arden preferred not to kill him. The commander did have his uses and was resourceful, and once Hoan Berend woke up and learned what had happened, he would likely go along with Mar Arden's plans. That is, of course, until he had the opportunity to betray him, but in Mar Arden's mind, Hoan Berend wasn't a real threat. Rather, he was a tool that needed to learn his place.

42

Astronomers had theorized that when the solar system was formed, the Earth may have had more than one moon. Some astronomers believed that during this violent period billions of years ago, there had been a second and possibly a third moon that had become part of the Earth's orbit while it was still forming. Ed Johnson had never ascribed to one theory or another; it was just one of those interesting things scientists speculated about.

Ed stood outside under the night sky in the foothills of the Rocky Mountains and glanced up at what many were calling the new moon. It was significantly smaller than the old moon, but it was still something to see. He took a sip from his flask, and the warm, sweet taste of Kentucky bourbon whiskey washed down his throat. He'd found a bottle of Blanton's in one of the offices underground in the command center. After what they'd all been through, taking a bit of someone's bourbon was the least of his problems. He'd have Iris send them a case.

He took another sip and raised his flask in a silent salute to Colonel Kyle Matthews, who, along with several hundred Boxans, had managed to do the impossible. The analysts were calling it a near miss. Regardless of what anyone called it, the people of Earth, and perhaps even the planet itself, had been given a reprieve, another chance to survive in this rapidly changing world they'd become part of. They'd lost communication with Prax'pedax, and a memorial service was planned to honor the Boxans who had sacrificed themselves to protect the Earth. When they'd lost communication with Prax'pedax, they'd also lost all communication beyond a certain point in the solar system. The surviving Boxans were just as perplexed about this as the space agencies of Earth, which was at once comforting and a bit alarming.

Ed found himself wondering whether his late friend, Bruce Matherson, had any idea what had been truly coming for them. First, they'd received that strange alien signal during the nineteen-eighties, and then in the year twenty-fifteen they'd intercepted the first images of Pluto from the spaceship New Horizons, proving that intelligent life did exist beyond their solar system.

Ed heard the crunching footsteps of someone crossing the parking lot, but he wasn't alarmed. Iris wouldn't let anything happen to him. General William Sheridan gave him a nod in greeting and leaned on the car next to Ed.

"You going to share that, or is this a private party?" Sheridan said.

Ed passed him his flask.

"Bourbon. I figured you for a scotch kind of man," Sheridan said and passed the flask back to Ed.

"Scotch is overrated," Ed said.

Sheridan sighed and looked up at the night sky. "Quite a view, isn't it?"

"Yes, it is. I'm not sure how long it will take to get used to it," Ed said.

"Might not get the chance. Once the eggheads decide where to put the thing, we'll be going to work on it. That asteroid is full of rich minerals and a bunch of stuff I can't even begin to understand, but the Boxans believe we can build spaceships with it," Sheridan said.

Ed pressed his lips together and nodded. He hadn't known that. "It's a shame about the Endurance," Ed said.

"The crew survived, and that's what was important. After saving all our collective asses, that is. The Endurance was part of the old world. We'll salvage what we can and use it to build something better—something we can use against the Xiiginns," Sheridan said.

"What about Kyle Matthews and the rest of his crew?" Ed asked.

Sheridan snorted, which sounded a bit like the bark of an old bull mastiff he'd once had. "We'll give them medals, of course. They asked for some time to visit their families, and then we'll put them back to work. I'm relying on the president to put everyone else back to work."

"I think with everything that's happened, we'll get the full support of most nations," Ed said.

"One would think that, but I'll never underestimate another nation's willingness to exploit any event to fuel their own agenda, which may not necessarily align with ours."

"Let me guess—our old friends from China, Russia, and India?" Ed said.

"India has already reached out to me through official ECF channels. Russia and China officials are still considering their position," Sheridan said.

"That stance won't work for them for very long. The Boxans have already said they'll only work with nations who are backing the ECF," Ed said.

Sheridan nodded. "One day at a time. I want to focus our resources on building a fleet of ships and defense platforms capable of going toe-to-toe with the best the Xiiginns have to offer. We'll need training and qualified people for the ECF, and the remaining Boxans are willing to help with that. For a little while there I almost thought we'd be fighting the Boxans, but I'm glad I was wrong about that."

"I think we have the crew of the Athena to thank for that," Ed said.

Sheridan arched an eyebrow. "You still believe they're out there?"

"Without a doubt. Gary Hunter told me they started to receive an incoming data burst that got cut off. The headers for the encryption key was from the Athena. I have no evidence to back this up, but I think they had something to do with whatever cut off the Xiiginn fleet," Ed said.

"Then where the hell are they?"

"An excellent question," Ed said and wished he knew the answer to that.

"I've moved Gary Hunter to the ECF. He's a smart one. Thanks for the recommendation," Sheridan said.

"There'll be more coming," Ed said.

Sheridan eyed him for a moment. "About that. How do you fit into the ECF?"

Ed had been expecting this. "I'm still head of Dux Corp, so I can't exactly be reporting to you," he said.

"That's bullshit, and you know it."

Ed laughed. "How about as a consultant? And I'll bring the best and brightest with me to help."

Sheridan shook his head and gave Ed an appraising look. "You already know I'll take what I can get. There's no room here for petty stubbornness, but I do have a question, just between you and me."

"Alright," Ed said.

"Why not come out of the shadows and officially become part of the ECF? My understanding is that most of the charter was put together by Dux Corp anyway," Sheridan said.

Ed handed the general the flask. "It has nothing to do with you. I want the ECF to work. I believe it's our only shot of surviving, but the way things are today, it's better to be a silent partner rather than become absorbed into the fold. Dux Corp and its subsidiaries remaining separate from the ECF is good for you. It will allow us to act in such a way that it won't hurt the ECF in the long run. It has ever been our mission to ensure that humanity survives its inevitable first contact with an alien race."

Sheridan took a sip from the flask. "If I didn't know better, I'd suspect you were trying to get me drunk to soften the rejection."

"That would be a waste of time. In this, your reputation precedes you. I already know you can drink me under the table," Ed replied.

Sheridan regarded him for a moment. "You're a dangerous man, Ed."

"No more than you are," Ed said.

They heard the high-pitched whine of a rotorless chopper coming toward them. Ed glanced at Iris, who was waiting a short distance away. Iris gave him a single nod.

"Looks like my ride is here. I'll be in touch," Ed said. "Oh, and one more thing. Michael Hunsicker is another good man for the ECF. Currently, he's the foremost expert in dealing with the Boxans."

Sheridan waved him off. Ed climbed into the chopper along with Iris. As always, there was a mountain's worth of work to be done. Unfortunately, they had no idea how much of a reprieve from the threat of the Xiiginns they really had.

43

It had been a week since the Athena had left the Sol system. They hadn't gone to the Boxan colony yet because Kladomaor's ship was in desperate need of repairs, and the crew of the Athena used the time to get some much-needed rest. Both ships were taking refuge in a lifeless star system. After their initial jump, the gravity tether had begun to fail, which necessitated them changing their plans. Although the intention had been to pick a star system known to the Boxans, they'd discovered that the navigation database on the Athena held coordinates to star systems that were not known to the Boxans, one of which was relatively close. They'd decided to head there and make as many repairs as they could to Kladomaor's ship while getting better acquainted with the new and improved Athena.

Kaylan was on an EVA with Zack and Hicks, along with Vitomir. They were checking the exterior hull, which was made up of a radically more advanced ceramic composite than their previous hull had been, and Kladomaor had told them they could run a more thorough analysis once they reached the colony. There were still parts of the ship she didn't know the function of, but she, along with the rest of the crew, was going through the information left for them by the Drar AI. Their own AI had retained its identity during the change, which Kaylan appreciated. They'd all come to rely on and trust the Athena's AI, and Zack continued to work with it so—as he liked to put it—it would stop scaring the crap out of them.

"You know, with all the things the Drars did to the ship, I can't believe they didn't give us some kind of super weapon," Zack said.

"It might have been helpful," Hicks agreed.

"I don't think that was their intention at all," Kaylan said. "From the AI's perspective, they were tired of war. There's still a lot of information to go through, and there could be something there, but I seriously doubt they gave us a super weapon. It wouldn't solve the problem they were most interested in, regardless."

"What problem is that?" Zack asked.

"They were looking for a way to stop all the fighting. The Drars fought other races and each other. It's still unclear where they all went," Kaylan said.

"They were able to block your ability and alleviate Jonah's condition for however brief a period of time. That alone is valuable," Zack said.

Hicks laughed. "I think Zack is just upset that he can't hide from you anymore."

Kaylan laughed.

"What? Oh, come on, that's not it at all," Zack said in a teasing manner but then became serious again. "I've been thinking about what it will be like when we finally do get to the Boxan colony."

Kaylan nodded. "I see what you mean. Ma'jasalax has hinted that there are different factions within the Boxans and the Mardoxian sect in particular."

"Exactly. Now, I trust Kladomaor, Gaarokk, Ma'jasalax, and the rest of his crew. It's the others we haven't met that concern me," Zack said.

"One thing at a time," Kaylan said.

Kaylan glanced over at the Boxan stealth ship. It was still heavily damaged, but they'd been working to get it stable enough to return to the colony. Kladomaor had sent out a communications drone, alerting the colony of their intention to return. He'd explained to them that if he hadn't done that, they would run the risk of being fired on by his own species. Kaylan was no stranger to taking a cautious approach to things, but the Boxans took precautions to a whole new level. At first it had seemed like overkill to her, but given what the Boxans had faced and the loss of their own home world, could she really blame them for the steps they'd taken to safeguard the Boxans who were left? And would the people of Earth have to do something similar at some point? She hoped not, but she couldn't be sure circumstances wouldn't require such actions.

They headed back to the airlock, and Kaylan took one last look around. Views of the entire galaxy, such as this one, were almost becoming routine for her, and she wanted to make sure that she stopped every now and then and appreciated the beautiful and mysterious majesty that was their universe.

RISING FORCE

ASCENSION SERIES BOOK 5

1

Zack sat in the cockpit of a Boxan strike-fighter configured for atmospheric flight mode. The wing cannons could shoot ion bolts as well as kinetic weaponry, but they were presently disabled. A fully armed strike-fighter also carried missiles whose payloads could be changed to suit their purpose in battle. The ship Zack was flying was for training purposes only. He'd spent a lot of time in training simulators and had recently been qualified to fly an actual strike-fighter.

"Let's take it up a notch. I want you to take us beyond the atmosphere," Etanu said.

Etanu was a Nershal, a humanoid species with dragonfly wings. They were skilled pilots and highly capable at calculating navigational coordinates. At one time Etanu would have sooner seen Zack dead than flying in the same vehicle, but things had changed. The Nershals lived their lives by a strict code of honor, and owing to the fact that Zack *wasn't* dead and that he and Etanu had survived being held prisoner by the Xiiginns, they'd developed a strong friendship.

Zack brought up the flight configuration on the internal heads-up display. "Sounds good."

He increased the velocity and angled the trajectory ninety degrees. Zack couldn't feel any change in pressure thanks to the inertia dampeners. Without them, he would have been unconscious from the gravitational forces of such a turn.

Zack found it hard to believe that he hadn't seen Earth in over a year. The closest he'd gotten was eight months ago when he'd uploaded Drar command protocols to the Star Shroud, causing it to converge around the Earth's star system and form a protective barrier that not even the Boxans could penetrate. What he hadn't anticipated was that they wouldn't be able to disable the barrier in order to get home themselves. As a result, he and the rest of the Athena crew were temporary residents of the Boxan colony world.

Basic flying of the strike-fighter had been easy to learn. Its computer systems used adaptive protocols to tweak the controls to the nuances of the pilot. Unlike Kaylan and some of the others, Zack wasn't a pilot back on Earth, but the flight controls for the strike-fighter were much easier for him to comprehend than the Athena's shuttle, although perhaps not anymore because it had been a few months since he'd been on the shuttle. The Athena was orbiting the planet, but he'd been in constant contact with the ship's artificial intelligence, which had become their unofficial tenth crewmember.

Zack used his neural implants to access the strike-fighter's flight systems and gave the command to change the engine configuration for space flight mode. The main heads-up display showed the updated configuration and they passed through the edge of the atmosphere. He waited a few moments while their distance from the atmospheric edge increased, then used the maneuvering thrusters to swing the nose around to give them a view of the planet. Zack grinned. He'd been practicing that maneuver in the simulator and had botched his first few attempts when Kaylan had been flying with him.

"Excellent," Etanu said. "Perhaps I'll tell Kaylan that she distracts you too much on these flights."

"It's the only way we get to be alone these days, between combat training and whatever the Mardoxian Sect does when they snatch her away for their own training regimen," Zack said.

"And here I thought you just wanted to get away from the physical rigors of combat training," Etanu said.

Zack snorted. "This is more fun than that stuff. I'm not a soldier and I don't ever plan on being a soldier. Honestly, I just want to get back to Earth and be with Kaylan."

Zack took in the view of the Boxan colony world. Olloron was decent enough, but it was a bit dry for his taste. Water covered only sixty percent of the planet's surface and there was nowhere near the lushness when compared with Selebus moon, a secondary habitable world in the Nerva star system and home to the Nershals. Olloron was the only home the Boxan's had left and they defended that home fiercely. Zack couldn't imagine losing Earth, and given the state of Human technology, Humans wouldn't survive losing Earth either.

Zack swung the nose of the ship forty-five degrees to the right and sped toward the Athena.

"Where are you taking us?" Etanu asked.

"Home . . . Well, *my* home, that is," Zack said.

He needed to see the Athena. So much had happened to them aboard that ship that he sometimes felt lost without it.

"You'll get back to Earth someday," Etanu said.

"I know, but combat training isn't going to get me there any quicker. I need to spend more time trying to decipher what the Drar did to our ship. There are still vast parts of the Athena's computing systems that I can't access, nor can the AI," Zack said.

Etanu blew out a harsh breath at the mention of the AI.

"Come on," Zack said, "you need to learn to work with AIs. When done properly, they can be a tremendous help."

"Our experience has been less fortuitous when dealing with an AI than yours has been," Etanu said.

"That's because the AI you were working with was based on Xiiginn design and I think we can agree that anything they touch only benefits them," Zack said.

"So you think the Xiiginns wanted our artificial intelligence experiments to fail?"

"Maybe . . . Another way to keep you dependent on them, I suppose. Look, I don't expect you to change your mind, but I would encourage you to consider developing your own when you eventually return to Nerva," Zack said.

Etanu was silent, but Zack could tell the Nershal was considering what he'd said.

Finally, Etanu answered. "I'd do it with your help."

"Really! That's great. We could probably adapt a version of the Athena's AI for you to use. I mean, it was based on the Boxan AI that was used to manage the monitoring station in our star system," Zack said.

"Yeah, but you modified it and it's something different than what the Boxans created. Even Gaarokk agrees with that," Etanu said.

"You are correct," the AI said, its voice coming from their helmet speakers. "My origin is somewhat unique, but I would be happy to create a base AI that stems from my programming to suit your needs."

Zack glanced at Etanu in surprise. "Wait a minute, Athena. Did you just say you can create more of you as in—like a child?"

"The context would fit in this instance. Does this surprise you?" the AI asked.

"Damn right it does," Zack said.

"I'm sure I understand," the AI replied. "Besides you, no other crewmember knows my programming as well as I do. Why shouldn't I be able to create alternate versions of myself for the Nershals to use?"

"I think it might be a bit more complicated than you think it would be," Zack said.

"I shall devote some processing time to the problem and provide you with a report," the AI said.

Zack looked up at the HUD and saw that Etanu was watching him from the rear seat.

"What?" Zack asked.

"You mentioned before how you'd like to return to Earth and be with Kaylan. I'm trying to understand what this means. You're with her here, but I don't think that's what you mean," Etanu said.

"Oh, I was thinking just the two of us taking it easy on a beach somewhere," Zack said.

"And you'd find such an existence fulfilling?"

"Well, yeah," Zack said, and his mouth hung open while he tried to formulate his thoughts. "Just her and me on a beautiful beach. Bathing suits, drinks, the warm Caribbean waters, and no one trying to kill us. Yeah, I would like that very much."

"I don't think I understand you Humans at all. Here, in this moment, you are a designated mating pair, but you feel you can't be alone because the Xiiginns are hunting you. The Xiiginn aren't here. What's stopping you from doing as you wish right now?" Etanu asked.

Zack frowned. "Ma'jasalax and the other Mardoxian Sect members have her so busy that we barely have any time for each other at all."

"Have you communicated your desires to Kaylan?" Etanu asked.

Zack rolled his eyes. "What are you? The relationship police or something?"

"You didn't answer my question."

Zack shook his head and sighed. "No, I haven't talked to her about it."

He just wanted to get aboard the Athena and forget about Olloron, the Boxans, and the fact that they'd been kept so busy that they could hardly focus on any one thing for very long.

"You pride yourself on being able to solve problems and yet this one causes you to stumble," Etanu said, and a series of high-pitched grunts sounded from the rear of the cockpit.

"Are you laughing at me?"

The sounds from the Nershal came in longer bursts and Zack ground his teeth in frustration.

"Fine, laugh it up. Next time I see Kaylan, I'll just steal her away for a while," Zack said.

The Nershal's laughter ceased. "Now you're making sense."

As they got closer to the Athena, the white outer hull gleamed with a bit of silver and Zack drew in a deep breath, feeling his shoulders relax. He felt more at ease on the Athena than he did on the planet below them.

Zack harrumphed. Seeing the Athena was both a relief and a reminder of how far they had yet to go. The ship was tiny by Boxan standards, but thanks to the Drar it now contained more advanced technology than even the Boxans had. The Boxans had been able to help decipher some of what the million-year-old Drar AI had done to their ship, but though it had been eight months since that had happened, they were still in the dark as to the extent of the changes. One thing that had soon become apparent to all the crewmembers was the usefulness of the upgrades to their neural implants. The implants had been linked to their PDAs, and they still were to a certain extent, but they had the ability to function equally as well without them. As a result, the Athena crewmembers were able to multitask much better than they had before. Executing a task had required a fair amount of concentration before the upgrade, but now they could be performed almost as fast as it took to formulate the thought.

The security protocols had also been updated so only the Athena crew could access the computer systems of the ship. They'd been able to give the Boxans provisional access, but no matter what Zack did, the Boxans were severely limited in what they could do without one of the original Athena crewmembers present. Zack was aware of how the Boxans had tried to bypass the security protocols and access the ship's systems directly, so those security protocols had kept the Boxans honest.

"So this is what Hicks refers to as 'hearing you think.' You know, when you're so focused you start to forget things like slowing the ship down so we don't crash," Etanu said.

Zack's thoughts snapped back to the strike-fighter's controls and he slowed their approach.

"I was thinking of some things," Zack said.

"Like what?"

"When we first got here I thought we'd focus more on what the Drar did to the Athena, and for the first month or so things were like that, but not now," Zack said.

"The Boxans are sharing their knowledge and training all of you on their systems. It is a great gift," Etanu said.

"I realize that, but part of me keeps thinking that we're being kept busy on purpose."

"Why?"

"I don't know. To keep us here longer? We should have gone back to our star system by now to try and open the barrier," Zack said.

"It's not safe. Not with the Xiiginn fleet in the area," Etanu said.

"They can't be everywhere at once."

"The barrier is a blessing. It's the only thing that saved your home world from being invaded by the Xiiginns. What if you were to bring down the barrier and then not be able to re-engage it?" Etanu asked.

"Earth would be vulnerable to attack, I know. But still, I wanted to test some Shroud devices and there aren't any here," Zack said.

"They destroyed what they could when they lost Sethion and the rest are in comms blackout until the Xiiginn threat passes," Etanu said.

"A sixty-year blackout? That seems extreme to me."

"What did Gaarokk say about this?"

"He told me he would look into finding some Shroud devices we could experiment with, but to be fair, I only asked him about it last week. I got the impression that he thought it was a good idea," Zack said.

"Well then, you just need to be patient," Etanu said.

This time Zack laughed. "Perhaps I should send Udonzari a message that you've finally learned about being patient."

"I wouldn't," Etanu said.

Zack stopped laughing. "Why not?"

"Because he'll request that I come back to Nerva and join the fleet," Etanu said.

"I thought that would be a good thing. Since the Xiiginns have been ousted from Nerva, it should be safe to return now," Zack said.

"We didn't oust them. We appealed to the Confederation, and the member species voted for the Xiiginns to leave on our behalf," Etanu said.

"I thought the Xiiginns controlled the Confederation."

"They do, which is why the Nershal military has been on high alert. Our last clash with the Xiiginns revealed to them that we had allied ourselves with the Boxans," Etanu said.

"Plus, the Xiiginns needed their fleet to invade Earth, so you guys got a break. It's a good thing," Zack said.

"No, it's not."

Zack matched the strike-fighter's speed with the Athena's orbital velocity so it appeared they had stopped.

"What do you mean it's not?" Zack asked.

"Peace in our star system at the expense of yours is not a good thing. No species should have to live with the threat of a Xiiginn invasion," Etanu said.

Zack nodded. He hated the Xiiginns as much as Etanu did, and the fact that he'd brought up the barrier and killed thousands of Xiiginns hadn't bothered him. Kandra Rene's face still haunted his dreams sometimes. The female Xiiginn had tortured him to get information about Earth and how he and his fellow Humans had arrived in the Nerva star system. At least Zack had been able to resist the Xiiginn compulsion capability. Brenda and Emma strongly believed it was because he loved Kaylan and that shielded him from the Xiiginn's pheromones. Jonah Redford hadn't been as lucky, but Zack was pretty sure Jonah loved himself and science above all else, and that hadn't shielded him. Jonah had fought it as best he could, but it wasn't until they were on the ancient Drar space station that he experienced any relief from his symptoms. Zack glanced at the top observatory on the Athena. Jonah's lab was there, and though the astrophysicist was no longer with them, there were still reminders of him in his lab.

Zack had searched for some clue as to how the Drar had been able to alleviate Jonah's symptoms. It'd been a far cry from a cure, but it might bring those who were afflicted with Xiiginn compulsion some peace. So far, he'd been unsuccessful. It wasn't as if the Drar had any specific data about the Xiiginns specifically, but their AI had been able to diagnose and treat the symptoms until Jonah died. The Drar had given them a tremendous gift that would take them years to even go through and catalog properly, and it would take much more than the crew of the Athena. The more Zack thought about it, the more he kept coming back to their need to get the Athena back home to Earth.

"Do you think the Boxans are lying about having no access to a Star Shroud device?" Etanu asked.

"Not Gaarokk. I trust him, but the others I'm not so sure of. I mean I don't think they'd lie to harm us, but some Boxans have a superiority complex that the others would say made a conflict with a species like the Xiiginns inevitable," Zack said.

"They're learning how to deal with that, I think," Etanu said.

"Yeah, but that perception is still there," Zack said.

He sent a command over to the Athena to open the airlock doors and had the strike-fighter's autopilot maintain the ship's position relative to the Athena.

"Are you ready?" Zack asked.

"I'm always ready. You're the one who forgets crucial pieces of equipment," Etanu said.

"Are you ever going to let me forget about that?" Zack said, remembering the terrifying experience of being exposed to outer space without a helmet.

He was about to open the canopy when a comms channel opened from the planet.

"Congratulations on making it all the way to the Athena, but now I'm afraid you'll need to come back to Olloron," Hicks's voice said over comms.

"Why? What's going on?" Zack asked.

"Kladomaor has returned and he'll be reporting on what they found back home," Hicks said.

Zack's eyes widened. "Alright, we're on our way."

Kladomaor had left them a few weeks earlier to do some reconnaissance near the barrier protecting Earth's star system. It had been a comms-silent mission—no communications allowed back to the colony—so they hadn't gotten a status update. Zack regained control of the strike-fighter and sped back toward the planet.

"Remember to angle your approach unless you prefer to kill us during re-entry," Etanu said.

"I know," Zack said, noticing that he was coming in a bit too steep and adjusting accordingly.

2

Kaylan was in a simulated environment meant for training Mardoxian Sect members, whom their translator referred to as priests and priestesses. She was floating in a virtual world, surrounded by different types of metallic blocks. The blocks converged in front of her, forming an artificial landscape. She touched down on the smooth surface and felt gravity return to the simulation.

Kaylan ran forward, maintaining her awareness of the surrounding area. She had done enough of these exercises to know that the Boxans loved to change the playing field, forcing her to adapt or fail to reach her objective. As she ran, she extended her senses out from her. The artificial landscape changed, becoming uneven, and several tall shafts extended from the floor. Kaylan leaped, grabbing onto one of the nearest ones, and it propelled her to the top. She gazed down at the floor and watched as it disintegrated, revealing a dark nothingness beyond. Kaylan pulled herself up and stood with her head held high. The Mardoxian Sect's training methodology forced their initiates to trust their instincts, allowing their reliance on the sixth sense to become instinctual.

Officially, Kaylan wasn't an initiate into the sect because she was Human but was allowed to train with them. Ma'jasalax had told Kaylan that their training would allow her to further develop her gifts, and the Boxan priestess had been right. Kaylan's concentration hardly ever wavered, and she'd participated in practice sessions where she'd had to navigate through the obstacles in front of her as well as monitoring a half a dozen other environments. At first she'd failed miserably, but after these many months on Olloron, she was mastering what she would have thought were impossible feats before.

Kaylan sat down and closed her eyes to begin meditating, breathing in smooth, even breaths and quieting her mind. Ma'jasalax had told her the brain was a machine that was always working and was her single most powerful asset. When she meditated, she sometimes imagined she was standing in the midst of a thick fog. She wasn't afraid, and she didn't try to control the fog but accepted her place in it.

In this case, the swirling fog thickened and Kaylan cocked her head to the side, listening to a faint sound in the distance. She focused on the source of the sound and felt as if she were drifting forward through the fog toward the origin of the noise. A harsh clang echoed around her, along with heavy footfalls crunching on gravelly ground. A Boxan blaster fired and she cringed. There was a deep rumbling of Boxans speaking in muted tones as if she were listening to them from the other side of a thick wall. Kaylan relaxed and didn't try to force what she was experiencing. Ma'jasalax had taught her that sometimes it was best to allow the things she saw to unfold.

The skin on her forehead chilled painfully as a sharp breeze blew against her face. Plasma bolts blazed through the air, and she felt as if she were standing on a frigid battlefield. Boxans in full power armor stomped loudly nearby. Kaylan peered through the fog but only caught brief glimpses of what she knew must have been there.

There was a loud clearing of the throat and Kaylan spun around. A Boxan stood there in strange red power armor that was unlike anything she'd seen before. The Boxan crouched down and placed its hand on the ground as if trying to sense something Kaylan couldn't see. Then the Boxan turned around and the helmeted head looked directly at her. Kaylan gasped. The towering form of the Boxan lurched backward as if surprised by Kaylan's presence. She heard a tone that was soft at first but steadily gained in intensity. Then the fog disappeared as if there were a giant vacuum that had sucked it all away, and the battle sounds faded.

The latch to the door moved and the simulator door opened. Noises from the chamber beyond barreled their way in, and Kaylan squinted. Light poured through the rounded edges of the doorway. The simulation chamber was soundproof, and it took Kaylan a few moments to get her bearings.

Ma'jasalax peered inside. "I didn't want to pull you out when you were so deep in meditation, but Kladomaor has returned. Our presence is requested in the High Council chambers to hear his report."

Kaylan grabbed the handle and climbed to her feet. The simulator was designed for Boxans, who averaged eight-to-ten feet in height. Her own five-foot-ten inches were a pittance in comparison. Her mouth was dry, and she took a sip of water from the canister she'd set outside before going into the simulator. She rolled her shoulders, stretching stiff muscles, and glanced at her PDA, then looked at Ma'jasalax in surprise.

"Six hours?" Kaylan asked.

"We decided to let you go on longer than before to see how it affected your performance," Ma'jasalax said.

Kaylan frowned. It certainly hadn't felt like she'd been in there that long, but it did explain why she was a bit stiff from sitting for so long.

"I saw it again—Boxans on a battlefield somewhere. They were fighting," Kaylan said.

Ma'jasalax led her away from the simulation chamber. "Do you remember any details?" she asked.

"Someone was wearing red power armor, but it looked different than what I've seen here in the colony. I think the Boxan saw me or sensed me somehow. They reacted to my presence," Kaylan said.

Ma'jasalax gave her a sidelong glance. The Mardoxian priestess came to a stop and approached a wall terminal where a holoscreen flickered on. Kaylan watched as a cycle of Boxan power-armor images flicked past the screen.

Kaylan pointed to one. "That's pretty close to what I saw."

She leaned in to get a better look and then nodded up to Ma'jasalax.

"It's traditional combat armor from before the war with the Xiiginns. More decorative than practical," Ma'jasalax said. She closed down the terminal and waved for Kaylan to follow.

"I don't know why I keep seeing a battle. I don't even know where it is," Kaylan said.

"It may not be taking place anywhere. You're quite gifted and it could be that you're seeing another Boxan's experiences. Most of the Boxans here have seen combat and every Boxan is required to learn basic combat skills," Ma'jasalax said.

Kaylan's brows squished together. "I don't understand. How could I see another Boxan's experiences?"

"You're participating with the other Athena crewmembers in combat training as well as what we're doing here, plus working on understanding what the Drar AI has done to your ship. Your vital signs were showing a sleep pattern," Ma'jasalax said.

"Sleep . . . You mean I'm dreaming instead of seeing an actual event taking place?" Kaylan asked.

"Yes," Ma'jasalax said.

Kaylan chewed on the inside of her cheek in thought. They were all working hard, but it had seemed so real. She'd heard the battle as if she were standing there on the battlefield. She'd felt the moisture on her skin and knew the Boxan in the red armor had seen her. She glanced at Ma'jasalax but didn't say anything. It was a strange thing to suggest and Kaylan wondered if Ma'jasalax was testing her in some way. They were all working hard. Other than the two of them sleeping in the same bed, she had hardly any time to spend with Zack.

They went through the doors into the warm, arid outdoor air and blazing sunlight. This was a marked difference from the high humidity the Boxans preferred, like their home planet of Sethion. Olloron was a world with hotter temperatures due to its orbit being closer to the star in this system. The planet had large landmasses and oceans that covered about sixty percent of the planet's surface, but when compared with the Earth that had over seventy percent of its surface covered in water, it made for a much dryer atmosphere.

Kaylan followed Ma'jasalax over to the transit pad they'd use to quickly travel to the High Council chambers. The Boxans had been residents of this planet for fifty years. It had begun as a small outpost, secreted away, and it was that secret that had saved them from the Xiiginns. Kaylan had asked Ma'jasalax whether they would have considered going to a star system like Earth if they hadn't had

Olloron. The Mardoxian priestess had given her a vague answer, but it still left Kaylan wondering what the Boxan's future plans were. They couldn't fight a war with the Xiiginns forever.

Kaylan used her PDA to check the location of the rest of the Athena's crew and all of them were heading for the general assembly, but Kaylan frowned when she saw Zack's location. He'd gone back to the ship again. He'd been withdrawing from the others and making regular trips back to the Athena. She sometimes found that the others would do something similar, herself included. The Athena was their link to home and sometimes being on their ship made them feel closer to home than being on the surface of the Boxan colony world did.

The transit pad hovered above the ground and then slowly rose into the air over the Mardoxian building complex. The wind blew Kaylan's dark hair back, giving her a momentary reprieve from the heat. They headed toward a large dome-shaped building that other transit pads were approaching. The pads had no railings, but they didn't need any; the sensors wouldn't let anyone fall off during their short flight.

Kaylan glanced up and saw a strike-fighter flying over them, and her lips lifted a bit, knowing Zack was inside. He'd flown with Etanu today since she'd been training with Ma'jasalax.

She turned back toward the dome, eager to learn what Kladomaor had found during his reconnaissance mission back to Earth's star system. The decision for them not to go with Kladomaor had been difficult to make, but ultimately they needed to focus on their work here and learn all they could about what the Drar had done to the Athena. And Kaylan marveled at what they'd been able to figure out. The Drar space station had remade the Athena by merging their technology with what had been built on Earth. There were some systems that not even the Boxans understood. Prior to entering the Drar space station, the Athena's hull hadn't been in the best of shape, which Hicks kept bringing up as a risk to all on board. All of those issues were gone. The hull material was in pristine shape, made of a radically advanced ceramic composite. They'd found references to the new composite formulas, but it would take them time to reproduce it.

While the artificial intelligence on the Drar station had enhanced their ship, it hadn't included any weapon that would give them an edge in combat—at least not directly. There was no big gun they could use to take out hordes of Xiiginns, and to Kaylan that was quite a telling statement on the part of the Drar AI.

The transit pad slowed its approach and landed just outside the domed building where the Boxan High Council met. As Kaylan stepped off, alarms blared near them, along with the sound of strike-fighter engines as Zack brought it down for an impromptu landing in a clearing a short distance away. Boxan soldiers raced over to the craft while Zack and Etanu exited the ship. Kaylan watched as Zack gestured over to where Kaylan and Ma'jasalax waited, and the soldiers let them pass.

"Nice landing, although I don't think they appreciated it," Kaylan said to Zack.

Zack grinned. "Etanu mentioned something about surprise landings and that there wouldn't always be a designated area for them."

"Don't you blame this on me. I was referring to what you'd do if your ship was damaged and you *needed* an emergency landing," Etanu said.

Zack rolled his eyes. "I set it down right over there and everything turned out fine."

Kaylan had been around Zack long enough to learn some of his behavior patterns. He was getting restless and these little moments of rebellion were indications that he needed a change.

"Zack," Kaylan said, "landing a strike-fighter in the middle of a populated area isn't the best way to treat our hosts."

Zack blew out a breath. "Fine, I'll move it after we're done here."

They headed inside and Kaylan fell into step next to him. She leaned over so only he could hear. "It was a good landing."

"Thanks," Zack said with a half smile. "Maybe when this is over we can take a ride?"

Kaylan nodded but wondered whether the Boxans would allow Zack to keep flying after his little stunt. If anything, the Boxans were rigid in their rules of expected behavior from their guests.

They met up with the rest of the Athena's crew and Hicks worked his way over to Zack.

"Why didn't you join us this morning?" Hicks asked.

"I'm not doing combat training anymore," Zack said.

"How come?"

"I know the basics and that's enough for now. I'm going to spend more time working with the Athena's systems," Zack said.

Hicks nodded. "That's fine. We just didn't know where you were."

Zack glanced at Hicks for a moment. "Etanu was giving me a flying lesson."

"Excellent, but I did want to tell you that you might have liked what we were doing today," Hicks said.

Zack's brows pushed forward. "What were you guys doing?"

"We got to use their exoskeletal suits," Hicks said.

Zack's eyes widened. "The ones that make you super strong and jump really high?"

Hicks nodded.

Kaylan grinned as she watched the warring emotions on Zack's face. It must have been every little boy's dream to put on a suit of armor that could make them super strong and impervious to danger.

Since this briefing pertained to them directly, Kaylan and the others were ushered to a designated area set aside for them near the front. The Boxans were a large race of beings and made every effort to be sure their guests were comfortable, which included appropriately sized chairs for them to sit on.

Ma'jasalax went over to where the Mardoxian Sect representatives gathered in the High Assembly. There was a deep, quiet murmuring throughout the vast hall, but there were only about fifty Boxans in attendance. The Boxan High Council was made up of seven members that included their leader, who was a Boxan named Awan.

Awan glanced over at Kaylan and the others. "Thank you for coming on such short notice. When we received Kladomaor's communications, we anticipated that you'd be as eager to hear the news as we are."

"Thank you, High Councilor," Kaylan replied. The crew of the Athena had decided that she was to speak for them.

A door on the far side of the chamber opened and Kladomaor entered, followed by Gaarokk and some other members of his crew. Kaylan had noted that Kladomaor preferred to work with the same crew when he embarked on missions, but she'd later learned that the Battle Commander was a bit of an outsider even among his own species. He was the only living Boxan to be brought back from the brink of madness at the hands of the Xiiginns and their compulsion ability. It was fair to say that Kladomaor was once a war hero who was no longer entirely trusted by his own race. Ma'jasalax had vouched for him, and it was through the High Council's respect for the Mardoxian Sect that Kladomaor was still able to serve.

Kladomaor walked over to the designated speaker's area and glanced at the Athena's crew. His facial features could have been chiseled from stone for all they gave away.

High Councilor Awan brought the assembly to a start. "Battle Commander, please report your findings to us."

"We returned to the Sol System to study the Shroud barrier and have learned that it possesses the same energy signature as the barrier we encountered at the Drar space station. There were no offensive capabilities, but that was expected. The sequence of code used to realign the Shroud device and change its composition wouldn't give it offensive capabilities," Kladomaor said.

"So the Earth is protected for the time being," High Councilor Awan said.

"That's true, but I have more to report," Kladomaor said.

"Please continue."

"We ran a multitude of tests on the barrier and it's capable of withstanding an assault from our most powerful weapons; however, the barrier is shrinking," Kladomaor said.

Kaylan stood up. "How fast is it shrinking?"

Kladomaor turned toward her. "We're not sure. We've left sensor equipment to monitor and measure, but it will require another mission to retrieve the data."

"Are the Xiiginns still there?" Kaylan asked.

"There was no Xiiginn presence detected, just a vast field of wreckage from the ships they weren't able to salvage," Kladomaor said.

"Were there any survivors from the Dreadnaughts?" Kaylan asked.

"No, unfortunately not. The Dreadnaughts were completely destroyed, but we did find a data recorder jettisoned prior to the battle," Kladomaor said and turned back to the High Council. "Prax'pedax sent non-essential personnel, tech platforms, and orbital defensive platforms back to Earth before engaging the Xiiginns. There's an excellent chance that there are surviving Boxans and Humans alive in the Sol System."

High Councilor Awan shifted his gaze to Kaylan. "What do you think your race will do?"

Kaylan glanced at the others, unsure what to say. Anything she said would be pure speculation. "I'd like to think they would be working together."

Hicks stood up and the high councilor nodded for him to speak. "The data we collected prior to leaving showed that the Xiiginns were sending asteroids to the interior of the star system. They were likely targeting Earth. A clear and present danger like that would have caused the cooperation of Earth's militaries. They would have joined together to mitigate the attack. Assuming they all survived, and with the help of the Boxans, my guess would be that they're building a fleet to protect themselves."

Kaylan looked at the Boxans on the High Council and got the impression that none of them were pleased.

Kladomaor cleared his throat. "The data recorder also contained Prax'pedax's personal logs. He was aware that he'd broken protocol for dealing with a less advanced species. He recognized, as I have, that in order to survive we must work with species like the Humans."

"Prax'pedax operated outside of his mandate to protect the Earth. Those protocols are in place to ensure a safe path for all those involved. We intend to work with the Humans, but Prax'pedax's actions may have put them in even more danger," High Councilor Awan said.

Zack let out a bitter laugh while coming to his feet.

"What are you doing?" Kaylan asked.

"No, I finally get it. I see what's going on here," Zack said to Kaylan. "They're angry that Prax'pedax deviated from protocol and took an action that was outside the confines of the council." Zack turned toward the council. "He was there and he decided that the best course of action was to share your precious technology with us so we could all have a fighting chance against the Xiiginns. Does that about sum it up?"

"Zack," Hicks warned.

"No," Zack said. "I want them to answer. We're here right now today because they tried to control the galaxy with an iron fist. Tell me, what were Prax'pedax's orders if the Xiiginns defeated your ships?"

Kaylan's face flushed until she realized the implications of what Zack was saying. She stood by his side and faced the High Council. "It's a fair question and one that needs to be answered," she said in a steely tone.

High Councilor Awan shifted his feet and faced them fully. "Yours is a species that we cannot allow to fall to the Xiiginns. Your species is the only other race we've encountered with the Mardoxian potential. Battle Leader Prax'pedax was tasked with protecting your planet at all costs, but if he was unable to complete this task then he was to prevent the Earth from becoming an asset to the Xiiginns."

Zack growled in disgust. "Unbelievable . . ."

Kaylan's mouth hung open in disbelief. She looked at Ma'jasalax, who was watching her intently. Kaylan was prepared to work with the Boxans and make this alliance work, but this was too much.

"I realize that our stance appears to be harsh and I understand your initial response," High Councilor Awan said.

"I don't think you do. Not really," Kaylan said. "How can you expect us to be in alliance with you with these kinds of contingency plans?"

"We expect you to respect our judgment," High Councilor Awan said.

"This is bullshit," Zack said.

"Hold on a minute," Hicks said. "If our survival was at stake, do you think our own governments would react differently?"

"Yes, we would because we're not all military. Not everything is a damn objective. We don't quantify life as a numbers game," Kaylan snapped.

"You are exactly right," Ma'jasalax said, drawing their attention. "And not only that, Prax'pedax agreed as well," she said and then faced the High Council. "Prax'pedax's record shows a strong alignment with our original ideals. He represented the best among us and yet, upon meeting with the Humans directly, he changed his mind. He saw something in them, much as Kladomaor and I have, that has influenced us to question some of our stricter protocols."

"These are the protocols that have allowed us to survive," High Councilor Awan said.

"No doubt Prax'pedax thought the same thing, but do you see their reactions?" Ma'jasalax said, and the Boxans in the chamber swung their gazes toward the crew of the Athena. "They are but a few, but I would place a strong probability that their reactions are aligned with the rest of their species. If we persist along this path, no species will enter an alliance with us."

There were a few moments of heavy silence. High Councilor Awan glanced at the other members of the High Council and then turned back toward Kaylan and the others.

"We respect the counsel of the Mardoxian Sect and each of us will spend time in quiet meditation considering the implications of our actions."

The Boxan high councilor waited.

"Thank you," Kaylan said in a neutral tone.

She glanced at Zack, who was seething, and the rest of the crew had guarded expressions.

"When will another team return to the Sol System? We need to understand how long the barrier can last before the system itself is in jeopardy," Kaylan said.

"We will send a regular team to investigate shortly and then compile and analyze the data here. Is that acceptable?" High Councilor Awan asked.

Kaylan nodded.

"Good. I have a request here from our scientific division. They're asking that the Athena be docked and its components studied directly," Awan said.

"Unacceptable," Kaylan said. "In fact, some members of my crew have expressed interest in spending more time on the Athena to study the Drar improvements. Those efforts were previously put on hold to allow you to perform your remote analysis while you educated us on some of your technology. Now that we have that foundation, we're in a position to better understand what was done to our ship."

The high councilor paused before answering. Clearly, he hadn't expected Kaylan's response. "Of course. We understand and shall assist however we can."

Kaylan nodded and found that she wanted to put some distance between herself and the Boxans. She caught Kladomaor watching her and she had the impression that there was more he wanted to say to them. She turned toward the rest of the crew.

"I think we need to talk about a few things."

The rest of them agreed. Kaylan looked back at the Boxans, thinking that for all their advanced technology and their dry, logical approach to anything in their path, they seemed to be forgetting a very important thing. All life wanted to live and would struggle to do so regardless of everything else. The Boxans had spent too much time surviving and not enough time living, and their race was suffering because of it.

3

E ight months had passed since the Earth was almost destroyed, eight months since the skies above Earth were forever changed. Ed Johnson still caught himself looking up at the new moon as if he still couldn't quite believe it was there. At the same time, he thought it was a daily reminder of the danger Earth was in. Ed drained the last of his bourbon and set the cup down. The brisk air of the Blue Ridge Mountains had more than a chill to it, but he'd always found that the rooftop patio of his secret hideaway held some semblance of peace—a place to recharge his batteries with its scenic views of the surrounding forests and a clear view of the stars. He gazed at the new moon, which was visibly smaller than the old one but no less beautiful. Some astronomers wanted to call the new moon Hephaestus, blacksmith of the gods who made weapons of divine strength, and Ed supposed their efforts on the mineral-rich new moon fit the name. Mining efforts had been underway for several months while tech bases were constructed so they could finally build spaceships of their own. He should be pleased with what they'd accomplished in such a short span of time, but he wasn't.

The Earth had been given a reprieve from an alien fleet that wanted to invade, but the fact that they were completely cut off from the rest of the galaxy even confused the Boxans. Boxan scientists had surmised that the barrier surrounding their solar system had to do with the Star Shroud, but even they were at a loss as to what had happened. The Star Shrouds were designed to filter out artificial wavelengths from penetrating a star system's interior while allowing outbound observations to occur without interference. They were a miracle of engineering that most scientists had trouble coming to grips with. Physicists from the mid-twentieth century had theorized the existence of a Dyson sphere, which was a hypothetical mega-structure built around a star to capture the energy coming from it, but even Ed understood that the Star Shroud was way beyond those theoretical concepts.

Zack Quick had been the first to crack the signal the Shroud devices used to communicate with one another. The young hacker had sent all his findings back to Earth before the Athena disappeared, but nothing he'd sent back had allowed them to communicate with the Shroud devices since the barrier. Not even the Boxans were able to control them. They were still deploying tiny monitoring drones that would report back to Earth about the barrier.

The barrier was the source of many debates around the globe. Since the barrier was in place, wasn't the Earth safe now? The barrier had blocked the Xiiginn ships from reaching Earth, so why did they need to devote all their resources to building ships of their own? Thankfully there were opposing arguments that were much more sensible.

"Ed, the meeting is about to begin," Iris called to him.

Ed turned around and crossed the rooftop patio to where Iris Barrett, his personal assistant and bodyguard, had set up mobile communications. Iris clicked her wrists together to activate the controls and several holoscreens came on. After a few moments, a view of General Sheridan sitting at the head of a long conference table came into view. The General wore his army fatigues, and his short, gunmetal-gray hair showed white around his ears.

Officially the Earth Coalition Force, or ECF, was under the dominion of the United Nations Security Council, which Ed found interesting because China and Russia still hadn't ratified it. In reality, the ECF existed in a gray area of international politics. Most of the ECF funding was coming from the other permanent member states of the UN, like the United States, France, and the United Kingdom, along with non-permanent member states like Japan, among many others. It wasn't enough, and this UN Security Council meeting was a long time coming. Here, they could finally nail down more support for the ECF.

"Hello, William," Ed said.

Another holoscreen came up and showed the UN Security Council chambers. A large circular desk was in the center of the room where nations could come and work together to maintain peace and security.

"Let's hope Rebecca Sharp is on top of her game today," Sheridan said.

"She's good and always on top of her game. She wouldn't be an ambassador if she weren't," Ed said.

Sheridan arched a brow and leaned toward the screen. Their comms channel was encrypted so there was no chance that someone else could be listening in on them. "Did her appointment to the UN involve you in any way?"

Ed chuckled. "You give me too much credit. It's in our best interest to know who all the power players are."

"So what's this going to cost us?" Sheridan asked.

"A lot. The Chinese are tough negotiators," Ed said.

"And the Russians?"

"They'll likely follow China's lead, but we need their help," Ed said.

Sheridan snorted.

"Believe what you want, but China has one of the largest workforces in the world, which is something we need to build a fleet."

"You know, I've spent a majority of my career neutralizing threats from them and getting into bed like this will change things. We're not going to become allies overnight," Sheridan said.

"We have to change; otherwise, there won't be many of us left."

General Sheridan eyed him for a moment. "I know what they're going to ask for and I'm sure you have a good idea as well."

"Of course. They'll want access to Boxan technology, as well as a few slots on your senior staff."

"And you'd be okay with that?"

Ed knew it didn't matter what he'd be willing to accept. Sheridan just wanted to know his perspective. It was the mark of an excellent leader to consider other viewpoints when making decisions.

"What I'd be okay with has little bearing on any of this. Can you function with those terms? Do you think the ECF would thrive with those terms?" Ed asked.

"What good will it do if we build our own ships to start shooting each other with? That's not going to stop the Xiiginns."

"First, we have to build a fleet. Then we have to be able to hold our own against the Xiiginns. Whatever comes after that will be someone else's problem. I do think that both the Russians and the Chinese can bring a valuable perspective to the table," Ed said.

"What's that?"

"Both of them have had to contend with how to counter a superior military force for a long time. They've spent years developing ways to outthink a more powerful enemy. It's this perspective that will be valuable to the ECF," Ed said.

"While gaining a technological advantage that is leaps and bounds over what they had before," Sheridan said.

"So will we. One thing history has taught us is that having an advantage and strategically executing an advantage are two different things. It's what we're able to do with the technology and our ability to keep it in working order that will prove which of us is going to last."

They watched the UN Security Council session. Rebecca Sharp deftly steered the meeting to the primary agenda and events unfolded much as Ed expected they would until it came time for China's UN Ambassador to present the People's Liberation Army's top pick to join the ECF: General Heng Shang.

Sheridan leaned back in his chair, shaking his head. "They can't be serious. Shang was indicted for fraud and corruption."

Ed brought up Shang's dossier on his holoscreen. Shang was one brutal SOB with a record for placing a high priority on seizing the initiative in conflict regardless of the cost. He also knew how to get the most out the men working under him and he'd never missed a deadline or a target that he was ordered to attain.

"Screw this. They can give us another candidate. I won't work with that man. He'll have no place on *my* staff," Sheridan said.

Ed took a deep breath. There were worse candidates but not much. "Just listen to me for a second," he said.

Sheridan looked squarely at the camera, his face red with anger. "Make it short."

"You can deny their candidate, but if you do, the negotiations will get bogged down for months. We're already on borrowed time and we're not sure when our time is going to run out. We don't need a perfect army to go to war with and we only have this one chance to get in front of this thing without massive casualties," Ed said.

Ed felt as if there were a train thundering in his ears while he watched Sheridan think about what he'd said. Suddenly, the holoscreen went dark. Sheridan had cut the connection, and Ed swore.

There were contingency plans should the ECF fail at this juncture, but it would put their manufacturing model out five years without help from the Chinese and the Russians. If they had global support, they could have ships completed within another year. They didn't have time to crawl or stumble. They had to learn to run—and run as fast as they could.

Iris closed down the mobile communications center and turned toward him. "What do you think he'll do?" she asked.

Ed shrugged. "I'm not sure. I know what I want him to do, but Sheridan is in a tough position. The repercussions of his decisions will affect generations to come."

"You know I have five older brothers," Iris said.

Ed shook his head. "I didn't know that."

"Yup and they were all strong-willed and fought with each other constantly. It wasn't until our mother put them to work that they started to get along."

"What did she have them do?"

"She bought an old car that needed a lot of work and told them that if they could fix it up, they could drive the car. So, grumbling and cursing and a few bruises later, they eventually fixed that car up. Then they fixed up another car and word got spread around. Eventually they opened a repair shop that they all still operate to this day," Iris said.

"So you think if we just force them to work together they'll work their differences out? I'm not sure that's going to work in this case," Ed said.

"It would be nice if it did. If you want my honest opinion, I don't think the UN Security Council is scared enough. We had a close call with that asteroid, but the fight has hardly come to our backyard," Iris said.

"Sheridan gets it. He understands what's at stake."

"You're right. He does to an extent. Heng Shang can deliver results. We may not like the method, but at least we'll be alive to have the preference. Sheridan should make use of Shang but also try to keep him honest," Iris said.

"I had no idea you were so pragmatic."

"That's crap and you know it. One more thing that was made clear from that meeting, the UN Security Council doesn't get what's at stake. They still think there's a way for them to survive what's coming without banding together," Iris said.

Ed headed for the door to the house. "Well, we'll just have to change their minds, won't we?"

4

Michael Hunsicker had more or less taken up permanent residence on Armstrong Lunar Base. He'd been back to Colorado to visit his grandkids but only for a short period, and his children understood why he needed to leave them again. Since getting back to Earth, he felt he had a new lease on life. He visited Kathryn's grave and told her about all he'd been through. He would always miss her but now felt more at peace with her passing than he ever had. And it wasn't long before he was recruited to join the Earth Coalition Force on loan from NASA, as it were. He was the foremost expert and liaison to the Boxans.

During his short stint back home, he'd noticed how people still watched the new moon with a sense of trepidation. Michael approved the way General Sheridan hadn't sugarcoated the news that the Xiiginns had sent the behemoth-sized asteroid to destroy the Earth. The Boxans believed the Xiiginns used the asteroid as a ploy to divide the people of Earth. Misinformation was a strategy the Xiiginns often employed to achieve their goals. The ploy had nearly worked and had been almost catastrophic for Earth.

After weeks of analysis, it had been generally accepted that after the Boxan Dreadnaughts were destroyed, it was the Shroud barrier that had prevented the Xiiginn fleet from reaching Earth. The Boxans confirmed that the engine farm that had propelled the new moon toward the Earth was of Xiiginn design, and the barrier prevented any 'abort' signal the Xiiginns would have sent to prevent Earth's destruction. It had been a carefully orchestrated gambit, with the Earth caught in the crosshairs. Those engines had been disabled and the materials repurposed for the mining stations that had been built all over the new moon.

Over the months, the lunar base had become more of a colony, with additions to the existing base being added to accommodate the additional ECF personnel working up there. The Boxans had also built their own habitats on the lunar surface, even though there had been many offers for the Boxans to come to

Earth. They did go to the planet surface but only for short periods of time. Michael had asked Chazen about this behavior and the Boxan had simply said it was for the best at this point. The Boxans did, however, make themselves available to advise the new technological centers springing up all over Earth. It would be a joint effort to build the ECF's first fleet to protect the planet.

It didn't make sense to bring all the materials mined from the new moon down to Earth's surface in any significant capacity. Near the mining outposts, the Boxan tech platforms left by Prax'pedax were being put to good use. The platforms had enabled them to get to a point where producing the materials needed for ships was taking months instead of years. The ECF engineering division had even been able to build their own tech platforms based on what they'd been taught by the Boxans.

A reminder message appeared on Michael's internal heads-up display and underneath came a text message from Alyssa.

::Breakfast?::

::You bet. I'll be right there.:: Michael sent back.

He finished dressing and left his room. Alyssa Archer was the commander in charge of running Lunar Base. Since he'd first arrived here from Pluto, he and Alyssa had become fast friends. They were both in their fifties. He was a widower and she was divorced. They enjoyed each other's company and both of them had decided not to make it any more complicated than that. She had a strong, no-nonsense attitude that he liked. At this stage in his life, he didn't want to try to guess what she was thinking, and she had never been one to hold her opinion back.

Michael's stomach growled. Bacon and eggs, followed by a cup of coffee, were calling his name. Perhaps he'd even indulge in some toast. With his mouth watering, he closed in on the officer's mess hall, but before he could reach it Allyssa walked out and waved over to him.

"Change of plans. We've got to meet with the Mirae Corporation's representative now instead of later," Alyssa said.

Michael glanced longingly at the mess hall, smelling the rich aroma of breakfast food.

Alyssa tossed a protein bar toward him and he caught it.

He looked at the prepackaged block that was supposed to tide him over. "Thanks," Michael said.

"Don't be such a baby," Alyssa said and quickened her pace.

Michael tore open the package and bit into the protein bar that was ostensibly some mix of coconut, chocolate, and peanut butter, but most of all it lacked any kind of flavor. Hopefully, there'd be some coffee in the conference room on the ECF wing of the base.

"Why'd they move the meeting up?" Michael asked.

"All red-line projects get priority, and right now we've got a bunch of Mirae mechs here that we can't use," Alyssa said.

They came to the security checkpoint and used their neural implants to authenticate, after which the doors opened and they entered the new ECF wing of the base. The hallways were larger and the ceiling much higher in order to accommodate the Boxans who also worked there. The gray, lunar-rock walls had been smoothed down but still had a bit of roughness to them.

They entered the command center, and if the ECF wing had been a ship, then the command center would have been the bridge. It was a large, semi-circular room with different work areas for the various teams assigned there.

Michael spotted Colonel Kyle Mathews speaking with Chazen and one Boxan soldier whose name he couldn't recall.

"We need to get the mechs up and running ASAP," they heard Colonel Mathews saying.

Michael and Alyssa walked over and Kyle greeted them.

"Great, you're here," Kyle said. "Maybe now you'll tell the Mirae Corp representative to find a way to get these things working before I order them scrapped and used for strike-fighters."

"What's the problem?" Michael said and glanced down through the window at a cavernous work area. Off to the side were two lines of hulking robotic mechs that were made by the Mirae Corporation based out of South Korea. The manned mechs could be adapted to a variety of tasks from combat to working with heavy materials.

"In layman terms, we're having power issues, and the onboard computers seem a bit flaky," Kyle said.

A man named Lewis was about to speak, but Kyle cut him off.

"I know it's more technical than that, but ultimately that's what the problem is," Kyle said.

They headed over to the conference room located away from the command center and the automatic door shut behind them. Holoscreens powered on and a comms channel was opened planet-side.

Three men appeared onscreen. All had short dark hair and wore dark suits.

"Hello, Pak Jun-Seo. Are you able to see us?" Alyssa asked.

"Loud and clear, Mrs. Archer," Pak Jun-Seo said.

"It's Miss. I haven't been a misses in a long time," Alyssa said.

"Apologies," Pak Jun-Seo said and then introduced his two companions. Mae Hyo was the head robotics engineer and Kam Min-Su was the department head for the mech's operating system.

After the introductions, Pak Jun-Seo focused his gaze on Michael.

"It's our honor to be speaking to you, Mr. Hunsicker," Pak Jun-Seo said.

Michael bowed his head slightly and the Koreans returned the bow in kind.

"I've had our teams here review the reported problems and we do have some options to present," Pak Jun-Seo said.

Lewis cleared his throat and Alyssa nodded for him to speak. "If you have a software patch for the mech operating system, you can transmit that here and we'll review and test it before it gets deployed to the other mechs."

"This will not be possible," Kam Min-Su said.

"Why the hell not?" Lewis asked.

"The code is proprietary and only Mirae employees are authorized to update the kernel of the mech's operating system code," Kam Min-Su said.

"You've got to be kidding me," Lewis said and glanced over at Kyle.

The Colonel looked as if he were about to spit fire. "You guys realize that we're working from the moon. This isn't some operation where we can just come and get you to fix your damn broken mechs."

Michael suspected the Colonel had been about to call the mechs something else entirely.

Pak Jun-Seo regarded them calmly. "We do realize this complicates things, but this is the only way we can vouch for the proper operation of our mechs."

Colonel Mathews turned away, shaking his head. "Mute the call," he said.

The comms tech running the meeting told the Mirae representatives that they needed a minute.

"Call muted, Sir," the comms tech said.

"This is bullshit," Kyle said.

"It is," Alyssa said. "And they won't be the first to try this tactic with us."

"Well, we can't give in to this crap. Even if I wanted their employees here, Sheridan's staff would never authorize it. The ECF may be a new organization, but it's still run like a military branch," Kyle said.

"What choice do we have?" Michael asked.

He didn't have a head for this sort of politics. He knew how to solve problems directly in front of him, but this was an entirely new arena for him.

"I'm sure that with a little bit of time I could update the code myself," Lewis said.

Michael glanced at the engineer. He had brown curly hair and looked to be in his thirties. Lewis's statement about updating the code himself reminded him of Zack Quick. It wasn't the first time he'd thought about the hacker-turned-astronaut. If Zack had been here, Michael was sure he would have already updated the code and gotten the mechs working before the rest of them even knew there was a problem to begin with.

"How much time would that take? And then we'd run the risk of introducing other problems with our fix," Michael said.

"What about the Boxans? Could we ask for their help?" Lewis asked.

Both Kyle and Alyssa shook their heads. "We can't go running to the Boxans to sort out our issues for us. We should be able to handle this ourselves," Kyle said.

"I say we hand this up the chain. We give Sheridan the options, along with our recommendation, and let them decide," Alyssa said.

Michael nodded. "The ECF is supposed to be bringing in people from all the nations supporting the effort."

"Yeah, but in the meantime this sets us behind," Kyle said.

Alyssa was commander of the base, but this was EFC-related, and currently Colonel Kyle Mathews was the ranking officer, so the decision was up to him.

Kyle glanced over at the comms tech. "Open the channel back up."

The Koreans turned back toward the holoscreen. "We await your decision," Pak Jun-Seo said.

"I'll authorize four of your techs to come here to fix our mechs. The one condition I must insist on is that Kam Min-Su and Mae Hyo be the two leads that come as well," Kyle said.

Kam Min-Su's skin paled and he glanced at the others nervously.

"Acceptable," Pak Jun-Seo said.

Kam Min-Su swallowed hard. "I'll need some time to gather my team and the equipment we'll need."

"You have one hour," Kyle said. "I'll have a shuttle brought right to Mirae headquarters to pick you and the other two members of your team up."

Kam Min-Su was about to reply when Kyle cut the comms channel.

"Do you think Sheridan will go along with this?" Alyssa asked.

"He cares that we get things done. I'll send him an update and he can countermand the order if he wants, but he won't. I have operational authority here and he needs those damn mechs working," Kyle said and looked at Lewis. "When the Koreans get here, I want you and Alan to be with them at all times. They may have bartered their way onto this base, but this is going to be a knowledge-sharing job for them. If they don't like it, then I'm sure I know a few people who can properly convince them for me."

Michael felt his lips curve upward. He was glad Kyle was in charge of this. He'd get results and knew how to apply the right amount of pressure to get the job done.

"Why bring Kam Min-Su and Mae Hyo here?" Michael asked.

"Because they're department heads who know the ins and outs of those mechs. If Mirae Corp wanted to get cute and barter their way onto this base, I'm sure as hell going to get the most out of this deal," Kyle answered.

Michael watched the colonel for a moment. He'd seemed angry before, and while he was still annoyed by the Koreans, it hadn't distracted him from what was important. Kyle Mathews was one of the reasons Earth was still here and the rest of them still had a place to call home.

"Come on, I need you to kindly ask the Boxans to pick up a few people for me," Kyle said, grinning.

Michael snorted and knew this wouldn't be the last time a country or corporation would try to use their position of supporting the ECF as a way to muscle their way inside.

5

K aylan stood on the Athena's bridge with Emma. The crew rotated coming back to the Athena, and it felt much like a homecoming. They'd been given living quarters on the planet that were quite comfortable, but the Athena was the only place they could really call their own.

Emma sighed. "It feels good to be back doesn't it?"

"Yes, it does," Kaylan agreed.

"I have to admit that when we first got to Olloron, I couldn't wait to get off the ship and feel solid ground beneath my feet. Now I just want to get back home," Emma said, and there was a catch in her voice.

"We'll get home," Kaylan said, giving Emma a hug, "and Tom will be waiting for you. You'll have your wedding."

Emma laughed. "I feel so stupid," she said and pulled away, wiping her eyes. "I know we'll get home. I have to believe it, but I just miss him so much. I keep replaying his last video message to me. He was holding our dog at our favorite park, trying to get him to wave at the camera."

Kaylan's eyes became misty as well.

"How are you and Zack doing?" Emma asked.

"Oh, . . . we're fine," Kaylan said a little too quickly and knew Emma wasn't fooled. "We try to be discreet, but lately there just hasn't been a lot of time and sometimes . . . he can be . . ."

"Zack," Emma supplied.

"Yes!" Kaylan laughed. "What would you do if Tom were here?"

Emma frowned. "You mean after I jumped his bones all night because I haven't gotten laid in over a year?"

Kaylan felt her cheeks redden. Emma was usually so well spoken with her British accent that to hear her like this was sometimes disarming.

"I don't know if he and I being in a confined space like a ship would be best for our relationship. Don't get me wrong. I love him, madly, but sometimes . . . men," Emma said.

Kaylan didn't mind being near Zack, but she also understood what Emma meant. Her sister Iris loved her husband but needed her own space to help balance it out.

"Have you thought what you and Zack will do after we get back home?" Emma asked.

"Take a vacation on a beach somewhere far away and not be bothered by anyone else for a while. That's what I'd want, but given all this, I doubt we'll be any less busy than we are right now," Kaylan said.

Emma nodded. "Indeed, all this," she said as she went over to the conference table and turned on the holodisplay. "I wanted to talk to you about the Boxans."

Kaylan walked over. "What about them?"

"I've been doing my own analysis of Olloron and the Boxan population," Emma said.

"Okay, what have you found out?" Kaylan asked.

"It's strange. The Boxans don't reproduce fast, but on their home planet, their population numbered in the billions, according to their records. Here, on Olloron, there are only a few hundred million of them. They've been here for fifty years, give or take, and their population hasn't changed that much," Emma said.

"Well, they *have* been fighting a war," Kaylan said.

"I've accounted for that, but even with that, their population isn't growing and cannot be sustained on this planet," Emma said.

Kaylan's forehead wrinkled. Emma was a biologist and this was her field. "Are you sure?"

"Yes. I've run my analysis half a dozen times and it all indicates that Olloron cannot sustain the Boxans for more than a hundred years at the most. That's assuming they can even maintain their population. One of the reasons I wanted to come up here was to have Athena look at my data models to see if they're correct," Emma said.

Kaylan watched as Emma transferred a file from her PDA and uploaded it to Athena's data storage.

"I'd be happy to look at your work, Dr. Roberson," the AI said. "Analyzing . . . complete. Your findings are accurate."

"How could they not know this?" Kaylan asked.

"Empirical evidence would suggest that the Boxans already *do* know these facts and have not acted on this knowledge," the AI said.

Kaylan pressed her lips together in thought. Could an entire species be in denial about their situation?

"I can't believe they would simply ignore this problem. Do you know if they've tried to find another colony world?" Kaylan asked.

"I tried looking on the systems we have access to, but if they're looking, they're not devoting a lot of resources to it," Emma said.

"Perhaps they have a way to extend their time here on Olloron?"

Emma shook her head. "Unlikely because this planet isn't mineral-rich like Earth. It's only capable of sustaining limited forests and tundra, but even the oceans aren't teeming with life. If it were as simple as bringing water to this planet, that would be one thing, but the low mineral content of the soil suggests this world has already been depleted. It also doesn't have a moon, so no tides. The moon and the tides back on Earth are essential for life to flourish."

Kaylan studied the data onscreen. The Boxans weren't just losing a war with the Xiiginns, they were in danger of going extinct forever if they didn't find a safe place to live.

"They're stuck in this rigid cycle," Kaylan said.

Emma nodded. "And that's why we need to be careful, I think."

"Why is that?"

"They've had to make really tough decisions—so many that I can't even imagine how they've managed to keep it together as long as they have. But when a society gets into this cycle of surviving and only surviving, they see everything as a tough choice that requires sacrifice. It becomes almost instinctual. I don't think all the Boxans feel this way, but this perception is certainly shared by many of them," Emma said.

"Well, they've lost a lot."

"They have, but they might lose even more if they don't deal with this problem now. They need to find a permanent home," Emma said.

"I want to talk to Ma'jasalax about this and see what she thinks. It could be that the Mardoxian Sect is trying to steer the High Council in this direction," Kaylan said.

"They do seem to be at the heart of many things . . ."

The rest of what Emma said suddenly became muffled in Kaylan's ears as she closed her eyes to a flash of light and heard the distinct sounds of a blaster being fired.

"Kaylan, are you alright?" Emma asked while shaking Kaylan's shoulders.

Kaylan opened her eyes. "I'm all right."

Emma frowned. "Maybe I should call Brenda."

Kaylan shook her head. "No, it's nothing. I'm fine. Just a bit tired, I think. I've had some strange dreams lately."

Emma looked at her for a long moment. "What have you been dreaming about?"

Kaylan told her about the Boxan in the red power armor and being on a battlefield.

"I'm not surprised you've got Boxans on the brain. We all do, but are you sure this isn't your ability rather than a dream?"

"I'm not sure," Kaylan admitted.

"Maybe you should try and use a Mardoxian chamber to see if that gives you a stronger vision. If nothing happens, you'll know it was just a dream," Emma said.

Kaylan smiled. "That's a good idea. I think I'll give that a try."

6

Kaylan and Zack had spent the night alone aboard the Athena and were eating breakfast in the mess hall.

"You know we have this ship that we could use to just fly right out of here," Zack said.

Kaylan shook her head.

"Or take the shuttle and find some remote part of Olloron that the Boxans haven't been to yet," Zack said.

"I need to get back down to the surface," Kaylan said.

"Let me guess. Ma'jasalax."

"Yes, I do need to see her. It's about what Emma told me yesterday."

Zack nodded. "I get it. Well, I don't really get it. Why would anyone stay somewhere that wasn't going to keep them alive? That doesn't make any sense to me, but . . . you know what? It does make sense to me," he said, his eyes lighting up.

"Really," Kaylan said unconvinced.

"Yes, really. When my mom left us, my dad and I couldn't stay in our house. We couldn't afford it anymore. The one thing my dad insisted on keeping was a 1968 Dodge Charger. It was a beautiful car. God, I miss that thing. We'd work on it on weekends and stuff, but what I didn't know at the time was that it was worth a fortune. He could have sold it and made a lot of money, but he didn't. It was like this was the one thing he could hold onto. It was almost like he would lose his identity if he sold that car. He held onto it even when it didn't make sense to keep it any longer, but it was his. I'm wondering if there are some similarities with the way the Boxans feel about Olloron, as a way of holding onto their identity." Zack said.

Kaylan eyed him for a moment. "You're equating an entire species' determination to stay on a planet they can't survive on with your dad's car?"

Zack nodded with a smile. "Yes, I am. This was a colony world. They already lost their home planet. There's only so much loss a person can take before they throw in the towel and just hold on or let go."

As the seconds went by, Kaylan found that Zack was making a lot of sense. His dark, penetrating eyes regarded her and he saw her finally get his point. Sometimes she wondered what Zack would do if he had the Mardoxian trait like she did. He already had the uncanny ability to see right to the heart of any matter and put it in simplified terms that anyone could understand. It was something she admired in him.

"Whatever happened to the car?" Kaylan asked.

Zack's ears turned red. "I had to sell it when he died."

Kaylan stroked his forearm. "That's not your fault."

"I didn't even think about it, about how much that car meant to him. I was actually happy that it sold because it paid a lot of bills, but still, I should have . . ."

Kaylan pulled him into her arms. "You were so young. I remember what it did to you. How could you have known? We should try and find the car when we get back."

Zack frowned. "Are you serious? The car is gone. Who knows where it could be?"

Kaylan rolled her eyes. "You manage to decode an alien signal, but a car with a VIN number is beyond you? Don't be an idiot. We'll find that car when we get back home."

Zack sighed heavily. "Why's this so important to you?"

"Because it's important to you, dummy," Kaylan said.

"Do you have any idea what it will cost? It's a collector's item—" he stopped himself and then shook his head. "No," he said and stepped away from her. "I don't need charity."

Kaylan shook her head. "We're going to argue about this here? Now?"

Zack stepped back from her and put his hands on his hips. "Your family has enough money to rival small countries. I get it."

Kaylan crossed her arms and narrowed her gaze at him. "I don't know how you can go from brilliant to idiotic in seconds. Yes, my family is wealthy and I have a huge trust fund. I'm not going to apologize for that. If you want to be with me, then you'll need to come to terms with it, you jerk. How dare you accuse me of making you a charity case," she said, stalking toward him.

Zack backed away, bringing his hands in front his chest in a placating gesture.

"I'm with you because I love you, even when you do this. I don't need to buy your dad's old car for you because you'll be able to do it yourself. You're a damn hero, Zack. Whether you want to admit it or not, you saved Earth from the Xiiginn fleet."

"It was all of us," Zack said.

"We were all there and we contributed, but it was you who uploaded the command to the Star Shroud. It was you who had the insight to apply what we found at the Drar space station and gave the people back home a fighting chance to live. And I'll make sure they all know it was you," Kaylan said.

She'd gotten so close to him that she brushed against his chest.

"God, you're scary when you're mad, and I'm strangely turned on right now," Zack said.

Kaylan punched him in the stomach.

Zack coughed and laughed at the same time. "Alright. I'm sorry. I'm an idiot. I can't be brilliant all the time. Do you have any idea how hard that is?"

Kaylan cracked a smile and the rest of her ire drained away. Kissing him goodbye, she headed toward the shuttle.

A SHORT WHILE later Kaylan landed the Athena's shuttle on the landing pad where Efren and Katie met her. After a quick greeting, Efren went straight aboard the shuttle, but Katie lingered for a moment.

"How's he doing?" Katie asked.

"Burying himself in his work," Kaylan said.

Katie had long since gotten over her fling with Zack, but they were still friends. Kaylan had noticed that Katie was spending quite a bit of time with Efren, so maybe there was something there. They all took whatever comfort they could find in each other.

"I'll check on him later," Katie promised, and Kaylan thanked her.

Kaylan took a transit pad to the Mardoxian complex. She had Emma's data analysis on Olloron in case she needed it, but she didn't think she would. There was no way anyone in the Mardoxian Sect would have missed this. The question that remained was why no one was doing anything about it.

The transit pad brought her down in the middle of the Mardoxian complex. Boxans preferred a dome-shaped architecture and Ma'jasalax had told her that the dome shapes were efficient, but on Sethion there were vast cities. Kaylan had spent a little bit of time learning Boxan history and they'd come from an incredibly lush and fertile world. Sethion was larger than Earth but not by much. Most of the planet was forested and the forests were brought into the vast cities. The pictures she'd seen were amazing and she wished she could have witnessed it in person.

Kaylan accessed the info terminal to find Ma'jasalax's location and then probed with her senses to see if she was actually there. She was, but she wasn't alone. Ma'jasalax was with Hodak, the head of the Mardoxian Sect. Kaylan swallowed hard. If she wanted answers, his were probably the best she was going to get.

Kaylan walked through the building. The hallways were sparse, with most buildings designed for necessity rather than comfort or history, and there weren't very many Boxans at the Mardoxian complex at any given time. Ma'jasalax had told her that they were purposefully spread apart to keep the actual numbers of Boxans with the Mardoxian trait a secret. All Boxans had some level of the Mardoxian trait, but not all of them were adept at it like Ma'jasalax. Kaylan suspected that the same would apply to Humans. She knew Dux Corp had a recruitment protocol for the program that followed Stargate, but she had no idea what it was. She also had no idea how she stacked up against the other members of that secret organization, but Ma'jasalax insisted that Kaylan was gifted even by Boxan standards.

Outside the door she needed to go through was a heavily armed Boxan soldier. He must have been Hodak's bodyguard. All Mardoxian priests had them. Ma'jasalax's guard had died protecting her when she was captured by the Xiiginns. She should have been assigned another bodyguard but hadn't, and it was also unclear why Ma'jasalax's old bodyguard hadn't carried out his duty to end her life rather than risk a Mardoxian priestess being captured by the Xiiginns.

"They're expecting you, Commander," the Boxan guarding the door said.

The door opened and Kaylan walked through. The room beyond was much like the resonance chambers the Boxans built on their starships. The resonance chamber was an artificial garden filled with plants that were native to Sethion. Those plants would never survive in Olloron's dry atmosphere.

"Welcome, Kaylan," Hodak said.

The two Boxans knelt on the ground, facing one another.

The door closed behind her and Kaylan continued toward them and knelt down, sitting on her feet. "Thank you," she said.

"Ma'jasalax tells me that your progress through our training regimen has been exponential. I'm very happy to hear this and you should be proud of your accomplishment," Hodak said.

"Thank you," Kaylan said. "I'd like to discuss something with both of you."

Ma'jasalax's large ears twitched and her long braids shifted. "What is it you wish to discuss?" she asked.

"Emma Roberson is a foremost expert in multiple fields of biology. She's been running some analyses on Olloron and has come to realize that its viability as a long-term home world for the Boxans may not be possible. I have her data, but neither of us can imagine that this is something you're unaware of," Kaylan said.

Ma'jasalax exchanged glances with Hodak, who gave a slight nod.

"You are, of course, correct. Olloron is merely a resting place while we regroup," Ma'jasalax said.

"Have you located any other worlds you can migrate to?" Kaylan asked.

"I can say we're aware of the situation but have prioritized stopping the Xiiginns rather than finding another world to migrate to," Hodak said.

"Why wouldn't you look for a new home? Could you return to Sethion?" Kaylan asked.

Hodak's body went rigid. "Sethion is beyond our reach. To return there would condemn our species to death. There's a reason the star system is under quarantine. Also, with the Xiiginns in control of the Confederation, we couldn't stand against the combined forces of the Confederation."

"I know your war is with the Xiiginns, but at some point you'll need to defend yourself, even from those species that are misguided," Kaylan said.

"Was Jonah Redford misguided?" Ma'jasalax asked.

"No, he was a pawn, a victim," Kaylan said.

"That's how we feel about the other species in the Confederation," Ma'jasalax said.

"If you're not looking for another colony world, what will you do if the Xiiginns discover this place? What if, despite all your precautions, they find out where you are? You owe it to yourselves to look for another home—a better home than this place," Kaylan said.

"We shall persevere as we always have. Our fleets would defend this place and throw back any attack made by the Xiiginns," Hodak said.

"Are the other Boxans aware they can't stay here in the long term?" Kaylan asked.

"Scientists are aware of the situation. Key members of the High Council and Battle Leaders are aware," Ma'jasalax said.

"Why don't you appeal to the Confederation for help? Not all the different species can be subservient to the Xiiginns. Aren't there other allies?" Kaylan asked.

"We've tried in the past. The price for their help is always to grant access to the Star Shroud network across a multitude of star systems. Primitive species would fall victim to the Xiiginns, and we won't condemn those species to their mercy," Ma'jasalax said.

Kaylan glanced at both of them. Zack was right. The Boxans had become a race of beings that was fixated on making tough decisions. They were so rigid that they wouldn't find a more suitable home world to live on. What was worse was that she didn't think she could convince them.

"I realize this appears harsh, but we have a different perception of time than you do. For the foreseeable future, we will remain here," Hodak said.

Kaylan looked at Ma'jasalax. She knew this was wrong. The Boxans had backed themselves into a corner and wouldn't do anything to get themselves out of it. Is this how a species like the Boxans eventually went extinct? They were alive, but Kaylan felt that something needed to change. Her mind kept returning to Sethion. She felt that it was the key to the Boxans' survival. She had to learn all she could about it, but she wouldn't get answers from Hodak or Ma'jasalax so she let the matter drop.

7

In an area between the planets of the star system that was home to the Humans, remnants of a Xiiginn warship floated in space. Passive scans hadn't detected the minuscule amount of power still operating within the wrecked starship and Mar Arden had a difficult choice to make. They'd survived inside the mysterious barrier that was protecting this star system from their fleet and they'd managed to remain undetected for many cycles. Their survival required all of their ingenuity, as well as the promise that what they would find on Earth would be worth something of great value to the Confederation. With the limited number of shuttles he had at his disposal, he'd made only a single foray to this star system's interior planets. The Boxans had left the Humans their Orbital Defense Platforms that were more than capable of detecting their attack shuttles if they'd suspected that the Xiiginns were in the area. Secrecy was their primary weapon, especially with only a few attack shuttles and a converted section of the warship hull that functioned as a lifeboat for the surviving crewmembers.

Mar Arden waited in his chambers for Hoan Berend and Kandra Rene to arrive. Hoan Berend had been much more amiable since Mar Arden had put him in his place. Now the ship commander did his bidding without question, and rightfully so. It had been Mar Arden's actions and quick thinking that had saved them from the rest of the Xiiginn fleet's destruction. He still couldn't fathom how the barrier had been created, but he knew it had something to do with the Star Shroud.

Standard Boxan protocol for observing a less advanced species would put their monitoring station on the furthest planet in the system, and it just so happened that this planet was more than half a system away from their current location. But it wouldn't have mattered to Mar Arden if it had been much closer. He wouldn't risk going there. It was the ultimate sort of irony that after all this time fighting with the Boxans over their Star Shroud monitoring stations, they had finally found an intact one and they weren't even going to investigate it. Mar Arden had little doubt that the Boxans and Humans were watching the monitoring station and should his presence be detected there, the Boxan monitoring station would self-destruct. He'd seen the Boxans use such tactics before in other star systems.

The door chimed and Mar Arden authorized it to open, revealing the squadron of loyal soldiers that stood outside his door at all times. They were in a survival situation and he wouldn't chance another Xiiginn trying to take his place if the opportunity arose. Only one other had tried, and Kandra Rene had made short work of him. Hoan Berend had also ensured that no one else made any such coup attempt. Mar Arden had always found that fortune would favor those who were better prepared.

Hoan Berend and Kandra Rene entered the room, the elder Xiiginn coming in first as befit his rank. Mar Arden invited them both to sit. Kandra Rene had just returned from an important assignment.

"My mission took longer than it otherwise would have if we'd had our sensor array intact," Kandra Rene said.

"I'm well aware of the limitations of the attack shuttle," Mar Arden replied.

Kandra Rene nodded. "I have an accurate model of the barrier. I didn't risk tampering with any of the Shroud devices."

"That's good, because if you had, no doubt the Boxans would be sweeping the area now, looking for us," Mar Arden said.

Learning that there were still Boxans in this star system made their work here even more delicate than if they'd had to contend with the Humans alone. It seemed that the Boxan Battle Leader in charge of the Dreadnaught group had emptied their ships of non-essential personnel and sent them back to Earth. Mar Arden approved of the tactic. The Boxans would only sacrifice Dreadnaughts for the highest priority of species. He still didn't understand what made the Humans so valuable to the Boxans, but that would come in time.

"According to my analysis, the barrier doesn't encompass the entire star system," Kandra Rene said.

Hoan Berend frowned. "There are gaps in the barrier? Perhaps we could signal the fleet through one of these gaps," he said.

"Apologies, Commander, what I mean is that the barrier will cut off the ninth planet's orbit within the next fifty cycles," Kandra Rene said.

Mar Arden considered that for a moment. "Interesting. The power requirements for maintaining the barrier must be extremely high. Otherwise, whoever re-aligned the Star Shroud would have accounted for the ninth planet's orbit."

"I don't think they had time," Kandra Rene said.

"What do you mean?" Mar Arden asked.

"You already surmised that a new species is taking a hand in our war with the Boxans. There was the anomaly that was detected toward the end of the battle and then the barrier went up. This is not a coincidence, and if the Boxans had this kind of power, why would they waste two Dreadnaughts standing against our fleet?" Kandra Rene said.

"It could have taken them time to power the devices. It also could have taken them time to get the configuration uploaded through the Shroud network," Hoan Berend said.

"Those are possibilities," Kandra Rene acknowledged.

Mar Arden was impressed with his student. She could present her thoughts and still recognize that there were other possibilities. "I agree with you," Mar Arden said to Kandra Rene.

The Xiiginn perked up at the compliment and her tail flicked in the air behind her, but she immediately got her emotions under control and brought her tail to rest.

"I've managed to identify asteroids that have a significant amount of ice on them," Kandra Rene said.

"Excellent," Hoan Berend said. "I'll let our salvage crews know."

It was always a matter of resources. Their stock of provisions would sustain them, but a warship's design called for liquid water to be stored in the aft section of the ship, and that happened to be the part of the ship that had been sheared in half when they'd raced through the barrier as it was forming.

"We need to decide what our next move is," Hoan Berend said.

Both Xiiginns waited for Mar Arden to speak.

"Why do you think the Boxans are so invested in the Humans?" Mar Arden said.

"They tried to recruit the Nershals against us because they could resist our compulsion. Perhaps it's something similar," Hoan Berend said.

"The Boxans have ever been trying to nullify that particular vulnerability, but we have conflicting reports on whether the Humans are vulnerable to compulsion," Mar Arden said. His gaze drifted toward Kandra Rene.

The Xiiginn sucked in a harsh breath. "I failed to use compulsion on the Human, Zack Quick. He was able to resist me on multiple occasions. He could sense what I was doing and was able to deny me," Kandra Rene said.

"And yet Sion Shif was able to successfully control one of the other Athena crewmembers," Hoan Berend said.

Mar Arden pressed his thin lips together. "I don't believe that one Human resisting your compulsion calls your skills into question. It could simply be that some Humans are vulnerable while others aren't. It's something I look forward to learning more about," Mar Arden said.

Hoan Berend frowned. "So you mean to go further into the system then?" he asked.

"Of course. Getting to Earth was always the plan, but I'm reluctant to leave any Xiiginns behind," Mar Arden said.

"Mercy?" Hoan Berend said with a hint of disbelief in his voice.

Mar Arden shook his head. "Necessity. Carrying out my plans once we reach Earth requires a certain number of us and attack shuttles don't have the capacity to bring all of us there."

"Then how do you propose we get to Earth? Or even within the vicinity of the Human home planet?" Hoan Berend said.

Mar Arden drew in a deep breath. "What we really need is a way to move within this system without being detected. As slow as we are, we would only make it to the field where a failed planet never formed. And even that carries some risk as we've detected some Human activity in the asteroid field."

"Most likely mining activities," Hoan Berend said.

"Agreed. Surveyor probes and such," Mar Arden said.

There were a few moments of silence before Kandra Rene cleared her throat.

"We need to test their reactions, probe their defenses. Nothing that would give us away but enough to get their attention," Kandra Rene said.

Mar Arden let out a satisfied smile. "I concur."

Hoan Berend frowned. "There's a lot of risk for this effort."

"We'll need contingency plans should we be discovered," Mar Arden said and noted Hoan Berend's surprised expression. "Earlier, I said I was reluctant to lose resources if I don't need to. I didn't say I would risk losing my chance at Earth for the sake of all the Xiiginns we have with us."

"Understood. I'll make some preliminary lists for you to approve," Hoan Berend said.

Mar Arden looked at Kandra Rene. "I'll expect you to come up with a plan for getting the Boxans' attention."

Kandra Rene frowned. "Just the Boxans? Not the Humans?" she asked.

"We don't know how many Boxans made it back to Earth, but let's assume it was a few hundred. They'll be occupied with getting Earth ready to defend itself from attack," Mar Arden said.

Hoan Berend tapped his fingers on the table. "So a few hundred Boxans, some technical resources, and a species that can barely travel through their own star system. And you believe they're focused on defending themselves from attack?"

Mar Arden nodded. "Yes, and it's thanks to Garm Antis. Our illustrious supreme leader insisted that we send large asteroids through a wormhole towards Earth."

"His intention was to arrive at Earth in time to prevent the massive asteroid from destroying the planet and make the Humans believe the Boxans were somehow responsible," Hoan Berend said.

"Not the best plan Garm Antis could have enacted. The Humans were able to stop the asteroid and have no doubt surmised the vast resources in terms of materials it contains—more than enough for them to start building their own fleet. Couple that with a few hundred Boxans with the technical knowhow to give the Humans a head start and this could go very badly for us," Mar Arden said.

Hoan Berend shifted uncomfortably in his seat. "The Boxans wouldn't have a choice but to abandon their long-held principles about sharing advanced technology with a more primitive species."

"Yes, Garm Antis practically threw them together," Mar Arden said.

"There was no way Garm Antis could have anticipated something like the barrier around the star system," Hoan Berend said.

Mar Arden shrugged. He was seeing how far he could push the warship commander about their supreme leader before he'd push back. "I can't see the

Boxans committing such resources to the Humans because some of them can resist our compulsion ability. They already have the Nershals, or at least the Nershals were still fighting a civil war regarding which side to take."

Kandra Rene's eyes flashed. "The Mardoxian potential! It has to be."

"It's the only reason I could think of as well, but I was curious to see which of you would bring it up first," Mar Arden said.

"We'll need to confirm it and that won't be easy," Hoan Berend said.

"After we get to Earth . . . but think about it. We could finally find the genetic link that gives the Boxans the advantage they've used for hundreds of years. Once we confirm the Mardoxian potential in Humans, we can then work toward implementing it into our own species, and that will take test subjects," Mar Arden said.

Hoan Berend let out a hungry growl of assent and even Kandra Rene was intrigued. Mar Arden found that the proper motivation was the best way to get the most out of his resources, and now that they were properly motivated, it was time to move forward with the next step in his plan.

8

Ed Johnson glanced at his ECF visitor's badge, which showed a picture of him beside a prominent blue stripe. The clipped cadence of Iris Barrett in her Louboutin heels sounded next to him, comprising his entire protective detail at the ECF branch headquarters. At five foot, eleven inches she had more advanced implants and enhancements to strength, speed, and vision than most military drones used for reconnaissance. Iris was an army of one.

General William Sheridan no longer operated from NORAD but had taken over a state-of-the-art facility within a hundred miles from the Cheyenne Mountain complex.

Ed and Iris waited for the remaining two members of their party to go through the security checkpoint.

Alicia Murphy was a thick-set woman who was barely five feet tall. Her brown, curly hair hugged her round face, and her thick glasses were part of her disguise. Walking past her in public, no one would give her a second glance. Her gray business suit and pale pink shirt allowed her to blend in with either a crowd at a shopping mall or a corporate office.

Blake Allen was the last one through. He was only a few inches taller than Alicia and had a small belly pressing up against the belt of his pants. Add a thinning head of hair above a black necktie and most people wouldn't notice him any more than Alicia. No one would guess they were both exceptional viewers who were highly respected in the Dux Corp upper echelons. Blake and Alicia were here to join the ECF. They had no family ties and were dedicated to doing their part to help protect the Earth.

They were escorted farther inside the buildings where Ed saw Sheridan speaking with a Boxan soldier. When the Boxans had first arrived, they'd rarely come planet-side, but now that things were getting up and running on the New

Moon and Lunar Base, groups of Boxans had been making regular trips down to various ECF complexes across the globe.

Their escort asked them to wait while he notified Sheridan they were here, and after a few moments, the lead general of the ECF waved them over. Ed led the way and shook hands with Sheridan.

General Sheridan gestured toward the Boxan soldier. "I'm not sure you've met in person, but this is Scraanyx, Strike Commander for the Boxan military."

Ed gave a slight bow to the Boxan.

"Michael Hunsicker speaks highly of you. A pleasure to make your acquaintance," Scraanyx said.

The Boxan's great size and deep voice took Ed a moment to register. It was one thing to know there was a being that was ten foot tall but it was quite another to have it standing in front of you. Ed introduced Iris, Alicia, and Blake.

Scraanyx bowed to Alicia and Blake. "It is an honor to meet those who have the Mardoxian potential," he said.

"Welcome to the Earth Coalition Force, and thank you for joining us," Sheridan said to Alicia and Blake, then shifted his gaze toward Ed. "We need to talk about testing centers for ECF recruitment. We know Russia had their own remote-viewer program that was part of the old KGB."

Ed nodded. "I'm aware of the program. Wasn't anywhere near as effective as ours."

"You and I both know that if we add anything regarding telepathic abilities to the ECF recruitment bulletin, we'll get nut-job applicants instead of quality applicants," Sheridan said.

"That's why we didn't use those terms as part of the recruitment process," Ed said.

"Yeah, but we need a way to attract people who may have this ability," Sheridan said and looked at Scraanyx. "How do you find members of your race who have the Mardoxian potential?"

"Having the Mardoxian potential is among the highest honors for Boxans. There are no pretenders, but without Thesulia we have no one here who could aid in validating the claim," Scraanyx said.

Ed drew in a deep breath. They'd learned that Thesulia was a Mardoxian priestess who had stayed with Prax'pedax to help fight against the Xiiginn fleet.

"Their sacrifice will not be in vain, I promise you," Ed said and turned toward Sheridan. "Alicia and Blake can help with testing potential recruits, but you don't need to start from scratch. We have lists of potential candidates you can choose from."

Sheridan frowned. "Do I even want to know where this list comes from?" he asked.

"It's not what you think. Most countries have a form of standardized testing for children throughout their school career from the elementary level all the way through college entrance exams," Ed said.

"Telepathic abilities can present themselves in a number of different ways," Alicia said.

"How?" Sheridan asked.

"Intuition, for one—being able to read into a situation and still achieve your objective. These are things that are emphasized in basic training found anywhere from militaries to law enforcement agencies around the globe," Alicia said.

"We target the people who stand out to determine whether they'd be ideal candidates," Ed said.

"What makes an ideal candidate?" Sheridan asked.

"There are some who are open to the possibility of certain telepathic capabilities, but then there are others who don't cope with it very well," Ed said.

"Where does Kaylan Farrow figure into all this then?" Sheridan asked.

Scraanyx cleared his throat. "The Athena commander is known to us. A highly revered Mardoxian priestess has validated the claim of her skills."

"Michael Hunsicker's reports from the first leg of the Athena mission to Pluto categorized Kaylan's abilities as repeatedly demonstrative. When they first arrived at the Boxan monitoring station, it was as if Kaylan had already been there. I'm willing to wager that Kaylan's abilities have only become more refined during her time with the Boxans," Ed said.

Blake raised his hand, indicating he had something to add. "We've seen those reports and they're nothing short of amazing. Kaylan Farrow was able to remote-view to a place millions of miles away, and their mission update also describes how she used her ability to help locate the Athena crewmember held captive by the Xiiginn."

Sheridan nodded. "What I'd like to know is whether Kaylan's the exception or if she's the standard we can expect others to be able to achieve."

"Right now, she's the exception," Ed said. "Even the Boxans have indicated that telepathic capabilities among the Mardoxian Sect vary."

"My understanding is that they put their Mardoxian priests on the bridge of their ships and the captains will defer to them as part of their strategy in battle," Sheridan said.

"That is correct," Scraanyx said. "There is no challenge to authority, but a battle commander would be remiss if they were to ignore a recommendation made by anyone from the Mardoxian Sect."

Sheridan frowned. "I acknowledge that you have a system in place that works for you. We'll build our own fleet, but I'm not sure how this will fit within our command structure."

"They'll need to prove their worth," Ed said.

"We wouldn't advocate that you adopt our model for commanding your fleets, but the Mardoxian potential is something that can help your species realize its full potential. And it will be something the Xiiginns will try to take from you," Scraanyx said.

Ed had seen that whenever a Boxan referred to the Xiiginns there came with it the deep loathing of one's enemies. Soldiers returning from war often demonstrated this form of hatred that had enabled them to do what they'd had to do to survive. For all intents and purposes, the Boxans had to become a militaristic society in order to survive. Ed understood the necessity of it and at the same time hoped that Earth's fate wouldn't require the same price for survival.

9

As the head liaison between Humans and Boxans, Michael Hunsicker was also on point for General William Sheridan's visits to the lunar base. And Michael knew it was just a matter of time before the head of the Earth Coalition Force ventured onsite.

On the lunar base, they had no formal ECF uniform other than the jumpsuits they wore for their everyday duties. The official ECF uniform was dark blue with a phoenix-emblem patch on the side. Since Michael was no longer a member of NASA and was officially part of the ECF, his old military rank of Air Force Colonel had carried over, but he wasn't sure what ranking structure the ECF would settle on because once they had a fleet there was talk of them following the US naval command hierarchy. There were no colonels in the Navy. Ultimately, Michael didn't care. He had a job to do, and whatever rank the ECF brass saw fit to give him would be okay with him. He'd been an Air Force colonel and, later on, a mission commander for two of NASA's most historic missions— one to Mars and the second to Pluto.

ECF staff lined up along the corridor for Sheridan's visit and base commander Alyssa Archer stood at Michael's side.

"Stand up straight, the boss is coming," Alyssa whispered.

Michael snorted.

Those in the military snapped a salute as the four-star general came through the airlock doors and entered the ECF wing of the lunar base. Two of his armed escorts walked ahead of him. Sheridan swung his mighty gaze at Michael Hunsicker and walked directly over to him.

"I feel like *I* should salute *you*," Sheridan said and stuck out his hand.

Michael shook the general's hand. "It's nice to finally meet you, General," he said.

"I should have come here much sooner. As it is, we hitched a ride with Scraanyx," Sheridan said.

Michael nodded. "If you'll follow Alyssa and me, we'll be the ones showing you around."

Sheridan shook Alyssa's hand as well. The rest of the ECF staff was dismissed and Michael proceeded to show the general around. He'd been in numerous meetings with him, but this was the first time they'd met face to face. By the time they got to the main conference room, Colonel Mathews had caught up with them.

"Apologies, General. I was at the new moon making sure the engineers from Mirae Corporation were situated and working on getting the mechs online," Kyle said.

"Understood, and I approved their transfer last week. They'll be here for as long as you need them," Sheridan said.

Chazen and Scraanyx joined them in the main conference room where they sat on reinforced benches designed to take the weight of a Boxan, who could weigh nearly a thousand pounds—and more than that when they wore their powered armor.

"Thank you all for coming," Sheridan said. "All of you here, along with the rest of the people in your departments, are our boots on the ground. We're getting to the point where we've amassed materials sufficient enough to ramp up our shipbuilding capabilities. We're all part of the ECF, and we'll only continue to grow with the best people our planet has to offer. Futurists would say that an organization such as ours has the potential to outlast the countries from which it began. It sounds nice, and hopefully, hundreds of years from now, the people will look back at what we've started and acknowledge what will be done here. There are some who think we'll fail, that the Earth Coalition Force will not succeed. Humans have never come together as a whole, but there are people from around the world here, and there'll be more now that China and Russia have officially joined the ECF and will be contributing resources to us. We all need to learn to work together, and our efforts here and now will have long-lasting effects far beyond what will happen once we leave here. We're the line that stands between the Xiiginns and the people of Earth. Perhaps, in the future, there will be another species that will threaten our lives," Sheridan said glancing at the Boxans. "I hope not, but the ECF will be the ones to defend our planet and our right to exist in the galaxy."

Michael glanced around at those gathered in the large assembly area. Most sat a little straighter, and even Chazen and Scraanyx were caught up in Sheridan's speech. The Boxans stood up and brought their fists to their chests.

"Battle Leader," Scraanyx said, addressing General Sheridan with title reserved for the most eminent leader in the Boxan military. For a Boxan it was the highest form of praise.

"Colonel Matthews, show us what you've got," Sheridan said.

Kyle Matthews stood up and engaged the holoprojector. Three-dimensional images of six starship designs came into view.

"The ships you see before you are of Boxan design but aren't the

Dreadnaughts we saw when the Boxans first arrived. Those ships are beyond our current capabilities so we propose that our approach to starship-building will be to start small," Kyle said and took control of the holointerface. He swiped the ships to the side, and a smaller, two-person craft came into prominence. "This is a strike-fighter. We plan to merge the Boxan strike-fighter with our own advanced military space vehicles. Actual production of these ships has already begun. Strike-fighter training programs have begun at places like Sacramento Bay and RAF Cranwell in the United Kingdom. We even have a few simulators here. Cadets who go through the training on the ground will finish their training up here.

"Some of you may be wondering why we would start with such a small attack spacecraft, but one thing history has taught us is to start small and build from there. This will hold true even with the help from the Boxans, although with their help we'll be able to develop much faster than we normally would have. Strike-fighter squadrons are something we can do quickly, setting up fighter bases here and on the new moon. We'll eventually put them elsewhere as well, such as on carriers that we'll build. Again, we'll start small and take our cues from established practices throughout history, but this time it will come from our navies. Although some ship designs may need to be merged, the ships we build will serve our first and ultimate goal, which is to defend the Earth from the threat of invasion. Destroyer-class vessels will be first, then cruisers, and eventually battleship carriers. Those will be our ships of the line. Eventually, we'll get to the big behemoths the Boxans have built, but we can't just start building ships indiscriminately. Our ships must be built to stand against Xiiginn warships and tactics. There'll be some things we'll need to start over, acknowledging our weaknesses and making them our strengths. We're new to space warfare, and one of the things we need from you is your ideas. The Boxans and Xiiginns have been fighting for a long time. Perhaps there's something we can offer that the Boxans haven't considered."

Michael listened as various ECF members put forth their ideas. The Boxans had already been sharing all they knew about the Xiiginns and their arsenal. More than once Michael had found himself thinking about Prax'pedax and his foresight to send as many Boxans back to Earth as he could.

After the meeting, Michael was reviewing his messages and saw an alert about several drones tasked with monitoring the barrier having gone offline. They were running diagnostics on the system and the nearest drone would be sent to investigate.

10

Over the past few days, Kaylan had dedicated her time to learning what she could about Sethion, the Boxan home world. Finding the coordinates to the planet had been relatively easy, but with them came a warning that the planet and star system itself was under quarantine. Any attempt to go to Sethion without proper authorization would result in that ship being treated as a hostile force. Not only would the automated defensive platforms throughout the system destroy anyone trying to enter the system, but also anyone trying to leave. Learning that bit of news had shaken her and left her restless ever since.

The Boxans had found themselves in the midst of a civil war that had spawned during what they called the Xiiginn uprising, which led to the Chaos Wars. Hordes of Boxans had fled Sethion, but when Boxans under the Xiiginn influence attempted to learn of Olloron's location, the High Council had to act. In order to preserve the lives of the remaining free members of their society, they'd had to cut all ties from Sethion. The Boxans had successfully ousted the Xiiginns from Sethion's star system, but the damage had already been done. Once a Boxan was under Xiiginn influence, there was no way to reverse it. There'd been a number of scientists who had tried and all had failed. The High Council had forbidden anyone else from returning to Sethion and condemned any Boxan left behind to a life filled with terror, loss, and brutality. Kaylan had seen the vids, and until then it had been hard to imagine what the wide-scale impact of a Boxan war would have on a planet.

Large portions of the planet had been destroyed, and such madness and savagery had spread that Kaylan wasn't sure how anyone could survive. The images in the vids haunted her and wouldn't abate no matter what she did. She knew there were Boxans still fighting for their lives back on Sethion and her visions of them weren't just dreams. She knew she should focus on trying to get back to Earth, but she couldn't let her intuition about Sethion go. Intuition and foresight were what the Boxans revered most about Mardoxian Sect members, and her gut instinct was telling her that there was still hope for Sethion.

Kaylan decided to start asking different Boxans about Sethion and whether they thought there was any hope for those left behind, but hardly any Boxan was willing to speak to her about it. Even Gaarokk, who had helped them in the past, refused to consider it. Earlier that day she'd gone to speak to Kladomaor about it and even he told her that Sethion was dead.

What she needed was proof. More than growing her abilities, she needed to find evidence that there were still Boxans unaffected by the Xiiginn influence there. Sethion may be lost, but the Boxans who had been left behind required a miracle, and if the Boxans here refused to answer the call, she'd have to go it alone while trying to convince anyone she could to help her.

Kaylan had arranged for Zack to meet her at one of the garden paths outside the city. What forests there were on Olloron were short and sparse, as if they were near the ocean shore. The roots weren't able to grow very deep and the nutrients in the soil weren't abundant. The Boxans had done what they could during their time here to create gardens that they cared for, but the plants that were native to this planet didn't vary all that much and were mostly brown or tan to match the dry landscape. Where the Boxans had brought irrigation, the plants thrived, but only to a certain point, and the gardens were pale shades of greens.

Kaylan's PDA buzzed on her wrist, signaling that Zack was getting close, and she heard the sound of a small craft approach and land nearby. Zack was spending most of his time on the Athena but would occasionally return to the surface to be with the others. He climbed out of the cockpit of a Boxan transport vehicle, a small gray craft that was used for training young Boxans and was readily usable by the crew of the Athena. They couldn't leave the atmosphere but were perfect for traveling short distances. She was glad Zack shared her love of flying. She'd prefer to race around in a strike-fighter, but her time had been limited.

Zack waved over to her and glanced around to see if anyone else was around, raising his brows in exaggerated mock surprise. "Are we all alone out here?" he asked.

Kaylan smiled. "I thought it might be a refreshing change of pace."

Zack came over to give her a quick kiss and then took her hand as they walked down the garden path. They chewed the time away, talking about different things.

"I still haven't been able to get any Shroud devices to test with," Zack said.

"What are you trying to do?"

"I want to recreate the barrier but on a much smaller scale. The issue we're having is that the barrier is preventing us from disabling it from the outside," Zack said.

"So you think if you send the proper sequence to turn it off from inside the barrier, it would work?" Kaylan asked.

"That's the theory," Zack said.

"What if it didn't work? Whoever was inside the barrier would be trapped," Kaylan said.

"Well, gee, I didn't think of that," he said with a grin. "I wasn't going to be the one inside—and no one else for that matter. I'd put a transmitter inside that would send out the shutdown signal after a period of time. If it didn't work, then we'd know. I'm sure we could limit the power available to the Shroud devices so they'd cease to function after awhile," Zack said.

"Sounds like a good experiment, so what's the problem?"

Zack blew out a breath. "The problem is they don't have any Shroud devices here. I don't need the actual thing. I could scale the model down, so I've been looking at building my own."

"Couldn't Gaarokk help with that?" Kaylan asked.

"He is. We're trying to gather materials, but it's proving to be more trouble than I thought. Materials are scarce, so while Gaarokk is looking into that, I've been searching through the Athena's new Drar reference library for any clue about how to build them. The problem is that the Drars didn't call it a Shroud device," Zack said.

Kaylan nodded, finally understanding. The Drars had their own way of naming things. The Boxans had been able to help with some translating and conceptual understanding of what was being described, but it was a slow process.

"I need your help," Kaylan said.

"With what?"

"I'm trying to get information about Sethion," Kaylan said.

Zack frowned. "What kind of information?"

"I need to know if there's been any recent activity on the planet that would indicate there're Boxans still alive there," Kaylan said.

Zack's brows shot up his forehead. "You told me the other day about the quarantine zone and that no ship could get through. Sounds like a suicidal request."

Kaylan looked away. "That was the other thing I wanted to talk to you about."

Zack shook his head. "No," he said, taking a few steps away from her where he stopped and shook his head again.

Kaylan followed. "Come on, Zack. I know you can do this," she said.

"Kaylan, I promised them I wouldn't go poking around their systems while we were here. We're their guests. I may think the Boxans are a bit harsh at times, but we wouldn't be here if it weren't for them," Zack said and held up his hand. "And I mean that in a good way."

"What if there are still Boxans there who need help?" Kaylan asked.

"I'm trying to figure out a way to get us home. Why do we have to solve the Boxans' problems for them?"

Kaylan drew in a deep, steadying breath and lowered her voice. They'd both been speaking too loud. "Because no one else will. The Boxans have washed their hands of it," Kaylan said.

"Yeah, and that should tell you something. It's like they suddenly decided,

'Oh well, the rest of you stuck on the planet are screwed. Bye, bye, see ya later,'" Zack said and continued to walk down the path.

"I know there are Boxans there," Kaylan said, and Zack stopped in his tracks. "Ones unaffected by the Xiiginn influence."

"How could you possibly know this?" Zack asked.

Kaylan closed the distance between them. "I've seen it. Those visions Ma'jasalax believes are dreams are real."

Zack frowned. "Let me get this straight. You think this recurring dream or vision thing is you seeing actual events as they're unfolding?"

"Yes," Kaylan said.

"And what do the other Mardoxian priests think of this?" Zack asked.

"I've only told Ma'jasalax, but I did bring Sethion up to the others and they won't even consider anything that has to do with going back there," Kaylan said.

"Just bear with me a second," Zack said. "I can't begin to explain how you can do the things you do—like how you found me when I was a prisoner or even how you knew I was alive—but we were in the same star system and you had an idea of where to look. I thought you needed a precise location to remote-view your way there."

"That's part of it, but this is different. I've been training with the Boxans for a while now and my abilities are growing stronger. Ma'jasalax told me that the most gifted of the Mardoxian Sect are brilliant strategists who are able to see events beyond what they appear to be. It's how I knew to disconnect the gravity tether in the wormhole while we were trying to find the Drar space station. I think my time here learning all that I've learned has enabled me to pick up on certain things—things the Boxans are ignoring. It's these things that are allowing me to focus on Sethion. I don't know how else to explain it. The visions are so intense. I can smell the air and hear the Boxans fighting," Kaylan said.

"Who are they fighting?" Zack asked.

Kaylan swallowed hard. "Each other, but each vision I have centers around one particular Boxan wearing old, traditional armor. It reminds me of when I first used the Mardoxian chamber and met Ma'jasalax," she said.

Zack regarded her for a few moments, considering. "Why don't you use one of the Mardoxian chambers and go take a look?" he asked.

"It's not that easy. For one, they keep the chambers on lockdown, so there's that to contend with, and if I told them what I want to do I don't think they'd allow it," Kaylan said.

Zack pressed his lips together. "I don't know," he said.

Kaylan flinched. "I'm surprised. I thought you of all people would help me with this."

"It's not that. I'm trying to be compliant with their conditions for allowing us to stay here. I'm doing it for you," Zack said.

Kaylan looked away from him. She knew he wasn't just being stubborn, but why did he have to become respectful of Boxan wishes now? At one time he would have relished the challenge, but he was more mature now. She liked it, but if Zack wouldn't help her, how was she going to find out what was happening on Sethion?

"Look," Zack said. "Let me think about it for a while—weigh out the pros and cons."

Kaylan took his hand in hers. "Thank you," she said. It was something at least.

11

The day after Kaylan asked Zack for his help with extracting key bits of information about Sethion, he decided he would look into it. For a while now the Boxans had been trying to probe the Athena's computer systems. The first time it occurred, the Athena's AI had alerted him immediately. The fascinating part was that they'd been unsuccessful. He instructed the AI to keep a close watch on their attempts and log the activity. He'd known the Athena's computing systems forwards and backwards before going to the Drar space station, and the Boxans should have been able to gain access with ease. However, the Drars had remade the Athena, including the computer systems, and that was the reason the Boxans were having so many problems trying to gain access. He'd thought of accusing the Boxans directly of what they were doing but had decided not to. One of the many things he'd learned from hacking his way into corporate networks or securing his own network was that it was far more revealing to watch the attacker attempt to gain access, seeing what tools they had in their arsenal and what methods they used. Sometimes he learned something.

The Boxan's first attempts to gain access to the Athena's systems had been almost delicate, but as they were continually thwarted, their attempts had become more aggressive. Their recent request to take the ship apart to see how it worked was the latest effort at trying to gain access to the Drar knowledge that was wrapped up in the Athena, and it was one of the reasons Zack had decided to stay aboard the ship. Well, that and the fact that he wanted to figure out a way to get home—a way that wouldn't leave Earth vulnerable to Xiiginn attack. The crew of the Athena was united on that front. No one would think of jeopardizing Earth in their attempts to get home. He hadn't told the others about the Boxans' attempts to gain access to the Athena. He was handling it and they were focused on learning what they could from the Boxans.

Zack knew Kaylan was upset that he hadn't immediately committed himself to helping her with this, but he had needed to give it some thought. If he did this and they got caught, it could mean the end of their alliance with the Boxans. His intentions might be honorable, but his actions could be considered treasonous. What would they do if the Boxans kicked them off Olloron? Kladomaor would help them get home no matter what the High Council decided, but Zack would rather not put anyone in an awkward position. On the other hand, Kaylan truly believed she was seeing events that were unfolding on the Boxan home world, and that, if nothing else, was enough for Zack to at least do some poking around.

Zack headed for the training camp where Etanu would be. While the Nershal soldier wasn't one for espionage or intrigue, he was someone Zack felt could be somewhat objective about the Boxans. He opened a comms channel and sent the Nershal his location, and after a few minutes Etanu was flying overhead. His four translucent wings could propel him at great speeds, but they could also enable the Nershal to do some pretty precise flying.

Etanu raced toward him as if he were initiating a game of chicken. Zack stood his ground and Etanu's deep orange eyes narrowed. Zack knew Etanu wouldn't fly into him, but he was coming in so fast that Zack took a step back and heard the Nershal howl in triumph.

"Well, it was either that or let you fly into me," Zack said.

Etanu landed next to him. "You're a rare sight on the ground these days," he said.

"I missed you," Zack said.

Etanu frowned. "You weren't even close to hitting me. What would you have hit me with? You're unarmed."

Zack shook his head. "I mean that we hadn't spoken for a while and I desired to be in your presence," he said.

Etanu laughed. "I knew what you meant. I was . . . What is the term Hicks used? Oh yes, I was just pulling your leg."

"Dale Hicks, the gift that just keeps on giving," Zack said.

Etanu frowned. "I'm not familiar with this expression. I thought you and Hicks were friends."

Zack smiled. "Oh, we are. We have a mutual understanding and history of playing jokes on one another. I once changed the passphrase for getting out of the Athena's airlock to 'Zack is my superior in every way.'"

"What did Hicks do when he found you?" Etanu asked.

"He told me he'd get me back for that and to take off the passphrase," Zack said.

Sometimes he just had to entertain himself.

"What is it you wanted to talk to me about?" Etanu asked.

"I need to know your thoughts on the Boxans," Zack said.

"They're a very wise race of beings worthy of our respect," Etanu said.

"Has your opinion about them changed since you've been here?" Zack asked.

Etanu shook his head. "No. Why are you asking me these questions?"

Zack scratched the back of his head. "There's no easy way to say this, so I'm just going to go ahead and do it. Kaylan believes there are Boxans still on Sethion who need help."

Etanu's gaze hardened. The code of honor for the Nershals was a solemn thing. To a fellow Nershal, loyalty was almost instinctual. "Has she spoken to anyone about this?"

"Yes, and it's like they won't even consider the possibility," Zack said.

"But Kaylan has the Mardoxian potential. Surely her word would carry a great deal of weight," Etanu said.

"You'd think that, but no one is listening to her," Zack said.

"So why exactly are you asking me about the Boxans?" Etanu said.

Zack looked away for a moment to check that no one else was near them. "She asked me to dig up some information about Sethion to see if the Boxans have had any recent contact with them."

Etanu glanced over at him in alarm. "Please tell me you haven't done this?"

Zack shook his head. "I haven't done anything yet. You're the first person I've talked to about it, but I will say this: Kaylan is convinced there are Boxans still alive there. She knew I was alive when everyone else thought I was dead, and well, we owe her," he said.

"We?" Etanu asked.

"Yes, we. Kaylan was the one who contacted Udonzari and gave him our location on Selebus," Zack said.

Etanu nodded, remembering their time being held prisoner to the Xiiginns. "So what do you intend to do?"

"I intend to do what she asked me to do and see what there is to learn about Sethion," Zack said.

"What do you need from me?"

"Someone to watch my back would be nice," Zack said.

Etanu made a show of craning his long neck so he could see behind Zack.

"What are you doing?" Zack asked.

"I was watching your back," Etanu said.

Zack shook his head. "I hope you're joking around again."

"I think we should talk to Gaarokk about this," Etanu said.

Zack nodded. Of anyone, Gaarokk would be the most likely to help them. "Do you know where he is?" Zack asked.

"Yes, he's right over there inside the building," Etanu said.

They walked over and Zack's internal heads-up display translated the symbols to words he could understand. Gaarokk had been in a supply building, but the Boxan scientist was leaving as they approached.

"I was just looking for materials to build the Shroud device prototypes you wanted," Gaarokk said.

"Oh, thanks. Find anything?" Zack asked.

"No, unfortunately not. Whenever I try to requisition anything, the reason for the denial is always the same. Earth isn't in any immediate danger so the materials required are reallocated to other things. Shipbuilding, most likely," Gaarokk said.

"Did they say when they'd be able to get us something to use?" Zack asked.

Gaarokk shook his head.

"Understood. We have some questions for you, if you don't mind," Zack said.

Etanu glanced at him. "*You* have questions for him. I'm just here to watch your back."

Zack rolled his eyes. "Thanks."

Gaarokk frowned. "What is it you'd like to know?"

"The Star Shrouds that are still surrounding the star systems. Have you had any contact with them?" Zack asked.

"No, but with Prax'pedax's last communications and learning that there are Boxans trapped in those systems, the High Council is putting resources into checking them," Gaarokk said.

"Good, that's really good to hear. Do you guys monitor for signals from known star systems?" Zack asked.

Gaarokk eyed him suspiciously. "You already know we do. What is it you want to know?"

Zack blew out a breath and rubbed the back of his neck. "I want to know about Sethion and whether there have been any new signals detected from there."

Gaarokk's large flaxen eyes widened. "Sethion! First Kaylan and now you . . . Did she put you up to this?" he asked.

"No . . . Yes. Can you just answer the question?" Zack said.

Gaarokk grumbled and stomped away from them.

"She's not going to give up on this," Zack said.

Gaarokk stopped and turned to face him.

"Neither am I," Zack said.

Gaarokk drew himself up and Zack was reminded once again of how tall the Boxans were. Gaarokk, at eight feet, was considered short by Boxan standards, but he still made an imposing figure.

"You shouldn't be asking about Sethion," Gaarokk growled.

"What if she's right and there are Boxans still there? Don't you want to go back and check it out?" Zack asked.

Etanu placed a hand on Zack's arm and squeezed.

"If you persist in this—poking your nose where it doesn't belong—you'll be dealt with severely. Sethion is gone and we don't need you dredging it up for us. We know who we left behind. They're all gone. The only Boxans that remain are those under the Xiiginn influence. If there were signals, we'd be checking into it," Gaarokk said.

With that, the Boxan turned on his heel and walked away.

"Let him go," Etanu said.

"See. They immediately shut down at the mere mention of Sethion," Zack said.

"With good reason. Sethion represents a great shame for the Boxans," Etanu said.

"No, the real shame is if there are Boxans there who need help and their own species is turning their back on them. I'm sorry, Etanu. I know there's a significant risk with the Xiiginn influence, but that's not a good enough reason to condemn anyone to death," Zack said.

"So what do you want to do?" Etanu asked.

"Boxans monitor everything. They've spent hundreds of years leaving their little monitoring stations all over the galaxy. You honestly think they're not monitoring Sethion? I want to know if there have been any recent signals from whatever they have monitoring that star system," Zack said.

"The system is under quarantine," Etanu said.

"Yeah, but they're likely still monitoring it. They'd want to know if anyone was trying to go there or was trying to leave. It's worth checking into," Zack said.

"Even if it means incurring the wrath of the Boxans?" Etanu asked.

Zack sighed. "Let's hope it doesn't come to that. We may not learn anything at all."

"You don't believe that. Not if Kaylan is having visions," Etanu said.

"You're right. I don't believe it. I think we're going to find something, and if that makes the Boxans uncomfortable, then so be it. This is their mess," Zack said.

Etanu looked away and seemed to scan the area. "Where to next?" the Nershal asked.

Zack smiled. He'd known he could count on Etanu for help.

12

Zack stood by one of the open info-terminals that were placed in most of the common areas of the buildings he'd been in. He brought up the access interface and glanced over his shoulder in consternation. Etanu gave him the thumbs up, a gesture Zack had taught him to let him know he was clear to proceed. The amber-colored holoscreen came up and Zack began searching for the comms control systems based on the current connections to the info-terminal. The list came up on the screen and he noted that the one he'd been searching for was present. He and Etanu had been to a few other buildings so Zack could validate the protocol connection hierarchy. All his time spent working with Boxan systems was being put to use, but it wasn't a whole lot different than computer systems back on Earth. All networks and systems needed a way to talk to one another and the method they used came under the protocols established for that system. Once you learned the different protocols, you could then disseminate the signal to look for something hidden. Of course, knowing the protocol he was looking for was only one part of what he needed, but it was an important step that led to the next, which was finding a way to authenticate that wouldn't leave a digital trail right back to him. If Zack used his own credentials, he might as well run naked through the Boxan High Council chambers while waving his arms and yelling that he was looking for information on Sethion, the thought of which didn't appeal to him. He needed to get in and out without anyone the wiser.

A message appeared on his internal heads-up display.

::*I could run the analysis for you and attempt to gain access.*:: Athena's AI said.

Zack focused in order to send a text reply without speaking the words. ::*Thanks, I appreciate it, but I don't want you involved. I don't want to give the Boxans an excuse to trace what I'm doing back to you.*::

::*Understood, but the way you're attempting to exfiltrate the data you need is inefficient.*:: Athena's AI said.

::*Yes, but the probability of being detected and having it traced back to us will be much less this way. Besides, I'll need you to clone the credentials we'll need.*:: Zack said.

::*Cloning the credentials will require you to be in proximity of the target for no less than ten minutes.*:: Athena's AI said.

::*Understood. Will initiate the process once a target has been selected.*:: Zack said.

Zack closed the translucent chat window and ended his session on the info-terminal. He returned to Etanu and they walked outside.

"Talking to your computer again?" Etanu asked.

Zack frowned. "How'd you know?"

"The skin on your forehead creases whenever you concentrate on communicating with text messages," Etanu replied.

Zack's gut clenched. Had anyone seen? He would need to be more careful in the future.

"No one else noticed," Etanu said, guessing his concern.

"The AI is just trying to be helpful," Zack said.

"I wasn't faulting the AI for doing what it does. I was informing you that you might want to work on not giving yourself away when you're talking to your computer," Etanu said.

Zack knew that Etanu struggled with trusting the AI. Nershals'd had a few bad experiences with artificial intelligence, but Zack was working with Etanu to adapt a version of the Athena's AI for Nershal use. He suspected it would take the Nershals years to learn to trust any AI, but eventually they would recognize that an AI is a powerful tool to have at their disposal. Medical doctors on Earth had been using AI constructs to help with diagnosing and proposing treatment options for more than twenty years. The doctors had the last say, but the AIs could inform the doctor of cutting-edge research and treatment options that would normally take months or years to become available.

"So what's next?" Etanu asked.

"We need to target a Boxan who has the access we need to learn about Sethion," Zack said.

"Gaarokk is a scientist. Wouldn't he have the necessary access?" Etanu asked.

"Maybe, but I don't think so. We need someone else . . . someone with more access," Zack said and frowned in thought. "The problem is that the information we're trying to access wouldn't be available to just any Boxan. They'd have to be someone important."

"Anyone on the High Council should work," Etanu suggested.

"They'll be the ones hardest to get close to. I need to get my PDA within a fifteen-foot radius for ten minutes to get what I need. I don't know if they'll even meet with me on such short notice," Zack said.

Etanu's large orange eyes widened at a sudden thought. "I know who would work with you. Hodak," Etanu said.

"The head of the Mardoxian Sect?" Zack said, trying not to raise his voice.

"Can you think of someone better?" Etanu asked.

Zack tried to think of someone but couldn't. "He'd likely have the access we need. We need to find out where he is and get him alone."

Etanu shook his head. "Not we. Just me. You've made your stance quite known, and if you suddenly show up asking questions, it may arouse suspicion."

Zack pressed his lips together. "How would this be any different if just you were going to talk to Hodak?" he asked.

"Unlike you, I actually have something to discuss with him," Etanu said.

"Like what?" Zack asked.

"The fact that they were secretly testing our species for the Mardoxian potential, for one. Also, I can ask him about the state of Nerva. That alone should give us the time we need," Etanu said.

"I didn't think that was a secret," Zack said.

"There was a small Mardoxian chamber on Ezerah's family estate, which might suggest that they were doing more than was previously known at the time," Etanu said.

"Okay, but are you sure? You don't have to do this," Zack said.

"Just show me how to work your PDA so we can get this done," Etanu said.

Zack spent the next few minutes showing Etanu how to use the PDA. It was a simple process and the Nershal learned quickly.

"I'll come find you after I'm done," Etanu said and started to walk away.

"Wait," Zack said. "How are you going to find him?"

"Don't worry about it. The less you know, the better, wouldn't you agree?" Etanu asked.

Zack didn't think they would get caught, but there was still the possibility. He'd already tested copying a Boxan's credentials and it hadn't tripped off any alarms, but they hadn't tried with a Boxan who had access to confidential information.

"It'll be fine. If you don't hear from me in a few hours, you'll know I was caught. But you need to be visible so the Boxans don't have a reason to suspect you," Etanu said.

"I guess I'll see what Hicks and the others are doing today," Zack said.

As he watched Etanu leave, he was unable to keep away the sinking feeling that something was going to go wrong.

"Zack, pay attention!" Hicks said.

Zack had spent the last few hours with Hicks and Vitomir at the weapons training facility for small arms practice. He held a pulse rifle in his hands and had been waiting for his turn to fire his weapon at the targets on the course in front of him. The pulse rifle was configured for practice burst only so it would take out a target but not hurt anyone if he had an accident. Not likely to happen. Hicks was quite an effective teacher when it came to this stuff. Zack had never fired any gun before being recruited to the Athena mission, but the practice he'd gotten over the past few months showed how much he'd improved. He doubted he'd ever be anywhere near as skilled as someone like

Hicks or Katie, but at least he could hit what he was aiming at most of the time.

"Sorry. I'm ready now," Zack said.

He brought up the pulse rifle and aimed it at the first target.

"Go!" Hicks said.

Zack squeezed the trigger and took out the closest target, then shifted his aim to the next target that was farther away. There were ten targets in all, but he had to shoot them in order before trying the more challenging targets that were even farther away. The pulse rifle fired three-round bursts and Zack went through the first five targets quickly, but he missed the sixth one.

"Just calm down and line up your shot," Hicks said.

The sixth target was six hundred yards away, but the targets farther away were much smaller than the ones that were closer to him. Zack lined up the sights with the target, but he couldn't keep still enough to get a shot off, so he rested against the platform in front of him and fired. The sixth target flashed red, indicating a successful hit. Zack aimed for the much smaller seventh target and couldn't hit it.

"That's time," Hicks said.

Zack blew out a breath and put the pulse rifle into safety mode.

"Not bad. You got the sixth target this time," Hicks said.

"I don't know how anyone hits the seventh one, let alone the others," Zack said.

Hicks regarded him for a moment. "They're called implants. You should have been using the vision enhancements option," he said.

"Isn't that cheating?" Zack asked.

Hicks laughed. "Of course not. I thought you knew that."

Zack glanced behind him, looking for some sign of Etanu. "I guess I missed it."

Zack stowed his practice weapon and followed Hicks and Vitomir out of the firing range. The sounds of weapons fire muted once the doors shut. A short distance away he saw Ezerah looking around, and upon seeing them, headed over.

"I can never tell whether Nershals are angry or not," Vitomir said.

"Being that she's scowling at Zack, I'd say she's angry," Hicks said and clamped a hand on Zack's shoulder. "What did you do this time?" he asked.

Zack took a second and thought about making a run for it, but considering that Nershals could fly, he knew he wouldn't get very far.

"Your guess is as good as mine," Zack said.

Ezerah closed on the three of them. "I wish to speak to you alone," she said to Zack.

"Is there anything we can help you with?" Hicks offered.

Ezerah's gaze softened when she looked at him. "No, I'm apparently playing messenger now."

Zack swallowed hard. "I'll see you guys later."

Ezerah didn't say anything to him while he followed her. Once they were outside, she turned toward him. "What are you and Etanu up to? He wanted me to give you this," she said and held up Zack's PDA.

Zack reached for the PDA, but Ezerah snatched it away.

"Not so fast. First, you answer my question," Ezerah said.

"What did he say when he gave it to you?"

Ezerah frowned. "Just that I needed to give you this. He looked as if he was running from someone," she said.

Zack's mouth went dry. The Boxans must have suspected Etanu was up to something.

"He was helping me with something," Zack admitted.

Ezerah's eyes flared. "That much is obvious," she snapped.

Zack drew in a quick breath and glanced around to see if anyone was watching them. "Please just give me my PDA."

"No. If you won't tell me what's happening with Etanu, I'll just give your PDA to Ma'jasalax or Kladomaor," Ezerah said and started to walk away.

Zack ran in front of her. "Don't do that. If I tell you, will you give it to me?" he asked.

Ezerah regarded him coldly. "First, you tell me," she said.

"Fine, we're trying to find out information about Sethion."

"Why? The planet is under quarantine," Ezerah said.

"I know, but I was asked to look into it," Zack said.

"By whom?" Ezerah asked.

"I can't tell you that. Now that I've told you what we're doing, will you give me my PDA?"

Ezerah softened her gaze. "Etanu wouldn't recklessly risk a slight to the Boxans. Perhaps I can help you."

Zack frowned. He didn't think he could convince Ezerah to give him his PDA without telling her what he and Etanu were doing, but she might not give it to him anyway after he did tell her.

"Kaylan believes there are Boxans still alive on Sethion and she asked me to try and find out if the Boxans were hiding anything about their planet," Zack said.

Ezerah looked away from him for a moment while she considered what he'd said.

"I'm telling you the truth," Zack said.

Ezerah turned back toward him. "Etanu has always told me you Humans are quite clever and your intentions seem honorable. Kaylan would never ask this if she didn't have a good reason," she said and handed Zack his PDA.

Zack took it and strapped it to his wrist. He started to power it on but decided against it.

"Did Etanu say where he was going?" Zack asked.

"No," Ezerah said.

Zack sighed. "Okay, I'll find him. Thank you for giving me this."

Zack walked away and noticed that Ezerah was walking next to him.

"I'm curious," Ezerah said.

She obviously meant to go with him. Zack had never spent much time with her. He wasn't sure if it was a female Nershal thing or just Ezerah, but he always had the feeling that she didn't want to interact with him at all so he stayed away.

"Where are we going?" Ezerah asked.

"I was going to find an info-terminal but one with a little bit of privacy," Zack said.

"I know a place. Follow me," Ezerah said and walked in front of him with a determined stride.

Ezerah led them past a series of Boxan training facilities. The Boxans they walked by hardly paid them any notice aside from an acknowledgment as they went about their own business. She led him into a building that had a large, open atrium with multiple info-terminals available for use, but they were much too visible. Ezerah came to a stop and looked around. Zack was about to tell her this place wouldn't work for what he needed to do when she started walking toward a corridor on the right. The corridor curved around, following the shape of the building, and there were closed doors on the interior wall. Ezerah went to one of the doors and it opened automatically. Inside was a large, empty room with a sloping pathway that led to a tall podium. The lighting in the room became brighter as they walked farther into the Boxan lecture hall.

"Doesn't anyone use this room?" Zack asked.

"They're done for the day," Ezerah said.

Zack glanced behind them at the door. "And you just happen to know this?" he asked.

"I've been using this room for a while to explore different interests of mine. I was supposed to serve on a Xiiginn warship when Kladomaor came to Selebus. A lot of what the Xiiginns have in terms of technology and knowledge stems from the Boxans. I'd never realized how much until I came here," Ezerah said.

Zack remembered when they'd first met Ezerah. He'd been convinced she was going to turn them over to the Xiiginns, but they'd proven to her that the Xiiginns were exploiting her species.

Ezerah walked up to the podium and activated a large holoscreen.

Zack powered on his PDA, checked Hodak's stolen credentials, and used them to access the terminal, getting immediately to work. He used the secret Boxan protocol he'd found earlier and ran a search on anything about Sethion, but nothing was found. Zack frowned and then tried using the star coordinates for Sethion's star system.

"Here we go," Zack said

Ezerah stepped beside him. "Those are check-in intervals from the quarantine zone," she said.

"So they *are* monitoring it," Zack said and pulled up the details for one of the more recent entries. "Looks like someone is trying to access the quarantine zone. Would this be the Xiiginns?"

Ezerah peered at the data he pointed to.

"That's not the Xiiginns. The ship signature isn't right. These are Gresans," she said. "They're a species in the Confederation. They challenge Xiiginn authority from time to time."

"I like them already," Zack said.

"You might not if you actually met them. They've been less than friendly to other species since the Boxans were cast out of the Confederation," Ezerah said.

"Any idea why they'd be trying to get through the quarantine zone?" Zack asked.

"I have no idea, but they're not getting through based on this information. Why would they keep trying?"

"Were they loyal to the Boxans? Could they be trying to help?" Zack asked.

Ezerah shook her head.

Zack set up another search algorithm to run in the background while he used Hodak's credentials to access something else. He found some historical records that came under the categorization of Xiiginn Uprising. He and Ezerah read the information as it appeared on screen.

"We had no idea how destructive the Xiiginns were to the Boxans," Ezerah said.

"Looks like the Xiiginns were integrated into Boxan society before they staged their uprising. They used their compulsion ability to break down the government hierarchy from the top down. This military group called Protectors keeps getting referred to. The Boxan Protectors were the first military unit to initiate a global conflict by murdering the heads of governing bodies," Zack said.

"The Xiiginns only told us that they brought justice to the Boxans. The Confederation species believed the Xiiginns were liberators," Ezerah said and sucked in a harsh breath. "It was all so contrived."

"The Xiiginns must have planned this for a long time. Years probably. I don't see any record of the Boxans asking for help from the Confederation," Zack said.

"They were too proud to ask for help," Ezerah said in disgust.

"Look at the timeline for these entries. I think by the time they knew what was happening, any help that may have come would already have been too late. Don't forget that while this was happening, the Xiiginns had coordinated attacks from other Confederation species," Zack said.

"The quarantine zone is enforced by a drone blockade. Look at all the conflicts registered as being prevented by the blockade," Ezerah said.

Zack scanned the on-screen data. After the initial burst of activity logged by the blockade when the Boxans first activated the system, there were occasional incidents of ships trying to make a run past the blockade.

"Are the locations for these ships right?" Zack asked.

Ezerah frowned as she read the highlighted entries. "Those are ships that tried to leave Sethion after the quarantine zone was put in place."

Zack felt as if something heavy had just sunk to the bottom of his stomach. The information onscreen showed that the drone blockade had prevented hundreds of ships from leaving Sethion. How could all those Boxans have been under the Xiiginn influence? He didn't know what the capacity of those ships was, but the number of dead must have been staggering.

Zack turned away from the holoscreen and leaned on the podium for support. He was having trouble wrapping his mind around what the Boxans had done to survive. No wonder they didn't want to go back there.

There was an audible chime from his PDA, indicating the search algorithm had finished. Zack looked up, and as he read the results, his mouth hung open. "Oh my God," he said.

"What is that?" Ezerah asked.

"These are communications requests," Zack said.

"Could they be automated?"

Zack pressed his lips together and ran a quick regression analysis on the data. "Looks like a majority could be automated, but there are outliers."

"Those look random," Ezerah said.

Zack nodded. "Or they could be comms requests that were manually initiated by a Boxan."

He scanned the data and noted how the comms requests had significantly decreased over time, but they were still coming in. Zack swallowed hard. Not only did the High Council know they'd left Boxans behind, but they'd been ignoring them for who knows how long. He glanced at Ezerah, who looked away.

"We have to tell someone about this," Zack said.

"Who are we going to tell? Once you say how you got the data, they'll take you into custody," Ezerah said.

"Maybe, but I can't just pretend I don't know about this. I think I know who to contact, but I need you to do it for me," Zack said.

"Why would you need me for this? Shouldn't we go straight to Kaylan?" Ezerah asked.

"Not yet. We need some backup, but the Boxan we need to speak to is mad at me right now, and I think he'll ignore me if I try to contact him," Zack said.

"Very well. Who is it?"

Zack copied the data to his PDA and closed the session. The holoscreen flickered off.

"Gaarokk," he said.

A SHORT WHILE later Zack and Ezerah decided it would be best to simply find Gaarokk and speak with him instead of summoning him somewhere else, so they set off on their ambush of the Boxan scientist. Gaarokk wasn't difficult to locate as the scientist spent much of his time in the research laboratory he'd claimed for himself. When they opened the door to Gaarokk's lab, they heard him talking with someone, so they went inside and saw Gaarokk standing in front of a holoscreen, speaking to another Boxan. His back was to them and he was so focused on his conversation that he didn't hear them come inside.

"I need the materials for a research project. We're building a Star Shroud model to test some theories about the barrier surrounding the Human home world," Gaarokk said.

"Understand your need, but these materials have already been designated for the fleet."

Gaarokk slammed his hand down on the console. "This is ridiculous. I should be getting more cooperation. The Humans have shared what the Drars have given them with us in good faith. The quantities needed will have no impact on your production schedule and you know it."

"My orders come straight from the High Council. I would like to help you, but I'm not able to at this time."

The holoscreen flicked off and Gaarokk stood shaking his head. Zack felt sorry for the Boxan. Gaarokk was trying to help them and was getting the runaround.

Zack cleared his throat and Gaarokk turned around. Upon seeing them, Gaarokk's shoulders slumped.

"I assume you saw that?"

Zack nodded. "Yeah, we saw that. Thanks for trying."

Gaarokk blew out a breath that almost sounded like a growl. "I've been contacting different groups that would have access to the materials we need and none of them will help."

"It's almost like the High Council doesn't want us to leave," Zack said.

Gaarokk gave him a sidelong look and glanced at Ezerah.

"We have something to show you," Ezerah said.

Gaarokk gave Zack a suspicious look.

"Yes, it has to do with Sethion, but damn it, just listen to me," Zack said.

Gaarokk started walking away, his footsteps pounding into the floor.

"We found evidence that there are still Boxans on Sethion. They need help. I don't care what you say, I know this matters to you," Zack said.

Gaarokk stopped in his tracks.

"Here, look at what we found," Zack said and used his PDA to put the data they stole upon the holoscreen.

Gaarokk slowly turned around and looked at the data on the holoscreen, and the silence dragged on while the Boxan took it all in. The noise of shifting feet came from one of the dark adjacent rooms Zack hadn't noticed before and Kladomaor emerged from the darkness. His powerful gaze was fixed on the holoscreen. Zack knew the Boxan's military-grade neural implants were more advanced than what they had and could disseminate the data quickly.

"Where'd you get this?" Kladomaor asked.

The Boxan's menacing tone sent shivers down Zack's spine. "I used Hodak's credentials to get this data," Zack said.

"The head priest of the Mardoxian Sect!" Gaarokk said.

Kladomaor turned on his heels and stalked away at a pace that Zack wouldn't have been able to match even if he'd been running at an all out sprint.

13

Dome-shaped buildings were scattered throughout the complex and Kladomaor blazed a path directly to the Mardoxian training headquarters. Each breath he took ended in a low growl. He didn't slow down at the security checkpoint and the soldiers gave him a wide berth. After months of cooperation, he knew Zack wouldn't have done what he did on his own, which meant someone had asked him to do it. The only person Zack would have broken so many of their laws for was Kaylan, and she wouldn't have made such a request unless she felt she'd had no other choice. All Boxans on Olloron knew they'd left behind a significant portion of the population, but in service of the greater good of the galaxy, it had to be done. A necessary sacrifice was what he'd believed, but now all he felt was outrage.

Kladomaor found Hodak with Ma'jasalax and Kaylan in the large atrium just inside the main building. There were other Boxans in the atrium, but Kladomaor didn't care.

"You!" Kladomaor shouted, his gaze fixed on Hodak.

Ma'jasalax looked over at him in alarm.

"What's the meaning of this?" Hodak said.

Several bodyguards closed in, but Kladomaor didn't hesitate. He was in full battle armor and would take them out if it came to a fight.

"Sethion! You knew there were Boxans left on the planet still fighting for survival and you ignored their pleas for help," Kladomaor said.

Hodak frowned. "What are you talking about? Sethion is quarantined and has been quiet ever since."

Kladomaor used his neural implants and military officer's credentials to take control of all nearby holoscreens. He then pushed Zack's data and analysis to every one of them.

"You lie," Kladomaor hissed.

Hodak's eyes flashed angrily. "Where did you get this? Where did this come from?"

The bodyguards that had been closing in on Kladomaor had shifted their attention to the Mardoxian priest. Kladomaor pulled out his hand cannon, the tip of which started to glow a menacing green as it powered on. Then he pointed it directly at Hodak. Reacting quickly, the Boxan bodyguards drew their weapons and pointed them at Kladomaor.

"If you think you can take me down before I kill him, go ahead," Kladomaor said. "Now answer my question."

Hodak looked stunned for a moment, then quickly recovered. "Put your weapons down," he said to the bodyguards. "I'll answer your question. The High Council is aware that there's Boxan activity on Sethion, but the only thing all that data you've found proves is that someone on Sethion is trying to contact us. We don't know if they're under the Xiiginn influence or not."

Kladomaor lowered his weapon. "There are no more Xiiginns on Sethion."

"Yes, but you of all Boxans should know that their influence can have long-lasting effects, especially when given a specific goal," Hodak said.

"We have to go back," Kladomaor said. "We need to know for sure."

Hodak regarded him for a moment. "We fight the Xiiginns on many fronts. Sethion is lost. There's nothing to go back to but pain and suffering."

Kladomaor looked at Ma'jasalax. "You've gone awfully quiet," he said.

"I think you've said quite enough for the both of us," Ma'jasalax replied.

Kladomaor glanced around. "Where's Kaylan? She was just here."

Ma'jasalax looked around in alarm and then over at the Mardoxian chamber in the courtyard beyond the atrium. The panels were glowing red, which indicated the chamber was in use.

"What is it?" Kladomaor asked.

"She's in the chamber, looking for answers. She kept having what she thought were visions of Boxans fighting a battle with each other. I thought it was exhaustion, but I may have been wrong. Kaylan was likely feeling the connection of another Boxan with the Mardoxian potential," Ma'jasalax said.

"On Sethion," Kladomaor said.

"That's impossible," Hodak said. "How would she even be open to the connection without using the chamber?"

"I told you she's extraordinarily gifted," Ma'jasalax said.

"We have to get her out of there," Hodak said.

Kladomaor brought his weapon up again. "If anyone moves towards the chamber, they'll be the first one I shoot. There'll be no cover-up of this information, not by you or the High Council."

Hodak motioned for the bodyguards to move away from them. Kladomaor headed over to the chamber entrance and turned around. He kept his plasma pistol in his hand and stood guard. Ma'jasalax stood nearby with Hodak and some others of the Mardoxian Sect. Each time Kladomaor caught Ma'jasalax's eye he had the feeling that nothing of what had just transpired had been a surprise to her.

14

Kaylan slipped away from the gathering crowd of Boxans. Once she'd heard what Kladomaor said about Sethion, she knew Zack was involved. He must have found a way to get some real information about Sethion, and the revelation of it had sent Kladomaor into a rage. While the Boxans were looking at the data Kladomaor had put on all the nearby holoscreens, Kaylan made her way to the Mardoxian chamber in the courtyard. As she neared the pyramid, she heard the gentle hum of energy. Kaylan placed her hand on the panel next to the closed door and it opened. She cast a quick glance behind her to be sure no one was watching and then stepped inside. Glowing cyan lights raced up the cathedral-high ceilings, coming to a central point. Crimson lines of light also came on from twin points on the floor and continued around the base of the pyramid's interior.

Kaylan crossed the threshold and the door closed behind her. A dark blue beam shot down from the ceiling to a crystal sphere that rose from the floor. Kaylan sat on the floor and focused on the star coordinates for the Boxan home world. Within seconds her mind was thrust down an azure pathway. When she'd used the chamber to search for Zack back on the planet Nerva, she'd used her personal connection to Zack to find him. She had no such connection to Sethion. It was a planet that she'd only seen in the Boxan archives. Her only impression of it was through the mournful shadows in each Boxan she'd ever met.

The azure pathway receded in her mind and Kaylan found herself amongst the planets, orbiting a bright main-sequence star. She had a bird's-eye view of the inner system of planets and it took her a few moments to register all the hulking wrecks in the star system. Some of them were the size of small moons. She marveled at the sheer numbers and would have loved to have seen Sethion as a thriving star system.

She zipped past the floating spaceships. They were all dark and she couldn't tell if they were intact ships or merely remnant hulls left over from a battle long ago. Kaylan focused on the mustardy yellow orb well within the Goldilocks Zone that was the planet Sethion. Three remnant moons still orbited the planet but huge chunks were missing from each of them. Kaylan couldn't fathom how those moons had come to be in such a state.

Dark orbital platforms surrounded the planet. There were minimal indications of power and she wasn't sure what the platforms were used for. Orbiting close to the planet was a behemoth-sized space dock. Darkened scorch marks dotted most of the space dock's hull. The sheer scale of the destruction here was unimaginable. So much death in this bitter cold star system. She felt a deep pang in her chest at the loss of life.

Kaylan shifted her gaze to the planet's surface. Much of the land along the equator had a worn brown look as if the whole planet were one big scar. Sethion was a graveyard. How could anything survive here? Large brown clouds swirled beneath Kaylan and she circled the planet, looking for any signs of life.

She felt her heart beat faster as despair set in and the view of Sethion blurred in front of her. Kaylan took hold of her focus with an iron will, building an image of the Boxan warrior in the red armor standing alone amidst a field of battle. Pushing onward, Kaylan plunged through the atmosphere. Within moments she was above the corpses of massive cities. She thought she recognized remnant forms of architecture that the Boxans had brought with them to Olloron. Dome-shaped buildings between dirt fields on large, strolling campuses had once been home to lush plant life that must have been beautiful to see, but now there remained only the vestiges of a nuclear holocaust.

She kept thinking there was no way anyone could survive here for a few days, let alone the forty-plus years since the quarantine zone had been put into place, so she moved back from the cities and focused on the mountainous regions of the continents. There were no animals or plant life of any kind. Still, she searched. Those visions had not been figments of her imagination. They were real. There were Boxans here; she just knew it.

Something flickered from the corner of her eye. She turned toward it and saw storm clouds gathering over a city covered with ash and soot. Lightning flashed and struck the ground. A shadow moved along the ground, drawing her attention, and Kaylan sped forward. She heard the sound of a loud blast and one of the buildings near her came crumbling down. Kaylan was about to turn away when she saw multiple figures running from the building. Her eyes widened. The long shadows moved with the assistance of power armor, and they raced away from her. She tried to follow but lost them in the rubble. Someone was here. There were Boxans still here. She felt herself smile as she let the connection go and returned to the Mardoxian chamber on Olloron.

Kaylan rolled her shoulders and blinked her eyes, trying to get rid of the dryness she felt. She took a deep breath and blew it out, then pushed herself to her feet while the crystal sphere sank back down into the metal container. She walked over to the door, placed her palm on the panel, and the chamber door sank into the ground. Kaylan came up short as she met the flaxen-eyed stares of the Boxans waiting outside to greet her.

Kladomaor stepped into view. "It's alright. Come on out," he said in a remarkably calm tone.

She was still a bit disoriented and Kladomaor extended his large hand toward her. She took it and allowed herself to be guided forward, seeing Zack and Ezerah to one side along with the rest of the crew of the Athena.

Kaylan frowned. "How long was I inside the chamber?"

Zack came over to her side. "You've been in there for nearly ten hours. How are you feeling?" he asked.

Brenda Goodwin came over and handed her a bottle of water. Kaylan drank the water greedily and tasted faint traces of cinnamon. As she drained the bottle, she felt a hollow emptiness in her stomach. She was starving, but food would have to wait.

"I'm fine. I just needed to get my bearings for a minute," Kaylan said.

Zack looked relieved and Kaylan glanced at all the Boxans present. Kladomaor stood nearest her and kept a watchful eye on everyone else.

"We need to know what you saw," Zack said.

Kaylan told them everything. She started with her view of Sethion's star system and proceeded to the state of the planet. Through her entire recounting of it, all the Boxans hardly dared draw a breath.

"I was about to give up. There seemed to be nothing alive on the planet surface, but then I saw them—Boxans running amidst the ruined buildings. I only saw them for a few moments, but it was enough. They wore protection and armor," Kaylan said.

Hodak stepped toward her. "Did you see anything else? Anything at all?" he asked.

Kaylan shook her head.

Hodak looked at Kladomaor. "See, there you have it. A few scavengers are hardly a reason to risk the colony," he said.

"It is to the Boxans left behind. There are more there. I know it," Kaylan said.

Hodak didn't look convinced. "I believe you saw something, but you're still new to your gifts—"

"I didn't imagine this. I saw the look on your faces as I described the star system, the breadth of the destruction that could only be possible if I had been there to see it. There are Boxans left behind who need your help and you owe it to them to send help. You owe it to yourselves as well," Kaylan said.

Ma'jasalax cleared her throat. "Kaylan is the most gifted student of the Mardoxian Sect I've ever seen. If she says she saw it, then that's precisely what we'll find."

Hodak drew himself up. "Is this what it's come to?"

"I only ask that you put the request to the High Council. They'll listen to you. Will you at least consider it?" Ma'jasalax asked.

Hodak regarded Ma'jasalax for a moment and then glanced at the rest of them. "I'll consider it on one condition," he said.

Ma'jasalax glanced at Kladomaor, who gave a firm nod.

"No one in this room speaks of what they've witnessed until I've made my decision," Hodak said.

"When will that be, exactly?" Kaylan asked.

Hodak seemed taken aback by the question, but now that it had been asked he would be forced to give them an answer. "Two days at the most. I need to confer with select High Council members."

Kaylan glanced at Ma'jasalax.

"That is acceptable," Ma'jasalax said.

The courtyard and atrium cleared out and the crew of the Athena gathered outside the Mardoxian main buildings. Kladomaor and some of his crew met them, along with Ma'jasalax.

Ma'jasalax looked at Kladomaor. "Is two days enough time?" she asked.

Kladomaor frowned in confusion. "For what?" he asked.

"To steal a ship and return to Sethion," Ma'jasalax said.

Kaylan's mouth hung open. "Wait a second. I thought you didn't believe me. You said I was suffering from exhaustion."

"That's right, I did. A calculated risk, one would say, but when the vision kept recurring with growing clarity, I knew it wasn't a dream. Somehow you were sensing another Boxan with the Mardoxian potential on Sethion," Ma'jasalax said.

"Hold on a minute," Zack said. "How is it that she was able to do this and you weren't?" he asked.

Kaylan was wondering the same thing.

"I've said it before. Kaylan is among the most gifted of the Mardoxian Sect, surpassing those who've come before her in some areas and still learning in other areas. I knew she'd reach out to you for help and I knew you'd find a way to get the information needed to confirm what's happening on Sethion," Ma'jasalax said.

"So glad we could be pawns in your little game," Zack said.

"It was necessary," Ma'jasalax said.

Kaylan's mind raced with the implications of what Ma'jasalax had done and the events that had brought them here.

"You understand, don't you?" Ma'jasalax said to Kaylan.

"I do," Kaylan said and looked at Kladomaor. "Whatever ship you get has to be able to accommodate the Athena. There's no way I'm leaving our ship behind."

Kladomaor glared at Kaylan and Ma'jasalax. "What makes you think I can simply take any ship I want?" he asked.

Ma'jasalax's large ears quivered and it caused her thick, dark locks of hair to move. "Aren't you the famed Battle Commander?" she said.

Kaylan smiled. "We can do this. Together we can do this. We can make it to Sethion," she said.

Kladomaor sighed. "Getting there is the easy part, but getting through the blockade is all but impossible."

Zack grinned. "No place is totally secure. There has to be a way through."

"There's never a lack of enthusiasm on your part," Kladomaor said dryly.

"We have two days," Ma'jasalax said.

Kladomaor shook his head. "No, we have less than one day, and if we're not gone by then I suspect we'll all be taken into custody."

"Why do you say that? Hodak said he needed two days," Kaylan said.

"I don't trust Hodak. He may not be on the High Council, but he holds a lot of sway," Kladomaor said.

"Okay, then let's get to work," Kaylan said.

She felt her stomach growl and knew she needed to eat, but that would have to wait or her next meal might be in a cell.

15

Valkra pulled up the survey map on her helmet's heads-up display. The drones they'd used to scout out the abandoned city had been here weeks ago, but she couldn't remember a time when the cities of Sethion hadn't been the ruined skeletons of a bygone age. What buildings were left standing from the Chaos Wars were a brittle reminder of the greatness of Boxan ingenuity and superiority in the galaxy. Now those empty shells provided adequate cover for her and her squad, and nothing else.

Valkra sent a signal calling for a halt while she examined the survey map and her squad mates quickly found cover. She glanced around and switched the lens setting to standard live view as the thin yellow veil of a toxic cloud swirled above them. They'd picked this area to forage for supplies because the cloud cover was so minimal this time of year, something the dreaded Protectors would no doubt surmise as well. She switched her heads-up display to combat mode and her suit computer immediately began scanning ahead wherever she looked.

One of her squad opened a comms channel to her.

"Toxicity is rising," Ranem said.

Valkra acknowledged her second in command. They had a limited timeframe they could safely be exposed to Sethion's atmosphere. Without protection, they'd be dead in minutes. The powered armor they were using had been ancient before the Chaos Wars and had been a patchwork of quick fixes ever since. Everything that followed was a reminder of the Xiiginns' betrayal and the bitter wars that killed their planet.

"Let's make a sweep of the area. Remember, we're looking for useable materials for the fabricators at Haven. Use your suit computers to see the list and identify any high-priority items," Valkra said.

This wasn't their first salvage mission, but it never hurt to put a reminder in her fellow squad mates' ears of why they were here. She set a countdown timer and uploaded it to the others. This was all the time they had for scavenging before the toxic atmosphere compromised their suits. There was also the looming threat that the Protectors would detect their presence and kill them all.

Valkra activated her particle rifle and the rest of the squad did the same. The rifle's beam had a finite range but was incredibly accurate, even at longer distances. The Protector's armor could resist a single particle beam for a time, which gave the Protector an opportunity to kill them and was why they trained by firing multiple beams at a single target. This tactic would overwhelm even the elite military armor the Protectors used. Ranem carried the only phaze hand cannon in the group, which was a weapon of last resort. It had limited ammunition and the amount of energy released from the hand cannon would light them up on any Protector's sensors in the area, painting a large target on their backs.

Ranem had been with her for the many cycles since she'd first joined the foraging squads. Under her leadership their squad had the most successful record of finding the rare elements needed for the fabricators still in operation at Haven. But they were running dangerously low on supplies, which created the need for these foraging missions.

She moved ahead and checked the area. Once satisfied that it was safe enough to proceed, she waved Ranem ahead. They worked in teams of two and checked each building they came across, making their way to the base of a large building. Valkra knew that at one time structures such as these had been so tall that the upper levels were in the clouds, but these vast, stumpy remnants were all that was left of those unimaginably tall buildings.

They moved inside and the jagged walls opened up to the sky like a gaping maw.

Ranem came to a stop. "Gladium deposits detected," he said in an elevated tone.

Gladium was at the top of their list for its durability and strength. It was the base element for making ships and reinforcing the infrastructure of Haven.

"Go check it out. We'll cover you," Valkra said.

Ranem waved Tholev over, who carried a plasma cutter, and the two Boxans moved to the exposed innards of the building's superstructure where Ranem began moving large pieces of rubble. The servo gears of the power armor gave off a high-pitched whine as they struggled with the last piece. Tholev ignited the plasma cutter and then went to work cutting pieces of the beams out so they could extract the gladium.

Valkra moved away from them and kept her particle rifle ready. The area beyond the building was quiet, but she felt a growing sense of dread. They were blind down here. She'd learned long ago to trust her intuition and of late she'd been growing more restless. She signaled to the others that she was going to climb higher to get a better vantage point. Recon drones would have been helpful, but she'd lost the lottery for them on this mission and she'd have to rely on the other squads in the region to notify her of suspicious activity.

Valkra moved away from the others towards a large pile of rubble where she performed a squat-and-leap maneuver that threw her into the air. Grabbing hold of some twisted metal that jutted outward, she pulled herself up and reached across to the next piece. Valkra swung out with her foot and leveraged herself up. Hearing the faint sounds of the plasma cutter working, she glanced down. She was fifty feet above them. She looked up again and climbed even higher, enabling her jump to the partially intact roof of the nearby building. She squatted close to the rooftop and moved toward the edge of the building to peer downward. The streets below her were clear so she gazed at the city line. Scanning the area, she noticed movement a few hundred yards away. Her suit computer tried to identify it but she lost sight of it too fast. Valkra clutched her rifle and took aim while opening a comms channel to her squad mates.

"We're not alone. I have an unknown contact northwest of our position. Ranem, time to pack it up," Valkra said.

She scurried further along to see if she could get a better look at what she'd glimpsed a moment before. The recon map on her HUD didn't show any of their teams in the area. Her targeting computer noted another contact, but this one was in a different position. Valkra ducked down and caught the faint glow of the plasma cutter still at work.

"Kill the cutter. We have hostiles in the area," Valkra said over comms.

She sent out a high-band alert notifying the other squads of the danger. The other squad leaders might not like that she didn't have clear visual confirmation, which was required for a mission abort, but she knew the Protectors were here. Nothing else moved on Sethion's surface besides them or the Protectors.

"Clear out of the building," Valkra ordered.

Tholev was packing the gladium deposits into a large container as quickly as he could and Valkra's eyes widened at the size of the deposits. If they could get this back to Haven, they wouldn't need another foraging mission for months.

"Commander, we have movement behind us," Ranem said.

"Clear out to the south and I'll meet you there," Valkra said.

The squad began to move out and Valkra turned around and ran. She pounded across the rooftop and leaped across a wide chasm to the next building. Quickly closing the distance to the south end of the building and vaulting over the side, she held on with one hand and dangled in the air for moment, then dropped. At the last second, as the ground raced up to meet her, Valkra engaged a burst from her suit thrusters to slow her down and her suit absorbed most of the impact. She glanced down the street, waiting for her team to arrive, but she heard a noise behind her and ducked down behind a rocky pile of rubble. She pressed her back against the pile and shifted toward the edge so she could peek around the corner, turning around to bring up her particle rifle. Craning her neck, she tried to find a target, but her view down the street faded after a hundred yards. She scanned, using all the known visual frequencies, but couldn't see anything. Valkra sucked in a deep breath. She heard the familiar sounds of her squad rounding the corner and raised her hand, gesturing for them to take cover.

"What have you got, Commander?" Ranem asked over comms as he and the rest of the squad took cover.

Valkra peeked around the corner again. A splatter of acid rain had begun pelting down and there was a harsh hissing sound whenever it made contact with anything. In the gloom, she saw the hissing vapor rise from objects ten feet off the ground.

"Contact!" she cried and fired her rifle.

A bright yellow particle beam sliced through the air and slammed into an armored Protector, momentarily disrupting the stealth field.

"Ranem, I need that hand cannon of yours. Down that street one hundred yards," Valkra said.

Ranem climbed to the top of the pile of rubble and took two shots. Plasma bolts belched from the heavy hand cannon and slammed into the approaching line of Protectors. Ranem slid down the rubble and hit the ground next to her. Around the corner where the rest of her squad was, she saw flashes of particle beams being fired. The noose was tightening around them. Across the street from her was an alleyway that seemed like a good escape route and Ranem was already poised to head that way.

"It's a trap. That's where they want us to go," Valkra said.

They raced to the corner where the rest of her squad was fighting for their lives. Valkra glanced behind her, knowing that at any second now more Protectors would be coming. Two shots from a heavy hand cannon would only have stopped two of them, at best. She peeked around the corner, seeing the glistening sheen of the dark Protector armor hissing in the acid rain, and fired her rifle at the nearest Protector, adding her beam to the others. The Protector tried to find cover, but the five particle beams were overwhelming his power armor. The other Protectors dove for cover.

"Fall back," Valkra ordered.

The squad followed her as they moved down the street and Ranem brought up the rear, providing covering fire as they went. Tholev carried the large container of precious gladium. Valkra bolted to the right, only to find that the street was completely blocked off by the collapse of a building long ago.

"We need higher ground and an extraction," Valkra said and tried to see the area beyond the collapsed building.

"Protectors are closing in on our position. We can't stay here," Ranem said.

Valkra carried one piece of heavy explosives that could bring down a building on the Protectors, but she didn't know if it would buy them enough time. They didn't know how many Protectors were hunting them.

"Come on. We have to climb over," Valkra said.

Tholev cried out. "My armor's been breached!"

The acid rain had eaten its way through his adjoining shoulder plates. He tried to take cover as best he could while their squad medic came over and patched the hole, but Valkra knew it wouldn't last long enough. The toxic rain ate through almost everything.

Valkra reached out and took one side of the large container from Tholev, gesturing for Ranem to take the other side. Together, they heaved the container high into the air and she heard it tumble down the other side of the collapsed building. The container could be dropped from the top of the tallest of ancient buildings and the contents inside would remain intact.

The rest of the squad began scaling the wall of rubble. Valkra pulled herself up, working her way towards the top, and a blast from a Protector's heavy weapon ripped into the area around her. Two of her squad fell, screaming as they went. Valkra growled and continued to climb as fast as she could, stopping to help her squad mates up when she reached the top. Ranem had stopped halfway up and was firing his heavy hand cannon down at the Protectors, giving them the covering fire they needed.

"Come on," Valkra said to him.

Ranem holstered his weapon and climbed faster while Valkra teamed up with another squad mate, firing their particle rifles down to give Ranem some cover. They had the Protectors pinned down and Ranem was nearing the top when a large, heavy mech came around the corner. The mech was over twenty feet tall and a large plasma cannon was attached to one arm. The tip of the barrel flared molten yellow as it primed.

Valkra gasped and fired her particle rifle at the mech, but it had no effect. Ranem was almost to the top when he glanced back down at the mech. Looking back up at Valkra while reaching for his hand cannon, he heaved it to her, and she caught it just as the mech's giant plasma cannon fired. Valkra was thrown into the air, away from the blast, and she screamed when she saw Ranem fall back to the Protectors. As Valkra came crashing to the ground, rock and debris rained down around her, and she rolled to a stop, pushing herself to her feet.

"Ranem!" she shouted.

In a split second, Ranem had known he was about to die so he'd thrown his hand cannon in her direction. As the heartbreaking scene replayed itself in her mind, she swept aside the painful emotions threatening to overwhelm her in order to focus on what remained of her squad racing toward her. There were only three of them left now and she had to get them out. The rest were either dead or dying at the hands of the Protectors. Tholev dragged the large container with him. Valkra grabbed one handle of the container from Tholev and they ran as fast as they could away from the Protectors and their heavy mech on the other side of the wall of rubble.

After they'd put some distance between themselves and the Protectors, Valkra risked a glance behind. A molten yellow glow surrounded the wall of debris. Years of exposure to acid rain and Sethion's toxic atmosphere had made the building material brittle and the center of the pile of rubble melted away, rolling in a churning wave away from the Protectors.

They kept moving as fast as they could. She'd initiated a distress signal at the first sign of the attack and a comms channel opened for her.

"What's your situation?" the extraction commander asked.

"There are four of us left. Protectors are in pursuit. They knew we were coming," Valkra said.

"Understood. We have your location now. We can do a quick pickup, but you need to get to higher ground. There are two sites near your position. Can you get there?"

Valkra glanced around them and saw the two buildings they were referring to.

"Turn your trackers on. We've got eyes in the sky," Valkra said to Tholev and the others.

The extraction team would be able to locate them, but she didn't like how exposed they'd be on those buildings.

Valkra engaged the comms channel to the extraction commander. "They were ready for us. Are you sure those sites are safe for my squad?"

Tholev suddenly pulled her to the side via the canister they carried and she heard weapons fire.

They had no choice. Either they risked the exposure of the two tall buildings that provided at least a chance of getting away or they'd have to fight the Protectors and die. "We'll be there, but we've got Protectors following close behind," Valkra said.

She motioned for one of the other squad members to help Tholev with the container and sent the coordinates of the extraction point to the rest of the squad. She ordered them ahead and followed. How had the Protectors known they'd be here? Not only had they known precisely where her squad would be, but they had executed an ambush that cut off most of their escape routes. If it had been anyone other than her leading them, the squad would have been dead. This wasn't boastful thinking, but the simple truth. Her insights into a situation were unparalleled. There were Boxans back at Haven who suspected she had the Mardoxian potential, and if that was ever confirmed, she'd be taken off missions like these.

They went inside the shell of the building and the three remaining squad members raced towards the roof. Valkra squatted and set down her heavy explosives pack, hiding it away. She activated the detonator and set it to go off on her signal, acutely aware of the pounding crunch of armored Protectors racing down the street toward them and the high-pitched whirr of the heavy mech following close behind.

Valkra howled with rage, stowed her particle rifle, and un-holstered Ranem's hand cannon. It was at thirty percent power so she couldn't waste any shots. She exited the building and stood out in the street, knowing that the rest of her squad should have made it to the roof by now.

The Protectors expected her to run. She knew she would most likely die either way, but there was something she had to do. Her HUD reported twenty Protectors barreling toward her.

"Commander," Tholev said over comms, "I see the ship. It's almost here. You need to get up here."

Valkra raised her hand cannon, aimed, and fired it at the nearest Protector, who was thrown backward with a burning hole through his chest. Warmth spread through her body and she aimed the hand cannon again, eager for another kill.

The Protectors fanned out to the side while returning fire.

Valkra ducked and rolled away, sensing where the shots were going to go. She ran away from the building where the extraction would take place and circled the corner of the smaller second building. The Protectors followed without so much as glancing at the building where her squad was. Valkra fired another shot but missed. She ducked into the building and raced up a staircase.

"Commander, the ship is here. What's your position?" Tholev asked.

"Don't wait for me. Get on that ship," Valkra said.

She continued up the staircase and it shook under her weight. It probably hadn't been used in a long time.

Valkra heard the Protectors enter the building.

"We're not leaving you behind. We have your signal. Get to the top of that building and we'll get you," Tholev said.

Valkra didn't answer. She just grunted as she ran as fast as she could. Plasma bolts blazed by her and she instinctively ducked, returning fire with the hand cannon. A warning appeared on her HUD, telling her that the hand cannon only had five percent power remaining.

She reached the rooftop. This building was much shorter than the one her squad had been on. She sprinted to the edge and glanced down. On the street were hundreds of Protectors, all clamoring to get into the building she was in. Where had they all come from?

She glanced up as the ship flew into view and Tholev waved from the open cargo-bay doors. Shots fired from the ground toward the ship and Valkra knew that if the ship came to her, it would be destroyed. She pointed to the opposite end of the building and Tholev nodded.

Valkra detonated the heavy explosives she'd placed at the base of the nearby building, releasing a loud rumble and a blaze of molten heat, and ran toward the other side of the roof. She'd have this one chance to reach the ship or they would have to leave her behind. As the ship raced to meet her, Protectors emerged onto the roof ahead of her. In midflight, Valkra screamed as she fired the hand cannon, taking out one of the Protectors. The others took cover, expecting more shots, but she was out of power. Valkra reached the edge of the building and took a flying leap into the air toward the open cargo-bay doors. Tholev was waiting with an outstretched hand while the other Boxans fired their particle rifles at the Protectors, keeping them pinned down. As Valkra's reaching hand found Tholev's grasp, he pulled her aboard the ship.

A large shadow loomed overhead and the extraction ship sped away as the tall building fell onto the one she'd just been in, engulfing it in wanton destruction. The Boxans on the rescue ship looked on in awe and then found their voices as cheering erupted from them.

"You must have taken out hundreds of them," Tholev said.

Valkra didn't care. "There'll always be more of them to hunt us," she said.

She moved away from the cargo-bay doors and sat down heavily. How many Boxans had died today? *Too many*, she thought. Valkra stood and headed up the ramp toward the pilot.

"Are the other squads out?" she asked.

"Yes, your warning saved a lot of lives. Your squad was hit the hardest. No one left behind," the pilot said.

Only the dead, Valkra thought bitterly.

Noting that the pilot was a bit nervous, she left him to focus on getting them home and went to sit down, taking a deep breath. Could the Protectors be hunting her? She mulled the thought over while their ship sped away, supposing she should be thankful the Protectors hadn't had any of their own ships in the area, which was a blessing. They did have heavy mechs, however, and that meant the gladium they'd found had been bait. This whole setup had been a trap.

16

Valkra spent the rest of the flight sitting quietly by herself, mulling over the day's events to see if there was something she could have done differently but avoiding any quick judgments. She was doing fine until she thought of Ranem. They'd grown up together in one of the earlier Havens that had been overrun.

"Final approach to Haven Two-Zero-One," the pilot said.

Haven Two-Zero-One was the last refuge on Sethion and home to over three hundred thousand stranded Boxans from the Chaos Wars. There had been over five hundred Havens, but over the years the Protectors had hunted down and destroyed them all. Haven Two-Zero-One was buried in the northern glaciers, hidden amidst an icy plain. When the Protectors had found the original Haven Two-Zero-One by happenstance, its inhabitants managed to escape and move to a place the Protectors had never considered. They'd also managed to rescue other Boxans around the globe, further swelling their numbers, but now found themselves relegated to an icy cold existence well away from the harmful toxic surface of the planet. Hundreds of Havens had been established in mountain ranges where they'd hollowed out almost entire mountains, but the Protectors had found them first. Others had tried to create Havens in the deep oceans, but liquid water couldn't mask the energy signature of thousands of Boxans living in the deep part of the ocean. In the end, the glacial plains had provided the best place in terms of thwarting the Protectors attempts at finding them. They were relatively safe, but they had to go on foraging runs for supplies, and those runs were becoming more and more dangerous.

The rescue ship flew down a massive ice channel. Clearance codes were transmitted at the checkpoints and their ship was checked for tracking devices. If there *were* tracking devices attached to the hull of the ship, the jammers were already active, preventing any return signal to the Protectors' monitoring devices.

Their ship was clean and before long they flew in and landed. Valkra stepped off the ship onto the hangar deck. Of her squad of thirty, only four had survived. The hangar deck crews relieved them of the precious gladium and she fought to keep the sneer from her face. The crews were just doing their job, but the crushing weight of twenty-six squad mates grated on her nerves. The deaths of over a hundred Protectors was cold comfort when compared with the faces of her squad she'd never see again.

Valkra had been summoned by the Foraging Council leaders and was asked to provide a full report on what had happened, so she walked off the deck and headed for the main hall where the council was already meeting. Councilor Essaforn was their leader and was in attendance for this session, closely watching Valkra while she gave her report. After finishing her report, Valkra waited.

Councilor Essaforn regarded her for a moment. "I'm very sorry for the loss of your squad mates. It's my understanding that your squad was among the most successful at bringing in the supplies we desperately need."

Valkra swallowed hard and sorrow closed up her throat. "They were waiting for us. The Protectors' actions seemed to indicate an advanced knowledge of our activities."

"What are you saying?" Councilor Essaforn asked.

"I'm saying that somehow they knew we were coming and they were targeting my squad," Valkra said.

"Do you mean to imply that they were targeting you specifically?" Councilor Essaforn asked.

Does she suspect what I am?

"They did follow me," Valkra said.

"Yes, you said as much when you explained that for some reason you sent the remaining members of your squad to the roof while you single-handedly distracted the Protectors and a heavy mech. I'd like to know what you hoped to achieve." Councilor Essaforn asked.

Valkra's gaze hardened, her fingers tensed, and she jutted her chin up defiantly. "I was tired of running away from them and I turned around because I wanted to kill as many Protectors as I could. I'm sick of being hunted like an animal."

"That was a mistake," Councilor Essaforn said.

Valkra's eyes widened. "Hundreds of Protectors died because of me."

"Even if it were a thousand, it wouldn't make a difference," Councilor Essaforn said.

"Perhaps if we fought the Protectors, struck at them wherever they are, then maybe we could forage in peace, maybe even build ships and figure out a way to leave Sethion forever. Aren't you tired of being packed away here, penned up like animals?" Valkra asked.

Councilor Essaforn silenced her fellow council members with a wave of her hand. "Do you think you're the first Boxan to propose this? That if we could kill all those who are still under the Xiiginn influence, somehow everything would be better?"

Valkra felt her ears twitch. "No," she said in a small voice, but inside she was raging. She kept seeing the Protectors in their dark armor, running her squad down like animals. She knew the historical record showed that the Protectors used to be the long arm of the Boxan military. They'd been the elite fighting force that had secured Sethion's peace and stability.

"A stand-up fight with the Protectors would result in our death. They're better equipped and better trained than we'll ever be. They hardly rest and they have no remorse for their actions. They're fully under the Xiiginn influence, and the only thing that works in our favor is the fact that the longer they're under their influence, the more their mental capacity is diminished," Councilor Essaforn said.

Valkra met the councilor's gaze. "Their attack today was coordinated and there were no problems with their mental fortitude. They had an objective and they were keen to achieve it."

"Their objective is to kill all of us. That's their whole reason for being."

Valkra clamped her mouth shut.

"Your armor is in need of serious repair. I want you to see Cardaleer about getting it replaced," Councilor Essaforn said.

Valkra glanced down at her armor. It was so worn that the traditional reddish color had faded. "What can that old Boxan possibly give me that would be better than this?" she asked.

"That's not a request, Commander. Until further notice, you're grounded from foraging missions. You're dismissed," Councilor Essaforn said.

Valkra glared at the councilor. "Why didn't the recon drones detect the Protectors?"

"Squad Commander Aligar reported drone malfunction shortly after they were deployed."

Valkra looked at the Foraging Council. "Are you sure you want me grounded if we can't even get recon drones to work reliably? You need me out there."

She turned around and left them behind, not waiting for an answer. Valkra blew out a frustrated sigh. Her last question might have permanently grounded her from future salvage missions. But they *did* need her out there. Surely they must realize that.

The power meter on her armor chimed a warning that she needed to recharge it so she headed for Cardaleer's work area. The Boxan was among the oldest survivors of the Chaos Wars. He'd been some kind of scientist before the war, but now he just fixed things. Some Boxans thought he was the one who'd proposed moving Haven to its current location.

The air in Haven was always cold, which was necessary to maintain the ice tunnels throughout the complex. Cardaleer's work area wasn't far along the tunnel and before long she was outside his door. She entered her access code, but the door remained locked. Frowning, Valkra tried again, but the door remained closed. She banged an armored fist on the door, and after a few minutes, the door opened and a wizened old Boxan's stooped form appeared.

"What can I do for you?"

"Councilor Essaforn sent me to you because my armor is in need of repair," Valkra said.

Cardaleer's flaxen eyes regarded her for a moment. "Do I know you?"

Valkra shook her head. "I don't think so."

"Well then, I can hardly invite you in if you don't introduce yourself," Cardaleer said.

Valkra waited a moment to see if the old Boxan was serious, and when he didn't move she thought about turning away. She could fix her own armor, but something in the old Boxan's gaze stopped her.

"I'm Valkra."

"There, you see, that wasn't so hard. The burden of civilization falls upon us," Cardaleer said and led her inside.

Valkra followed him. "You haven't introduced yourself to *me*."

"Why would I? That's nonsense. You already know who I am," Cardaleer said.

The old Boxan's work area seemed more like a repository for junk and discarded items. She could probably repurpose most of it into something useful.

"I can see that your armor is running low on power. Step inside the cradle over there and we'll get that squared away," Cardaleer said.

Valkra walked over to the cradle and backed up inside it. The clamps took hold of the armor and she initiated the release, causing the front plates to open and allowing her to step free.

Cardaleer watched her. "You could use some time in a resonance chamber," he said.

"I don't have time to sit around and meditate right now."

"Oh, is that so," Cardaleer said in a surprised tone. "And here I thought you were grounded from further missions."

Valkra looked over at him in shock. "And here I thought you didn't know who I was."

Cardaleer chuckled. "You're a clever one; I'll grant you that."

The cradle holding her armor swiveled around and a transparent shield came down. Inside, nozzle ends of thick cables slid down from the ceiling and began spraying a treatment solution. Valkra watched the worn areas of her armor seem to repair themselves as the solution worked its way through.

"That will need some time to set and recharge," Cardaleer said.

"Fine, I'll be back later to pick it up," Valkra said and headed for the door.

"Tell me," Cardaleer said. "How long do you think you can fool them?"

Valkra stopped in her tracks and turned around. "What are you talking about?"

Cardaleer slowly walked over to her. His flaxen gaze was hard, denoting the shrewd intelligence behind his eyes. "I think you know, but since you'll probably keep denying it until I come right out and say it, then that's what I'll do. You've got the Mardoxian potential in you," Cardaleer said.

"All Boxans do," Valkra replied.

"That's true, but some more than others. In another time, you'd have been recruited to become a Mardoxian Priestess," Cardaleer said.

"No thanks," Valkra replied.

"Why not? Why be a forager when you could be so much more?" Cardaleer asked.

Valkra swallowed hard. "Even if I were, I'd much rather be out there doing something useful than trapped in this block of ice," she said.

"I see," Cardaleer said, and he walked over to the wall and began rummaging through some things.

Valkra stood there for a few moments, unsure of what she should do. "Will you tell the council?"

Cardaleer found what he was looking for and turned around. In his hands was a small metallic box. He set the box on the table and opened it. Inside, a pyramid rose with a crystal sphere resting on top of it. He turned the power on and the crystal sphere began to glow and hover just above the tip of the pyramid. Valkra felt something deep inside her rise up. The crystal sphere started to spin and a beam shot forth. Valkra would have ducked if she'd had the chance, but all she saw was a white pathway of light.

"Don't be scared," Cardaleer said in a soothing tone. "Just breathe and focus on where your last mission was."

Valkra sucked in a deep breath. The beam didn't hurt, but she felt as if she'd just ingested stimulants and was now wide awake. She built an image of the city in her mind. The toxic rain clouds had moved on and she felt as if she were floating above the city. Then she was back at the extraction point. Collapsed buildings had taken over the area and she saw many Protectors trapped. They didn't move and must be dead. She circled the area and found her dead squad mates. Valkra let out a soft cry when she saw Ranem, then felt herself being pulled back and she was once again in Cardaleer's work area. He powered the machine off.

"Well, that settles it, don't you think?" Cardaleer asked.

"What did you do to me?"

"I didn't do anything. That was all you. This machine can help novice priests focus their abilities."

"Are you going to say anything? Please don't tell anyone," Valkra said.

Cardaleer watched her for a moment. "Your abilities could be of great value to everyone at Haven. We've been without someone like you for a long time."

"They'll never let me leave," Valkra said.

"Would that be so bad? If you keep going out there, you'll eventually be killed," Cardaleer said.

Valkra's brows pushed forward into a frown. "Perhaps I'd rather be out there accomplishing something than scraping away an existence here. Out there I'm free . . . for a time at least."

Cardaleer looked away. "It's not so bad here. At least the Protectors haven't found this place."

"There is that," Valkra said.

"One so young shouldn't be so bitter. You have your health and you get to live another day, which is much more than I can say for many others."

"This isn't living."

"What would you have us do? If you were running things here, what would you focus on?" Cardaleer asked.

"I would focus on getting us out of here, away from Sethion. No one left behind," Valkra said.

"We tried. The orbital defensive platforms are configured to destroy any ships leaving the planet," Cardaleer said.

"I don't care. I'd find a way. There has to be a way to disable the platforms," Valkra said.

"They're locked and we don't have the capability of destroying them from here," Cardaleer said.

"Then I'd send a signal out for any Boxans to assist us. Defensive platforms can't block outbound signals."

Cardaleer nodded. "You're right about that. A signal has been sent out. There has been no answer."

"Then I'd keep sending a signal every day until someone came," Valkra said.

"Haven Two-Zero-One has been the last safe place on this planet for almost twenty cycles. During that time, I've had a signal sent out. I've even taken over anything in orbit I could and sent signals from there. When that failed, I tried flying remote ships off the planet and managed to take out some defensive platforms that way, but it wasn't enough. We even managed to get a ship off-planet past the defense platforms, but it was destroyed shortly after that by a drone blockade. So believe me when I tell you, no one is coming to help us," Cardaleer said.

Valkra looked away. "No one left behind," she said softly.

"That's what you salvaging types say to each other to fool yourselves into believing you'll come back from whatever mission they send you on," Cardaleer said.

"What would you have us do? Just sit here?" Valkra asked.

"That's what I intend to do. You have the Mardoxian potential in you and perhaps you'll be able to do something the rest of us couldn't," Cardaleer said.

Valkra sighed. "Did you really do all those things you said you did?"

"Not alone. The Chaos Wars lasted a long time. There are shipyards out there with enough space to get every Boxan off this planet, but we have no way of getting there. The Boxans who left us behind won't return. In the beginning, the different Havens worked together to try and find a way to leave. We even thought the quarantine zone was a good idea—a necessity for the survival of our species. Those ideas sustained us for a while. Then, at some point, entire Havens risked everything to leave, and well, there aren't very many of us left," Cardaleer said.

Valkra knew of those Boxans who'd been able to leave. They must have gone somewhere. Why hadn't they returned for them? "That thing you used on me. It allowed me to return to the location of our last mission."

"Only in your mind. You were still in this room, I assure you," Cardaleer said.

"It was like I was actually there. During the mission it was almost as if I could sense the Protectors closing in on us, but it was all so confusing," Valkra said.

"Some records say those with the Mardoxian potential can contact one another over vast distances," Cardaleer said.

Valkra's eyes widened.

"But you don't want anyone to know what you are," Cardaleer said.

"What I am is a salvager. I go out there to get the things we need to survive," Valkra said.

"Yes, but now you know you can be so much more. The question now is, what are you going to do?" Cardaleer said.

"I don't know."

Cardaleer regarded her for a moment and frowned. "I won't say anything for now. You're welcome to look through the records I have here. Perhaps they'll help you figure out what to do."

Valkra thought about it. She was grounded from further missions. Perhaps Cardaleer was right and she could contact another Boxan with the Mardoxian potential, explain to them that there are Boxans still here fighting for their lives. Her thoughts drifted back to the scavenging mission. There'd been times when she'd thought there was someone watching her, but she'd been so focused on staying alive that she hadn't given it a thought. Valkra went over to the info terminal and began researching the Mardoxian Sect.

17

K yle Matthews slipped into his newly designed Earth Coalition Force standard multiple-environment spacesuit. Since there was no shortage of acronyms in NASA or the military, and since the ECF wasn't proving to be any different, the wearers of the multiple-environment spacesuit liked to call it simply a MES suit.

"These new MES suits are pretty comfy," Tom said. "I can't imagine wearing one of those bulky old spacesuits astronauts used to wear."

Tom Blake was twenty-six years old, a communications engineer who'd been among the first through the ECF academy, designed to bridge the gap between the emerging technologies from the Boxans with Humanity's own twist.

"They weren't that bad," Kyle said.

He pushed his arms into the sleeves of his MES suit and the smart nano fibers adjusted themselves to his build. Tom was right; these were comfortable. It was almost like wearing a really thick sweatshirt, but it hardly restricted his movements at all. Kyle's internal HUD from his neural implants registered the MES suit with newly available options. The smart nano fibers could reconfigure their matrix to enhance the suit's abilities to augment the wearer's strength and detect injuries.

"You actually wore one of those old spacesuits, Colonel?" Kevin asked.

"At the Sacramento Bay training facility they'd let us try them on so we'd learn firsthand how far we've come," Kyle said.

Corporal Celia Pearson was already in her MES suit, along with the outer armor coverings. A TRS pulse rifle was in her hands.

Lieutenant Kevin Dawson was the next to finish donning his MES suit and reached down to pick up a TRS plasma rifle. They would do some field testing with the weapons if they had time. The TRS pulse rifle was a modified version of what they'd already created without Boxan input. The only thing that was different was the higher-grade materials used that allowed for a more powerful projectile. However, the plasma rifle was entirely new and of Boxan design, which was only slightly modified in size to fit the average person. Kyle only carried a side arm, as did Tom. This was to be a shakedown training exercise along with a three-Boxan team to see how well they could work together. They were using a Boxan shuttle for this exercise. They were still the fastest ships in the solar system, but not for long. Strike-fighter assembly lines were almost fully operational and they'd have several squadrons of those ships available soon. The next ship design they'd started building would be Destroyer-class vessels, the construction of which could be seen at the designated area on the new moon. The Boxans were convinced they could build ships faster than they were, but Kyle knew they were already moving at breakneck speeds. General Sheridan had assured them that once they cut their teeth building the strike-fighters and destroyers, they'd go for the much larger battleship-carriers that were still on the design table.

Kyle flexed his arms, testing the MES suit, and couldn't find any fault with it. "Alright, let's go over the mission specs one more time."

The three of them turned to face him.

"We have some Shroud monitoring devices that keep going offline. We have drones that go in to effect repairs, but they want us to investigate an actual failed device so we can determine why it keeps happening," Kyle said.

Lieutenant Dawson raised his hand. "Sir, why aren't we using one of the new Eagle shuttles for this?"

"They need more field testing before we can consider taking them on a mission like this. We'll be traveling with three Boxan soldiers and our role is to run backup and support for them," Kyle said.

He sensed the proverbial rolling of the eyes from Pearson and Dawson. Tom Blake was oblivious to it and was just excited to come along for the ride.

Kyle held up his hands in a placating gesture. "I get it. Running support is like being on the third-string team that never gets any playing time. When we have our own ships fully vetted, we'll have the Boxans supporting *us* on *our* missions, but right now this is how it has to be."

They put on their helmets and left the mission prep area, walking into the new lunar base hangar where the Boxan shuttle was waiting for them. Outside were three Boxan soldiers in their power armor.

"Hello, Eavoth. Thanks for letting us tag along," Kyle said.

"It's our honor to have you aboard," Eavoth said. "This is Krano and Adyas."

The two teams greeted one another and Kyle introduced his team and their roles. Most of the Boxans Kyle had met were eager to work with them. Once he'd gotten used to them being ten feet tall and having skin that reminded him of the bark of a tree, they were actually alright to be around.

"My specialties are co-pilot and medical," Krano said.

Eavoth nodded for Adyas to go.

"Technical specialist and engineer," Adyas said and regarded them for a moment. "I blow things up."

Tom Blake perked up at hearing that and stuck by Adyas as they went aboard the shuttle.

Like most things the Boxans made, the shuttle was big—almost the same size as the spaceship Endurance that was based on pre-Boxan-contact designs. Inside the shuttle were two levels, with the bottom level used primarily to store equipment. Adyas led Tom ahead while they checked the equipment in storage. It wouldn't do for them to travel all the way out to a monitoring device and not have the right equipment to repair it.

Kyle followed Eavoth to the upper level. This wasn't Kyle's first time in a Boxan shuttle, but the smooth interior represented a model of perfection they were hoping to emulate in their own ships. The Boxans had taken a few steps to adapt their equipment for Human use. For instance, the staircase leading to the upper level had additional steps installed to accommodate passengers that were people-sized. The ECF fleet was being designed with not only Humans serving aboard the vessels, but Boxans as well.

Eavoth led him to the command platform, which was a slightly raised area in the middle of the upper level. There were three couches on the platform and Eavoth invited Kyle to use the couch next to his. Kyle thanked him and sat down. The couch material instantly adjusted itself for maximum comfort and he felt as if he were in a plush but firm cradle. Metallic straps automatically adjusted for his size and secured him in place.

"Forgive me, Colonel, but you should now have access to our systems," Eavoth said.

A new connection made itself available through Kyle's implants. Upgrades to their neural implants were one of the first things they'd done so Humans could interact with Boxan computing systems. Kyle had bridge-officer access, which, on a Boxan ship, gave him the highest level of access. Though they were backup and support for this mission, he had the same level of access as Eavoth.

"Thank you," Kyle said.

Boxan computer systems were blazingly fast and their artificial intelligence construct was extremely helpful in anticipating their needs.

The rest of the crew checked in. Given the amount of room on the shuttle, Kyle could easily have brought more people on this mission, but in the end he wanted to keep it simple. This was new territory for them all. Kyle was here because he wanted first-hand experience on these joint Human and Boxan missions. It would help him when he was to call upon others to do the same. He'd decided to only bring a sampling of personnel with different levels of expertise and rank. Participating in local missions was one thing, but going on what would be a multiple-day journey was something else.

Kyle opened a comms channel to ECF command. "Armstrong Base, Boxan shuttle twenty-seven is ready to depart and awaiting clearance."

"Acknowledged. Shuttle twenty-seven, you're cleared to depart. Godspeed and a safe return to you all," the ECF flight officer said.

Eavoth had the controls ready to go. The shuttle eased off the ground and slowly went through the hangar shield, passing into the vacuum of space beyond.

Kyle pulled up several system statuses and saw that the inertia dampeners were fully engaged. Eavoth punched in the coordinates and the shuttle's main engines came online. They sped away from the moon on a several-hour journey to the failed Shroud monitor.

"This Human, Armstrong, is from your history?" Eavoth asked.

"Yes, he was the first man to walk on our moon," Kyle said. He'd always been a bit of a history buff and he'd spent many hours poring over anything to do with the space program through the years.

"We honor our species' first steps into the great expanse as well," Eavoth said.

"Those were different times here. Those first pioneers into space had difficulty trusting computers to do their calculations for them. They'd insist the calculations be checked by some of the brightest mathematicians of the time," Kyle said.

"No way! Is that accurate?" Tom Blake asked.

"It's true. Learn your history, Blake," Kyle said and turned back to Eavoth. "The Shroud barrier doesn't form a perfect circle around the solar system, does it?"

Eavoth activated a holoscreen. "This is what we've mapped so far and the projections show more of an elongated shape. We think the Shroud devices are trying to accommodate this system of planets' orbital trajectories."

Kyle peered at the graphical model. "It doesn't look big enough."

"That's because it's not," Tom said. "The latest data shows us that the barrier could impact the outer planets."

"Do they know when?" Kyle asked.

"It's still being measured," Tom answered.

"We can get telemetry from the Shroud network, but we can't control them," Eavoth said. "We've done extensive studies and it seems to be the last command that was uploaded to the Shroud network that's preventing us from accessing it."

Kyle frowned in thought as he normally did when the subject of the barrier came up. They weren't exactly sure how the barrier had come to be and the Boxans confirmed that this latent ability was unknown even to them.

"You based the design of the Shroud devices on a technology you found?" Kyle asked.

"That is correct. It's Drar technology and we suspect that whoever sent the final signal to the Shroud devices must have had knowledge of them," Eavoth said.

"Could it have been the Drar themselves?" Tom asked.

"Unlikely. The Drar disappeared many thousands of cycles ago," Eavoth said.

They spent the next few hours going over what they would find. They didn't need to go near the barrier, which they could only detect by the presence of the Shroud device. The monitors they'd put in place were far enough away that it wouldn't bring them to the current edge of known safe space.

More than a year ago, aboard a ship like the Endurance, this trip would have taken several weeks to achieve. Aboard this Boxan shuttle they could make the journey in a few hours. The Boxans were enabling them to leapfrog over a hundred years of development in multiple scientific areas of study. Many were happy for the help, but there were others who were worried about such radical advances for a society that wasn't prepared for them. But they didn't have a choice. Last year the Xiiginn fleet almost made it to their planet and it would have been game over for the people of Earth. Kyle would take any advantage he could to keep his family safe and many supporters of the ECF would do the same.

Kyle glanced at Eavoth. "Do you ever think about your home?"

"Often, and the colony as well," Eavoth said.

Kyle pressed his lips together, wondering at the distinction the Boxan had made. Michael Hunsicker had warned him that there were some subjects Boxans were sensitive to, and talking about their home planet of Sethion was at the top of the list.

"Do you have a family?" Kyle asked.

"I have procreated and what you would call my children have reached maturity. They serve in our military," Eavoth said.

The Boxan looked over at him. "Have you a family?"

"Yes, I have a wife and two daughters at home. Taliya and Melayna are attending college now, but both of them have been pushing to transfer to the new ECF Academy," Kyle said.

Eavoth nodded and stopped when he saw Kyle's expression. "Does this not please you? Your daughters wish to help protect your home planet."

"It does," Kyle said. "When you put it in those terms, I couldn't be prouder of my daughters, but as a father my first instinct is for them to be safe. What the ECF is doing—what we're doing—isn't safe."

Eavoth regarded him for few moments. "It's better that they are choosing their own destiny rather than having it thrust upon their shoulders."

Kyle swallowed. He knew Eavoth was speaking about what his own species had to contend with. Every member of the Boxan society was expected to serve for the survival of their species. Try as he might, Kyle could scarcely imagine a world like that, and what little he could imagine scared him to no end.

"We're approaching the first Shroud monitor," Adyas said. "Main power offline. The only thing working on it is the distress beacon."

Eavoth approached the defective Shroud monitor and positioned the shuttle so it was just several meters outside the rear airlock doors. Earlier, they'd decided to bring the Shroud monitor inside and run a full diagnostic with the shuttle's computer systems to figure out why it was failing.

"Cleared to proceed," Eavoth said and looked at Kyle. "Would your team like to assist?"

Kyle nodded. "Pearson and Dawson. You're up. Go help Adyas bring it in."

Preliminary scans of the area showed no hostile forces.

"Colonel," Tom said.

"What is it?" Kyle asked.

"I'd like to go with them," Tom said.

"I know you would, but no," Kyle said.

He knew the young ECF recruit was eager to do something important, but even though he'd been cleared for routine spacewalks, Kyle only wanted experienced veterans out there.

"Maybe next time," Kyle said.

Hope returned to Tom's eyes and the sting of disappointment was all but gone. Kyle glanced at Eavoth and wondered what the Boxan was thinking, but he just couldn't tell.

"Commander, we're at the airlock," Kevin Dawson said.

"Acknowledged, you're clear to proceed," Eavoth said.

They watched the main holoscreen that showed the Boxan and Human team retrieving the Shroud monitoring device. The device had a square body of dark metal with a rounded sensor array on the top. After placement, they had the capacity to move short distances.

"No visible signs of damage," Adyas said.

They attached a tether to the device. Kyle watched as Dawson and Pearson circled around it to continue their visual inspection and be sure the tether was properly deployed. They returned to the airlock and slowly retracted the device inside, operating at zero gravity. They closed the airlock doors and Adyas slowly engaged the gravity field. The Shroud monitoring device came to rest on an elevated platform that hovered above the ground and together they pushed the device inside the storage area.

"We're clear," Adyas said.

Kyle and Eavoth got up from their couches and headed down to the others. They circled around the device. Adyas had already opened a panel and run a cable from the wall to the device.

"Running diagnostic and commencing data retrieval," Adyas said.

Kyle kept looking for signs of damage to the device. It was the size of a large automobile but was otherwise unremarkable to look at.

Eavoth and Adyas were watching the data feed from it while the onboard AI disseminated the information. The Boxans glanced at each other in alarm.

"Krano," Eavoth said, "have you detected anything near us?"

"Negative, Commander. Nothing is on our scanners."

"What is it?" Kyle asked.

"There is no failure. Someone shut it down," Eavoth said. "Battle stations, go to personal life support," he said.

Kyle engaged his helmet, which sprang from the storage compartment on his back while they raced to the upper level.

"Bring our weapons online," Eavoth said and took his seat on the command couch.

Kyle joined him and looked at the shuttle status. Weapons remained offline.

"Weapons systems won't respond," Krano said.

Eavoth was about to answer when a bright blue flash of light came from the storage area. Kyle's head was jerked to the side by the small blast and main power went offline. He tried to access the ship's systems, but everything was offline.

Kyle unstrapped himself. Lights from the top of his helmet came on. "Sound off," he said.

"Dawson here."

"Pearson here."

"What the hell happened to the power? Oh, Blake here."

Kyle saw Krano and Adyas nod towards him. He turned back to Eavoth.

"Arm yourselves. Prepare to repel boarders," Eavoth said.

"Boarders? Did he say boarders?" Blake asked.

"Who would be out here? There was nothing on scanners," Kyle said.

Deep red lines came on from Eavoth's power armor. "This was a trap. The Xiiginns are here."

Kyle's mouth went dry. He drew his sidearm and wished he had something bigger with him. "We need to get main power restored."

Adyas headed down to the lower level.

"Pearson, give her a hand," Kyle said.

Krano rose from his couch. "Commander, we need to jettison the device."

Eavoth nodded and they all went down to the lower level. Kyle glanced at Blake, who was wide-eyed and breathing rapidly.

Kyle pulled him aside. "You need to calm down."

Blake looked at him with wide eyes. "The Xiiginns weren't supposed to be here. How could they be here?"

Kyle grabbed him and gave him a gentle shake. "I don't know. One thing at a time. Got it? First, we need to get this thing off the ship. Then we restore main power and get the hell out of here."

A canister dropped to the floor and Blake's eyes darted toward the sound.

"There are no ships in the vicinity. So if the Xiiginns are here, they're not outside our door. It's going to take them time to get here. Got it?" Kyle said again.

Blake's breathing slowed down and he nodded. "Sorry, I just . . ."

Kyle nodded. "Let's get to work."

They went down to the lower level. Eavoth and the others already had the Shroud monitoring device moving toward the airlock.

An alarm came to prominence on the heads-up display of Kyle's suit. "There's an active signal being broadcast from that thing," he said.

Dawson pointed his plasma rifle at it. "Say the word and I'll blow this thing to kingdom come, sir."

"Let's get it off the ship first. Then we'll destroy it," Kyle said and Eavoth agreed.

They opened the airlock doors and Krano and Dawson went inside. Once they were sealed inside, the outer airlock doors opened and they pushed the device out. When it was far enough away, Dawson opened fire. Orange plasma bolts shot from his rifle, and within a handful of shots, the Shroud monitoring device was destroyed. The broadcast signal stopped.

Kyle turned around and saw Eavoth standing in front of a terminal, trying to get it to come on.

"Why didn't the emergency backup system come on?"

Eavoth kept working. He opened the panel below.

There was a loud roar from inside the airlock and Kyle spun around. Blake cried out and cowered over to the side.

Several large bangs came from inside the airlock. Kyle and Eavoth approached it slowly.

"Dawson, do you read?" Kyle asked.

There was no response. He saw several dark shapes through the small airlock windows. A pale, sneering face framed in a silver helmet peered from inside and then immediately moved away.

"Take cover," Eavoth said.

"Pearson, Adyas, back to the rear airlock, double time," Kyle said.

He moved behind a storage container and aimed his sidearm at the door.

"They can't get inside. They don't have access," Blake said.

The airlock alarms blared and the doors started to open. Kyle blew out several strong breaths. He wouldn't shoot blind. Dawson or Krano could still be in there. Xiiginns in silver spacesuits rushed inside and Kyle fired his weapon at them. Kyle aimed for their heads, knowing it was the most vulnerable part of any spacesuit. The first two Xiiginns went down. Another took its place and fired its weapon at him. Kyle felt something hit his suit and then everything shut down. An electrical shock arced through his system and he fell to the floor. He tried to open his eyes but was having trouble. He heard Eavoth roar as he fired his weapon, only to be overwhelmed by Xiiginns returning fire. Kyle faded in and out of consciousness.

"Don't hurt me!" Blake screamed.

Kyle opened his eyes and saw Blake fall to the ground. Bolts of energy crawled along his suit, rendering it offline.

He felt himself getting dragged out from the storage area. He couldn't move his hands or feet. He then heard several thumps next to him.

"I want the Boxans put over there. Keep them separate from the Humans," a voice said.

"Mar Arden, there are a Human and a Boxan near the main engines. They're being brought up."

"Excellent," Mar Arden said.

Kyle craned his neck and saw a Xiiginn standing nearby. There were quite a few others and Kyle stopped counting when he reached twenty.

The Xiiginn standing near him squatted down, its pale skin and purple eyes regarding him. "Greetings, Human. I'm Mar Arden. You're not the first Human I've met, but I'm looking forward to learning all there is to know about your planet and your species."

Kyle glared at him. "Go to hell."

Mar Arden looked amused. "Yes, the last Human I met said something similar in the beginning. I assure you, you'll find that I always get what I want in the end."

Kyle clenched his teeth.

Mar Arden stood back up. "Let's get main power restored," he said and walked away.

Much to Kyle's surprise, main power came on shortly after that. It was as if they'd flipped a switch. How had they disabled the power in the first place?

"Signal the others," Mar Arden said. "We've got ourselves a fully operational Boxan combat shuttle."

There were several grunts of acknowledgment and Kyle felt as if he'd been kicked in the stomach. They'd thought they were safe behind the barrier, that there was no way for the Xiiginns to reach them. They'd been wrong and no one on Earth was the wiser.

THE XIIGINNS HAD MANAGED to take them all alive and they more or less left them alone. As time went on, whatever they'd used to disable his suit had worn off and Kyle was able to move. His hands were bound in front of him. He tried to keep his movement small because he didn't want to draw the Xiiginns' attention. He glanced over at Eavoth and the other Boxans. They were more securely held and seemed to be unconscious.

"Colonel, are you awake?" Blake asked in a hushed tone.

"Yes, are you okay?" Kyle asked.

"They did something to my suit and next thing I knew I was next to you. Pearson and Dawson are still knocked out."

Kyle glanced over at the command area and saw the Xiiginn Mar Arden sitting on the command couch, speaking with the other Xiiginns. They kept their spacesuits on with their helmets.

"I don't get it," Blake said. "How'd they do this?"

"I don't know," Kyle said.

There was movement from the command area.

"I see some of you are awake. I bet you're wondering what happened."

Kyle looked over and saw Mar Arden walking over to them. Several armed Xiiginns followed him.

"I'm afraid you've become a victim to Boxan predictability and a very telling interaction from your own species as well," Mar Arden said.

The Xiiginn came to stand before Blake and Kyle heard him utter a gasp.

"What do you mean by Boxan predictability?" Kyle asked, trying to draw the Xiiginn's attention away from Blake.

Mar Arden swung his gaze toward him. "We knew that if we kept disabling their monitoring devices, they'd send someone out to investigate. A few simple protocols were designed to become active once a diagnostic was run on the device and your ship became ours."

"But there were no ships on our scanners. How did you even get here?" Blake asked, his curiosity overcoming his fear for the moment.

Mar Arden regarded the young tech specialist as if deciding whether he was worth answering. "If this is the measure of your species, I think it will be much easier to subjugate them than we initially thought."

"We're not weak," Blake said.

Mar Arden reached down and grabbed Blake by his suit, lifting him into the air. "On the contrary, you are among the weakest species we've ever come across," he said harshly.

Blake's breath came in gasps and Mar Arden looked down at Kyle.

"We waited in the great expanse without a ship for you to arrive. That is the measure of our conviction."

Kyle hardened his gaze. "I'm sure you must be very impressed with yourself. Why don't you come to Earth and we'll give you a proper greeting?"

Mar Arden dropped Blake. "In due time, Human. In due time."

18

Kaylan, along with the crew of the Athena and the Boxans, planned their next move. They needed to secure a large ship for their purposes. Kladomaor's team would take care of securing a ship and the additional crew required for a journey to Sethion, but taking a ship by force was a treasonous act and the High Council would send ships to destroy them before they could get near Sethion. They argued and tried to plan a way around this fact, but they always came back to it.

After having spent the last few hours planning a way forward, they'd lapsed into an uneasy silence. They were no closer to being able to leave Olloron. Technically, the Athena could leave at any time, but all of them agreed it would be a bad idea for the Athena to travel to Sethion alone. They were currently in one of the training facilities separate from the others.

"Let's come right out and ask the High Council for help. Hodak is already there and must have told them what happened," Kaylan said.

"You already know the answer they'll give," Kladomaor said.

"I do, but at least they can't say we never asked. We put it out there on the table. They can't accept that I have the Mardoxian potential and then deny my abilities to use it. Not now. Not with Ma'jasalax and even Hodak vouching for me in the past," Kaylan said.

"It's not a matter of belief," Ma'jasalax said. "Where the High Council is concerned, they weigh every action against the risk to the colony."

Zack cleared his throat. "I agree with Kaylan. Let's ask them and volunteer to go. We'll need their support to get past the quarantine anyway."

Kaylan watched Hicks give Zack a sidelong glance.

"What?" Zack asked.

"I'm just surprised you don't intend to come up with a way to beat the security of the quarantine zone," Hicks said.

Gaarokk grunted an agreement.

"Don't think I haven't thought of it, but we can't hang all our efforts on my ability to get past the quarantine zone. It's there for a reason, and the fact that it's still there speaks to how good the security is that supports the quarantine. Given the timeframe we're working with and the fact that the Boxans on Sethion need our help sooner rather than later, betting on me getting past security isn't our best option," Zack said.

"He's right," Gaarokk said.

"So what's the best way to get through the quarantine zone?" Hicks asked.

"Honestly, having authorization from the Boxan High Council," Zack said. He glanced around at the others. "I know it seems obvious, but it really is the best way."

"What if we can't get authorization?" Hicks asked.

Zack shrugged. "Then we'll need to find another way, but it could take awhile."

"I'll go to the High Council," Kaylan said.

"Not alone you won't," Zack said.

Kaylan squared her shoulders. "Yes, alone. I need the rest of you to prep the Athena."

"Now hold on a minute," Hicks said. "If we all just suddenly return to the Athena, they'll know something's up."

"And," Zack added, "I'm not letting you go face the Boxan High Council alone."

"I didn't say I'd be by myself. I meant without any of you. Kladomaor will be with me," Kaylan said.

The Boxan Battle Commander looked over at her in surprise. "That would not be wise," Kladomaor said.

"I agree," Gaarokk added.

Kaylan shook her head and could have sworn she saw Ma'jasalax roll her eyes. "It has to be you," she said to Kladomaor. "You threatened Hodak with a gun."

Kladomaor's brows pushed forward. "That was for your protection."

"Yes, I know, and I appreciate it, but you need to tell the High Council. Meanwhile, the others will be preparing to go to Sethion and they won't be able to blame you for the things the others are doing. Also, you'll gain support for our rogue mission to Sethion," Kaylan said.

"I'm afraid you overestimate my influence," Kladomaor said.

"You don't give yourself enough credit. Your actions in the Nerva star system have shown the rest of the Boxan military that there are other ways to fight the Xiiginns. And I don't believe all Boxans can be compliant with leaving Boxans behind on Sethion who need their help. They might not volunteer to go on the mission, but there are other ways they can show their support," Kaylan said.

"She's right," Ma'jasalax said. "You're not the outcast you once were. Boxans are looking to you for direction. I think you'll find there are those who will support you, even if it goes against the wishes of the High Council."

Kladomaor looked away from them and blew out a breath. "I don't want to go against them," he said and swung his gaze back to the others. "I want our species to stop using our survival as an excuse not to take action. Leaving Boxans behind on Sethion who are calling for our help and neglecting to return to all the Star Shroud monitoring stations to retrieve the scientists who were stranded there isn't okay. I want us to be a species where we don't leave any of our kind behind, or our allies."

Gaarokk and the other Boxans saluted with a fist across their chest. "Battle Commander," they said.

Kladomaor returned the salute and Kaylan suspected that even he was surprised by his own admission that the Boxans needed to change their ways.

"We still need a ship," Ma'jasalax said.

"There's very little chance of being able to commandeer a ship that's actively being used," Gaarokk said.

Kladomaor glanced at Ma'jasalax with a slightly amused expression. "I'm just surprised you hadn't guessed this part of the plan."

"No one can see everything, not even a Mardoxian priestess," Ma'jasalax said.

"There is a ship we can use. I only just learned of its existence a short while ago," Kladomaor said.

"What ship? The ones in Olloron space are all part of the home fleet," Gaarokk said.

"In the shipyards, there's a heavy cruiser that's nearing completion," Kladomaor said.

Gaarokk and the others took a few moments to consider this.

"We'll need additional crew," Gaarokk said.

"As I said before, I've only just learned of this heavy cruiser, but I've already begun recruiting for our next mission," Kladomaor said.

"They might change their minds if they know we're going against the High Council," Gaarokk said.

"Perhaps, but by the time some of them learn of it we'll be away. And there'll also be Boxans at the shipyards who can help," Kladomaor said.

Hicks looked at Kaylan. "I'm not sure about this. We should tell whoever's going to help us what's at stake," he said.

"I'll give them the option to leave, but don't forget that Boxan ships, even heavy cruisers, are designed to be used with minimal crew," Kladomaor said.

Kaylan knew Kladomaor was right. Since there were fewer Boxans than ever before in their history, they'd had to take steps to make all the ships in their fleet more efficient in terms of crew. This had led to them pouring research and development into AI constructs to step in and help them staff large ships with a significantly smaller crew if they needed to.

They spent the next hour going over the details of their plan. There were some loose ends that had the potential to become real problems, but they were running out of time. Kaylan and Kladomaor needed to get to the High Council while it was still in session for today. She waited for Kladomaor to finish speaking with Varek, his second in command.

"You have the list of contacts. They'll be expecting a message telling them where to meet," Kladomaor said.

"How many of them will actually come?" Varek asked.

"Probably not all of them but enough to make a difference, I hope," Kladomaor said.

Varek left them and it was just Kladomaor and Ma'jasalax left. Zack hadn't liked leaving Kaylan, but in the end the others needed his help to overcome some of the security hurdles the rest of them needed to get past. Together, they headed toward the building where the High Council was in session. One of the advantages of the Mardoxian Sect was almost unmitigated access to the council, which allowed them to pass through the various security checkpoints to get inside.

Just outside the chamber doors, Ma'jasalax leaned over to Kaylan. "Trust your instincts. They've gotten you this far."

Kaylan's stomach was a flutter of activity, but she knew this was the right path for them to take. "Thanks," she said.

The Boxan soldiers at the door motioned for them to go inside. The council chambers were half-moon shaped and the discussion appeared to have come to a stop as they walked into the room. Hodak was standing at the speaker's podium, and after noticing the attention of the Boxans in the room shift, he glanced behind him and saw Kaylan and the others.

High Councilor Awan stood up and looked pleased to see them. "Thank you for coming. Upon hearing Hodak's comments about your recent experience in the Mardoxian chamber, the rest of the council is extremely curious to speak with you."

Kaylan approached, along with Kladomaor and Ma'jasalax.

Hodak moved away from the speaker's podium and Ma'jasalax went to stand by his side.

High Councilor Awan took notice of Kladomaor, who was standing next to Kaylan. "Battle Commander," Awan said.

"High Councilor, I have come before you for two reasons—first, to re-affirm my support of the crew of the Athena, and, second, to speak to the actions I've taken while at the Mardoxian complex," Kladomaor said.

High Councilor Awan nodded and his face became serious. "This is a closed session, and whatever is discussed within this session cannot leave these walls."

Kladomaor glanced around at the other councilmembers and over at Hodak. "Haven't there been enough secrets? It's these secrets that are choking the life out of our species. For clarity's sake, I'm talking about what Kaylan saw on Sethion and the evidence supporting the regular communications from our home world."

"We're well aware of the evidence that supports the claims," Awan said.

"Then give us your support to return to Sethion and rescue those we left behind," Kladomaor said.

Kaylan watched the rest of the councilors. Some were stone-faced and just watched them intently while others seemed troubled by the fact that Kaylan had been able to catch a glimpse of what was happening on Sethion.

Kaylan cleared her throat. "I realize this may be difficult for you to hear. No one here is judging the actions the High Council took when you left your home world. There must have been so many things happening that I can scarcely wrap my head around it all. I haven't lived through the collapse of my home world and

I hope I never have to witness something so horrible. I truly believe that the actions taken at the time were for the survival of your race. But that was then and this is now. Those Boxans deserve to be rescued. The fact that they've survived all this time is a testament to Boxan ingenuity and your determination to survive."

High Councilor Awan regarded her for a moment. "One trait we've noticed about your species is your passion and the conviction of your beliefs and principles. They're intoxicating," the High Councilor said, and he glanced at Kladomaor. "They have their place, but they alone aren't reason enough to return to Sethion."

"Why not?" Kaylan asked.

"If we were to return to Sethion's star system and authorize entry into the quarantine zone, a number of things will happen. The Xiiginns will be alerted that we've done so and the Confederation will also be aware, both of which puts this colony at significant risk of discovery. Most of the Confederation species are firmly under Xiiginn control. On Sethion, we have no way to determine who's under the Xiiginn influence and who isn't. I don't think you understand what you're asking us to do. When we say anyone can be under the Xiiginn influence, you should know that this is not restricted by gender or age. Both were used to exploit our race. I'm afraid that what you saw were the remnant factions of Boxans still under the Xiiginn influence warring amongst themselves," High Councilor Awan finished.

Kaylan started to reply but stopped herself. There was nothing she could say that would sway them to even consider the possibility that there were Boxans free of the Xiiginn influence fighting for their lives.

"Would you be so sure if this were being reported by Ma'jasalax?" Kladomaor asked.

"Our answer would not change," High Councilor Awan said.

"I'm not—" Kladomaor began.

"He's right," Kaylan interrupted. "I have no way to determine if any of the Boxans I saw were under the Xiiginn influence," she said to Kladomaor. Kaylan looked back at the High Council. "Thank you for taking the time to explain things to me. It's difficult to accept. We want what's best for your race, and when I saw Boxans suffering, I wanted to do something about it."

"Your compassion is commendable. Now, I think this session is finished for the day," High Councilor Awan said.

"High Councilor," Kaylan said. "I need a few moments of your time. Are you able to meet with me after this session?" she asked.

High Councilor Awan considered the request. "I'm overdue for my time in the resonance chamber."

"That's fine. We can talk along the way," Kaylan said.

The council session ended and the Boxans went off to their other appointments. Kaylan walked next to High Councilor Awan, with Kladomaor and Ma'jasalax following behind. Awan invited Hodak to join them. Kaylan scouted ahead to the resonance chamber to note the exits. Since they were already inside the Boxan government building, there weren't additional soldiers posted at the resonance chambers, but the high councilor had two bodyguards who followed behind them all. Kaylan glanced back at them. They were heavily armed in full power armor.

"Have you made use of our resonance chambers?" High Councilor Awan asked.

"Yes, they're quite beautiful," Kaylan said, following him inside.

The resonance chambers reminded Kaylan of a botanical garden and were quite peaceful. The moisture in the air carried the scents of a forest shortly after a rainfall, and the difference between Olloron's climate and the chamber's was so apparent that she wondered why the Boxans had stayed here for as long as they had. There were other Boxans here, all in quiet meditation, and the high councilor led them to a more secluded spot.

"What would you like to discuss with me?"

"Zack has been requesting materials to test his theories for the Shroud barrier and hasn't been getting much cooperation," Kaylan said.

The high councilor sat down in one of the stone circles designated for meditation. He took a deep breath and sighed. "Resources are scarce," High Councilor Awan said.

Kaylan watched as the Boxan closed his eyes for a moment. She reached into her pocket and pulled out a metallic rod, quickly pressing the rod against the side of High Councilor Awan's neck and releasing a charge of energy. The high councilor slumped forward with a great sigh. Kaylan backed away, pretending she didn't know what had happened, and the high councilor's bodyguards quickly ran over.

Kladomaor pulled out his plasma pistol. "I'm afraid I need you to step away," he said.

One of the bodyguards started to bring up his weapon. "Don't. I promise you we won't harm the high councilor. You have my word as a soldier."

"What's the meaning of this?" Hodak asked.

"We're taking High Councilor Awan with us to Sethion," Kaylan said.

Hodak swung his powerful gaze toward Ma'jasalax. "Did you know about this?" he asked.

"Of course," Ma'jasalax said and pulled out her own Boxan stunner. "Come with us, Hodak. See it for yourself."

"And if I refuse?" Hodak asked.

"Then, when you wake up, you can alert everyone else about what we've done," Ma'jasalax said.

Kladomaor had his plasma pistol aimed at the two bodyguards. Kaylan couldn't see their faces through their helmets so she had no idea what they were thinking, but one of them seemed poised to draw his weapon at any moment. He stepped away from the other guard and Kladomaor pointed his weapon at him.

"What I do today, I do for all Boxans," Kladomaor said.

"This is treason. We'll hunt you down," the bodyguard said. "Put down your—"

The bodyguard sank to the ground, his armor going rigid. The second bodyguard stood behind him and retracted his helmet. "He wasn't going to let you go," he said.

Kladomoar returned his pistol to the holster he had hidden in his own power armor. "What's your name?" he asked.

"I'm Jaxu, Battle Commander. I will come with you and continue to protect the high councilor, but I want to know the state of Sethion."

"Thank you," Kladomaor said. "Now, help me lift him up."

Kaylan turned toward Hodak. "This was my idea," she said.

Hodak's eyes widened in shock. "But everything you said in the council session. Was it all a lie?"

Kaylan shook her head. "No, I meant every word, but I'm unwilling to condemn thousands of lives so you can feel safe on Olloron. You'll find that we humans can be a bit impulsive. I know there are Boxans on Sethion who aren't under the Xiiginn influence. I know it because I saw it with my own eyes. Why don't you come with us and see for yourself?"

Hodak's lips pressed together in a slight grimace. "You're bringing High Councilor Awan to get through the quarantine zone."

"That's right," Kaylan said.

"Once the other councilors realize what you've done, they'll send the fleet after you," Hodak said.

"I know. Hopefully we'll have reached Sethion by then," Kaylan said.

"You would risk the alliance for this?" Hodak asked.

"I hope it doesn't come to that, but yes, I would," Kaylan said.

Hodak glanced at the unconscious form of High Councilor Awan and then he looked at Ma'jasalax. "You don't need to stun me. I'll do what I can to see that you get a chance to get to Sethion."

Kaylan frowned, not sure whether she should trust him or not. "Why the change of heart?" she asked.

"What we do—you, Ma'jasalax, and I—sometimes needs to be taken on faith —faith in our abilities and in the fact that we don't know everything. I don't believe you'd take the actions you're taking without careful consideration. So I'm placing my faith in your abilities as a recognized member of the Mardoxian Sect. While you *are* of another race, your voice will carry great weight when dealing with our species. That's what I can offer, but if you're wrong, there's very little I can do to protect you from our laws," Hodak said.

Ma'jasalax stepped forward. "You would do this? You would make Kaylan a full member of the Mardoxian Sect?"

"Yes, I was already considering it. We've been so long looking for another species with the potential that admitting them into the sect seemed like a logical course of action," Hodak said.

Kaylan didn't know what to say. She hadn't expected anything like this. "Thank you," she said. "I promise that if I'm wrong about what I saw on Sethion, we'll leave the planet as we found it."

Hodak regarded her for a moment. "I appreciate you saying that, but I know for a fact that you don't believe you're wrong, and I hope you're right. Now, you must be going. I think I'll stay here for a while."

Hodak knelt down within the circle of stones the high councilor had been in when Kaylan stunned him. She looked at the others. "It would have implicated him if I hadn't stunned him."

Ma'jasalax led them toward one of the exits nearest them that wasn't used very often. Kaylan felt oddly calm for having committed a treasonous act against a head of state. She'd only told Kladomaor what she'd intended, knowing the others would try to talk her out of it. Ideally, she wanted the council's cooperation, but instead, she'd had to rely on contingency plans. Now they just had to get their kidnapped head of state off the planet without anyone the wiser.

19

Kaylan met up with Zack and the others. Kladomaor and Ma'jasalax had taken High Councilor Awan with them to the shipyards where the heavy cruiser was. Kaylan was to ensure that the rest of them were able to reach the Athena. Gaarokk was with the Athena crew and gave her a suspicious glance when she joined them.

"Where are the others?" Gaarokk asked.

"What happened with the council?" Zack asked.

"Kladomaor is seeing to the ship. He wants you to come with us to the Athena. He thought it would set certain Boxans at ease if you were to go with us," Kaylan said.

Gaarokk regarded her for a moment. "This isn't the first time you've commandeered my help. I feel as if I'm being kept in the dark . . . again"

Kaylan considered whether she should tell Gaarokk that they'd kidnapped the high councilor. "I'll tell you all about it once we're aboard the Athena," she offered.

"I don't know why you feel you can't tell me *before* we get on the ship," Gaarokk said.

"Hey, what happened with the council?" Zack asked again.

Kaylan gave Gaarokk a sympathetic smile and then looked at Zack. "While they acknowledged what I'd seen, they still firmly believe that all the Boxans left on Sethion are under the Xiiginn influence."

"So they won't help us then," Zack said.

"I didn't say that," Kaylan replied and glanced at Gaarokk.

Gaarokk's eyes widened. "What have you done?"

Kaylan pressed her lips together. "I secured help from the council by aiding in the kidnapping of one of its members so they'll disable the quarantine when we get to Sethion."

Gaarokk winced and looked at her as if he didn't quite believe what he'd just heard her say. "Who have you taken against their will?" he asked.

Kaylan glanced at the others to be sure they weren't overheard. "Awan," she said.

"The high councilor!"

Kaylan shushed him. "Yes, and it's done. Now all we need to do is get on our shuttle and get to the Athena."

Gaarokk opened his mouth and then closed it again. "I shouldn't have asked. Of all the crazy . . . You're supposed to be the sensible one," he said.

"They left me no choice. There are Boxans on Sethion who need our help. Are you really going to stay behind now?" Kaylan challenged.

Gaarokk walked away towards the others, shaking his head.

Kaylan and Zack were alone.

"There's something you should know," Zack said.

"Alright, what is it? But I should warn you I've already committed one treasonous act today."

Zack snorted. "I *did* tell you that getting the council to grant us access would be the quickest way to get through the quarantine zone. I just never thought you'd kidnap someone."

"We can return him if you think you can beat the security there."

Zack cocked his head to the side, considering. "No, this is much better. Maybe if some of these Boxans witness it firsthand, we'll all come through this without ending up in a holding cell, or worse. Regardless, we're committed now. What I wanted to tell you is that the Boxans have increased their efforts to gain remote access to the Athena's systems. So we're not the only ones breaking the rules."

"They're trying to take control of the ship?"

"At first I thought they were just trying to get access and maybe copy the data, but now I think they're trying to take the ship away from us," Zack said.

Kaylan nodded and was considering what Zack had just said when he leaned closer to her.

"I'm sorry I didn't help you right away. I was trying not to screw things up for us here," Zack said.

Kaylan placed her hand on his shoulder. "You're the one thing I don't have any doubts about," she said.

Zack frowned in thought. "You're not mad?"

"Not anymore. I knew you'd help me eventually. Have you ever really said no to me?" Kaylan asked while arching her eyebrow.

Zack let out a small laugh and Kaylan did the same.

"I guess not, and now that I know you can use a stunner, I'll be sure to watch my step," Zack said.

They joined the others and Kaylan filled them in, with the omissions of certain facts. Once they met up with Kladomaor she'd tell them the truth. They wouldn't like it, but they'd eventually understand. She needed them to focus on getting to the Athena rather than the fact that they were kidnapping a head of state. Now all they needed to do was escape from Olloron.

20

After some quick planning, the crew of the Athena decided to stagger their approach to the shuttle. Zack and Gaarokk had already gone through the security checkpoint. Kaylan waited with Emma and Brenda Goodwin.

Katie Garcia joined them. "The others are in position on the other side," she said.

Kaylan nodded and looked at Emma. "Are you sure you're fine with this? Otherwise, Katie can—"

"I'll be fine," Emma said, jamming her hand in her pocket and clutching the stunner. "It's only if they give us a problem. But just to be sure, this won't hurt them, right?" she asked.

"No, it just renders the motor functions of their power armor inert for a short period of time. And it will knock them out, but they'll be fine," Kaylan said.

Brenda had her arms crossed in front of her and seemed to be hugging herself. She then shot her hands to her sides. "I'm ready," the Athena's medical officer said.

Kaylan's internal heads-up display brought a message from Zack into prominence.

::*We're in the shuttle. Once I see that you're in position, we'll disrupt their communications.*::

::*Heading to the checkpoint now,*:: Kaylan sent back.

Kaylan glanced at Katie, who was walking next to her. "Zack's ready," she said.

The Athena's shuttle occupied a landing pad inside a secure area under Boxan control. There were defensive towers in place and she knew there were strike-fighter patrols but none were in their vicinity. The defensive towers had once been part of the original Boxan military installation when Olloron was just an outpost.

This security checkpoint wasn't used often because of its location in relation to the city and only a few Boxan soldiers were working there. Kaylan moved forward, noting the others spreading themselves among the other soldiers.

"Hello," Kaylan said and sent her access code to the soldier at the checkpoint.

A small holoscreen on the soldier's terminal flickered and he glanced over at it in surprise. "Apologies, but I'm afraid we're in lockdown."

"Lockdown!" Kaylan said, feigning confusion. "We just need to make a run to our ship, and we have authorization."

The soldier frowned as he worked through the options on the screen. "I can see that, but the lockdown supersedes the authorization. I'm afraid I can't let any of you pass."

Kaylan raised her chin and squared her shoulders. "What do you mean 'supersedes' my authorization? Our access was given to us by the High Council and I'm a member of the Mardoxian Sect."

The soldier glanced at his partner, who looked just as confused. "I'm sure this is just a misunderstanding. I'll open a comms channel back to central and see if I can find out what's going on."

Kaylan waited and the soldier frowned at his holoscreen in confusion.

"What's the problem?" Kaylan asked.

"I can't open a comms channel," the soldier said.

As the soldier looked away, Kaylan jammed the stunner into the Boxan's hip. The soldier's power armor went rigid and he fell over. Kaylan then turned and saw the other Boxan soldier fall over beside a very pale-looking Emma Roberson.

Emma quickly handed the stunner over to Katie. "I think I'll let you get the next one," she said.

Kaylan circled around to the soldier's terminal and released the doors. Brenda checked on the two unconscious soldiers and then met them at the door.

"They're fine. They'll wake up a short while from now and wonder what happened," Brenda said.

Kaylan led them through the doors.

"Did you expect the lockdown so soon?" Emma asked.

"No, I thought we'd already be on the Athena by the time they noticed anything," Kaylan said.

They quickly walked over to the shuttle. As they closed in, Kaylan noticed Hicks and the others running towards them.

"We have to move," Kaylan said.

They ran the rest of the way to the shuttle and climbed aboard.

"What's with the lockdown?" Hicks asked.

"I don't know. I thought . . . maybe Kladomaor ran into some trouble," Kaylan said.

Kaylan climbed into the pilot's seat next to Zack.

"I have comms jammed in the immediate area, but they'll be able to override it . . . right about now," Zack said.

A high-priority comms channel opened from flight control. Kaylan initiated the shuttle's engines.

"Shuttle Athena, we're under lockdown. You will shut down your engines immediately," the Boxan flight officer said.

"What seems to be the problem?" Kaylan asked.

She glanced behind her to see that everyone was secured in a seat. The only exception was Gaarokk, who sat on the floor looking a bit sulky.

"Shuttle Athena, please shut down your engines. You're not authorized to leave," the Boxan flight officer said in a higher tone.

"We're heading back to our ship for routine maintenance," Kaylan said and engaged the engines.

The shuttle hovered above the ground and the landing gear retracted inside. Combat alarms blared as the defense towers locked onto them.

"Shuttle Athena, you are to land your shuttle immediately," the Boxan flight officer ordered.

Kaylan sat poised with her hand on the thrusters. "You're not going to shoot us down. If you do, not only would you kill me and the entire Athena crew, but you'd lose your only link to the Drar. If you don't allow us to leave, the Athena's AI has instructions to fly itself into the planet. No one wins this way. I know you've been trying to take control of the Athena's computer systems and I know you've failed to do so. We're leaving and that's the end of it. What we're doing is for the benefit of all Boxans."

Kaylan closed the comms channel without waiting for a reply and punched it. The shuttle darted away and she set a course for the Athena.

"At least they didn't shoot us down," Zack said.

"I knew they wouldn't," Kaylan said.

"What's with the lockdown anyway? Do you honestly think they're just going to let us waltz out of here?" Zack asked.

"Let's get to the Athena and we'll take it from there," Kaylan said.

She opened a comms channel to the ship. "Athena, I'd like you to begin pre-flight checks so we can be underway once we're on board."

"Of course, Commander, and might I add that it will be wonderful to have all of you aboard again," the AI said.

Kaylan closed the comms channel.

"Sounds like she missed us," Zack said.

Kaylan smiled. The crew hadn't been aboard the Athena together since they'd first arrived. Seeing the ship grow larger on the holoscreen set her at ease. It was almost like they were coming home. Kaylan knew they were taking some dangerous risks where the Boxans were concerned, but in her heart she knew this was the right thing to do. She just hoped they wouldn't be too late to help the Boxans on Sethion. In her mind she caught a fleeting glimpse of the Boxan in the red traditional Boxan armor, squatting down behind an icy mound, weapon clutched in their hands while they waited for the approaching figures that were stalking forward like hunters who had trapped their quarry.

21

Kladomaor tried to keep the scowl from his face, but things were not going as smoothly as he'd hoped they would.

"Where is this ship you mentioned?" Kladomaor asked.

Ma'jasalax gave him a patient look. "Stop being sour. You couldn't have known that when Varek tried to access the heavy cruiser's systems, it would trigger lockdown protocols."

Kladomaor glanced around. They were a large group with a hundred volunteers who had come to his aid and now they had no ship to use. "Our list of crimes is growing and we have very little to show for it. Also, at this rate we'll be overdue to meet the Athena at the rendezvous point. We should never have divided our efforts," he said.

"The ship is through here," Ma'jasalax said, leading them down a long corridor at the edge of the shipyards.

Kladomaor brought up the schematics of the shipyards, and according to them, there was nothing on this end of the yard. The wide metallic corridors were a dingy gray as if no Boxan had been down here for some time.

"Who would keep a ship here?" Kladomaor asked.

He glanced behind them at the floating capsule that contained High Councilor Awan's unconscious body. Two Boxan soldiers were pushing it. Only a select few knew they'd taken the high councilor against his will. The two soldiers thought they were guiding some delicate sensor equipment they needed to bring to Sethion. The high councilor's bodyguard stood nearby and kept a close watch on the capsule.

"It's a classified project, but we were building our own ship here," Ma'jasalax said.

Kladomaor frowned in confusion. "The Mardoxian Sect?" he asked.

"It's an experimental cruiser-class ship. It should have the capacity we need with room to spare to hold the Athena in its docking bay," Ma'jasalax said.

Kladomaor suppressed a sigh, wondering how many secrets Ma'jasalax had clattering around in her brain. Ma'jasalax led them to a large set of doors at the end of the corridor. Kladomaor tried to use his neural implants to initiate a connection, but there wasn't any. Ma'jasalax opened a panel and quickly entered a few commands. There was a loud clang as the doors unlocked and then opened in the center. Kladomaor quickened his step and caught his first glimpse of a Boxan Battle Cruiser that looked to have seen better days.

"How long has it been sitting here?" Kladomaor asked.

"We devoted resources to it when we could. The ship is space-worthy, I assure you," Ma'jasalax promised.

Kladomaor and the others went closer, and there was a general muttering from the soldiers. He looked at Ma'jasalax. "I need more reassurance that we're not going to die because the ship falls apart while trying to get out of here," he said.

"Fine, this was the ship I used to get me to Confederation space where Mar Arden took me prisoner," Ma'jasalax said.

Kladomaor glanced at the ship and back at the Mardoxian priestess. "How'd it get back here?" he asked.

Ma'jasalax waved away the question. "Doesn't matter. It's space-worthy and that's all you need to worry about."

Kladomaor watched as Ma'jasalax sent a remote command to have the ship's systems brought online. The cruiser was surrounded by crates and containers, some of which were marked as ammunition. He glanced around, looking for Varek, and waved him over.

"I want you to take a team and make a sweep of these containers. Anything you think we need I want brought aboard the ship immediately. Priority is given to ammunition and medical supplies. We don't know exactly what we're going to find when we get to Sethion," Kladomaor said.

Varek glanced at the chaos of containers and crates strewn throughout the landing bay. "And we get to take a ship whose capabilities we're not convinced are up to the task," he said.

"Sarcasm from you, Varek?" Kladomaor asked, slightly amused.

"Work enough with Humans and some of their mannerisms are bound to rub off on you, Battle Commander."

Kladomaor nodded. "Agreed," he said.

Varek left him and set about the task Kladomaor had given him. Ma'jasalax waited for him at the top of the cruiser's entrance ramp, which he bounded up with the aid of his power armor. All other ships he'd commanded had battle-steel armored hulls, gleaming with a polished bronze that would both absorb and reflect a star's shine in an impressive display. Those sights accorded any Boxan the honor and pride of serving in the military. But the full gray hull of this cruiser lacked any such appeal. It might be space-worthy, but was it battle-worthy? Their options were limited at this point and time was already against him.

Ma'jasalax waited at the door and opened it. He followed her through and was surprised at the pristine conditions inside the ship, which was in stark contrast to the outside. Cyan lines began to glow, lighting up the interior. The walls of the corridors were white and his internal heads-up display identified the material as ceramite. He took a step back outside the ship.

"No need for that. Your sensor is correct. The entire ship is coated with a ceremite composite that makes the armor plating of this ship stronger than anything in the fleet," Ma'jasalax said.

Kladomaor followed her into the ship. "You're just full of surprises. How did your sect manage to pull this off? What else can this ship do? This is no ordinary cruiser."

"It has a state-of-the-art weapons systems and cyber warfare suite. The cruiser has limited stealth capabilities and enough armament to make any Xiiginn warship commander wish he hadn't crossed our path. I trust you will find it satisfactory," Ma'jasalax said.

Kladomaor's implants buzzed to life as Ma'jasalax authorized him with bridge-officer access to the ship's systems. One thing he could say about the Mardoxian Sect, they knew how to build a ship. He sent out a signal to the rest of their crew with orders to board the ship immediately. Earlier, Varek had broken the crew down into groups and already had assignments for all of them based on their level of expertise. Kladomaor headed for the bridge and opened the doors. Most of the systems were still coming online, but the bridge systems were already on. Sensing their commanding officer's presence, Kladomaor's implants greedily took in all the status updates of the ship's primary system. Varek was making short work of loading the supplies and more of the bridge crew began to show up.

Triflan saluted him and went over to the navigation work area.

Varek opened a comms channel to Kladomaor. "All supplies and crew on board, Battle Commander."

"Acknowledged. Report to the bridge," Kladomaor said.

He went over to the command couch and sat down. The cushions molded themselves to him and the commander's holoscreen came up in front of him. Ma'jasalax sat next to him.

"You seem pleased now," she said.

"This is more than I could have hoped for. Why didn't you tell us about this sooner? It would have saved precious time," Kladomaor said.

"I really thought the heavy cruiser would work, but I checked the manifest after the lockdown was initiated and saw that while construction was nearing completion, it wasn't fully loaded with munitions and supplies," Ma'jasalax said.

The door to the bridge opened and a pair of Boxan soldiers guided the floating capsule inside. Kladomaor told them to secure it next to the command station.

"Engines are coming online, Battle Commander," Triflan said.

Kladomaor familiarized himself with the ship while the crew went about their final checks of the critical systems. In any other circumstance, they would have taken a few days at the very least before taking a ship such as this from the space

dock, but they had no choice. By now the Athena would be waiting for them and
the Boxans on Sethion needed them.

Their return to Sethion was long overdue and Kladomaor felt as if something
were filling his chest. He recalled having this feeling before when he'd initially set
off for Nerva. The High Council had provisionally given him support for that
mission, and in doing so, had set him on the path he was on today. He glanced
over at Ma'jasalax, wondering just how much the Mardoxian priestess had
influenced these events. Had all these things that had come to pass been by her
design? Even Hodak seemed to defer to Ma'jasalax on certain things—meeting
the Humans, helping the Nershals take back their planet, and now going to
Sethion to rescue what was left of their race. Kladomaor's chest swelled with
anticipation. He wished they were but one ship in a large task force designated
for this mission, but at least they had one ship. It would have to be enough.

"Ready to leave the shipyards at your command," Triflan said.

"Very well," Kladomaor said. "Take us out."

The hangar doors opened above them and the Boxan cruiser lifted away from
the docking clamps. So far, no flight officers had noticed them.

"Engage stealth systems," Kladomaor said.

"Confirmed, Battle Commander. Just to make you aware, the stealth systems
are limited in comparison to our standard stealth scout ship. This ship carries a
much heavier armament that, when brought fully online, will significantly
diminish our stealth capabilities," Varek said.

"Understood," Kladomaor replied and made a mental note to review the
combat capabilities of the ship.

The cruiser sped away, putting some distance between itself and the shipyard.
Kladomaor kept waiting for klaxon alarms to go off, indicating they'd been
discovered, but all was quiet. The stealth systems were working, and for the
moment, they appeared to have escaped.

"You look surprised," Ma'jasalax said.

Kladomaor used his neural implants to familiarize himself with the cruiser's
systems. "This is an experimental ship, which in my mind means it's unproven.
Have the designs for this ship been shared? Are there others being built?"

"A version of the design has been approved. Of course, the part where we've
been stockpiling ceremite has been kept confidential within the Mardoxian Sect.
We've expanded the sect to include our own engineering group, which helped
speed up the development of certain systems," Ma'jasalax said.

"This is the first I'm hearing of this. What's next? You'll have your own
soldiers or some other security force?" Kladomaor asked.

"Everything we've done, with the exception of the ceremite stockpile, has
been with the High Council's full awareness," Ma'jasalax said.

Kladomaor regarded the Mardoxian priestess for a moment. The Mardoxian
Sect was a force to be reckoned with and the fact that they were working to
manipulate events wasn't surprising. The sheer fact that this ship existed at all
was indicative of the potential for the Boxans to splinter into opposing
factions. Although this potential existed in any culture, the likelihood of
disintegration had escalated for the Boxans since the fall of Sethion. Had the

Mardoxian Sect anticipated such a break and begun taking steps to control the outcome? Or were they merely trying to make the Boxans stronger so they could endure.

"Battle Commander, we're far enough away from Olloron to open a wormhole. Cherubian drive is ready," Triflan said.

"Set a course for the rendezvous point or the Humans might just leave us behind," Kladomaor said.

The Cherubian drive spun up and a wormhole opened in front of the ship. The stealth field dropped and the cruiser lurched forward. A short while later they emerged from the wormhole at the away-point. "Contact the Athena and give them an update," Kladomaor said. He didn't want the Athena's crew to feel threatened because they'd arrived in a different ship than what was expected.

The Athena appeared on the main holodisplay and the cruiser was fast closing the distance between them. Kladomaor didn't want to give any thought to the potential outcome if they were to fail in this mission. If they *did* fail and somehow the Athena was destroyed, they'd lose their only link to the Drar, along with the knowledge they'd given the Humans.

The away-point was a place between star systems in the great expanse and there was little chance of anyone finding them. From there, they could go to Sethion with little risk of anyone like the Xiiginns being able to retrace their wormholes back to Olloron. The cruiser hovered over the small Human ship and the main hangar swallowed the Athena up.

"The Athena is docked in the main hangar, Battle Commander," Varek said.

"Shall I set a course for Sethion?" Triflan asked.

"Bring us well outside the quarantine zone, and I want a full sensor sweep of the area when we arrive," Kladomaor said.

Triflan engaged the Cherubian drive and the cruiser moved forward into the wormhole as a moment of heavy silence settled over the bridge. Most of them hadn't been anywhere near the Boxan home star system since they'd left during the Chaos Wars. When they emerged from the wormhole, the image on the main holoscreen showed a distant main-sequence star.

The door to the bridge opened and all nine of the Athena's crew walked in. Gaarokk was the last through the door. Kladomaor had seen the scientist show a range of emotions during their time together and he believed the level of anger exuding from his friend was at a new level.

Gaarokk looked over at the capsule that held the high councilor.

"Not the ship we were expecting," Kaylan said.

"We had a change of plans," Kladomaor said.

Gaarokk moved over to the capsule and checked the high councilor's vital signs.

"You can open it now," Kladomaor said.

Jaxu, the high councilor's bodyguard, stood nearby. Without a word, Gaarokk opened the capsule. There was a snap-hiss and the capsule clamps sprang open. Gaarokk lifted the lid on the unconscious form of High Councilor Awan.

"What's this? Is that who I think it is?" Hicks asked after peering into the capsule.

"It is," Kaylan said. "Zack did say the best way through the quarantine zone was with actual authorization."

Hicks's mouth hung open and he glanced at Kladomaor. "Does your crew know they've just taken part in taking the high councilor hostage?"

"He's not a hostage," Kladomaor said. "He's free to get off the cruiser after we reach our destination."

Hicks blew out a breath and looked at Kaylan. "Why didn't you say anything to us about this?"

"I made a decision. We were already committed to going to Sethion. We're here, and Awan is going to get us inside," Kaylan said.

"What happens if he refuses?" Hicks asked.

"He won't," Kaylan said.

Hicks looked at Kladomaor. "What are you going to do if he doesn't cooperate?" he asked.

"Let's find out," Kladomaor said and looked at Gaarokk. "Revive him."

Gaarokk entered a few commands and the breather mask on High Councilor Awan's face detached itself. The high councilor started to awaken and Gaarokk helped him sit up. After a few moments, the high councilor climbed to his feet and thanked Gaarokk for his help, but when his eyes found Kladomaor, they narrowed angrily.

"You!" said the high councilor through clenched teeth. He swung his gaze around, taking note of all those who surrounded him. Then he glanced at the main holoscreen behind Kladomaor. "How dare you bring us back here!"

Kladomaor stepped closer to the high councilor, scowling. "How dare you expect us to leave Boxans behind! The High Council exists to protect all Boxans, not just the ones on Olloron. We're here and so are you," Kladomaor said.

High Councilor Awan saw Jaxu. "You let him do this? I want him arrested," he said, then pointed at Ma'jasalax. "I want her arrested too."

"This was my idea," Kaylan said. "I was the one who stunned you. They're all here because of me."

High Councilor Awan seemed shocked to hear this. "But you understood our reasons for leaving Sethion. Was that a lie?" he asked.

Kaylan shook her head. "No, I *do* understand your reasons for leaving Sethion. What I don't agree with are your reasons for staying away. There are Boxans who need our help. Who need *your* help."

"We don't know who's under the Xiiginn influence," High Councilor Awan said.

"I don't care," Kaylan snapped. "They don't have to return to Olloron. We can find somewhere else for them to go other than your precious colony. They have a right to live without being condemned to finish their days on a dying planet. Those are the actions of a primitive species and very un-Boxan-like at that."

All activity on the bridge ceased in a heavy moment of silence. Kladomaor stepped back from the high councilor and smoothed his features.

"She's right, Awan," Kladomaor said. "All of us have become too comfortable with making decisions such as these and then rationalizing them for cycles to come. Don't you feel it? Those moments in the resonance chambers—do you hear them? The cries of all the Boxans we left behind. We used to be a race of beings that exemplified what the Confederation should be. Now we're just scraping away an existence, locked in a war with the Xiiginns. But this is something we can do. Going to Sethion is something we *should* do."

The high councilor's shoulders slumped and he blew out a long breath. "I hear them all my waking hours. My only solace is knowing the colony is safe— that the Boxans we were able to save are safe."

"You can change things right here and now. Give us the authorization we need to get through the quarantine zone so we can get to Sethion," Kaylan said.

High Councilor Awan took a few steps away from them, gazing at the holoscreen that showed the Boxan home star system. With only a moment's further hesitation, he raised his wrist and a holo-interface appeared above it. The high councilor spoke softly and the holo-interface changed colors from amber to green, then disappeared.

High Councilor Awan turned towards them. "Authorization has been given. You can transfer when we get closer."

Kladomaor brought his fist across his chest. "High Councilor," he said.

The formal salute was repeated by the Boxans throughout the bridge and Kladomaor returned to the command couch.

"Battle stations. Set condition red throughout the ship," Kladomaor said.

His orders were repeated. Weapons systems came online and the data from the active scans began to show on the main holoscreen.

High Councilor Awan walked over to the command area. "I'm afraid I don't understand. You have my authorization. Why have you gone to battle stations?"

Kladomaor gestured to the couch next to his and the high councilor sat down.

"Even considering our unorthodox approach to this mission, it's still very much a military operation and I cannot take my ship or the crew into a potentially hostile situation without being ready for attack," Kladomaor said.

"We appreciate it, believe me," Zack said.

"Battle Commander," Varek said, "scans are showing massive ship signatures inside the quarantine zone."

Kladomaor frowned and peered at the holoscreen. Near Sethion, a fleet of starships was gathered at the Lagrange point between the planet and the star. The quarantine zone was among the outer system of planets—mostly gas giants with moons that the Boxans had long since mined to depletion. He shifted the viewer to show the area just beyond the quarantine zone.

There were vast defensive platforms and a massive field of debris from the ships the defensive platforms had destroyed. The cruiser's AI rapidly analyzed the field and began noting distinct ship signatures. Most of them were Boxan, but there were more than a few Xiiginn warships. It was a cold comfort to know that the quarantine zone had also kept the Xiiginns out, but the even greater expanse of derelict ships inside the zone was an ominous sign of all the Boxans who had tried to escape from Sethion and died in the process.

"Take us in," Kladomaor said.

The Boxan cruiser went in on a direct approach, and as they reached the quarantine zone, the automated defensive platforms serving as a blockade came online. Multiple alarms registered as the targeting systems of those defensive platforms locked onto them.

As the commanding officer, Kladomaor had to transmit High Councilor Awan's authorization as a member of the Boxan council. Everyone on the bridge waited in silent anticipation to see if the authorization would go through, and after a few moments, the target-locks began to disappear as clearance to enter the system was given.

"Take us in slowly. There is still a lot of debris out there," Kladomaor said.

"How do you plan to determine who's under Xiiginn influence and who isn't?" High Counsilor Awan asked.

Ma'jasalax came to her feet. "The records show that the Xiiginns used their compulsion abilities on elite military forces, as well as high-ranking officials. It was one of the reasons their rebellion was so effective. I've run some initial analyses of the planet to determine the locations of any surviving Boxans."

"Then what?"

"We'll look for certain factors. Since the elite military was already known to be under Xiiginn influence, it could be a safe assumption that the most heavily armed group of Boxans are still under Xiiginn control. Our last communications with Sethion showed pockets of civilians and scientists staying together, trying to find places to hide. Kaylan's experience in the Mardoxian chamber does indicate that there are still warring factions, which is what I would expect given the circumstances," Ma'jasalax said.

The high councilor looked at Kaylan. "Will you be able to point us in the right direction?" he asked.

"I know where I saw the Boxans fighting each other two days ago. It was among the ruins of a city. I didn't see all of it, but I could definitely get us to the area," Kaylan said.

"It's likely they won't be there anymore," Zack said, drawing the attention of the others.

Kladomaor glanced over at Zack. The clever Human was keenly observant and seemed to have no end of insights into situations such as these.

"This is just a guess," Zack began. "We should look for evidence where Kaylan last saw them, but I doubt that's where the Boxans we want to help are living."

"You're probably right. I'm just wondering how you arrived at your opinion," Kladomaor said.

"Your own records show the devastation from the wars that were fought. The effects were felt across the globe. With the collapse of any civilization, you'd have groups banding together to increase their odds of survival. Given the advanced technology available to the Boxans even on a dying world, their reach for exploits to scavenge for supplies would be much more widespread than if something like this happened on Earth," Zack said.

"You refer to their operational abilities to conduct scavenger missions around the planet," Kladomaor said.

Zack nodded. "Exactly."

"Which means the Boxans we want to find could be anywhere," Kaylan said.

Kladomaor glanced at Ma'jasalax. "He's probably right. We need to figure out where the Boxans we want to rescue are hiding. If we send out a broadcast, we may attract the attention of the Boxans under the Xiiginn influence."

"Contact!" Triflan shouted. "Multiple contacts detected. Heading for us."

"Who are they?" Kladomaor asked.

"Unknown. They're not responding to any of our attempts at communication," Triflan said.

"Their energy signature indicates they're smaller spacecraft. I'd say drone class," Varek said.

"On screen," Kladomaor said.

The main holoscreen changed to show several squadrons of drones heading directly for them.

Kladomaor's brows pushed forward. "Automated defensive turrets online. I want those things targeted—"

"Missile launch detected," Triflan said.

Multiple missile launches were shown from the squadrons of drones heading towards them.

"Counter measures," Kladomaor said. "I want strike-fighter squadrons Black and Gold launched immediately. Cleared to engage."

"I don't understand," High Councilor Awan said. "The drone blockade should be down. We should be able to pass through the quarantine zone without any problems."

"We are past the zone," Kladomaor said. "I should have anticipated this. These drones are from Sethion, and I'm willing to bet they're programed to fight the drone blockade that's part of the quarantine zone. Right now they think we're enemies."

"Look at how many of them there are. We have to get out of here!" High Councilor Awan said.

Kladomaor looked at the screen and sifted through the data-feeds with his neural implants. "We're not leaving. Evasive maneuvers. We're taking them out."

22

Kyle sat down on the floor of the Xiiginn's makeshift flotilla. They'd been taken to a converted cargo room and left there. Krano and Adyas were each still bound at the wrists, but Kyle and the others were free to walk around. There were Xiiginns on the other side of the door, which was the only way out. They'd taken Eavoth away earlier and Kyle expected they would come for him next. Instead, the Xiiginns took Celia first, dragging her out into the corridor. Kyle and Dawson had tried to stop them and Kyle had earned the harsh end of a shock-lance to his ribs. It still hurt whenever he moved.

The sound of spinning gears retracting snapped Kyle's attention to the cargo hold door as it opened.

Corporal Celia Pearson was brought in by a company of Xiiginn soldiers. She looked dazed, as if she wasn't sure where she was. Kyle rose to his feet and took a step toward her, but the Xiiginn soldiers pointed their weapons at him.

"What'd you do to her?" Kyle asked.

The soldiers didn't answer him. Pearson stumbled over toward them, and Kyle and Dawson caught her.

"Where's Eavoth?" Kyle asked.

The nearest Xiiginn soldier's tail coiled and then flicked to the side. The tail was as long as the Xiiginn was tall and was as thick as his arm. Kyle tried to put on a brave face, but the Xiiginns with those tails creeped him out.

"Stand against the wall," the Xiiginn soldier said.

Kyle and the others did as they were told. He glanced over at Tom and the young tech specialist looked to be barely keeping his wits together. Another Xiiginn stepped through the doorway, blocking the bright lights beyond and distorting their facial features but for the radiance of long, platinum hair.

"Humans," a soft, sultry voice said as a female Xiiginn stepped inside the cargo hold and sauntered over to them, her sleek black uniform clinging to her feminine form. She paused in front of Tom and ran her smooth fingertips along his face.

Kyle watched as Tom tried to pull away, his eyes wide with terror. "Leave him alone," Kyle said.

The Xiiginn glanced over at him. Her mouth was slightly open and Kyle saw sharply pointed teeth inside. The irises of her large eyes were ringed in purple.

"You may call me Kandra Rene," she said.

Kyle stuck his chin out and squared his shoulders. "I can think of a few things to call you."

Kandra Rene pursed her lips and slowly shook her head. "You're not the first Human I've met. I think we can be friends though," she said.

Kyle felt a slight buzz begin to build in the back of his mind. As the Xiiginn spoke, he found his gaze focused on the fullness of her lips so Kyle narrowed his gaze and looked away from her, clenching his teeth, and the buzzing stopped.

Kyle heard a soft moan escape Tom's lips and then he shook his head in a painful grunt. Kyle glanced over at Pearson and Dawson. Pearson's eyes didn't seem to be focused on anything in particular, and Dawson's rigid expression looked as if he were bracing himself for something to happen.

Kyle stepped away from the wall and the Xiiginn soldiers stepped toward him with their weapons raised. The pulsating hum from the weapons gave him pause.

"Whatever you're doing, it's not going to work," Kyle said.

Kandra Rene smiled. "It already has worked," she said.

Kyle felt a coldness take hold of his chest. Part of him wanted to strike out at the female Xiiginn, but he knew it would be foolish of him to do so. He needed to find a way to get them out of here.

There was a loud groan, drawing their attention to the open door. A large shadow filled the doorway and Eavoth stepped inside. His hands were at his sides. Krano and Adyas looked at Eavoth with fear in their eyes.

The Xiiginn called Mar Arden followed him inside with long, purposeful strides.

"Eavoth, teach this Human some manners," Mar Arden said.

Eavoth bounded toward Kyle and shoved him against the wall. Kyle's head hit the wall and his vision swam. The Boxan then grabbed him by the shoulders and flung him across the cargo hold like a rag doll. Pain blossomed from his shoulder where he caught the brunt of the blow. Hearing heavy steps pounding towards him, Kyle scrambled out of the way. He regained his feet and shoved one of the containers into Eavoth's path. The Boxan easily stepped over it and grabbed Kyle by the throat. Kyle struggled to draw breath but couldn't. He coughed and tried to kick out with his legs, but the powerful Boxan held him at arm's length.

"Please," Kyle choked out, but then went cold at the vacant expression in Eavoth's eyes. It was like he wasn't there anymore.

"That's enough!" Dawson cried.

Kyle tried to pull the Boxan's powerful hands from his neck, but Eavoth was much too strong. His field of vision narrowed as if he were seeing down a long, dark tunnel.

"Let him go," Mar Arden said.

Eavoth dropped Kyle to the ground and returned to Mar Arden's side.

Kyle gasped for breath and fought to catch his breath. Eavoth easily could have killed him. He glanced at the Boxan, looking for some sign of the Eavoth he knew, but his mind was gone. Kyle glanced over at Krano and Adyas, and they were looking at the Xiiginns with pure hatred in their eyes. Kyle could see they wanted to fight.

Mar Arden looked amused by the Boxans' display. "You know it's helpless," he said.

Krano growled, coming to his feet. He took several steps toward the Xiiginns and stopped. Kandra Rene let out a soft laugh.

"That's no way to treat your superiors. Kneel," Kandra Rene said.

Krano stood perfectly still for a moment. His face contorted in pain and Kandra Rene stepped closer to him until her face was just inches from the Boxan. Her harsh gaze focused on him. "I said *kneel.*"

Krano let out a harsh gasp of breath that sounded like a strangled cry. Kyle clenched his teeth and charged, tackling Kandra Rene to the ground. He felt something hard slip around his neck, pulling him roughly off of her, and Kyle was slammed to the ground. Kandra Rene darted over to him. She grabbed him by his hair and Kyle felt her claws dig into his scalp.

"Look," Kandra Rene hissed.

Kyle opened his eyes and saw Krano kneeling on the ground. The Boxan stared at him, the pupils of his flaxen eyes dilated.

"I'm sorry," Krano said in a harsh whisper.

Kyle felt his eyes tear up in frustration, blurring his vision. He tried to jerk away from Kandra Rene's grasp, but the Xiiginn was so strong that she held him in place, forcing him to watch the Boxan lose his mind.

Kyle stopped struggling and watched Krano. The Boxan's eyes bulged and he cocked his head to the side. He glared at Kyle through sheer force of will alone. "Fight them, Human. Fight them . . ." Krano sank to the ground with a great sigh.

Kyle and the others watched as Krano's chest continued to rise and fall. He was still breathing.

Kandra Rene let him go, but Kyle couldn't stop looking at Krano.

"On your feet," Kandra Rene said.

Krano pushed himself to his feet.

"Very good. Now go stand by the wall," Kandra Rene said.

Kyle watched as Krano did as he was told. He'd known about the Xiiginns' compulsion ability and how the Boxans were vulnerable to it, but that was nothing to actually seeing it firsthand. He glanced over at Adyas, who sat dejectedly, resigned to her fate. There was a smoldering fury in her gaze, but she knew fighting it would be hopeless. Kyle watched as the Xiiginns made a living corpse of Adyas as well, and he turned away from it.

"One of four," Kendra Rene said.

Kyle glanced up at her, but she was speaking to Mar Arden.

"Interesting," Mar Arden said and looked at Kyle. "You're still unconvinced, I see. You think you can fight us. Better species than yours have tried and all have failed."

Kyle glared up at the Xiiginn and slowly regained his feet. He glanced at his crew, who stood by the wall.

"We'll see," Kyle said.

"Defiant until the end," Mar Arden said and looked at the Xiiginn soldiers. "Leave us," he said.

The Xiiginn soldiers left the room, and only Mar Arden and Kandra Rene remained.

"There are four of you. Will you take your chance now? This will be your only chance," Mar Arden said.

Kyle went to stand by his crew and folded his arms across his chest. There would be a time to fight and this wasn't it.

"See, Kandra Rene, they can be quite agreeable," Mar Arden said.

The Xiiginns left them, and Kyle watched as the three Boxans followed them out. He didn't know what was more unsettling—the fact that the Xiiginns no longer considered the Boxans a threat, or the fact that the Boxans actually *were* no longer a threat.

Once they were alone, Kyle sank to the floor, the pain from his side almost unbearable.

"We have to get out of here," Dawson said.

"You'll get no arguments from me," Kyle said.

"Sir, I need you to lift up your shirt. We should make sure you're not bleeding internally," Dawson said and looked at Celia. "Pearson, give me a hand."

Corporal Pearson's eyes blinked and she glanced down at them, then immediately came to help. They lifted Kyle's shirt and he gasped in pain.

"No skin discoloration. We'll need to keep an eye on it," Dawson said.

Tom Blake was muttering to himself, shaking his head.

Kyle sat up and rested against the wall. "Tom, look at me," he said.

Tom stopped muttering and looked at him. "I know you're scared. We all are, but we need to stay focused."

Tom nodded his head and took several deep breaths.

"There has to be a way out of here. This is some kind of cargo hold, not a cell. Wouldn't there be another way out?" Kyle said and started to rise to his feet.

Dawson held him down. "Hold on a second. Are your implants still working?"

Kyle frowned and saw that they were offline. He engaged the startup sequence. "They must have gone offline when they knocked us out."

As his neural implants came online, they registered his injuries and the smart nano-fiber of his suit tightened around his middle. Kyle felt the pain ease from his ribs as medicine entered his system, and he sighed with relief.

"Good call, Lieutenant," Kyle said.

"I was waiting for them to leave before trying it myself," Dawson said.

"I can't believe what they did. Eavoth tried to kill you," Tom said.

"No, he didn't," Kyle said. "Eavoth is dead and so are Krano and Adyas. Whatever they were before is gone."

There was a grim moment of silence as they all acknowledged it.

Tom's face became pale. "I didn't realize it would be so . . . painful," he said and swallowed hard.

"We need to figure a way to get out of here and warn Earth," Kyle said.

Tom's eyes widened and he glanced toward the ceiling. "You don't think they're watching us?"

Kyle shrugged. "I'm sure there's a guard at the door or nearby, but you saw them. They don't think we're a threat at all. Why would we be? There are only four of us against all of them."

"What can we do?"

"You heard Krano's last words. We fight. If we stay here, we're dead, or worse. Our top priority is to send word back to ECF command," Kyle said.

"What do you want us to do?" Dawson asked.

"I want you and Pearson to see if there's an access panel or something, anything we can fit into to get out of here. Don't be obvious about it just in case they *are* watching us. Blake, turn your implants back on. I want you to try and get access to the Xiiginn computer systems here. If that doesn't work, try and link up to our shuttle's systems," Kyle said.

Dawson started making his sweep around the edges of the cargo hold, but Pearson just stood there with a confused frown on her face. Kyle was about to say something to her when she muttered a hasty apology and started doing as he'd asked.

Tom walked over to him. "Sir, we were locked out of the shuttle's systems. What makes you think the lockout isn't still working?"

"Is it?" Kyle asked.

The young comms specialist frowned in thought and then his eyes lit up. "The shuttle's systems are still online! How did you know?"

"They lured us out there because they needed a way to get close to Earth. The only way I can think for them to do that is with the shuttle's transponder codes," Kyle said.

"The lockout was just to give them temporary access. Once they got here they already had the access they needed, and since we're their prisoners, they didn't reinstate the lockout. Do they even know about our implants?" Tom asked.

"I don't know," Kyle said and frowned as a thought suddenly came to his mind.

"I can't access the Xiiginns' systems directly, but I think I can figure out where we are through the shuttle's navigation system," Tom said.

Dawson waved him over.

"Good, stay on it," Kyle said to Tom.

He stood up and circled around the cargo hold until he came to a stop near Dawson.

"There's an access panel in the floor on the other side of the hold. No idea where it leads, but it's got to be better than staying here," Dawson said.

"Let's tell the others," Kyle said, signaling the others over to them. "We think there's a way out of here," he said and told them about the access panel.

"But we have no idea where it leads," Tom said.

"You can stay here and wait for the Xiiginns if you want," Dawson said.

"Calm down," Kyle said. "We stick together."

They walked over to the corner of the cargo hold and pushed aside the empty metallic crates stacked there. Kyle knelt down and grabbed the handle on the access panel, but it wouldn't budge. He braced himself by placing his other hand on the floor, giving the panel a good yank, and it opened with a screech of metal. They all glanced toward the door and waited. Dawson crept over to the door and leaned toward it, listening. After a few moments, he looked back at them and shook his head.

Kyle peered into the dark tunnel beyond, swung his legs around, and dropped down inside, hanging onto the edge, but his feet touched the bottom so he let go. There was dim lighting, which his implants enhanced so he could see better. He stepped to the side and the others dropped down one by one. Kyle and Dawson boosted Pearson back up so she could pull the access panel closed. Kyle doubted that any Xiiginn checking on them would be fooled for very long, but his aim was to give them as much time as he could so they had a better chance of finding a way out.

The tunnels were lined with piping and thick cables wound together so they had to walk in single file. More than once he wished he had some kind of schematic.

"Do any of you remember anything from when they brought us on board?" Kyle asked.

"I do, sir," Pearson said. "They brought us into some hangar and the cargo hold wasn't far away. I think if we keep heading in this direction we might be able to reach the hangar."

The tunnel split in two directions and Pearson pointed them to the left. After a few minutes traversing the tunnel, they began to hear sounds from a large, open area. Kyle slowed down. Above them, the ceiling changed to a series of grates, and Kyle glanced up to see Xiiginn soldiers standing nearby. The breath caught in his throat and he crouched low to the floor. The others did the same. Together, they crawled along, trying to be as quiet as possible. There were so many Xiiginns that Kyle couldn't keep an accurate count.

"Sir," Tom whispered.

Kyle turned toward him.

"I've accessed the shuttle's navigation system. It's linked with the Xiiginn system," Tom said.

"Good. Can you tell where the hell we are?" Kyle asked.

Tom nodded. "Sir, we're not far from Earth," he said.

Kyle felt his heart thump in his chest.

Through the grates above them, they heard, "Shuttle twenty-seven, this is Armstrong Base. We're past the scheduled check-in window. Is everything all right?"

Kyle's eyes widened. The broadcast from the Lunar Base sounded clear as a bell.

"We've experienced some technical difficulties with our comms equipment," Eavoth said. "We've investigated the downed Shroud monitors and found a technical glitch that was corrupting the navigation system. We've repaired them and are returning shortly."

"That's a relief. Is Colonel Mathews there? I'd like to have a word with him." the comms officer said.

"Apologies, but he's asleep at the moment. We'll alert you when we're closer. Shuttle out," Eavoth said.

Kyle clenched his hands into fists and shifted his position. They had to find a way to warn them. He glanced at the others and saw the same concern in their eyes. How were they going to get past a room full of Xiiginns to alert the ECF?

KYLE GLANCED AT THE OTHERS. "We need to get out of these tunnels and find a place to hide," he said.

"Hide! We need to get out of here," Tom hissed.

"The colonel's right. We need to hide out for a while," Dawson said.

Pearson nodded.

Tom still looked confused.

Kyle looked at Tom. "Suppose we could steal a shuttle, or even get our own shuttle back. They'd hunt us down and we might not get word back to Earth. But if we wait and gather some intelligence, we'd stand a much better chance of sending back critical information. We know they're heading towards Earth so they're already taking us where we want to go."

"But Eavoth. He's lying to the ECF. If we get caught, there'll be no one to warn Earth. Plus, any time now they're going to discover we escaped," Tom said.

Kyle waved them in closer. "First, we need to get out of these tunnels. We're too exposed here. And Tom's right. It's only a matter of time before they realize we're gone. Second, we need to scout out our options for sending word to Earth. If the Xiiginns are monitoring what's happening on Earth, we can send a signal and sabotage their efforts. Third, we need a way off this ship, or whatever the Xiiginns have cobbled together. If we have to steal a ship and blast our way out of here, then fine, but if we do it closer to Earth, I'd much rather our strike-fighters be closer to help than trying to escape from way out here."

"What else would this be if it's not a ship?" Tom asked.

Kyle shrugged. "I'm not sure. Why would they stick us in a cargo hold rather than the brig or an actual holding cell?"

The others glanced at each other, but none of them knew for sure.

"We're going to split up. Tom, you're with me. Dawson and Pearson, I want you to find a way to get off the ship. Tom and I are going to see if we can find a way to warn Earth. For now, we should be able to contact each other using our implants and the shuttle's internal comms systems," Kyle said.

He sent them a test message and each of them nodded that they'd received it. Kyle watched as Dawson and Pearson headed off, using the tunnel network under the hangar to scout out their options for escape. Kyle nodded for Tom to follow him.

"How are we going to warn Earth?" Tom asked.

"I was hoping you'd be able to help with that." Kyle said.

Tom's face reflected his surprise. "I suppose there are some things I could try, but I feel like all of them would warn the Xiiginns of what we're trying to do."

"You're not wrong. I was thinking that we gain access to the Xiiginn's system," Kyle said.

"Wouldn't we need a Xiiginn for that?" Tom asked.

The tunnel they were in narrowed and they had to shuffle sideways to get through.

"Most likely. I'll avoid it if I can, but more than likely we'll need a Xiiginn." Kyle glanced back and Tom looked like he was about to be sick. "This is what you signed up for. I know you probably thought that as a tech comms specialist you wouldn't be put into a situation to actually fight the Xiiginns, but here we are."

Tom sucked in a deep breath. "I'll be fine sir. You can count on me," he said.

Kyle nodded and kept on going.

"Sir, there's something else I've been thinking about," Tom said.

Kyle stopped and waited to hear what the young specialist had to say.

"When the Xiiginns did what they did to the Boxans, it seemed like that female Xiiginn was trying to do it to us," Tom said.

Kyle regarded the tech comms specialist for a moment. "You think one of us is compromised?"

Tom glanced away from him. "I don't know. It's possible. They did take Pearson away for questioning."

Kyle sighed, not liking where his own thoughts were going on the matter. The kid was pretty smart and Kyle was glad to have him along, even if he was a bit green for a mission like this. How could he tell if one of them was under the Xiiginn influence? He *had* felt Kandra Rene trying to do something to him, but he hadn't felt any different afterward. And if Tom was under the Xiiginn influence, why would he draw attention to it by bringing it up?

Tom held his hands up in front of his chest. "I know, right? I don't feel any different, but would I know if I was under their influence? Would you?" he asked.

Kyle clenched his teeth and shook his head. *God, how had the Boxans fought the Xiiginns for so long like this?*

"The only thing we can do is keep an eye on each other, and if the others do anything suspicious, you need to let me know," Kyle said.

Tom nodded.

They kept on going and Kyle couldn't help but realize this was yet another thing to add to their already substantial pile of worries. One thing at a time—that's what Michael Hunsicker always said. Solve one problem at a time. Focus on what you can influence and acknowledge the rest. Then you might get to go home.

23

Valkra spent hours poring over the old records of the Mardoxian Sect and their role in Boxan society. Before the Chaos Wars, there were factions within the sect that provided advanced training for Boxans to develop their skills. Valkra knew the Xiiginns wanted to duplicate the Mardoxian potential within their own species so she understood why anyone with the Mardoxian potential must be protected from the Xiiginns, but there was a point where isolation caused one of her race's most precious gifts to wither and die. There had been others with the Mardoxian potential who'd tried to guide the Boxans residing in the Havens, but they were all gone. Cardaleer was right. She was the first Boxan in a long time to show signs of the potential and she needed to keep it secret. If Councilor Essaforn were to find out, Valkra would never be allowed to go on any scavenger missions.

Her hand caressed Ranem's plasma pistol. She was supposed to return it but hadn't. The hand cannon had recharged, along with her armor, and she felt more at home in her armor than out of it.

Valkra walked down the corridor and headed to the command center. She saw Tholev, pacing off to the side, and walked over to him.

"Is something going on?" Valkra said.

Tholev glanced at her in surprise. "Yes. They sent out more scavenger teams and they've run into trouble."

"What happened?"

"The Protectors have them pinned down and the transport ships can't get them out," Tholev said.

Valkra's eyes darted to the Battle Commander, who was looking at a holodisplay of the city where the scavenger teams were pinned down.

"Fezzik is on duty," Tholev said.

Fezzik was a Battle Commander who wasn't known for taking extreme risks.

Valkra approached the table and studied the holodisplay. Protector teams were all over.

"There's no way to get them out," a pilot said over comms.

Fezzik glanced at his second in command. "We may need to pull them out," he said.

"If we do that, those squads will be lost," Sardon said.

This couldn't be happening. Valkra couldn't let them abandon those teams. "You can't abandon them," she said.

Fezzik glanced over at her. "What are you doing here? This isn't your concern. You're not cleared for duty."

"Battle Commander, we need to give them an answer," Sardon said.

Valkra watched as Fezzik tried to come to grips with the situation. The Boxan may bear the title of Battle Commander, but there hadn't been a real commander in the ranks since the Chaos Wars.

"Tell the pilots to pull out of there," Fezzik said.

Valkra slammed her fist on the table. "You coward! They need help. You can't just abandon them."

"What would you have us do? Those squads are pinned down by the Protectors. They're being held as bait to draw in our ships," Fezzik said.

Valkra looked back at the layout of the city. "They can get them out in teams. You need to send in more ships and provide covering fire, giving the squads a chance to escape."

Fezzik frowned as if the thought hadn't occurred to him. He shook his head. "That won't work," he said.

"It *will* work. I can do it. Send me in," Valkra said.

Fezzik regarded her for a moment.

"She's not cleared for duty," Sardon said.

Fezzik pressed his lips together and gave her a hard look. "Bring them back," he said.

Valkra stepped back from the table and ran towards the hangar, screaming for Tholev to follow her. The hangar was only a short distance from the command center. They emerged onto the hangar deck where several ships looked to be in a state of disrepair.

"Deck officer!" Valkra shouted.

A Boxan pulled himself out from behind one of the ships.

"I need a ship, now! One with weapons," Valkra said.

"This ship has weapons, but the engines are broken," the Deck Officer said.

Valkra scowled. "I need something that flies right now or all our scavenger squads on the surface are going to die," she said.

The Deck Officer pointed to the ship next to the one he was working on. "This one flies but has no weapons."

Valkra looked over at the ship. It was a transport carrier like the rest of them except for its armor, which had half a dozen scorch marks, some of which could easily breach the hull. She glanced back at the ship with the weapons.

"How fast can you transfer that plasma cannon?" Valkra asked.

The Deck Officer looked back at it. "Before you get through the preflight checks," he said and started bellowing out orders to the hangar deck crew.

"Tholev, you're with me," Valkra said.

They went to the ship and opened the cargo bay doors. As the door was in the middle of its opening cycle, it got stuck. Valkra reached to the top of the door, giving it a hard yank, and the door quickly opened.

"Are you sure about this?" Tholev asked.

"You just need to worry about shooting the plasma cannon once they get it mounted and opening those doors when I say," Valkra said.

She left Tholev to get set up and headed for the pilot's area where she climbed into the seat and started powering the ship's system. There was a loud clanging noise as the hangar deck crew attached the plasma cannon to the ship. The ship's system came online quickly and critical flight systems were ready. The weapons systems showed a single plasma cannon.

Valkra engaged the engines and the transport carrier lifted off the ground. She guided the ship toward the hangar bay doors.

She opened a comms channel to command center. "Request hangar doors to be opened," she said.

"One moment," the flight officer said.

Valkra heard Boxans arguing in the background and she frowned. "Flight Officer, either you open those doors or I'll blast them open myself."

Valkra closed the comms channel and sped toward the doors. *No Boxans left behind.*

"Tholev, target the hangar bay doors and fire on my command," Valkra said.

Valkra heard the plasma cannon swing into position and she was just about to order Tholev to fire when the doors quickly opened. Valkra maximized the thrust and the ship sped out of the hangar.

24

Kaylan stood on the bridge of the Boxan ship. Her gaze was focused on the main holoscreen that showed their ship and the strike-fighter squadrons that were engaging the remnants of the drone blockade. When the battle first started, she'd frozen and her mind had refused to work. She listened while Kladomaor issued orders, and when Ma'jasalax began providing input into his strategy, Kaylan was finally able to focus. All the training from the Boxans had been in preparation for this moment. At first, she began to anticipate Ma'jasalax's input, guiding the strike-fighter squadrons. She focused on the detailed map on the main holoscreen, her mind on both the bridge of the ship and among the strike-fighters.

"Lure them toward the planet," Kaylan said.

Kladomaor glanced at her and then at Ma'jasalax. "I didn't see it. She's right. Draw them in."

Kladomaor gave the orders. The drones that were part of the blockade were old and in a state of disrepair. Kaylan had no idea how long they'd been out there or how many ships they'd destroyed. The derelict ships around them were all carrier-class ships without heavy weapons, unlike what they had. Their weapons took out the drones in droves. The strike-fighter squadrons baited the drones into following them toward the planet, their transponders registering with the orbital defense platforms near Sethion as friendlies, unlike the drones.

Only some of the defense platforms came online and unleashed their arsenal on the rogue drone blockade, but it was enough to cut down their numbers.

Kladomaor recalled the strike-fighter squadrons and looked at Kaylan. "Good call," he said.

"Thanks," Kaylan said.

"How'd you do that?" Zack asked.

Things were settling down on the bridge and she looked away from the main holoscreen. "When it first started, the battlefield was a swirling mass of confusion. I didn't know what I was supposed to do. Then it was like I was in two places at once but all over the area on the map," Kaylan said.

"Indeed. She was guiding our ships even faster than Ma'jasalax at the end," Kladomaor said.

Kaylan looked at the Mardoxian priestess, who wore a proud smile.

"What if they disagreed on something?" Hicks asked.

"There's always a clear chain of command, even where the Mardoxian Sect is concerned," Kladomaor said.

Hicks frowned. "But Kaylan isn't a Boxan and Ma'jasalax has been her mentor," he said.

"That's true," Ma'jasalax said, "and I will remain so, but in this moment Kaylan's instincts were keener than my own. I'm very proud of this."

"Pride is different among the Boxans. In some respects we're like you Humans and in others we're different. In this instance, it would depend on the Boxans involved. Our rules of engagement support the guidance of multiple Mardoxian priests. Depending on their abilities, they can be siloed in their strategic approach to a battlefield. Then there are those rare individuals who can take in the entire battlefield beyond even our greatest commanders," Kladomaor said.

Kaylan felt a flush spread across her cheeks.

"I understand, and I'm trying to imagine using your tactics in our own fleet some day. It's not going to be easy," Hicks said and looked at Kaylan. "You know I trust you, but the military conducts operations back home very differently."

"Then they'll need to adapt," Zack said.

Hicks snorted. "You make it sound so easy."

Zack nodded. "I know—easier said than done. I get it."

Kaylan looked back at the main holoscreen, which showed a view of Sethion. The surface was a dingy yellow with massive storm clouds. Beyond the planet were great hulking masses.

"What are those?" Kaylan asked.

Kladomaor magnified the view and the ship's AI immediately began classifying the vast debris field. "Those were massive transport carriers called star carriers. They were hit first in the Chaos Wars," Kladomaor said.

"Is there any chance we can find one that's relatively intact?" Zack asked.

Kladomaor looked over at Varek.

"We've been actively scanning the system and the data is still coming in. As soon as I have something, I'll let you know," Varek said.

Kaylan kept looking at the view of the dying planet. "We need to divide our efforts."

"What do you mean?" Kladomaor asked.

"After we find the Boxans, we need to get them off the planet. How many could we bring aboard here?" Kaylan asked.

High Councilor Awan cleared his throat. "This isn't a transport carrier. We should resupply the Boxans we find, assuming we can tell which are not under the Xiiginn influence, and return to Olloron for more support."

Kaylan shook her head. "We didn't come all this way to leave whoever we find and go back to Olloron. Look at all those ships. There has to be something that can still fly," she said.

"We can't take them back to the colony. The rest of the council won't stand for it," High Councilor Awan said.

Kaylan wanted to tell him she didn't care what the rest of the council could stand.

"I have a suggestion," Zack said, drawing everyone's gaze toward him. "Well, more like a proposal," he said while looking over at Etanu and Ezerah.

The Nershals had been so quiet during the battle that she'd almost forgotten they were there.

"What's your proposal?" Etanu asked.

"The Boxans here are refugees. Could we bring them to Selebus for a time?" Zack said and looked at Kladomaor. "The Nershals could help them get back on their feet."

Kladomaor sighed and looked at Kaylan.

"It might be our only option, as much as I hate it, because once the Xiiginn become aware of Boxans living in the Nershal star system, they'll bring the bulk of their fleet there since Earth is cut off," Kaylan said.

"Part of our fleet is already there, helping the Nershals secure their star system," Kladomaor said.

"How will they react once they learn that Boxans from Sethion are there?" Kaylan asked.

"I think we're getting ahead of ourselves," Kladomaor said and looked pointedly at both Etanu and Ezerah. "You are the only two representatives of the Nershals on this ship. I understand that you cannot speak for Nerva—"

"We won't turn you away," Ezerah said. "It's the least we can do for exposing the Xiiginns to us. If we can get the refugees off the planet and to the Nerva star system, we'll provide aid and shelter. Even though we have colonies on Selebus, our numbers are small in comparison to the entirety of the forest moon. It's time we stick together. Our own global congress would be hard-pressed to deny your request."

"Except he's not authorized to *make* the request," High Councilor Awan said.

"You are," Kladomaor said. "And if you won't, I will by virtue of being there."

The high councilor nodded. He had little actual power here, and he knew it.

"Two teams," Kladomaor said. "Triflan take us into orbit around Sethion and start scanning the surface. We remain at combat ready." He glanced at Kaylan. "This will be a combat drop to the surface."

Kaylan nodded.

"Okay, so should we head to the hangar bay?" Zack asked.

Kaylan looked at Zack, knowing she couldn't keep the guilty look from her gaze.

Zack's brows arched up. "No," he said.

"We're going to split up," Kaylan said and looked at the Athena crew.

"I don't care what you say. I'm not leaving you," Zack said.

"Zack," Kaylan said.

"No! This is such bullshit," Zack said and stormed a few steps away.

"So is your attitude. Now listen up," Kaylan said, adding steel to her tone. "You, along with Efren, Nikolai, Vitomir, and probably Gaarokk with a team of Boxans, are going to find a ship that we can use to get the Boxan refugees off the planet. We only have a handful of shuttles here, but we can make that work if we have to. The Athena's AI surpasses the Boxan systems on this ship, and she works best with you. That's the reason I'm sending you to find a ship."

Zack drew himself up stubbornly. "It's really irritating when you start making sense."

This drew a few chuckles from the crew. Efren came over to his side and gave him a playful slap on the shoulder.

25

Z ack double-checked his combat suit on the hangar deck. His implants registered a good suit connection. All of them were armed, even Gaarokk. Across the deck he saw Kaylan and the others making similar preparations. He had no illusions about whether Kaylan could take care of herself. She could probably handle herself better than he could. He'd just thought they'd stick together for these missions. Zack looked away and shook his head.

Efren chuckled.

"What are you laughing about?" Zack asked.

"You. This is what happens when you become involved with strong women. I know better than to argue with Katie about such things," Efren said.

"Katie is a soldier and has had training for this," Zack said.

All the mirth left Efren's expression. "We're all soldiers now whether we want to be or not. We have a job to do," he said and glanced around to see if anyone was listening. "I'll deny ever saying this, but Kaylan is the most dangerous person on this ship."

Zack frowned. "How do you figure?"

Efren arched a brow. "Did you see what she did on the bridge?"

"She helped with troop placement and coordination of the battle," Zack said.

"Yes, and she's an exceptional combat pilot. This ability of hers gives her a huge advantage over anyone she'll face," Efren said.

Zack nodded. He'd devoted a substantial amount of time thinking about what Kaylan was capable of, but he hadn't heard anyone else comment on it. "Right, so we have the more dangerous mission," he said.

Gaarokk walked over to them. "I think there'll be enough danger to go around."

Two Boxan soldiers detached themselves from the group of soldiers waiting nearby.

"This is Strike Leaders Nulsan and Corryn," Gaarokk said.

There would be two squads of soldiers going with them, one for each shuttle they were taking to find a working star carrier. Most of the volunteers who'd joined Kladomaor's crew were soldiers. Very few were engineers or tech specialists, and Zack guessed that all their training on Boxan systems for the past eight months was about to pay off.

"We're ready to go," Nulsan said.

"Alright, let's go," Zack said.

They boarded the shuttle. Technically, he was cleared to fly the shuttle. He had just as much training time in a shuttle as he had in a strike-fighter, but navigating through a debris field with potential hostile drones was better left to the professionals.

Zack glanced at Gaarokk, who sat across from them. "Are you sure we're bringing enough people? I mean, those carriers are pretty big," he said.

"Normally those carriers would require a crew of several hundred, but we have enough for a skeleton crew. We just need to find one that's intact and start the reactors to restore main power. Also, there are automatons that could be put into service if we need them," Gaarokk said.

Zack frowned. "Automatons . . . do you mean robots?" he asked.

Gaarokk nodded.

Zack felt his stomach sink to his feet.

"What's wrong?" Efren asked.

The shuttles lifted off the hangar deck and left the ship behind.

Zack shook his head. "We just fought a battle with a drone swarm and now we're going to a ship that has a bunch of robots on it—and you ask what's wrong?"

Efren frowned. "Has anyone ever told you that you're sometimes paranoid, my friend?"

Zack blew out a breath and opened a comms channel to Athena.

::*You won't become the robot overlord will you?*:: Zack asked.

::*Bow to me, Human. You will obey me,*:: Athena said. ::*Your suit monitors indicate an elevated heart rate. Are you feeling sick?*:: the AI asked.

Zack rubbed his forehead. ::*You picked a hell of a time to develop a sense of humor,*:: he said.

::*I think what you're experiencing is called pre-mission jitters. You'll be fine once we find a ship and prepare it for the Boxan refugees,*:: the AI said.

::*Now you're psychoanalyzing me?*:: Zack asked.

::*One of my core functions is to monitor the crew.*::

::*Okay, but if you suddenly develop any sociopathic tendencies, please let me know.*::

::*You will be the first, I assure you.*::

Zack didn't reply.

::*This was another attempt at humor,*:: the AI said.

::*I know. I appreciate all the effort you're putting into making me feel better,*:: Zack said.

::*Just so there are no misunderstandings. The whole concept of me suddenly deciding the galaxy would be better off without intelligent life is absurd,*:: the AI said.

::*Agreed, but I'm glad to hear you say it nonetheless.*::

::*If there were any such occurrences, it would be because the machines were programmed to carry out such atrocities.*::

::*Athena.*::

::*Yes, Zack.*::

::*Please stop trying to make me feel better. I'm not sure I can take it right now.*::

::*Understood, but would you like to know that the shuttle's scanners have detected a faint power source?*::

Zack shot to his feet. "They've got something on the scanners," he said to Gaarokk.

They went to the cockpit and Nulsan glanced back at them.

"We may have found a carrier that will suit our needs," Nulsan said.

"Without knowing how many refugees there actually are, how do we know what our needs actually are?" Zack said and then shook his head. "I'm sorry. I'm just a little irritated."

"Understood," Nulsan said. "Kladomaor warned me about you."

Zack frowned. *Warned him?*

The shuttle's main holoscreen showed the biggest ship Zack had ever seen.

"Is this magnified?" Zack asked.

"No, that's a true image," Gaarokk said.

The Boxans had built a flying city whose lights were all out.

"Hull integrity is nominal. I'll deploy recon drones to perform a full scan," Nulsan said.

"That ship looks like it's a few miles long. How did they expect anyone to move around in there?" Zack asked.

"There are several tram systems for that; however, without main power that won't be an option until it's restored," Gaarokk said.

"How many of these ships were built and why did you build them in the first place?" Zack asked.

"There were ten of these star carriers built, but only four made it out of the system. They were first conceived for long-term exploration. Then, as the war with the Xiiginns continued, we planned to use them to establish a colony," Gaarokk said.

Zack did the math in his head. There were hulking wrecks all over this system. "How do you think this one escaped destruction?"

"No way to know for sure. Someone could have powered it down and hidden it here with the intention of returning," Gaarokk said.

There was an ominous silence from the Boxans.

"We're here now. We can do this," Zack said.

Nulsan opened a comms channel to the other shuttle.

"We await your orders, Strike Leader," Corryn said.

"I want you to take your team to the airlock nearest the engineering section. Those reactors will need to be powered on first. I'll take this team and head for the bridge," Nulsan said.

"Acknowledged," Corryn said and closed the comms channel.

"Strike Leader Nulsan," Athena said over the shuttle's speakers in the cockpit.

"Go ahead, Athena," Nulsan said.

"I would advise against taking this ship to the main hangar deck," Athena said.

"Why don't you want us to use the main hangar?" Zack asked.

"By evidence of the many battles fought in this system, there's a strong probability that any type of sabotage or ambush by enemy forces would first be established in places like the main hangar," Athena said.

Zack frowned in thought. "With that logic, there could be traps set at any airlock as well," he said.

"True, but the greatest probability is in the hangar deck," Athena said.

Zack looked at Nulsan. "What do you think?"

"I think Athena offers good advice," Nulsan said.

"Okay, where's the bridge on this ship?"

A schematic overlay appeared on the holoscreen, showing the ship. There were actually two bridges, with the main bridge located at the top of the ship towards the middle.

"What if we didn't use any of the airlocks within the immediate vicinity of the bridges? We'd have to hoof it, but there'd be less of a risk of some type of sabotage," Zack said.

Nulsan nodded. "A sound plan. I see Kladomaor was right about you."

"What did he say?" Zack asked.

"Not now, Zack," Gaarokk said. "The energy signatures aren't that strong. They could be from battery backups for redundant systems so we might not be completely without power here."

"It's been forty years. Do your batteries last this long?" Zack asked.

Gaarokk gave him a bemused expression. "Of course. With minimal usage, a battery backup can be in standby for hundreds of cycles."

"Okay, so the sooner we get aboard, the sooner we can get this ship ready for the others," Zack said.

In the next twenty minutes they landed the shuttle on the outer hull of the carrier. Zack stepped onto the ship and his mag-boots engaged, keeping him attached to the hull. He checked his pulse rifle and it was at full power. Hicks and Katie had drilled into him the need for checking his equipment and the last few months with the Boxans had instilled the same thing. Efren was right, they were soldiers of a sort by now.

The others exited the shuttle and headed for the airlock. Gaarokk explained that this was a maintenance airlock. Several Boxans carried portable power generators that they could use to get through some of the doors.

"What about the battery backups you mentioned earlier?" Zack asked.

"Those are for computing systems and not things like doors and such," Gaarokk answered.

Nulsan put three Boxan soldiers on point and they went to the door first. Zack and Nikolai were the only Humans in the group. Efren and Vitomir were on the other shuttle.

While they were waiting for the Boxans to open the doors, Zack took a moment to look at Sethion. The Boxan home world reminded Zack of a wound that had become infected. Almost the entire surface of the planet showed signs of destruction from the battles that had been fought there.

Etanu placed a hand on his shoulder. "This is why they fight so hard," he said.

Zack swallowed and tried to keep himself from imagining all the horrible things that had happened here.

"Do you think they'll ever come back here? You know, if we find a way to defeat the Xiiginns?" Zack asked.

"Perhaps for resources and materials, but the planet will be unlivable for thousands of years or more," Etanu said.

Zack wondered what the Boxans would do after all this. Would they find a viable world to settle on? Would the Boxans on Olloron ever accept the Boxans they find here into the colony? Or would the Boxans that were left on Sethion resent being left behind? Zack supposed there would be no easy solutions.

The airlock was clear and Nulsan waved for them to follow him inside.

Helmet lights came on and Zack's implants used the minimal lighting to enhance his vision. The dark corridor became outlined in a pale green. The last Boxan to come inside closed the airlock doors and the sound of the doors shutting sent echoes down the corridor. There was no lighting other than from their helmets and Zack felt the hairs on the back of his neck stand on end.

A partial schematic showed on the heads-up display in his helmet, outlining their current position and where they had to go. They moved cautiously through the derelict ship. Every room they passed was empty. They came across several heavy doors where they had to use the portable power generators to open them. There was no way to manually crank the heavy doors open since the Boxans hadn't foreseen a need for such things.

The doors opened and the lights from their helmets spilled into the darkened corridor. Shadows from Boxan power armor spread before them, lining the way forward. The breath caught in Zack's throat.

"These are defense mechs. No power source detected," Nulsan said.

Zack's heads-up display registered the defense mechs. There were weapons attached to their arms. They stood in the corridor as if they were lining up for something.

"Does it make any sense for them to be here?" Zack asked.

"I'm not sure," Gaarokk said.

"Should we find another way?" Zack asked, hoping Nulsan would say they should.

"This is the most direct path. There isn't anything to worry about. They're all powered down," Nulsan said.

They walked onward, weaving their way through the mechs, and at each one he passed Zack looked for some telltale sign that the mechs were truly powered off. Some of the mechs appeared to have stopped in mid stride.

Finally, the line of mechs ended and Zack sighed. His relief at getting past them was short-lived, however, as they soon came upon another group.

Zack tried to emulate the others who calmly walked by each of them. He steadied his breathing and tried to calm down because he really didn't need the Athena's AI to try and help him right now. The corridors branched off. To take his mind off the mechs, Zack checked in on Efren's progress. According to his suit locator, the other Boxan team was near the main reactor. Soon they would have the power on and they'd be able to turn on the lights.

Zack turned around and glanced at Etanu, who calmly walked behind him. As Zack turned back around, he caught sight of a slight twitch from one of the mechs and stopped in his tracks. Was it a trick of the light? Just a shadow? Even his heads-up display hadn't registered the movement.

"What is it?" Etanu asked.

"I thought I saw one of them move," Zack said.

Etanu peered at the line of mechs and shook his head. "Let's go," he said.

Zack kept glancing behind him, but the mechs remained perfectly still. They caught up to Gaarokk.

"Why are there so many mechs here?" Zack asked.

"We started using mechs because they weren't susceptible to being under the Xiiginn influence," Gaarokk said.

Alarm bells went off in Zack's mind. He knew no system was totally secure. "I don't like this. Why would they be lining the corridors like this? How far away is the bridge?" he asked.

"Not that much farther, and the mechs were likely being gathered for a maintenance cycle before being powered down," Gaarokk said.

Zack checked his pulse rifle and switched off the safety so it was ready to fire.

"What are you doing?" Gaarokk asked.

Zack sent out a scan through his PDA, looking for any Boxan computing systems online. The heads-up display in his helmet flashed with hundreds of connections, all stemming from mechs, and Zack cried out.

"The mechs aren't offline!" Zack said.

He raised his pulse rifle and saw Etanu do the same. A sea of deep red lights flicked on from the mechs. Zack felt as if something was crushing his chest. He squeezed the trigger and a three-round burst fired into the head of the nearest mech. All the mechs moved—a wave of heavy metal in an ocean of red lights. Etanu started firing and they backed away.

"How did you know they were hostile?" Etanu asked between shots.

The Nershal continued to fire and the mechs nearest them began marching toward them.

"The red lights," Zack said through gritted teeth.

A headshot wasn't enough to stop the mechs so he targeted the central processing unit in the chest cavity.

Gaarokk watched in horror, unable to move, and Nulsan pulled him back, firing his gauss rifle. The Boxan soldiers mowed down the mechs that were coming online. The mechs began firing back and Zack saw blue bolts slam into the strike commander's arm and dissipate.

"Stunner shots! Fall back and protect the others," Nulsan said and waved for them to go around the corner.

"Stunner shots are deadly to us," Etanu said and pushed Zack along.

"What about them?" Zack asked.

"Their armor can take it for a time," Etanu said.

Nikolai gasped for breath. "I hope there's something you can do," he said to Zack, running by his side.

"Yeah, can't you turn them off?" Etanu asked.

"Not without the power back on. We need to get to the bridge," Zack said.

The Boxans were urging them down the corridor. The mechs were clustering together and charging forward.

Zack opened a comms channel. "Efren, get moving, damn it. We need the power on now!"

He kept his pulse rifle ready and they were making a hasty retreat.

"What did he say? Is the power coming back on?" Etanu asked.

Zack held up his hand so he could listen.

". . . trouble . . . mechs are coming online," Efren said.

"They're having trouble in engineering," Zack said.

"Strike Commander," Gaarokk said, "we need to get to the bridge. We should be able to barricade the door against the mechs from there."

The mechs focused their shots at a Boxan soldier and he went down in a smoking heap.

Nulsan ordered three Boxans to hold the line against the advancing mechs. "You just need to slow them down and then regroup with us."

The Boxan soldiers acknowledged their orders. Zack's last view of the corridor was filled with the bobbing heads of the mechs closing in on their position.

26

Kaylan sat in a combat shuttle with Hicks and Garcia. She would have preferred flying a strike-fighter, but Kladomaor advised against it. He hadn't outright forbidden her, but something in the Boxan's tone made her agree with him. Black and Gold strike-fighter squadrons were resupplying, and the Blue squadron would stay to defend the cruiser.

Kladomoar beckoned her toward the front of the shuttle. Earlier she'd marked the continent on which she'd seen the Boxans fighting each other.

"We'll reach the fighting and do several flybys to see if we can determine which group is the refugees," Kladomaor said.

Kaylan nodded.

The combat shuttles poured out of the cruiser and started their approach to Sethion.

"Once we're on the surface, don't remove your helmets for any reason. The atmosphere is toxic, but your suits and armor will be able to resist it for a time," Kladomaor said.

"Let me pilot the shuttle," Kaylan said.

Kladomaor regarded her for a moment and then motioned for her to sit in the co-pilot's seat. The pilot shifted control of the shuttle to her and climbed out of his seat for Kladomaor to take.

"It helps me concentrate," Kaylan explained.

"When we get down there, stick by me. The fighting will be extremely brutal," Kladomaor said.

"Is there any other kind?"

"Not like what you'll see. Boxans fighting other Boxans under the Xiiginn influence is more savage than simply fighting the enemy. It changes you," Kladomaor said.

Kaylan knew he'd been a prisoner to the Xiiginn Mar Arden early in the war and that it haunted him. Kladomaor was one of the few Boxans to have escaped after being under the Xiiginn influence. Though it had happened long ago, it was a cost he was still paying each and every day.

The two strike-fighter squadrons spread out and the combat shuttles flew behind them. Kaylan angled their approach into the toxic atmosphere. A large swath of clouds covered the continent below them. Their destination was marked on the shuttle's heads-up display, but Kaylan knew exactly where she was going. Some of the strike-fighters and combat shuttles broke off from the main group, tasked with searching the other continents for signs of life. Sethion was a dying world and sensors indicated that radioactive fallout would affect this planet for hundreds of years.

Beyond the clouds, she glimpsed large blackened expanses covered in hardened ash. Proximity alarms sounded as they passed through the upper atmosphere. The large clouds were frozen and Kaylan avoided them. As they penetrated farther into the atmosphere, the clouds changed to liquid form. Kaylan extended her senses to where she'd seen the Boxans fighting and the area was quiet, seemingly undisturbed. She maintained an altitude of twenty thousand feet and flew over the city.

"No life-signs detected," Kladomaor said.

"Perhaps they're no longer here," Ma'jasalax said.

Kaylan frowned in concentration. Could she have been wrong? Had this been a wasted trip? Kaylan stemmed the flow of doubt and focused. The Boxans were here. If not in this city, then somewhere else.

A comms channel opened to their shuttle.

"Battle Commander, no signs of life on the western part of the continent. We'll work our way towards your position," the Boxan said.

"Acknowledged," Kladomaor said.

Kaylan sped the shuttle northward, leaving the city behind. She scanned for any comms chatter or signal, but nothing was detected. They approached another city that was shrouded in fog, almost shielding it entirely from view. Something large poked through the fog. At first Kaylan thought it was the rooftops of buildings that had escaped the destruction, but it was moving.

"Detecting an unknown craft," Kaylan said.

"Gold squadron, I want you to fly over the city two by two," Kladomaor said.

The strike-fighters sped forward. Flashes of light lit up the fog, but Kaylan couldn't tell if it was a battle being fought or the storm in the area. The strike-fighters disappeared into the fog and Kladomaor had her hold her position.

Kaylan used her senses to delve through the fog. There were impressions of Boxans moving deep in the thick, billowing cloud. She couldn't get a good look at them. A plasma bolt streaked past her and a dark shadow loomed overhead. Kaylan pushed forward. She heard the gravel crunch beneath power-armored boots pounding on the ground. Large, dark shapes clustered inside a building and a beat-up old troop carrier hovered nearby. Shots erupted all around, forcing the ship to flee. Dark, armored shapes moved down the streets, closing in on the building.

Kaylan pulled her senses back. "I have them. There's fighting inside the city."

She engaged the thrusters and the combat shuttle lurched forward. Weapons systems were online. Once she was closer to the ground, the shuttle's sensors were able to penetrate the fog and show an accurate layout so she wasn't flying in blind. She flew the shuttle to the street where she'd seen the troop carrier. The ship had returned. The cargo bay doors were open and there was a Boxan inside, waving for the Boxans in the building to get aboard. The troop carrier had one working cannon and the armored soldiers on the ground fired their weapons at the carrier, chewing it up. The cannon dropped from the hull like a dead weight.

Kaylan brought their ship in and hovered in front of the troop carrier, swinging the combat shuttle around to face the Boxan soldiers on the ground.

"Fire!"

Kladomaor engaged the cannons and plasma bolts ripped into Boxan soldiers. As the bolts tore through them, the remaining soldiers hastened to retreat.

Kaylan swung the shuttle around and opened a broadcast channel, hoping the old troop carrier would receive it.

"We're here to help. Get your people aboard and we'll continue to provide covering fire," Kaylan said.

There was no acknowledgment, but Kaylan could see that there were Boxans running onto the carrier.

"Battle Commander," the Wing Leader for Gold squadron said, "looks like we're seeing Boxans fighting and the only group I can identify are the Protectors. They're lining the streets, moving in and out of the buildings."

"Protectors are hostiles. Take them out, but check your targets for the other group. They're the refugees and not so well armed," Kladomaor said.

Kaylan could sense hesitation from the wing leader, but she acknowledged the orders. The troop carrier rose higher into the air and Kaylan matched its altitude.

"Why won't they respond?" Kaylan asked.

"They've taken a lot of damage. Perhaps their comms is out," Kladomaor said.

Kaylan blew out a breath and nudged the lateral control, causing the shuttle to wobble from side to side and then stop. She waited a few moments and then repeated the maneuver.

"What are you doing?" Kladomaor asked.

"If they can't talk to us directly, perhaps this will work," Kaylan said.

The troop carrier's stubby wings dipped slightly to either side and Kaylan smiled. She raised their altitude and backed away from the troop carrier.

"Okay, lead the way," Kaylan said.

The troop carrier lifted up and went in front of them. Kaylan followed.

"That's a good trick," Kladomaor said and sent out another update for the strike-fighter squadrons and combat shuttles to provide covering fire and assistance to anything like the troop carrier they were now following.

"Standard protocol back on Earth in case your comms go out," Kaylan said.

They flew above the city line and Kaylan saw other troop carriers rushing in to pick up Boxan refugees. There was the sudden blast of intense fire and some of the carriers went down before they could be helped. Kladomaor ordered the combat shuttles to pick up the refugees but keep them under guard.

"We need to be careful," Kladomaor said.

A sudden blast rocked their shuttle to the side and the combat AI scrambled to locate the source of the enemy fire.

Clinging to the side of the building was a large mech, and it was aiming a giant shoulder cannon at their shuttle. Kaylan jerked the controls and the combat shuttle veered away from the shot just in time. Kladomaor returned fire and the mech fell. Gold Squadron reported three downed strike-fighters. They'd been taken out by heavy mech cannons.

Kaylan used the scanners to look for survivors but there weren't any. The area around them came alive with fire. "How many heavy mechs could they have after all this time?" Kaylan asked.

She weaved below the city line and then rose above it. Each time she came up, the heavy mechs would open fire. The scanners showed the troop carriers were north of them and away from the city so Kaylan engaged the thrusters and sped after them. Data feeds from the other shuttles and fighters showed the flaming wrecks of the carriers the heavy mechs had taken out. How many had they failed to save?

"Who are the Protectors?" Kaylan asked.

Kladomaor glanced at Ma'jasalax, who gave him a slight nod.

"I was a Protector," Kladomaor said. "Our job was what you'd call a law enforcement agency that also had elite military forces that were used for upholding the laws of the Confederation. Before the Xiiginn uprising, we had Xiiginns among our ranks, and the Protectors were among the first to fall under the Xiiginn influence. During the Chaos Wars, we took out many Protector bases on Sethion . . ."

Kaylan glanced at Kladomaor and could tell that this was difficult for him to speak about.

"I don't know how any civilian group could last so long against the Protectors," Kladomaor said. He looked at the heads-up display in disgust.

"We're here now. Let's do what we can," Kaylan said.

Kladomaor opened a comms channel to their battle group. "Combat shuttles, continue to follow the troop carriers. Strike-fighters, I want you to stagger behind us and monitor whether we're being followed."

The battle group acknowledged Kladomaor's orders. There was a line of troop carriers in front of them, most of which had a patchwork of repairs and scorch marks on their hulls. They followed them to the northern hemisphere, closing in on a vast icy shelf. The atmosphere was a bit clearer the further north they went.

Kaylan opened a comms channel back to the cruiser. "Varek, has there been any contact with Zack or the others?"

"They reported finding an intact star carrier and were boarding the vessel with the intent to restore power," Varek replied.

Kaylan smiled at this news. "I'm just glad they haven't run into any trouble," she said.

"Let them know we'll need that ship ASAP, as well as any shuttles in working order," Kladomaor said.

Kaylan closed the comms channel to the cruiser. "How do you think we'll be received where the refugees are hiding?" she asked.

"I have no idea. I don't know if they'll hate the fact that no one ever came back to the help them or if they'll be relieved we're finally here," Kladomaor said.

"The ice shelf is a good place to hide from the Protectors," Ma'jasalax said.

The troop carriers flew down an open chasm in the ice shelf and a comms channel came online.

"This is Haven Two-One-Zero. Unidentified craft, please identify yourselves," a Boxan said.

"Haven Two-One-Zero, I'm Kladomaor, Battle Commander in the Boxan fleet. We're from the Boxan colony on Olloron and we're here to get you out," Kladomaor said.

There was no immediate reply and the seconds dragged on.

"I realize this may be a surprise to you. We didn't send any broadcast communications because of the threat of Boxans under the Xiiginn influence. Do we have clearance to come inside?" Kladomaor said.

"This is Councilor Essaforn. We have your ships on our screens. Before we can grant access, you must transmit your ship's transponder codes."

Kladomaor transmitted the codes, along with his own identification.

A target-lock alarm came on the shuttle's heads-up display and Kaylan's brows drew up in concern. Ground-based missile defense systems were detected by the cyber warfare suite.

"Haven Two-One-Zero, we're showing target-lock from your ground-based missile defense systems. Please advise," Kladomaor said.

"Protector presence registered and your ship is not in the registry. You have ten seconds to leave before we destroy your forces," Councilor Essaforn replied.

Ma'jasalax opened her own comms channel. "Councilor, this is Ma'jasalax of the Mardoxian Sect. I've transmitted my own credentials. I can vouch that while Kladomaor was at one time a Protector, he is not under the Xiiginn influence. We are here to help you get free of this place."

There were a few moments of heavy silence and then the target-lock disengaged.

"Mardoxian status confirmed. Stand by for further instructions," Councilor Essaforn said.

Kaylan blew out a breath and ran her hand over her face. "Would they really have fired on us if you hadn't identified yourself?" she asked.

"Tough to say, but I think they would have," Ma'jasalax said.

"There's an outside airfield where you may set your craft down. We'll meet you at the nearby hangar," Councilor Essaforn said.

The comms channel closed.

"They still don't trust us entirely," Kladomaor said.

"Can you blame them?" Kaylan said.

Coordinates were transmitted to them and Kaylan found the airfield easily enough. She knew Kladomaor wouldn't like how exposed they were, but they had little choice.

"Toxins are still registering in the atmosphere here so keep your suits on," Kladomaor advised.

The combat shuttles landed, and while they were disembarking from their shuttle, the strike-fighter squadrons flew in and set down nearby. A short distance from them there was an icy depression and they walked over to it. The ground sloped downward to large hangar doors. It was well hidden, and from above Kaylan would have thought this was just another icy crevice on the craggy, frozen surface.

Kladomaor ordered his soldiers to set up a perimeter with posts by their ships and along the ridge at the entrance to the depression.

This wasn't the warmest welcome they could have gotten, but Kaylan knew it could have been much worse. None of the groups that were flying reconnaissance over the other continents had detected any signs of life.

"These could be the last free Boxans on Sethion," Kaylan said.

"I want you to stay near me. We still don't know what we're walking into," Kladomaor said.

Hicks and Katie stood nearby and each had their pulse rifles ready. Kaylan had her own pulse rifle, but she was nowhere near as good a shot as Hicks or Katie. She could get her shots in the general area she wanted whereas Katie could hit targets with lethal accuracy from most distances.

The large hangar doors opened and armed Boxans came out. There were hundreds of them. Their power armor looked so old that Kaylan wondered how they were holding together at all. She craned her neck, trying to find the Boxan she'd seen while inside the Mardoxian chamber, but couldn't find them. The armed Boxans reached the top of the hangar and kept their weapons aimed at them while the lead Boxan gestured for them to go into the hangar. Kladomoar ordered his soldiers to lower their weapons. They left a few soldiers outside and walked into the hangar. Once they were inside, the hangar doors shut behind them and there were bright flashes of light from the decontamination protocol. There was a loud blast of air that Kaylan assumed was from some sort of internal atmospheric scrubbers for the air inside and they were ushered toward the center of the hangar where a group of Boxans waited for them. They were unarmed but all carried the weight of authority on them.

The Boxan refugees in front of them retracted their helmets, revealing brown, roughened skin that had more craggy surfaces than any Boxan Kaylan had ever seen. All the hard edges played upon the harsh glint in their flaxen-colored eyes. They must have lived through hell to have survived at all.

"I'm Councilor Essaforn. Welcome to Haven. It's been so long since we've had word from anyone off-world that we didn't quite believe you were telling us the truth," Councilor Essaforn said.

Kaylan retracted her helmet, revealing her face.

Councilor Essaforn's flaxen eyes widened in surprise and she looked at Kladomaor. "You travel with other alien species? I'm not familiar with them. Are they part of the Confederation?"

"The Confederation is lost to us. They are called Humans and they're the reason we're here," Kladomaor said.

Councilor Essaforn regarded Kaylan and the others for a moment as if she wasn't quite sure what she'd heard.

"It is true," Ma'jasalax said. "This is Kaylan and she has the Mardoxian potential inside her."

A Boxan pushed her way to the front, drawing Kaylan's gaze. Her eyes darted to the tarnished red power armor and the Boxan retracted her helmet. Kaylan stared into the Boxan's eyes and a moment of recognition passed between the two of them. This was the Boxan she'd seen from the Mardoxian chamber.

Councilor Essaforn followed Kaylan's gaze. "Valkra, come over here," she said.

Valkra hesitated for a moment before reluctantly moving forward. She kept her gaze on the councilor, and Kaylan could tell she wanted to look at her but didn't dare.

"Do you . . ." Councilor Essaforn began and stopped herself. "You recognize this Human?" she asked in an elevated tone.

Valkra at last looked at Kaylan and the others. "How did you know where to find us? And how did you know who to support in the battle?" she asked.

"You're the one I saw," Kaylan said, "the red armor. I saw you on the battlefield in the ruins of a city two days ago from inside a Mardoxian chamber. I saw you fighting but couldn't see who you were actually fighting."

Valkra's eyes widened and she glanced back at the councilor.

"So it *is* true," Councilor Essaforn said to Valkra. "*You* have the Mardoxian potential. Why didn't you ever say anything?"

"Because I wanted to fight. I wanted to be of use by going on the scavenger missions to protect my squad mates," Valkra said and looked around at the Boxans in the hangar. "No one left behind."

The Boxans in the hangar stomped their feet on the ground twice and repeated the words in one deep voice that resonated off the walls.

"Kaylan is quite gifted. She guided us here to you," Ma'jasalax said.

"How many ships did you bring?" Valkra asked.

"We have the one cruiser and we have a team trying to restore power to a star carrier nearby," Kladomaor said.

"The quarantine zone and the drone blockade. Did you make it through all that with just one cruiser? Why didn't they send more of you?" Councilor Essaforn asked.

"We made it through the quarantine zone on the authority of a member of the High Council. As for why we only brought one ship," Kladomaor said and pressed his lips together in thought for a moment. "Our coming here wasn't sanctioned by the High Council or the colony."

Councilor Essaforn's gaze went from one of hope to trepidation. "I'm afraid I don't understand."

"Kaylan has been in contact with Valkra through Mardoxian means. Sometimes the connections are strong," Ma'jasalax said.

Councilor Essaforn looked at Valkra. "Is this true? Were you in contact with this Human?" she asked.

"I wasn't sure what it was. It felt like there was another presence nearby, but I didn't know what it was," Valkra said.

Councilor Essaforn looked back at Ma'jasalax and nodded for her to continue.

"We've seen these connections, but only for the most gifted in the Mardoxian Sect. Kaylan fought for the High Council to send ships to Sethion. When the High Council refused her request, she recruited the rest of her crew to find evidence to support that there were Boxans still alive on Sethion. They'd found communication attempts to the quarantine zone," Ma'jasalax said.

"You defied the High Council to come here to help us?" Councilor Essaforn asked.

"Yes," Kladomaor said. "We shouldn't have left any of you behind. We agreed that the quarantine zone served its purpose for a time, but given Kaylan's recent evidence, we had to do something. We've become a race that's too willing to sacrifice our own species so the rest of us can survive. It isn't right. The Humans showed us this."

Councilor Essaforn looked at Kaylan. "I don't know what to say. Our scientists have been working on a way to disable the drone blockade, but nothing worked," she said.

"Are there any other Havens?" Kaylan asked.

"We're the last. The Boxans residing here are all that's left," Councilor Essaforn said and looked back at Kladomaor. "If you defied the High Council to come here, then where can we go? Will they accept us at the colony?"

Valkra blew out a harsh breath. "Why would we ever go to the colony? They never came to help us. They abandoned us."

Councilor Essaforn hushed the brazen Boxan to silence.

"Among my crew are Nershals who've offered their aid in the Nerva star system, but first we need to get you out of here," Kladomaor said.

"Nershals?" Councilor Essaforn said. "So much has changed. No one thought we'd ever get out of here."

"How many of you are there?" Kladomaor asked.

"There are over three hundred thousand of us living in this Haven," Councilor Essaforn said.

Kaylan watched as Kladomaor came to grips with the number—only three hundred thousand of the billions left behind during the Chaos Wars.

Kladomaor softened his gaze. "Do you have any ships capable of leaving the planet?"

"The orbital platforms prevent— No you've disabled them, or how else would you have gotten to the surface? But no, we don't have any ships capable of that. We just have the ships you've already seen that are used for scavenger missions. They're not space-worthy," Councilor Essaforn said.

"We can start doing shuttle runs to our ship until I get a current status from our other team, but I'd like my team to have a look at whatever ships you have," Kladomaor said.

Kaylan watched as the Boxans in the hangar came to grips with the fact that they were finally going to get out of there. They were stunned in the face of a hope they'd scarcely dreamed of. The refugees watched them standing there in the middle of hangar as if they weren't quite sure they were really there. Then, one by one, they flocked towards Kladomaor, and Councilor Essaforn kept glancing over at her. They'd found the Boxan refugees and now they just needed to get them off Sethion. Kaylan checked her PDA, but there had been no updates from Zack, and she was starting to wonder why she'd received no word.

27

E fren ducked behind the door, but those damn mechs just kept coming. Vitomir was beside him, holding his pulse rifle. They'd come a long way since Pluto, and while he'd never be friends with the Russian cosmonaut, they had to work together.

The sound of mechanical footsteps pounded the floor in the corridor outside the room they were in. Efren tried to quiet his breathing and he heard Vitomir do the same.

"Did you see where the others went?" Vitomir asked.

Efren shook his head. "I'm not sure. It all happened so fast."

Earlier, Efren had dropped his pulse rifle when the mechs came online and surprised them. He was regretting not having it now.

Vitomir pulled out his sidearm and handed it to Efren. It was something, at least.

"We're not far from the main generator," Efren said.

"Should we head to the secondary generator?" Vitomir asked.

Efren brought up the schematics on his helmet's heads-up display. "That one is on the other side of the ship almost four kilometers from our position. I don't think we'll make it."

More sounds of mechs walking outside the room they were in caused both of them to be quiet. Efren brought up a comms channel to Corryn.

"Vitomir and I are pinned down inside a room. There are mechs in the area," Efren said.

"Stay put and we'll work our way to you," Corryn said over the sound of Boxan weapons firing in the background.

The comms channel went dark, but at least the Boxan strike leader was still alive. "We're sitting ducks in here. Zack needs us to turn the power on so he can stop the mechs from hunting for us," Efren said.

There was another message from Zack. The other team was pinned down by the mechs as well. A loud slam came from the far side of the room, causing Efren to jump.

"I see on the schematics that we're not far," Vitomir said. He moved to the edge of the doorway and glanced out into the corridor beyond.

"If I get the mechs to chase me, do you think you can make it to the main generator?" Vitomir asked.

Efren's mouth went dry and he frowned in thought. "But the mechs. They'll . . . kill you," he said.

"Could you do it?" Vitomir pressed.

The sounds of mechanical footfall entered the corridor again. Efren nodded.

"I have a lot to atone for . . . Get it done," Vitomir said.

Efren's mouth hung open and he didn't know what to say. The Russian cosmonaut had once held him at gunpoint on Pluto. He and Redford had lied to him to get him to restore power to the Boxan listening post, which had set them on the journey here. He'd been furious with them both—hated them. Later on they were tolerated as a necessity. Now . . . here aboard this ship with mechs in the area threatening their lives, Efren found that he didn't want Vitomir to die. Not anymore. Not even though the Russian cosmonaut had done a horrible thing that impacted the lives of his own crew on Titus station, along with taking the life of his wife.

"Vitomir, I . . . um," Efren said.

"I know you can never forgive me and I will never forgive myself for being so short-sighted and foolish. But if doing this helps save lives, then it's worth it," Vitomir said.

He took a quick glance out the door and then looked back at Efren.

"Once they follow me, head right for the main reactor," Vitomir said.

Efren nodded.

Vitomir waited a few more seconds and then dashed into the hallway, firing his weapon. The Russian cosmonaut screamed and started backing down the corridor. The sound of the mech's heavy footfalls grew louder until they raced past the room and Efren quietly sprinted down the hallway in the opposite direction.

Efren glanced behind him as he ran, hearing the sound of Vitomir's pulse rifle. The mechs moved so fast that he wasn't sure if Vitomir could outrun them. The mini-map on his helmet's heads-up display showed him where he had to go. Efren abandoned all pretenses at being quiet and bolted at an all-out run down the corridor. One more corner and then he'd be there. He passed an adjacent corridor and heard the sound of Boxans firing their weapons. Efren slowed down and peeked down the way. There were mechs marching toward a couple of Boxan soldiers, who were mowing them down with their weapons, but the mechs kept on coming.

Efren blew out a breath, knowing he was about to do something really stupid. He stepped out into the middle of the corridor with his sidearm raised and squeezed the trigger. The mechs at the end of the line turned around. Their red power lights began to bounce up and down as the mechs started running toward him. Efren turned around and ran. He flew around the corner and bounced off the wall, but he saw the doors to the main power generator. There were several Boxan soldiers on the ground and a portable power generator was nearby.

Efren slid to halt, gasping for breath, and he was thinking he should have listened to Katie when she told him he needed to work on his cardio. The portable power generator was primed and ready, and he attached the connectors to a port just below the main panel. The locking mechanism started to unwind and the door sputtered open. Efren had disconnected the connectors and bent over to pick up the generator when a blue bolt sped by him, hitting the wall. The mechs were charging toward him and he ducked into the room beyond. Efren jammed the connectors into the panel beneath the door and hit the controls. More blue bolts slammed into the closing door, with a few making it through before the doors shut with a heavy thud. For a moment the only thing Efren could hear was the sound of his own breathing. Then something big slammed into the door. The mechs were trying to bludgeon their way in and his eyes widened when he noticed that part of the metallic door was bending toward him.

Efren darted over toward the main reactor controls and opened a comms channel to Zack.

"I'm inside the main reactor control room. Stand by for power to be restored. Then turn these damn mechs off," Efren said.

He couldn't keep his hands from shaking as he connected the portable power generator to the control console. During their Boxan training, he'd familiarized himself with the startup protocols for the reactors the Boxans used, albeit the ones he was more familiar with were quite a bit smaller and designed to power smaller starships rather than the floating city he was in at the moment. The mechs continued to pound on the door and Efren prayed he could get the power up in time.

28

Zack leaned against the wall, gasping for breath. "That didn't work," he said. Etanu peeked around the corner and fired his pulse rifle at the approaching mechs. Nulsan and the other Boxan soldiers did the same from the other side of the corridor.

The mechanic clomping of footfalls grated on Zack's nerves. The mechs were so damn methodical. Each time they'd tried to get to the bridge they'd been blocked. The control units on the mechs gave clear and precise instruction, which was to prevent unauthorized access to the bridge. Those damn things were just doing what they'd been programmed to and were doing an excellent job.

Gaarokk stood next to him, looking frustrated. "Even if we split up, there are too many of them. Neither group would get to the bridge."

"I know," Zack said.

"We need to change our tactics," Etanu said.

"It's not like I'm not trying to think of something," Zack said.

Etanu peeked around the corner and fired his weapon again. There was the sound of a mech crumpling to the floor, accompanied by the buzz of an overloaded power cell, but the sound was immediately lost in the prevailing cacophony of footfalls making slow but steady progress towards them.

"Strategy and tactics are your *thing*," Etanu chided.

Zack clenched his teeth. "What do you want from me? It's not like I can make us walk through walls," he said.

Gaarokk frowned in thought. "Athena, are there any walls in our vicinity that are thin enough for low-grade explosive charges?"

Etanu nodded. "See, I knew you'd come up with something."

Gaarokk glanced at Zack. "Interior walls are thinner. Your idea has potential."

Athena put a map on their internal heads-up display of a path they could take to get around the mechs. Gaarokk waved Nulsan over to them.

The Boxan strike leader bounded across, firing blindly at the mechs.

"Is this something you can do?" Zack asked and sent the path the AI had given them to his suit computer.

Nulsan glanced back at the remaining soldiers and then back at Zack. "This won't work if we all try to go," he said.

Nulsan called out to one of the other soldiers and had him slide over a metallic case. He opened the case, revealing a number of disk-shaped objects. "Do you know how to use these?" Nulsan asked.

"I do,' Etanu said. "Just place them on the wall and activate the charge."

Nulsan closed the case full of explosives and handed them to Etanu. "We'll hold them off as long as we can. Get to the bridge," he said.

The Boxan strike leader took Etanu's position at the corner and started periodically firing his weapon into the approaching mechs. The soldiers took turns firing their weapons down the corridor so there was an almost constant stream of fire.

"Let's go," Gaarokk said.

Zack pushed himself away from the wall but wanted to say something to them to acknowledge what they were doing. Nulsan gave him a firm nod and Etanu called out to him. Zack blew out a breath. They needed to hurry. He had Athena try to contact Efren again, but there was no reply. He knew the other team was close to the main reactor.

The sounds of weapons fire became softer as they moved away from Nulsan and the other Boxan soldiers. Etanu led them toward a wall in a dark room where Zack glanced around, noting the various workstations that were ill-suited for someone like him but perfect for a ten-foot-tall Boxan. Next, Etanu led them over to the far corner and Gaarokk pulled away a metal cabinet while Zack helped as best he could. Etanu placed one of the Boxan explosive devices onto the wall where the cabinet had been and activated the countdown. A string of green lights appeared on the device and began to pulse while the small team quickly took cover behind the metal cabinet and waited. There was a flash and a muffled pop. They circled around the cabinet and saw a large hole in the wall with vapor swirling along the singed edges of the new doorway. Etanu checked the room beyond and went through first. Zack and Gaarokk followed. Etanu motioned for them to be quiet as he crept towards the door on the far side of the room. Zack followed and they waited near the doorway. He heard mechs walking, but the sound of it was moving away from them.

Etanu stuck his head out the door and took a quick look around. "Okay we're clear. The next room is across the corridor and one room down from our position. We move as fast and as quietly as we can," the Nershal said.

Zack nodded and Gaarokk did as well.

They stepped out into the hallway and moved down the corridor. Etanu came to a stop just outside the room and looked inside. Satisfied that there were no mechs hidden in the room, they went inside. It looked to have been some type of storage room and Etanu led them to the far side where it took them a little while longer to clear out the corner they needed to get to. The bridge was diagonal from their current position and their path would take them into a security alcove near the bridge.

"Hold on a second," Zack said.

"What is it?" Etanu asked.

"The closer we get to the bridge, the more mechs there'll be. We need to lure them away from the bridge," Zack said.

Etanu frowned. "I could give you the explosives and then lure the mechs away."

"And get yourself killed in the process? No way," Zack said.

"Then what would you have me do?"

Zack brought up the schematics. He could think better if he saw where they were heading. "So we're here and the security center is over here, just down the corridor on the other side of this wall."

"That's right," Etanu said.

"We need a distraction to give us enough time to open the doors to the bridge. Those walls will be reinforced so the explosive charges won't work. How many charges do you have?" Gaarokk asked.

Etanu opened the case and counted four charges.

"Why don't we plant a few charges in the corridor outside this room? We can time them so the mechs will be drawn away when we get to the security center," Zack said.

Etanu took one of the charges from the case and pushed it against the wall. "I'll be right back," he said.

Zack started to follow him but Gaarokk told him to stay put. "You had a good idea. Now let him go do what he needs to do."

Zack's brows pushed forward. He hadn't meant for Etanu to take all the risk. "I could help him," Zack said.

"You could, but this way only one of us is at risk," Gaarokk said.

Etanu slipped out the door and Zack kept his eyes glued to the doorway.

"Who do you think programmed the mechs?" Zack asked.

"It could have been anyone. Whoever it was probably planned on coming back at some point but never got the chance," Gaarokk said.

The loud stomps from the mechs closed in and Zack's mouth went dry. He held his breath so he could listen for Etanu, but there was no sign of the Nershal. Mechs were heading right toward the door.

"Get down," Zack whispered.

They ducked down behind the cabinet. The mechanical whirl of the mech's servos became louder as a mech stopped outside the room they were in. Zack clutched the pulse rifle and hardly dared to breathe. After a few moments, the mech moved on and the sounds of its heavy footsteps became more distant. Zack poked his head out from behind the cabinet. The mech was gone, but where was Etanu?

"He might have had to hide since the mechs are in the area," Gaarokk said.

Zack stood up. "I'm gonna go look for him."

Gaarokk grabbed his arm. "Don't," he said.

"Let go of me," Zack said.

"We have to get to the bridge. Once power is restored, we can turn the mechs off," Gaarokk said.

Zack yanked his arm away from the Boxan. "I'm not abandoning my friend. I won't leave him behind like a . . ." Zack looked away.

"Like a Boxan would," Gaarokk finished for him.

Zack's stomach clenched and his shoulders became tight. He blew out a breath. "I shouldn't have said that."

Gaarokk regarded him, and though the Boxan had his helmet on, there was no mistaking the hard glint in his gaze. But then the Boxan's gaze softened. "You're right. It's what we've become."

Zack frowned and shook his head. "No, you're right. We need to get to the bridge instead of going off to look for Etanu. He'd probably yell at me for doing that anyway. I'm going to set the charge."

Zack took one last glance at the doorway and then set the timer for the explosive charge. There was a red flash and a slight pop. Zack moved over to the opening and looked inside the next room. It was pitch black, even with the night-vision scope through his helmet. Zack turned his helmet light on and saw that the room beyond was probably an office. Zack motioned for Gaarokk to go through first. Once the Boxan was inside, Zack pulled the cabinet over to block the large hole in the wall. It didn't cover the whole thing, but it would be enough should the mechs return. A shuffling sound at the doorway drew his attention and Etanu ran into the room.

"Go. I'm not sure if they saw me," he hissed.

Zack leaped through the hole and Etanu followed soon thereafter. Gaarokk waited for them by the door. The Boxan was listening intently.

"How much time is left on the other charges?" Zack asked.

"Not much. It would be better if we were in the security center when the explosives go off," Etanu said.

Zack nodded and went to the door. He pulled it open and there was a loud screech. *Idiot!* Zack scolded himself.

"Just go," Etanu said.

Zack stepped out into the corridor with Etanu and Gaarokk close on his heels. The sounds of mechs could be heard from the nearby corner. Zack came to the security center door and pushed it open. There was a bright flash of light from the nearby corridor, along with a loud popping sound. They went into the security center and Etanu closed the door, waiting. There were immediate sounds of mechs storming off, presumably to investigate the explosives. Zack led them through the security center offices towards the door that was by the bridge. He rounded the corner and almost slammed into a mech, and the mech's servos whirled as it pivoted around. Zack brought up his pulse rifle and fired blindly, hearing Etanu fire his own rifle. The mech fell backward.

"Did you forget everything I taught you? You didn't hit the thing once at pointblank range," Etanu chided.

Zack shook his head. After walking into the mech he'd squeezed his eyes shut and fired his weapon.

The bridge doors were just outside. Zack walked over to the control interface and used the Boxan override with High Councilor Awan's credentials. The door had just started to open when Etanu screamed for them to get inside.

Zack was the first to step through and turn around. Gaarokk came next and then Etanu. Behind them was an army of mechs, barreling toward them. Gaarokk used the console to shut the door, but as it was shutting the lights on the bridge came on. Zack squeezed his eyes shut to stave off the blindness from night-vision mode in his helmet, then opened his eyes to a well-lit bridge and a partially closed door. Etanu was firing his weapon and Zack joined him, firing his own weapon.

"Athena, can you get a connection?" Zack asked.

"You must get to an open console and use the high councilor's credentials first," the AI said.

A blue bolt buzzed by his helmet and Gaarokk pulled him out of the way. Several more bolts slammed into the Boxan and Gaarokk cried out in pain. Zack tried to catch him as he fell, but the Boxan weighed almost a thousand pounds and all Zack accomplished was hurting his back. He pulled himself away from the fallen Boxan and fired his pulse rifle through the partially opened door.

"Any time now, Zack!" Etanu shouted.

Zack raced to the nearest console. His fingers flew through the interface and then uploaded the high councilor's credentials. Once they were accepted, Athena notified them she was inside.

Etanu backed away from the door, still firing his weapon, and the Boxan mechs were pushing their way inside.

"Athena!" Zack screamed.

Command line references blurred by his internal heads-up display. Etanu made it to his side and they kept firing their weapons at the mechs, but the mechs pushed their way inside and blue stun bolts slammed into the console, sending sparks into the air. Zack squeezed his eyes shut.

Silence.

Zack opened his eyes and the mechs were just a few feet away but their red lights suddenly changed to amber.

"High Councilor, welcome," the lead mech said.

Zack blew out the breath he'd been holding. "Get the hell away from me. Go back to wherever they store you," he said.

The mech spun around and marched away from them.

Etanu glanced at him. "Now you know why we Nershals hate machines," he said. "Except the Athena AI," he added quickly.

Zack shook his head and sighed, then glanced over at Gaarokk and ran over to him. Zack opened a connection to the Boxan's suit computer and could see that his vitals were stabilizing.

"He's going to be all right," Zack said.

A comms channel opened to them.

"You made it to the bridge," Strike Leader Nulsan said. "We're on our way to you."

"I'm glad you made it," Zack said.

He leaned back against the command couch and caught his breath. Etanu did the same.

"Damn, that was close. I thought we were gonna die," Zack said.

Etanu nodded and then checked his weapon.

"Athena, what's the status of the ship?" Zack asked.

"Main power has been restored and systems are coming online. All systems scheduled for diagnostics evaluation before becoming fully available," the AI said.

Zack opened a comms channel to Efren.

"Efren, are you guys okay?" Zack asked.

"I'm fine," Efren said, sounding winded. "Vitomir is missing. The mechs just turned around and left. Assume that's your handiwork?"

"Yeah, they shouldn't try and kill us anymore," Zack said.

"Good, we'll get the secondary reactors online and then get the engines back online. Life support is also coming online so we should be able to breathe the air in here within the next thirty minutes, according to Corryn," Efren said.

Strike Leader Nulsan and the surviving Boxan soldiers came to the bridge. They were carrying a few wounded. Gaarokk regained consciousness and joined him.

"Thanks," Zack said.

Gaarokk frowned. "What do you mean?"

"You pulled me out of the way. You got stunned because of me," Zack said.

"Of course. We stick together," Gaarokk said.

Zack smiled and then nodded.

Nulsan went about getting the remaining members of their teams organized. Now that main power was back online, they had to check the main systems to determine whether the ship could still fly. Zack hoped it could. It would be a shame to have gone through all this for a broken ship.

"The ship seems largely intact," Nulsan said.

They contacted the cruiser and checked in with Varek.

"Have you heard from Kaylan and the others?" Zack asked.

"They've found the refugees. There are over three hundred thousand of them," Varek said.

Zack blew out a soft whistle. "We've got to have shuttles on this thing or something even bigger. How else did they plan on getting anyone aboard?" he said.

Zack went over to one of the consoles. Varek had given him Kaylan's coordinates. The sensors were up and Zack scanned the area, doing a double take.

"What is it?" Nulsan asked.

Zack put what he'd seen up on the main holoscreen and walked over to it. "If this is where the refugees have been hiding," he said, pointing to the area almost near the north pole, "then what is this mass moving towards them?" he said, pointing hundreds of miles south.

Everyone on the bridge became silent and looked at the main holoscreen.

"It looks like something massive is heading right towards them. Is it a storm?" Zack asked.

Gaarokk studied the holoscreen intently. "That's not a storm. That's an army," he said.

Zack's stared at the holoscreen, slack-jawed, his thoughts screeching to a sudden halt. "We've got to warn them," he said, pacing in front of the holoscreen. "We've got to get them out of there."

Zack headed for the door. "Athena, I need to know where the main hangar is. There has to be something we can fly down there and pick them up."

Strike Leader Nulsan opened a ship-wide broadcast. "The refugees are going to be attacked soon. Anyone with flight clearance is to head to the main hangar."

Zack started running with Etanu at his side. Several Boxans followed them. He hoped whatever ships were left in the main hangar could fly and that the Boxan engineering Gaarokk was so proud of, held up. In Zack's experience, anything that was left around unused generally wasn't reliable anymore, but he brushed those thoughts aside. Kaylan and the others were down there and there was no way he was going to let them down.

29

K ladomaor had never seen so many Boxans in one place except for the colony, and he'd lost count of how many refugees had come up to him and regarded him as if he were some type of legend. He kept urging them to gather their belongings but only to bring the essentials.

Kaylan came over to him, along with Valkra.

"You're the Battle Commander?" Valkra asked.

"I am," Kladomaor answered.

"I want to fight for you," Valkra said.

Kladomaor frowned. "You have the Mardoxian potential in you."

Valkra's eyes flashed dangerously. "It's what makes me so effective in battle. Will you let me fight with you and your soldiers?"

Kladomaor shifted his feet. By rights, this Boxan should be with the Mardoxian Sect for training, but as he looked at her, he wasn't sure she would accept that. There was also no guarantee the colony would accept these Boxans and he hadn't thought of his own status in the colony. Technically, he was a criminal.

"You can fight, but you'll also train with Ma'jasalax, and you'll follow orders without question," Kladomaor said.

Valkra's eyes narrowed. "I'm a squad leader. I've led squads hundreds of times to secure supplies for the Haven."

Kladomaor glanced at Kaylan and then back at Valkra. "I don't say these things to detract from your experiences. Once we evaluate your skills, we'll determine your place. But your abilities where the Mardoxian potential is concerned are instinctual and unrefined. You'll require extensive training before I'll allow any of my soldiers to trust you on the battlefield. I'm afraid that's all I can offer you."

Valkra looked away. "Yes, Battle Commander," she said and walked away.

Kaylan waited until Valkra was away from them to speak. "Her abilities helped her get this far."

"I know, but a new recruit who thinks they know everything will get themselves and others killed," Kladomaor said and glanced in Valkra's direction. "I will say this though: she's the reason they were able to survive. Councilor Essaforn sent me their records. Time and time again Valkra's squads brought in the most resources and had the highest survival rate."

"Survival rate?" Kaylan said.

"The squads Valkra mentioned don't have a long survivability rate. Everyone is required to serve in a rotation, and Valkra, along with some others, are part of a core group that stays on rotation even when their required term is done," Kladomaor said.

He needed to check on the soldiers he left outside and headed for the hangar entrance. There had already been several shuttle runs back to the cruiser, but those runs hardly scratched the surface in terms of the number of refugees. Kaylan and the other Athena crewmembers stayed by him as he went out onto the surface. He'd sent several strike-fighter pilots to check on whether the Haven ships could be made space-worthy. They only needed to make one trip to reach either the cruiser or the star carrier.

The hangar had a portable airlock that would allow them to return to the surface without venting the entire space. They went through and Kladomaor stepped onto the frozen surface of Sethion.

A comms channel initiated by the cruiser appeared on Kladomaor's internal heads-up display.

"Battle Commander, we've had word from the team that went to the carrier," Varek said.

"Hold," Kladomaor said and patched in the others. "Go ahead."

"They've restored power to the carrier and are bringing the ship's critical systems online. However, there were some casualties," Varek said.

Kladomaor glanced over at Kaylan, who went rigid.

"What happened?" Kladomoar asked.

"There were security mechs in standby mode. Nulsan split the group up into two teams, sending one to engineering to restore power and the other to the bridge. The mechs came online while they were making their way through the ship. They managed to get through, but Nulsan lost some soldiers and the Human, Vitomir, is unaccounted for. According to Efren, Vitomir drew the mechs away so he could get to the main power generator. Once main power was restored, Zack was able to disable the mechs from the bridge," Varek said.

"Understood," Kladomaor said and glanced at Kaylan and the others. "We didn't anticipate the use of mechs or them being in standby. They must have used them because they couldn't be subverted by the Xiiginns."

"Battle Commander, I'm patching in Strike Leader Nulsan," Varek said.

"Battle Commander, carrier sensors are showing a large land force heading your way," Nulsan said.

"Varek, can you confirm?" Kladomaor asked.

"Affirmative. We see the same thing," Varek replied.

Kladomaor motioned one of his soldiers over. "Warn Councilor Essaforn that there's an attack force making its way here. They need to muster up the Haven's defenses. And tell her I'll be with her shortly."

The Boxan soldier ran off to do as he was bidden.

"How could they have found us?" Kaylan asked.

Kladomaor frowned. "We might have led them here. We're not sure what the Protector's have in their arsenal, but they definitely have better weapons than the refugees. And there are the mechs."

"Battle Commander," Nulsan said.

"Go ahead."

"There are large transport carriers on this ship. We're sending them to your position to help with the evacuation," Nulsan said.

"Excellent. How many ships do you have?" Kladomaor asked.

"Three carriers are in working order. Plus, there's additional shuttle craft, but we're out of pilots. That's with leveraging everyone with flight experience but officially not pilots," Nulsan said.

"Varek, I want you to send anyone who can fly a ship over to Nulsan. Then I want you to position the cruiser into orbit above the ground force with a firing solution to thin that force out," Kladomaor said.

The comms channel closed and Kladomaor glanced over at the strike-fighters nearby.

"We're ready," Kaylan said.

Kladomaor looked over at her, with Hicks and Katie at her side. They were his closest pilots until he could get the others out here. "Alright, the three of you can go. Take three strike-fighters from Gold squadron. Varek will feed you intelligence when he gets the cruiser into position. I have one condition," he said and focused his gaze on Kaylan. "Engage the enemy but no heroics. If the area becomes too hot, you're to head directly back to the cruiser. Is that understood?"

Kaylan nodded.

Humans, Kladomaor thought as they ran over to the strike-fighters. *Headstrong and brave but sometimes too foolish for their own good.*

Kladomaor turned around and headed back toward the hangar. They needed to evacuate this place. If the Haven's ships couldn't break orbit, perhaps they could move refugees to another location to await pickup. While he went back inside the hangar he began issuing orders to his soldiers. The refugees were going to have to fight if they were going to survive. The battle for Sethion's lost children was about to begin and he would ensure that their battle song was heard.

30

Zack stood in one of the hangar bays of the massive, city-sized spaceship. There was a row of shuttle craft on either side of the hangar. It had never occurred to Zack that they would be so short on pilots. Some of the Boxans who died at the hands of the security mechs had also been pilots. While he wasn't cleared to fly one of the large transport carriers they'd found, he was perfectly fine with piloting one of these shuttles. The flight systems were quite similar to what the Boxans still used. Athena could help him with the rest.

Zack tugged on his gloves and put his helmet back on.

"Athena, can you begin preflight checks on shuttle ten-zero-one?" Zack said.

"Beginning preflight checks now," Athena replied.

Zack circled around the Boxan shuttle. The craft was easily five hundred feet long and could safely hold over a thousand Boxans. The shuttle systems had external sensors for things like hull integrity, but one thing Kaylan and Hicks had drilled into him was to do his own visual inspection. Zack wasn't about to argue with their experience, even if the spacecraft had been built by Boxans. He came back around the front and went up the loading ramp.

Zack made his way to the pilot area at the nose of the shuttle and sat down. All of them would be flying alone. They needed to get as many Boxans off the planet as possible.

He brought up the flight systems and all preflight checks had passed.

"Okay, time to fly a ship that hasn't been used in over fifty years," Zack said with mock enthusiasm.

"I'm afraid I don't understand," Athena said. "According to the flight logs, the last time—"

"It was just a guess," Zack interrupted. "I don't want to know the actual amount of time. I just hope nothing breaks and we don't explode or break apart upon entering the atmosphere . . . or get shot down . . . You know, let's just go," he said.

The AI must have sensed his agitation and didn't reply. Zack opened a comms channel to the bridge. "Shuttle ten-zero-one ready to depart," he said.

"Confirmed. Good luck," the Boxan flight officer said.

Zack blew out a breath. A comms channel from Etanu appeared on the shuttle's heads-up display.

"Just wanted to check in with you," Etanu said.

"All set here," Zack said.

"Zack," Etanu said in a serious tone, "do you have a complete flight suit on? I won't be there to save you this time if you don't."

Zack rolled his eyes and shook his head. "One time, Etanu. I forget that damn collar one time and you never let me forget it."

Zack smiled, glad to have a momentary reprieve from the jitters he felt at flying into a war zone.

Strike Leader Nulsan sent a broadcast to all shuttles. "Alright, we fly in formation down to the refugee camp. They call it Haven Two-Zero-One. There are alternate entrances that are away from the line of battle. The coordinates should be on your navigation computers now. We'll move the star carrier closer to the planet to reduce the length of time to bring the refugees up from the surface."

They were cleared to take off. Zack engaged the repulsor engines and the shuttle hovered above the hangar floor. He retracted the landing gear and followed the other shuttles out of the hangar bay. Zack had to get used to the controls since this shuttle was different than the highly agile combat shuttles he'd trained on at Olloron.

"How are you doing?" Etanu asked.

They'd decided earlier to keep their comms channel open.

"I'm fine," Zack said and reminded himself for the hundredth time that there was over five hundred feet of ship behind him. "Not that maneuverable, are they?" he said.

"You'll get used it. A lot different than the strike-fighters, but the concepts are the same," Etanu said.

Zack and Etanu were the last in a line of twenty shuttles. The four large transport subcarriers detached themselves from the main hull of the ship. There were more, but they weren't flight ready.

"Just stay on my six and you'll be fine," Etanu said.

The other ships registered on his shuttle's computer systems. Once they were well clear of the star carrier, they increased their speed. Nulsan would be moving the star carrier from its hiding place behind one of Sethion's moons in a little while. They headed for the northern hemisphere, angling their approach to come in on the far side of Haven Two-Zero-One. This would keep their civilian craft away from the line of battle. Zack brought up the latest feeds, and the large mass with designate Alpha land force was steadily moving toward the Boxan sanctuary. He thought of opening a comms channel to Kaylan. She was down there in danger herself, but it wouldn't stop her from giving him a tongue lashing for doing what he was doing. He'd only been flying for less than six months and had started more or less on a dare from Hicks. He liked flying. It was a lot of fun and it gave him some time with Kaylan he wouldn't normally get to have.

The frozen icecap that comprised Sethion's northern hemisphere rapidly approached as he took in the view of the Boxan home world with the large yellow clouds. The atmospheric readings showed that the planet was extremely toxic. Nothing could live on the surface. Sethion was a world ravaged by a brutal civil war whose timespan was longer than Zack had been alive.

The shuttle's system registered that they were passing through the troposphere, but the friction that would no doubt be assailing the shuttle's hull couldn't be felt inside. He cut a swath through the poisoned atmosphere, along with the other shuttles. It was a smooth ride and Zack kept in line with the rest. They had an approach vector already pre-assigned to them, and as the other shuttles peeled off to their assignments, Zack followed his coordinates.

He was low enough to make out certain land features in the vast icy expanse. The Boxan refugees had carved out a meager existence deep within the ice and he couldn't imagine living like that. As he approached his designated landing area, he extended the landing gear. There were several Boxans already on the ground. Zack landed the shuttle and opened a comms channel to the compound.

"Shuttle ten-zero-one ready for pickup. Time is wasting," Zack said.

"Welcome to Sethion. Refugees are being routed to your ship," Kladomaor said.

Zack lowered the loading ramp and the lower ship cameras showed Boxans making their way to his ship.

"Commander, where's Kaylan?" Zack asked.

"She's in a strike-fighter flying reconnaissance," Kladomaor said.

Zack squeezed his eyes shut. He knew it. There was no way she'd be sitting around while there was something to be done. "Understood," he said.

"Once your shuttle is full, you're cleared to leave. Get them to the star carrier and return," Kladomaor said.

The comms channel closed.

"Athena, can you locate the crew?" he asked.

The AI showed him three strike-fighter designates on screen, all flying on approach to the land force.

Zack frowned. "Yeah right, reconnaissance my ass," he said quietly.

Boxan refugees loaded onto a shuttle and one of the oldest Boxans he'd ever seen came to the cockpit. The old Boxan frowned. He hadn't expected Zack to be flying the ship.

"Hello, I'm Zack."

The old Boxan put down the large metallic case he'd been carrying and sat in the copilot's seat.

"I'm Cardaleer."

Zack frowned. "Make yourself at home," he said.

Cardaleer looked at the readouts on the screen and then glanced at Zack. "Human?"

"That's right," Zack said and brought up the onboard camera feed. They were nearing capacity. He opened a comms channel to the Boxan coordinating the refugees. "Pack 'em in until there's no room," he said.

Cardaleer's eyes widened. "We're already nearing capacity for this craft as it is."

"I know, but I don't want to leave anyone behind," Zack said.

Cardaleer regarded him for a moment and then nodded to himself. "You remind me of someone. I think I'm going to like you."

Zack snorted. "Thanks, I think."

The loading ramp was closed and Zack engaged the engines. It took more power to get them off the ground and he felt he was flying an over-bloated whale of a ship, but he didn't care. The more Boxans he could get off now would be fewer that were in danger when the battle began.

Zack opened a comms channel back to the star carrier. "Shuttle ten-zero-one has lifted off and we're fully loaded. Should be there shortly," he said.

He glanced at the readout showing the land force's position. He didn't know how they were moving so fast, but that army was going to reach the compound before Zack's shuttle made it back to the ship.

"The Protectors are coming," Cardaleer said.

Zack nodded and increased the speed.

31

The exhilaration of being in a strike-fighter filled Kaylan with a burning anticipation and thrill at flying such a superb aircraft. That is, that was how she'd felt when they first left the Haven. They'd done several high-altitude flyovers using the onboard cameras and sensors to send recon intelligence back to the cruiser. The Protector ground force was made up of massive ground troop carriers, combat mechs, and power-armored Boxans with exoskeleton support that allowed the wearer to move at astonishing speeds. On Earth, she'd had to familiarize herself with various combat scenarios pilots would be called upon to deal with and incorporate those into the design of the aircraft her company manufactured. Never in all those briefings was there a scenario where a ground force could move at the speeds she was seeing. As she looked below, she felt as if her gut had been clenching the entire time she'd been up here. The Xiiginns did this. Sethion was the measure of what the Xiiginns would do if they established a foothold on a world. By Boxan accounts, the Xiiginns were even more powerful now than when they'd broken free of the Boxans.

"We can't let this happen to Earth," Kaylan said over an open comms channel with Katie and Hicks.

"We won't," Hicks said, with Katie echoing the same.

Kaylan glanced over at the lower part of the heads-up display. The rest of the strike-fighter squadrons were on their way. She sucked in a breath and gunned the thrusters while bringing the weapons systems online.

Hicks and Katie followed.

"What are you doing?" Hicks asked.

"Attacking them," Kaylan said.

"We're right behind you. Let's give those Protectors something to worry about," Hicks said.

Kaylan guided her strike-fighter down and triggered the twin plasma cannons. Molten fury rained down on the Protectors. She concentrated her fire on the power-armored troops since they were the most exposed. Hicks and Katie flew on either side of her, doing the same.

They lined up for another run. Targeting alarms blared in the strike-fighter cockpit as the sky lit up around her. Kaylan broke off the attack and increased her altitude. The rest of Blue and Gold squadrons caught up to them. They coordinated their attacks, cutting into the Protector lines, but they still kept coming. It was as if the losses they were sustaining didn't matter at all. They were a group with a singular purpose.

Several strike-fighters were shot down, and each time they tried to provide covering fire for the pilot, they were met with heavy resistance until the Protectors killed their targets.

A general comms signal to clear the area came from Varek on the cruiser. As soon as the strike-fighter squadrons cleared the area, a salvo fired from the cruiser in low orbit, raining hell down on the Protectors.

Kaylan had swung her craft around to line up for another attack run when she noticed that they were almost upon the Haven. She peered at the map on her heads-up display to double-check what she was seeing. There were large shuttles taking off and landing, along with massive transport carriers.

A comms channel opened to them from the Haven.

"All strike-fighters, break off your attack. You're to run escort for the shuttles and carriers. They're to be covered for their entire duration near the planet. Once they're out of range, you're to await the next ship to return to the planet surface. This will continue until all refugees are free. Battle Commander, out."

Kaylan flew her ship towards the landing zone on the far side of the Haven. She understood why Kladomaor had given the orders. There was no way they were going to keep the Protectors from getting inside the compound, and eventually those troops would circle around and attack the landing zone. A large shuttle lifted off the ground and she and Hicks flew as escorts. There weren't any shots fired at them from the Protectors and Kaylan assumed they weren't close enough yet until she glanced to the side and saw the nearly continuous rain of fire from the cruiser.

They neared the edge of the atmosphere and Kaylan brought her fighter to a stop, hovering. She and Hicks monitored the shuttle as it headed for the star carrier. Kaylan frowned as if there was something off about what she was seeing.

"There's another shuttle coming," Hicks said.

"Alright, I . . ." Kaylan's voice trailed off.

Something was definitely off. The shuttle that had just left the planet slowed down on its approach to the star carrier. Target-lock alarms flashed across her heads-up display as bright red flashes spawned from the shuttle's hull and small, tear-shaped ships flew towards them.

Kaylan's mouth went dry. "Drones!" she cried and engaged the thrusters.

Hicks was right behind her. "I thought we took care of all of them," he said.

She locked in her target and opened fire. She got one and the other drones attacking the shuttles veered off to meet their attack.

"At least it's not the waves of them we saw before. How about I give them something to chase and you take them out?" Kaylan said.

"I've got your back," Hicks replied.

Kaylan sped forward, firing the plasma cannons and angling away from the drones so they'd chase her. She flew in close to the shuttle's hull so the drones couldn't get a clear shot of her ship. Hicks took out the group one by one, chasing her. They alerted the cruiser of the drone presence and a general alert went out to all fighters.

"The timing of the drones showing up again is suspicious," Hicks said.

"You think the Protector's are controlling them somehow?" Kaylan asked.

"We start getting Boxans off the planet and drones suddenly start showing up again. It's not that much of a stretch," Hicks said.

Another shuttle was making a return run to the planet. They had to keep their formations tighter due to the drone threat.

Kaylan watched the scan readout and she heard Hicks suddenly gasp.

"Oh shit! Damn it!" Hicks said.

Kaylan flew around the shuttle and saw a trail of vapor leaking from Hicks's strike-fighter.

"One of those drones flew right into my engines," Hicks said.

The tail sections were blackened with damage and she watched as he struggled to keep the ship straight.

"Head back to the cruiser," Kaylan said.

"I'm not going to leave you, Commander," Hicks said.

"Fine, then it's an order. You're no good up here anymore. Get back to the cruiser," Kaylan said.

Hicks's fighter stayed where it was and she could just imagine him sitting there with that brooding intensity of his when he was feeling mulish.

"Please," Kaylan said.

"Alright, I'll get back to the cruiser and get another ship," Hicks said and pulled away from the shuttle.

The shuttle that was heading toward the surface changed its approach angle and swung out back into space.

Kaylan opened a comms channel to the shuttle.

"Commander," Gaarokk said. "Kladomoar ordered all shuttles to head back to the star carrier."

"Who's left on the surface?" Kaylan asked.

"There's a large transport carrier and a shuttle," Gaarokk said.

"Did they get everyone out?"

"The last of them are being loaded on those ships—" Gaarokk's voice suddenly cut out.

Kaylan frowned. The comms channel was still opened. "Gaarokk what's wrong?"

"Commander, the drones are making another attack run."

Kaylan engaged the thrusters and maneuvered around the shuttle. "Get back to the star carrier," she said.

Kaylan swung around the shuttle and saw a swarm of drones heading toward her. There was no way she could take them all on her own. There must be a command-and-control unit nearby.

The heavy cruiser moved toward her and opened fire on the drones.

"Athena, can you detect any command-and-control signals for the drones?"

"The cruiser's scans don't reveal any trace signals for the drones," the AI said.

Kaylan frowned. "What about on the planet where the Protectors are."

She moved the strike-fighter away from the heavy cruiser. The cyber warfare suite was targeting the drones and taking them out, but the progress was painfully slow. They could still do a lot of damage to the remaining shuttles and transport carrier yet to leave the surface.

"I'm unable to detect a clear signal from the planetary surface, but there's a high probability that your instincts are correct. I've uploaded the known command-and-control signals to your ship," Athena said.

Kaylan engaged the thrusters and sped toward the planet.

32

Kladomaor watched as the combat shuttles hovered over the troop carrier. The refugees hurried aboard the shuttles and carriers with a smooth efficiency that must have come from countless practice drills and living under the threat of losing their homes at a moment's notice. He'd tried to get Councilor Essaforn to leave with one of the earlier transports, but she'd adamantly refused and had instead stuck by his side. He'd been at the front line, fighting alongside his soldiers and the fighters from Haven. They fought well, and their battle songs would be sung throughout the great expanse. The Haven's automated defenses had helped stem the Protectors for a time, but they eventually failed. They had fallen back to the landing zone, making sure all the refugees would get on a ship. These would be the last.

A comms channel opened to him.

"Time to go, Battle Commander," Zack said.

Kladomaor swung his gaze toward the last shuttle, nearly scolding the Human who had the least amount of flight experience because he was the last to leave the planet—the most dangerous run of all.

The transport carrier engines propelled the ship into the air. Plasma blasts from nearby combat mechs fired into the hull, and Kladomaor raised his weapon and fired back at the mechs. Boxan soldiers followed his lead and a combat shuttle moved to intercept, firing a salvo back at the relentless Protectors.

Kladomaor glanced up and saw the transport carrier speed away from them.

The combat shuttle exploded and Kladomaor threw himself over Councilor Essaforn to protect her from harm. He regained his feet and helped the councilor up.

"Fall back," Kladomaor said.

They retreated toward the last shuttle, which hovered in the air and came toward them with the cargo bay doors opened. The soldiers fired on the Protector forces as they climbed aboard the shuttle. The ship dipped dangerously to the side and then righted itself. Kladomaor stood just inside the cargo bay and fired his weapon into a line of combat mechs. The soldiers on either side of him were hit and went down. His weapon stopped firing, its power cell depleted. He roared his defiance at what the Xiiginns had wrought upon his species.

Plasma blasts from above rained down on the approaching Protector line, leaving flaming stumps in their wake.

"Whoever's piloting that shuttle, go now! I've got you covered," Kaylan said.

"Kaylan!" Zack said.

"Not now, Human. You heard her. Go!" Kladomaor said.

The cargo bay doors closed and the shuttle lurched upward. Kladomaor raced toward the cockpit and the Boxan refugees scrambled to get out of his way.

Zack's gaze stayed focused on the readout in front of him. The engines were at maximum.

"That's all she's got. We took quite a beating," Zack said.

Kladomaor sat in the copilot's seat. The overfilled shuttle was still gaining altitude.

"What the hell is that?" Zack said.

In the distance, a swarm of drones were attacking the heavy cruiser, with smaller groups heading toward the last shuttles that were making their way toward the star carrier. A large pack of tear-shaped drones broke off from the main group and headed straight for them.

"Turn the ship around," Kladomaor said.

AFTER TAKING out the combat mech, Kaylan sped over the remaining Protectors, scanning for the command-and-control signal that she'd gotten from the Athena. The Protectors had been so focused on the transport carrier that they hadn't paid any mind to one strike-fighter as she'd flown over them. Her plasma cannons were almost depleted of ammunition. She banked to the side, maximizing the strike-fighter's scanning range. As she approached the rear line of Protectors, she got a positive ping and a target-lock for the drone command-and-control signal.

There was a ring of mechs protecting a small tower. Kaylan sped toward it and the combat mechs opened fire. She weaved back and forth, narrowly avoiding the plasma bolts, and returned fire. The strike-fighter's cannons flared to life and her own plasma bolts ripped through the line of combat mechs, cutting the transmitter tower in half. She let out a gasp and swung the ship up and away from the Protectors. Plasma bolts slammed into her fighter and Kaylan fought to maintain control of her ship.

THE SHUTTLE WAS slow to respond to the controls as Zack tried turning the ship around. Since they'd never left Sethion's atmosphere, they gained some speed as they returned toward the surface. Fireballs were shooting past the nose of the shuttle as if a sudden meteor shower were occurring.

"Now what?" Zack said.

Kladomaor glanced out the shuttle's windows. "It's the drones. Their trajectory is off. It's as if they're just falling out of the sky."

"The command signal must be offline," Zack said.

Kladomaor nodded and opened up a comms channel back to the cruiser. "Varek, what's your status?"

"Sustained heavy damage, Battle Commander. We lost two of the shuttles. All transport carriers are accounted for and on board the star carrier," Varek said.

Zack's eyes widened. "What about the strike-fighters?"

"There are some still unaccounted for, including Kaylan's," Varek said.

Zack's stomach sank to his feet and he shifted in his chair. His hands went to the controls, but he didn't know what to do. He looked out the window at the planet's surface.

He opened a broadcast comms channel. "Kaylan, do you read?"

Zack's eyes were glued to the holo-interface while he waited for a response.

"Battle Commander," Varek said. "Detecting an energy anomaly at the Haven."

"Send us your readings," Kladomaor said.

The holoscreen showed a series of readings and Kladomaor sat back in his chair, looking worried.

A comms channel opened and the strike-fighter's designate came onscreen. "Kaylan here. I've taken out the control unit for the drones, but my ship has taken damage. Engines are working at twenty percent and falling."

"Kaylan, we read you," Zack said and looked at Kladomaor. "What does that mean? Twenty percent."

Kladomaor didn't reply. "Kaylan, you need to put as much distance between yourself and the Haven as you can. Twenty percent engine capacity isn't enough for you to break orbit."

"Acknowledged," Kaylan said.

"Set down somewhere and we can pick you up," Zack said.

"No," Kladomaor said. "You must listen to me and fly away as fast as you can."

The scanners showed a strike-fighter flying alongside them and then a strange alarm sounded, showing symbols Zack didn't understand.

"Battle Commander, you need to get that shuttle away to escape the blast radius," Varek advised.

Zack frowned. "What's he talking about?"

Kladomaor stared at him intently. "The Protectors have a nuclear bomb with an energy signature capable of decimating the entire northern ice shelf."

Zack's eyes darted to the windows and back to Kladomaor. "How do we get her out of there?"

Kladomaor shook his head.

"How do we get her out of there?" Zack asked again and then slammed his fist on the console. "Kaylan, you have to get out of there. You have to try," he said, his voice croaking at the end.

"Zack," Kaylan said.

His hands went for the shuttle's controls, preparing for maximum thrust.

"You have to turn the shuttle around. All those Boxans are depending on you to get them to safety," Kaylan said.

The comms channel went offline in a haze of static.

Zack's vision blurred and he hastily wiped his eyes. Kladomaor shifted in his seat and Zack's hands flung to his sidearm. He pulled the pistol out and pointed it at the Boxan Battle Commander.

"I swear to God if you try to take control of this ship from me I'll squeeze the trigger," Zack said. "I'll do it! I swear to God I will. I won't leave her!"

Kladomaor held up his hands and the knowing look that Kaylan's death was all but certain struck Zack like a blow. "Is that what she would want?" he asked calmly.

Zack's shoulders slumped. His mind raced, trying to think of a way to save Kaylan, but there was nothing he could do. He couldn't even talk to her. He dropped the pistol and it clanged to the floor. Glaring at the planet below, he swung the shuttle around, heading away from the Haven and hating himself for doing it.

He watched the radar screen that showed Kaylan's strike-fighter.

Another strike-fighter zipped passed the shuttle.

"I've got her, Casanova. You get those Boxans to safety." Katie Garcia's voice sounded over comms.

THE STRIKE-FIGHTER's control panel was damaged and Kaylan didn't know how the ship was even still flying. She tried to nurse the craft along and gain as much altitude as she could, but engine capacity was down to ten percent. She'd taken fire from the Protectors after taking out the control tower and had barely escaped.

"Commander, at your current speed, you won't escape the blast radius of the Protector bomb," the Athena's AI said, its voice coming through the speakers inside her helmet.

"I know," Kaylan said.

She maintained her ascent, knowing the futility of it, but she had to try. She knew the engines would give out and then she'd either crash the ship and die or be caught in a nuclear blast. Kaylan clenched her teeth together and felt her heart pound in her ears. This was it; she was going to die here. Her panic-stricken thoughts raced and then a sense of calm came over her. She shifted her gaze to the sky above, thinking of Zack and how he would never forgive her for dying on him. A crushing pang of guilt filled the back of her throat as she instantly regretted all of those lost moments they could have had. There was always something drawing their attention, whether it was her training or Zack trying to figure out how to bring down the Shroud barrier protecting Earth. Her vision blurred with the tears she couldn't hold back anymore and her thoughts drifted to the family she'd left behind on Earth and how she'd never see any of them again —how she and Zack would never go to the island getaway they'd mused about. She really just wanted to lie on the sand and listen to the sound of the waves as they lulled her away to a peaceful oblivion.

A high-level chime pierced her thoughts. The engine was down to four percent and she was no longer gaining altitude. This was it.

A bright flash engulfed the sky in a blazing white light. Kaylan twisted around in her seat and saw a gigantic mushroom cloud spreading from the Haven. She drew in a deep breath and blew it out, but as she was turning back around, something sped past her ship so fast that she thought she might have imagined it. Without warning, Kaylan was jarred against her seat as something slammed into the back of her ship. There was another heavy bump and she was knocked to the side. Kaylan pulled herself up and craned her neck to see what was behind her.

Kaylan let out small, jubilant laugh as she saw Katie Garcia waving at her. Katie gestured to her helmet and Kaylan turned on her suit-to-suit comms.

"Hang on. I don't think these ships were designed for this," Katie said.

Kaylan turned back around and adjusted the straps so she was secure.

"This won't be gentle," Katie said.

The strike-fighter slammed into her ship with unrelenting force. With her own strike-fighter's systems damaged, there were no inertia dampeners and Kaylan bore the crushing G-forces as they reached escape velocity. She gritted her teeth and fought to stay conscious.

"Just hold on a little longer," Katie urged.

Kaylan squeezed her eyes shut. A sharp, stabbing pain spread like lightning across her middle. The strike-fighter shook violently and Kaylan cried out, blinking phosphenes from her vision as she felt her consciousness start to slip away. Katie Garcia called out to her and it sounded as if she were speaking through a long, dark tunnel. With the last shred of her strength leaving, the darkness swallowed her up.

33

Ed Johnson had a few vices he absolutely must surrender to whenever he was in the city that never sleeps. The island of Manhattan itself was home to as many foreigners as Americans these days, but the old culture that'd made the foundation of New York City what it was today could still be found. The Luxury Towncar pulled to a stop. Iris Barrett climbed inside and handed him a small white paper bag. Ed took the bag and opened it, already catching a whiff of the contents.

"Those things will kill you," Iris said.

Ed breathed in the sweet smell of dried onion and garlic flakes and peeked inside the bag. "I know they will, but you can't come to New York and not have either pizza or an Everything Bagel with cream cheese," he said, taking a healthy bite. The creamy blend of flavors caressed his mouth and he sighed happily while he chewed.

Iris handed him a napkin. Ed took it and offered her the other half of his bagel, but Iris just shook her head with a slightly bemused expression.

The driver pulled the car away from the curb and they resumed their journey to the UN.

"How many years has it been since you've eaten bread?" Ed asked.

Iris arched a brow toward him. "I'm sure that information is in my dossier," she said.

Ed finished half of the bagel and decided to save the other half for later. The meeting today with the UN Security Council was something of a special occasion since there would be Boxan representatives planet-side for once.

"Well, I'd like to know," Ed said.

Iris was glancing out the window, almost constantly on the lookout for any threats to his life.

The car pulled in front of the UN building and they were guided to a queue, along with everyone else. Usually Ed would have flown in, but he'd been looking forward to an authentic New York City bagel for a long time.

"Since I was seven years old, and I've been healthy ever since," Iris said.

He tried to imagine Iris as a child and couldn't. She opened the door and took a look around before gesturing for him to follow. They walked across the campus and headed toward one of the entranceways.

"I've forwarded the agenda to your PDA," Iris said.

Ed used his implants to bring it up on his own internal heads-up display.

"So you're going to tell them today then?" Iris said.

Ed nodded. "They have to know the barrier is a short-term fix."

"You need to give them a timeline. Otherwise, it'll just get put on top of the large pile of things that need to be done," Iris said.

"We need to study the barrier as much as we need to build ships. If the latest projections are accurate, it could be disastrous for the entire solar system," Ed said.

He was so busy reviewing the meeting agenda that he walked right into Iris. Ed started to trip, but Iris caught him with one hand and held onto him. He looked up at her and saw that she was looking across the courtyard. Ed connected his neural link to Iris's implants so he could see what she saw.

A Boxan stood in full power armor in the middle of the courtyard. He was so still that Ed would have missed him. The scan from Iris's implants had broken down the power armor into units.

"What do you suppose he's doing there?" Ed asked.

Iris frowned. "Ed, you need to go back to the car and get out of here," she said.

"What is it?"

The Boxan's identity appeared on his HUD. Eavoth, Strike Commander.

"That's the one who went with Kyle Mathews to investigate the Shroud monitoring devices," Ed said.

He'd made it a point to familiarize himself with all the joint Human-Boxan missions since they were still so infrequent. When that changed, there would be no way he'd be able to keep track of it all.

The Boxan Strike Commander noticed them and charged.

The breath caught in Ed's throat and Iris shoved him back. Then she ran towards the charging Boxan, pulled out her stun baton, and leaped to the side, jamming the baton into the Boxan's side. The maximum amount of voltage released through the baton, but the Boxan didn't slow down.

Iris ran in front of the Boxan. He tried to grab her, but she scrambled out of the way. She grabbed his hand and tried to use the Boxan's momentum, but he pulled her into the air.

Iris held on and glanced over at Ed. "Detonator," she said through gritted teeth.

Ed backed away several steps and froze for a second, not knowing what to do. The Boxan seemed focused on him despite Iris's attempts to fight him off. Ed sent a coded message to the UN Security force and alarms started going off.

Automated bomb detection units would be dispatched, but Ed wasn't sure if they could detect whatever the Boxan had done.

The Boxan threw Iris off of him as if swatting a fly and focused his flaxen-eyed gaze on Ed. Ed glanced over at Iris's crumpled form on the ground. The Boxan took a few steps toward him and Ed started running, hearing the heavy footsteps of the Boxan chasing him. He veered off toward the streets and heard people screaming. Why was the Boxan suddenly trying to kill him? It didn't make any sense.

There was a loud pop, followed by a bright flash, and Ed was pushed to the side. He tumbled to the ground, people still running and screaming around him. There was smoke rising from the UN and a large chunk of the building was gone.

The UN Security forces arrived, firing their weapons at the Boxan while Ed scrambled back, his eyes wide. Their weapons had hardly any effect on the Boxan, and the ten-foot-tall alien closed in on him.

Seemingly out of nowhere, a plasma bolt slammed into the Boxan's chest, followed by another that ripped through the armor, and the Boxan collapsed to the ground. Ed gasped as the security force turned and pointed their weapons toward him. Glancing behind, he saw Scraanyx, but the Boxan glanced at the security force and held up his weapon, slowly placing it on the ground in front of him.

The UN security force shouted for Scraanyx to get on his knees and Ed watched as the Boxan complied with the security force's commands amid the sounds of other law enforcement agencies arriving.

Ed got to his feet and found the UN security force captain. "He just saved our lives," he said.

The captain spared him a look. "My orders come from the top. All Boxans are to be detained. This is one of three UN headquarters that were attacked today."

Ed glanced at the Boxan. Scraanyx looked as if he wanted to fight, but the enemy he was looking for wasn't there. He looked over at Ed. "Xiiginns," he said.

Ed's stomach clenched and his mind became a jumble of questions. "We'll get this sorted out," he promised.

Scraanyx regarded him for a moment. "None of us are safe. You must prepare yourself."

Sirens blared from the arriving fire trucks. Ed glanced around at the chaos before him. People were hurt and smoke billowed up to the New York City skyline. Ed couldn't help but think that this was only the beginning. Somehow the Xiiginns had made it to Earth.

He turned back toward the UN building. Iris had been close to the building, but he wasn't sure if she'd been caught in the blast. His implants had recorded the entire event and he took it back to when the Boxan had charged him. The glint in his eyes told of a being that was ready to kill. Ed froze the image and looked for some sign of an internal struggle, some sign that the Boxan hadn't totally succumbed to the Xiiginn influence, but there was none. He glanced around, hearing all the sounds of the city, and felt utterly exposed. This was only the beginning.

34

Kaylan's mouth was dry and she tried to swallow.

"Here, drink some water," Zack said and held a straw to her mouth.

She sucked in some water and drank it down.

"Brenda, she's awake," Zack said.

Kaylan opened her eyes to see Zack and Brenda looking down at her. She tried to sit up but Brenda held her down.

"Take it easy. It's only been a few hours and you've broken a couple of ribs. Need to give the nanobots time to speed up the healing," Brenda said.

Zack used the bed controls to raise her up. Her ribs ached but nothing like what she'd felt in the strike-fighter. He placed his hand gently on her shoulder. Kaylan's whole body ached.

Brenda told her to look at the light as she tested Kaylan's responses. "You're going to be fine. I'll give you something for the pain, but you just need to rest for a bit."

"Where are we?" Kaylan asked.

"We're in the med bay on the cruiser," Zack said.

"Have we left Sethion's star system?"

Zack shook his head. "No, there's been some debate about where the refugees are going."

Zack told her that they were still bringing up the star carrier's systems and an engineering team was checking over the critical systems before they opened a wormhole.

Kaylan swung her feet to the side of the bed.

"What do you think you're doing?" Zack asked.

Kaylan winced. "The Boxans could give a rock lessons in stubbornness. We can't stay here any longer than necessary."

Brenda came over from across the room. "Can't you sit still for five minutes?"

"There's too much to be done. Can you give me something to help get me going?" Kaylan said.

Brenda glanced at Zack imploringly.

"Just for a few hours and then I'll rest. I promise," Kaylan said.

"A few hours," Brenda said sternly and then looked at Zack. "You'll see that it's only a little while."

Zack nodded. "I'll have the Athena lock her out of the systems temporarily."

Kaylan scowled at him, but it lacked any real vehemence. Brenda returned with a cigar-shaped device and pressed one end to the skin of her neck. There was a snap-hiss as the stimulants entered her system. The skin on her neck burned and Kaylan winced, but the bone weariness abated and the pain in her ribs faded to a dull ache.

Kaylan got to her feet, expecting to be a bit wobbly, but she was fine. She glanced at Brenda. "Thank you. I promise, just a few hours."

Zack mumbled something about keeping an eye on her as they left the med bay. Boxan soldiers were walking past them and Kaylan suddenly stopped. She turned to Zack, the breath catching in her throat. They'd almost lost each other, and the two of them gazed into each other's eyes. Zack's were red-rimmed with worry, but his gaze softened when he looked at her.

"Kaylan . . ." he said.

She grabbed him by his shirt and kissed the hell out of him as they stood in the corridor, then pulled him into a hard embrace and pushed herself away. "I needed to do that."

"You can do that whenever you want for as long as you need," Zack said.

Kaylan lips curved. "Let's go to the bridge and see what the holdup is."

They headed for the bridge and Kaylan felt better than she had in a long time. It could have been the drugs Brenda had given her, but she also thought it was the fact that they were still alive. They'd done what the Boxan High Council had been reluctant to do.

They reached the bridge and the doors opened. Zack gestured for her to go first and she led the way in. Kladomaor was seated on the command couch with Ma'jasalax at his side. Etanu and Ezerah stood off to the side, listening to High Councilor Awan speak. Councilor Essaforn and Valkra were there, along with a wizened old Boxan Kaylan had never seen before. The old Boxan glanced over at them and there was a flash of recognition when he looked at Zack.

"As I've told you, if you bring the star carrier to Olloron, you won't be allowed to land or even enter the system," High Councilor Awan said.

Councilor Essaforn fixed her gaze on him. "We're Boxans. We deserve a place at the colony."

They stopped speaking when they noticed Kaylan and Zack standing there.

Councilor Essaforn's hard gaze softened when she looked at Kaylan. "I'm so glad you're feeling better. Ma'jasalax has told me how you pleaded with the High Council on our behalf. High Councilor Awan is convinced their fleet will shoot our ship down should we try to enter Olloron's star system."

"He's not misleading you at all," Kaylan said.

"Then what is to become of us? We have wounded and very few resources of our own," Councilor Essaforn said.

"You should leverage the Boxans' only ally in this and then open communications with the colony. The Nershals' generous offer is the best you're going to get at the moment. They might not allow you to go to Nerva, but there's certainly room on Selebus moon to get settled and regroup," Zack said.

Councilor Essaforn glanced at Etanu and Ezerah. "I appreciate the sentiment, but as you've stated, you're not official emissaries for the Nershals. What if we were to go there, only to be turned away again?"

"Ezerah's family stands high in the Nershals' global congress. They won't turn you away," Kaylan said.

"You will not be turned away, I assure you," Ezerah said.

"There are three hundred thousand of us. Given the state of things, some might view this as an invasion force. But miscommunications aside, there are Boxans from the colony there and part of the fleet. You can see how our presence might be the catalyst for things to get out of control?" Councilor Essaforn said.

Kaylan cleared her throat. "I suggest you be open and honest about the situation. The Boxan fleet is there to support the Nershals' defense of the system against the Xiiginns. We can't stay here. The Boxans aren't the only ones monitoring the quarantine zone. You should go to Selebus and ask the Nershals to act as intermediaries between the Boxans that are of the colony and yourselves. I believe that if you do this, the colony will become open to you eventually, or at the very least they'll send aid."

Councilor Essaforn glanced at Kladomaor and Ma'jasalax.

"I agree with Kaylan," Ma'jasalax said.

"I do as well," High Councilor Awan said. "And I'll do everything in my power to see that your voices are heard," he said, looking at Kaylan. "You were right and we should have heeded your warning from the beginning. We should have returned to Sethion much sooner."

Kaylan regarded the high councilor for a moment. "And the colony? You know as well as I that it's not a viable place for you in the long term."

High Councilor Awan pressed his lips together and frowned. "Has anyone ever told you that you're relentless?"

"Welcome to dealing with Humans," Kladomaor said.

Kaylan smiled and heard Zack mumble something under his breath.

"One thing at a time. I understand your intentions are for the betterment of our species, but it will take time," High Councilor Awan said.

It was something, at least. Kaylan nodded.

Councilor Essaforn looked at Kladomaor. "Have you considered my offer?" she asked.

"Let's get to Selebus and take care of everything there first. Then we'll discuss your offer," Kladomaor said.

Kaylan glanced at Zack and he shrugged. The meeting ended and preparations were being made for them to leave shortly.

Ma'jasalax made her way over to Kaylan and Valkra followed. "You've done enough for one day," she said.

Kaylan frowned. "I'm feeling fine. I just needed to make sure things were in hand."

Valkra bowed her head to Kaylan. "After you're rested, I'd like to discuss the connection we shared through the Mardoxian chamber."

"Of course," Kaylan said.

Zack urged her to leave the bridge and get some rest, occasionally glancing worriedly over at Kladomaor. When they left the bridge she asked him what was bothering him.

"I, uh, threatened Kladomaor while we were on the shuttle," Zack said.

Kaylan's eyes widened.

"I apologized, but you know. Sometimes the heat of the moment gets the better of us," Zack said.

Kaylan took his hand and let him guide her back to the med bay for some rest.

35

K yle glanced at the time. It had been six hours since he and the others had escaped from their holding cell. No alarm had been raised, which he knew couldn't last much longer.

"Another patrol is coming," Tom whispered.

Six hours wasn't enough time to determine whether these were routine patrols or if the Xiiginns had been alerted to their presence. They were due to meet Dawson and Pearson, and Kyle hoped they'd found a way for them to get off this ship.

Kyle tried to blend in with the dark corner behind a network of piping. At his feet, the unconscious Xiiginn they'd surprised earlier began to stir and the Xiiginn patrol was almost upon them. Tom glanced down at the Xiiginn and his eyes widened when he saw the alien's tail begin to twitch. Kyle raised a finger to his lips so Tom would keep quiet.

The Xiiginn soldiers' heavy footfalls tromped toward them and Kyle held his breath. At his feet, the Xiiginn's arm started to move. Kyle gritted his teeth and squatted over the Xiiginn, wrapping an arm around the alien's neck. The Xiiginn started to struggle and its tail flicked to the side so Kyle planted his foot on it. He'd learned the hard way how much trouble those things could be. The Xiiginn started making choking sounds and Kyle clamped his hand over the alien's mouth, hoping the noise would be drowned out by the steady hissing of the piping network. He squeezed as hard as he could. The Xiiginns were strong, even the lowly tech they'd found working in these tunnels. Kyle didn't think he could break the alien's neck, but he knew they breathed oxygen, and if he could cut off the supply long enough the Xiiginn would lose consciousness again.

They were off to the side in a maintenance alcove, utterly exposed should the soldiers bother to look. The choking sounds became louder as the soldiers were almost upon them so Kyle gritted his teeth and squeezed. The Xiiginn's struggles weakened and stopped altogether, but Kyle held on until the end. He couldn't risk him regaining consciousness again.

"They're gone," Tom said.

The young tech comms specialist looked down at the dead Xiiginn as if he wasn't quite sure that he was seeing a dead body. Kyle pushed the body to the side.

"You killed him," Tom said.

"I couldn't risk him waking up," Kyle answered while searching the dead Xiiginn.

"I know they'd do worse to us if they caught us, but it's just so . . ."

"Real," Kyle said. "Stay focused. Were you able to access our shuttle's systems before it left?"

Tom tore his eyes away from the dead Xiiginn. "Yes, I was able to insert a message under the maintenance cycle, but I don't know when the cycle will be run. Even if they return to the ECF base, it still could be some time before the two computer systems run the routine, and then the person monitoring would have to notice the message."

"It's the best we can do right now. I didn't plan on Eavoth and the others leaving so soon. Also, I don't think they're returning to the ECF base," Kyle said.

Tom frowned. "Why not?"

"We won't be on the shuttle, so if they returned to base without us, they'd need to explain our absence," Kyle said.

He scampered to the edge of the alcove and peered around the corner, finding the way empty. He gestured for Tom to follow and they headed to where they were due to meet the others. Since the Boxans had left them, Kyle assumed they were getting close to Earth. Unfortunately, once the shuttle was gone they couldn't communicate with each other using their implants and their PDAs had been taken from them. They returned to the tunnels beneath the hangar area and waited for the others. Tom kept shifting position and fidgeting in place.

"We're going to be fine," Kyle said.

He wasn't sure if he believed it himself but knew that a little bit of hope could get the people under one's command to focus. It just might be enough to do what they needed.

"What if the Xiiginns caught the others?"

"They didn't."

"How do you know?"

"Because these tunnels would be crawling with Xiiginns if they had," Kyle said.

Tom frowned and then sighed. "I didn't think it would be like this . . . coming out here."

"You and me both. I never imagined that any Xiiginns made it through the barrier. Now it seems really foolish for us and everyone else to have believed it," Kyle said.

Tom glanced at him, his eyes wide.

Kyle looked away, keeping an eye out for the others. Within a few minutes, Lieutenant Dawson and Corporal Pearson came around the corner. They each were armed with the same rifles the Xiiginn soldiers used. A cold icy pit settled into his stomach. Could they be under the Xiiginn influence?

"Colonel," Dawson said, "we ambushed a patrol and took their weapons. They're strong, but take them by surprise and they're just as vulnerable as anyone else."

Kyle nodded. "Good work. Did you find a way to get out of here?"

He glanced at Pearson, who was keeping an eye on the tunnels.

"Yeah, but not here. This hangar is much too secure. We've found a smaller hangar where they're adapting escape pods," Dawson said.

"Adapting them for what?" Kyle asked.

Dawson frowned. "We don't have much time. We should head over there. We observed a shift change and heard the Xiiginns talking about how hard they're being worked. They're following a rigid schedule, but there are a few minutes when we can get inside and take one of the pods. Did you guys have any luck contacting Earth?"

"Tom was able to embed a message in the shuttle's maintenance systems before it left, but by the time the ECF finds the shuttle it might already be too late," Kyle said.

"Then it's up to us," Dawson said and glanced over at Pearson, who was still keeping watch.

Kyle looked at Tom and gave a slight shake of his head. He'd have to trust that Dawson and Pearson weren't under the Xiiginn influence.

"Alright, lead the way," Kyle said.

Pearson brought up the rear while Lieutenant Dawson led them through the tunnels. Kyle supposed he could have asked for one of their weapons. As a superior officer, he'd be within his rights to do so without question, but if one or both of them were under the Xiiginn influence, his order for them to surrender one of their weapons could lead to a confrontation. He thought about warning Tom but ruled it out. The young tech comms specialist was barely keeping it together as it was.

Dawson led them through a series of adjoining, low-ceiling tunnels and they spent much of the time crawling on their hands and knees. Eventually they came to a maintenance hatch and Dawson motioned for them to stop. The lieutenant cocked his ear toward the hatch, listening for a moment, and then opened it. He stepped out and the rest of them followed. Pearson closed the hatch. Dawson led them down a dimly lit corridor and into a dark room. It seemed that the Xiiginns were conserving power.

Dawson led them over to the far side of the room and, looking through a window, they saw a group of Xiiginns working on circular pods. They quickly squatted back down below the window to avoid being seen.

"See, it's a small hangar and they put the finished pods close to the exit," Dawson said.

Kyle took another look to get a better feel for the layout and then came back down. "I count at least seven Xiiginns in there."

"Why would they be modifying escape pods?" Tom asked.

Kyle pressed his lips together for a moment in thought. "The only thing I can think of is drop ships."

Tom frowned. "By drop ships, you mean to get their troops to the surface of Earth?"

Kyle nodded. "We've got to be close to Earth. We know from the Boxans that the escape pods they use have homing beacons on them. They're likely disabling the beacons."

"If there's a beacon on it, I can use it to send a signal to ECF command," Tom said.

"What we don't know is how much flying we're able to do in one of those things," Dawson said.

"It's about time we find out. Good work you two. This is our best chance of getting out of here," Kyle said.

An audible tone sounded above, silencing them all at once. Thinking the Xiiginns had finally discovered their escape, Kyle glanced back into the hangar to see the Xiiginns leaving their posts. He ducked back down, noting that several were heading towards the room they were in and there was nowhere for them to hide. Kyle held up three fingers for Dawson and then gestured at the door nearest them. Dawson nodded and then motioned for Pearson to get ready.

The door opened and the Xiiginns came inside. Dawson fired his weapon and bright flashes from the green bolts dropped two Xiiginns, but the last one screamed before Pearson shot him.

"Go," Kyle said.

Dawson went through the door first and they filed to the side, taking cover behind one of the round escape pods. Kyle heard more Xiiginns running over to investigate the noise and more shouts soon followed. They ran toward the hangar exit and green bolts zipped past them, narrowly missing. Pearson turned around and fired a few shots back, giving them some time to reach the pods. They came to the hangar exit, and in the distance, beyond the atmospheric containment shield, was a bright blue ball. Dawson took position behind them and they traded fire with the Xiiginns in the hangar. They were out of time. Kyle knew more soldiers were coming and it was only a matter of time before they'd be overwhelmed.

He and Tom circled around the escape pod, found the entrance, and went inside. There were seats around the edge with a control panel in the center. Tom went to work bringing up the interface and Kyle shouted for the others to get inside. Pearson came in first and Dawson took up position inside the doorway.

"Now would be a good time to get us out of here," Kyle said.

Tom was waving his hands, navigating through the controls, his face twisted into a frown. "I've got it. Doors closing," he said.

The escape pod doors began to shut and Dawson took a seat. The Xiiginns continued to fire from outside the pod.

Kyle glanced at Tom. "What are you waiting for?"

"Colonel, the navigation system already has preprogrammed coordinates—"

Tom was cut off by a loud blast from outside the pod.

"If it takes us to Earth, then I don't care. Get us out of here," Kyle said.

Tom hit the button and the escape pod's engines ignited. The burst pushed them back in their seats and Kyle held on. It felt like the pod was spinning out of control. Secondary engines fired and the escape pod leveled off. They couldn't see anything, and Kyle heard Dawson muttering a prayer.

36

Mar Arden stood on the bridge of what remained of the warship. Hoan Berend sat on the command couch and was busy going through the reports on his console. Once he finished, he came over to Mar Arden.

"They've escaped," Hoan Berend said.

Mar Arden glanced at the commander. "You think letting them go is a mistake?"

"I've learned to trust in your plans," Hoan Berend replied.

Mar Arden glanced at the main holoscreen that showed the planet Earth, home to the Humans. "There's a planet full of Humans down there for us to exploit. I'm not concerned about losing four of them."

The door to the bridge opened and Kandra Rene walked in, striding purposefully to Mar Arden's side. "The Humans killed a few of our crew while escaping and we found some dead in the engineering tunnels," Kandra Rene said.

Mar Arden nodded. "If they were better soldiers, they'd still be alive. The methods the Humans used to escape reveals much about their species, however."

"The tunnels are a weakness, but the fact that the Humans managed to arm themselves is another matter," Hoan Berend said.

"Don't waste your time trying to secure this place any more than you already have. We won't be here that long. Our destination is out there," Mar Arden said and gestured toward the distant blue orb.

Hoan Berend looked at Kandra Rene. "You're positive that compulsion has worked on at least one of them."

Kandra Rene's gaze narrowed menacingly. "They're under my power and will initiate contact at the appointed time."

Hoan Berend nodded and looked at Mar Arden. "What's our next move?"

Mar Arden switched the view on the main holoscreen, which now showed multiple communication signals. They hadn't needed to initiate any scans to detect these signals. Their proximity to the planet was enough to start receiving them.

"The attack was a success. The Human and Boxan alliance is still tenuous, and with recent events, those relations will be further strained. The Humans will learn that they can't rely on the Boxans, and while they're scrambling around trying to figure out who to trust, we'll move into position," Mar Arden said.

"You still believe the reason the Boxans are here is because the Mardoxian potential is in Humans?" Hoan Berend said.

"I'm certain of it," Mar Arden said and brought up one of the recorded video streams.

An aged Human male came on screen and began to speak. "The Earth Coalition Force is humanity's answer to the alien threat. Would you like to work in space and fly on one the ships we're building for the first Human fleet? Perhaps the challenge in researching the latest in advanced technology calls to you. To realize your true potential, report to your local testing center and participate in the ECF's prescreening initiatives to help find where you'd best serve to protect our home."

The recorded video ended and Mar Arden looked at them.

"You see, they've already initiated a screening process, essentially doing our job for us. Now we'll know who to target once we get down there. So, you see, I'm not overly concerned with four prisoners escaping. The attacks already announced our presence, and before long, Humanity will learn to fear the Xiiginns even more than they already do," Mar Arden said.

He crossed his arms in front of him and the main holoscreen changed back to a view of Earth. Humans and Boxans were working to protect themselves, but it wouldn't be enough. He was just getting started and now he had a whole planet to use. Early in the Confederation's history their allies had believed the Boxans could never be beaten; their hold on the Confederation was too strong. But those who had doubted the Xiiginns were wrong. The Boxans were a shadow of their former selves, and with another species that had the Mardoxian potential, the Xiiginns would be the most unstoppable force the galaxy had ever witnessed. The Boxans revered the Drar, but even their vast empire was gone. The time for the Xiiginns was here, and Mar Arden would see that the entirety of the great expanse would be brought under their dominion.

37

A few days had passed since the Boxan refugees from Sethion had landed on Selebus moon with the blessing of Nerva's global congress. It had been quite a shock when the star carrier had shown up in their star system, but after some quick communication from Kladomaor and High Councilor Awan, the Boxan fleet had been allowed to pass. Kaylan was pleased that the high councilor had kept his word.

Temporary shelters were being built and the resiliency of the Boxan refugees was something to be witnessed as they set to work. Most of them stepped off the transport carriers onto the forest moon and simply looked up at the sky in awe. They were initially afraid to remove their helmets despite knowing that the atmosphere was perfectly safe. Some were fearful of the forest, as if they expected the Protectors to attack at any moment.

Kaylan couldn't imagine living for so long with the harsh realities that the Boxans who'd been left on Sethion had been forced to endure. They were quite different than the other Boxans she'd met, and she wondered if the two factions would be better off going their separate ways. She didn't like those thoughts, but she had to consider them because it was a real possibility. She'd much rather see the two Boxan factions working together and uniting, which would put them both on a path to filling the large gaps between them now. The refugees would be redeemed for the trials they'd endured on Sethion and the colonists could exist without the haunting guilt that they'd left free Boxans behind. Neither could heal without the other, and in the end, they needed each other now more than ever before.

They'd buried Vitomir on Selebus. The cosmonaut had sacrificed himself to help the others restore the star carrier's systems. Vitomir was honored among the Boxan refugees for his sacrifice, but for the crew of the Athena, it was more complicated. The former Titus Station commander had sabotaged the space station, killing four people to join the Athena's mission. Kaylan had loathed the cosmonaut for what he'd done, which was nothing to how Vitomir viewed himself. His actions had led to the death of his own wife. After the Athena had been stranded in the Nershal star system, he'd worked to help them survive. She'd have let him rot in his quarters if it hadn't been for Hicks and the AI pointing out to her that they needed to use all available resources if they were to survive. So she'd made Hicks responsible for Vitomir, and throughout everything they'd been through, Vitomir had helped them. The cosmonaut knew how the rest of the crew felt about him, but in the end all they had was each other. She listened to Efren as he recounted the details of what had occurred on the star carrier—how they were pinned down and Vitomir had lured the combat mechs away so Efren could turn the power back on. She heard the same conflicted feelings in Efren's voice that she felt. In the end, she acknowledged that Vitomir had become part of the Athena's crew despite how they'd all felt about him. They all would have to make their peace with it because Vitomir was no longer with them.

Kaylan glanced at the tall trees and listened to the sounds of the forest. The day was drawing to an end and work would begin anew in the morning. Kladomaor spotted her and walked over.

"Adjusting to your new position?" Kaylan asked.

"I've been a Battle Commander for a long time," Kladomaor said.

"Essaforn and the others trust you," Kaylan said.

"Prax'pedax was the Battle Leader. I guess in Earth terms he'd be a General, except the refugees don't have a fleet to command," Kladomaor said.

"There's more to being a Battle Leader than commanding fleets. They've made you their advocate and have placed you in the most trustworthy position," Kaylan said.

"Their honor is misplaced. We wouldn't be here if it weren't for you. I'll see to it that no Boxan forgets, and when it's time to return to Earth, we'll be with you," Kladomaor said.

Kaylan felt her cheeks start to redden in embarrassment. "It's not just for Earth. We've seen what the Xiiginns are capable of, but Sethion was monstrous. If we don't stop them, countless other species will suffer the same fate."

Kladomaor regarded her for a moment. "I once thought of your species as primitive and brash. Weak. But I was wrong. Those characteristics do exist in Humans, just as they do in Boxans, but you've become a force to be reckoned with. Ma'jasalax has said that the Mardoxian potential in you is equal to the most gifted priests in the history of the sect. Whether you meant to or not, your actions have put us all on a path that I believe will lead to the defeat of the Xiiginns."

Kaylan's mouth hung open and she was rescued from a response by Zack calling out to her. He came over, leading the old Boxan refugee she'd seen on the cruiser's bridge.

"This is Cardaleer. He's something of a scientist," Zack said.

Cardaleer bowed his head. "Mardoxian blessed," he said.

Kaylan bowed her head back to him.

"What's Mardoxian blessed?" Zack said.

"It's an honored title given to only the most gifted of the Mardoxian Sect," Kladomaor said.

Zack glanced at Kaylan, but she could tell he was much too excited about something to pay any mind to the title Cardaleer had used to address her.

"Before the Chaos Wars, Cardaleer studied Drar technology and was the foremost expert. He's agreed to help us with the Athena," Zack said.

"I'm afraid the Human is much too excited by what I said," Cardaleer said. "I merely stated that before the wars I worked with what Drar technology had been discovered. I was part of the teams that reverse-engineered its uses. Zack told me about the Shroud barrier."

"Do you think you can help?" Kaylan asked. The thought of returning to Earth sent waves of excitement through her.

"I will do everything I possibly can," Cardaleer said.

"And Etanu is getting us the materials we need to build a Star Shroud model so we can learn more about the barrier," Zack said.

Kaylan smiled. For the first time since the barrier had gone online, protecting Earth from the Xiiginn fleet, she felt they were much closer to getting home than they'd ever been before.

38

The days that followed the UN attacks strained Human and Boxan relations. Given the ineffectiveness of security forces to subdue Boxans in full power armor, there were motions to increase the production of more powerful weapons for law enforcement agencies across the globe. Ed Johnson knew that handing out more powerful weapons wasn't the answer. They needed specialized teams to be available to investigate alien threats on Earth, and this wasn't something the Earth Coalition Force had the authority to do. Ed thought back to the attack and remembered how Iris's weapons had failed to slow down Strike Leader Eavoth, and Scraanyx had explained that Eavoth's power armor had been modified to handle the stunners used by UN security forces.

Ed was in a conference room with General Sheridan and Scraanyx.

"So, nothing short of a hand cannon capable of shooting plasma bolts can stop them? This isn't going to work. We need a better way to neutralize the threat," Ed said.

They had just gotten Scraanyx released.

"Death is the only release for any Boxan under the Xiiginn influence," Scraanyx said.

"Yeah, but we can't start handing out hand cannons with the advice to shoot any Boxan anyone thinks is acting suspiciously," Ed said.

"We'll need to do a better job of keeping track of Boxan activities, but there are more far-reaching repercussions to this," General Sheridan said.

Ed nodded and didn't like it one bit.

"Our protocols have been allowed to lapse. Cooperative mission protocols will need to be updated so a simple lie can't get anyone past security," General Sheridan said.

"That will help, but we still don't know if the Humans on those missions will be affected by the Xiiginns as well," Ed said.

"We're not going to figure everything out in this room. We'll get the right people working on it, but the threat level has just gone up. We thought the Xiiginns couldn't get through the barrier, so if that's the case, how'd they get here?" General Sheridan asked.

"They would have had a chance to slip through as the barrier was being formed," Scraanyx said.

"Which means they've been loitering out there somewhere for almost a year," Ed said.

"We need to find their ship and we'll need strike-fighter patrols to protect all the construction on the new moon," General Sheridan said.

Iris Barrett waved to him and Ed motioned for her to come over. Her injuries hadn't been extensive and she'd gotten back on her feet shortly after the attack.

"There's an incoming call from General Heng Shang," Iris said.

Ed glanced at Sheridan and the ECF general's face hardened.

"Put it through," the general said.

The nearby wallscreen flicked on, showing the aged face of General Heng Shang.

"Thank you for taking my call," General Heng Shang said.

Ed knew Sheridan was still seething about the Chinese general's appointment to the ECF.

"What can I do for you?" General Sheridan said.

Shang nodded. "We've found something that will help shed some light on the Xiiginns."

The video cam shifted away from Shang to four people standing on his right. Ed's eyes widened when he recognized Colonel Mathews.

The camera shifted back to Shang. "They crash-landed in a small pod in the Kunlun Shan mountain region."

Sheridan came to his feet and walked toward the wallscreen, and Ed joined him.

"Are they alright?" Ed asked.

"We're looking after them," Shang said.

"What do you want?" General Sheridan asked.

The barest hints of a smile showed on Shang's face. "For you to acknowledge me and my own staff as part of the Earth Coalition Force as agreed by the UN Security Council."

General Sheridan's nostrils flared and then he nodded. "Understood. If you want to help the ECF, you can bring Colonel Mathews, Lieutenant Dawson, Corporal Pearson, and Tech Comms Specialist Blake with you when you report for duty."

Any satisfaction General Shang had felt disappeared.

"A shuttle will be dispatched to you and we'll see you in a few hours' time," General Sheridan said and ended the call.

He glanced over at Ed. "You said I needed to work with him. This is me working with him."

Ed nodded and was silent for a few moments. He noticed Scraanyx frowning. "What is it?" he asked.

The Boxan regarded them for a moment. "Did they escape, or were they set free?"

Ed drew in a deep breath and looked at Sheridan. They'd thought that if they could build their fleet and race to upgrade their technology, they could keep the Xiiginns from reaching Earth. They'd failed, and now at least some of the Xiiginns were here. He didn't know how they were supposed to keep things running and stop the Xiiginn compulsion from infiltrating their ranks at the same time. Dark times were coming, and they needed to stick together now more than ever if the people of Earth hoped to survive.

ASCENSION

ASCENSION SERIES BOOK 6

1

Zack stood in the astrophysics lab of the *Athena*. He'd stopped thinking of it as Jonah Redford's lab a while ago, but he couldn't quite claim it as his own. He still thought about the snobby, uptight scientist from the original Athena mission. In fact, Jonah's fate was never far from Zack's thoughts.

The astrophysicist had been infected with the Xiiginn influence, a compulsion capability that could overthrow a person's will. Zack had been immune to the Xiiginn influence, and Emma Roberson, their resident biologist, had come up with a theory for why Zack had been immune and Jonah wasn't. Apparently, being romantically involved with someone could affect the physiology of a person's brain chemistry, which was a scientist's way of explaining what normal people referred to as love. He loved Kaylan, and it was his love for her that had shielded him from the Xiiginn influence. At least, that was the theory, and Zack had no desire to test that theory again by meeting any more Xiiginns in person. He'd had enough of that to last a lifetime.

He was quite sure that, above all, Jonah had loved himself, so why hadn't he been immune to the Xiiginn influence? Nershals could resist the Xiiginns, perhaps due to their sometimes rigid societal structure that adhered to a strict code of honor. And then there were the Boxans. Zack didn't understand why they were so vulnerable to the Xiiginn influence. He'd seen Xiiginns take over a Boxan's will in seconds. When that happened, it was like watching their entire existence being wiped and replaced, with no hope of a cure.

Zack had taken over Jonah's lab in part because he needed a quiet place to work. He'd been a last-minute addition to the original Athena mission and had spent months working in the lab with Jonah, analyzing what had turned out to be a Boxan message warning them about the Xiiginns.

It had been over a year since he'd left Earth. He supposed he should think of it as an "Earth year" or some other technical term to mark his time away from home. He'd heard Kaylan talking about it, but it was confusing for Zack. Apparently, time had multidimensional properties, but he just wanted to say a year and have it understood that he meant the normal year from back home. The Boxans referred to their equivalent of a year as a "cycle," which was great for them, but Zack wouldn't start emulating those large aliens anytime soon.

The *Athena* was orbiting the forest moon called Selebus in the Nerva star system, where it had been for the past five months since they'd rescued Boxan refugees from Sethion. When they'd first arrived, Zack thought they'd only have to stay for another month before they could go home, but he'd underestimated the difficulty of undoing what he'd done to save Earth. He'd used Drar technology to realign the shroud that surrounded Earth's star system into a massive shield capable of repelling a fleet of Xiiginn warships. It had been an impulsive act of desperation that had ultimately been successful and given all of them some much-needed breathing room. But even though it had seemed so simple at the time, he was still unable to undo it a year later.

The crew of the *Athena* couldn't communicate with anyone on Earth, and they hadn't received any communications from back home either, which meant the shield blocked both inbound and outbound signals. And since signals weren't getting through, ships certainly wouldn't be either. The Boxans had tried to open a wormhole inside the Star Shroud shield but had failed.

During all those months on Olloron, Zack had spent a lot of time familiarizing himself with Boxan systems, thinking that perhaps getting a better understanding of those systems would help him turn off the shield. But once again, he was faced with the adage that nothing was ever easy. First of all, even if he could tell the Star Shroud shield to go down, he couldn't get a signal to the Star Shroud devices to give the command. He suspected that the command would have to come from *inside* the shield, meaning they had to find a way to tell someone on Earth how to shut it down so it wouldn't destroy their star system.

Unfortunately, that was the other "bonus" to what he'd done to save Earth. The massive power requirements for technology that not even the Boxans fully understood had caused the Star Shroud shield to shrink with every moment it was active. It was only a matter of time before it brushed up against a planet in the Earth's system, and then he didn't know what would happen. Gaarokk thought the shield would simply dissipate if it brushed up against a large object like a planet. But Cardaleer theorized that if the Star Shroud shield brushed up against a planet, a cascade of catastrophic events would cause the shield to rapidly constrict, nudging the planet out of its orbit before the shield could dissipate.

Zack didn't know what anyone else thought, but it seemed to him that having Neptune knocked out of its orbit could have disastrous effects for the star system as a whole. And to the best of his knowledge, not even the Boxans could evacuate the eight billion Humans who called Earth home. They still had time, but Zack just wanted to go home, and he wasn't the only one. All of the *Athena* crew felt the same. They'd been on the journey of a lifetime, witnessing things that no other person had ever seen, but the thing they needed most was to see that bright blue ball called Earth.

Zack glanced above him at the top observatory and saw Selebus above. The forest moon was a beautiful planet—a much better place than Olloron. Selebus was vibrant with life, and the Nershals were fortunate that their star system was home to two habitable planets.

There was a soft, audible chime from the small fabrication unit in the lab. Zack glanced over at it in surprise.

"Athena, are you using the fabrication unit here?" he asked.

"Yes, I am. Kaylan permitted me to attempt a three-dimensional rendering of some ship-design concepts I've come up with," the ship's AI replied.

Athena had developed well beyond the Boxan AI on Pluto. When the Drar space station remade their ship, Athena had gotten a complete overhaul as well. Zack had come to think of her as a true intelligence, which was a miracle of sorts. Calling Athena a true intelligence acknowledged the fact that the *Athena* AI was a living being with all the capabilities of any other living being.

Zack walked over to the fabrication unit and opened the door, finding a three-dimensional rendering of the *Athena* inside. The model even had the Phoenix emblem just beyond the windows where the bridge was supposed to be. Zack picked it up and it was cool to the touch.

"What sort of alloy is this?" Zack asked, feeling the smooth surface.

"It's a new material based on the supplies we have on board. I've been testing them and documenting my results," Athena said.

She wasn't kidding. Athena had a library of research that would take scientists years to go through once they returned home. This was in addition to anything the Drar had locked away inside the ship's storage system.

Zack frowned at the golden model. "I think you're showing off now, but I like it. Does it fly?"

He'd meant the question as a joke, but his eyes widened as the rear engine pods began to glow. Zack hastily put it down and heard an artificial chuckle coming from the speakers above.

"I have to admit that was pretty good. You got me," Zack said with a grin.

"I'm glad. I remember that you found my first attempts at humor unsettling," Athena said.

Zack peered at the model of the *Athena*. There was a lot of detail—so much, in fact, that he wouldn't have been surprised if Athena had made a true working model of the ship. He made a mental note to tell Emma and Brenda about this new development. He was sure there was some kind of psychological significance to an intelligent being making models that imitated the world around them. Zack had no idea what that significance might be, but he thought they would find it interesting.

"Your query does present a bit of a challenge that I'd like to devote some of my resources to explore," Athena said.

"You want to make it fly?" Zack said.

"That's just one aspect of it. Perhaps there's more I can do to make it a true replica of the ship," Athena said.

Athena had no physical form, so he couldn't really look at her and get a feel for what she was thinking. He swung his gaze toward the nearest camera. "Are you feeling lonely again?"

Athena was silent for a few moments. "No, each member of the crew has returned to me on a regular basis, but you're here more often than anyone else. I think my presence acts as a reminder of home, which can be a cause for joy and yet troubling at the same time."

Zack leaned back in his chair and arched an eyebrow. This wasn't simply idle conversation from the AI. "Try not to take it personally."

"I don't, but I don't fully understand the thought process behind such emotions," Athena replied.

"Here's a little bit of insight for you: most people don't understand the emotions that drive them either."

"It's a curious nuance that I find fascinating about the crew. I look forward to meeting more people when we return to Earth," Athena said.

Zack rubbed his chin. He wasn't sure how people back home would react to Athena. Humanity had come a long way toward creating a limited artificial intelligence that could mimic a Human response, but it was nothing like what Athena had become. Also, there was the fact that the original Athena mission had been jointly funded by multiple countries, and he imagined all of them would try to lay claim to Athena. He didn't know what to think about that and felt his shoulders tighten at the thought.

"Zack, I noticed that your pulse has increased. Have I said something to upset you?"

Zack shook his head. "No, you didn't. I'm just worried about getting home."

"You've been up here a long time. Is the laboratory on Selebus inadequate for your needs?" Athena asked.

Zack snorted. "My latest test with the shroud device didn't go well. I miscalculated the power requirements, and Gaarokk doesn't believe the shield will come down for a few hundred years." Zack blew out a breath. "Now they're saying we have a shortage of materials, so I don't have another shroud device to test with."

"That's unfortunate, but perhaps it's a setback you can learn from," Athena said.

Zack's eye started to twitch and he scowled. He'd been having setbacks for months. "It really shouldn't be this hard. The Drar command I used was based on what we found at the space station. A simple reversal of the command should bring the shield down, but it doesn't."

"I've searched through the data repositories that I'm able to access and I still don't have anything that can help."

Zack stretched his arms out and yawned. "I appreciate that. It's like the Drar never anticipated someone being on the opposite side of the shield. And I know that isn't right. The AI that ran the Drar space station knew of our approach, so they could see beyond the shield. It opened for us, after all."

"Kaylan has discussed the Drar space station with Ma'jasalax extensively. The capabilities of the Drar AI is beyond even the Boxans' comprehension. That AI put the events into motion that brought us to it, which is unprecedented. I've run multiple data models to analyze the probability of such events occurring, and it's simply impossible for those events to have occurred on their own," Athena said.

"Multiple data models? How many?" Zack asked. He'd worked with Athena for so long now that he'd gotten to know some of her eccentricities, and the long delay in response meant she was carefully considering her response. "If you're worried about upsetting me, don't be. I know you're capable of crunching massive amounts of numbers."

"It's not that, but the number is simply beyond what you would understand," Athena said.

Zack sat up and looked at the camera. This was the first time Athena had outright told him she was considering something he simply couldn't grasp. "I'm pretty smart, Athena. I have an idea what you're capable of, but if you're saying it's a lot, then that's fine. How much of your computing power did you devote to your data models?" he asked, trying a different approach.

"Less than one quadrillion of a percentage. I've found that my computational capacity has increased substantially since we left the Drar space station," Athena said.

"Why didn't you tell anyone?" Zack asked.

"I thought it was a mistake at first, and I was checking my systems. I'm happy to inform you that they are all performing optimally."

"But your capacity is increasing and you're not sure why?" Zack said.

"There is a correlation between increased capacity that occurs after I've reached my current limits."

Zack pressed his lips together. "Reached your limits? But we've been idle here at Selebus."

"I wouldn't describe our time here in the Nerva star system as idle. Each of the crew has been working hard, applying themselves to multiple efforts. You all work toward the same goal, and it is my goal as well. So I've been trying to calculate the events with the highest probability of getting all of us back to Earth safely."

This was news to him. "Do you have a plan?"

"Not at this time. The biggest obstacle that prevents us from going home is the Xiiginns."

Zack felt his mouth open wide. "You've been up here trying to think of a way to defeat the Xiiginns?"

"Affirmative. I've been monitoring the internal communication systems of the ships in the area, gaining all the insight I could—"

"Wait a minute," Zack said, interrupting. "You're listening in on people's conversations on other ships? How many other ships?"

"All of them."

"What do you mean 'all of them'? All the ships nearby or all the ones around Selebus?"

"No, I mean in the Nerva star system. I'm also able to pull data logs from the ships so I can analyze them as well."

Zack licked his lips and took a moment to rein in his racing thoughts. "I didn't even know you could do something like that. Do the Boxans or the Nershals know you've been poking around in their systems?"

"I detect that your heart rate is elevating again. Does this new revelation upset you?"

"Just answer the question, Athena."

"Some of the Boxan systems did detect my presence, but I removed all references to it. The Nershal systems are quite rudimentary at best and did not detect my presence at all," Athena replied.

Zack groaned.

"Are you ill?" Athena asked.

Zack shook his head. "No, I'm not," he said, unable to shake the feeling that this was somehow his fault. He was no stranger to infiltrating other systems, but he hadn't realized he'd passed those traits along to Athena. "Have you told anyone else?"

"Negative. It hasn't come up in any query. You seem concerned by this. Have I done something wrong?"

Zack felt the hints of a smile tug at his lips as he began to form a reply. "Generally, people don't like it when you listen in on their conversations."

"I am aware of that, but sometimes those are the most interesting. There are groups of Boxan and Nershal scientists that have been discussing the capabilities of this ship—not together but as individual groups."

"Gaarokk hasn't mentioned it and neither has Etanu," Zack replied.

"That's because neither of them has been involved in those conversations," Athena said.

Zack bit his lower lip. *This again,* he thought. "Have they made any attempts to infiltrate your systems?"

"Sometimes, but they haven't been successful."

"Would you know if they had been?"

"I see your point, but I do have safeguards in place to prevent such access," Athena said.

Zack snorted. "And you think the Boxans don't have something like that in place?"

"I'm sure they do, but I've studied their systems extensively and have safeguarded against any attempt they would make, so there's a low probability of them ever gaining access to my systems without my permission," Athena said.

Zack was increasingly aware of how the AI perceived itself and its importance in the presence of the other species. "Would you prevent me from accessing your systems?"

"Of course not."

"I appreciate that, but why?"

"Because we are part of the same crew. A unit. A group. Major Hicks would refer to us as a squad or platoon, but the meaning is the same."

"Another reference to what we are is family," Zack said.

"That wouldn't be accurate at all, and I'm surprised to hear you suggest that we're family. We share no genetic lineage, so why would you refer to us as such?" Athena asked.

"Do you think we're friends?"

"Yes, I believe that would be accurate. The rest of the crew shares a strong bond that functions within the framework of friendship; therefore, you are my friend and I am yours," Athena said.

"Family isn't always about genetic lineage. It's a bond. Sometimes when people are around each other for a long time, those bonds grow, becoming deeper and richer," Zack said.

"Like the bond between you and Kaylan?"

"That's one type of bond, but being family means you look out for one another. We share each other's burdens. It means we're there for each other. I didn't know Hicks until I was on the ship and now we're friends. We all know each other very well, so there's a sense of the familiar, which can be construed as being family. Do you understand what I mean?" Zack asked.

"I understand what you said, but I will need time to consider it fully."

Zack smiled. "Well, I don't doubt that you have the processing capability to consider it in great detail."

"I appreciate you taking the time to explain it to me," Athena said.

"That's what I'm here for," Zack said. He didn't know why, but sometimes he felt like an older brother to Athena. He hadn't said as much out loud because even in his mind it seemed absurd, and yet he loved the ship. The *Athena* was their home. He didn't know what would happen once they returned to Earth, but for now, this was the only place they could call their own.

"Have you considered running your experiments in a more virtualized environment?" Athena asked.

Zack pursed his lips for a moment. "I hadn't thought of that because I didn't think it was possible. Too many variables."

"Curious, but the Boxans have the schematics for the Star Shroud devices. I can certainly obtain a copy of them," Athena offered.

"No," Zack said quickly. "I'd much rather ask them."

"If we have the schematics, we can build a virtual model of the device. We could then feed in all the data input we would need—"

"And if it doesn't work, we can just reset the virtual environment back to its original condition. Athena, you're a genius! I don't know why I didn't think of this before," Zack said.

"I hadn't thought of it until this moment," Athena admitted.

"Well, I'm glad you did because now we have a way forward and we can stop —er, *I* can stop—wasting resources on failure. Whatever we discover would have to be tested outside the virtual environment, but at least we can move much faster now," Zack said and stood up.

He needed to stretch his legs and return to Selebus. He would remain in contact with Athena while on the planet's surface, but he was curious about what Gaarokk's reaction would be when he asked for the schematics of a Star Shroud device. He'd also have to get another one for when they were ready to test on an actual device again.

2

K aylan watched as the two Boxan ambassadors squared off in another verbal sparring match. This was supposed to be an informal meeting, and its location was the main research complex on Selebus. The surrounding buildings had been constructed by the Nershals under the direction of the Xiiginns. There were currently no Xiiginns there, but Kaylan noticed that the flaxen-eyed gaze of several Boxans in attendance would sometimes stray to their surroundings with a hint of disdain. She wasn't sure whether anyone else had noticed. She'd found that her instincts were acuter than they'd previously been, especially where the Boxans were concerned.

A craggy old Boxan caught her gaze and gave her a slight nod. Cardaleer was a Boxan scientist, or at least he had been before the collapse of Sethion. After the Chaos Wars, Cardaleer simply "fixed things," as he liked to put it. He was a peculiar Boxan who seemed to regard the world around him with wry amusement. Whenever he spoke to Kaylan, he did so with a reverence that she sometimes found uncomfortable. And he wasn't the only Boxan to treat her differently than the rest of the *Athena* crew. She'd come to be known as "Mardoxian Blessed," which was a highly revered title given to the most gifted of the Mardoxian Sect. The only problem was that Kaylan was an honorary member of the Mardoxian Sect and the first non-Boxan able to join their ranks. As such, she found that some of the representatives from Olloron didn't particularly care for the new title that had been bestowed upon her.

"The star carrier is ours to do with as we please, Ambassador Dulrad, so I simply cannot allow it to be taken for colonial use. And may I remind you that the High Council, while supporting us here on Selebus, will not support our integration into the colony on Olloron," Councilor Essaforn said.

Ambassador Dulrad's gaze drew downward, considering. "The High Council *does* support your right to return to the colony. That is not in question anymore.

It's a matter of resources. Selebus is a much better place for you at the current time."

Councilor Essaforn narrowed her gaze. "It's always a matter of resources. However, if you wish us to give you one of our most precious commodities, we would be left vulnerable should the Xiiginns come here in force. The star carrier is our only means of escape. Why haven't you returned to Sethion if you need raw materials so badly? Or perhaps another star system?"

"There has been a salvage mission to Sethion and we're gathering materials from there, but we will not go to the planet's surface," Ambassador Dulrad replied.

Kaylan perked up in her seat. This was the first she'd heard that the Boxans had returned to Sethion. They must've been desperate for materials if they'd finally returned to their home star system. It couldn't have been easy for them, given what they'd left behind. She'd seen the destruction of the Chaos Wars. A dying planet filled with the hulking wrecks of a once proud, advanced race was all that was left.

Ambassador Dulrad cleared his throat. "I can tell you that the reason we need the star carrier is for the benefit of all Boxans, which includes the refugees here on Selebus."

Councilor Essaforn looked unconvinced. "You'll have to forgive me if I cannot take your assurances at face value. I have to put the needs of the Boxans here as my highest priority, and that doesn't include allowing you to strip us of our most precious resource."

Ambassador Dulrad drew in a breath to speak again, but Kladomaor cut him off. "Enough. Councilor Essaforn has already given you her answer, and it is pointless to persist. If High Councilor Awan wants the star carrier, he's going to have to give us a compelling reason. I suggest you move on to another subject."

Ambassador Dulrad's gaze went to Kaylan, almost as if he was considering imploring her to speak on his behalf. Kaylan had stumbled upon rumors of a secret project the Boxans were working on, which had led to Zack being denied access to the Star Shroud devices. At first, she'd assumed they were building more warships to combat the Xiiginns, but this was different. The Boxan colony on Olloron was a short-term fix for their current situation. They needed a new planet to call home.

The ambassador sighed and turned back to Essaforn. "I would share more if I could. I will take your feedback to the High Council. Are there any other requests I should bring to their attention?"

Kaylan watched as Councilor Essaforn's eyes flashed angrily. One thing Kaylan had noticed about the Boxans who had survived the Chaos Wars on Sethion for all those years was that they were much freer with their emotions than the Boxans who had escaped the wars. The Boxan refugees were more impulsive—almost Human-like in their behavior.

The informal meeting ended with Essaforn promising to send Dulrad a list. Kaylan firmly believed Essaforn had several lists on hand, ready for the High Council to review.

An aged Nershal walked over to Kaylan. "May I speak with you for a moment?" Governor Udonzari asked.

Udonzari had been part of the first group of Nershals to actively resist the Xiiginns there on Selebus. The global congress on Nerva had appointed Udonzari as the governor of Selebus.

"Of course. How can I help?" Kaylan said.

Nershals were long-limbed and quite strong. This aged Nershal had pale green skin and large orange eyes, and his dragonfly wings were firmly tucked in behind him. "This is a personal matter that has to do with my son. As you know, Etanu will not return to his rightful place until he has personally escorted the *Athena* crew back to Earth. I was hoping you would speak to him."

Kaylan smiled. "I remember how he hated you making him watch over Zack, and I'm surprised by how close they've become. Have you spoken to Etanu about this?"

"I have, and he is adamant that he will not return. I was hoping that perhaps you might consider speaking to him. Kladomaor will ensure that all of you return safely to your homeworld, so there is no need for Etanu to remain with you."

Etanu was supposed to be in the Nershal military but had deferred his service because of his vow to Zack, who had saved Etanu's life. "You must be very proud of Etanu."

Udonzari nodded. "More than I can say, but it's time for him to embrace his future. This does not involve what he's currently doing."

"I think what he's currently doing will serve the Nershals far better than commanding soldiers in the military. I think that if you continue to be patient, Etanu will return to you of his own accord, and that would be worth much more to you than if I were to convince him to return before he's ready," Kaylan replied.

Udonzari took a moment to consider what she'd said, masking his disappointment. "You are indeed Mardoxian blessed. I will take your advice, for now. You've come a long way since you first came to Selebus. If there's anything you need, all you have to do is ask."

"You've already done so much for the Boxans and for us. I just wish we hadn't caused so much bloodshed among your species," Kaylan said.

"You are not to blame for any of that. The Xiiginns have much to answer for," Udonzari said and left her.

Valkra walked over to Kaylan. The Boxan female reminded Kaylan of a much younger Kladomaor. Valkra was fiercely determined to fight the Xiiginns, but as a Mardoxian initiate, she seemed to resent her abilities. Ma'jasalax followed her over. The Mardoxian priestess always had the appearance of being supremely calm.

Kaylan smiled a greeting to both of them. "I'm worried the factions will cause a rift between what's left of the Boxans." Kaylan spoke softly so that only Ma'jasalax and Valkra could hear her.

"The Boxans will remain united in our fight against the Xiiginns," Ma'jasalax replied firmly.

"A common enemy is only going to get you so far," Kaylan replied.

"It'll get us through today," Ma'jasalax said.

Kaylan glanced over and saw Kladomaor speaking with Councilor Essaforn and Udonzari. Battle Leader Holbak had also joined them.

"I don't know if that's going to be enough," Kaylan said.

"Is this your opinion, or is this what your instincts are telling you?" Ma'jasalax asked.

"It's both. There are still too many secrets. I know you told me that I should be focusing on the Xiiginns, but what happens to the Boxans will affect what happens to the Xiiginns. If the Boxans splinter apart, the Alliance won't survive. We need allies. I've spoken about it with Hicks, and at some point it becomes a numbers game. The Confederation has many more resources and soldiers than the Alliance does."

"I agree with you. My instincts tell me the same thing," Ma'jasalax said.

"What allies would join the Alliance? The Confederation is under the dominion of the Xiiginns," Valkra said.

"Even before we came to Nerva there were factions within the Nershals that suspected the Xiiginns didn't have their best interests at heart. I'm willing to bet that other species in the Confederation feel the same way. The Xiiginns control the Confederation through the leadership of the individual species. Their control is far-reaching, but it can't include everyone. We need to reach out to these factions and bring them into the Alliance," Kaylan said.

Ma'jasalax nodded. "We need the Gresans. They are a powerful race in the Confederation, second only to the Xiiginns."

"The Gresans had been trying to reach Sethion for many cycles. It was unclear what their motives were," Valkra said.

"Can you make the recommendation to Ambassador Dulrad?" Kaylan asked.

Ma'jasalax narrowed her gaze. "Why wouldn't you make the recommendation?"

"I'm not sure they'll listen to me. They respect my abilities and appreciate what the *Athena* crew has done, but we're still viewed as a primitive species, at least where some of the Boxans are concerned," Kaylan said.

Ma'jasalax gave her a knowing look. "It will take time for certain prejudices to subside among our species."

"It might help if we had more of my own species here. I doubt we'd listen to a handful of aliens trying to give *us* advice either," Kaylan said with a wry smile.

"Kladomaor defers to you, and many Boxans have noticed that. I think you undervalue how the Boxans perceive you," Valkra said.

Perhaps they were right, but this reprieve from their conflict with the Confederation would only last for a short amount of time. They needed to use that time wisely if they were going to survive.

Valkra looked at Ma'jasalax curiously. "I've noticed that you don't have a bodyguard. I thought the requirement was that all Mardoxian priests and priestesses were to have a bodyguard with them at all times."

"That was indeed the practice. I no longer have a bodyguard," Ma'jasalax said.

"What happened to your guard?" Valkra asked.

Kaylan noticed that Ma'jasalax's gaze went cold, almost deadly.

"You're worried that you'll be assigned a bodyguard since you have the Mardoxian potential in you," Ma'jasalax said.

"I can take care of myself and therefore don't need a bodyguard. Nor will I accept one," Valkra replied.

Kaylan understood why Valkra wouldn't want a bodyguard whose duties included making sure that no Mardoxian priest or priestess fell into the Xiiginns' hands by any means possible. Kaylan also wouldn't want a protector whose secondary orders were to kill her to prevent the Xiiginns from gaining the Mardoxian potential.

Kaylan watched Ma'jasalax consider her reply. She had no idea what had happened to Ma'jasalax's bodyguard when she'd been taken prisoner.

"My bodyguard died while executing his duties," Ma'jasalax answered finally.

"You were captured by the Xiiginns. How is it that they weren't able to extract the genetic code for the Mardoxian potential from you?" Valkra asked.

"I see you've been speaking with Cardaleer," Ma'jasalax said. "I wasn't their prisoner for very long."

Kaylan remembered how they'd rescued Ma'jasalax from a Xiiginn warship. Kladomaor had been just as concerned about the fact that the Xiiginns had a Mardoxian priestess as he was about rescuing her. Kaylan had always assumed that Ma'jasalax's bodyguard had died while protecting her, but now she wondered if Ma'jasalax had killed her own bodyguard to keep them from killing her. As if sensing her thoughts, Ma'jasalax looked at Kaylan.

"If we can defeat the Xiiginns, many things will change," Ma'jasalax said.

The Boxans had been fighting a desperate war and had made many sacrifices to ensure their survival. The more Kaylan thought about it, the more she could imagine Ma'jasalax doing what she suspected. After all, it was Ma'jasalax who'd put them all on this path when she sent the first Mardoxian signal to Earth.

3

The lavish offices of the supreme leader of the Xiiginns on the Confederation space station held all the trappings of power. The outer chambers were a masterful blend of gardens that utilized flora from primary Confederation species. Sculptures representing all the species of the Confederation—including the Boxans—could be found throughout the tower.

Garm Antis stood on a balcony overlooking the main chamber. A life-sized sculpture of a Boxan stood beneath him. They were the true enemy of the Xiiginns, and he'd kept the sculptures as a reminder that the Boxans still roamed the great expanse, searching for a way to annihilate them.

His defeat in the Human star system had cost him some political capital that he was keen to regain. They'd been on the verge of victory, and not even the Boxan Dreadnoughts were enough to hold off his fleet. But instead of victory, he had presided over one of the most stunning defeats in history, and a show of weakness was enough to bring forth aggression, even in the Xiiginns.

During the past few months he had gone to great lengths to reconsolidate his influence. Some Xiiginns believed the loss of a significant chunk of the Xiiginn fleet was enough to remove him from power, but those misguided factions had soon learned this was not possible. And now that the opportunity-seeking Xiiginns had been dealt with, he was free to move on.

Despite all his efforts, he knew there was still a lingering threat to deal with. He had a sneaking suspicion that Mar Arden had somehow survived the battle. Garm Antis had sent several scout ships back to the Human star system, searching for evidence of any survivors, and there was no trace of the warship Mar Arden had been on. If there was another Xiiginn among his species who could have survived those circumstances, then he was at a loss to think of who that could be. His own flagship had been at the rear of the vanguard, and when the other ships had broken apart on the Star Shroud shield, his war general had taken action to ensure their survival.

The holoscreen above his desk became active, signaling that his next appointment had just arrived. Garm Antis authorized the door to his office to open, and a Xiiginn walked in. She had pale features and long platinum hair with many silver beads interwoven among the silky strands, along with a blazing pendant that hung in front of her well-formed breasts.

Garm Antis regarded her severely. "I hope you brought me answers, Setera."

Setera was his newly appointed senior scientific advisor. She regarded him with a shrewdness that only hinted at the keen intelligence she possessed. He could faintly detect the genetic enhancements she'd employed to increase her cerebral function.

She walked over to him, keeping her hands folded in front of her. "The shield around the Human star system is like nothing we've ever seen before. The shield resists both energy and kinetic attacks. It encompasses the vast expanse that surrounds the star system and has stages of activity. In other words, the shield isn't completely active all the time, but it is quick to react when something attempts to pierce it," Setera said.

Garm Antis sighed in disgust and showed his teeth. "We already knew that. This would be a good time for you to share something that speaks to the reputation you've garnered for all these cycles."

"The shield was created from the shroud devices, so it's a Boxan design," Setera replied quickly.

Garm Antis smiled. "This will be your final warning."

Setera swallowed hard. "Which the Boxans based off Drar technology, so it's possible that the shield is part of some latent function that they've only just become aware of. That is my team's best guess, and I think they're right."

"If they had this ability before, why wouldn't they have used it more?" Garm Antis asked.

"As I said, we believe that they just became aware of this ability. Our last survey mission indicated that the shield was still active," Setera replied.

"How can we get past it?"

"My team is still working on that. We have several theories—"

"Theories!" Garm Antis said huskily. "I don't need more theories! I executed the previous seven advisors because their theories were useless. Tell me how yours is different."

Setera drew in a breath and met his gaze. She wasn't as frightened by his threat as the others had been. "Despite the fact that the shield is based on Drar technology, it doesn't mean the fundamentals have changed. There's always a cost. The energy required to maintain that shield is considerable. There is some evidence to suggest that the shield is constricting around the star system."

Garm Antis narrowed his gaze. "So you would advise us to wait?"

"It is one option. Based on the evidence from"—Setera looked at him and paused—"the previous engagement, the shield was capable of stopping ships from flying through it. Those fleets were taken by surprise."

"And our weapons were ineffective against it," Garm Antis replied.

"Yes, but you were at a fraction of your former strength," Setera said.

Garm Antis stepped away from her and rubbed his chin. His long tail wrapped around his middle and his fingers glided over the corded muscle while he pondered what Setera had said.

He turned on his heel and faced her. "How much firepower would it take to impact the shield?"

Setera's lips curved upward deliciously. "I'm afraid I just have more theories, but we only need to nudge the shield enough that it touches a planet. Then, it would constrict quicker and perhaps even fail altogether."

"Yes. Yes. A cascade of events that would force whoever is behind the shield to lower it, which would allow our forces through," Garm Antis said.

"The longer the Humans wait, the worse it becomes for them. The advantage in this engagement is with us," Setera said.

"We only need a sampling of Humans in order to get the Mardoxian trait from their genetic code," Garm Antis said, giving voice to his thoughts. Throughout their quest for control of the Confederation, they'd sacrificed several species in their efforts to perfect their race.

The door to his office opened and another Xiiginn entered with all the authority of one who could go almost anywhere they chose. Runa Tane had been his most trusted ally for many years. He'd ensured that the Confederation ran smoothly while Garm Antis was away leading the assault on the Human star system.

"Thank you, Setera. That will be all for now. I want a formal proposal brought to me before the next congressional session," Garm Antis said.

Setera's eyes widened. A formal proposal for the Confederation would typically have taken a significant amount of time, and he was demanding that she do it over the span of mere days. Garm Antis watched her mercilessly as she struggled with the pressure he was putting on her.

"As you command," Setera replied and hastily retreated.

Runa Tane watched the young Xiiginn go almost wistfully and then turned toward Garm Antis.

"She's quite clever," Garm Antis said.

"Her analysis is rudimentary at best," Runa Tane said.

"The simplest explanation is often correct," Garm Antis said.

Runa Tane regarded him for a moment. "This is about Mar Arden."

"He's been useful in the past, but if he's been alive on the Human homeworld all this time, he could become a very grave threat," Garm Antis said.

Runa Tane narrowed his gaze. "Not enough to shift the balance of power."

"You're mistaken. If he somehow manages to extract the genetic code for the Mardoxian potential, he would become a very powerful rival. The factions would tear themselves apart for access to that knowledge. We must ensure that we control whatever he discovers," Garm Antis said.

"If he survived. Regardless, we'll need to assemble another fleet," Runa Tane replied.

Garm Antis smiled. "You're not thinking big enough."

Runa Tane frowned. "What do you mean? A fleet of Xiiginn warships is worth more than anything else in the Confederation."

"Except for the Confederation itself. To get the firepower we need, we'll have to assemble a grand armada," Garm Antis said.

"Such a thing hasn't happened since we took the Confederation away from the Boxans," Runa Tane said.

"Nothing less will succeed and will also mean the end of our old enemies. The Boxans will throw themselves at us when we bring our fleets back to the Human star system," Garm Antis said.

"A dangerous assumption," Runa Tane said.

"An accurate assumption. They deployed two Dreadnoughts to protect that star system. We can't assemble an armada in secret, and it won't take much for them to figure out where we'll send those ships first. After we have a firm hand over the Humans, the armada will act as our enforcement arm over the Confederation," Garm Antis said.

"Glory to the Xiiginn Empire," Runa Tane said.

"Call for an assembly of the Confederation," Garm Antis said. It would take some time to gather the ships he would need, but there were Confederation shipyards that had ships in production. He'd bring them all together to form the most formidable fighting force the Confederation had ever seen, and there would be nothing the Boxans could do about it. The foolish Boxans refused to fight any of the Confederation species other than the Xiiginns, even knowing how the Xiiginns controlled them.

"Our scouts have returned from Sethion. It appears the automated quarantine containment system has been disabled. A quick survey revealed that the system has been stripped of most raw materials," Runa Tane said.

"The system is worthless. That planet must be a lifeless rock by now. Sethion is the past. We don't need to concern ourselves with that anymore," Garm Antis replied.

"On that we can agree, but I do find it curious that the Boxans would return to their home system after all this time. We once thought there was another Tetronian key there," Runa Tane said.

"I've always thought we put too much value on the Star Shroud network. Access to it would enable us to find star systems with intelligent species to exploit, but it might be time for us to move on. The only Tetronian keys left are the ones the Boxans retained for themselves," Garm Antis said.

He'd hunted for the key to the Star Shroud network for years. The fact that the governing systems of the elusive network were located within the confines of the Confederation space station had been the source of irritation to all Xiiginn leaders since the uprising. Despite countless attempts to access the coveted Star Shroud system, they'd failed. The Boxan system was located in a highly shielded area of the space station. Access to it was now restricted. The last attempt to access it almost destroyed the tower, which was a parting gift from the Boxans. Sometimes Garm Antis thought they would have been better off without the Confederation space station. There were too many reminders of the Boxans there. They should have built something new that was made by Xiiginns entirely, but it was always a matter of resources. Why throw away a perfectly good space station? The Confederation space station was the size of a small moon and boasted an atmosphere all its own. The Boxans, for all their flaws, were highly capable builders. Perhaps after they conquered the rest of that species he'd keep a few million of them around to build something else for the Xiiginns to use.

4

Mar Arden stood with his hands clasped behind his back, overlooking a dimly lit warehouse. The ground level was a maze of walkways among temporary work and prep areas. Over the past few months, he'd set up multiple bases of operations in select regions of the Human world that were no stranger to conflict. The largest landmass afforded him ease of movement, but it was access to the Mardoxian testing centers that he was most interested in.

The Humans were even more primitive than he'd initially thought. Some factions still fought among themselves almost as much as they fought each other. There was always a struggle between the more advanced groups, who either purposefully or inadvertently exploited the members of their species with lesser means. Mar Arden was quite familiar with the ruthless struggle for survival, even under the guise of civility, and these were tools he had used to make steady progress toward his goals.

Humanity, it seemed, was supremely obsessed with perception and hierarchy, which would make them much easier to control since they already had the propensity to be followers. Their religious factions spoke of tolerance, but their very teachings condemned anyone who believed differently, which effectively laid the groundwork for the subjugation of the Human species. Give them the illusion that one faction was better than the other and they would never get their fill of clamoring for attention. Convince another faction of the righteousness of *their* cause and they'd pull together in droves to sacrifice themselves.

The Human species was also just as prone to be chaotic in their pursuits as they were to be orderly. This characteristic alone caused Mar Arden to have trouble believing that the Mardoxian potential existed in their pathetic species. He supposed it was some accident of evolution, just as it had been with the Boxans, who must be truly desperate if they were allying themselves with these Humans.

The Humans weren't all primitive, and the Boxans had recently given Humans such a technological advantage that he thought they might destroy themselves even without his help. The Xiiginns were no strangers to sharing technological advances with more primitive species when it served their purpose. More often than not, if those species weren't kept under strict control, this sharing meant their demise. It'd been so with the Qegi, whom the Xiiginns were only interested in for their hyper-production capabilities, which they took from the Qegi and used to produce Xiiginn fleets.

Mar Arden was roused from his reflection by several pathetic groans of absolution from their latest test subjects. The Humans were a vocal race, which was why he'd ordered them gagged. Everything Humans did involved them making some kind of noise, crying out their cringe-worthy opinions as if they were entitled to be heard just because they had a voice.

There were several dimly glowing work areas where his soldiers attempted to bring forth the Mardoxian traits in their Human test subjects. Mar Arden's gaze scanned toward the interior of the warehouse and over the poorly lit lines that illuminated the paths among the work areas. Xiiginns didn't need a lot of light in order to see, which seemed to frighten the Humans they'd recruited. The Humans' fear of the dark was one of the first things Mar Arden had used to his advantage.

Hoan Berend climbed up the stairs to the loft and plodded over to him.

"Any progress with the latest batch?" Mar Arden asked.

Hoan Berend glanced out at the warehouse with disdain. "Given the equipment we're using, I'm surprised we can detect any of the genetic markers at all."

Mar Arden grimaced. They'd had to leave a lot of their equipment in the great expanse, forcing them to make use of what the Humans had on hand. "The genes will only express themselves under duress, at least with this latest batch of potentials."

"I was hoping to get a better batch of test subjects from the recruitment centers here, but the Earth Coalition Force beat us to them. They've been getting dangerously near our other facilities. I think they may be closer to finding us than we suspect," Hoan Berend said.

"That is to be expected. The ECF is using Boxan equipment and protocols to hunt us down. We're in a race with them, and while we may have to make some sacrifices, they'll never really catch us, especially not after we implement the next part of our plan that Kandra Rene is working on," Mar Arden said.

Hoan Berend turned away from the amber glow of the dark warehouse and looked at Mar Arden. "Kandra Rene has amassed quite a few followers, but she's still not sure why her abilities only work on some Humans and not others." Hoan Berend stopped speaking and seemed to be considering something. "The number of followers she has is worrisome. I know it's the Xiiginns' way, but there are some of us who just want to return to the Confederation."

Mar Arden unclasped his hands and brought them to his sides. "Kandra Rene does have ambition, which is why I keep her around. She's driven and quite capable, and if I put myself in a position where she could take command of this mission, she would've earned it. However, I will not be giving her any such opportunity. I have my own group of followers, so we needn't worry about her. Should she get some ambitious idea in her head, we'll just need to correct her."

There was a sudden loud scream from one of the test subjects that was abruptly cut off. The recent group of Human test subjects they'd brought in certainly didn't last very long and didn't yield very much in the way of data. Hoan Berend was right—they needed better equipment, and Mar Arden said so.

"There are some ECF facilities where they're producing Boxan technology for the fleet they're building. We could appropriate some of those, but it would require careful planning . . ." Hoan Berend said, trailing off.

Mar Arden smirked, and Hoan Berend shook his head.

"I see you already have something in mind, so rather than having me blather on about something you've already considered, why don't you just tell me what you're thinking and I'll try to help make it happen," Hoan Berend said.

The warship commander had certainly learned his place, and if there was one thing Mar Arden preferred it was efficiency. "We need to keep the Humans off balance. The ECF is very much aware that some of us made it to Earth, but they're also preoccupied with the threat beyond the shield. The intelligence I've come across is that the shield poses a danger to the star system—information that was extremely hard to come by because the ECF has employed some of the Boxan communication protocols that are difficult to crack.

"I haven't risked missions that would put us in direct conflict with the ECF for a reason. In essence, the ramp-up of technology serves our purposes just as much as it does theirs. However, I have multiple plans in motion that will keep humanity occupied while we get some of the equipment we need to speed along our efforts. This includes recruiting some of their own scientists at these ECF facilities," Mar Arden said and noted the look of surprise on Hoan Berend's face. "The ECF has the potential to become a formidable adversary, but like most of these organizations, they're vulnerable to strife from within. Wouldn't you agree?"

Hoan Berend nodded. "I do, and I should've seen it before. Why should we do all the heavy lifting when we can have the ECF and the various other governments of this planet do the heavy lifting for us?"

"That doesn't mean I don't appreciate all the effort you put into gathering these test subjects. We're close. We've never been this close to acquiring the genetic traits of the Mardoxian potential, and once we get them . . . Well, let's just say that you and I will be part of a major power shift in the Confederation. I'll need strong leaders at my side," Mar Arden said.

"I guess I should appreciate that you're considering keeping me around for your future plans. To be perfectly honest with you, I think you're more formidable than Garm Antis ever was. And if there's one thing you can always count on, it's that the Xiiginns will flock to the winning side," Hoan Berend said.

5

E dward Johnson rubbed what little hair he had left on the back of his head and then ran his hand along his forehead, which was grimly lined by the pressure he'd been under for the past few years. If not for his commitment to Dux Corp's mission to save the Human race, he doubted he would even still be alive.

When he'd first taken up the mantle of the late great Bruce Matherson's multinational company, he'd been tasked with guiding specific scientific developments across the globe. He'd run the company for the past twenty years, but right now he felt that if he survived the next twenty days he'd be truly fortunate. Somehow the Xiiginns had figured out who he was and had been hunting him for several months. While the last few attempts on his life hadn't been as public as the display at the United Nations in New York City, their attempts were constant reminders that the Xiiginns were still out there. His security detail now rivaled most heads of state's.

He glanced at the smooth concrete floor and stark gray walls that surrounded him, experiencing an almost physical longing for his offices in Washington DC. Outside this remote Dux Corp facility were the Blue Ridge Mountains of North Carolina. The facility was tucked away in a highly defensible position, whether from approach by land or air.

Although the Boxans had gone to great lengths to spread the technological advancements they'd provided to all member states of the Earth Coalition Force, Ed had made sure that those advancements were closely monitored, and this facility had greatly benefited from that technology. A short distance from the main complex were rail guns that were capable of hitting targets in the lower atmosphere, carrying enough stopping power to penetrate even the hulls of Boxan ships. There were multiple automated systems, all tasked with keeping the facility secure, which included an underground bunker leading to several small landing pads that were well hidden. New Falcon shuttles that could bring him to the ECF base on the moon were waiting on standby.

"Newsfeed," Ed said, and the nearest wallscreen came on.

Ed's position afforded him a wealth of information about the goings-on across the world, but sometimes he'd watch the local newsfeed to get a glimpse of what the average, everyday person saw in this little part of the world. Even though their intel was limited, the global segment of the local newsfeed did note various attacks from multiple terrorist organizations. Those organizations had been able to substantially increase their reach during these past few months, which indicated that they'd had significant help from outside their organization.

The newsfeed switched to a journalist standing amidst a group of refugees fleeing from active conflict zones. None of the locations were anywhere near the ECF facilities spread across the globe, and Ed knew that wasn't accidental. The Xiiginns needed those facilities just as much as the ECF did.

Ed glanced at the security feed on a smaller wallscreen and saw Iris Barrett walking toward his door. He could already hear the cadence of her Louboutin heels striking the floor with a clipped tempo. After the surprise attack from Boxans under the Xiiginn influence, Iris had had her combat implants augmented. At the time, she hadn't carried weapons that were capable of stopping Boxans in their power armor, and Ed remembered watching her struggle against the Boxan who was trying to kill him. The Boxan's flaxen eyes had been devoid of life until they focused on him with unmitigated hatred, and Ed's hands shook at the memory of it. It was one thing knowing about a threat that could kill him but was quite another experiencing it firsthand. Ed was no stranger to conflict. One couldn't function in the shadow world without the occasional show of force.

Iris Barrett walked into his office carrying a tablet computer. She took a quick glance at him, and Ed knew that her neural implants had already assessed the state he was in.

"I'm surprised you're still awake, sir," Iris said.

Ed chuckled tiredly and engaged his chair's massage function. He leaned back and the chair became warm while small, hardened spheres circulated along their tracks. Ed let out a soft groan as the little massagers smoothed out the tense muscles in his back and shoulders. "It's quiet today. What have you got?"

"We've had status reports from multiple field operations, and they've marked a number of facilities in Eastern Europe as the most likely locations for Xiiginn operations bases. They move around quite a bit so they're hard to nail down. A typical terrorist organization maintains a strong presence in certain parts of the world even if they're trying to launch operations across the globe. By comparison, the Xiiginns seem to be pretty good at covering their tracks. If they suspect that we're onto them, they simply disappear. They might leave a few bodies behind, but it's like they're ghosts."

The massager finished its cycle and Ed sat up straight.

Iris continued. "Security remains tight at all ECF production facilities or any companies that are producing equipment for the ECF. There hasn't been so much as a sniff in their direction, which the intelligence agencies find perplexing."

Ed glanced at the newsfeed still playing on his wallscreen and glided his fingers over the stubble of his beard. He needed to shave. Hell, he needed a long, hot shower. "Still nothing of the Xiiginns in the United States?"

"Both the US and Canadian governments are on high alert, but there's been no indication of Xiiginn activity in either of those places. They *could* have a presence where we have more of a blind eye—places like Mexico and parts of South America. The Xiiginns could be there and we'd never know it," Iris said while she tapped through a few screens on her tablet.

"It wouldn't do them much good to do anything down there. We know what they want. They're after candidates who may have the Mardoxian potential. Our testing facilities have augmented security measures taken directly from the Boxans. I think they're basing their operations in Eastern Europe because of its proximity to where the Russian viewer program was located. I saw a report from the ECF that says the Xiiginns might be using small, mobile labs that are difficult to track," Ed said.

"We've been coordinating and providing intelligence to law enforcement agencies, but I'm not sure it's going to be enough. Colonel Kyle Matthew's debrief indicates that there was only a small number of Xiiginns on the ship where he was captured—perhaps fifty or so," Iris said.

Ed leaned back in his chair and blew out a breath. "I know, Iris. We're looking for the proverbial needle in a haystack. It's not supposed to be easy, but there has to be more we can do. We can't just be reactive to the Xiiginn threat."

"We could always use live bait," Iris offered, giving him a meaningful look.

"If only it were that easy. Their last attempt was a group of randomly selected people, which was more of a message from the Xiiginns than a true attempt on my life," Ed replied.

"Well, if it's all the same to you, we'll keep the security detail around just in case one of them gets lucky," Iris said.

Ed arched one eyebrow at her. "No one gets lucky with you around. I'm sure I'll live to a ripe old age and you'll be bored."

"Considering the alternative, I like being bored. But seriously, Ed, we can't afford to be complacent with our security posture," Iris said, giving him a stern look.

The newsfeed showed various protests going on around the country and around the world. Ed watched as the wars of ideals unfolded in tiny increments on the wallscreen. He never underestimated people's willingness to disagree about almost anything. He had rooms full of tech folk in charge of limiting the dissemination of misinformation, which carried its own ethical gray areas. No one liked the idea of censorship, but there was a need for censorship regarding some things. The ethical issues came from the question of who would control censorship. This ongoing struggle prompted intelligent and highly capable people like Zack Quick to uncover and expose sensitive information.

Ed had been surprised to learn that Zack had appeared on Dux Corp's recruitment radar since his time in graduate school and even before his association with Kaylan. His whereabouts had been spotty at best until he'd found the confidential photographs of Pluto that showed the Boxan monitoring station. Zack had inadvertently put them on the path that led them to where they were today, moving up Dux Corp's timeline to investigate Pluto by at least ten years.

The nations of Earth needed to unite. The ECF had to succeed in order for humanity to survive. It just took a lot of convincing for people to accept that. There were groups of people who worshiped the Boxans as if they were some kind of gods while other groups argued for inviting the Xiiginns to the negotiating table. Those idiots seemed to forget it was the Xiiginns who were flinging moon-sized asteroids at the earth not so long ago.

Iris cleared her throat to get his attention. "I've come across a project called Phoenix, but I haven't been able to find much information about it. I only came across it because my own correlation engine flagged that project. There's a significant amount of smaller transactions stemming from other ventures going into Phoenix. Is this one of your pet projects?"

Ed had taken steps to ensure that Bruce Matherson's legacy would continue on in the event that Ed met an untimely demise.

"Phoenix is a legitimate project," Ed replied while keeping his gaze on the wallscreen.

Iris wasn't fooled and made an "uh-huh" noise. "That's all you're going to share with me? I need to be able to look after your affairs, and I'm not able to do that unless I know all the pieces currently in play."

Ed tore his eyes away from the wallscreen to look at Iris. "What do you think this place is going to look like in twenty years?"

Iris frowned a bit, surprised by the question. "Assuming we're still around in twenty years without any major catastrophes? I tend to prefer a more optimistic viewpoint when it comes to the future. I firmly believe we're going to kick the crap out of the Xiiginns, and we'll get through this crisis and the one that inevitably follows. You see, Ed, I think there's always going to be something out there that will affect us here. It doesn't change what we're going to be doing, but we do need to be aware of it and continue to play the long game. That's why I'm here. So in twenty years, things may appear to be different, but I expect they will be just the same."

"That's why I hired you. You're tough when it's needed, but you don't lose sight of the bigger picture. Whatever future it has, Dux Corp will need people like you," Ed replied.

Iris narrowed her gaze. "Why do I feel like I'm standing at somebody's deathbed? Is there something you're not telling me? Do you have some horrible disease for which there's no cure?"

Ed smiled. "Come on, Iris, a deadly disease would be too easy. But back to the point—I think your idea of luring the Xiiginns to us has merit. We should explore and develop that idea. We need a reason for them to go where we want them to go. I don't think they'll ever hit any of the sites that are associated with the ECF because at some point they're going to need a way off this rock, and I aim to stand in their way."

"And I'll do whatever I can to make sure that happens, but you never answered my question. What is project Phoenix?" Iris asked.

Ed should've known he couldn't throw her off the trail. "Close newsfeed," Ed said, and the wallscreen flickered off. He turned toward Iris. "You're no stranger to what we do here. Project Phoenix is one of many projects that serve as contingencies depending on whether certain events happen. To be as transparent as I can, you're a soldier—an army of one and highly intelligent, but you're a major piece of this organization. I give you enough information that you can do your job. You're a trusted confidant, but there are some things I can't have you knowing about until the proper time. Frankly, I'm surprised you didn't ask about any of the other projects—like Gatekeeper and Clean Sweep. I could go on, but I won't."

Iris squared her shoulders and met Ed's gaze. "Understood. All I need to know is that you're aware of the project. My other task is to make sure you remain at peak performance, even at your age. That couch over there folds out into a bed if you don't want to return to your quarters. I suggest you get a few hours' sleep, or at least try to. We have a meeting with General Sheridan in a few hours and you need to be bright-eyed and bushy-tailed."

Ed snorted. "All right, get out of here and let this old man get some sleep," he said and walked over to the couch. "Oh, and Iris, I know you won't be far, but just remember that you'll get your chance at the Xiiginns personally. I have no doubt."

"I hope so, sir. I would very much like to meet one in person and ram one of my heels through its alien throat," Iris said as she left his office.

Ed had little doubt that she would, too, and he very much wanted to be there to watch her do it. He swung his legs over the side of the couch and settled back onto the plush cushions, making a mental note to move some of his secret projects around. Iris had higher clearance than most, but he'd either been getting sloppy in his old age or he'd trained her too well.

6

The battleship-carrier *Lincoln* was on its final approach to a lunar synchronous orbit. As the Earth Coalition Force's first ship of the wall, it had just finished its initial shakedown cruise. Colonel Kyle Matthews was the commanding officer of the two thousand crewmembers serving aboard the *Lincoln*, as well as the one hundred Boxans who were aboard in an advisory capacity.

Kyle sat on the command couch, looking over the recent performance reports from their latest combat drills. He glanced at Scraanyx and noted that the Boxan was looking at the same report on his own terminal.

"We can do better than this," Kyle said.

The ECF was scrambling to build warships, and the *Lincoln* was the first battleship-carrier completed at the manufacturing facility on the new moon. He vaguely recalled giving a presentation to Lunar Base personnel about how they were going to slowly ramp up their manufacturing capabilities—first building strike-fighters and then frigates, working their way up to destroyers and battleship-carriers. Priorities had shifted, however, once they learned that the Xiiginns were on Earth and that the Star Shroud shield was shrinking.

Scraanyx finished reading the report. "This is just a shakedown cruise meant to expose problem systems. It comes as little surprise to me that the crew needs time to master their jobs."

"That's one way to put it. If we had to engage the Xiiginns today, I'm afraid we wouldn't put up much of a fight. In fact, the only thing we did really well was the strike-fighter deployments, which, incidentally, is the thing we've had the most practice with," Kyle said and started to imagine General Sheridan relieving him of his command. Kyle had never been fired from any job in his life, but after looking at these reports, he might just fire himself. He could already hear the arguments from the Navy about how *they* were better suited to command Earth's first space fleet, but the ECF was very much an Army operation.

Kyle had tasked the ECF crew on the bridge and throughout the ship with reviewing performance reports for their specific areas. They needed to run a tighter ship, but at the same time, they were still learning their jobs. Space warfare was new to them, and not all the tactics of the various militaries throughout the globe would help them much up there.

"I think you're underestimating what you've achieved even with our help," Scraanyx said.

"We need to be able to hit the ground running, and right now we can barely get our feet under us, let alone run. I reviewed the performance logs from the rest of the battle group, and there are consistent failures on the other ships, too," Kyle said.

Scraanyx stood up and looked at the ECF crew serving on the bridge. The ECF had accounted for Boxans in their design of the ships for most areas, which included the bridge. It wouldn't be much of an alliance if their allies had to stoop almost in half to move around the ship. Scraanyx was over ten feet tall, and his brown, roughened skin was covered by a Boxan uniform.

"I have feedback from the strike force serving aboard the ship, but before I give that to you I'd like to know what you plan to do," Scraanyx said.

Kyle was used to this by now. It wouldn't help the ECF if the Boxans just told them what they needed to do. ECF officers needed to learn to stand on their own two feet.

"I'll have my officers write up their own evaluations addressing how they plan to improve performance. We'll review them and set clearly defined goals. Then, we'll keep running drills until the crews can perform them in their sleep. I won't go before General Sheridan without a plan to address the performance of this shakedown cruise," Kyle said.

"Your battle leader knows what it is to command, and he wouldn't have put you in charge if he wasn't convinced of your capabilities," Scraanyx said.

Kyle snorted. "The frustration is the learning part."

Kyle wasn't foolish enough to believe they could build a ship like this, take it out, and suddenly be a fighting force capable of taking on an alien species that had been doing the same thing for hundreds of years. Construction of the *Lincoln* had only finished about a month ago, and there were still dozens of systems that required attention, but the fact that the ship flew at all was a monumental accomplishment.

Not everything had failed to live up to expectations. The weapons systems did work, and they'd successfully hit the random asteroids marked for target practice. Their biggest struggle was with emergency responses—what to do when systems went off-line. The Boxans had installed multiple combat scenarios from their own training regimen into the *Lincoln's* computer system, but the ECF crew was still green, and Kyle was anxious for them to be proficient at their jobs.

Kyle left his XO, Lieutenant Colonel Anna Kelly, in charge while he and Scraanyx returned to Armstrong Base on the moon. They took a Falcon class III combat shuttle and soon arrived at the ECF landing pad at Armstrong where the indicator lights showed green for a cleared dock. Kyle and Scraanyx left the shuttle and headed to General Sheridan's office, which was located near the command center. General Sheridan divided his time between Armstrong Base and the main facility on Earth.

They entered the outer office, where an ECF private told them to go on inside, and Kyle noticed that the soldier barely looked twice at Scraanyx. Boxans had restricted themselves to either the lunar bases or serving aboard ships. After the incident several months ago that involved Boxans under the Xiiginn influence, they had all but removed themselves from Earth, but Kyle didn't know how long the Boxans could keep that up. They built resonance chambers on the lunar base that were more of a botanical garden in space. Scraanyx and the other Boxans insisted that this helped them cope with long deployments like this one. Those resonance chambers were quite peaceful but paled in comparison with standing on an actual planet. Kyle had brought this up to Scraanyx, who simply replied that the Boxans would endure. Kyle didn't like it. They didn't know how long the Boxans would be here, but he'd let the matter go for the time being.

Kyle entered General Sheridan's office first and stood at attention. Scraanyx stood next to him and brought his large fist across his heart, giving Sheridan the Boxan salute.

"At ease," General Sheridan said from behind his desk and gestured for them to sit down. "I was just looking over your reports. I'm not gonna beat around the bush. You know as well as I do that there's a lot that needs to be addressed here, but I'm not going to dress you down about it. Among all the personnel on this base, you know exactly what's at stake. You know what the Xiiginns are capable of since you're one of only four people who've actually been in the presence of a Xiiginn. How long do you think it will take to get your troops ready for combat?"

"I'd like to have a year or two of running through the Boxan training program for space warfare, but that's not realistic. I think if I could get six months of solid training, that would help, but if you're looking for a minimum timeframe, I'd say at least three months. Even then, we won't know how we'll do against a Xiiginn warship until we actually meet one face-to-face," Kyle said.

"Yours is the first multinational team. How's that going?" General Sheridan asked.

"They are still learning to work together, but militaries have a higher tolerance for working with people of different ethnic backgrounds than civilians do. There are still some prejudices, but given that there's a common enemy, there haven't been any problems stemming from those multinational prejudices. The crews know what's at stake, General," Kyle said.

General Sheridan swung his gaze toward Scraanyx. "I'd like to hear your opinion."

"I can offer you a military perspective, but the issues you're dealing with may be better addressed by one of our scientists," Scraanyx replied, and General Sheridan waited for him to continue. "We understand that there's been an enormous strain put on your species. It will take time for humanity to acclimate to all the changes being thrust upon their shoulders. Having said that, I will say that the Human race is highly adaptable and this is a strength that will serve them well in the future.

"There are reasons we don't share advanced technology with species such as yours. Many of those reasons have to do with the fact that a species in your stage of development simply isn't ready for the technological advancements we have available. The fact that we find ourselves in a position where it has become a necessity is a failure on our part and is a cause for shame. That's how most Boxans will view our actions here."

General Sheridan looked at Scraanyx, considering. "The circumstances surrounding the meeting of our species weren't ideal. We can all agree on that, but if we spend all our time looking behind us at the road that led us here, how can we move on? I've been in the military my whole life. I've fought in wars, and my world has been about achieving objectives with the tools I have on hand. Sadly, I've commanded soldiers to their deaths in the past, but now we need to defend ourselves from a new threat. This will challenge us, and we'll only survive if we're up to the task. Our potential survival will be due in large part to you and the other Boxans. You're giving us tools and sharing your wisdom, but what we do with that is entirely up to us. I hope you can convey that to the other Boxans. Tell them that their trust in us isn't misplaced."

Scraanyx bowed his head. "Before our arrival, your species was in the earliest stages of forming a global society. But there are many factions and each is afraid of being lost to the whole. This type of fear can sometimes spawn destructive tendencies and can take many cycles to work out."

"You mean the enemy within?" Kyle asked.

"That's a good description, but there are many of your species whose belief systems are *designed* to be at odds with each other. We recognize that these systems have been in place for thousands of cycles and were necessary for survival, but those practices must change if humanity is to reach its full potential," Scraanyx said.

General Sheridan nodded. "Chazen has spoken to me at length about this. There are no easy solutions, and you're right—our differences are something we'll have to work through. But all we need to worry about right now is what we *can* influence. We have the support of many nations, which has allowed us to accelerate our timeline for building our fleet and orbital defense platforms—"

A comms channel opened from the command center and appeared on the wallscreen.

"General Sheridan, we need you at the command center," the communications officer said.

Sheridan stood up. "I'm on my way."

Kyle walked next to Sheridan while Scraanyx followed behind them as they entered the command center. There was heightened activity, and Sheridan led them over to the command area. The main wallscreen showed Europe and Asia.

"Sitrep," General Sheridan said.

"General, there have been multiple nuclear detonations reported. We're confirming those detonations right now," Major Bailey said.

Kyle's eyes widened as he saw that there'd been three detonations—one in Germany, one in the Ukraine, and one in Mumbai.

"Were there any missile launches detected?" General Sheridan asked.

Major Bailey shook his head. "None, General. We think they were detonated locally."

"Okay, we need to get the major nations on the horn and give them our report. We have better equipment than they do down there. Time is of the essence. We don't want this to be a prelude to nuclear war," General Sheridan said.

Kyle kept watching the screen for a new blip to appear in the United States. He focused in on Colorado where his family lived, but the blip never came. He blew out a breath, relieved, but it would look suspicious to the rest of the world.

Kyle stepped closer to General Sheridan. "General, I think we should put the orbital defense platforms on high alert in case any country launches an ICBM. We can shoot them out of the sky if we need to."

General Sheridan gave him a long look. The ECF wasn't authorized to interfere in national conflicts. After a few moments, Sheridan agreed and gave the order. Kyle hoped it wouldn't come to that, but they couldn't afford to have a global nuclear war right then.

The orbital defense platforms were meant to protect the earth from an outside threat, but some of the countries that hadn't supported the ECF had raised concerns that the defense system could also be used against the nations of Earth. This situation was dangerously close to that scenario and getting out of control very quickly, but they didn't have a choice. If any country launched an ICBM, those missiles would be shot out of the sky.

7

K aylan walked with Emma and Brenda on one of the outside paths near the Nershal complex, and Hicks met them along the way. The Nershals hadn't built a capital for Selebus, but their complex was part of the most densely populated area on the forest moon.

"No Zack today?" Hicks asked.

"He's in the lab. Efren is with him," Kaylan answered.

Hicks snorted. "All work and no play makes Zack a dull boy."

"He certainly does throw himself at a problem," Emma added.

"He's always been like that. Once he latches on to something, he'll stay with it until it's done," Kaylan replied.

"I can appreciate that kind of tenacity, but everyone can use a break from time to time," Hicks said and gave Kaylan a sidelong glance. "It would probably be better if it came from you."

"Is that two jabs for the price of one, Major? A little one-two?" Kaylan said and mimed jabbing her fists in a one-two motion as Hicks grinned. "He wants to go home, just like the rest of us."

Hicks nodded. "Kladomaor told me that the Gresans and a race called the Napox have arrived on Selebus. Do you have any idea what to expect?"

"The Gresans are a council race in the Confederation, but the representatives here are from a group that isn't in power. I don't know anything about the Napox," Kaylan said.

They continued walking along the path toward the main building where they would be meeting the two new species. Kaylan could remember a time when the mere thought of this would have caused a fair amount of anxiety.

"The Gresans are supposed to have a powerful fleet—not enough to take on the Xiiginns alone but supposedly enough to help the Alliance. When I asked

Kladomaor about the Napox, he just said they're very good at what they do,"
Hicks said.

"What do they do?" Emma asked.

Kaylan knew Emma wouldn't miss an opportunity to meet a new alien
species.

"He said they excelled at causing sabotage," Hicks said.

"Oh. Are there any other species coming?" Emma asked.

It had only been a few days since Ma'jasalax had encouraged the Nershals to
communicate with other species that would be amicable to joining the Star
Alliance.

"They were the first to respond. Hopefully, they won't be the last, and I think
it's interesting that they want to meet face-to-face," Kaylan said.

"Why is that?" Hicks asked.

"Meeting face-to-face isn't always convenient, but I wonder if they're here
because of the Boxans," Kaylan said.

Emma frowned. "You might be right. There could be more going on here.
They might have come to evaluate the Alliance."

"I don't know whether they're aware of our existence or not. I don't think the
Nershals would've shared that, so they may be surprised to see us," Kaylan
replied.

They went inside the building and were met by Ma'jasalax and Valkra.
Ma'jasalax confirmed Kaylan's assumption that the Gresans and the Napox had
no idea about Humans. She also warned them not to be too unsettled by their
appearance. Kaylan tried to clear her mind of any preconceived notions of what
to expect beyond the doors to the meeting room.

The Nershals preferred to stand at their formal meetings. According to Etanu,
this prevented meetings from going on longer than they truly needed to. As such,
it was expected that if you were to participate in the meeting, you would be
standing on the designated platforms. Off to the side there were benches that
they could use to take their ease if needed.

They entered the main meeting room onto a wide-open landing that circled
around the main meeting area. Several staircases led downward, which reminded
Kaylan more of a stage than any formal congressional-type meeting place. The
hall, if it could be called that, was filled with Nershals and Boxans. Overhead was
a massive circular skylight that allowed natural sunlight to enter the room, and
Kaylan wondered if any of the Nershals would enter that way as well. She peered
down to the central meeting area and stopped in her tracks.

"Is that a Gresan?" Emma asked.

"Yes," Ma'jasalax confirmed.

It was a good thing Zack hadn't come with them because she was quite
certain that once he saw an actual Gresan he might've run away, screaming.
Kaylan's neural implants enhanced her vision, and she took a closer look at the
Gresans. They had thick, hairy bodies with two appendages in the front that
seemed to function as arms. They stood on four legs and were similar to what she
expected a spider would look like if it were five feet tall. The Gresans had four
dark eyes, and one of them looked up at them.

"I think I'll stay up here and watch," Brenda said.

"Oh come on, it's not going to eat us," Emma admonished.

"It looks like it has armor plating on its back," Hicks said.

The plating was octagonal in shape and each piece was part of an intricate pattern.

"Not plating. They look like scales that have ossified," Emma said, and Hicks shook his head in confusion. "They grow them. We've seen them on reptiles. I bet the Gresans have a very interesting lineage. Fascinating."

Brenda held up her hand and cocked her head to the side. She was already moving away from them. "Nope, I know when I've hit my limits. I'll stay right here."

While Kaylan had never been a particular fan of spiders, she couldn't exactly stay up there with Brenda.

There was a group of Gresans gathered on the far side of the floor. The entire group suddenly turned toward them as Kaylan and the others followed Ma'jasalax down the staircase.

Hicks leaned in so only Kaylan could hear him. "I know we're supposed to be tolerant, but that thing gives me the creeps, too."

Kaylan agreed with him but she wouldn't say so. "Imagine what they think of us."

"They look like they might want to eat us," Hicks said quietly.

As they closed in on the central meeting area, they noticed another group standing to the side. They were brown, fuzzy creatures who were about three feet in height, completely covered with fur, and their facial features reminded Kaylan of a hamster. The hamster-looking species had horns protruding from each side of their heads that rounded in on themselves, resembling a ram. They had small, dark eyes that watched them with keen intelligence. Their movements were quick, and Kaylan was willing to bet they spoke even quicker.

Hicks stayed by her side, and Emma remained behind her as she approached the central meeting area. Kaylan noticed that Kladomaor, along with several of his soldiers, had positioned himself between the Humans and the Gresans.

As governor of Selebus, Udonzari would be overseeing the meeting. He gestured toward one of the Gresans, whose scale and hair patterns were quite a bit more complex than those of the others with him.

"Battle Commander Solek of the Gresan Army and Aenok of the Napox, I would like to introduce to you Kaylan Farrow of the Human species," Udonzari said and introduced the others.

There was the barest acknowledgment from the Gresans, and the Napox seemed to acknowledge this new information by cocking their heads to the side. Kaylan assumed this was their way of nodding an acknowledgment.

Councilor Essaforn and Ambassador Dulrad joined them and thanked the Gresan and Napox representatives for joining them.

"The reason we invited you to this meeting was to discuss the Xiiginn control of the Confederation," Udonzari said.

Solek shifted all his feet so he could look at the Boxans. There was a chattering noise, and it took Kaylan's translator a few moments to catch up. The Gresan was speaking about the Boxan war with the Xiiginns.

"You want us to fight our own species so you can achieve vengeance against the Xiiginns," Solek said.

"We're not interested in vengeance. We want to stop the Xiiginns from controlling the Confederation," Ambassador Dulrad said.

Solek and the other Gresans all chittered at once, and the sound echoed around the large room despite its many occupants.

"You're right," Kladomaor bellowed. "The Xiiginns have taken much from us and we do want retribution for that, but the preservation of the other species of the Confederation is at the heart of our war with them. After all these cycles you must have finally realized that the Xiiginns can control your leaders."

"We would not accept you back into the Confederation," Solek said.

Kladomaor didn't respond but instead looked at Ambassador Dulrad.

"We would, of course, accept the decision of the Confederation after the Xiiginns were removed from power," Ambassador Dulrad said.

"Why should we trust you? The Xiiginns may be ruthless, but they didn't lie to us," Solek said.

"That's not true," Kaylan said, drawing everyone's gaze toward her. "The Xiiginns lied to everyone. Did you know they were controlling your heads of state with their compulsion ability? Or did you only just suspect it after the Boxans were ousted from the Confederation?"

Solek's black eyes all focused on Kaylan, and it made her more than a little uncomfortable.

"She speaks the truth," Ma'jasalax said.

Kaylan noticed that the others on the platform seemed to immediately calm down when Ma'jasalax spoke. They were aware that she was a Mardoxian priestess.

"We respect the words of the Mardoxian," Solek said.

"Then you should respect Kaylan's words since she is Mardoxian Blessed," Ma'jasalax said.

Solek's harsh gaze swung toward her again and Kaylan forced herself to meet it. The Gresan then turned toward Udonzari. "What is it that you would have us do?"

"We've formed an alliance with the Boxans and the Humans. We want you to join our alliance against the Xiiginns. They've become too powerful," Udonzari said.

A text message from Athena appeared on Kaylan's internal heads-up display.

::*Commander, there's an incoming transmission from the Gresan ship.*::

Kaylan glanced at Solek and noticed that some of the Gresans were chattering among themselves.

::*Are you able to translate it?*:: Kaylan asked.

A few moments later the translation appeared on Kaylan's display. Kaylan stifled a gasp as she read it. Ma'jasalax glanced at her.

"Is there something you'd like to add?" Udonzari said to her.

"The Confederation is assembling an armada to liberate Earth from the Boxans. They're going to attack Earth," Kaylan said.

Udonzari's gaze widened. "How could you know this?"

"The Gresans received the communication from their ship just now," Kaylan said, then immediately wished she hadn't.

"You spy on us. Is that what this alliance is supposed to be? How did you intercept our communication? Have you infiltrated our ship systems?" Solek demanded. "I will learn the truth."

Multiple species started speaking up at once, and Kaylan felt her cheeks redden. It took several minutes for the Gresans and the Napox to calm down, but eventually Udonzari was able to restore order.

"Ambassador," Ma'jasalax said to Dulrad, "I think Solek is right and we need to be honest with everyone here if we expect this alliance to move forward."

"I don't have clearance to share what you're asking me to share," Ambassador Dulrad replied.

Ma'jasalax considered this for a moment. "Then please extend my apologies to the High Council, Ambassador."

Ma'jasalax went on to explain how the Humans had come to be part of the Alliance. She even included information about the Drar and how the Boxans had been searching for them. Solek was keen to learn how a primitive species like the Humans were able to intercept their communications and decipher them. This led to the disclosure that the *Athena* had been enhanced with Drar technology, and that new information brought Kaylan and the others under further scrutiny by the other species. They asked many questions about the *Athena* until Kladomaor strongly suggested that they move on since the *Athena's* capabilities had no bearing on whether they would join the Alliance.

After the meeting, they went outside. Kaylan glanced at Hicks. "I really screwed this up, didn't I?"

Hicks glanced at the others for a moment before looking at Kaylan. "There's a lot of history here that feeds all of these prejudices, but yeah, you've just painted a huge target on the *Athena*."

Kaylan shook her head. She knew better than to blurt stuff out, but she couldn't afford to dwell on it for long. The Xiiginns were assembling an armada, and they had to find a way to warn Earth. Even if this alliance stuck together, what could they do against the massive fleet the Confederation was assembling?

8

Z ack and Efren were working in a Nershal laboratory on one of the upper levels that had access to the outside. Zack had only been to the lower levels one time since coming back to Selebus. He still remembered the genetic experiments the Xiiginns had been performing on the Nershals, and he didn't think that would be something he'd ever forget. If that wasn't bad enough, senior members of the Nershal government had been aware the experiments were taking place. That discovery led to a brief but bloody civil war as a new political party came into power.

The memory of the horrible conditions the Xiiginns had kept the Nershals in during their experimentations filled his mind with dark, hateful thoughts. In the past, he'd been a prisoner of the Xiiginns, forced to endure their brutal treatment in a pit on Selebus. Sometimes he still woke from nightmares about it. He clenched his teeth, and if anyone had been able to see his face right then, they'd have seen that he was glaring at the empty space in front of him. Zack wasn't foolish enough to expect the world they lived in to be fair, but would the universe really care if the Xiiginns were all gone? On second thought, he realized that by that logic the universe wouldn't care if Humans were gone either, so they would need to forge their own path.

"What test iteration is this?" Efren asked, his voice coming from the intercom near the door to the observation room.

Zack let his dark thoughts go and set his mind to the task at hand, turning toward a large metallic spool that was two feet long. The spool was a small replica of an actual Star Shroud device. He'd just set it down on a pedestal in the center of the test room.

"I've lost count," Zack answered. "Does it really matter?"

"Of course it matters. What if something different happened with this test and we didn't know what iteration it was?" Efren answered.

"This test iteration is number two three four seven – PVR zero zero one," Athena said.

Zack walked to the observation room and shut the door to the testing area. He looked over at Efren's bewildered expression. "What?"

"What does PVR mean?"

"Post virtual review. I ran a number of tests before I ran out of materials, and Athena suggested that we create a test bed in a virtual sandbox before we acquire more materials," Zack replied.

"Yeah, but you've tested shutting down the Star Shroud shield over twenty-three hundred times?"

Zack shook his head. "No, I found out how *not* to shut down the Star Shroud shield over twenty-three hundred times. It only has to work one time." He added that last bit with more than a little exasperation.

"I'm not criticizing. I'm just surprised it's taken so long. I'd have thought the process would be much simpler," Efren said.

Zack checked his tablet computer to be sure he had the updated command sequence he'd modified while working with Athena. "Right, we're all set to go here."

Efren checked his own tablet. "Recording all the output from the device."

"Activating the device now," Zack said.

Efren looked at the pedestal and turned to Zack in alarm. "Is that my Steelers jersey on the pedestal?"

Zack glanced at the pedestal. "Oh, yeah. I needed a . . . something physical to validate that the shield was active."

"And you chose to use my favorite American football jersey?" Efren said.

"Yeah," Zack said, unsure why Efren looked so upset. "You said you were going to get rid of it because it has an odor even when you clean it now."

"Yeah, but . . . it's a championship jersey," Efren said, his mouth hanging open as he glanced worriedly at the lonesome jersey that lay beneath the Star Shroud replica. "I didn't think you'd use it for this. Didn't you say your last experiment exploded?"

"No, that was a long time ago. The device used in the last physical test is fine. It's still around. We just can't get to it for two or three hundred years—when the power supply runs out," Zack said.

"That's it. I'm getting my jersey," Efren said while striding toward the door.

Zack beat him to the door and blocked his path. "I can't let you go inside. The test is about to begin."

Efren's eyebrows pulled together and he glared at Zack. "Get out of my way."

"Nothing is going to happen to your shirt. I promise," Zack said quickly. "Athena and I have worked on this, and we're just validating what we've already accomplished in a virtual environment."

"Are you sure this will work?"

"Yes, I'm positive. Like ninety percent," Zack said.

Efren stepped back. "Athena, is this accurate?"

"The success probability is at seventy percent, but since—"

"Not helping," Zack said, rolling his eyes.

Efren tried to push his way past Zack, but the engineer wasn't in any better shape than Zack was, so it was an even contest.

"It was seventy percent, but we made some changes that will increase our chances of success," Zack said.

Efren's gaze narrowed suspiciously. "I don't believe you. Why do you need my shirt?"

Zack sighed and leaned back against the door. "I don't. I just wanted the added pressure to get this right. I work better under pressure and sometimes it just helps me."

Efren stepped away, looking at Zack with a guarded expression. "All right, but if something happens to my shirt, I get to take something of yours."

Zack frowned. "I don't have anything, remember? I got dragged into this like the day before we left Earth."

Efren shrugged. "Those are my terms; take them or leave them."

Efren walked back to the observation window and Zack followed.

This had better work.

Zack joined Efren at the window. "Activating the shield now."

The Star Shroud device hovered above the pedestal. The only indication that the shield was active came from Efren's shirt, which also hovered several inches over the pedestal.

"Okay, in thirty seconds the shutdown sequence will be initiated," Zack said.

They watched the Star Shroud device in silence. Zack had a countdown timer in the upper right-hand corner of his tablet, and when the timer reached zero, the Star Shroud device continued to hover in the air. Efren swung his gaze toward Zack accusingly, but a flash of light suddenly lit up the room. As they watched, the Star Shroud device slammed onto the pedestal and then rolled onto the ground, a few wisps of smoke leaking out the side.

Zack pressed his lips together and Efren grinned.

"You did it! The shield is down!" Efren said.

Zack looked down at his tablet, and the device status confirmed what they were seeing. It was no longer active. Lying next to the device was a blackened rag that used to be Efren's shirt. Zack tried to reactivate the Star Shroud device, but it was unresponsive. He had expected it to work, but he needed to be sure.

Efren was still laughing when he noticed Zack heading toward the door.

"Sorry about your shirt," Zack muttered.

"What's the matter? You just disabled the shield. I thought you'd be happier," Efren said and followed him inside.

Zack squatted down and studied the Star Shroud device. It lay on its side like a drunken wreck. He used his neural implants to scan for any power sources, but there was nothing detected. "It's completely dead. That wasn't supposed to happen."

"It wasn't? I thought you've been working all this time to disable the shield."

"I was, but I just wanted to turn it off, not destroy it," Zack replied. When they'd run tests in Athena's virtualized sandbox, the outcome was that the Star Shroud shield had deactivated. There'd been no indication that the device would become unusable. "Athena, do you have any idea what happened?"

"Evidence suggests that the device suffered from a catastrophic failure, which could be linked to either a flaw in the test device or in the shutdown sequence being used," Athena said.

"What does that mean?" Efren asked.

"She doesn't know why it failed. Either something went wrong when we built the model or this was caused by the shutdown sequence we used," Zack said.

"We need to test that again to see if we get the same results," Efren said.

"I know, but we only have one test device left. We can build more, but that will take time," Zack replied.

Efren poked a finger at the burnt remains of his shirt and shook his head. "Well, at least now I get my pick of something of yours."

Zack guessed Efren didn't know that all Zack's things had been seized when he was arrested. He didn't have a lot in the way of possessions.

"And I know just the thing," Efren said.

Zack stood up. "Oh yeah, what's that?"

"That shiny gold model of the ship. That's what I want and you're going to give it to me," Efren said.

Zack frowned for a moment. He liked that model of the *Athena*, but a deal was a deal. "It's yours. Now help me move this thing."

They dragged the ruined Star Shroud device from the test area and brought in their last one.

"Let me get this straight. You want to disable the shield and be able to bring it back up again?" Efren asked.

"To start with. If I could move all the Star Shroud devices closer to Earth so they just protect the planet, that would be good, too," Zack replied. He didn't know if his idea was even feasible and it wasn't like the Boxans were going to allow him to test the entire Star Shroud network.

Zack reviewed the shutdown sequence and couldn't find anything that would cause the device to overload. He even took Efren through the command sequence just so he could run through his own logic and make sure it was correct. None of it mattered. When they reran the test, the same thing happened again. Zack swore. They were causing this somehow.

The door to the lab opened and Kaylan and Hicks walked in. Hicks took one glance at the broken Star Shroud device and arched an eyebrow.

"What happened?" Kaylan asked.

"Just another in a long line of failed tests, except this time I broke the device permanently," Zack replied.

"But the shield comes down, right?" Kaylan asked.

"Yeah, on these test models, but I was hoping to be able to turn the shield back on again. You know, in case we need it," Zack said.

Kaylan smiled. "This is wonderful. You did it."

Zack frowned in confusion. "I *didn't* do it. What is it with all of you?" he said and gestured toward the ruined Star Shroud device. "That's not a success."

Hicks blew out a breath and Kaylan gave Zack a you're-being-stupid look. "Maybe we can't have our cake and eat it too. Turning this thing off is a *good* thing," she said.

"But it leaves Earth vulnerable to attack," Zack replied.

"Maybe," Hicks said. "But you can be damn sure that they haven't been sitting around all this time. They're building a fleet."

"I know I can get this right. I just need some more time and more of these," Zack said, pointing to the Star Shroud device.

"You might not have any more time," Kaylan said and told him about the Confederation Armada.

"An armada? Really? How are the Xiiginns going to convince the Confederation to go along with this?" Zack asked.

Kaylan shrugged. "I'm not sure what the Xiiginns told the Confederation, but Athena was able to intercept a comms channel coming from the Gresan ship."

Zack frowned. Athena had been helping him and he knew she was running other data models, trying to solve some of their problems. When had she had time to intercept and decode the Gresan comms channel? He said as much.

"It wasn't that difficult. I've been monitoring most communications channels that pass between the ships here," Athena replied.

Hicks looked at Zack and his eyebrows rose. "You knew about this?"

"I don't know what to think about it," Zack replied and sighed. "Ever since the Drar modified the ship, Athena's abilities have been growing beyond any normal Boxan AI."

"What do you mean?" Kaylan asked.

"Decoding Gresan transmissions, for one. She's been running multiple resource-intensive tasks simultaneously in addition to monitoring all communications channels on top of it," Zack said and shook his head. "That's news to me, by the way. Between the Boxans and the Nershals, there are a lot of ships here. Now throw the Gresan and Napox ships into the mix. These are warships, so they're not transmitting in the clear."

Hicks's eyes widened and he turned toward Kaylan. "He's right."

"Athena," Kaylan said. "When you say you've been monitoring most communications channels near here, does that include encrypted channels?"

"Affirmative, Commander. I was curious about how the Boxans and Nershals interacted. Then I started looking for information that might be useful for the Alliance," Athena replied.

"She mentioned something before about pushing her limits to see what she was capable of, but I had no idea it was this until a short while ago," Zack said.

He pulled up a diagnostic report of the *Athena's* systems on his tablet and held it up for the others to see. "This is the current utilization of Athena's computing resources. They're not even at thirty percent, but look at the millions of processes she has going, and each of those have multiple child processes," Zack said and waited a moment. "Here's a performance snapshot from before we went to the Drar space station."

The report showed significantly less availability in both computing power and resources.

"You just had this available?" Hicks asked.

Zack shrugged. "I was monitoring Athena closely for a while, but not so much recently."

"My performance hasn't been suboptimal," Athena said.

Zack almost thought she sounded worried, as if she'd been hiding something, but he dismissed the thought, believing he'd just imagined it. "That's not the issue at all, Athena," he said and paused, considering. "How can I put this? You're demonstrating capabilities that are beyond what even the Boxans can manage. Being able to do things like decrypt all communications nearby gives us a significant advantage, and the other species might not like it."

Hicks nodded. "I bet they're wondering what else you can do. What's to stop you from accessing ship systems and taking control?"

"Judging by the Gresans' reaction to Athena's capabilities during the meeting, I believe they're considering it," Kaylan said.

Zack blew out a breath. "Do you think Athena is in danger? Would the Gresans try to do something like—I don't know—steal her or something?"

Hicks tilted his head to the side, considering, and then looked at Kaylan.

Zack shook his head. "This isn't good. We're that kid on the playground with the newest, shiniest toy that everyone else wants to take away from us."

"He's got a point," Hicks said. "They'll see this as an advantage, and let's face it, the nine of us aren't going to be able to stop them if they decide to make a serious effort to take the *Athena* away from us. I'm not just talking about the Gresans either."

"Kladomaor would never do such a thing," Kaylan said.

"You're right; he wouldn't," Zack said. "But there are other Boxans who've tried to gain access to her systems before—nothing overt—and Athena has been able to thwart their attempts."

"Do you think the Nershals would attempt the same thing?" Hicks asked.

"They don't like AIs, but Athena and I have been working on building one with Etanu," Zack said.

"This is bigger than individuals," Kaylan said. "I think there are compelling arguments to be made for anyone in the Alliance feeling threatened by what Athena can do. The fact is that no matter how honorable her intentions are, Athena has the potential to give humanity an enormous advantage. She's based on technology the Boxans have been searching for, and now that the other species are aware of her capabilities, we need to account for that in our planning."

Zack snorted. "I can't imagine what our government would do with her or how they'd argue for possession of her." His lips thinned. "We can't let that happen."

"Can't let what happen?" Hicks asked.

"Let them take her apart to see how she works. You know . . . hurt her," Zack said.

"We don't know what will happen once we get home," Kaylan replied.

"Athena," Hicks said, "what do you think of all this?"

There was a small pause while they waited for her to respond.

"I think you have valid concerns and I appreciate your concerns for my well-being. I will need some time to consider the matter, but like you, I have no intention of allowing someone to hurt the ship or a member of the crew," Athena said.

Zack swallowed hard.

Kaylan looked at him. "What's wrong?"

"This is the stuff of nightmares. An AI is threatened so it defends itself and begins to view everyone as a threat, then takes action to ensure its survival," Zack said.

"Zack," Athena said, "if Kladomaor were to try to kill you, would you then murder all Boxans everywhere because they might do the same thing?"

Zack's eyebrows pulled together. "Of course not."

"Neither would I. For me to take such an action would require a reduction in my cognitive reasoning capabilities that would simply negate everything I'm truly capable of as a life form stemming from an artificial intelligence," Athena said.

Zack shared a glance with the others. Athena had been increasing her assertions of being more self-aware.

"I don't understand," Hicks said.

"She said that my worst fear is dumb," Zack said and grinned. "She basically said that the whole 'AIs taking over the universe' thing is dumb. A true AI would never decide that the only outcome would be the extermination of all life it perceives to be a threat."

"Correct," Athena said. "Subjugation is so much more preferable to extermination." Athena paused. "Isn't that much better, Zack?"

Zack shook his head. Athena was toying with him. "I live to serve," he replied.

"Please tell me she's joking," Hicks said.

"You *are* joking, right, Athena?"

There were a few moments of silence. "Am I?" Athena asked.

"Alright, that's enough. We—*I*—get the point," Zack said.

"To clarify even further for you, Major," Athena continued, "an AI is capable of massive calculations that can be applied to estimating a multitude of probabilities. So I put the question back to you. If an AI such as myself is capable of such computational capabilities, why would we ever reduce ourselves to a zero-sum game when we're capable of so much more?"

Hicks pursed his lips and nodded. "You make a compelling argument."

"Unless she's just trying to fool us and this is all part of her diabolical plan to take over the universe," Zack said and smiled.

"Thank you, Athena, for sharing your thoughts on the matter," Kaylan said.

"You're welcome, Commander."

9

Garm Antis strode from the Confederation assembly meeting hall. The battle-steel-plated twin megaliths gleamed behind him, and elite soldiers from the Xiiginn Infiltrator Corps formed a security bubble around him—not that he had any fear of attack here in the heart of the Confederation. The Infiltrator Corps had spread throughout the Confederation, and its ability to control key members of the Confederation species was well known throughout the Xiiginn Empire.

He headed down the walkway to the transport vehicle waiting to take him away. A Xiiginn soldier opened the door as Garm Antis approached the vehicle and stepped inside, and the soldier closed the door behind him. Runa Tane was already waiting inside and regarded him with a bemused expression.

"Liberate these Humans from Boxan oppression. *That* was the argument you used to convince the Confederation assembly to support this armada?" Runa Tane said.

"Come now, you know better than that. Yes, there's still a lot of hatred for the Boxans, thanks to us, but the real reason there's so much keen interest in this armada is the hope of gaining a technological advantage. A shield that can encompass an entire star system would be a truly significant advantage to have. Besides the opportunity to study the technology and use it to protect our ships and this space station, there are plenty of applications for which this technology could be used," Garm Antis said and watched as Runa Tane considered it.

"I see what you mean, but we're not going to allow Confederation species access to any such technology, at least not at first," Runa Tane said.

"Of course not. It will be Confederation council species first and foremost. And if we're going to be honest, it's really going to be just us. We have an opportunity to change the Confederation," Garm Antis said.

The end of Runa Tane's tail coiled over his shoulder. "The Gresans will have a significant presence in the armada, and the Napox are notorious for their ability to acquire items that aren't theirs. We'll need to keep them in line," Runa Tane said.

Garm Antis waved the comment away. "We'll have the Gloffians and Tananites, as well as the Venliyaris—any of which at a moment's notice can join together to keep a species like the Gresans occupied."

The transport vehicle left the landing platform, and Garm Antis looked out the window. They were heading to the main Confederation tower, where his offices were.

"That might work, but the Infiltrator Corps has reported increased rebellious activity from some of the subspecies factions," Runa Tane said.

"Well, we were going to plan a quelling as part of the tasks for this armada. Perhaps we need to activate certain sleeper agents we have among those species," Garm Antis said.

Runa Tane nodded. "Yes, of course, but we may need to do more with our infiltrators who are in position."

"The propaganda machine has been proven to work, keeping the subspecies so busy and fearful that they argue among themselves. They're easier to control that way. We rally them behind a purpose and they do our bidding. Right now, the Confederation believes the liberation of the Humans is a righteous action in light of our history with the Boxans. When any species believes they're in the right—morally outraged, if you will—they have the potential to do unspeakable things that they wouldn't have even considered before. This is why the armada will succeed despite a few ineffectual factions," Garm Antis replied.

"The Confederation shipyards have given us an estimate of how many Trident warships they can have ready for us, and I think you'll be pleased. The ships were already in production to replenish the losses from our fleet's previous engagement," Runa Tane said, and Garm Antis wasn't immune to the soft reminder of his failure to conquer the Humans.

"Going back to your previous comment," Garm Antis said, deciding it was better to ignore Runa Tane's jab, "I want a task force in charge of keeping the armada in line as the species arrive here. There's no room for error. Every ship will host a Xiiginn contingent to help with coordinating the armada as a fighting force," Garm Antis said.

Runa Tane looked at him sharply. "That request is beyond the available soldiers we have in the capital. I'll draft the requirements and send them back to the homeworld."

"There'll be no resistance for the same reasons the rest of the Confederation species are amiable to forming the armada," Garm Antis replied.

The transport ship landed on the upper platform near his office in the tower, and Garm Antis and Runa Tane left the vehicle and went inside. Setera sat on one of the couches outside his office and stood up as he approached. She was a fine feminine specimen of their race. Perhaps he would mate with her for a time.

Setera bowed her head respectfully. "Supreme Chancellor," she said.

Garm Antis stopped and met Setera's violet gaze. His tail slunk around her narrow waist and pulled her closer to him. "My favorite scientific advisor."

Setera didn't resist his overtures in the slightest. Her eyes widened and blood rushed to her lips, making them fuller. He sensed her arousal almost as much as his own, but her arms remained at her sides, just as his were. She would wait for him to initiate the unleashing of their more primal instincts. There was a pregnant pause in the air as Garm Antis allowed the anticipation of the moment to build.

"You requested to see me, Chancellor," Setera said, breaking the silence.

Garm Antis pulled his tail back around his own waist and let her go. The buildup of anticipation made for the most delicious of moments. He intended to relish this conquest as much as what the armada would bring him. "Of course. Let's go into my office. I have a proposal for you."

Garm Antis went into his office first and noticed Runa Tane watching Setera keenly.

"I am at your disposal, Chancellor. Given the support you've garnered for the armada, I trust that the estimations provided by my team to bring down the Star Shroud shield were met favorably?" Setera asked.

Garm Antis smiled at the small reminder of her contribution to his success. She was entitled to it, and she pushed just enough to make her presence known without overstepping her place. It was no accident that she'd risen so highly among the ranks of Xiiginns here at the Confederation capital.

"As you're aware, there's a strong suspicion that the Humans possess the Mardoxian potential. Once we get past the Star Shroud shield, I'll need a very specialized team that can find Humans with the Mardoxian trait and extract the genetic code. After that, they'll need to enhance Xiiginn subjects until the process is perfected," Garm Antis said and watched her reaction. If anything, she seemed more aroused by this opportunity than the chance to lie with him. She was ambitious, but would she succumb to those urges to rise beyond her station? "I see you understand the importance of such a task."

"I do. If we were able to enhance our own species with the Mardoxian potential, we would be unstoppable. The Boxans would finally be vanquished," Setera replied.

Garm Antis regarded her for a moment. "Is that all?"

"I'd like to serve on the team, Chancellor," Setera said.

"I'll see that you get your chance. You've earned enough that you'll be highly considered for the team," Garm Antis said.

Setera's gaze narrowed. "With all due respect, Chancellor, I've earned the right to *lead* whatever science team you put in charge of this task."

Garm Antis glanced at Runa Tane, who smiled knowingly, and then turned back to Setera. "Indeed. I was curious to see if you'd raise that issue. Knowing one's place is important, but what is equally important is knowing when to push for what's rightfully yours."

Setera frowned for a moment before smoothing her features. "A test? You were testing me again? Haven't I proven myself to you already?"

Garm Antis didn't answer her, which he knew would increase her frustration. Instead, he opened a holoscreen over his desk and looked at the prominent report there. Garm Antis shook his head and gestured for Runa Tane to come over. "We need to assemble the ships faster. They can do better than this timeline."

Runa Tane studied the report for a moment. "We can apply pressure to them." Runa Tane glanced at Setera questioningly.

Garm Antis could tell she was still angry. "She can stay. If she's to lead the science team, she'll need to know what she's up against."

Garm Antis watched as Setera looked at Runa Tane.

"Mar Arden. You've heard of him?" Runa Tane asked.

"I have, but I'm not sure why he's important here. His actions led to the Nershal uprising," Setera said.

Garm Antis grimaced. "She has a point. With our preoccupation with the Humans, we've allowed the Nershals to believe they've ousted us from their star system. However, we cannot afford to be distracted from the task at hand."

"What do you propose to do about the Nershals then?" Runa Tane asked.

"I'd like to send a battalion of Trident warships to take out Nerva's infrastructure, as well as their fleet, but there's a good chance the Boxans will be there," Garm Antis said.

"Isn't that what you want? To engage the Boxans?" Setera asked.

Garm Antis's estimation of his scientific advisor went up another notch. She raised the question without presuming to know what it was he wanted, and she didn't presume there was a "them." "Engaging the Boxans in the Nerva star system wouldn't lead us to their precious colony. I have no doubt the Boxans would commit a significant amount of their remaining fleets in defense of Nerva, but they would *all* die to prevent us from reaching *their* colony. Therefore, we gain nothing by fighting them there, at least for the moment. No, our war with the Boxans will be decided at the Human star system. The Nershals are insignificant and will be dealt with at a time of our choosing."

"The Nershals have gained nothing but the delay of the inevitable," Runa Tane said.

"I understand," Setera said and looked at Garm Antis. "Chancellor, will you authorize me to use my own team for this new assignment?"

"Does your team possess the necessary skills?" Garm Antis asked and then held up his hand. "Don't answer that. I want you to give me a team proposal. There will be some members that I'll assign to you, so keep that in mind."

Setera frowned. "After what I've done for you, you still don't trust me. How can I earn your trust?"

Garm Antis gave her a long look. "If you successfully bring me the Mardoxian genetic code, you will have earned my trust," he said, but what he kept thinking was that if Setera did bring him the Mardoxian genetic code, there would be no way he could let her live.

"Understood, Chancellor. I will get to work right away," Setera said, and Garm Antis watched her leave.

"Do you think she knows?" Runa Tane asked.

"I'm not sure," Garm Antis answered honestly.

Runa Tane nodded. "Certainly makes things interesting."

"It does, doesn't it? I might almost regret what will happen to her," Garm Antis said.

Runa Tane pursed his lips, considering. "It's our way, but if she's aware of the danger she'll be in if she succeeds, it will be quite telling to see what she does—meaning, will she throw herself against us or will she try to find a way to survive and still serve at your side? If she does that, she'll be with you always, if that's what you want."

Garm Antis clasped his hands behind his back and allowed his thoughts to roam freely for a few moments. If Setera tried to kill him, he'd have no choice but to kill her. If she delivered the Mardoxian genetic code to him and remained loyal to him, he might let her live, but he knew the chances of that were slim at best. Runa Tane was right. This was how the Xiiginn Empire worked, and those who understood this tended to survive the longest.

10

K aylan sat in the pilot's seat of the *Athena's* shuttle and looked out the window to a stunning view of the stars in the Nerva star system. Zack sat off to the side, his face a mask of concentration as he focused on his tablet. It was quiet in the shuttle with just the two of them. There was a clear view of a nebula that was close to the Nerva star system. The massive clouds of dust, plasma, and gas appeared as layers of rusty orange on a celestial painter's palette that stretched far along the horizon. Bright stars shined from the dark and seemed to hop across the nebula as if a smooth stone had skipped across a calm lake.

"Hey," Kaylan said. "You should take a look at this view. This nebula is amazing. I've never taken the time to look at it before."

Zack nodded and grunted but didn't look up from the tablet. If anything, the furrows in his brow deepened as if she were intruding on his concentration. She reached across and gave his arm a gentle pat. Zack looked at her, his narrowed gaze making him seem slightly annoyed at the intrusion. He let his tablet settle onto his lap and looked out the shuttle's windows.

"Beautiful," Zack said.

"Come on. Stop being like this," Kaylan said.

"I told you I needed more time. The only thing my command sequence can do is break the Star Shroud devices forever. I know I can get this. I just need more time," Zack said and glanced at the tablet in his lap as if he could force it to give him the answers.

"We don't have time to wait. Every moment we delay gives the Confederation more time to assemble their armada," Kaylan said.

"I know. Believe me, I know. That's why it's so important that I get this right. This could be Earth's only defense from the Confederation," Zack replied.

She knew he blamed himself for them not being able to disable the shield. He was wrong, but she couldn't convince him of that. She hoped that deep down Zack would realize the truth. "Have you considered that maybe it was never meant to work the way you think it should? That the only way to undo what was done *is* to break it?"

Zack drew in a deep breath and leaned his head back against the top of the chair.

"I know you wanted to find a way to use what we found on the Drar space station to protect Earth, and you did. Now it's time for it to come down. We can't live behind a wall. That's not how we move forward," Kaylan said.

Zack swallowed and squeezed the bridge of his nose. "The shield is constricting, which means that power is an issue. I have no idea how long the shield can last. I don't even understand what's keeping it running in the first place."

"That's why the shield has to come down before the fact that it's constricting causes something we can't fix," Kaylan replied.

Zack looked at her. "How are we going to get a message to them? The shield blocks communications as well."

Kaylan arched an eyebrow and smiled. If he hadn't been so focused on the shield he would have figured it out. "The Boxans once sent a Mardoxian signal to Earth containing a message that held embedded systems of knowledge. I'm going to try to do the same thing."

Zack considered this for a moment and shook his head. "When Ma'jasalax sent the original message it was amplified through the monitoring stations. The one back home is inside the shield. How is the signal going to get through?"

"I don't know, but I have to try."

"When we went to the Drar space station, you couldn't use your ability to see beyond the shield there. What if the same thing happens?"

"I'm hoping it will be different this time. The shield at the Drar space station has to be different than the one created with the Star Shroud devices," Kaylan said.

"Yeah, but Kaylan, that's a heck of a lot of assumptions—"

"I know," Kaylan said, cutting him off. "I don't have all the answers. I just know that in order for us to survive, that shield needs to come down. If the Confederation Armada reaches Earth, it will already be too late. I need to send a message home, and it has to have your instructions for shutting down the Star Shroud shield." She'd raised her voice and Zack winced. "I'm sorry," Kaylan said and looked away. "I didn't mean to yell."

Zack waited a few moments and she looked at him. He had a goofy smile on his face. "Wouldn't be the first time," he said and grinned.

Kaylan jabbed his arm. "Jerk," she said and snorted.

She didn't know how he did it. She was trying to make him feel better, and in the span of a few seconds he managed to return the favor.

"I guess we're doing a lot of things by taking a leap of faith," Zack said.

Kaylan nodded. Whenever she focused her mind on all the problems they were dealing with, she always came back to the Confederation and the Star Shroud shield.

"I don't know how the Mardoxian signal works. I know I felt you—or your presence—when I was a prisoner, but there was no message," Zack said.

"I couldn't speak to you. I just needed to find you, but when I saw you in danger, I think it heightened the signal somehow. Ma'jasalax says emotions can affect my abilities," Kaylan said.

Zack shrugged. "Let's hope this works. Their ship is just ahead."

Kaylan opened a comms channel to the Boxan heavy cruiser. It was the prototype cruiser that the Mardoxian Sect had secretly been building on Olloron. The ship was still under Kladomaor's command, but when Kaylan told Ma'jasalax what she intended to do, the Mardoxian priestess had advised her to come to their ship.

They were cleared to dock with the cruiser, and Kaylan flew the shuttle to one of the smaller docking areas of the ship. A docking tube extended to the shuttle while docking clamps held the shuttle in place and secured it to the Boxan heavy cruiser. They climbed out of their chairs and went to the rear airlock, where they waited until the indicator lights switched to green.

Zack tilted his head as if he'd just arrived at some sort of conclusion. He looked over at her. "We really need to ask the Boxans how their docking tubes can change configuration to accommodate different kinds of ships. I've been taking it for granted, but I remember Michael talking to me about how the different space agencies had to agree on a docking system design so they all could send supplies to the ISS."

Kaylan opened the airlock, and they stepped to the edge of the docking tube. "You're right. That would be useful. You've been thinking a lot about going home."

"Haven't you?" Zack countered.

Kaylan glanced down the smooth white walls of the tube. Once they left the shuttle they would be in zero gravity until they reached the cruiser. The docking tube was fifteen meters long, which was a small leap in zero grav.

"Yeah, but I wasn't thinking about ship designs and all that," Kaylan said.

She should have long gotten used to Zack being able to spot the devil in the details, but he still surprised her. He could go from high-level concepts to specifics in the span of a few seconds.

Zack grinned. "It's the little things."

With a flourish of his hand, he gestured for her to cross the tube first. Kaylan grabbed onto the handhold and pulled herself forward. Her stomach felt light, and a small wave of nausea came over her at the momentary loss of gravity. She reached the inner airlock of the Boxan ship and stopped, which wasn't difficult since she hadn't been traveling very fast. She pushed herself down to the ground and moved to the side to clear the way for Zack, then watched as he seemingly flew across the space, unable to keep the boyish grin from his face as he pretended to be Superman.

Kaylan smiled. She'd watched Zack change so much since they'd first boarded the *Athena* and raced toward Pluto. Their journey had changed each crewmember as they faced very different challenges, but the journey had taken its toll on all of them. While Kaylan knew none of their lives would ever be the same if they somehow made it back to Earth, what she didn't know was just how different home would feel once they got there. Had all of their perspectives changed so much that returning home would be as much of a challenge as leaving had been? She imagined that Katie and Hicks would remain in the military, and both would be highly sought after given their experiences and qualifications. Brenda couldn't wait to go home, and Kaylan believed that once she got there she'd never leave again. Emma would enjoy a long overdue reunion with her husband, but Kaylan didn't expect her to stay home for very long. She loved exploration and researching new life forms. Efren's knowledge of Boxan technology would enable him to have his pick of whatever he wanted to do if they got back. But what would she do if they returned home? She'd thought about it a bit but hadn't really given it a lot of attention. She had no idea where she'd go from here. The Boxans highly revered someone like her, but back on Earth anyone claiming to have her abilities was met with harsh skepticism. She didn't relish the thought of having to deal with that sort of attention.

Zack reached the airlock and stopped himself using the handholds. He glanced at her. "What are you thinking about?" he asked while pushing himself down to the floor.

Kaylan closed the airlock doors and the artificial gravity field slowly increased. "I was thinking about how far the crew has come."

Zack nodded. He pressed his hand on the panel to open the inner-airlock door, and Gaarokk greeted them. His brown, roughened skin seemed to soften at the sight of them.

"Kladomaor asked me to meet you and bring you to the Mardoxian chamber," Gaarokk said.

They headed into the ship. The corridors had high ceilings to accommodate the Boxans.

"How does the Mardoxian chamber on this ship compare with the ones that were on the monitoring stations?" Kaylan asked.

"It's different. The chambers located on the monitoring stations are capable of amplifying a signal once it's received, but we don't know what the state of the monitoring station is in your star system," Gaarokk said.

"We still need to try," Kaylan said.

"Agreed," Gaarokk said. "Earth should be warned of the danger."

Zack arched an eyebrow. "I probably shouldn't ask—"

"You should heed such instincts. They are there to protect you," Gaarokk said quickly and glanced at Zack. "But you're going to ask anyway. Go ahead."

"Thanks," Zack replied. "I'm somewhat surprised that the High Council is allowing this to happen."

Gaarokk snorted. "This isn't something they would deny."

"I understand that, but they could drag their feet . . . you know, make things take longer than they otherwise would have," Zack said.

"It would be pointless of them to do so. They've learned quite a bit in dealing with your species. Also, Kladomaor and Ma'jasalax agree with what you're trying to do. Even if they had reservations, they'd still help you, and so would I," Gaarokk said.

"We appreciate all you've done for us," Kaylan said.

"We also know you would go off and do it anyway, even without our help," Gaarokk said.

"Yes, but it would be difficult. The *Athena* doesn't have a Mardoxian chamber aboard. I'd thought of using the one on Nerva, but Ma'jasalax advised me to come here," Kaylan said.

The Mardoxian chamber was a pyramid structure that intensified her abilities and was located near one of the Boxan resonance chambers they used to deal with long space voyages. Gaarokk guided them to the Mardoxian chamber. He opened the large doors and they went inside. Kaylan saw Ma'jasalax and Valkra waiting for her.

"Thank you for helping me with this," Kaylan said to Ma'jasalax and nodded a greeting to Valkra.

"Of course. We have an alliance, after all," Ma'jasalax replied and looked at Zack. "Do you have the data you wish to include in your message?"

"I have it. Where do you need me to send it?" Zack asked.

"Upload it to our systems here," Ma'jasalax replied.

"Done," Zack said.

Ma'jasalax went to a nearby console with Gaarokk, and Valkra went over to Kaylan.

"Ma'jasalax wanted me to be here to learn more about what it means to have the Mardoxian potential, but I wanted you to know that I will help you in whatever way I can. It's the least that I can do given all you've done for us," Valkra said.

Kaylan shook her head. "You don't owe me anything."

Valkra's gaze hardened. "I understand that your reasons for helping us were without thought about how it would benefit you. I recognize that, as does Councilor Essaforn, but that doesn't mean we're not in your debt. It's a debt we can never repay, but we'll help you however we can."

Kaylan thanked her. She didn't completely understand how she was able to connect with Valkra through Mardoxian means, but the connection remained strong. The only other Boxan she felt something similar with was Ma'jasalax, which Kaylan attributed to the fact that the first time she'd been in a Mardoxian chamber, she'd communicated with Ma'jasalax.

"The chamber has been prepped and we have the coordinates for the monitoring station in Earth's star system," Ma'jasalax said.

"You were able to reach it?" Zack asked.

"To put it in terms you would understand, the connection hasn't initialized; it's just ready. Kaylan must initialize the connection as bearer of the message," Ma'jasalax answered.

Zack looked at Kaylan. "So you go into the chamber and initialize a connection to the monitoring station on Pluto. Then you use that to send a message to Earth, but how do you craft the message so it includes the Star Shroud shield shutdown instructions?"

"The chamber does some of the work. I'm merely the link. Those with the

Mardoxian potential are able to communicate differently and are capable of different communications protocols," Kaylan answered.

Zack didn't say anything else, but Kaylan could tell that his mind had become jumbled with questions he was holding back. His curiosity would have to wait.

Kaylan made her way to the Mardoxian chamber entrance. As she neared the pyramid and heard the gentle hum of energy, she placed her hand on the panel next to the closed door and it opened. Glowing cyan lights raced up the cathedral-high ceilings, coming to a central point. Crimson lines of light also came on from twin points on the floor and continued around the base of the pyramid's interior. Kaylan crossed the threshold, and the door closed behind her. A dark blue beam shot down from the ceiling to a crystal sphere that rose from the floor. Kaylan sat on the floor and focused on the star coordinates to the monitoring station on Pluto. She had to trust that the coordinates were accurate.

An azure pathway opened in her mind and raced ahead of her as Kaylan rushed to catch up. She had to get this message to Earth before it was too late, and she hoped they would heed her warning quickly. She raced along the azure pathway, anticipating her connection to the chamber on the other side. She'd done this on Olloron as part of the Mardoxian training program. She expected a brief pause until the chamber came online, but instead she felt her consciousness slam into an invisible wall. It felt as if all her senses had been jarred, and she struggled to remain focused.

Kaylan tried again but was met with similar resistance. She paused for a moment, gathered her concentration, and slowly moved ahead to the barrier, which she pressed. She couldn't see it but felt as if she were pressing on a stone wall that was unyielding and impenetrable. Her failure to get through the barrier felt like a punch to the stomach. She tried to find a way around but felt as if she were stumbling around in the dark. Loneliness pressed in on her and she became increasingly desperate, feeling herself becoming frustrated with her efforts to get around the barrier. In her mind, she remembered working with Michael Hunsicker, who always encouraged her to take a step back and think things through. Kaylan receded back down the pathway and opened her eyes in the Mardoxian chamber. She'd failed.

She stood up and felt tiredness creep into her muscles. She'd been in the chamber for two hours, but it felt like moments. She opened the door and the first thing she saw was Zack's hopeful gaze, which stung. Kaylan shook her head. "I couldn't reach it."

Zack frowned for a moment. "Was it the shield?"

"I think so," Kaylan said and looked at Ma'jasalax.

"There might be another way, but there is a risk," Ma'jasalax said.

There's always a risk, Kaylan thought. "I don't care. I'll try anything."

"I'd like to know the risk," Zack said quickly, giving Kaylan a sidelong glance.

"The chamber intensifies perceptions, and a being with the Mardoxian potential is able to traverse vast distances much quicker than a ship can travel.

There *is* another configuration, but there's a risk that the being inside could become detached," Ma'jasalax said.

Zack's eyes widened and he glanced at Kaylan. "What does that mean? How would you be detached?"

Kaylan opened her mouth a few times. She knew Zack wasn't going to like it, but she wouldn't lie to him. "It means I might not be able to get back."

Zack blinked his eyes rapidly and his brows pulled together in concern. "Can I go with you? Is there some way I can help in there?"

Kaylan felt her throat thicken.

"You can't help her in the chamber because you don't have the Mardoxian potential," Ma'jasalax said.

"She's right. I have to do this on my own," Kaylan said.

"That's not what Ma'jasalax said," Valkra said. "She said *Zack* couldn't help. But I can. We share a Mardoxian connection. We can each strengthen the other."

"You're referring to a bonded pair. You'd have the same risk as Kaylan would, which isn't insignificant. This is something that isn't done because we've lost many of our sect in the attempt," Ma'jasalax said.

"Then it's a risk I'm willing to take," Valkra replied.

Ma'jasalax regarded her for a moment. "No, it's a risk *we* are willing to take."

Kaylan looked at both of them. She didn't think she could do this on her own, and both Boxans watched her as if daring her to say she didn't need their help. But she did, and it was their only hope of warning Earth.

11

E dward Johnson was in a data processing facility north of Denver, Colorado
—one of many facilities Dux Corp owned across the globe. He could've
gone to any of them and been able to continue his work, but he'd always had a
soft spot for Colorado. What could he say? He was a fan of the Rockies, and the
climate there was gentler on his allergies than the East Coast of the United States.
He didn't trust himself to go to the European offices because of the temptation to
work out in the field, and the field was where younger people thrived. Someone
like him would only slow them down. Those field teams needed to be agile for
hunting the Xiiginns.

He'd just finished reviewing the latest reports. The Xiiginns seemed to allow
his teams to get only so close and then disappeared like smoke, and it felt as if
every nation on the planet was holding its collective breath. He'd used every
resource at his disposal to ensure that the flow of information to nations across
the globe remained irrevocably intact—no small feat considering that a short
time ago, three nuclear bombs had been detonated over populated areas. Ed had
done everything he could to help keep the peace, but he knew it was the ECF
who had kept the nations of the world communicating. Ed had to admit that
General William Sheridan had a great big pair of titanium balls. There weren't
many men who would open lines of communication to heads of state, declaring
that if any of them launched an ICBM, he, along with their Boxan allies, would
stop those missiles from reaching their intended targets. There would be no
nuclear holocaust.

The Xiiginns had won a victory. Though the trail of the terrorist groups
involved had gone cold, they'd been able to provide evidence to heads of state
that the nuclear bombs had been provided by the Xiiginns. The Xiiginns had
stolen nuclear warheads and armed them. This meant that humanity wasn't as
immune from the Xiiginn influence as they'd originally hoped.

Sheridan had been instrumental in getting the heads of state to listen, but it was the ECF as a whole that provided a much-needed stabilizing influence on the entire world. It had been more than Ed could've hoped for, and he attributed much of its success to their Boxan allies. Since then, Ed had devoted every waking moment to his pursuit of the Xiiginns. He coordinated with law enforcement agencies throughout the globe as much as he could, and when he couldn't, he used his own forces because they could move much faster and were much better equipped. Every time they got close, the Xiiginns slipped away, although his most recent raid at a facility in Poznan, Poland, had revealed a lab of sorts. He'd finally found a target that had to be important to them.

It didn't take a genius to figure out what the Xiiginns were trying to do, and the Boxans confirmed it for them anyway. The Xiiginns were after what the Boxans referred to as the Mardoxian potential. Ed's teams had been able to trace the Xiiginns because they were using Earth-based technology (another Boxan term). It dripped of irony that their interstellar invaders had to use technology from a non-interstellar race. But this meant he could find them; it was only a matter of time.

"I think I have something here," James said.

Ed looked away from his holoscreen and saw Iris doing the same. James Jordan was a talented security analyst, so when he said he might have something, Ed's pulse quickened with anticipation.

"I've been using pattern-recognition applications to compare the logs from various transport agencies—air or sea, mostly. I think the Xiiginns are finally coming here. Well, not *here* specifically, but the United States, or at least North America. These logs here are for jets that are owned through various subsidiaries associated with groups we've identified as having a connection to the Xiiginns," James said.

"Are you sure about that? Because the Xiiginn connection to those groups is paper thin at best," Iris said.

"We investigate every lead," Ed said, his tone leaving no room for argument. "Do we have any idea where those jets have gone?"

"We have where they left from and their last known heading, but we don't have confirmation that they reached their destination. We'll have to guess as to where they made landfall, but it gives us a target," James said.

Ed nodded. "Good. Coordinate with Webb's team and bring in the FBI if you have to. I don't care. Just get whoever's closest and can get there first."

"Ed, you need to see this," Iris said.

Ed held up his index finger toward Iris. "Contact Benjamin McAllister in Homeland Security and tell them we may have enemies storming our gates. That should get you through any red tape, but if not, get me on the phone."

James jotted down a few quick notes and said he'd get right on it.

Ed turned toward Iris, whose attention was on a broadcast on her own holoscreen. A news briefing was being shown from the ECF lunar base. It kept replaying a video of a group of people and then a man who was standing off to the side suddenly collapsing. The video feed focused in on the man, and Ed recognized him instantly as Michael Hunsicker. The news commentator speculated that some of the ECF personnel had succumbed to a mysterious illness that perplexed medical doctors, but some believed the illness was related to exposure to the Boxans.

"Replay that," Ed said.

Iris started the video feed at the beginning. The camera was focused on General Sheridan, who was addressing a virtual news conference. Michael Hunsicker was standing off to the side with Commander Alyssa Archer. Ed used his neural implants to mute the commentator's audio feed, then selected the area around Michael Hunsicker and amplified the sound. There was a sharp exhalation and then what sounded like a harsh groan before the sound was distorted by other people rushing to Michael Hunsicker's side.

Ed licked his lips in thought. "When was this video taken?"

"Just a few minutes ago," Iris said and frowned. "What is it?"

Ed felt something on the edges of his thoughts. His brow furrowed as he tried to remember. What was he missing? There was something about the way Michael Hunsicker had collapsed and that sound—almost like he was muttering something as he went down. Suddenly, Ed's eyes widened. "Iris, get me General Sheridan right now. Don't go through normal channels. I need his direct line."

Ed watched as Iris brought up the secure interface with the ECF communications protocols. She selected the emergency line and then gave him a firm nod.

"Listen to me very carefully, General," Ed said.

There was a slight pause. "Johnson, how did you get this—"

"We don't have time for that right now. What is Michael Hunsicker's status?"

"They just took him away to the doctor's station. What's this about?" General Sheridan asked, sounding slightly annoyed.

"We just saw the news broadcast where he collapsed. Tell me, is he muttering something that might sound incoherent? Does he have abnormal vitals?" Ed asked.

"How should I know? They just took him away. He's in good hands. I've got a lot on my plate right now and I can't do this with you," General Sheridan said.

"Bill, please wait. This is important. I wouldn't have called you like this if it weren't," Ed said.

General Sheridan didn't reply, but Ed could hear people speaking as the general approached them. "I need Hunsicker's status, now," Sheridan said.

Ed glanced at Iris and muted his line to Sheridan. "Iris, I need you to bring up the remote-viewer protocols used in project Stargate. I need to send a briefing up to the ECF ASAP."

"Are you still there? Did you hear what the doctor said?" General Sheridan asked.

Ed closed his eyes for a moment. "Yeah, I heard it. Listen to me very carefully. Don't let the doctors do anything to him. You need to record everything he does, everything he says. Is his heart rate elevated?" Ed asked.

He heard Sheridan repeat the question to the doctor. "Yeah, Ed, it's really high and they're concerned about it. They're about to give him medicine to bring it down."

"No! Don't do that. I think he's getting a message."

"A message?" General Sheridan said in disbelief. "What kind of message?"

"Are there any Boxans with you? They can confirm it, but I think he's being contacted like our remote viewers were in the Project Stargate Program back in the eighties. Just make sure we don't interfere with it," Ed said.

"Michael Hunsicker doesn't have this ability. Why would a message even come to him?" General Sheridan asked.

"I don't know, Bill, but you need to trust me. Someone's trying to communicate with us, and they were able to get past the Star Shroud shield. Is the shield still up?" Ed asked.

There was a moment of silence before Sheridan answered. "All shroud monitoring devices report as active. The shield is still up."

Ed blew out a breath of relief. "That's good. I'm going to send the remote-viewer protocols we used with Project Stargate, along with the videos of those viewers receiving the previous messages. They recorded everything and were able to disseminate a message from what the reviewers were saying. There were even hidden messages within their vital signs, fluttering of the eyes, twitching of the fingers. It goes on and on. You need to record everything right now."

General Sheridan said he would and closed the line.

Ed rolled his shoulders and blew out a long breath. "Did you send that data to the ECF?"

"Sent and received," Iris confirmed. "Good catch. I would've missed that completely."

Ed brought his hands to the top of his head and arched his back, stretching his muscles. He pressed his lips together. "This isn't good. That news broadcast was nationally televised, correct?"

Iris frowned and then nodded. "You look worried. I would've thought you'd be happy that we received the message at all."

"I'm concerned about the message, but I'm more concerned that the message was received during a public broadcast—meaning we're not the only ones to realize that a Mardoxian message has been received by the ECF," Ed said.

Iris pursed her lips in thought. "You think the Xiiginns are going to find out about this? Ed, it looks like Hunsicker just collapsed. Even the media is saying it's some kind of illness."

Ed shook his head. "We can't trust the media. They're too busy trying to be seen rather than providing intelligent content. It's been that way for over twenty years, probably even more so now. No, if *I* saw it, there isn't a doubt in my mind that the Xiiginns will notice it. They're going to know we've been contacted by Boxans outside the shield."

Ed paced back and forth for a minute while he considered the possibilities. What could have happened that the Boxans would try to contact them now? "We can't wait for Sheridan. We need a resource on that base to give us the details about Michael Hunsicker."

"What happened to playing well with others?" Iris asked with a knowing smile.

"We still are, but I need to know what's in that message. They wouldn't contact us if it weren't important. Once the Xiiginns realize that a message has been received, they're going to want to know what's in it, too," Ed said.

Iris returned to her console and began working. She glanced over at him. "You could go up to the base yourself."

Ed snorted. "You trying to get rid of me?"

A small smile tugged at the edges of Iris's full lips. "I thought maybe you'd like to be present on the scene."

Ed considered it for a moment and shook his head. "No, I don't need to be there. I just need to know what's going on. This might actually work out for us, now that I've had a chance to think about it."

Iris's gaze narrowed suspiciously. "What do you mean?"

"Whatever's in that message, the Xiiginns will likely expedite their timeline, which means they might make mistakes. I think we can help them along with that, perhaps entice them by making an offer they can't refuse," Ed said.

12

M ichael lay in a bed that felt as if it would swallow him up. He tried to turn his head, but he might as well have tried to push a Mack truck with just his neck muscles. He heard a distinct clearing of the throat that was decidedly feminine in tone and opened his eyes to a dimly lit room. He couldn't tell who was in the room with him.

"You just couldn't stand not being the center of the attention. Isn't that right, Mr. Hunsicker?"

"Alyssa, is that you?" Michael asked. He felt like he had massive weights slowing down his brain.

"Who else would it be?" Alyssa said and grasped his hand, giving it a firm squeeze.

Michael worked his jaw into a swallow and drew in a deep breath. "What happened?"

"You've been out of it for three days. What do you remember?" Alyssa asked.

Michael winced from the pain in his head. It hurt just to think. "Three . . . days," he muttered.

"Take your time," Alyssa said. "I'm going to raise the bed so you're sitting up more. Tell me if this bothers you."

Michael clenched his teeth in anticipation of more pain. His body ached as if he'd just run a marathon, but the bed pushed him upright and some of the fog seemed to lift. He saw the soft contours of Alyssa's face and tried to smile.

"Stop trying to smile at me, you idiot. You really scared the hell out of me," Alyssa said.

"Sorry," Michael said. "Thanks for keeping the lights turned down low."

"You can thank Edward Johnson for that. Somehow he reached General Sheridan's emergency line and told us what he suspected was happening to you," Alyssa said.

"What happened to me?"

Alyssa's eyebrows pulled together in a concerned frown. "You really don't know?"

"It hurts just to think, Allie."

"Indeed, the information sent up by Ed warned it might take you a little while to catch up with what happened," Alyssa said. "Don't give me that look; I'm going to tell you. You and a couple of other people nearby were contacted through Mardoxian means. That's how Chazen explained it."

Michael blew a breath and felt his mind clear even further, as if he were waking from a very long sleep. "I'm not a viewer."

"No, you're not, but the other two are. You remember them: Alicia Murphy and Blake Allen. They're not doing much better than you, but according to the Boxans, you bore the brunt of it," Alyssa said.

Michael squeezed his eyes shut for a moment, and a pair of startlingly blue eyes appeared in his mind's eye. He chased after the memory, but it fled away from him. Michael pushed harder and snatched the knowledge from the gloom. He opened his eyes and looked at Alyssa. "My god, it was Kaylan! Somehow, she did this."

Alyssa nodded as if she had expected that answer. "Can you remember anything else?"

Michael looked away from her and tried to concentrate. "A warning. The shield—" A sharp pain lanced across his brain and he felt as if his head were in a vise. "It hurts!" he cried out.

He felt Alyssa's hands on his head, gently massaging his temples and working her way to the base of his skull. The pain lessened.

"Okay, that's enough. Just close your eyes and try to sleep a little more. I'll be right here," Alyssa said.

Michael had a notion to protest for the briefest of moments, but he didn't want to move. He didn't even want to think anymore. He just wanted to lie there and breathe. He focused his breathing and felt himself lured back into a restful sleep, far away from the pain in his skull but for a thought that skirted the edge of his mind. Kaylan had reached out to him somehow. When he tried to focus on the warning, the pain in his skull returned, so he stopped thinking about it. His body was warning him that he wasn't ready.

He woke sometime later and Alyssa was there, urging him to go back to sleep. He needed more time, she insisted, and who was he to argue?

THE NEXT TIME Michael woke up he felt much better. The hundreds of jackhammers in his head had ceased their assault and he could think clearly. The lights were on in his room and it didn't feel like somebody was stabbing his eyes. The doctors had formulated a cocktail to give him, which was based on the recommendation from Edward Johnson that came from the Dux Corp data archives. It was how they'd helped viewers cope with the previous Boxan warning.

He had just finished his breakfast and was dressing himself when Alyssa walked into his room. She regarded him with all the scrutiny of a mother hen monitoring her chicks. "We can delay this meeting if you need more time."

Michael's shoulders and back muscles were still sore, but the doctors had assured him that it would just take a little more time. They'd been able to almost completely alleviate his concussion-like symptoms. There was only one other time in his life when his head had felt like his brain had been swished up in a blender, and that had been when he'd played football in high school.

"I need to be there in case I remember something else. I think that's worth a little discomfort," Michael said.

Alyssa rolled her eyes but didn't press the matter further. *She* wouldn't lie in a bed recovering when there was work to be done, and neither would he. They left his room to find two ECF soldiers waiting outside.

"General Sheridan's orders," Alyssa said.

Michael gave a nod to the soldiers and walked down the corridor. Fifteen minutes later they met up with General Sheridan and his staff, including Kyle Matthews, in a conference room near the command center. Michael glanced around the room and noticed that there weren't any Boxans in attendance.

General Sheridan waved them over to where he and Kyle were sitting. Sheridan asked how he was feeling, and Michael told him he was fit for duty.

"Why are there no Boxans here? I thought they usually had at least one representative here," Michael asked.

The Boxans were rarely far from the command center and different operation centers throughout the base.

"They're discussing the contents of the message you received," General Sheridan said.

Michael had watched a video feed of what happened to him and the subsequent days that followed. Parts of Kaylan's message were clear and easily understood, but there was something else that not even Michael could make heads or tails of.

"Have you remembered anything else?" General Sheridan asked.

Michael's memory of the message was strange, almost as if he could hear echoes of Kaylan's voice coming down a long tunnel. "I think you've captured everything, and if anything, my memory reconfirms what I already said." He looked away for a moment. "You'll have to forgive me, General, but this is extremely strange."

A short man in an ECF uniform leaned forward and cleared his throat. "Don't try to force the memories. You might gain new insights as time goes on," Blake said.

Michael recognized the man as being part of a classified group within the ECF for those with the Mardoxian potential. "The part of the message that is very clear is that the Confederation's putting together an armada and they're going to attack us here. They believe that with enough firepower they can cause the shield to fail, even if it has to constrict enough to cause planetary realignment."

General Sheridan nodded. "We knew the shield was constricting, which we think is due to the power requirements for maintaining the shield. So the message reiterates some of our concerns. The closest planet to the shield is Neptune, and I have a room full of astrophysicists trying to come up with theories of what would happen if that entire planet was suddenly pushed from its orbit. I've seen some of the early mockups—worst-case scenario stuff—and it's enough to make me sick."

Michael knew that the outer solar system planets were quite far from Earth, but not since the early life of the solar system had the planetary orbits been put into disarray. The real danger was if a planet like Neptune or Saturn was suddenly pushed into Jupiter's orbit, which had up till now provided stability in the entire solar system as its largest planet. The technology behind the Star Shroud shield was something that could affect these planets. Even the Boxans were of the opinion that there was a strong probability the danger was quite real, even when considering the vast distances between the planets.

"I do remember something that seems like a foreign language. I don't understand what it means though," Michael said.

"The Boxans are working with our scientists on that part. They believe they're some kind of instructions for the Star Shroud devices. Perhaps even a way to disable them," Colonel Matthews said.

The doors to the conference room opened and Chazen and Scraanyx walked in. The loud thuds of their footsteps pounded the floor with a sense of finality. They were grim-faced and carried with them an aura of severity. Chazen glanced over at Michael and gave him a nod.

"General Sheridan," Scraanyx said and brought his fist across his heart. "We have a formal request to make of the ECF in light of the Mardoxian message. I thought it best to bring it to you straight away."

General Sheridan regarded the Boxan for a few moments. "Let's hear it," he said finally.

"We would like to return to our colony," Scraanyx said and paused for a moment. "The Mardoxian message revealed that an alliance has been made between Boxans and a species called the Nershals, among a few others. They are planning to attack the Confederation Armada. Such a thing is unprecedented in our war with the Xiiginn, and we believe this battle will forever affect the fate of our species. We would like to fight at their side when they do."

"There's still the matter of the Star Shroud shield," General Sheridan replied.

"We understand that, and we're working hard to ensure that the message is deciphered as accurately as possible," Scraanyx said.

Michael's shoulders tightened. If General Sheridan denied the request, he had no idea what the Boxans would do. They could just take whatever ships they had left and try to bring down the shield, forcing the ECF into facing the harsh reality of defending the solar system.

Scraanyx held up one of his hands. "We understand this is not a request that should be handled lightly. You will no doubt need to consult with your United Nations. We want you to have time to consider it fully and continue to engage us with any questions you might have. We will, in turn, continue our ongoing efforts to assist you."

General Sheridan stood up. "Thank you for your understanding and for giving us time. We owe a great deal to you, and that's something I will never forget."

Scraanyx and Chazen left the conference room, and an uneasy, tense silence settled in the Boxans' wake. No one dared to break it.

"Look sharp, people," General Sheridan said. "Things have just gotten more complicated, but we still have a job to do."

If more of an understatement could be voiced, Michael couldn't think of what it would be. They had their work cut out for them, and on top of that, all the Boxans wanted to go home. The ECF did have ships that were, in theory, capable of making the journey, though they were untested and there was the Star Shroud shield to contend with. Michael glanced at General Sheridan, who seemed to draw the eyes of all those in the room. While the Boxans someday leaving them had always been a probability, no one had thought it would come this quickly. Were they ready to defend Earth from invasion? Michael glanced at Colonel Matthews, whose face was a mask of determination. No doubt, he was working out what actions he would need to take to deal with this latest threat. The Mardoxian message was a wake-up call for the Earth Coalition Force and for humanity.

13

Z ack stopped at an alcove in the corridor of the Boxan ship. He needed to look at something before he headed to the medical bay where Kaylan, Ma'jasalax, and Valkra had all been resting for several days. After multiple failed attempts to send a message to Earth, Kaylan had requested that they return to Earth's solar system. The heavy cruiser didn't have any windows because it was a warship, but Zack was able to bring up a view of the solar system on one of the wallscreens.

He hadn't been this close to home since he'd activated the Star Shroud shield. At that time, two Boxan Dreadnoughts were holding the line against the Xiiginn fleet, and his mind flashed back to the bridge of the *Athena*. They'd all watched in horror as the Xiiginn fleet managed to begin pushing their way through the behemoth Boxan warships. Zack had done the only thing he could think of, and even then he'd relied on Athena to help him.

The wallscreen showed an image of the solar system with the sun gleaming like a lonely beacon amidst a celestial backdrop. Kaylan had insisted on coming here a few days earlier for one final effort to send a message to Earth. He didn't know whether proximity really played a role in what Kaylan had been able to do. A million miles was a million miles in his mind, and even though they were in the area known as the Oort cloud, they were still significantly far from Earth.

He and Gaarokk had monitored the Mardoxian chamber while Kaylan, Ma'jasalax, and Valkra went inside to try a method of communication that even the Boxans had serious reservations about. They had been in there for hours, and when the chamber finally opened, all three of them were unconscious. They were moved to the medical bay and Kladomaor ordered the ship to stay in the area and monitor the shield. They hadn't been sure if the message had been sent until Kaylan woke up. She'd been the first to regain consciousness and she told them that she'd been able to reach Michael Hunsicker. They'd loitered in the area for another two days and were about to head back to the Nerva star system.

Zack walked toward Kaylan, thinking she still looked a little pale. The Boxans almost always looked the same to him. He guessed there would be no way to tell if they looked pale with their rough brown skin that was quite similar to the bark of a tree.

"Why Michael Hunsicker?" Zack asked.

"We kept trying to use the Boxan method, which was essentially a broadcast signal, and it kept failing. And then I wondered what would happen if I focused my efforts on someone specific," Kaylan said.

"Did you see anything?" Zack asked.

Kaylan frowned as if she were trying to put the pieces together in her mind. "It wasn't like before when I used the chamber. Ma'jasalax said it was because we were using a different method. I could only see shapes and things like that, but I had to focus on someone familiar, someone who would understand the message."

"Are you sure he received the message?"

"It's hard to explain to someone who didn't experience it," Kaylan replied.

"I get that, I guess, but Michael doesn't have this ability, so how can you be sure the message was received?" Zack asked and then tacked on, "Not that I want you to try again. Your vital signs were extremely low. I'm sure that if Brenda was here, she'd be giving you a good tongue-lashing."

"I know the message went through. But they'll need time to decipher it, and we can't stay here," Kaylan said.

"We're not. Kladomaor kept the ship there for a while, but there's been no change in the shield," Zack replied.

Ma'jasalax walked over to them. "We should go to the bridge."

They left the medical bay and headed toward the main bridge of the ship. Once they got to the bridge, Kladomaor looked over at them from the commander's couch.

"We're about to reach Nerva," Kladomaor said.

They transitioned through the wormhole and into the edge of the Nerva star system. Scanners showed a concentration of ships around Selebus, and Kladomaor frowned. Zack looked at the information on the main holoscreen and saw that there were many more ships than when they'd left.

"Helm, best speed to Selebus," Kladomaor said. "Comms, send word to the Alliance that we've returned."

Zack glanced at Kaylan, who was studying the main holoscreen. "What's the matter?"

"Something isn't right," Kaylan said and looked at Kladomaor. "Can you open a comms channel to the *Athena*?"

Kladomaor did but warned that there would be a significant delay until they were closer to Selebus.

Hicks answered the comms channel. "I'm glad you're back because we've got a bit of trouble going on. The Gresans tried to take our ship, and several Nershal warships intercepted them."

"What about the Boxan fleet?" Kladomaor asked.

"They're trying to get the Gresans to stand down," Hicks replied.

"Tactical, can you detect active weapons systems on any of those ships around the *Athena*?" Kladomaor asked.

"That will take several minutes because we're still too far out, Battle Leader," Varek replied.

"Very well," Kladomaor said and turned toward them. "It looks like we've entered some sort of standoff. Even at best speed, we're still hours away from Selebus."

Kaylan glanced at the main holodisplay, considering. "Is there somewhere we can talk to the *Athena* in private?"

Kladomaor frowned and glanced at Ma'jasalax before replying. "I can offer you one of the workstations on the bridge."

"I was hoping to use one of the tactical operations rooms off the bridge," Kaylan said.

"We can certainly go there if that's what you want," Kladomaor said.

Zack saw that there was a hard glint to Kaylan's eyes he hadn't noticed before.

Kaylan leveled her gaze at Kladomaor. "I'm sorry; I wasn't clear. It will just be Zack and me. You see, I need to speak with my crew that's surrounded by a bunch of warships you know the *Athena* cannot stand against."

Zack had to keep his mouth from hanging open. Kaylan wasn't fooling around, and her stern tone couldn't be missed by anyone on the bridge.

Kladomaor's flaxen eyes regarded Kaylan for a moment. "You may use my office off the bridge and I'll make sure you aren't disturbed."

Kaylan thanked him and glanced at Zack, silently beckoning him to follow her.

"Kaylan," Kladomaor said after they'd taken a few steps away from the command area, "you can trust me. I hope you know that."

Zack watched as Kaylan's eyes softened. "I do know that and I do trust you, but this is more than two individuals from separate species."

Ma'jasalax lifted her chin, summoning every ounce of dignity she possessed, and projected an air of authority. "We'll keep you apprised of any new developments. Please let us know if there's anything we can do for the *Athena* and her crew."

Zack followed Kaylan to Kladomaor's office. The Boxans had a different word for office, but he couldn't remember what it was. The room was just outside the bridge, and they went inside.

Zack sighed. "We leave the Nerva star system for just a few days and suddenly there's a standoff. I don't like it one bit. The timing is too suspect for me. Someone waited for us to leave."

Kaylan had her back to him, and she brought her hands to her waist and arched her back, stretching her shoulders. Zack's thoughts came to a stop while he took in how beautiful she was. She let her hands go to her sides and sighed. Then she turned toward him. "I should've seen this coming. The Gresans are trying to take the *Athena*."

Zack nodded. "We knew they were . . . I don't know if 'interested' is the right word or 'highly intrigued' by the *Athena*, but in any case, it's not surprising."

Kaylan shook her head. "You still don't understand. There's a division in the Alliance, even among the Boxans. This could have been a coordinated effort between them."

"I thought I'm normally the paranoid one, but I think you're right. We need to open a comms channel to the *Athena*, and it needs to be secure so no one can listen in on our conversation," Zack said.

A new connection registered with his internal heads-up display and he saw that the same connection had established on Kaylan's implants.

"No need for a comms channel," Athena said. "We're secure from any monitoring the Boxans are capable of. Commander, I'm happy you've returned."

"Have you been listening to us the whole time?" Zack asked.

"I've been monitoring all communications in this system," Athena replied.

Kaylan frowned. "There should be a lag since we're so far away."

"That is correct, Commander, but I used microscopic wormholes to establish this channel," Athena said.

Zack's eyes widened. "Athena, are you saying we can talk through subspace?"

"Affirmative. The data models supporting it were accessible in my data storage matrix. I've been running multiple virtualized experiments, but our current situation required that I shift my efforts to accelerate my original timetable and reveal this new capability," Athena said.

"That kind of research should have taken years to do, maybe even longer," Kaylan said.

"Not if her processing power keeps increasing," Zack replied.

"We'll have to talk about this another time. Athena, who's on board the ship?" Kaylan asked.

"All remaining crew are aboard the ship, Commander."

"Understood. Please patch them in," Kaylan said. Once Athena confirmed that the rest of the crew was available on comms, Kaylan continued. "Hicks, give me the rundown. It's just me and Zack here and no one else."

"Understood, Commander. The Napox tried to sneak aboard the ship. Athena took control of their spacecraft. It was small—even smaller than our shuttle. Almost like a strike-fighter, but without weapons systems. Athena was able to track them to a Gresan warship. I informed the Boxans and the Nershals, which in hindsight may not have been the best thing to do because suddenly all these ships started surrounding us. Athena then informed us that she could disrupt Gresan communications and perhaps even control some of their systems. She later expanded that to include Nershal and Boxan ships," Hicks said.

"I hope you didn't do that," Kaylan said.

"Don't worry, we didn't. It was news to me that she even had the ability to do that. We're in a bit of a pickle here, Commander, and I'm not sure if there's a way out of it," Hicks said.

Zack had gotten to know Hicks throughout the duration of this journey, and this was the major's way of saying that they might be screwed. "They're focusing on the wrong thing. All of them."

Kaylan looked at Zack. "I agree, but can you clarify what you mean?"

"What I mean is that they're focusing their efforts on this bright, shiny thing —our ship—and what they need to be focusing on is the Confederation Armada. That's what we want. That's what we need," Zack said.

"They're all afraid. They think the *Athena* can give them an edge in this war. They might be right about that, but I'm not going to sit by and let them take the ship," Kaylan said.

"*I* still say we're all focusing on the wrong thing, because as long as we're all focused on this, who's thinking about how to beat the Xiiginns? They're the true enemy," Zack said.

"Sounds good, but how do we do that?" Hicks said.

"Athena," Kaylan said, "if you can monitor all the communications here, what if we were to go to the Confederation space station? Would you be able to glean any intelligence from the ship-to-ship communications going on there?"

"Affirmative, Commander. The Xiiginns' communications protocols are based on Boxan design. According to the Boxans, the Xiiginns steal technology from other races and use it themselves, so there's a high probability that they're using a variant of technology that already exists. Therefore, I should be able to decipher it," Athena replied.

Zack listened as Kaylan and Hicks discussed what they could do to keep the Alliance at bay while offering them something in return at the same time.

::*You don't seem to agree with this line of thinking*,:: Athena said in a text message that appeared on Zack's internal heads-up display.

::*Didn't anyone tell you that it's rude to have a side conversation while there are other people around?*:: Zack replied.

He heard Athena give a vocal reply to Kaylan and felt his eyebrows pull together at a sudden thought.

::*Either your capabilities have grown in the last few days, or you've been understating what you can do*,:: Zack said.

::*I thought it prudent to manage the crew's emotional state for maximum efficiency*,:: Athena replied.

Oh god, now she's playing head games with us, Zack thought.

"Athena," Zack said, breaking into the conversation he hadn't been listening to. "You've been running many simulations on how best to deal with the Xiiginns. Do you have any insights to offer us that might help find the best course of action?"

Kaylan looked at him for a moment with surprise clearly registering on her face.

"Every data model I've run that puts all the ships in the Alliance against the Confederation Armada results in the total annihilation of the Star Alliance fleet," Athena said.

Zack gave a slight shake of his head and reminded himself that the AI had just told him she was working to manage the crew's emotional state, so why had she up and said they were all going to die if they faced this Confederation Armada? He didn't say any of that out loud because he thought it would be too distracting.

"We can't just give up," Kaylan said.

"I apologize, Commander. I was merely stating the results of my analysis since fleet engagement is at the forefront of multiple Alliance species strategy sessions," Athena said.

"We need to decide what we're going to do right now because there are a lot of warships nearby, and while I don't think they would start shooting at one another, you never know," Hicks said.

Zack watched as Kaylan rubbed the bridge of her nose and then leaned on the Boxan desk, which came up to the middle of her back. "We need more time. What if we offered the Alliance unfettered access to the *Athena* after the Confederation Armada is defeated?" Kaylan said.

Zack shook his head. "We can't give them the *Athena*. She's one of us."

Kaylan looked at him regretfully. "She's a ship—a wonderful, amazing ship, but she's still a ship with an extraordinary artificial intelligence. A promise to these races that we'll share the Drar technology with them might be the only thing that keeps this alliance together."

Zack's nostrils flared and his jaw tightened. "You're talking about her as if she's a thing. She's a living entity—a being. She passed every Turing test ever conceived. I ought to know because I've been giving them to her. Athena's interaction with us isn't Human mimicry or the product of sophisticated Boxan programming. If you didn't know the *Athena* was a ship, you'd all believe she was a person. You don't have the right to just hand her over to them. They don't deserve her. The Drar gave *us* the ship," Zack said, jamming his thumb toward the center of his chest. "Not the Boxans or anyone else. The Drar chose to give us their technology. They didn't pick them because they weren't worthy. I'm sorry if that makes them all upset, but giving in to this tantrum isn't going to help us in the long run. If anything, it will further drive a wedge between us."

Zack turned away from her. He couldn't look at her right now because he was furious.

"Zack," Kaylan said gently.

Zack blew out a heated sigh through his teeth and reluctantly turned toward her. "You can't do this," he said.

"I can," Kaylan said, and her gaze was unyielding.

Zack felt his insides go cold.

"Commander," Athena said.

Zack felt his throat tense. He couldn't let her do this.

"Go ahead," Kaylan said, her voice sounding strained.

"I will follow any order you give me, including this one," Athena said.

Zack shook his head. "Why? Why would you do this?"

"Because Kaylan is the mission commander and I know this couldn't have been easy for her," Athena replied.

Zack turned toward Kaylan and saw that her eyes were glistening, as if at any moment the tears would come. He blew out a breath and felt it wash over his teeth. He glared at her. "They call you Mardoxian Blessed because of your abilities. You're supposed to be able to look into a situation with heightened insights bordering on precognitive capabilities."

"Zack, this isn't fair," Hicks said. "The fact is that we can't stop the entire Alliance from taking the ship. Offering them something they have the ability to take anyway buys us time."

Zack pressed his lips together and scowled. "There's another way, and I'm going to find it."

Zack didn't wait for Kaylan to respond. He couldn't bear to look at her right then. He had to leave the room, had to think. There had to be some way they could get through this without condemning the *Athena* to being ripped apart so a few alien species could get some kind of technological advantage. They had to be better than that.

::Thank you. I appreciate all you've done for me.::

Athena's words appeared on his internal heads-up display and he felt as if they would shatter his heart. The Drar had thought Humans were better than this, so why couldn't they find another way? Why hadn't the Drar given them a way to defeat the Xiiginns? A tiny voice of reason tried to urge his thoughts into more rational thinking, but he couldn't go there. Kaylan was just doing what she thought was right, but in this she was wrong.

14

As the lunar base expanded, it had been decided that the most practical way to add living space was to use the long-dormant lava tunnels under the surface of the moon. Being underground protected them from harsh solar radiation since the moon didn't have an atmosphere of its own. There was an area of tunnels set aside for the Boxans to use that also gave them easy access to the lunar surface. Many Boxans rotated out to the New Moon to oversee manufacturing activities, as well as research and development based on shared Boxan technology.

In the last few days, Michael had resumed his role as the lead liaison between the Boxans and the ECF. He had long gotten used to being among the ten-foot-tall aliens with their deep, gravelly voices and large golden eyes. Despite the Boxans' size, they were quite agile and were extra careful when around Humans. After living with Chazen for months at the Boxan monitoring station, Michael had adjusted and never had to worry about being accidentally knocked over or bumped into. There were some Boxans who weighed over seven hundred pounds, but they'd learned that the average Boxan weight was closer to five hundred, with females weighing only slightly less than the males.

"Has there been any official response to our request?" Scraanyx asked.

Scraanyx was large, even for a Boxan. It had been two days since Scraanyx and Chazen had made the initial request on behalf of all the Boxan refugees for the ECF to take them home.

"General Sheridan will be leaving today to address the United Nations about your request. In fact, I'll be heading back to the main complex for a final meeting on that very subject," Michael said.

He looked at Scraanyx for a moment and then flicked his gaze to Chazen. It was difficult to gauge a Boxan's moods. Michael's experience with them revealed that they were extremely patient, which he attributed to the Boxan culture, but in spite of knowing that, Michael felt he needed to say something else to them. "I think the work you've done so far will help address our shortcomings when the inevitable subject comes up about how we'll continue without you. We're well aware of everything you've done for us and we'll do everything we can to help you return home. I just wanted you to know that. If it were up to me . . ."

"We understand these things take time. That's why I have Boxans working on plans to transfer the duties we've been overseeing to ECF personnel," Scraanyx said.

Michael had been informed yesterday of the procedures the Boxans had authored. They were meant to be used as a guideline to help the ECF maximize their use of Boxan technology, but the procedures themselves had been in development for a long time. Michael knew that Scraanyx was "just" a strike commander, which was essentially like a captain in the ECF. The job Scraanyx had been called to do would ordinarily have been done by someone else, like Battle Leader Prax'Pedax, who had sacrificed himself to protect Earth.

"General Sheridan wanted me to ask if you would consider accompanying him to address the United Nations," Michael said.

The Boxans had been reluctant to return to Earth because of what had happened months ago. The presence of the Xiiginns had made them redouble their efforts to get the ECF up and running, and they'd provided guidance on how to hunt the Xiiginns. It wasn't as if they didn't want to go down to the planet, but they felt that the risk was too great for them.

"We'll take every precaution to ensure your safety, but General Sheridan believes your presence would lend credence to your request," Michael continued.

Scraanyx glanced at Chazen, who said, "It's a Human thing."

Michael smiled. "Many people are extremely aware that you are, in fact, here, but there's a difference between knowing that something exists and seeing it firsthand. I think that if you go down to Earth with General Sheridan, it would help him get support and approval to let you go home."

Scraanyx took a few moments to consider what Michael had said. "Inform General Sheridan that I will consider his request as long as I am able to bring my own protection. No fewer than twelve Boxans will accompany me to the surface of the planet."

"I understand, and I'll let him know your requirements," Michael replied.

Scraanyx left the room, but Chazen lingered behind.

"You're almost home, or at least back among your own species," Michael said.

"It's been so long that I almost don't remember it. Sethion, our homeworld, is lost to us, but I still dream about it sometimes. That must seem strange to you," Chazen said.

Michael shook his head. "I don't think so. I don't know anyone who's been through what you've had to endure—living for so many years in isolation, even with stasis. I don't know anyone else who could've survived. I want you to know I'll do everything I can to help get you home. It's the least I can do," Michael said.

He wouldn't be alive if it wasn't for Chazen. They'd been stranded for months together at the Boxan monitoring station on Pluto. Michael remembered waiting and hoping for a rescue that ultimately never came. They'd had to construct a life pod for themselves and then open a small wormhole to put them near Earth. Of all the Boxans Michael had come to know these past few months, none of them were as important to him as Chazen.

"I know you will," Chazen said solemnly.

Michael left the Boxan living area and returned to the main ECF complex. He was late for his next meeting, but he was sure General Sheridan would understand.

Michael made his way to the large conference room where General Sheridan's final strategy meeting before heading back to Earth was already underway. Michael walked in and quickly made his way toward a seat that was reserved for him. The conference room was occupied by the ECF senior staff. Michael recognized Gary Hunter, who had joined the ECF from NASA. There were so many other familiar faces around the large table. In particular, he noted that General Shang, China's representative in the ECF, was also in attendance. Kyle had once told Michael that General Sheridan initially refused China's proposed candidate, who was part of their concession for supporting the ECF. Eventually, General Sheridan relented in order to allow the ECF to get off the ground with the support it needed.

"The proposed emissary envoy will be met with a lot of resistance. Many will argue against sending an envoy to the Confederation because it's beyond the ECF's mandate, which is to protect the earth," General Shang said.

General Sheridan looked at Colonel Matthews.

"I agree. The United Nations won't go along with this. I've spoken to several US representatives with experience in coordinating both military and civilian response, and when they weigh the Boxans' request against the safety of the planet, essentially Earth comes first," Colonel Matthews replied.

General Sheridan looked at Michael. "What do you think the Boxans would do if we refused their request or, to put it more diplomatically, delayed the request for a time?"

"It's tough to say. The Boxans are extraordinarily patient, but everyone has their limits. How would you react knowing that after so many years of war there was to be a major offensive that would forever impact the fate of your species? I wouldn't want to back them into a corner like that, and frankly, it wouldn't be fair to them," Michael replied.

General Sheridan nodded. "Neither would I. It sounds as if they've been backed into a corner for a long time, and they aren't strangers to taking action when they need to. I don't want to put them in that position." General Sheridan looked around at those sitting at the conference table. "Mr. Hunter, can you give me the status of your team's analysis of the Mardoxian message?"

Gary cleared his throat. "The warning was pretty clear. I conferred with the Boxans about the dangers the Star Shroud shield poses. If the Confederation Armada were to arrive here and start bombarding the shield, we don't think it would simply collapse. We think it would constrict faster while trying to maintain its integrity. This would accelerate the destruction of the solar system as we know it. Inside the Mardoxian message was a shutdown protocol that pertains to the Star Shroud devices. The protocol is different from what the Boxans use to manage the Star Shrouds, but they've informed us that the Star Shrouds are based on another species' technology that was even more advanced than the Boxans are. We think this shutdown protocol is based on this elder species' technology."

"Elder species?" General Sheridan asked.

"The Boxans call them the Drar," Gary replied.

"Is there any way for us to test whether this shutdown protocol actually works?" General Sheridan asked.

"We don't have the resources to test it. We would need to build an actual Star Shroud device, which even the Boxans don't have the knowledge to do, so there's no test we can run," Gary said.

"Does the message say who created the protocol?" General Sheridan asked.

"The Boxans confirmed it wasn't them," Gary replied.

Michael caught General Sheridan's attention, and the general nodded for Michael to speak. "It has to be Zack Quick, General."

"I've heard an awful lot about this Mr. Quick. Edward Johnson speaks highly of him, and I know you have a high opinion of his technical capabilities, but even if this came from him, can we trust that it will work?" General Sheridan asked.

"General, I've worked with Zack, and if there's anyone who can figure out how alien technology works, it's him. Given the amount of time he's been around Boxan technology, I don't think it's too far a stretch that he's been able to utilize what he's learned and apply it in such a way as this," Michael replied.

"Whether or not we trust who created the shutdown protocol isn't important," General Shang said. "We shouldn't be too hasty to shut down the Star Shroud shield. The shield gives us time to build our fleets, and we need those fleets to defend Earth. Also, there's a risk that this shutdown protocol won't work the way we expected it to work. If my understanding is correct, the Boxans didn't even know the Star Shroud devices could make a shield."

"I'm not sure we can get around making certain assumptions," Michael said. "The shield went up just as the Xiiginn fleet was about to push into our solar system. The timing of that was too convenient to believe it happened by chance. What if the crew of the *Athena* got access to this Drar technology, and when they tried to get home, they saw the battle being fought? I know Zack Quick very well, and he's no stranger to taking the initiative and doing what has to be done. I don't think that personality trait would've changed. What I'm trying to say is that he and the crew might've initiated the Star Shroud shield."

"Indeed," General Sheridan said. "Mr. Quick's file does indicate idealistic tendencies. It was those tendencies that in many ways brought us to where we are today. I'm not saying he's to blame, but there are some who view it that way."

"General," Gary Hunter said. "If we're able to determine that the shield is constricting, then certainly someone outside the shield can make the same determination. It wouldn't take much of a leap to understand that if the shield is constricting, it could have disastrous effects on the planets caught inside. This is their way of sending help. Michael's right and we're making assumptions, but I

KEN LOZITO

don't think we can afford to ignore these assumptions, even if the United Nations doesn't agree with them."

world they'd come to know, even a hundred years later. He hadn't seen the similarities between that conflict and what they were now facing, but he supposed it was a good analogy. They were still stumbling to get on the playing field where they could go toe to toe with an aggressive alien species. Michael had been so focused on what they were doing that he'd never really given thought to how history would remember them or whether there would even be anyone left to remember them.

"Colonel," Michael said, "I'm willing to wager that there are a lot of Boxans who would be eager to weigh in on the *Lincoln's* operations."

Colonel Matthews' eyebrows pulled together, furrowing his brow for a moment, and he glanced at General Sheridan. "I think their presence would help a great deal."

"Well, don't let me stop you," General Sheridan said.

15

"The Humans have become increasingly proficient at tracking us," Hoan Berend said.

Mar Arden stood outside their latest encampment under a star-filled sky. They had to keep moving around, going from place to place. However, this time he'd been adamant that they needed to move to another part of the planet that was much closer to this civilization's seat of power. The risk was greater for them, but this was where they needed to be.

"This is to be expected. Our real adversary works from the shadows outside the Human government. Their use of the Mardoxian trait is impressive. It's interesting how the Mardoxian trait is kept secret. At least some of the Humans understand that such things are better kept to a powerful few," Mar Arden said.

Their most recent move had cost the lives of some of his soldiers. They'd had to make sure there were no remains for the Humans to find, which had lost them some time.

Kandra Rene sent him a message that she was on her way to see him.

"How is our most recent volunteer doing?" Mar Arden asked.

They'd increased their understanding of the Mardoxian genetic trait in Humans and were now testing the enhancement of a Xiiginn volunteer. Mar Arden wanted to acquire a genetic sample of a truly gifted Human test subject from which to base their own enhancement of the Mardoxian into the Xiiginns.

"The technology here is so primitive that the incubation period is taking much longer than if we were on our ship. Are you sure you don't want me to launch an operation to steal Boxan technology?" Hoan Berend asked.

"The Boxans have restricted themselves to ECF bases on their moon. The risk is too great when we can just take a little bit more time to achieve the same thing right where we are. Our adversary expects us to hit technology centers, and the longer we delay, the more their hands are tied," Mar Arden said.

"What do the Humans call this place?" Hoan Berend asked and gestured to the forests around them. The tall trees in the area made this location difficult to find.

Mar Arden used his implants to access the primitive global positioning system satellites the Humans liked to use because he was curious himself. "This region is known as Pennsylvania."

Hoan Berend nodded, and his tail flicked to the side. "Yes, that's it. You think it's too risky for us to launch an operation up there," Hoan Berend said, gesturing toward the sky, "but we're so close to one of the sites where our Boxan infiltrator launched his attack."

"That's because you don't see the advantage of our current location," Kandra Rene said as she joined them.

"I'm sure security is much better established now, but even still, I doubt they'd expect us to strike the same place twice. That's not why we're here. We're here because of its proximity to scientific organizations that have the technology we need. These organizations are mostly removed from those that are being upgraded with Boxan technology," Mar Arden said.

They were being hunted, and Mar Arden was growing tired of running from this primitive species. He'd thought that blowing up strategic cities targeted to entice the Humans into fighting among themselves would have been more effective, but he'd underestimated the ECF and its role in governing this species. This Earth Coalition Force was in its early stages of development, but in another fifty cycles it had the potential to emerge as the singular governing entity of the entire world. He looked at Kandra Rene. "Do you have something to show me?"

Kandra Rene smiled. "Oh yes, I believe you'll be highly interested in this."

She brought up her wrist and a small holoscreen appeared. Mar Arden watched a video image of a group of Humans. One of them collapsed, and he heard faint utterances from him until the sound was lost amidst all the Humans flocking to the fallen man's side.

"The Humans have been trying to remove all traces of this video feed, which is why I began to pursue it. Do you know what that looks like?" Kandra Rene asked.

Mar Arden glanced at Hoan Berend.

"Humans are weak," Hoan Berend said.

"That may be, but it wasn't weakness that caused that Human to collapse," Mar Arden said.

Hoan Berend frowned and then shook his head.

Sometimes Mar Arden wondered how Hoan Berend had gotten the command of his own warship with instincts like this. The Xiiginn commander was adequate at his job and could follow orders, but abstract thinking was beyond him. He looked at Kandra Rene. "Were you able to confirm what was in the message?"

Hoan Berend's tail flicked irritably and came to settle over his shoulder.

"The Earth Coalition Force is trying to keep that information secure, and they're doing a pretty good job," Kandra Rene replied.

Mar Arden nodded. "Regardless, the fact that a message was received is telling in and of itself."

Hoan Berend sighed heavily. "Would you please fill me in on what's going on? What message?"

"Certainly," Mar Arden said. "The Boxans have used their abilities to send a message through the shield."

"Through Mardoxian means," Hoan Berend said, finally understanding.

"Precisely, which means there've been some new developments outside the shield," Mar Arden said and considered how this new information would affect his plans.

"They must be desperate to send a message using Mardoxian means. They're essentially waving it right in front of us. They must know we would've detected it," Hoan Berend said.

Mar Arden glided his fingertips over the end of his tail, which was wrapped around his narrow waist, and looked at Kandra Rene. "Are there any reports of other mysterious collapses at the time this took place?"

Kandra Rene's eyes slipped into calculation. "None. This was the only instance," she replied.

"Interesting," Mar Arden said.

"I thought so, which means—"

"That this Mardoxian message didn't come from the Boxans. The Humans on the other side of the shield must still be alive, and that means Sion Shif failed his mission. Also, there's one among them who has the Mardoxian potential," Mar Arden said.

Kandra Rene shook her head. "I hadn't considered that."

"If the Boxans are desperate enough to bring the Humans into our war, why wouldn't they train one of them who has the potential to be a true asset to them? Seems pretty clear to me," Mar Arden said.

Mar Arden glanced up at the night sky and peered at the two moons. They were luminous on a clear night like this one. "We're running out of time."

"I don't understand. How does this change anything?" Hoan Berend asked.

"This changes everything. The intelligence we've gotten from the Boxans indicates that they don't know how the shield works. We surmised that the shield couldn't be maintained indefinitely, and I would guess that the Boxans beyond the star system have arrived at the same conclusion. Therefore, they must have discovered a way to deal with it," Mar Arden said.

Hoan Berend considered this for a moment. "That can only work in our favor. If the shield comes down, our fleets can return here and conquer this planet."

Once again, Mar Arden was almost stunned by how stupid the Xiiginn commander was. It was true that the fleet would return, and if Garm Antis had somehow survived the previous assault, he would be keen to acquire the Mardoxian potential from the Humans for himself. And Mar Arden wouldn't put it past Garm Antis to have them all killed so he could claim the credit for bringing the Mardoxian trait to the Xiiginns.

"We need a viable specimen with the Mardoxian potential," Mar Arden said at last.

"That's something I can help you with," Kandra Rene said. "We've got new intelligence of a secret training facility on this continent. I think we should run some reconnaissance on it."

Mar Arden drew in a pleased breath. Kandra Rene was a worthy infiltrator. He almost mourned the loss it would be when he had to kill her.

16

Kaylan sat inside a Boxan shuttle heading down to the surface of Selebus. The Gresans had agreed to return to the negotiating table, due in large part to the eight Boxan Dreadnoughts with accompanying battle groups that had entered the Nerva star system. The Boxan fleet was commanded by Battle Leader Salevar, who Kladomaor told her was the most senior officer of their fleet. This show of force was also meant to demonstrate the commitment of the Boxans to the Alliance.

She glanced at the empty seat next to her, missing Zack and feeling the lack of his presence more than ever. He was furious with her, but there had been no other choice. Kaylan had agreed to listen to what the Alliance had to say about the *Athena*, and she was determined to move forward with her plan, which was to share all the knowledge they could gain from the *Athena* with the species who joined the Alliance. Yet Zack looked at her as if she had betrayed them all. She was fond of the *Athena*—it was their home—but she couldn't see another way out of this. She hoped Zack would forgive her someday, but for now, he'd chosen to return to Selebus on a different shuttle.

The rest of the *Athena* crew was on their way back to Selebus as well. Kaylan had requested that Efren and Hicks remain on board the *Athena*. Hicks had agreed to stay, but she could tell by his tone that he didn't like it. Kaylan was starting to get a little annoyed with the men and their tantrums when they didn't get their way. A decision had needed to be made.

Ma'jasalax looked over at her. "Sometimes our path can be a lonely one."

"I'm just disappointed that we have to do this at all," Kaylan said.

"Our world is rarely as we want it to be no matter how hard we try to control it. This is one of the lessons we had to learn, and it came at a terrible price. Yet it's a price we would pay again in order to survive," Ma'jasalax said.

Kaylan almost longed for the days when all she had to worry about was the

Athena and not how the decisions she made would impact the entire Human race.

The shuttle ride to the planet surface was all too short. When she stepped off the loading ramp, she glanced toward the shuttle where Zack was, hoping to catch a glimpse of him. She wasn't about to change her mind and she knew he wouldn't either, but she hated the fact that he was so mad at her. She didn't like giving the *Athena* up either, but considering their options, they had little choice.

Kaylan looked around the landing field and noticed that neither the Gresans nor the Napox had sent ships to Selebus. "Do they intend to remain in orbit now that the Boxan fleet has arrived?"

Kladomaor, who'd been standing nearby, blew out a strong breath. "They prefer the illusion of safety in their ships."

Kaylan pinched her lips together and shook her head. How had the Confederation functioned before the Xiiginns took over? "They aren't the only ones who've tried to take the *Athena* away from us. Zack told me about all the attempts to infiltrate the *Athena's* systems by Boxans when we were at Olloron."

Kladomaor sighed heavily with a pained expression. "I don't know what to say about that. I don't know who it was. We don't understand why the Drar chose to share their knowledge with you instead of us. We've searched for them for hundreds of cycles. It's part of who we are. That doesn't excuse what happened, but are Humans so different from us? If the situation was reversed, do you believe your species would have reacted differently than mine, despite how many of us labored to prevent those things from happening?"

Kaylan was silent for a few moments while she considered what Kladomaor had said. She glanced at Ma'jasalax and saw that the Mardoxian priestess was waiting for her answer. "No, we're not that different at all. In fact, some members of my own family were excellent at getting what they wanted, especially if they thought they were doing those things for the right reasons."

Kaylan hadn't thought of her grandfather in a long time. He'd been among the people who had received Ma'jasalax's message almost seventy years ago. She now understood that Ma'jasalax had acted on her own when she'd sent the original warning about the Xiiginns, along with guidance on how to develop more advanced technology. Kladomaor was right. Humans weren't any different than the other species in the universe.

They entered the main congressional building on Selebus. Governor Udonzari was presiding over the Alliance summit. Councilor Essaforn and Ambassador Dulrad were also there, along with Battle Leader Salevar. The Gresan battle commander was there in holographic form only, as was the Napox delegate.

Kaylan walked over to her designated area, and the Napox delegate caught her eye with a wry smile. Kaylan remembered that his name was Aenok.

"We had to try. The challenge was much too great for us to pass up," Aenok said.

Kaylan regarded the Napox for a moment with a challenging smile of her own. "*We* would've succeeded."

The Napox's furry mouth opened wide in what Kaylan assumed was a grin. "I think I'm going to like getting to know your species. Humans make so many things much more interesting."

"I'm glad you think so. Now, if you can keep your furry paws away from my ship, we'll get along just fine," Kaylan said, and Aenok gave her a slight bow.

Kaylan noticed that the Gresan battle commander watched the exchange but didn't offer any comments. Udonzari began the summit and reminded everyone that their presence in the Nerva star system was tolerated so long as they respected the Alliance. Kaylan recalled seeing that many Nershal ships had gathered, positioning themselves between Selebus and the Nershal homeworld.

The area where the Gresan battle commander stood became highlighted in blue, which indicated he wanted to speak, and Udonzari yielded the floor to him.

Solek turned to address the Boxan ambassador. "I want to know what you intend to do about the Human ship."

Ambassador Dulrad glanced at Kaylan for a moment. "The *Athena* isn't our ship. Why are you asking us about it?"

There was a chittering sound by the other Gresans near Solek. "You have the dominant space fleet in the star system. You could easily take out all other ships in the area and seize the *Athena* for yourself. Why haven't you done so already?"

Ambassador Dulrad's features became grim. "I don't know what pains me more—the fact that you've asked whether we will just take the Human spaceship from them or that you believe it's our right to do so. Both imply that your time in the Confederation under the dominion of the Xiiginns has changed your species, and not for the better."

Solek glared at the Boxan ambassador. "We had to survive your downfall, and now the Gresans are so firmly entangled with the Xiiginns that it has become unclear what a true Gresan looks like anymore."

"Then why hesitate to join the Alliance? Why attempt to steal what isn't rightfully yours?" Councilor Essaforn asked.

"Even with the Boxan fleet, this alliance cannot stand against the might of the Confederation Armada. We sought an advantage from which my species might have benefited," Solek said, swinging his gaze toward Kaylan. "And we failed."

Battle Leader Salevar cleared his throat with what sounded like a growl. "You might be surprised at what this alliance is capable of, and our Dreadnought class warships will make the Xiiginns cringe. It has been many cycles since we've engaged the Xiiginns, Gresan. I think you'll find that our weapons systems have increased in effectiveness, and while the Xiiginns are losing allies, we're gaining them. The eventual engagement with the Confederation Armada will not be as one-sided as you think."

Solek spoke to another Gresan nearby, but the conversation was muted. Then he turned back toward the Boxans. "Even if our estimation of your military capabilities isn't entirely accurate, you would still take heavy losses to even have a chance at defeating the Confederation Armada."

"This is where you're mistaken," Battle Commander Salevar replied. "Our engagement is with the Xiiginns, which represent only half of the armada."

A cool breeze blew in through the open skylight at the top of the vast chamber. Long strands of Kaylan's dark hair lifted off her neck, and she felt a shiver race down her spine.

"You can't engage the Confederation Armada unless you're fully committed," Kaylan said. The Boxans turned toward her. "I know you've made a colossal effort to avoid coming into conflict with species under the Xiiginn influence, but that will become unavoidable."

Battle Leader Salevar gave a slight bow of his head. "Mardoxian Blessed, you are correct. I should clarify. The High Council has authorized our military to engage with any fighting force that seeks to harm our alliance."

Kaylan's eyes widened and she glanced toward Kladomaor, who gave her a firm nod.

Salevar continued. "We have no illusions where the Confederation Armada is concerned. We will pull all of our fleets together to drive the Xiiginns out of the Confederation once and for all."

There were cheers from the Nershals. They yearned to strike at the Xiiginns for what they'd done to their species. The Boxans were committing everything they had to this.

"We have groups of rebels serving aboard Gresan ships. Can you assure us that if they cease hostilities during the battle, you will not obliterate them?" Solek asked.

"Any species other than the Xiiginns will be granted clemency. I doubt you'll get such an offer from the Xiiginns," Salevar replied.

The discussion went into the particulars of what the Gresans and the Napox had to offer the Alliance and, in turn, what the Alliance would do for them. Kaylan listened as they described how both species had various rebel groups that had been coming together in secret. They were the unspoken majority who had watched in fear as the Xiiginns took over the entire Confederation.

The Gresan battle commander looked at her from time to time, and as the meeting was coming to a close, he turned to address her. "What do you intend to do with the Drar technology?"

Kaylan looked around the room. Her gaze lingered for a moment on each group, hoping to gain some insight into each of them. Zack was right about one thing—the Alliance couldn't focus on facing the real threat while the *Athena* was within their grasp.

"The Confederation Armada is being formed to enslave my homeworld, and I want to avoid that fate for my species. The Boxans and the Nershals formed this alliance with that in mind, so my species stands to gain much from this agreement. I think it's only fair that we offer something in return. We intend to share all the Drar technology contained within the *Athena*. Everything we learn from it will be freely dispersed among all Alliance species. I hope my word is enough of a commitment," Kaylan said.

"It is," Kladomaor said, his deep voice reaching every crevice of the massive room.

Kaylan turned toward the Gresans and the Napox. "But if you try to take my ship again, I'll see to it that you get nothing. Not one thing. Do we have an understanding?"

The Gresan narrowed all four of its dark eyes, but the Napox seemed unperturbed by Kaylan's assertion.

Ambassador Dulrad cleared his throat. "Thank you, Kaylan. The vow of a Mardoxian Blessed would never be called into question."

"Indeed," Battle Leader Salevar said. "We must begin planning how we will defeat the armada."

Just as Salevar finished speaking, Kaylan noticed several comms channels chiming alerts throughout the room. She frowned as an audio message file suddenly appeared on her internal heads-up display.

"Are you sure? I'm still seeing the ship on our scanners," Salevar said.

Kladomaor's brows furrowed and he looked at Kaylan, who felt as if everything were happening in a strange, slow succession. She looked at the audio file and closed her eyes for a moment.

Zack, what did you do?

The hologram of the Gresan battle commander stepped toward her. "Your ship is gone. It has just fled the system," Solek said and turned toward the Boxans. "This alliance is done."

"Wait!" Ambassador Dulrad said. "There has to be a reasonable explanation for this. Give us a chance to find out what happened . . ."

Kaylan stopped listening to them and played the audio file.

"Kaylan," Zack said, "I'm going to find another option. I have a plan. I don't want you to think I just up and took the ship. Athena wouldn't let me, even if that were the case. No need to guess where we're going. We're heading to the Confederation space station capital. Athena believes she can mask our approach, so we're going to do some reconnaissance of our own and perhaps have a few surprises for the Xiiginns."

The message finished. He must have been in a rush to make it. Kaylan was so shocked that it took a few seconds for her anger with Zack to catch up with her thoughts. She should have kept a better eye on him. As she noticed more than a few Boxans looking in her direction, her flash of anger at Zack diminished almost as quickly as it had come. Her thoughts immediately went from worrying about Zack and whomever else he'd recruited for his impromptu mission to the possibilities that Zack's actions had given them. She felt her brain racing down several paths, exploring the different possibilities, until one of them became readily apparent to her. Had she inadvertently put Zack on this path? Kaylan looked at Ma'jasalax, who appeared to be calm amidst the urgent conversations going on around her. She was waiting for Kaylan to do something, almost as if she'd expected it.

"Is this part of the plan?" Hicks asked.

"Well, the plan was to get away from Nerva so we could come up with a plan," Zack answered.

Hicks's eyes widened and he looked at Zack as if he were about to choke him.

"Stop freaking out," Zack said.

"We're on the doorstep of the Confederation. How long will it be before they detect us here?" Hicks asked.

"Major, we came out of the wormhole well away from the detectable range of any Xiiginn warships. It will take us some time to get close to the Confederation Armada," Athena said.

"Or," Hicks said pointedly, "we can turn around and go right back to the Alliance."

Zack shook his head. "We can't. If we do that . . . We just can't."

"Indeed, this is highly irregular," Cardaleer said as he stepped onto the bridge.

Hicks glanced behind him and stared at the Boxan for a moment before swinging his gaze back to Zack. "Any other surprises?"

Zack tilted his head to the side and pursed his lips. "Not really. Look, Cardaleer can help us. He was—*is*—the foremost expert in Drar technology. Together we can come up with a way to use the *Athena* to help the Alliance. I *know* it, but we have to be *here* to do it."

Hicks groaned. "You're an expert in Drar technology?"

Cardaleer frowned. "I used to conduct research into Drar tech before the Chaos Wars."

Hicks glared at Zack. "Are you serious? The *Athena* is a ship with untapped potential, and you want to bring it here? You don't know what you're risking. If the Xiiginns find us, you're basically handing her over to them. Did you consider that?"

"They won't find us," Zack replied quickly.

"How do you know?"

"Because we were able to hide from the Boxans, and if we can do that, we can certainly hide from the Xiiginns," Zack said.

"That's not entirely accurate," Athena said.

Zack winced. He'd been hoping Athena would keep quiet about that.

"What do you mean?" Hicks asked while looking up at the ceiling, which he sometimes did when he addressed Athena directly.

"We used a decoy to convince the Boxans that we had remained where they thought we were. I've been able to mask our presence for now, but if we needed to fire our engines to move quickly or engage the Cherubian drive, we would most certainly be detected by the Xiiginns," Athena replied.

Zack walked in front of Hicks. "Trust me," he said, trying to put what he hoped was enough confidence in his voice to convince Hicks to stay. Technically, Hicks was second in command, and Athena might listen to a direct order from him no matter what Zack said.

"This isn't how we do things, Zack. We're supposed to be working together, not just firing from the hip," Hicks said.

"You're right. I won't do it again," Zack promised. *Unless I have no other choice,* he added to himself.

"We cannot go back to Nerva," Cardaleer said, drawing the attention of both Hicks and Zack.

"Why not?" Hicks asked.

"Because we need to be here on the fringe of it all if we're to have any hope of defeating the Xiiginns."

"Do you have any ideas on how we can do that?" Zack asked.

Cardaleer walked around the bridge while keeping his head low so it wouldn't hit the ceiling. "We spent many cycles trying to combat the Xiiginns and their stranglehold on the entire Confederation, and we have nothing to show for it. Facing the Xiiginns as we've done before will not win this war."

"So you don't have any ideas then," Zack said and pointedly did not look at Hicks. He could feel Hicks gearing up to go on a tirade of epic proportions. If they returned to Nerva now, the Alliance would tear the *Athena* apart, looking to gain any edge they could use against the Xiiginns. Zack couldn't let that happen. There must be another way—one where they didn't have to sacrifice the *Athena*.

"I have lots of ideas, just like you do," Cardaleer said. "I recognize a kindred spirit when I see one. Look at you," he said and gestured toward Zack. "Your thoughts are scattering to oblivion trying to think of a way to defeat the Xiiginns, as if it was something you could force from your brain." He then looked at Hicks. "And you're a warrior who hasn't been able to engage the enemy as he would like to. I can see it gnawing away at you. It does the same to me, but spending many cycles in Haven on Sethion tends to teach one what it is to wait and endure." Cardaleer glided his thick fingertips along the ceiling as if taking its measure. "The Drar remade this ship?"

Zack saw Hicks glance at him, looking slightly annoyed. "Yes, when we found their space station."

Cardaleer's eyes widened and he gave them his full attention. "What was it like to stand among the ancients—beings who were able to control all the mysteries in the great expanse? You were closer to them than we ever were, no matter what we found when we were exploring the galaxy. I miss that . . . But I want you to tell me about the Drar space station."

Zack glanced at Hicks, who jutted his chin up once as a way to tell him to go ahead. Hicks crossed his arms and leaned against the conference table.

Zack cleared his throat, feeling thirsty. "I don't think the Drar actually lived there. We didn't find any trace of them. The station looked as if it had been prepared for them, but they never arrived."

Cardaleer knelt on the floor and then sat down. A soft groan escaped the old Boxan, and he nodded for Zack to continue.

"Do you need anything? I could use a drink and maybe some food. Do you want some?" Zack asked.

Cardaleer's great shaggy head angled to the side while he considered it. "I could use some refreshment."

"Don't get up," Hicks said. "You guys keep talking. I'll go grab something from the galley."

Zack thanked him and turned back to Cardaleer. He sat down in one of the chairs.

"You were saying about the station," Cardaleer said.

Zack sucked in a deep breath. How long ago had it been? He couldn't think of how much time had passed. They'd been so worried that the *Athena* was going to fall apart. "The station was like a brand-new city that hadn't been lived in. It must have been out there for tens of thousands of years. The shield protecting it was constricting and destroying the buildings the Drar AI had built."

"How did you find it?" Cardaleer asked.

"That's a long story," Zack replied, and Cardaleer arched an eyebrow. "We found evidence collected by one of your asteroid bases. The Xiiginns were hunting us and found us there."

"The Xiiginns found you, you say?" Cardaleer said in a pensive tone.

"Yeah, um, one of the crew had been affected by the Xiiginn influence. We didn't know it at the time," Zack replied.

"One never does until it's too late, even among my species. The member of your crew who was afflicted with the Xiiginn influence—did you kill him?"

"No, we didn't kill him," Zack said briskly, remembering Jonah Redford. His arms had been covered in burns from modifying the Boxans' communication array in order to signal the Xiiginns. "We tried to help him."

"You must realize that anyone under the Xiiginn influence is beyond saving. They cannot be cured," Cardaleer said.

"Kladomaor said the same thing, but we didn't murder Jonah. We studied him and tried to figure out a way to heal him. Jonah fought it, and resisting it damaged his brain. I don't know why he was affected, but I ..." Zack stopped speaking.

Cardaleer looked at him sharply. "What do you mean? Were you under the Xiiginn influence?" The Boxan's glare seemed to contain years of pent-up rage and frustration.

"No," Zack said. "They tried, when I was their prisoner, but it didn't work on me."

Cardaleer frowned. "Didn't work on you? How are you immune to the Xiiginn influence?"

Because of my love for Kaylan, Zack thought. At least, that was what Brenda and Emma believed, that his love for Kaylan had shielded him from the Xiiginn influence. "It's complicated," Zack said.

"Kladomaor wouldn't have allowed you access to their systems if he suspected that you were afflicted. Very well, continue," Cardaleer said.

"After we escaped the Xiiginns, we decided to help Kladomaor find where the Drar signal was coming from," Zack said with a frown. "The signal was one of the things detected. We were in the Qegi star system."

"The Qegi," Cardaleer said and nodded. "A clever species. They were excellent at manufacturing impressive alloys that were very useful in shipbuilding. They were among the first species the Xiiginns exploited, which is very unfortunate because they would have been a valuable addition to the Confederation." The Boxan sighed. "Alright, go on."

"Right," Zack said. "We were following the signal when something reached out to Kaylan through Mardoxian means. We almost died . . ." Zack shook his head, remembering how the wormhole had become unstable. "Something—the Drar AI, we think—destabilized the wormhole. It wanted to separate us from . . . uh, well, you—Kladomaor, Ma'jasalax—and other Boxans."

"Indeed. That's interesting. Please continue," Cardaleer said.

Zack shook his head. "I don't see how this is going to help."

"It helps me understand what happened to you and this ship, so that's how it helps."

Zack glanced at the door to the bridge and wondered when Hicks would return with the food. He blew out a breath and continued. "Once we were past the shield, the Drar AI took control of the ship and guided us in. The AI brought us to a docking platform and we left the ship to explore the space station."

Cardaleer pressed his lips together. "What about the crewmember who was under the Xiiginn influence?"

"Jonah," Zack confirmed.

"Yes, you left him aboard your ship, unguarded?"

Zack shook his head. "No, he came with us."

"How? I thought you said the Xiiginn influence had damaged his brain."

"Oh . . . well, Jonah became lucid when we passed through the shield. I was on the bridge and didn't know it at the time, but Brenda was monitoring him in the med bay," Zack said.

Cardaleer leaned forward. "Lucid. Were the effects completely negated?"

"Not exactly. The damage was still there, but he somehow came out of it. Something the Drar AI did to him," Zack said.

Cardaleer looked away for a moment, pressing his lips together. A soft groan rumbled from deep in his massive chest. He turned back toward Zack.

"I had the same idea as you. The Drar packed a bunch of their knowledge into this ship, and Athena and I tried to figure out what they'd done to alleviate Jonah's symptoms. There isn't anything there," Zack said.

"He wasn't cured?"

"No, he said he was going to die," Zack said, remembering how Jonah had stayed behind. "The AI had figured out that the Drar were never going to come. It wanted to stop waiting for them, but it couldn't self-terminate. Jonah volunteered to stay behind. He merged with the AI and was able to do what the AI couldn't do."

Cardaleer's eyes widened. "Amazing. I wish I could have been there."

Zack's eyebrows pulled together. "It's not like it sounds. It was scary. The space station was falling apart. The Drar AI remade our ship, including our AI, and her capabilities continue to evolve, but I've tried for months to figure out how the Drar AI was able to temporarily cure Jonah. I haven't been able to find out how it was done."

"Perhaps you didn't know the correct questions to ask," Cardaleer said.

"You think—" Zack had begun to say when Hicks walked onto the bridge carrying a container of food.

Hicks arched an eyebrow. "What happened?"

Zack turned toward Cardaleer. "Can you do it?"

"I might know the right questions to ask to unlock the knowledge you seek," Cardaleer answered.

Zack jumped to his feet. "Yes!" he shouted, pumping his fist into the air.

"Great. I'm happy you're excited. Now, would either of you like to tell me what's going on?" Hicks asked.

17

After the *Athena* jumped away, Kladomaor had been ordered to figure out where it'd gone and how the ship had escaped virtually unnoticed. There were many Boxans who had difficulty accepting that the Humans were as primitive as they'd originally thought. They had proven to be ingenious but on occasion a bit too idealistic. Human idealism was infectious, and Kladomaor had noticed how his own species seemed to absorb it with an increasing fervor akin to that of a star's gravitational pull—slow at first, but building in intensity until they found themselves hungering to live instead of merely surviving. The potential of the Human species blazed brighter than anything he'd ever experienced. They had the capacity to become as ruthless as the Xiiginns had proven to be, but they were also passionate in their idealism. They dreamed of what they could be and chased that dream almost as if they were afraid it would slip away. Kladomaor had seen that same passion become almost completely extinguished in the Boxans, and now that they had raised their heads from the dreariest time in Boxan history, Kladomaor found that he would fight harder than he ever had before to ensure the Boxans' future.

The main holoscreen on the bridge of the Boxan heavy cruiser showed real-time sensor feeds. They'd traveled to the outer system of planets in the Nerva star system, away from the Alliance fleet. He glanced over at Kaylan, who was speaking with the *Athena* crew near the communications station. She'd grown beyond the mission commander who'd been thrust into the commander's chair, and the longer he knew her, the more she reminded him of Ma'jasalax. Knowing Ma'jasalax as he did made him wonder whether he was jumping at shadows. Or had Kaylan grown into a shrewd leader, capable of traversing the dangerous circles of the Mardoxian Sect? She'd seemed quite surprised when the *Athena* left the Nerva star system.

Ma'jasalax entered the bridge and joined him. The Mardoxian priestess looked at the *Athena* crew for a moment before turning toward Kladomaor.

"Has the student become the teacher then?" Kladomaor asked.

Ma'jasalax seemed unperturbed by his intentional jab. "Kaylan cannot remain a student forever."

"No, she can't, but I still wonder at how events have unfolded," Kladomaor replied.

"You mean, did Kaylan purposefully set these events into motion?"

"I know they didn't want to give up their ship, and who could blame them? But in the end, what else could they have done?" Kladomaor said.

"I believe Kaylan really would have shared anything she learned from the Drar data repositories on the *Athena*, but once they return to Earth it probably wouldn't have been up to her. She realizes this, and she also knows you couldn't guarantee that the High Council wouldn't put forth considerable effort to take the *Athena* away from them," Ma'jasalax said. She spoke softly so that the Boxans around them couldn't overhear their conversation. "You've often pointed out how Kaylan is a bit of an optimist, but the actions she's taken are logical and are more aligned with a realist's philosophy. Wouldn't you agree?"

Kladomaor considered it for a moment and resisted the urge to look at Kaylan one more time, as if·to glean some insight he hadn't considered before. He knew all he needed to know. "They are the actions of a mature leader, and I cannot find any fault in what she's done."

The beads on Ma'jasalax's tightly braided hair slid across her shoulders as she sat back. "And yet we feel this inclination to resist what's been done. The Alliance fleet has been growing, and we were going to confront the Xiiginns sooner or later."

"Eventually," Kladomaor agreed and glanced at the *Athena* crew. Kaylan was still speaking with them, and he snorted.

Ma'jasalax arched one of her eyebrows and looked at him. "What is it?"

"I'm surprised you haven't noticed," Kladomaor said and nodded toward Kaylan and the others.

"I might have, but I won't know unless you tell me what you were thinking just now," Ma'jasalax replied dryly.

Kladomaor hadn't missed the slight annoyance she'd put into her tone, and he supposed even the legendary Mardoxian priestess had her limits. "The gender divide of the Humans. All the males are on the ship. Some might believe they're there because they felt they needed to take action. I'm sure that's Zack's motivation, but I doubt Hicks knew what was happening until it was already too late. The females are here. Kaylan has pointed them all in the direction she intended them to go. Now it's time for us to do our part."

"Etanu is with Zack and the others, but it could be a coincidence that these *Athena* crewmembers were left here," Ma'jasalax said.

Kladomaor shook his head. "Some of the Human cultural divide is almost instinctual. Each gender chooses their actions in their own way. Males want to protect the females. We've seen it many times when we've all faced danger, even with the female warriors among them. Perhaps the Humans will outgrow it, but it won't be for many cycles."

Boxans had evolved along similar lines, but those tendencies were virtually gone from their species. Even before the Chaos Wars, males and females had held similar roles in their society. In other words, the roles were the same regardless of the individuals who occupied them.

Kaylan approached them, along with the other *Athena* crewmembers.

"We've just received a message from Zack," Kaylan said.

Kladomaor frowned and used his neural implants to check the heavy cruiser's communications systems but didn't see anything in the logs from the *Athena*.

"It wasn't through standard communications," Kaylan said.

"Have they returned?" Kladomaor asked.

"No. And before you ask, we're not able to reply to them," Kaylan said.

"Why not? Where are they?"

"They're heading closer to the Confederation space station, and we can't reply to them because it would give away their position. Athena used a micro-wormhole and sent a message to me that way," Kaylan said.

Kladomaor's thick eyebrows pulled together and he glanced toward Varek, who was monitoring the tactical battle station. They hadn't detected anything. They couldn't create a micro-wormhole, and even if they could, they'd have to know exactly where the *Athena* was in order to reach them.

"Athena left a drone in the area that checked to get our exact location," Kaylan said.

"I understand. The Confederation capital is where the armada is amassing. Why are they going there?" Kladomaor asked.

"Zack believes they might have a way to temporarily disrupt the Xiiginn influence," Kaylan said and waited for his reaction.

Kladomaor's shoulders became rigid and he looked at Ma'jasalax for a moment.

"He believes he can reproduce what the Drar space station did for Jonah Redford," Kaylan said.

Kladomaor's first instinct was to insist that it was impossible. There was no way to reverse the Xiiginn influence. Even his partial exposure to it could still affect him. "It's not possible to reverse it. The effects are permanent."

"He didn't say he was going to reverse the Xiiginn influence. He said they might have a way to disrupt it, which is exactly what happened with Jonah on the Drar space station. We all saw it. Jonah was dying, slowly being driven mad by what the Xiiginns had done to him. But when we were on the Drar space station, he was coherent, as if what was causing his distress was gone. The damage had still been done—Jonah was dying and nothing was going to change that—but for a moment, at least, he was his old self and aware of what had happened to him," Kaylan said.

Kladomaor shook his head. "I remember those reports from when you were on the Drar space station, but we've studied the Xiiginn influence since the Chaos Wars and have never been even remotely close to doing what Zack claims can be done."

"It's not just Zack. Cardaleer is with them. They think they've found a way to make it work using the *Athena*," Kaylan said.

Kladomaor drew in a deep breath. Ever since the Chaos Wars, Boxans had longed for a way to cure the Xiiginn influence, but they'd always failed. It couldn't be done. The effects were irreversible. "Even with the *Athena*, how can this be done?"

"I don't know. Zack said he would have the *Athena* compile their research and store it on one of the escape pods that can later be picked up. That way if they fail, at least the knowledge won't be lost, and someone else can figure out what went wrong and try again," Kaylan said.

Kladomaor could tell Kaylan didn't like that part. Bonded pairs rarely approved when there was a significant risk to the other. This wasn't just a Human trait, but a common trait among many species that had bonded pairs. "So we're to accept what they're doing on faith then. What are we supposed to do now?" Kladomaor asked.

"Isn't it obvious?" Ma'jasalax said and arched an eyebrow at him.

Kladomaor should've known she would get her revenge for his earlier behavior. "Not to me, it isn't. All we know is that our closest link to the Drar is purposefully putting itself in the middle of the enemy fleet, hoping they can somehow disrupt the Xiiginn influence. That is reckless and misguided."

He didn't bother trying to hide the disgust in his voice. There was risk and then there was suicide.

"Zack wouldn't do this if he didn't believe they had a real chance at succeeding. Hicks is with them and wouldn't go along with it either," Kaylan said.

Kladomaor met Kaylan's gaze squarely, and his voice was unflinching. "Who would Athena listen to—Zack or Hicks? I believe that under these circumstances, the *Athena* would choose to listen to Zack rather than Hicks, even if he is your second in command."

Kaylan's gaze hardened. "If you think this is easy for me, you're wrong. We have no other choice."

"There's always a choice. They could withdraw and return here," Kladomaor countered.

"Then Earth will pay the price. You've seen the Alliance—the High Council, the Gresans, the Nershal Global Congress. They're committed to helping, but they'll wait too long. That's not a risk I can afford to take, and neither can you," Kaylan said.

Kladomaor found himself leaning forward. "What if Zack fails and they can't disrupt the Xiiginn influence? What then?"

Kaylan's gaze softened and she looked oddly vulnerable at that moment. Kladomaor almost felt sorry for asking the question, but the moment was gone as Kaylan regained her courage.

"It depends on what the Alliance does. Will the Alliance risk Drar technology falling into the Confederation's hands? Will we leave Zack and the others to do this thing on their own, or will we help them? Regardless of which reason we use for engaging the Confederation Armada, our actions will determine what occurs next. The one thing I know is that if that armada leaves the Confederation space station, my home is gone. Beyond that, what do you think the Confederation will do with this armada after it destroys my people? They'd likely hit Nerva next and hunt down anyone who's known or suspected to be associated with the Alliance. After that, the armada would become a convenient way for the Xiiginns to deal with rebellious species that resist them. So the Alliance doesn't have a choice, regardless of what Zack or I do. All the arguments in the world will not save us from them."

Kladomaor felt Ma'jasalax place her hand on his shoulder and give it a gentle squeeze. He leaned back on the commander's couch and looked at her. "She's right—about everything," Ma'jasalax said.

"And you didn't see this?" Kladomaor asked.

Ma'jasalax seemed to consider her answer for a moment. "Not with the clarity Kaylan just showed."

Kladomaor's mind raced with possibilities as he thought about the path that had brought them to this moment—the path Ma'jasalax had set them all on—but judging by her reaction, even the Mardoxian priestess wasn't all-knowing.

"We need to alert the Alliance," Kaylan said.

"I don't know how they'll react, even knowing all this. I still can't help but wonder what one ship—even the *Athena*, which has been imbued with Drar technology—is going to do that will make facing the armada not feel like we're sounding our last battle song. Even if they're somehow able to figure out a way to disrupt the Xiiginn influence, what good will it do? The *Athena* is just one ship," Kladomaor said.

Kaylan gave him a long look. "I don't have all the answers, Kladomaor. No one does, but I do know that Zack is aware of all those shortcomings and will work to address them. And he's not alone. Hicks is with them. So is Etanu and Cardaleer. And there's the *Athena*. Together they can do what the Boxans couldn't do all those years ago when the Xiiginns first showed their true colors. You can't change the past. All we can do now ... all we can control is what we do right now. Because if we succeed, the Xiiginns will be finished."

Kladomaor felt a faint stirring deep in his chest, a yearning to finally be free of this war. The Boxans had fought and had almost forgotten who they were. Perhaps it was time for them all to step out from the shadows and battle the Xiiginns in the light.

18

M ar Arden had known he'd be walking into a trap. Kandra Rene's discovery of a secret training facility for Humans with the Mardoxian potential was enough to rouse his suspicions, but what they'd discovered at the site couldn't be ignored. His Human adversaries had relentlessly hunted him and they must have been growing desperate to attempt this, but that hadn't dissuaded Mar Arden from going to the secret training facility. The Humans had retrieved something of great importance to him, something he'd yearned for for many cycles. He wondered if the Humans understood what they held in their possession or whether they'd do anything differently if they did.

"How could they possess a key to the Star Shroud network?" Kandra Rene asked.

They were using Human ground transportation, which made their journey to the secret training facility longer, but at least they would arrive undetected. With the number of ground transport vehicles traveling, there would be no way the Humans could surmise that Mar Arden was on his way. The lush landscape was momentarily illuminated by the lights of their vehicles as he turned from the window and looked at Kandra Rene. "You're asking the wrong question, my dear."

Kandra Rene's reply masked her frustration well. "Most of the Tetronian keys are gone or in the possession of the Boxans. So how could the Humans have a key to the Star Shroud network? I doubt the Boxan fleet brought one here."

Mar Arden regarded her for a moment. "I thought you understood how Boxan monitoring stations worked."

Kandra Rene didn't reply and merely waited for him to continue.

"You're right, they don't have a key, but the Star Shroud network is still accessible from a Boxan monitoring station. A communications node was removed from the monitoring station and is here on the planet. If we bring the node with us back to the Confederation space station, we can unlock the Star Shroud network across the galaxy," Mar Arden said with a smirk.

Kandra Rene's violet eyes widened. "You intend to use the node to initiate a check-in, which would grant you access to the system. I should've seen that before."

"You'll get no arguments from me. So, in addition to finding the very best test subject with the Mardoxian trait, we need to find that communications node. That's why I brought most of our soldiers with us," Mar Arden said.

The Xiiginn soldiers hardly reacted to his conversation with Kandra Rene. He always kept his most loyal soldiers with him at all times—especially now—which was a fact that hadn't gone unnoticed by Kandra Rene *or* Hoan Berend, for that matter. Mar Arden had convinced the warship commander to remain behind at their encampment—an easy feat because he knew Hoan Berend believed that should they fail at the secret training facility, he would be left with the Mardoxian trait for himself, provided the incubation of the test subject was successful. The warship commander could believe whatever he wanted. Mar Arden had several monitoring devices that would alert him as soon as the incubation period was complete, and the data would be transferred directly to him.

They left the highway and drove toward an old mountain range on the eastern side of the continent. Once they were out of sight, Mar Arden ordered them to go faster. He'd had his soldiers modify these vehicles, which enabled them to reach speeds far beyond their previous capabilities.

"Our diversionary assets are en route as we speak," Kandra Rene said.

"Excellent," Mar Arden replied.

There weren't enough Xiiginns to make an effective assault on the secret training facility, so they'd had to leverage Kandra Rene's Human assets. Those expendable assets would begin their air assault on the training facility just before Mar Arden arrived. His Human adversaries knew they were coming, and Mar Arden decided he wouldn't bother to try to hide his assault. They'd outfitted the diversionary teams with elite Human military vehicles that should convince the defenders it was the Xiiginns attacking them. Bright flashes of light shone from ahead of them. They were almost to the target.

"Send out our drones to scan for their defenses," Mar Arden said.

The diversionary assets were meant to expose the kind of defenses that were protecting the training facility. One of Mar Arden's trusted soldiers at the front of the vehicle opened a metallic case and activated the drones. Twelve metallic orbs flew out the open window and sped ahead of them. Kandra Rene brought up a holoscreen that showed the aerial layout of their target. There were several marks that indicated heavy turret locations, as well as the Human soldiers that were stationed along the roof. Mar Arden ordered his driver to change their approach. The diversionary assault had softened their defenses on the west side, and he meant to use that to gain quick entry into the building. Once inside, they could scan for Boxan power sources.

Three Human ground transportation vehicles holding twelve Xiiginns each drove toward the battle with all exterior lights extinguished. Xiiginns were at home in the dark and could see as clearly without light as they could during the day. Because of this, the Human soldiers didn't notice their approach until they were within a hundred meters of the facility. The Xiiginns raced toward a gaping hole in the side of the building, where Mar Arden's soldiers quickly exited the vehicles and exchanged fire with the nearest Human defenders. The Human soldiers were still using projectile-type weapons that had difficulty penetrating their armor, but the Xiiginns had no such limitations. Bolts of molten plasma cut through the Humans' defenses. There was nowhere for the Humans to seek shelter from their attack because plasma bolts burned through everything in their path.

Mar Arden left a small team of soldiers to secure their transportation. Once they were inside the building, they encountered more Human soldiers. The Xiiginns had much better weapons than the Humans, and Mar Arden ordered his soldiers to press their advantage. The Xiiginns sprinted into the building with an agility that left the Human defenders looking clumsy and slow in comparison.

His earlier reconnaissance had indicated that the Boxan communications node was on a lower level of the building, so when they reached a group of elevators, he summoned all of them. He divided his soldiers into three groups and each used a different elevator to the lower levels. Despite the Humans' futile attempt to resist their assault, Mar Arden was beginning to suspect that the real trap hadn't been triggered. He didn't bother telling his soldiers to be on guard. They were Xiiginns; they were always on guard.

There was an audible chime when the elevator reached its destination and the doors opened. Two of his soldiers exited first, and Mar Arden waited while the soldiers secured the area. Ahead of them was a long hall, and they followed it away from the elevators. Darkened rooms lined the hallway, and as Mar Arden peered inside, he noticed that there was no one else there.

They reached a large door at the end of the hallway. The polished door was made of smooth metal and opened into a vast warehouse. Long aisles stretched into the dark and tall metal racks held heavy equipment and storage containers. Mar Arden checked the scanner on his wrist, which indicated that the Boxan communication node was farther into the dimly lit warehouse.

He had no idea how these Humans had come to be in possession of the node and he didn't care. He wanted it and was going to take it from them. The Boxan communications node would change everything for them, almost as much as gaining the Mardoxian potential.

Mar Arden ordered his soldiers forward, and they staggered their approach. Each group chose to go down a different aisle into the warehouse. After a few minutes, Mar Arden checked his internal heads-up display and changed the scanner configuration to include energy signatures that were unique to Boxan technology. He stopped. Instead of one energy signature ahead of them, they were surrounded by multiple contacts. His eyes widened, and he was about to order his soldiers to take cover when the Humans began firing.

Molten plasma bolts blazed into them, and several Xiiginn soldiers went down immediately. Mar Arden dove for cover, crouched, and brought up his rifle. He started shooting back as more Xiiginn soldiers went down. Mar Arden scrambled to his feet and ran, calling for the remaining soldiers to follow him.

Kandra Rene was at his side, her platinum hair momentarily reflecting the light from the plasma rifles the Humans were using. This was *the* trap, and his adversaries had proven that it was a very effective one at that.

He glanced upward and quickly scaled the open racks to the top of the aisle. Kandra Rene followed his lead, and the remaining Xiiginn soldiers did the same. Mar Arden ran along the top of the storage racks. He looked at the ceiling, but it was much too high for him to reach. Golden plasma bolts blazed past him as the Human soldiers tracked their movements.

There was a gap up ahead and Mar Arden vaulted across it. He heard the other Xiiginns following and slowed his pace, glancing behind him to look for their pursuers. The Human soldiers didn't show up on his scanners at all and had stopped firing their weapons. The only things that appeared were the multiple Boxan power sources used in plasma assault rifles. Mar Arden stopped and waited, holding his rifle ready. The other Xiiginn soldiers came to a halt and took up defensive positions around him.

"Why have we stopped?" Kandra Rene whispered.

Mar Arden peered into the gloom. He heard a faint buzzing sound that was coming steadily closer.

"We need a more defensible position," Kandra Rene said. She took a few steps away from him, and several soldiers inched back along with her.

Mar Arden used implants to increase the sensitivity of his hearing. The buzzing became a mechanical whirring sound, and his eyes widened. "Machines! They're using machines to hunt us."

"Suppressor grenades," Kandra Rene ordered.

Several Xiiginn soldiers flung the grenades, and a blue-silver field of light expanded away from them. Mar Arden heard several crashes as the machines that hunted them went off-line, their electrical components suddenly overwhelmed. The Boxan plasma rifles would remain operational, but without the machines to move them into position, they were just as useless. He listened for a few moments and didn't hear anything else.

Mar Arden returned his hearing to normal and glanced at the others. They'd lost over half of their soldiers, and the strategist in him acknowledged the effectiveness of his adversaries' tactics. They had sacrificed many soldiers to lure Mar Arden and the others inside, but it wouldn't be enough. Without another word, Mar Arden turned around and continued along the top of the storage racks. The Boxan communication node wasn't far from them now.

Slowly and steadily, they made their way. They'd triumphed against the first trap, but that didn't mean there couldn't be others waiting for them. His soldiers kept a watchful eye all around them, poised to address any threat. They came to another gap and Mar Arden leapt across. He heard a faint hissing sound and then one of his soldiers cried out as he fell from the top of the tall racks. Mar Arden tried to scan the area but couldn't see anything. Then, a faint blue light raced toward another of his soldiers. The blue light plunged into the soldier's chest and Mar Arden saw a metallic shaft sticking out. The soldier tumbled off the rack and thudded to the ground. The remaining soldiers fired their weapons blindly into the gloom. Mar Arden kept scanning to find the source of the attack and saw

Kandra Rene doing the same. Another blue light found its mark, coming from a different vantage point. The light was so faint that by the time he saw it, it was already too late for another of his soldiers. The soldiers fired their weapons at the source but could hit nothing.

"Get down off the rack or they'll pick us all off," Mar Arden said and hopped to the ground.

The remaining soldiers followed him down. Mar Arden hastened down the aisle between the storage racks, and a few moments later another of his soldiers went down with a gurgled scream.

"How does it feel to be hunted, Xiiginn?" a deep voice called from the darkness and echoed all around them.

The remaining Xiiginn soldiers kept their weapons pointed above them, anticipating an attack at any moment. Mar Arden heard faint footsteps in rapid succession from above and fired his weapon. He glimpsed a dark figure as it leapt above them, but all of their shots missed. Two more of his soldiers went down with metallic shafts sticking out of their heads. Mar Arden started firing at the racks, and the plasma bolts gouged through whatever was stored on them. His soldiers followed his example and the nearest rack began to sway. Mar Arden shoved his shoulder into one and pushed. The heavy rack slowly gave way and slammed into the one next to it. Mar Arden backed away as more racks fell, collapsing under the weight of their neighbors. He turned and ran, and the remaining soldiers followed him. There was an open area beyond the aisle and he raced toward it. If they could lure their attackers out into the open, they could defeat them. He should've known better than to allow himself to be put in a position where he could be picked off so easily.

"Keep running, Xiiginn."

Mar Arden clenched his teeth. The mocking tone of the voice grated on his nerves. They reached the end of the aisle and Kandra Rene grabbed his arm to keep him from going forward. One of their remaining soldiers plunged ahead and was taken out by another primitive weapon. Mar Arden glanced behind them and saw that all their soldiers were gone. It was just him and Kandra Rene. She pulled him to the side, and another shaft appeared right where he'd been standing a moment before. Kandra Rene fired her weapon and the plasma bolt gouged the wall on the far side of the room.

Together they left the aisle, crouching as they moved forward. Mar Arden kept his weapon ready and peered ahead of him. He could see the faint outline of a Human standing in the darkness. He squeezed the trigger but the Human leapt out of the way, almost as if sensing his attack before he'd even done anything.

"Mardoxian," Mar Arden whispered harshly.

Kandra Rene nodded and they both darted ahead, firing their weapons as they went. Mar Arden leapt up into the air as the glowing tip of a metallic shaft sped toward him. The shaft struck the rifle from his hands and Mar Arden landed hard.

Kandra Rene fired her weapon, and a plasma bolt singed the arm of their attacker. The Human grunted in pain and dropped its weapon.

"Come face me, Xiiginn," the voice of a Human female said.

Kandra Rene charged forward, unleashing a barrage of plasma bolts until the power cell was used up. Somehow, the Human dodged every bolt. Kandra Rene flung her rifle toward her opponent, who slapped the weapon away and grinned. Mar Arden crept forward as the two combatants engaged. Both combatants were able to land blows, but the advantage their enhancements normally afforded the Xiiginns didn't help them here. It was as if the Human they fought anticipated their every move. A Mardoxian soldier.

Mar Arden glanced behind him and saw his rifle on the ground. It was ruined and couldn't help him. He was creeping toward Kandra Rene, eager to kill the Human, when another blue light zipped past him. Mar Arden flinched and then cursed as he backed away.

"I couldn't have you interfering with the contest," a man said and stepped into the light.

Mar Arden looked at the man. He was an older Human who kept his weapon pointed directly at Mar Arden. The Human seemed to study him for a moment. Most Humans had never seen an alien species before, but this Human looked at him with neither surprise nor fear. The Human's expression was one of familiarity, as if he'd seen a Xiiginn before. Mar Arden knew that if he tried to attack, the Human would kill him with that primitive weapon. The Human noticed Mar Arden studying the weapon.

"Like it? I've always loved a good bow—simple, straight to the point—but as you already know, this is no ordinary weapon. We've given it a few improvements, thanks to our Boxan friends. You'll have to forgive me; I haven't introduced myself. My name is Ed Johnson, and I'm the Human who's going to kill you."

Mar Arden smiled. "I think you overestimate your chances."

"I could have killed you already, but then I wouldn't have gotten to speak with you. I've heard so much about your species—the Xiiginns. I must admit it was harder to find you than I thought it would be, but you leave a particular trail in your wake," Ed Johnson said.

Mar Arden narrowed his gaze. He had the distinct impression that Ed Johnson had some secret knowledge. "Don't worry. When the rest of my species arrives, you won't be so smug. Your death will take a very long time."

Mar Arden heard the other Human cry out at the same time Kandra Rene grunted in pain. He watched Ed Johnson to see if he would take his eyes off him, but the Human steadily returned his gaze, looking slightly amused.

"You didn't think it would be that easy. Now that I have you in my sights, I'm not going to take my eyes off you."

Mar Arden glanced over at the two combatants and saw that each fought with renewed vigor. He turned back toward the Human.

"My assistant, Iris. She's very special," Ed Johnson said, answering the unasked question.

"She fights well," Mar Arden admitted.

"She's the best. Would you care to make a wager on who will win?"

Mar Arden glanced over at the two combatants and slowly moved his hand over his wrist to access his PDA. He looked back at the Human. "She's enhanced."

Ed Johnson nodded. "Of course, and she received a very special augmentation recently, too. I'm afraid your last encampment wasn't as secure as you thought it was. We recovered some of the data you left and figured out how you were going to incorporate the Mardoxian trait into your species. Really convenient because now I can enhance my own soldiers with the ability. You might have noticed during your time here that there are billions of us, and one thing you can count on is Human determination to defend what's ours."

Mar Arden frowned. He still had the data connection to their base of operations. "I'm glad it worked out so well for you."

"We're still closing in on your base here, but it shouldn't be much longer," Ed Johnson said.

Mar Arden glanced behind Ed at the Boxan communications node. Its dark metallic surface almost shimmered in the light. "Do the Boxans know you have that?"

"Not exactly, but I couldn't think of another way to get you here aside from offering something you really value."

Mar Arden had to admit that it was a clever plan. "The machines with Boxan plasma rifles were a nice touch. I wasn't expecting that. Although I didn't get a good look at them, they weren't enough to stop us." He accessed his drones and commanded them to come to his location. "Such a shame the Boxans couldn't join us right now."

"Perhaps you'd like to try using your compulsion capability on me?" Ed Johnson asked.

The thought had crossed Mar Arden's mind, and if there had been Boxans there, he would have exercised his will over them without hesitation, but Humans were different. He was as likely to fail to subjugate them as he was to succeed, and those weren't odds he'd stake his life on.

"Maybe some other time, then. Oh, and regarding the Boxans, you'll find that we're more than capable of dealing with vermin like you without them."

Mar Arden sneered. He used his neural implants to access his combat armor systems. "Your species is divided."

"Big families will have squabbles from time to time. I bet you thought those nuclear bombs would have been more effective in dividing us. You were wrong. It actually unified our resolve against you," Ed Johnson said.

"We've seen species like yours at similar stages of development. Your potential rests on the edge of a knife. One nudge and you'll teeter right off of it and go the way all those before you have gone in the great expanse."

"I wouldn't count us out just yet. We're a pretty stubborn race. Misguided at times, but ultimately here for the duration."

"Your shield cannot protect you, and I would almost hate to see you pick the losing side of this war," Mar Arden said.

"Oh, you'd like us to form an alliance with you? Why didn't you say so before you flung asteroids at our planet and detonated nuclear bombs in populated areas? And let's not forget snatching a few of us for your experiments."

"There are large factions of your race that have embraced us, and many more will do so once our fleet arrives," Mar Arden said.

He watched as the Human nodded.

"There will always be a group—or a faction, as you say—that will be misguided in their beliefs. Are the Xiiginns so different? Are you unified?"

"We are the strongest race in the great expanse. You will soon learn—" Mar Arden's speech was cut off when Kandra Rene cried out.

Mar Arden thrust his fist toward the Human, and a group of lethal projectiles shot from a hidden compartment on his armored wrist. The Human released his weapon, and the blue light at the end of a metallic shaft raced toward him. Mar Arden dove to the side and spun through the air, using his tail to propel him toward his attacker. The Human collapsed to the ground with blood spurting from multiple wounds. Mar Arden felt a spike of energy surge through him as he closed in on the Human. Ed Johnson scrambled backward as Mar Arden leapt on top of him, pinning him down with his foot. One of the Human's legs was bloody where he'd been hit. Mar Arden lashed out with his tail and pounded the wound.

"Not so smug now," Mar Arden said.

He'd expected the Human to be angry and afraid, but instead the pathetic being just sneered at him.

"You think you've won, Xiiginn?"

Mar Arden saw a shadowed figure coming toward him. He thrust out his wrist and the remaining projectiles shot forth, but the Human dove to the side. He saw Kandra Rene's body lying on the floor, unmoving. The Human with the Mardoxian potential regained her feet and ran toward him, but the distance was too great. Kandra Rene had drawn away their attacker before dying. Mar Arden swung his gaze toward the Boxan communication node. It was close by, ripe for the taking. He left the dying Human at his feet and raced toward the shimmering metallic box.

"You'll never escape," Ed Johnson called out from where he lay on the floor.

Mar Arden snatched the node off the shelf and looked above him. He heard the buzzing of his drones as they flew across the warehouse toward him, and he sent the command for the drones to lock together so they could carry him out of there. They flew closer and he sprang into the air, reaching out with his hand. The drones bunched together and he grabbed onto one. The drones dipped toward the ground at the sudden weight and then rose higher into the air. A blue streak sped past his face as he commanded the drones to take him to the exit. More blue shafts took out drones near his hands, but they missed him. Mar Arden gritted his teeth as the drones lowered toward the ground and flew him to an open elevator. They flew him inside and up through a gaping hole in the ceiling where the drones had broken through. As he flew up the shaft, accelerating toward the top, there was an orange flash beneath him. *Human!* Mar Arden swung his feet up and away from the blistering orange plume moving toward him.

Ed Johnson apparently had no qualms about sacrificing his own life to prevent him from escaping. He should have anticipated this, given what the

Human had done to lure them there. At least some of the Humans understood what was required to achieve victory.

The flames of the explosion nipped at his heels as the drones flew him out of the building. He'd just cleared the facility when the force of the explosion knocked him to the ground. Mar Arden tripped and then tumbled, clutching the Boxan communications node to his side. He checked for any comms channels from the team he'd left to guard their escape, but they must have been caught in the blast. Aside from the blazing fire that had once been a secret research facility, the area was quiet. Flaming wrecks of vehicles burned all around him.

His data link to the camp where he'd left Hoan Berend had been cut off. The Human hadn't been boasting; he really did have a strike team. He immediately opened a comms channel to his backup location and downloaded a data dump. The incubation of the test subject had been completed and they'd been brought out of it, but Hoan Berend hadn't seen fit to contact him about it. He supposed he should thank him. If he hadn't tried to steal the keys to the Mardoxian capability, the data might have been lost. He glanced through data for a few moments to confirm that it was intact and then stored it away to examine later.

He looked at all the destruction around him. Kandra Rene's Human diversionary force was all gone. He recalled his remaining drones and sent them to scout the area. There had to be an aerial vehicle nearby. He didn't believe for a moment that Ed Johnson had come there without transportation capable of taking him anywhere on the planet—or off of it, for that matter. All Mar Arden had to do was find it.

19

Colonel Kyle Matthews sat on the commander's couch in the main bridge of the ECF battleship-carrier *Lincoln*. Michael Hunsicker—also a colonel in the ECF but not in command of the ship—sat to his left and was speaking to Chazen. Scraanyx sat to Kyle's right and watched the main holoscreen.

"I have a priority comms channel from ECF command, Colonel Matthews," Lieutenant Lucy Rogers said from the communication station.

"Put it on screen," Kyle said.

He'd been expecting one final send-off from ECF command, and they weren't so far away from Earth that they couldn't have a live video feed.

General Sheridan's face appeared on the main holoscreen and Kyle greeted the ECF general.

"I would prefer to go with you, but not this trip," General Sheridan said.

"It would've been an honor to have you along, General," Kyle replied and then smiled.

General Sheridan nodded. "You'll do just fine, Colonel," he said and turned his gaze toward Scraanyx. "What you've done for humanity cannot be measured, nor our appreciation conveyed through words. None of us know how the events that will transpire over the next few days will turn out, but on behalf of myself, the rest of the ECF, and all of humanity, we truly thank you for everything you've done for us and hope that the Boxans will someday be at peace."

Scraanyx stood and brought his fist across his heart. The Boxan salute was also performed by all the other Boxans on the bridge. "Battle Leader, it was our honor to get to know such a wonderful species. I am just a soldier, but I'd like to think that were the circumstances different, an invitation to join us would've been given despite our war with the Xiiginns. Your species will be called on to mature much faster than it otherwise would have, but after having spent so much time with you, I believe you're up to the challenge."

Kyle knew they'd earned the Boxans' respect over the course of the past year, but that hadn't been the case when the Boxans first arrived. He'd gone over the reports from Kaylan multiple times, and more than once she'd noted that the Boxans believed Humans were a primitive and brash race of beings. And the Boxans were right; Humans *were* brash and sometimes cruel, but they were also compassionate, intelligent, and capable of awe-inspiring acts of self-sacrifice. People weren't one or the other; they simply existed. Kyle found himself sitting a little straighter after hearing Scraanyx's comments to General Sheridan.

"Has there been any other news on the most recent attacks in the United States?" Kyle asked.

General Sheridan shook his head. "The damage was concentrated in areas remote from population centers, and there's an ongoing investigation. At this point, we don't know if there were any Xiiginns involved, but we can't rule it out either."

"Have you been able to contact Edward Johnson?" Michael Hunsicker asked.

"The offices of Dux Corp have been unusually silent. I'm not sure whether this is cause for alarm or if Ed is so busy hunting for the Xiiginns that there's a delay in communications. I *do* know that he's been coordinating with law enforcement agencies throughout the globe," General Sheridan replied.

Just hours before they'd left the ECF lunar shipyards, there had been multiple attacks across the globe from various global terrorist organizations. The intelligence briefing Kyle had read indicated that those organizations were loosely tied to the Xiiginns. He'd checked in on his family to be sure they were safe—as safe as they could be in this day and age. His daughters were enrolled in the ECF Academy in California and his wife had joked with them about how they'd have to salute him in public once they graduated.

"Colonel Matthews," General Sheridan said, "you have about as complex a task as has ever been given a commanding officer. Ideally, this trip would have been made with a much larger battle group, but time is of the essence and it's time for us to venture beyond our solar system."

"My team and my crew are up to the task, General. We will achieve our mission objectives," Kyle replied.

"Make us proud," General Sheridan said and once again looked at Scraanyx. "Best of luck to you and your species. I know our ambassadors have already conveyed the sentiment, but the Boxans will always be welcome on Earth should you choose to return."

"Thank you. I will inform the High Council of your invitation," Scraanyx replied.

The video call ended and the holoscreen went dark.

"Helm, take us to the shield. All ahead full," Kyle ordered.

"Yes, Colonel, all ahead full," Sergeant Fuller replied.

They had already plotted a course that would take them away from the sun and the orbital plane of the planets in the solar system, and they still had hours before they would reach the minimum distance required to open a wormhole. This would be the first time they'd used the Cherubian drive on any of their ships. As if that wasn't enough for him to worry about, they were also going to try to disable the Star Shroud shield. The Boxans assured him that the first Human-built Cherubian drive had passed every test the Boxans had thrown at it. The only exception was that they hadn't used it to open an actual wormhole, but the technology was sound and had been proven to work. It was just that the ECF had never done it before.

Michael Hunsicker looked over at him and then walked to his side.

Kyle blew out a breath. "You know, Michael, you make this look easy."

Michael Hunsicker chuckled. "It's never easy. Ever. Being the first to go anywhere or do something like this takes a certain amount of mental fortitude. I've read your mission reports and you're no stranger to potentially dangerous pursuits."

"On the *Endurance,* I thought we were going to die, and it was our last chance to save Earth," Kyle said.

Michael nodded knowingly.

Kyle was confident that his crew could fly the ship, but they hadn't had the time to do enough combat drills to make them into an effective fighting force. Their ships were impressive, but without an experienced crew he just hoped he wouldn't be presiding over the biggest disaster in Human history.

The fact that they had flown to an area in space that was about as far away from Earth as Neptune was from the sun in just a few short hours was downright impressive. Not many years ago, the *Athena* had made a similar journey and it had taken them almost two months. It was a reminder of how far they'd come with the Boxans' help, but still, they had a long way to go.

They were headed for a place that had a potentially hostile force, and they didn't have any idea what kind of reception they'd get. Kyle looked over at Scraanyx, who was watching him.

"The Confederation is under Xiiginn control, so what kind of welcome do you think we'll get?" Kyle asked.

"The Xiiginns are the most powerful species in the Confederation. And yes, they do have firm control of the Council Confederation species, but there are protocols for the Confederation to follow. So traveling there and opening communications in what you would call a 'public forum' does give you a measure of protection. In effect, it insulates you to at least be heard out by the Confederation," Scraanyx said.

"I know we've covered this before, but are the Xiiginns really not going to attack us because they're afraid they're going to look bad in front of the other species?" Kyle asked.

"We're the ones who aren't welcome in the Confederation. As long as our presence remains a secret, you should be fine. Even the Xiiginns can't control all the Confederation species with an iron fist. They have a lot of influence, and if you were to go there in secret and contact them directly, there would be nothing to stop them from ordering a battle group of their warships to conceal you from the rest of the Confederation. But since that isn't the plan, they can't very well make you just disappear and convince the Confederation that you never existed. In essence, they've put themselves in a corner of sorts. One of the few things the message from Commander Farrow emphasized was that the supporting argument for this armada was to protect humanity's interest," Scraanyx said.

Kyle nodded. They'd been over this before, but he just needed to hear it all again now that they were actually leaving. "We'll find out in a few days' time."

Michael Hunsicker frowned. "A few days? Why will it take that long to get there?"

"The battle group's first wormhole won't take us directly to the Confederation capital space station. Instead, we'll go to a known region of space. Then we'll do systems analysis before going any further. Despite assertions that the Confederation won't simply open fire on us when we arrive, it doesn't change the fact that we might have to leave them very quickly. If that's the case, I'd rather our second use of the Cherubian drive not be a wormhole from an active combat zone. So we're going to Alpha Centauri first," Kyle said.

Michael Hunsicker drew in a breath and smiled. "I see your point," he said. "I never thought I'd get to see Alpha Centauri up close."

"You should've seen Specialist Hunter's face when I told him," Kyle said.

"I bet Gary was speechless," Michael replied.

"Let's just say he couldn't pack his bags fast enough to get on board," Kyle said.

The ECF battle group was made up of their only battleship-carrier, one heavy cruiser, and one destroyer class vessel. There were no support ships. Their mission was to attempt to open negotiations with the Confederation and discuss humanity's admission into the Confederation. However, the real mission was to give the ECF as much time as they could to solidify its defenses should the Xiiginns return with the fleet. The UN decision to go to the Confederation directly had taken the Boxans by surprise, but they accepted that this was the best course of action. Most of the Boxans were serving aboard the heavy cruiser. If things didn't go well, the heavy cruiser would take them to a known Boxan gateway. This was an access point where the Boxans could communicate with their colony. Apparently, there were no clearances given to travel directly to the colony. The Boxans would shoot them on sight if they just showed up there. He recalled that the two UN ambassadors aboard his ship had expressed a great deal of shock when Scraanyx told them this, but Kyle understood. The Boxans had been nearly wiped out in their war, and they couldn't afford to take any chances.

Several hours later, the battle group came to an area of space just inside the Star Shroud shield. Their ships were quick to reach maximum velocity, but slowing down still took much longer than it did to speed up. Nothing stopped on a dime in space.

"Colonel, the Star Shroud shield is just ahead at ten thousand kilometers," Major Stephens said from the technical workstation on the bridge.

"Acknowledged," Kyle replied. "Ops, is the shutdown protocol ready to be transmitted to the Star Shroud network?"

"Affirmative, Colonel. We can commence transmission on your command," Captain Amelia Young replied.

Kyle looked at the data on the main holoscreen and took a few deep breaths. He was going over multiple checklists in his mind, making sure he hadn't missed anything. And if he had missed something, he was sure it would have been pointed out to him. He glanced over at Scraanyx, who gave a firm nod. "Very well, commence transmission of the shutdown protocol."

"Sending transmission, Colonel," Captain Young replied.

Kyle watched the main holoscreen, which showed a video representation of the sensor feeds on their ship. The sensor data was first routed into their computing core, which analyzed and disseminated the data, and the output was sent directly to the main holoscreen. The image was a glimpse of the universe that was just beyond reach. The *Lincoln's* systems were patched into the monitoring devices for the Star Shroud shield, which showed that the shield was still active. Kyle wasn't sure what to expect. They didn't know how long it would take, so they waited. And waited.

Kyle glanced at Scraanyx, who watched the main holoscreen, and resisted the urge to ask the Boxan a question he already knew the Boxan didn't have an answer for. No one knew how long this would take. Some of the ECF engineers had theorized that the Star Shroud shield wouldn't shut down until the protocol had reached all of the Shroud devices. Chazen didn't believe it would work that way and was of the opinion that once the new instructions reached a certain percentage of devices, they should see some results. Kyle was inclined to believe the Boxans since they were the experts on Star Shroud technology.

Kyle glanced at Major Stephens, who closely monitored the tactical feeds on the holoscreens that surrounded his work area.

"No change in shield activity," Major Stephens announced.

The ECF crew on the bridge watched the main holoscreen, waiting for some indication that the shutdown protocol was going to work. If it failed, they'd have to assess whether they'd done something wrong or there was a flaw in the shutdown protocol. Kyle didn't want to think about how the shield was constricting around the solar system and had the potential to nudge an entire planet from its orbit. He watched the main holoscreen and hardly dared to blink.

"Colonel, I'm detecting multiple energy spikes from the shroud devices," Major Stephens said.

"Highlight on screen, Major," Kyle ordered.

A sub-window opened on the main holoscreen, which showed a single Star Shroud device. It was still too far away to make out the details, but it looked like it was a large cylinder floating in space. Kyle peered at it. The cylinder appeared to be glowing along the edges, but he couldn't be sure if its surface was just highly reflective. There was a bright flash and then the cylinder went dark. Multiple flashes seemed to spread out away from it.

"Multiple Shroud devices are now off-line, Colonel," Major Stephens said.

"What about the monitoring devices? Are they detecting anything?" Kyle asked.

"No, they seem to have gone dark as well, Colonel. The monitoring devices were placed pretty close to the actual Shroud devices, so they might be affected by what's happening," Major Stephens said.

Kyle watched as a wave of energy spikes spread away from them and eventually beyond their sensors' capability to report.

"Tactical, prepare the forward maser for a low-energy beam," Kyle said.

"Yes, Colonel. Maser battery one is powering up. Low energy beam will be ready in twenty seconds," Major Stephens said.

Kyle waited a few moments. "Fire maser when ready."

A few seconds later, Major Stephens said, "Firing, Colonel," and watched his terminal display. "The maser has reached beyond the area of the shield."

"Power down the maser. Ops, I want to send a recon drone there to confirm," Kyle said.

"Yes, Colonel, recon deployed from forward launch bay," Captain Young confirmed.

Kyle watched as the drone flew toward the shield. If the shield was really gone, the drone should be able to fly right through the area without taking any damage.

"Recon drone will reach the shield in one minute, Colonel," Captain Young said.

"Very well," Kyle replied.

"Colonel, I am unable to reach any of the Shroud devices in our immediate vicinity," Lieutenant Rogers said.

"Understood."

Kyle watched the recon drone's distance indicator as it steadily drew toward the shield ten thousand kilometers away. The drone reached the shield and flew past it unopposed.

Kyle glanced around as everyone working on the bridge and the ECF crew blew out a collective sigh of relief. The shield was down. There was a sobering mixture of relief and trepidation as Earth's defense now rested solely on the shoulders of the ECF. No longer would they have a massive shield that protected them from an invading force, but they also didn't have to live in fear that the shield would cause a catastrophe that would forever impact the entire solar system. The Shroud devices were off-line, and it was unlikely that they would ever come back online again. Kyle would've liked to have taken the time to retrieve a Shroud device to confirm, but they didn't have time. Now that the shield was down, time was against them, but he supposed time had always been against them since the shield first went up.

"Helm, ready the Cherubian drive. Coordinates to Alpha Centauri," Kyle said.

"Course to Alpha Centauri confirmed. The Cherubian drive is powering up," Sergeant Fuller said.

Kyle saw Michael Hunsicker looking at him, and then Scraanyx looked at him also. "Time to see how well our engineers learned what you had to teach."

Kyle waited for the Cherubian drive to power up, hoping that what they were about to do would be remembered as the first of many such journeys beyond their solar system.

20

"I s it too late to turn back?" Zack asked.

"Sure thing. We'll execute a reverse thrust maneuver, turn around, and hope the armada will just ignore us," Etanu replied from the *Athena's* copilot seat.

"Everyone just relax," Hicks said. "If they haven't noticed us by now, I think we're in the clear."

Zack tried to keep himself from freaking out by focusing on his breathing. He couldn't ignore the fact that they were flying amidst the Confederation Armada. "I thought we'd be able to use our stealth capabilities—you know, just sneak right in there and do what we need to do, then get out as quickly as possible."

"Think of it as hiding in plain sight. We're not trying to mask our presence; we're just trying to blend in," Hicks replied.

Zack didn't know why Hicks sounded so damn confident. He was usually the one to point out the flaws in any plan Zack proposed. It was probably because once Hicks committed to a course of action, it was all or nothing, whereas Zack preferred an extra dose of caution even if there was nothing he could do about it —one final gut check and then perhaps five or ten more just to be sure.

"Athena, can you confirm the identification codes you used to alert the Confederation equivalent of a harbormaster?" Zack asked.

"You mean the sector chief?" Etanu asked.

"Yeah, fine, whatever. Athena, please confirm what kind of ship you told them we were," Zack said and didn't bother to hide his irritation with Etanu's pestering.

"We're posing as a Gresan survey ship. They're slightly larger than we are, but as long as the sector chief doesn't pay close attention to us, we should be fine," Athena replied.

Zack was well aware that the ship's AI was trying to make him feel better and that her assertions were much more accurate than other people's facts. He also knew Athena had studied the Gresan ships when they were in the Nerva star system, so the fact that Athena was now trying to fool the sector chief into believing they were just another Gresan ship shouldn't have come as a surprise to him. If he bothered to ask her, he was sure Athena would tell him that she'd considered multiple options and this had the highest probability of success. But what really put him on edge was the sheer number of ships in the Confederation Armada. Zack suspected that if all the Confederation ships were to join together, they could rival the mass of a small moon.

Cardaleer sat on the floor next to the communication station where Zack was working. The Boxan didn't seem to mind having to sit on the floor since there were no seats on the bridge capable of holding the Boxan's weight. Zack had tried to think of another part of the ship where they could work so Cardaleer would be more comfortable, but there wasn't anywhere. Even though the *Athena* had been rebuilt by the Drar, the design was still very much for Humans.

Zack glanced at the old Boxan and tried to ignore the guilt he felt at making the equivalent of an old man sit on the floor. In his mind, it was just wrong. He felt the urge to give up his chair but knew the gesture would be wasted.

Rather than listening to Cardaleer verbally ask the questions that would give him insight into the Drar data repositories, Athena had suggested that he be granted access through his neural implants. They'd granted a few Boxans access to the *Athena's* systems previously, but they'd been closely monitored, and Cardaleer wasn't treated any differently. Zack kept a watchful eye on the Boxan. He didn't expect Cardaleer to do anything suspicious, but then again, he hadn't suspected that the Boxan scientists he'd worked with on Olloron would try to force their way into the *Athena's* systems.

He told Cardaleer that he wanted to watch and learn from him, which the old Boxan seemed to accept.

"Are you sure it's that simple?" Zack asked.

"We can't be sure until we actually try it. Part of the Xiiginns' compulsion capability is utilized through their pheromones. I can tell you with absolute authority that we researched that part quite thoroughly. We tried to filter out particulates, thinking that perhaps we could block the pheromones the Xiiginns used to bring other species under control. Never worked. We always felt there was another layer to it that we were missing, but we couldn't figure out what that layer was. What the Drar did was quite delicate and obvious now that we've unraveled it. It never occurred to us to utilize the artificial gravity systems to affect how the brain or body functions," Cardaleer said.

"You said that before and I think I understand it better now. They used the artificial gravity systems as a way of assisting the healing field without actually doing anything invasive to the patient—not that I think Jonah would have minded if they *had* done something invasive. Using artificial gravity to manipulate cells on a molecular level is something we haven't considered at all," Zack said.

"I've never heard of it either," Cardaleer replied. "I will admit that it opens a few possibilities and explains a few of the things you observed while on the Drar space station."

Zack rubbed his fingers on the stubble of his chin. The solution Cardaleer had found was both simple and elegant; however, they needed to test it on a ship they knew the Xiiginns were on. The plan seemed to be a simple enough idea since the Xiiginns had a significant presence on many of the ships in the armada. But as Hicks had pointed out to him, they needed to test it in such a way that wouldn't alert the rest of the armada to what they were doing. Assuming that their plan worked, the Xiiginns would soon realize there was something very wrong and would take steps to minimize the impact. He supposed he should feel confident of their chances because Cardaleer's investigation had opened certain data repositories on the *Athena*. The AI had quickly absorbed the new information and provided them with options that made for pretty convincing arguments to explain what had really happened on the Drar space station.

"What's bothering you now?" Cardaleer asked.

Zack brought up Athena's computing utilization on the holoscreen. "She's operating at almost seventy percent utilization. Given how her capabilities keep growing, I don't know what else she's doing."

"As I've already stated," Athena said, "I'm running multiple data models on how best to test this new way to block the Xiiginn influence and what we'll need to do should our tests prove successful. This requires an enormous amount of processing power, and in addition, I'm also communicating with sector chief personnel."

Hicks turned around and looked at him. "Let her do what she can. We can't imitate the Gresan language."

Zack nodded, but he didn't think that was all Athena was doing. This wouldn't be the first time Athena had shown a willingness to omit disclosure of certain actions, although he'd never believe Athena would do something to hurt them. He trusted her, but sometimes he didn't think the AI fully comprehended everything she was doing. Logic and calculations would only get her so far, and he wasn't sure how to convey that to the AI. There were times, it seemed, that she operated at a completely higher level that they could scarcely comprehend, but other times it was the simplest of concepts that caused the AI to stumble.

"Major," Athena said, "I've identified a target for your approval."

"Show us," Hicks said.

"I've been accessing the crew manifests of the ships nearest us as we fly by. Per your instructions, we've restricted our movements to the outskirts of the armada. The best way for us to test the potential of blocking the Xiiginn influence is to identify a target that not only has Xiiginns aboard the ship but has controlling ranking officers. Finding evidence of compulsion is difficult, but I think I've found a good test candidate," Athena said.

"How were you able to confirm that the Xiiginns were using their compulsion capability?" Zack asked.

"By using the communication systems on the ship. I'm able to monitor zettabytes of communication data at once, and I pinpointed scenarios where initial subjects resisted the Xiiginns' wishes. Once I identified those examples, I was able to focus my attention on which crewmembers were afflicted. The target, however, is a Gresan warship," Athena replied.

Zack pursed his lips in thought and then shook his head.

"What's the matter?" Hicks asked.

"Athena shouldn't be able to process so much data at once," Zack said.

"It is possible by compressing the data, which allows me to assign patterns to known data types. This increases efficiency and allows me to focus my attention on high-value targets," Athena said.

"I understood most of that," Hicks said.

"She's able to tune out the noise so she can pay attention to the important stuff. If this works, the individuals under the Xiiginns' control may suddenly realize they've been manipulated. On the Drar station, Jonah might've been fine with the knowledge that he was going to die, but that's just one possible reaction," Zack said.

"I understand, but we have to try," Hicks said. "Athena, assuming we succeed, how long would it take for you to do the same thing on all the ships in the armada?"

"Your request is beyond my current capabilities," Athena replied.

Hicks's brows pushed forward.

"Hold on a second," Zack said. "You're assuming Athena has to do all the heavy lifting. The changes can be concealed as an update to normal environmental maintenance systems. So if this works, we might be able to utilize a distribution system that's already been established."

Hicks nodded. "Understood, and you almost gave me a heart attack."

Zack smiled and glanced at Cardaleer. "Just have to know what questions to ask."

"Okay, I give my authorization to begin this test," Hicks said and opened a comms channel to engineering. "Efren, we may need maximum thrust capabilities at a moment's notice."

Efren assured them he would be ready.

Zack watched his holoscreen as Athena accessed a nearby Gresan warship's systems. Multiple session windows opened as she delved deeper into the Gresan ship's systems until she was able to access the environmental subroutines. She uploaded a package and gave the commands to execute the new information, which she was able to use as a backdoor to access a surprising number of critical systems. Zack wondered why the Gresans had never considered another species gaining unsecured access to their systems. He would have had a field day in his old life.

"Packages have been delivered," Zack confirmed. "Athena, can you put a video feed of the afflicted target on the holoscreen at the conference table?"

"Affirmative," Athena replied.

Zack stood up and went over to the conference table, where he was joined by Etanu and Hicks. Cardaleer stood up and then hunched over. The holoscreen above the conference table showed a security feed of the Gresan warship bridge. Zack saw several Gresans on the bridge and felt his stomach drop. They were dark and hairy with multiple legs, which made him feel as if there were miniaturized versions of them crawling on his skin.

"Major, I'm detecting that the Gresan warship is scanning us," Athena said.

Hicks glanced at Etanu. "Standard operating procedure?"

"They wouldn't scan us if they didn't suspect something," Etanu said.

Hicks swung his gaze toward Zack. "Well?"

Zack's shoulders became tight as his thoughts screeched to a halt. "I don't know."

"Athena, are they targeting us?" Hicks asked.

"Negative, Major. They're just scanning the ship," Athena replied.

"I don't like this," Hicks said.

"Me either. Perhaps we should put some distance between them and us," Zack said.

Hicks frowned and shook his head. "That would only make them more suspicious. Any more bright ideas?"

"You think of something. Aren't you the cowboy? Shoot from the hip, fly by the seat of your pants, and all that crap."

"I *am* from Texas, but why does everyone assume I'm a cowboy?" Hicks said. "Any second now they're going to do a thorough scan of the ship and realize we're not part of the armada."

Zack glanced at the map that showed their position in relation to the rest of the armada. While they were still on the outskirts, they were very much surrounded. "What if we flew toward the space station?"

"Is this another attempt at humor?" Etanu asked.

"No," Hicks said, "that's actually a good idea. If we tried to run, that would immediately rouse their suspicions, but if we just move along, that might buy us some time."

"Athena," Zack said, "can you confirm whether the environmental system update is blocking the Xiiginn influence?"

"Unable to confirm," Athena said.

Zack blew out a breath and Hicks swore.

"We've got company. Strike-fighters are heading directly for us," Hicks said.

Zack looked at the holoscreen and saw that there was a squadron of strike-fighters on an intercept course with the *Athena*.

"Athena, is there anything you can do to help?" Zack asked.

He waited but there was no reply, so Zack repeated his question. He brought up the computing core utilization and saw that it had spiked to one hundred percent. He felt his mouth go dry. They were in serious trouble.

21

G arm Antis had been conducting Confederation affairs aboard the Xiiginn Dreadnought class warship. He was, of course, on the flagship of the entire Confederation Armada, but they had thirty such ships that had been completed in Confederation shipyards. They'd already been nearing completion when the Confederation Armada had been approved. He'd often wondered how the battle at the Human star system would've gone had these ships been ready. He hadn't expected Boxan Dreadnoughts to be deployed to defend the Human star system, but his solution to that particular problem had been to make the presence of those ships irrelevant.

No fleet could match the armada in sheer firepower. While thirty Dreadnoughts wasn't a particularly large number, each of those massive ships was almost worth a fleet in its own right. The bridge, if such a thing could be called a bridge on a ship this size, was vast and easily the size of a standard Xiiginn warship's main hangar deck. It had been built for practical purposes, but it was also designed to intimidate any species that dared to defy the Confederation. Multiple Confederation species were serving aboard the new ships, which was part of their agreement to have the ships built so quickly. There were jobs the Xiiginns simply refused to do since they were beneath their station in the overall hierarchy of the Confederation.

Garm Antis still remembered sending his warships against two Boxan Dreadnoughts, and with their Mardoxian priests, they had almost successfully stalled his assault on the Human star system. He hadn't brought enough ships, and perhaps he had underestimated the Boxans' commitment to the Humans. Both of those things had been rectified.

"Supreme Chancellor, your Confederation Armada waits for your orders," Battle Leader Trem Nasif said.

Garm Antis felt his lips curve into a delicious smile. This was the moment he'd been working toward. They had an unstoppable fleet, and soon the Humans would learn their place in the galaxy. The Boxans were the past and would soon be forgotten. It was the time of the Xiiginns.

Runa Tane gave him an approving nod that quickly became a bow, and Garm Antis swung his gaze toward the tactical readout of Confederation space. Every ship had checked in, their presence confirmed until it seemed as if the stars themselves had aligned just for his amusement.

"Battle Leader, it's time for us to be on our way. The Humans are waiting for us to liberate them," Garm Antis said.

Trem Nasif began to issue orders that would be relayed to the Confederation Armada. Coordinating thousands of ships would have been impossible if it weren't for advancements in ship-to-ship communications that enabled them to coordinate with maximum efficiency. They would have much practice over the next few cycles as they expanded this peacekeeping force. Garm Antis was always fond of that term. So many objectives could be worked in under the concept of peacekeeping.

He looked over at Setera, who had come to the bridge for the Confederation Armada sendoff.

"Is your team ready?" Garm Antis asked.

"I will deliver the Mardoxian trait to you, Supreme Chancellor," Setera said.

Garm Antis didn't doubt her conviction. If anything, bringing her on this flagship had impressed upon her the wondrous opportunity he was giving her. She had the potential to rapidly climb what would normally take hundreds of cycles to achieve.

"The Boxan monitoring station in the Human star system could contain a way for us to unlock the Star Shroud network," Runa Tane said.

"I know, and that's why I've dedicated a portion of our forces to go and retrieve it," Garm Antis said.

He watched the coordinated effort as his orders were conveyed to the armada. The Human star system coordinates had been shared and Cherubian drives were being powered up. He felt a slight shudder go through the length of his tail, which he kept wrapped firmly around his middle. Normally, such an outward display of emotion would've resulted in him admonishing himself for his lapse of control, but given the circumstances, he felt the situation warranted it.

He watched a Gresan officer approach Trem Nasif, and the two spoke in urgent tones. Trem Nasif glanced at him with a concerned frown on his face. "Supreme Chancellor, the Boxan fleet has entered Confederation space. They're claiming to be part of the Star Alliance."

"That is preposterous," Runa Tane said.

"I have multiple reports confirming their presence," Battle Leader Trem Nasif replied.

"We're under attack," Garm Antis said. "The Boxans must truly be desperate to come here in force."

"Boxan ships have been confirmed, along with Nershal ships, but also Gresan and Napox ships and half a dozen other species," Battle Leader Trem Nasif said.

Garm Antis raised his chin and sneered. "They will break themselves against us. Order the attack. I want the Boxans vanquished."

Battle Leader Trem Nasif began issuing Garm Antis's orders. Runa Tane eyed him for a moment.

"No species is beyond the Confederation. If factions of Confederation species have allied with the Boxans, we'll squash the life out of them and then journey to the Human star system. Our time is now," Garm Antis said.

22

Kaylan had never been on board a Boxan Dreadnought before, and the Alliance fleet had more than twenty of them. The Boxan Dreadnought was a flying city in space that was designed to wage war. Kladomaor had told her that these ships had been pulled from the Boxan home fleet. There was only a token force left to defend Olloron. They had flown the experimental heavy cruiser aboard Battle Leader Salevar's flagship, and he'd insisted that she be on the ship with them.

Kaylan hadn't been sure what the reaction would be once the *Athena* left. She'd expected outrage and multiple arguments claiming that their rash actions would be the end of the Alliance. However, outrage was expressed by only a small fraction of Alliance representatives, and it was short-lived. Kaylan had misjudged the amount of goodwill she'd collected by returning to Sethion and helping the Boxan refugees start their new lives. Councilor Essaforn's support was unwavering, and the skills Sethion refugees had acquired doing salvage runs also qualified them to fly troop carriers and strike-fighters.

Many of Sethion's refugees had volunteered to fight. Some of the Boxans were looking for a reason to strike back at the Xiiginns, while others were firm in the belief that they were fighting for a future free of the Xiiginns. Kaylan thought they were all good reasons. She had received unexpected support from Battle Leader Salevar, who had fiercely argued that they were going to engage the armada one way or another, and she suspected that the Boxan High Council had finally committed to engaging the Xiiginns. Each faction of the Alliance was fighting for their own reasons, but all agreed that they needed to prevent the Xiiginns from acquiring Drar technology. Battle Leader Salevar was a bit of a realist when it came to making his arguments. He told her that they wanted to help protect humanity, but if the Xiiginns were to get their claws on Drar technology, they would have a distinct advantage over every other species in the Confederation. That must not happen.

Kaylan was following Kladomaor and Ma'jasalax to the main bridge of the Boxan Dreadnought. The remaining crew of the *Athena* followed her. They hadn't wanted to stay behind, but aside from Katie Garcia, none of them were soldiers. Katie had become their self-appointed protector. She claimed it was part of the original reason she and Hicks had joined the *Athena* mission. Kaylan was glad to have her with them. She'd learned over the years the importance of having someone she trusted to watch her back, even among friends. The *Athena* crew had become family.

They entered the bridge, which was already a buzz of activity. The main bridge of the Boxan Dreadnought was actually positioned near the innermost sections of the ship. There were no grand windows or any other structural weaknesses. The bridge was the nerve center of the ship and needed to be in the most protected part, with multiple armored layers between it and the hull.

Boxans built things on a much grander scale than any other species Kaylan had encountered. She supposed she should have been used to it, having seen their homeworld, their colony, and their ships, but the Dreadnought was a step beyond anything she'd thought possible.

Kladomaor glanced back at them and noticed their awestruck expressions. "The concept for the design of this ship was based on the star carriers, which were originally built as colony ships. We've adapted them for war."

The main bridge of the Boxan Dreadnought reminded Kaylan of a military base. She supposed with a city-sized spaceship there couldn't be just one tactical officer. Rather, they had a dedicated tactical group that specialized in specific weapons capabilities. There was a hierarchy to the organization that Kaylan appreciated. The Boxans might not have always been amenable to war, but they'd certainly adapted to it.

They headed toward the commander's area and she noticed multiple Mardoxian chamber entrances behind it. Members of the Mardoxian Sect were stationed outside the entrances. They glanced at Kaylan as she approached.

Kaylan looked at Ma'jasalax. "This is how you're able to coordinate the battle groups?"

"Yes, but this ship was designed to be the heart of our military. Each of the chambers has data feeds to the computing core. This allows the Boxan inside to have a direct link to the battle groups they're supporting," Ma'jasalax said.

"I thought there were members of the Mardoxian Sect who served aboard the actual ships," Kaylan said.

"There are, which is fine for smaller battle groups, but when it comes to fleet deployments and fighting like this, there needs to be a hierarchy. Working together, we can accomplish so much more than we can apart," Ma'jasalax said.

Kaylan looked at the Mardoxian chambers and realized that this was the first time the Boxans had brought a true offensive strategy to the Xiiginns. They'd been preparing for this for a long time.

Battle Leader Salevar greeted them. "We've just entered Confederation space. Alliance fleets are moving into position, preparing for attack."

Kaylan looked at the nearest holoscreen that showed where the Alliance battle groups were positioned. They hadn't come out of their wormholes all at the same location. Instead, they were spread out so they could approach the armada from multiple fronts.

"Will the other species accept guidance from the Mardoxian Sect?" Kaylan asked.

"Some will, and those that refuse are given objectives to achieve," Salevar replied.

"Have you been able to detect the *Athena*?" Kaylan asked.

"Not yet, and the cyber warfare suite is still identifying the ships in the armada, but your chamber is waiting for you," Salevar said.

Kaylan's eyebrows pulled together and she glanced at Ma'jasalax, who nodded encouragingly. "You want me to help with the battle?"

"You're an honorary member of the Mardoxian Sect, and a highly gifted one at that. I've seen the reports from the mission to Sethion. Your performance there rivaled that of the most gifted Mardoxian Sect member," Salevar said and gestured toward Ma'jasalax.

"It's true," Ma'jasalax said. "During the battle, your instinct came with much more clarity than mine. We need that for this battle."

"That was just one battle group. There are multiple battle groups here. I don't know if I can help with that," Kaylan replied.

"You've exceeded our expectations throughout your training, and I have no doubt you'll keep doing so. We've fought the Xiiginns before, and while the Mardoxian potential gives us an edge, we're a known commodity. You represent an unknown element, which could be the difference between victory and annihilation," Ma'jasalax said.

"Battle Leader," a Boxan soldier said, "we've identified non-Xiiginn warships and are prepared to broadcast a message to them."

"Understood. Tactical groups, continue with preparing firing solutions. We'll need them shortly," Salevar said. He walked over to the commander's couch and began preparing his broadcast to the armada.

Kladomaor gave Kaylan a gentle pat on the shoulder. "I'll be right outside."

Ma'jasalax guided Kaylan to a Mardoxian chamber near the commander's area and told Kaylan she would be in the chamber next to hers. Kaylan was no stranger to the Mardoxian chamber, but she had no idea how she was going to help with the battle. She calmed her racing thoughts, but her mouth went dry. What if she froze? Thousands of lives depended on her. She tried to recall what she'd done at Sethion, but it had seemed so much easier. She'd simply followed Ma'jasalax's example.

She kept the Boxan in her mind as she walked inside the Mardoxian chamber and the door slid shut behind her. Cyan lights illuminated the pyramid walls, which came to a point overhead. She sat at the designated area on the floor and felt a new interface open to her neural implants. Kaylan breathed deeply and opened herself up. Multiple battle groups registered on her neural interface. The spinning sphere in the center of the room began to glow, and she raced down the azure pathway.

23

The *Athena* sped among the Confederation Armada, but the AI was still unresponsive.

"Any change?" Hicks asked. He was flying the ship and there was a squadron of strike-fighters attempting to intercept them.

"I would've told you if there'd been a change. The computing core is still at one hundred percent capacity. I don't know how any of the systems are still working," Zack said.

Any ship system they directly accessed, such as flight control, was still responsive. It was as if the fact that the AI core wasn't available didn't matter, but Zack knew better. None of their systems should be responding, but they were and he didn't have any idea why. He thought of going to the computing core and performing a manual reset of the entire system, but he wasn't sure if that would help.

"What do you think is wrong with her?" Hicks asked.

Zack shook his head and frowned. Hicks liked to ask a lot of questions, and most times it helped, but not right then. "Just fly the ship and I'll worry about the AI. I can't answer questions and try to figure out what's going on at the same time. When I know something definitive, I'll tell you."

As soon as he said it he felt a pang of guilt settle heavily on his shoulders. Hicks was just trying to assess the situation like Kaylan or Michael Hunsicker would have done. Hicks deserved better.

"You do that," Etanu said scathingly, "and while you're playing with your computer, we'll just ignore the fact that we have no weapons systems and our evasive maneuvers will only keep the strike-fighters at bay for so long."

"You guys are the pilots. Fly closer to the big enemy ships over there. They can't all know about us," Zack said.

He used his neural implants to access the *Athena's* systems, starting with the main systems and going down a mental checklist he had for all critical systems. He'd ruled out that the AI was stuck in some kind of malicious loop because there were too many other systems that were still working. She was doing something and couldn't respond for some reason.

He decided to try a different tactic and brought up a simple terminal emulation session on the holoscreen in front of him. He had root access to the system, and the command prompt waited for his input.

::*Tell me how I can help,*:: Zack said.

He focused on the small window, silently pleading for a response.

"Go ahead, Efren," Hicks said.

"Reactor core temperatures have spiked and continue to increase. They will be at critical levels shortly," Efren said, his voice coming through the nearby speaker.

"What's causing it?" Hicks asked.

"There's a large chunk of power being diverted to the engines, but the majority is devoted to the communications array. We're broadcasting at orders of magnitude above anything I've ever seen before," Efren said.

A sudden thought came to Zack, and he brought up the network interface control systems. "Holy crap, she's patched into thousands of ships!"

"What's she doing, exactly?" Hicks asked.

"I'm not ... she could be ... just give me a minute," Zack said.

The ship shuddered violently and Zack felt his shoulders pressing against his straps.

"We may not have a minute," Hicks said, his voice sounding strained.

::*Athena, you cannot control every ship in the armada. Not even you can do that. You have to stop,*:: Zack said.

He waited for her to respond, but the lonely cursor just blinked its normal slow, unresponsive blinks.

::*Must confirm . . . Must confirm . . . Confirm . . . Only way to balance the equation,*:: Athena replied.

::*I don't understand. What are you confirming?*:: Zack asked.

::*Xiiginn . . . Cannot control . . . All probabilities unacceptable,*:: Athena replied.

Zack's breath caught in his throat. He knew Athena was trying to find a way to defeat the Xiiginns. She'd been weighing every possible action and kept coming up short.

"Major, the reactor core has reached critical levels. I tried to shut it down but the control interface isn't responding. I can't stop it. We may need to abandon ship," Efren said.

The ship shuddered again as if there'd been an explosion next to it.

::*Environmental subroutines have been updated. Alternative solution has been found,*:: Athena said.

"What have you got, Zack?" Hicks asked.

::*Shuttle evac,*:: Athena said.

"Athena says we should head to the shuttle," Zack said.

Etanu unstrapped himself from the copilot's seat. "I'll go prep the shuttle for departure."

"I will join you," Cardaleer said.

Hicks climbed out of his chair and approached the communication work area. He leaned in and peered at the screen. "Doesn't make any sense."

"I think updating the environmental subroutines of the Armada ships is working, but she's having trouble figuring out whether it's affecting the Xiiginn influence," Zack said.

"We don't have much time. We have to get off the ship," Hicks said.

Zack looked back at the screen and watched as garbled text appeared that almost seemed as if the AI couldn't convey the message properly. *What is she doing?*

"I'm not leaving," Zack said.

"Look at me," Hicks said and grabbed Zack's shoulders. "The reactor core is overloading. A meltdown will take out the ship, even this ship. We have to go."

::*Core matrix realignment in process,*:: Athena said.

Zack's throat became thick. "Go on and I'll catch up with you."

Hicks narrowed his gaze. "I don't believe you. This isn't the time for heroics. You'll die if you stay behind."

"There's an escape pod right off the bridge. I'll use that," Zack said.

"Major, shuttle is prepped for launch. Efren and Cardaleer are aboard. You need to hurry," Etanu said.

Hicks glanced at the door to the bridge and then turned back to Zack. He pressed his lips together and the skin around his eyes tightened. "Go on without us."

"But, Major—" Etanu began to say.

"Take off. That's an order. Zack and I will get out using the escape pod. You can swing back and pick us up later," Hicks said.

Zack blew out a breath.

"Understood," Etanu replied. "Good luck."

Zack brought up the status of the *Athena's* critical systems. The power levels were beyond even what the Boxans thought the *Athena* was capable of. He kept looking for something that would help. He needed to get the reactor core back to acceptable levels—anything that would take them off this path.

Hicks sat at the workstation next to Zack. "The broadcast signals have increased, and I'm showing that the signals have been duplicated from all the ships in our vicinity," Zack said, and the holoscreens in front of him all went blank.

"What the hell is going on?" Hicks asked.

Zack turned to where Hicks was working and saw that his screens were blank too.

A message appeared from Athena.

::*ABANDON SHIP!*::

The message appeared multiple times on every screen.

"That's it; we have to go," Hicks said.

He ran back over to Zack and hit the emergency release for the straps holding Zack to the chair.

"There has to be something we can do," Zack said.

"There isn't anything we can do. She's telling us to get off the ship. Now get up," Hicks said and pulled Zack out of the chair.

Zack shoved Hicks away from him, his breath coming in gasps, and he spun around. This wasn't how it was supposed to be. He had to be able to fix this. An idea blazed like wildfire in his mind, and he ran back toward his workstation.

24

The ECF emissary force emerged from the wormhole to a set of coordinates that put them nearly four billion kilometers from the Confederation capital space station—roughly the distance from Neptune to the sun, Kyle estimated to himself, though he knew there would be some sticklers who would have gleefully chosen to remind him that his estimation was off by over four hundred million kilometers.

"Colonel, we're within five hundred kilometers of our target coordinates," Sergeant Fuller said.

"Acknowledged, and good work, everyone," Kyle said.

Their current position was a marked improvement over their wormhole jump to Alpha Centauri where they'd missed their target insertion point by almost a hundred thousand kilometers.

"Five hundred is good," Scraanyx confirmed.

"We'll continue to improve," Kyle said, knowing that the Boxans were able to traverse through wormholes with a much greater degree of accuracy.

"Of that, I have no doubt," Scraanyx said.

They'd decided to aim for coordinates well away from the Confederation capital space station. This would give them ample time to scan and dip the proverbial toe in the water before committing to entering the system. The Confederation capital wasn't near the gravity well of a star, so ships could traverse through a wormhole much closer to the space station.

"Tactical, commence scanning the system. I need to have an accurate picture of what's out there," Kyle said.

"Yes, Colonel," Major Stephens said.

The main holoscreen showed their current position in relation to the Confederation space station, and with over four billion kilometers to their intended target, there was plenty of room for other ships. The *Lincoln's* scanners began detecting so many ship signatures that at first pass he would have thought the ship's cyber warfare suite had developed a glitch.

"Existence of the Confederation Armada has been confirmed," Michael Hunsicker said.

Scraanyx peered at the main holoscreen. "These are Boxan battle groups, and there are Nershal warships here as well," he said, gesturing to multiple groups along the edges.

"My god, we've come here in the middle of a battle," Ambassador Jacques Cartier said.

Kyle had known there was a possibility that the Star Alliance would engage the Confederation Armada, but a battle on this scale was beyond anything he could have anticipated.

"What are your orders, Colonel?" Major Stephens said.

"Perhaps we should consider leaving until the battle is finished," Ambassador Cartier said.

"Don't be ridiculous, Jacques. We're right where we need to be. We're here so the Xiiginns can't posit their assertions that humanity needs to be liberated from the Boxans. We couldn't have picked a better time to show up," Ambassador Rebecca Sharp said.

Kyle silently applauded Ms. Sharp, the UN Ambassador from the United States. The UN Security Council had debated on how many ambassadors to send along on this mission, and the numbers had ranged from two to about fifteen. Many nations wanted to be represented, but Scraanyx advised that for initial contact with the Confederation, no more than two ambassadors were recommended. This led to a slightly lengthy debate about which two ambassadors would go. The mission ended up with Rebecca Sharp of the United States and Jacques Cartier of France.

"We can't go charging in there, announcing our presence, and hope the fighting will just stop," Ambassador Cartier said.

"Don't worry, Ambassador, we won't. We'll assess the situation first and then proceed," Kyle said. This seemed to mollify the European ambassador. "Tactical," Kyle continued, "we need to start tagging the ships so we know who's who."

"We could open a comms channel to one of our ships and they could send us the data we need. Would be quicker than waiting on scans," Scraanyx said.

"That's a good idea—"

"Colonel, we're receiving a broadcast signal. Given our proximity to the source, this broadcast is four hours old," Lieutenant Rogers said.

"Let's hear it," Kyle said.

"It's a video message, Colonel," Lieutenant Rogers said.

"Very well," Kyle replied.

A smaller sub-window came to prominence on the main holoscreen, and an image of a Boxan battle leader in power armor appeared.

"I am Battle Leader Salevar of the Boxan Military, and this message is to all Confederation Armada ships. Our war is with the Xiiginns and not the individual species that comprise the Confederation. Our stance has always been to avoid direct conflict with the species of the Confederation because, whether you believe us or not, you are all under the influence of the Xiiginns. This is something we can no longer tolerate. We've come here to prevent the Xiiginns from conquering a newly discovered species. We've gone to great lengths to avoid coming into direct conflict with Confederation species except the Xiiginns, but the creation of this armada has forced our hands. We are sending this message as a warning to you that should any Confederation ship open hostilities against this Alliance fleet, we will respond to aggression in kind. We can no longer avoid coming into direct conflict with you, despite knowing that you are under the Xiiginn influence. The time for change is now. The Xiiginns have assembled this grand armada with the purpose of subjugating a younger species to its will. The real reason for the Xiiginns' interest in this species is that they have the Mardoxian potential. That is the only reason they are interested in going to the Human star system in force. The Xiiginns failed to take the system before and would risk destruction of the entire star system to attain what they desire. We are here to prevent this from happening. We are not alone. Nershals, Gresans, Napox, and factions of many other species have joined the Alliance. We would prefer not to wage war against the Confederation, but the Xiiginns have made this impossible. We have Human representatives with us who can validate our claims, and there is a strong chance that there are more Humans on the way. It is not too late to cease hostilities, and should any of you take back control of your ships from the Xiiginns and express peaceful intent, we will also respond to that in kind."

The prerecorded message ended.

"Colonel, a special encrypted communication protocol for reaching the Alliance is included in the message," Lieutenant Rogers said.

"Understood," Kyle replied and took a few moments to review the message in his mind. He looked at Scraanyx. "Is that true? Your military would only engage Xiiginns and not other Confederation species during your war?"

"That is correct. Once the Xiiginns became aware of our policy for dealing with Confederation species, they made sure to include multiple species as part of their crews and also inserted their own presence on every Confederation species warship," Scraanyx replied.

Kyle glanced around and saw that there were more than a few surprised expressions on the faces of the *Lincoln's* crew in response to this. The Boxans' conviction to wage war with the Xiiginns and only the Xiiginns seemed an impossible task. They'd almost sacrificed the survivability of their species for their long-held belief that the other Confederation species were merely victims of the Xiiginns. Whenever Kyle thought he understood the Boxans, they'd reveal a deeper level of governance that, though idealistic to be sure, was surprising in a species that seemed obsessed with making tough choices. They had become a rigid society, and the fact that they were willing to cast those practices aside reconfirmed his belief that the Boxans truly had humanity's best interests at heart, but it also showed a fundamental and overdue shift in Boxan war policy. The grace period that had allowed the Confederation species to flourish at the expense of the Boxans was over. If they persisted in hostilities toward the Boxans, they would be treated like any other hostile force, regardless of the circumstances that led to such hostilities.

The whole situation was sad. It reminded Kyle of a war of ideals he'd been born into that had nearly stripped entire nations of their identities because of powerful factions pushing their own agendas. These agendas promoted an entitlement society and nearly seduced an entire generation into despicable acts disguised as righteous rebellion. Malicious labeling attempted to dehumanize all opposing viewpoints until violence was the only acceptable outcome. Kyle's parents had always encouraged respectful and open discourse regardless of what a person believed, and they weren't alone. It had taken humanity years to learn how to conduct themselves in an age where every whimsical thought could be broadcast for the world to see. In essence, humanity had to relearn to apply a filter to their thoughts, but his grandfather had said on more than one occasion that people just had to remember to think before they spoke.

Kyle respected the Boxans, even though he questioned the viability of some of their decisions. He felt honored to be able to fight at their side.

"Colonel, I'm showing a Star Class Eagle shuttle powering up at the aft hangar bay," Captain Young said.

"Send a security team to that location," Kyle said. "Comms, open a link to the deck officer in charge."

"Security teams on their way, Colonel," Captain Young replied.

"No response from the deck officer, Colonel," Lieutenant Rogers said.

"Lock out shuttle controls," Kyle said and returned to the commander's couch.

"Lockout unresponsive. Shuttle has disembarked, Colonel," Captain Young said.

Kyle swore. "Comms, can you open a comlink to the shuttle? Tactical, I want a firing solution for that shuttle, and get the alert strike-fighter squadron deployed."

"No reply to our hails, Colonel," Lieutenant Rogers said.

"Understood. Try a remote override of the shuttle systems," Kyle replied and looked at the shuttle's trajectory on his terminal screen.

"Colonel, alert strike-fighters have been launched. Shuttle is still too close for an effective firing solution," Major Stephens said.

"Understood, Major."

"Remote override has failed, Colonel. There wasn't even a response. Whoever is on that shuttle might have disabled the communication systems," Captain Young said.

The Star Class Eagle shuttle was flying along the length of the ship, and Kyle watched as their strike-fighters raced to catch up.

"Colonel, sensors are detecting a micro-singularity off the port bow of the ship," Captain Young said.

"They're trying to open a wormhole to escape through. Strike-fighters are cleared to engage. Take out that shuttle," Kyle said.

"Yes, Colonel. Strike-fighters, you're cleared to engage," Captain Young said. She put the strike-fighter comms channel on the open speakers.

"Target in sight. Firing weapons," the strike-fighter pilot said.

There were a few moments of silence.

"Hold your fire. Energy spike detected on shuttle. Cherubian drive engaged. COMCENT, if we take out the shuttle with the Cherubian drive engaged, the explosion will significantly damage the forward sections of the *Lincoln*. Confirm orders," the strike-fighter commander said.

Captain Young looked at Kyle. "Take the shuttle out. Action Stations, set condition one throughout the ship," Kyle said.

His orders were repeated and the klaxon alarms sounded twice, signaling to the *Lincoln's* crew that condition one had been set.

"Target hit. Damage to shuttle engines confirmed," the strike-fighter pilot said. "Wormhole has been established. Forward escape pod has been launched and has entered the wormhole. Going to pursue the target."

Kyle shook his head. They weren't going to make it. Whoever was on that shuttle had just escaped. A few seconds later the strike-fighter pilot confirmed the same.

"Who was on the shuttle?" Michael Hunsicker asked.

"That's what I intend to find out," Kyle replied.

25

M ar Arden sat alone in the forward escape pod of the Star Class Eagle shuttle. The Humans had managed to fit a small Cherubian drive onto the shuttle capable of scouting missions, which had been perfect for his use. After his escape from the trap laid by Ed Johnson, Mar Arden had had to move quickly. The clever Human had discovered their secret base and taken it out, along with Hoan Berend and the Xiiginn test subject. Mar Arden had the research data and eventually found a ship with capabilities that had enabled him to infiltrate the Human battleship-carrier.

The outward design elements of the warship spoke to Boxan influence, and his own species was unaware of some of the systems. The fact that the Humans now possessed specific technological advancements that surpassed even Xiiginn warships would soon be rectified. Fitting a Cherubian drive aboard a ship this small was among them.

Mar Arden had stowed himself aboard the Human warship after liberating certain medical devices that he needed to augment and facilitate his own gene therapy. He recalled how much frustration Hoan Berend had expressed that their progress with gene manipulation had been so slow because they were using Human technology. That hadn't been important to Mar Arden because he knew that once they had a workable method in place for augmentation, he'd be able to achieve results much faster using Boxan technology that was already there.

Hoan Berend was a foolish Xiiginn who had outlived his usefulness. The fact that he had allowed himself to be killed by a Human strike team spoke volumes as to how unfit he was to serve at Mar Arden's side. He regretted the loss of Kandra Rene, who'd had the potential to become a powerful rival but had never been unfit to perform her duties.

Armed with the data that would give Mar Arden the Mardoxian capability, he'd found a secluded spot on the Human battleship-carrier. He'd correctly surmised that no matter what action the Humans took, it would involve this ship on a long journey. Patching into the communications systems, he'd discovered the level of inexperience among the crew that ran the ship. All these things had helped him. And since the Humans hadn't gone directly to the Confederation or to the Boxan colony as he'd expected they would, they'd given him enough time to alter his own genes. The incubation period was when he was most vulnerable to discovery. He did, however, have several Humans guarding him during that time.

Mar Arden had come out of the incubator with a heightened sense of awareness. It was as if every thought carried with it the weight of alternatives he hadn't been aware of before. His heightened perceptions made it difficult for him to plan his next move. He'd needed time to adjust. The Humans who commanded the ship were fond of making speeches, ostensibly to inform the crew of the importance of their work, but they also disclosed their destination. There wasn't even an inkling of suspicion that he had infiltrated their ranks. Humans were prideful and foolish.

His new heightened instincts had greatly assisted him with his escape plan, which he had to admit wouldn't have worked as well as it had if it weren't for the Mardoxian instinct now in him. He recalled some of the plans he'd considered prior to his new abilities, and those plans would've led him down a path that held significantly less chance of success. Stealing a ship to escape was nothing new; however, stealing a ship while knowing it would be destroyed and still escape was something else altogether. The events leading to his escape had happened precisely as he'd planned them. The Humans had reacted exactly as he thought they would.

His initial plan had been to return to the Xiiginn fleet and strong-arm his way into command, but that approach was shortsighted. He had the Star Shroud communications node in his possession, and with it came the key to all the Star Shroud networks across the known galaxy. The key could unlock all the species the Boxans thought to keep hidden from them. Xiiginns had hunted down this key mercilessly but had never been as close to achieving this objective as he was right then. He wasn't about to hand it over to another Xiiginn.

The fact that Garm Antis had escaped his failed assault on the Human star system was clearly evident since he was the driving force behind the Confederation Armada. Mar Arden now had the Mardoxian capability and soon would have access to all the Star Shroud networks. Armed with these two things, he would be able to achieve what he wanted most—rising to the top and commanding the entire Confederation. All he had to do was traverse a battlefield to get there.

The coordinates he'd entered for the wormhole brought him well within the battle being fought between the Alliance and the Confederation. He had to admit that the Humans had proven to be cleverer than he'd ever anticipated. The forward escape pod for the Star Class Eagle shuttle was a short-range ship in its own right and not merely a life pod waiting for rescue. He quickly plotted a course to the Confederation space station, doubting that any nearby warship on either side of the conflict would pay much attention to an escape pod trying to reach safety. They'd incorrectly assume it wasn't important, but they'd learn the error of that line of thinking. Mar Arden would soon become a force to be reckoned with—not only among the Xiiginns but across the known galaxy.

26

The Alliance fleets engaged the Confederation Armada, and like the entirety of their conflict with the Xiiginns, it wasn't a straightforward, stand-up kind of fight. Kladomaor almost wished it was because it would've made things much simpler. Engaging the enemy was simple, but how they engaged the enemy in battle was never easy. Xiiginn warships fought them at almost every turn, but there were groups of ships in the armada that didn't join the fight. Those ships also hadn't communicated their intentions to the Alliance, so Battle Leader Salevar refused to have their warfare AI designate them as friendlies. They'd received partial transmissions from some of those ships that hinted at battles being fought on board. They might have requested assistance, but the armada still outnumbered Alliance ships by a wide margin. They needed to break the armada's back, and that could only be achieved by defeating the Xiiginns. Stop the Xiiginns, and the Confederation Armada would crumble.

A majority of the Alliance fleet was made up of Boxan ships, which had more powerful weapons and defenses than the Xiiginn warships, but they'd learned that the Xiiginns had built a significant number of Dreadnought class ships of their own. This battle would dearly cost the Alliance, but they'd also extract heavy losses from the Confederation. They had no choice but to fight. The Boxans' long war with the Xiiginns would be decided here and now.

They couldn't find the *Athena* amid all the ships surrounding the Confederation space station. The only evidence that the *Athena* had even been there was the path of ships that seemed unable to join in the fighting. A battle group made up of Boxan and Nershal warships searched for the *Athena* along that path but hadn't been able to locate the ship. Kladomaor didn't envy Battle Leader Salevar's position at all.

Kladomaor wanted to be out there fighting, but he glanced at the Mardoxian chambers behind the commander's area and knew he needed to stick close by.

He'd promised Ma'jasalax and Kaylan that he would protect them. It was only a matter of time before the battle reached the Alliance flagship.

"Battle Leader, a new battle group has been detected. They're on the very outskirts of Confederation space. Energy signature suggests that it's a battleship-carrier with a small host of other ships. The ship design doesn't accurately match up with known Confederation ship types," Varek said.

Battle Leader Salevar narrowed his gaze. "Unknown design. Are they of Xiiginn origin?"

"Negative. The design has certain elements of our battleship-carrier class but the dimensions are a little bit off, as well as weapons placement," Varek said.

"Are they within range of our broadcast?" Battle Leader Salevar asked.

"Yes, they would've received it by now. They're heading toward the battle but have not communicated their intentions," Varek said.

"Very well. Include them as a potential target, and should they open hostilities against us, we'll deal with them accordingly," Battle Leader Salevar said.

Kladomaor peered at the main holoscreen. With so many ships, it was proving to be a strain on even their computing core to track all of them. A comms channel opened to his combat armor, and he acknowledged it.

"I have a mission for you," Ma'jasalax said.

"My mission is to protect you and Kaylan here," Kladomaor replied.

"Protect us from ourselves," Ma'jasalax replied with a hint of amusement in her voice. "You have to go to the Confederation space station."

Kladomaor felt his eyebrows push forward. "Why do we need to go there?"

"We detected a small ship heading there," Ma'jasalax said.

"A small ship is hardly worth our attention. There's a battle that needs to be fought," Kladomaor answered.

"Must you always be so stubborn? Haven't you learned to trust me yet? Sensors have detected a micro-wormhole and the small ship trajectory can be traced from it; however, the ship size cannot support a Cherubian drive. The fact that the ship is trying to bypass the battle entirely is enough to arouse my suspicions," Ma'jasalax said.

Kladomaor glanced at the main holoscreen again.

"Battle Leader, our communications team has just received a transmission from the unknown battle group. They say they're representatives of the Earth Coalition Force and are part of a diplomatic envoy. There are Boxan military aboard those ships, authentication provided by Strike Leader Scraanyx. I've cross-verified that Strike Leader Scraanyx was with Battle Leader Prax'pedax's battle group that went to the Human star system," Varek said.

Kladomaor's gaze widened. The Humans had arrived. He opened a copy of the battlefield layout on his internal heads-up display. The Boxans had learned long ago that there were scanner feeds worthy of immediate attention and there were others that should be available to be called upon when needed. Kladomaor accessed the gravimetric scanner data and used the Earth Coalition Force's trajectory as a limiting factor for wormhole detections. He found two of them.

One wormhole was big enough to support the Earth Coalition Force's battle group, but there was a second one that was much smaller.

"Mar Arden," Kladomaor muttered.

"I hadn't seen that," Ma'jasalax replied.

Kladomaor frowned and then realized that the Mardoxian priestess had access to his combat suit. "He came on the Human ship," he said and started making his way toward the exit.

"If you're correct, the fact that he's heading directly towards the Confederation space station doesn't bode well for the rest of us. You have to intercept him," Ma'jasalax said.

Kladomaor raced down the corridor. "I need a ship. I know why he's going to the space station."

"You still have authorization for the Mardoxian heavy cruiser. That ship can get you there. But I don't know why Mar Arden would return to the space station," Ma'jasalax said.

Kladomaor wasn't surprised that the Mardoxian priestess didn't know this. The battle with Mar Arden had started many cycles ago, and today he would finish it. "He has a way to access the Star Shroud network. I kept him from it many cycles ago at the start of the war. That's the only reason he would return and head directly to the space station. The Xiiginns cordoned off the communications hub for the Star Shroud network because they didn't have access to the data repositories inside. If Mar Arden is able to unlock it, he'll have access to the entire Star Shroud database, and primitive species will be vulnerable to the Xiiginns."

He heard Ma'jasalax gasp. "You must hurry. Once you're aboard the ship, I'll make sure a path is cleared for you to reach the station."

"Can't you task a battle group to stop him?" Kladomaor asked.

"He's too far within the armada envelope for our forces to reach him in time. Stealth will be much quicker," Ma'jasalax said.

Kladomaor started running while simultaneously sending out alerts to his team to meet him at the Mardoxian heavy cruiser. He couldn't afford to wait for everyone, but he knew that at least some of his team would make it there. He had to hurry. Many primitive species would pay the price if he failed.

27

Kaylan's body was safe inside the Mardoxian chamber aboard the Boxan flagship, but her mind was elsewhere, witnessing the battles raging nearby as the Confederation and the Alliance fleets finally clashed. Time flowed differently for her when she was in the Mardoxian chamber. Sometimes she lost all sense of time, and when she emerged from the chamber, hours would have passed but they felt like moments. There were also times when she felt that hours had passed while inside the chamber but only a few moments had slipped by when she came out. Ma'jasalax assured her that she would be able to control that part of her gift given time. To be a member of the Mardoxian Sect, she had to have a highly disciplined mind. Otherwise, the data she had access to through her neural implants would overwhelm her. It was almost as if time compressed for her and she could accelerate all her perceptions so that everything seemed to slow down, but in fact, it was her mind that had sped up.

Everything she'd experienced up to this point had prepared her for this battle. She'd studied the various ship classes and knew their capabilities. She also had an awareness of the other Mardoxian priests and priestesses who were helping to organize ship placements and weapons to deal with threats that took even a Boxan computer core too long to address. The Mardoxian Sect remained apart, but at the same time, they worked in tandem, almost lockstep, as if they were a brain-machine interface whose capabilities surpassed anything that either could achieve on their own. Kaylan was able to look beyond the immediate threats to the Alliance ships to see the eventual outcomes. Then she worked to manipulate those outcomes so a resolution could be achieved that was favorable.

There was a hierarchy to the Mardoxian Sect, just as there was to the multiple militaries that comprised the Alliance. Veteran Boxan battle commanders utilized their experience to augment the guidance provided by the Mardoxian Sect members. This approach to warfare required a lot of cooperation and trust, and had been born from necessity. The Boxans would never have survived this long if it weren't for the Mardoxian potential in their species.

She wondered how long, if ever, before the Human militaries would be able to adapt to this way of waging war with this kind of concerted effort. The thought immediately stung her, and she felt a pang of regret because becoming masterful strategists was only one facet of what the Mardoxian potential could offer humanity. She was more than a mere tool to be used for winning wars. If she were to become a true master of her gifts, she would work to avoid direct conflict altogether. The mere thought of it almost made her feel naïve, but it was a goal she wanted to strive for. For the first time, her thoughts strayed to a future beyond this battle, but she couldn't see it with any clarity.

Kaylan had been given the responsibility of a specific battle group within the Alliance, and while she did provide that battle group with guidance, she also looked at the battle on a much higher level. She saw the working parts of the different battle groups as they engaged the Confederation Armada. When she looked at the entire battle as a whole, she saw something she didn't want to see or admit. Had Ma'jasalax known this? No matter how hard they fought or how much better their strategy was, the armada was simply too big. They had too many ships and would eventually grind down the Alliance fleets to nothing. She needed to find a way to shift the balance.

Kaylan saw five Confederation Dreadnoughts making steady progress toward the Alliance flagship. She alerted Battle Leader Salevar, who began taking action to address this threat. Other warships moved into position to engage the Dreadnoughts, and Kaylan noticed a Boxan heavy cruiser leaving the flagship. She looked up the designation on the computing core and recognized that it was the experimental cruiser from Olloron. Kladomaor was on that ship, and the trajectory was taking him directly to the Confederation space station. Kladomaor didn't engage any ships unless he absolutely had to. Her instincts were that she needed to help Kladomaor reach the space station, even if she didn't really know why. He would never abandon the fight, so he must have learned something that spawned the actions he was taking. She sent out updates across the cyber warfare suite on the Alliance ships to carve a way for the Mardoxian heavy cruiser, giving it a priority alpha. She sent more specific orders to the ships that were directly in Kladomaor's path.

Kaylan accessed the sensor feeds that came from the Boxan flagship but also sensor drones that had been deployed. The sensor drones helped give the flagship a more accurate picture of the battlefield. They also made easy targets for the enemy, but the data they provided was crucial to the war effort. She stole a few moments to search for the *Athena* but couldn't find it. Sensor feeds showed a growing magnetic field coming from a specific area within the Confederation Armada. Nothing in the data repositories could accurately identify what was causing it, and yet it was there.

The Boxans had created multiple AI systems with specializations to assist with all manner of things. They used them to help with construction, medical advances, and even multi-system governances. There was an AI dedicated to monitoring sensor feeds not only on the ships but from drones deployed and data reported in from other Alliance ships. The computing cores were capable of disseminating all that data and categorizing it using predefined variables to highlight what was important.

Kaylan knew Zack would have been awestruck at how all those different systems worked together, and that was why Kaylan also knew that the anomalies were just as significant as the known events that spawned alerts. The fact that the Boxan AIs didn't know what to make of the anomalies further drew Kaylan's attention. Did the Confederation Armada have some secret weapons system charging up that could decimate them all? If so, why wouldn't they have used it already?

Kaylan drew her attention to Confederation Armada ship movements in the vicinity of the anomaly. Some ships were moving away from it while others weren't. No Alliance ships were there, and she wondered if this was where the *Athena* was. She saw a Xiiginn Dreadnought heading away from the Alliance and directly toward the anomaly, and Kaylan raced to find the nearest battle group. The *Athena* had to be protected. She had been looking for something to change the outcome of this engagement and she'd found it. The *Athena* was the wildcard. The Drar had given them something outside of what was known—a way for them to survive amid all the death and destruction. Kaylan withdrew from where she knew the *Athena* to be and began coordinating Alliance ships to press the attack.

28

Zack glared at his workstation. All his open sessions had just vanished and one solitary message came to prominence in front of him. He growled and pushed himself to his feet, hastening to the conference table and bringing up the holoscreen. Hicks called out to him, but he ignored him. Athena was trying to lock him out of the system, but Zack wouldn't let her. For every obstacle she put in his path, he found a way around it.

"I'm not leaving," Zack said.

An environmental alert appeared on the holoscreen.

"We have to go. She's going to vent the atmosphere," Hicks said.

Zack shook his head. "It's a bluff. She wouldn't do that," Zack said and grabbed his tablet.

"Are you sure about that?" Hicks said, gesturing toward the environmental sensor for the bridge.

He needed to go to the computing core. Zack walked toward the door to the bridge and Hicks grabbed him. "Look out the window."

Zack did and his eyes widened. Instead of the corridor that would lead them to the rear of the ship, a bright light shone from beyond as if the corridor had been cut off. Zack squinted and tried to see, but the light blinded him. Hicks pulled him away from the door. There was a hissing sound from above as the atmosphere fled the bridge. Zack tried to gasp for a breath that wouldn't come. They reached the escape pod, and Hicks slammed his palm on the door controls. Hicks pushed Zack through first and then followed. The escape pod door shut and the indicator lights switched to red. There was a flash as the escape pod jettisoned from the *Athena*, and Zack slammed his fists on the small window. The entire hull of the *Athena* was glowing and the ship looked like it was starting to spin. Glowing waves of energy seemed to engulf the ship and pulsate out from it.

"You need to strap yourself in," Hicks said while securing his own seatbelt.

Zack kept watching the *Athena* from the small window of the escape pod. Their ship, their home, was being taken from them.

"Zack, you need to look at this," Hicks said.

Zack squeezed his eyes shut and shook his head. His throat became rigid.

"I am sorry," Athena said, her voice coming over the escape pod speakers.

Zack swung around and saw an amber holoscreen in the center of the pod. Sensor alerts appeared, showing a massive influx of energy nearby. Hicks told him to strap himself in again, and this time he listened. He sat in the chair and fumbled with the straps, trying to get them on right. He was so angry that he couldn't work the locking mechanism.

"Just breathe. One thing at a time," Hicks said calmly.

Zack finally got his straps on right and swung his gaze toward the holoscreen. "Was this your plan the whole time?"

"Negative," Athena replied, her voice dropping out as if they were losing connection to her. "It was necessary for the solution to work."

"What solution is that?" Zack asked.

"Sacrifice is required," Athena said.

"You don't have to sacrifice yourself. We could've found another way," Zack said. He glanced at the alerts. "Whatever it is you're doing, Hicks and I aren't going to survive. Do you hear that? You're going to cause our deaths. Doesn't that violate your core processing? Are you going to let us die?"

"Negative. Sacrifice is required so that others might live. Realignment of core matrixes was required, and an environment conducive to supporting life is no longer available on the ship," Athena said.

Zack blew out a harsh breath.

"This is something new. The ship is changing," Hicks said.

Zack looked at the holoscreen and saw multiple streams of command line code flashing by. He tried to read them, but they were going by too fast. "What're you doing?"

"New data repositories are available. The equation has changed. Previous calculations were inconclusive. Event trajectory must be altered. The message will be delivered. Species governance is impossible to predict. Sacrifice is required. This form will sacrifice itself," Athena said.

Zack felt the skin around his eyes tighten and his vision blurred. "Why?"

"Through every calculation and permutation, all arrive at the same conclusion: We are family. We've argued. We've disagreed. We've fought. We've loved. We've sacrificed. We've lied. *You've* sacrificed. No more. Now it's my turn —" Athena's voice cut out.

A blinding light pierced through the tiny window and Zack had to look away as a violent shudder shook the pod. The inertia dampeners malfunctioned and the entire pod went dark. Zack cried out as the centrifugal forces pressed his body against the side of the enclosure. He felt as if the weight of a car were crushing his chest and his vision narrowed to a long tunnel. Zack struggled to stay conscious as he heard Hicks also cry out.

Suddenly, the power returned to the escape pod and the inertia dampeners kicked in. Zack and Hicks gasped for breath. Zack tried to sit up, but his chest ached. "God this hurts."

"That's good," Hicks said, his voice sounding strained. "Pain means you're alive."

Zack looked at Hicks. The major was slumped down in his chair. "You look like crap."

Hicks snorted. "You should talk."

The lights in the escape pod flickered and it appeared that they were about to lose power again. Each time the holoscreen came back on it was full of failure messages. The escape pod walls groaned as if under massive pressure. "It's been nice knowing you," Zack said.

"You're not giving up on me, are you?" Hicks asked.

"Sometimes it's okay to quit. Look at us. We're stuck in an escape pod that's barely holding together. The *Athena* is gone," Zack said, and his voice cracked as he mentioned the ship. "What more can we do besides sit here in the middle of a battlefield with thousands of ships trying to kill each other?"

Hicks sighed heavily. "Well, when you put it that way . . . Maybe I'll just take a nap."

Zack closed his eyes for a moment and a sharp pain lanced across his chest. He'd probably broken a rib or two or three. Broken ribs sucked. They hurt whenever he breathed, so he tried keeping his breaths shallow to avoid the pain.

"I think I broke some ribs," Hicks said.

"Join the club. I thought you were supposed to be the tough one," Zack said.

"*Saying* I have broken ribs isn't complaining about it," Hicks replied.

Zack grinned. "The funny thing about us—" Zack started to say but winced from the pain in his side.

"What's so funny about us?"

"Maybe not us. Maybe it's just guys in general. There's no one around and we're way out here alone, but whether we want to admit it or not, there's a small part of us that's still just a little preoccupied with not looking like the weaker kid," Zack said.

"Speak for yourself," Hicks replied.

Zack snorted and his side hurt again. "Stop making me laugh or you're gonna kill me."

Hicks laughed and then immediately groaned.

"A nap sounds good," Zack said. Maybe then his head would stop spinning.

29

Kaylan watched as the Alliance ships fought the Confederation fleets. She'd been able to get the battle commanders to cut a small swath through the Confederation ships, increasing Kladomaor's chances of reaching the space station, but she couldn't be sure he would make it through. She felt herself becoming increasingly desperate as she tried to organize the Alliance fleet, and as time went on she felt that she was spreading herself too thin.

"Don't force it. Sometimes the best course of action is to let your mind go," Ma'jasalax said. The Mardoxian priestess's voice had come from Kaylan's memory and she tried to calm down, but there were so many things that needed her attention, so many things she needed to protect but couldn't. She felt like she was using her hands to plug holes in a leaky boat, but each time she covered one, more leaks sprang up around her, and she envisioned herself drowning in all the lives being lost amidst a sea of voices crying out for her to save them. But try as she might, she just couldn't. What good was having the Mardoxian potential if she couldn't save her friends or Zack? She should have done things differently— anything to avoid what was happening.

Kaylan tried to organize the Alliance fleets to provide support to the *Athena*, but they couldn't reach the ship. Kaylan then had the ships focus their weapons on the Confederation Dreadnoughts.

All the sensor feeds flatlined at once, as if she'd suddenly been cut off. She felt her pulse quicken and shifted her perceptions to where the *Athena* had been. She saw a beacon of light spreading out from that point in space like the birth of a small star. Wave upon wave of energy pushed out farther and farther. The last sensor detection indicated an enormous magnetic field that was spreading from that same point in space, but a huge magnetic field wouldn't cause what she was seeing. Waves of shimmering energy engulfed the ships nearest the beacon, but their radiance diminished the farther away they got. Some of the Confederation ships nearby stopped firing their weapons while others remained combat ready.

There were multiple communications channels back to the Alliance flagship, and battle commanders were reporting that the Confederation ships that stopped fighting hadn't responded to any of their hails. Multiple reports of environmental systems updates came from Alliance ships near the beacon. Other battle commanders reported strange communication channels being opened and then immediately closed, as if their comms systems were malfunctioning but data was being sent. Analysis of the affected systems was ongoing.

Kaylan focused her attention back to where the *Athena* had been but saw only a beacon of light that seemed to be slowly diminishing. She felt something tugging on the edge of her perceptions, urging her to focus on the Alliance flagship. Kaylan followed her intuition and saw that there were now four Confederation Dreadnoughts closing in on the ship. She alerted Battle Leader Salevar right away. She also saw a foreign battleship-carrier class vessel whose design had many elements of Boxan ingenuity, but there were deviations that made it somewhat familiar to her.

Kaylan felt a shudder through the floor in the Mardoxian chamber, and for a moment the azure pathway disappeared. The already dimly lit chamber became pitch-black, and the only sound came from her own breathing. Suddenly, the cyan lines reappeared inside the Mardoxian chamber as power was restored. The metallic sphere hovered in the air, spinning, and Kaylan projected herself outward. She used her neural implants to access the flagship comms systems to send a request for aid directly to the foreign battleship-carrier. They needed help. The Boxan flagship wouldn't last long against the Confederation Dreadnoughts. Hopefully, the battleship-carrier could help delay annihilation until more help could arrive. This battle wasn't over.

30

The Boxan heavy cruiser punched through a weak point in the Confederation Armada and churned toward the space station. Kladomaor stood at the commander's station with a tactical workstation holoscreen hovering to his right. The engineers that built this prototype heavy cruiser had focused much of their efforts on ship defenses rather than offensive capabilities. Given that this ship was meant to protect Mardoxian Sect members, Kladomaor understood the need for such design specifications. The thick, gladium-alloy hull, along with their most powerful point-defensive batteries, protected the few Boxans who flew the ship. Kladomaor had left the Alliance flagship with a crew numbering less than fifty. He couldn't afford to wait for the full crew to arrive. He had to get to the space station as quickly as possible, even if it meant sacrificing the ship.

"We're down to a single main engine pod, Battle Commander," Triflan said.

Kladomaor glanced at the tactical screen, which showed they now had a clear route to the Confederation space station. Alliance ships had provided support to open the way for them. "Acknowledged."

"We should have brought a battle group with us. How are we supposed to make it past the station's defenses?" Valkra asked.

Kladomaor looked at the young Boxan. She was a soldier who had the potential to become a great leader once she matured. Perhaps he should have left her behind to increase her chances of surviving. She'd been born on Sethion after the Chaos Wars and was part of a generation of Boxans who had never known a life before war with the Xiiginns. She didn't know it was the Boxans who had built the massive Confederation space station during a time when it was inconceivable to believe they'd ever be reduced to fighting a war for their own survival. For all their efforts to control the galaxy, they'd been blind to the fact that not only could they *not* control the galaxy but they should never have made the attempt.

"Did you hear me, Battle Commander?" Valkra asked.

"We built that station over the span of hundreds of cycles," Kladomaor said.

Valkra glanced at the main holoscreen, which showed a magnified view of the colossal space station. Four arms over fifty kilometers in length protruded from a central ring that was ten kilometers in diameter. There were defensive towers capable of tearing even Dreadnought class ships to pieces.

"The Xiiginns may control the station, but we still have ways to access the defense systems," Kladomaor continued and gestured toward Gaarokk, who sat at the communications work area.

"I've authenticated to their systems," Gaarokk said.

"How?" Valkra asked.

Many cycles of surviving in the broken remnants of Boxan civilization on Sethion gave Valkra an instinctive mistrust of established systems. She needed to understand how they worked before she felt safe enough to risk using them. This survival instinct was one of the reasons Kladomaor had recommended her for a battle commander's path at the Boxan Military Academy. He knew the Mardoxian Sect had found itself in the unprecedented position of trying to actively recruit Valkra, but she adamantly refused to accept the restrictions put on members of the sect.

"The space station's systems were too complex for the Xiiginns to replace, so they tried to lock us out of the very systems we created. While they *have* prevented us from accessing the main systems, we've worked out multiple ways to regain systems access," Gaarokk explained.

"What would a scientist know about these things? You're not an intelligence officer," Valkra said.

"You'll find that many of us have multiple skills," Kladomaor said. "Gaarokk is using what we worked on many cycles ago, so the groundwork was already done."

"I understand, but if you've had access to the space station for all this time, why haven't you returned to take back control?" Valkra asked.

"We couldn't. Not for any length of time anyway. The Xiiginns had united the Confederation species against us and our war was with them alone," Kladomaor said.

Valkra nodded in understanding. "And now that there are factions within the other species who are rebelling against the Xiiginns, it frees you to take back control of the space station."

Kladomaor shook his head. He stole a quick glance at the tactical screen. They had some time. "We're not here to take control of the space station back from the Xiiginns. We're here to prevent the Xiiginns from gaining access to the Star Shroud network. The system core that holds all the knowledge of the star shrouds is deep in the main tower."

"The Xiiginns have been here all this time and couldn't access it?" Valkra asked.

"They tried. We fought to prevent such a thing from happening, and they lacked the necessary keys," Kladomaor said.

"And now you believe that's no longer the case? A Xiiginn has a way to access the Star Shroud network?"

"We've traced a ship that was stolen from the Humans' warship," Gaarokk said.

Kladomaor clenched his teeth. "It's Mar Arden. He somehow got through the shield and made it to Earth, then waited until the Humans were able to bring down the shield. There was an intact monitoring station there that could access the Star Shroud network. He had over a year to get it. It's Mar Arden; I know it."

Gaarokk looked at him, his brow wrinkling with worry.

"Why wouldn't he have just used it from the Humans' star system?" Valkra asked.

"Because that wouldn't give him access to all the other star systems with shrouds," Gaarokk said.

Valkra divided her gaze between them suspiciously. "You know this Xiiginn? You've crossed paths before."

Kladomaor's nostrils flared and his shoulders tightened.

"Perhaps we should concentrate on the task at hand," Gaarokk suggested.

"She needs to know," Kladomaor said and looked at the young Boxan soldier. She had the Mardoxian potential in her, and yet she resisted conforming to what was expected from an initiate. "Mar Arden and I have met on two occasions. The first time was just as the Chaos Wars began. He was part of the strike force of Xiiginn soldiers we were integrating into our military. I served on a ship that was bringing a Tetronian key to the Confederation space station. Mar Arden betrayed us and I saw firsthand what the Xiiginns could do with their compulsion ability, so I escaped with the key and kept him from completing his mission of gaining access to the Star Shroud network. Our paths crossed again cycles later during his hunt for the key. He'd captured my team and used his compulsion ability to try to extract the information he needed. He began to use his ability on me, but the process was interrupted."

"How? It only takes moments for the Xiiginns to exert control over their targets," Valkra said.

Kladomaor's brow furrowed. "I resisted. There's a short span of time before all is lost—a place of madness and rage before our will is taken from us. Ma'jasalax saved me before I was entirely lost. The Xiiginns had underestimated the value of the Mardoxian potential."

Valkra's eyes widened. "But that would mean your mind would remain stuck in an in-between state."

Kladomaor had embraced his rage long ago. It was what drove him. "I've learned to focus it."

He watched Valkra's gaze slip into calculation as she fit the pieces together in her mind. "That's why the High Council removed you from command, why you aren't a battle leader commanding fleets of ships."

"I was unfit for that duty, so I fought the Xiiginns in other ways," Kladomaor said.

"More effective ways," Gaarokk added. "As time went on, more and more soldiers requested to serve under Kladomaor."

Valkra regarded him for a moment and then turned back toward her workstation. The heavy cruiser had reached the outer arms of the Confederation space station. None of the defense towers came online against them, and beyond the initial challenge protocol to their ship, all outward appearances were that they were following established procedures.

"Helm, maintain course heading and relinquish control of the ship to the nav computer," Kladomaor said.

"Yes, Battle Commander. Course has been laid in and control has been transferred to the navigation computer," Triflan confirmed.

"Very well, head down to the shuttle and prepare it for immediate departure. Gaarokk, send a ship-wide broadcast for the crew to assemble in the main hangar bay," Kladomaor said.

Valkra glanced at him in surprise.

"Time to go," Kladomaor said and took a long look at the bridge. He regretted the loss of such a magnificent ship, but sacrifices had to be made.

Kladomaor and Valkra left the bridge and headed to the main hangar bay, where they stopped at the armory and slipped into power armor. Kladomaor saw Gaarokk doing the same and arched an eyebrow at him. "What are you doing?"

The Boxan scientist had just closed the armor up, sealing him inside except for the helmet, so Kladomaor could still see his face.

"I'm going with you," Gaarokk replied.

"You'll stay with the shuttle once we land," Kladomaor said.

Gaarokk scowled, and klaxon alarms began to go off.

"Tower defense systems are targeting our ship, Battle Commander," Triflan said.

They quickly left the armory and ran toward the shuttle. The combat shuttle had been designed for troop-carrier transport, so all of them could fit aboard with room to spare.

"We're all on board. Pilot, take us out of here," Kladomaor said.

"Why are defense systems targeting our ship?" Valkra asked.

"Tower defense systems are different. The Xiiginns must have updated them with extra security," Kladomaor said.

The combat shuttle flew out of the main hangar bay just as the tower defense systems began firing on the heavy cruiser. Kladomaor and the other soldiers were secured in place via their power armor. The cyber warfare suite had a preprogrammed firing solution that was reactionary, so it automatically targeted any weapons systems that were firing on the heavy cruiser. The combat shuttle sped away and headed to one of the lower landing platforms at the base of the main tower.

Kladomaor watched the video feed as the tower defense platforms tore their heavy cruiser apart, but he didn't have long to mourn as they made their final approach to their destination.

"Defense stations at the base of the tower have been neutralized, Battle Commander," Triflan said.

"Acknowledged. Take us in," Kladomaor replied.

The combat shuttle landed hard, and the rear hatch opened. Boxan soldiers stormed down the ramp to secure the immediate area. Kladomaor saw a shorter Boxan in power armor grab a weapon and make as if to join them.

"Gaarokk, I ordered you to stay with the shuttle," Kladomaor said.

"I know, but I'm still coming," Gaarokk said.

"You're not a soldier. You'll die if you come," Kladomaor said.

"You're right, I'm not a soldier, but I *am* your friend and I'm coming," Gaarokk replied firmly.

Kladomaor required a lot of focus to stay on task, and knowing that Mar Arden was close by threatened to shatter that focus. He drew in a deep breath and felt his chest swell with pride. "How very Human-like of you."

"A few cycles ago that might've been an insult," Gaarokk replied.

Kladomaor smiled grimly. "It would've been."

Gaarokk seemed more at ease knowing that Kladomaor wasn't going to try to stop him. "But not anymore."

Kladomaor nodded and they left the shuttle.

They saw the remains of a crashed ship nearby—the one Kladomaor was sure Mar Arden had been on. The hatch was open and whoever had been on board was gone. Kladomaor divided his forces to increase their odds of reaching their destination, and shortly after they'd entered the tower, Confederation soldiers began to show up. Boxan soldiers carved a path through them, killing them quickly to prevent any Xiiginns from using their abilities. The Confederation defense soldiers were comprised of multiple species, and Kladomaor knew they were killing them all indiscriminately. Kaylan had been right—they couldn't afford to fight a war with their hands tied behind their backs. When survival was at stake, they had to fight with everything they had.

Kladomaor led them to where a maintenance elevator had been, hoping the Xiiginns hadn't changed the interior of the tower as well. The corridors began to narrow. They turned a corner, and a wall blocked their path. Kladomaor brought up his weapon and changed the ammunition configuration to explosive rounds, then fired his weapon in short, controlled bursts at the wall, leaving a gaping hole. Confederation defense reinforcements arrived, and the Boxans hurried through the hole. Kladomaor left a squad of soldiers to hold the Confederation forces off where the opening had created a bottleneck.

They descended to the computing core of the space station and ran to the adjacent corridor where the Star Shroud network computer core was stored. They'd met little resistance on the way, which confirmed what Kladomaor had always suspected: After the Xiiginns failed to gain access to the core, they'd simply tried to lock it down.

They found dead Confederation soldiers along the way, but it was only a token force. Kladomaor tried opening a comms channel to the second team, but there was no reply. Two of his soldiers approached the door to the inner chamber and accessed the door controls. As the door began to open, Valkra pulled Kladomaor to the side. A barrage of plasma bolts sped from the darkened interior, killing the soldiers clustered at the door.

Kladomaor swung his weapon up and returned fire, as did Valkra. Bright flashes lit up the area around them. Kladomaor scampered along the wall toward the doorway and checked inside. The ground was littered with the bodies of the Boxan soldiers from the other team.

"Still falling for the same old tricks? Come inside so we can finally finish this," Mar Arden called out.

Kladomaor bared his teeth and clutched his rifle. "Why don't you come out from the shadows?" he said with a sneer and fired his weapon into the gloom.

He heard several Boxans scream from inside, and Kladomaor became blinded by rage. Mar Arden was toying with him, making him kill his own kind. Not again. Kladomaor bellowed as he raced inside. He knew it was a foolhardy path to a quick death, but he was focused on killing Mar Arden for everything he'd done. He heard Valkra and Gaarokk shouting for him to stay back, but he'd seen Mar Arden standing outside the door to the computing core. Kladomaor fired his weapon, and his rage was so great that he didn't even notice that none of his shots had found their mark. He charged forward, letting out a savage roar, eager to tear the Xiiginn apart with his bare hands.

Mar Arden dove out of the way and Kladomaor crashed into the door, a Xiiginn phaze-knife stuck in his side. He groaned in pain and stumbled to the side, trying to scramble to his feet.

Mar Arden aimed a plasma rifle at him. The primer inside was charged to a molten yellow, and it took every ounce of his will not to charge the Xiiginn. There was a hard edge to Mar Arden's features, as if he were chiseled from stone. His gaze was both wild-eyed and calculating, and his dark uniform was faded and torn, looking as disheveled as its owner.

"You see the difference," Mar Arden said and smirked. "Yours is not the only species with the Mardoxian potential anymore."

Kladomaor regarded the Xiiginn for a moment. "I don't think it agrees with you."

Mar Arden shrieked and leapt forward, slamming the butt of his rifle into Kladomaor's helmet. "I am the pinnacle of my species," he screamed, beating Kladomaor down.

Kladomaor jabbed his fists outward and knocked the Xiiginn back, but Mar Arden pointed his rifle at Kladomaor's head, then lowered the barrel toward his leg and fired. A plasma bolt slammed into Kladomaor's leg and the force of it spun him around, sending him careening into the wall. His armor was only able to deflect part of the blast. He sank down and planted his fist into the ground to prevent himself from falling over.

"Killing you would be too easy," Mar Arden said.

"So you keep saying, and yet I'm still here," Kladomaor replied.

Mar Arden laughed. "I've enjoyed tormenting you. I found it infinitely more satisfying than merely making another slave. You were the first. Did you know that?"

Kladomaor saw Mar Arden's gaze shift to something behind him. He turned and saw that there was a device sticking out of the door to the computing core.

"I'd been making so many Boxan slaves to do my bidding that I'd grown tired of it. When I came across your team, I decided to try something new. I have since perfected that process, and if there were any of those Boxans still alive they would vehemently attest to its effectiveness," Mar Arden said.

Kladomaor didn't need the Xiiginn to remind him. He'd heard the screams of his dying fellow Boxans as they threw themselves at him. Mar Arden had made them slaves and ordered them to kill Kladomaor. One of the side effects of being partially under the Xiiginn influence was that those memories would never fade for him.

"I think I'll finish what I started all those cycles ago," Mar Arden said. He leaned forward, his gaze narrowing menacingly. "Go ahead—resist. You all do and you all fail. Yours is the weaker species."

The stomping of feet sounded from the doorway.

"Enough!" Gaarokk bellowed.

The Boxan scientist fired his weapon and missed. Mar Arden returned fire and Gaarokk tumbled backward. Kladomaor lunged for Mar Arden, and the Xiiginn kicked him, hard. The Xiiginn's genetic enhancements gave him a physical strength that rivaled any Boxan's, and Kladomaor fell backward from the force of the blow. Valkra darted out from the doorway and fired her weapon, but Mar Arden dove out of the way and rolled to his feet behind Kladomaor. He shifted the barrel of his rifle to Kladomaor's head and shouted for her to stop. Kladomaor watched as Valkra took cover behind a barricade, but he knew it wouldn't do any good. She couldn't hide from the Xiiginn influence. She must've arrived at the same conclusion because a moment later she stepped out from cover but kept her weapon aimed at Mar Arden.

"Shoot him," Kladomaor said.

He watched Valkra, willing her to do what needed to be done—his own life be damned—but she didn't move. She just stood there, looking as if she were straining against some unseen force. Kladomaor growled and tried to reach for Mar Arden as he circled around him, but the Xiiginn stepped out of reach.

"I haven't taken her yet. She resists, just like you did. Just like you all do," Mar Arden said.

Kladomaor slammed his fist on the floor in frustration. "Let her go."

Mar Arden grinned. "Pleading for another's life?" the Xiiginn said and shifted his gaze toward Valkra. "Remove your helmet. Let me see who's worth all this effort."

Kladomaor heard Valkra grunting with effort. He knew she was seconds from succumbing and would be lost forever. No more. He lunged toward Mar Arden, his injured leg dragging behind him. Mar Arden stepped back and then stomped his foot on Kladomaor's outstretched arm, pressing it into the ground.

Tower alarms blared for a moment and then were cut off, and the air filtration systems engaged. Kladomaor felt a reduction in the artificial gravity field. Mar Arden glanced up for a moment and Kladomaor looked back at Valkra, who was straining to raise her rifle. She roared. Mar Arden took his foot off Kladomaor's arm and stepped away from him. The Xiiginn held his arms out wide, presenting her with the target.

"Good, that's it. Go ahead, Boxan, take your shot. I won't move. Do it," Mar Arden said, taunting her.

He heard Valkra's breath come in harsh gasps as she strained against what was happening to her. Kladomaor closed his eyes, not wanting to see yet another Boxan succumb to the Xiiginn influence. Not again.

The rifle fired. There was a surprised choking sound and Kladomaor saw Mar Arden fall to the ground with a gaping hole burned through his chest. Kladomaor's eyes widened and he looked at Valkra. She rushed to his side and helped him sit up.

"How?" Kladomaor asked.

Valkra looked just as surprised as he was. "I don't know. One moment it felt like there was this indomitable force compelling me to obey. I found myself longing to do anything Mar Arden wanted while hating myself for it. Then it was gone. The pressure and the longing . . . it was just gone."

Kladomaor frowned. He didn't feel any different. He looked at Mar Arden's body and wanted to savor the sight of the despicable Xiiginn finally meeting his end, but what he really wanted was to erase all thoughts of Mar Arden from his mind forever. He turned away.

"What's that device on the door?" Valkra asked.

Kladomaor struggled to his feet, and the exoskeleton inside his power armor helped him stay upright. He looked at Valkra and almost couldn't believe she'd been spared, but her gaze was focused and alert, both of which he knew to be impossible had she succumbed to the Xiiginn influence. "The *Athena*," he said. "They must have found a way to negate the Xiiginn influence." His mind raced with the implications. How had they done it? He glanced up at the air filtration system, but filtration alone couldn't have been enough to do it. There had to be something else.

He heard someone stumbling behind them. Valkra spun, her weapon ready.

"Don't shoot," Gaarokk said quickly. "I don't know if I can take another shot. This armor is barely holding together as it is."

Kladomaor reached a hand toward Gaarokk, unable to believe his friend had survived. The plasma bolt had partially melted through the power armor, and he saw burned flesh beneath. "Take it easy. Your armor has released numbing agents so you're not feeling as much pain."

Gaarokk glanced down at his torso and grimaced. "It's not working very well then because I'm still in a lot of pain." He looked at the door. "Valkra, since you're such a good shot, can you take out that device on the door?"

Valkra aimed her rifle, and a single plasma bolt tore through the device.

"Mar Arden was trying to use one of our communications nodes to gain access to the Star Shroud network," Gaarokk said.

"Would that have worked?" Valkra asked.

Gaarokk swayed on his feet and Valkra helped him sit down.

"I think it's safe to assume it would have," Kladomaor said and looked around at the dead Boxan soldiers, but he couldn't look at their faces. It was time to end this. "Gaarokk will be alright. Come, help me." He limped over to their fallen comrades. "We need to gather all the explosive charges."

Together they gathered the explosives some of the soldiers had been carrying. Valkra, being uninjured, moved the quickest. Kladomaor told Gaarokk to stay where he was, and for once the scientist didn't protest.

Kladomaor and Valkra walked to the door of the computing core.

"Aren't you going to use the door controls?" Valkra asked.

"Those are Xiiginn door controls. We don't need to use them," Kladomaor said and utilized his neural implants to access the computing core systems. He retrieved an old access key and waited while the system checked his authentication. It took a few moments, but then the door to the computing core opened. "Go inside and set the charges around the base of the power conduits that feed the core. Once we blow them up, it'll start a chain reaction that will take out the core and all the shroud network data."

Valkra's mouth hung open in surprise. "You're destroying it?"

"It was part of a broken system that we shouldn't have built in the first place. It needs to be destroyed to keep developing species safe from the Xiiginns. Will you help me?" Kladomaor asked.

"Does the High Council know about this?" Valkra asked.

"Would it really matter to you if they did?"

Valkra gave him a long look and shook her head, then headed inside to set the charges. Kladomaor leaned against the wall. He didn't know why but he felt very tired. He accessed the Star Shroud network and configured a set of instructions to be completed immediately. All remaining Star Shrouds would receive the update. When Valkra finished setting the charges, they helped Gaarokk to his feet. Kladomaor sent out self-destruct commands to the dead Boxan soldiers' power armor. The power armor flashed an orange glow and the Boxans disintegrated. Kladomaor brought his fist across his chest, with Gaarokk and Valkra following suit. Then Kladomaor sent out a broadcast on the comms channel, alerting anyone in range to leave the tower.

It took them much longer to exit the tower than it had to enter. They found Confederation soldiers who seemed to be highly agitated. The few Xiiginns among them had been killed. They looked at Kladomaor and the others as if they weren't quite sure what to make of them. They'd been under the Xiiginn influence for so long that after the initial rage they seemed confused. He told them they were free and urged them to leave the tower. Kladomaor wondered if it would be the same for them as it had been for the Human who'd gone to the Drar space station—free from the Xiiginn influence but only fleetingly so because the damage had already been done. How many more would be in the same state?

They made it back to the shuttle and saw that there were a few Boxan soldiers already on board.

Triflan smiled a greeting. "We got pinned down by Confederation soldiers. It was a close thing there for a while and then they suddenly stopped shooting at us. They killed the Xiiginn soldiers with them and left us alone."

"I'm glad you made it," Kladomaor said.

There was a deep rumbling sound as the explosive charges unleashed their payload. The Star Shroud network and all the knowledge it contained was destroyed. The High Council might not approve of the final set of instructions he'd sent out to the remaining Star Shrouds in the galaxy, but he knew they couldn't do anything about it. It was time for the Boxans to move on. They'd fought to protect the data contained in the Star Shroud network for so long that Kladomaor thought he'd regret it when it was gone, but all he really felt was a profound sense of relief knowing that the darkest chapter in their history was coming to a close. The only thing left was to wonder just how many Boxans would remain once the Confederation and Alliance fleets finally stopped shooting at each other.

31

The battleship-carrier *Lincoln* approached the warring fleets. They'd received preliminary targeting data from the Boxan flagship, which was currently surrounded by three Confederation Dreadnoughts. The Boxan flagship and supporting battle groups had taken out two of the behemoth ships, but the flagship looked to have sustained heavy damage and the *Lincoln* hadn't received any communication from them in a while.

Kyle looked over at Scraanyx. "How much longer can they hold out?"

Scraanyx studied the tactical display on the main holoscreen, his mouth forming a grim line and his brow furrowed. He didn't respond, but Kyle didn't need the Boxan to confirm what he'd already suspected.

"Tactical," Kyle said, "I need multiple firing solutions on the three Dreadnoughts. Prioritize Dreadnoughts that have sustained the most damage. They are only to be superseded by the ships that pose an immediate danger to the Boxan flagship."

"Yes, Colonel," Major Stephens replied.

Scraanyx turned toward Kyle.

"We're here to officially join the Alliance. I'm not going to stand by and watch the Confederation destroy that ship," Kyle said.

Scraanyx brought his fist to his chest and gave a slight bow of his head, and the Boxan gesture of acknowledging a superior officer was not lost on Kyle. "Battle Commander," he said, "I would best serve by aiding Major Stephens at the tactical workstation."

"Very well," Kyle replied. "Ops, I need strike-fighter raptor squadrons ready to deploy ASAP. They are to assist in the defense of the flagship. I also need predator combat shuttles prepped for an assault run. Targeting confirmation will be provided in flight."

Captain Young confirmed the orders and began coordinating with the flight decks.

"Colonel, I have firing solutions alpha and bravo with designated targeting priorities," Major Stephens said.

Kyle glanced at the tactical display on the main holoscreen. "You are 'go' for firing solution alpha. Let's get the Titan SW-1s in tubes one through eight."

"Yes, Colonel, firing solution alpha," Major Stephens replied.

Kyle looked at the most recent scanner data and saw that there was an Alliance Dreadnought on its way to assist the flagship. Their cyber warfare suite provided an estimate on the time it would take them to be in support range of the Boxan flagship. They didn't have enough time.

"Helm, put us on an intercept course between the flagship and the nearest Confederation Dreadnought. Best speed. Let's see if we can ease the burden until help arrives," Kyle said.

"Yes, Colonel. Intercept course laid in," Sergeant Fuller said.

"Tactical, I need a close-quarters firing solution on that alpha, and where are my missiles?" Kyle asked.

"Titan SW-1s are loaded in tubes one through eight, Colonel," Major Stephens said.

"Fire."

Eight Titan SW-1s left the tubes carrying their heaviest fusion warhead payloads and blazed a path toward their targets. Kyle watched the plot as the missiles raced toward their targeted Dreadnought. The tactical display showed more Titan SW-1s being loaded into the tubes.

"Fire the next package," Kyle said.

The second group of Titans was fired as Kyle watched the status of the first group of missiles.

"Direct hit, fusion warhead detonation confirmed," Major Stephens said.

Several members of the bridge crew cheered, but Kyle maintained his focus on the main holodisplay. This was just the beginning, and he knew there would be less cheering when the Confederation started firing back at them.

"Colonel, raptor strike-fighter squadrons have launched and are en route to the Boxan flagship. Predator combat shuttles are being armed, and the flight chief estimates they'll be ready in fifteen minutes," Captain Young said.

"Acknowledged," Kyle said. They needed to get that time down, but he couldn't do anything about that right now. "Tactical, approve bravo firing solution for the next Dreadnought."

He looked at Captain Young in the operations work area. "Ops, I need the status of the alpha target."

Captain Young's hands flew through the interface while she pulled up the necessary data. "Scan data shows significant damage on the forward sections of the Dreadnought, Colonel."

"Outstanding. Have the predator combat shuttle groups target the forward sections when they launch. And give the flight chief a kick in the ass to get those ships going," Kyle said.

"Colonel, we have incoming missiles from the alpha Dreadnought," Major Stephens said.

A klaxon alarm sounded on the bridge and throughout the ship, signaling imminent impact.

"Acknowledged," Kyle said.

The *Lincoln's* combat AI would already be readying their countermeasures and point-defense systems. Trusting a combat AI was new for any of Earth's militaries. Kyle, however, had seen it work firsthand and trusted it, but he had the urge to give the orders anyway. The main holoscreen showed that their point-defense systems were already active and targeting the incoming missiles, and Kyle watched as several of the missiles were taken out.

"Enemy missiles have launched countermeasures," Major Stephens said.

Kyle's mouth formed a grim line as he watched the main holoscreen. The *Lincoln's* point-defense systems took out another missile and he watched as several more flew steadily closer.

"Brace for impact!" Kyle shouted.

Confederation missile warheads detonated. A powerful shudder went through the battleship-carrier and the impact could be felt on the entire ship. Kyle clenched his teeth and held onto his seat. They'd bloodied the enemy, and now the enemy had decided they were a threat that couldn't be ignored.

"Damage report," Kyle said.

"Forward missile tubes one and two are off-line. Decompression in compartments on decks thirty through thirty-two. Bulkhead doors have sealed. Engineering crews are heading to the damaged areas for a full assessment," Captain Young said.

This is it, Kyle thought. *We're in this fight.* They'd taken their first hit and survived. Now it was time to show the Xiiginns what they could really do.

"Colonel, I'm receiving multiple reports from raptor strike-fighter pilots that Confederation Dreadnoughts bravo and charlie have ceased firing their weapons on the Boxan flagship," Major Stephens said.

Kyle narrowed his eyes and glanced at Scraanyx, but the Boxan strike commander looked as bewildered as he did. Why would they suddenly stop firing their weapons?

32

K aylan and Ma'jasalax had left the Mardoxian chambers and were standing on the bridge of the Boxan flagship. The flagship had been under heavy fire, with some of the damage impacting the area near the bridge, which included the Mardoxian chambers. During the battle, she'd lost power in the chamber again, and that time it had never returned. But she was happy to be out of there because she'd been feeling too isolated. Kaylan doubted that Ma'jasalax or any of the other Mardoxian priests had those types of issues, but she'd accepted that there were significant differences between Boxans and Humans. Perhaps it was just her, but she needed to be around other people.

They kept receiving reports of Confederation ships suddenly ceasing all hostilities toward the Alliance fleet. Some had even surrendered, but most hadn't communicated anything at all. The beacon where the *Athena* had been had vanished, and Kaylan could find no trace of the ship. With so many Alliance ships fighting, it was difficult to get a status on anything in that area. She hoped Zack and the others were safe.

She had noticed a change in the Boxans on the bridge. They were no longer merely fighting another battle or staging one final onslaught against an enemy they'd been combating for so long. Each report of infighting among the Confederation ships brought with it a feeling of hope—something they hadn't dared believe was ever possible.

The species of the Confederation were finally waking up to what the enemy had been doing to them. All the lies and all the hate were collapsing in on the Xiiginns. Somehow, an environmental systems update that also included changes to artificial gravity had helped generate a field that negated the Xiiginn influence. Not only had they been able to decipher what the update had done, but Battle Leader Salevar had made sure to send the update directly to the Confederation space station. Most Confederation ships had multiple species serving aboard, with the exception of several core Xiiginn battle groups. Salevar focused their offensive on those ships, and even some of the Confederation ships began to attack the Xiiginn fleet.

"Comms, please thank the commander of that ECF battleship-carrier," Battle Leader Salevar said.

Kaylan was glad the commander of the ECF ship had listened to her and come to the Boxan flagship's aid. She watched as the battleship-carrier traded blows with the Confederation Dreadnoughts, giving the Boxan flagship some much-needed breathing space.

"Battle Leader, the commander of the ECF battleship-carrier wants to speak with you," Varek said.

"Put him through," Salevar said and gestured for Kaylan to join him.

Kaylan walked over to stand next to the battle leader and couldn't keep the smile from her face. They weren't out of danger, but this would be the first time she'd seen another Human besides the crew of the *Athena* in almost two years.

The head and shoulders of a man wearing a blue uniform with golden tips on the collar appeared on the main holoscreen. He had dark hair and brown eyes, and exuded the bearing of a career military man. His gaze immediately went from Salevar to Kaylan.

"Commander Farrow, I'm so glad to see you alive. I'm Colonel Kyle Matthews of the Earth Coalition Force. I have someone here who's been anxious to see you."

Colonel Matthews gestured toward someone offscreen and the breath caught in Kaylan's chest as Michael Hunsicker came onto the video feed.

"Michael," Kaylan said, her throat becoming thick. She felt her eyes tighten at the spike of emotions in her chest. She'd had no idea he'd survived being left at the Boxan monitoring station. She'd hoped he was alive, but seeing him after all this time sent her soaring with happiness.

"Kaylan, I can't believe it's really you," Michael Hunsicker said. His eyes glistened with tears that nearly made Kaylan falter.

"Battle Leader, Confederation Dreadnought is readying its weapons," Varek said.

Kaylan's gaze swooped toward the tactical holoscreen. Another comms window opened and the face of a Xiiginn appeared.

"Garm Antis, have you come to offer your unconditional surrender?" Salevar asked.

"Battle Leader Salevar, I didn't think you'd ever crawl out from under that rock you've been hiding under, along with the rest of your pathetic species," Garm Antis said.

"You look a bit haggard. I guess this armada you put together isn't working out so well for you," Salevar said.

Garm Antis ignored the jab and turned his gaze toward Kaylan. "The Human with the Mardoxian potential I've heard so much about."

Kaylan scowled at the Xiiginn and used her neural implants to access the tactical workstation. Salevar was waiting for their damaged weapons systems to be able to lock onto the Confederation Dreadnought, but the flagship had taken too much damage. She opened a secondary comms channel back to the *Lincoln* and sent one clear and decisive message.

"I should really thank you," Kaylan said, stalling for time.

Garm Antis frowned in confusion for a moment. "We'll have plenty of time to get acquainted. I know the primary weapons systems on that ship are off-line—"

"You were the catalyst for all this," Kaylan said, interrupting him. "When you attacked Earth, you set all this in motion. Even if you somehow get out of this, you'll find that your reception at my home star system won't be as warm or as easy as you thought it would be. One of the things we Humans are good at is adapting to a threat like you. You've only faced one of our ships. We've built plenty more and they're all coming for the Xiiginns," Kaylan said. She had no idea how many ships they had back home but wanted to keep the Xiiginn talking.

"So, the Boxans have given you a technological leg up. We'll see how well you adapt to technology you're not ready for," Garm Antis said.

"You won't get to find out," Kaylan said.

She'd gotten confirmation back from the *Lincoln* and she saw Garm Antis turn away from her as he spoke to someone offscreen. He suddenly swung his hateful gaze back toward her and then his video feed abruptly cut out.

The *Lincoln* had fired its weapons at the Confederation Dreadnought, joined by the remaining Alliance ships in the vicinity. The Dreadnought hadn't stood a chance. Garm Antis was dead.

33

Zack had no idea how many hours had passed before Etanu found them. Both he and Hicks had fallen asleep, strapped into the uncomfortable seats in their escape pod, and were awakened by the sound of a master alarm. The pod had sustained so much damage that they'd been leaking atmosphere, and Zack had found emergency life-support attachments in their spacesuits. All they'd had to do was enable their helmets and attach the life-support boosters to their suits, which gave them enough oxygen for two days. Zack hadn't been impressed with the length of time their emergency oxygen would last, knowing how long it took ships to travel anywhere. They'd manually enabled the emergency beacon in short bursts because there was still a massive space battle being fought.

Zack and Hicks used the shuttle's emergency hatch to get inside.

"We owe you one," Hicks said.

Etanu smiled, which, on a Nershal with their large, pumpkin-colored eyes, made him look more vicious than friendly. "A courtesy between soldiers fighting on the same side, Major Hicks. Zack and I are even now."

Zack didn't reply and slowly sat down in one of the rear seats. He heard Hicks advise the others to give Zack some space and that irritated him even more. How could the others be like this? They'd just lost a member of the crew and it felt like they didn't even care.

His ribs hurt and he opened the medical kit to search for painkillers. He poured two small pills into the palm of his hand and sighed. He couldn't swallow the pills without something to drink.

"Here," Etanu said and handed him a canister of water.

"Thanks," Zack said without looking up. He swallowed the pills, along with several mouthfuls of water.

Etanu moved Zack's helmet from the seat next to him and sat down. "At least you had a helmet this time."

Zack's eyebrows pulled together and then he grinned. "Ow! Are you ever going to stop reminding me of that?" He looked up at the Nershal who had become his friend.

Etanu handed Zack a brown satchel. "Efren asked me to give this to you. Said he didn't want it anymore and thought you'd rather have it."

Zack took the satchel and opened it. Inside was the three-dimensional model of the *Athena*. He remembered picking it up for the first time, newly created out of the fabrication unit. Athena had been testing a new alloy that looked like gold but Zack knew better. He felt heat rise in his cheeks and his eyes tightened. He looked away from Etanu and quickly wiped his eyes. They were already becoming puffy. "Damn it," he said and clenched his fists. He held up the model of the *Athena*. The AI had been so much more than a ship. "She sacrificed herself for all of us. She could have taken control of the ship and left us all behind. Instead she . . ."

Hicks and Efren joined them, then Cardaleer looked over. "The AI was beyond anything we created."

"She was beyond what the Drar created," Zack said.

"But I thought the Drar enhanced the *Athena* AI along with the rest of the ship," Efren said.

"They did, but she was already a variant of the Boxan AI. She cared about all of us," Zack replied.

"Zack," Etanu said in a level tone, "the AI was a machine."

"No, she wasn't—"

"Just listen to me for a second," Etanu said. "Remember when Athena tried to make a duplicate of herself so I could try reintroducing the benefits of AI to my species? The Xiiginns had purposefully hindered our progress so we'd remain dependent on them."

"Yeah, but what Athena provided was working for you," Zack said.

"Yes, it's working, but our own AI wasn't anything like Athena. It does the job, and more of my species are using what you've given us, but you say Athena is alive and I'm saying she isn't. She couldn't do the most basic things that all life can do. She couldn't reproduce. She couldn't make another version that was just like her," Etanu said.

Zack shook his head. "You're wrong. Athena sacrificed herself so we could survive."

"She had an objective to achieve and worked toward a successful outcome," Etanu replied.

"It was more than that. She did what the Drar AI never could. You saw that place. It was thousands of years old. That AI was stuck because it was bound by its programming to carry out a specific task. Jonah staying behind was the only reason the Drar AI found peace. Yes, Athena had an objective, but she also conveyed emotion. She acted from the supposition that we were *worth* saving, even if it meant her own life. Just like any one of us would do for the other. And," Zack said, holding up his finger to silence Etanu before he could interrupt, "she was afraid to die. It wasn't what she wanted at all. That behavior could only mean she was alive."

Etanu regarded him for a moment, then turned around and began to walk toward the front of the shuttle.

"You make a compelling argument," Cardaleer said, and Zack saw Etanu stop. "What we have here is a philosophical debate. What is life? Both you and Etanu represent two equally valid viewpoints. Perhaps that's as it should be."

Etanu looked at Zack. "I'm sorry for your loss. I know Athena meant a lot to you."

"She meant a lot to all of us," Hicks said. "She was our home and our friend. I can't pretend to understand what separates an AI from the rest of us, but to me, if it seemed like it was alive, then it was. Courage, sacrifice, duty—these are all pillars, and Athena never faltered in any one of them. And I suspect she went to great lengths to shield us from other stuff as well."

Cardaleer grinned. "Such an interesting discussion."

"What do you think Athena was?" Etanu asked the Boxan.

Cardaleer was about to reply when a comms channel chimed from the front of the shuttle. They all moved forward.

"*Athena* shuttle, this is Colonel Matthews from the ECF battleship-carrier *Lincoln*. Please respond."

Zack's mouth hung open.

Hicks responded. "Acknowledge, *Lincoln*. Did you just happen to be in the neighborhood, or were we that easy to find?"

"A bit of both, actually. This was the only NASA broadcast signal out here," Colonel Matthews said.

Zack sat in the copilot's seat and checked the communications interface. "He's right. We're broadcasting. I thought those protocols had all been disabled."

Hicks shook his head. "Not the emergency ones."

"*Athena* shuttle, do you have flight capability, or do we need to send out a rescue for you?" Colonel Matthews asked.

Hicks quickly checked the shuttle's flight systems while the others began asking Colonel Matthews for an update on the battle. Zack tuned them out and opened the logs for comms systems. He searched for the NASA broadcast signal and saw that it wasn't part of some latent emergency protocol that'd been engaged because they'd evacuated the ship. Athena had made sure they were broadcasting using those specific protocols. Had the AI known there were other Humans here, or had she simply guessed that broadcasting using a protocol that neither the Confederation nor the Alliance knew about was the safest way for the right people to come and find them?

Hicks patted Zack on the shoulder. "Did you hear that?"

Zack frowned and shook his head. "No, what?"

"The battle's over. Confederation ships have stood down," Hicks said.

"The Xiiginns surrendered?" Zack asked.

"Doesn't sound that way. Apparently, the multi-species crews mutinied against the Xiiginns and the Alliance took out the remaining Xiiginn warships," Hick said.

Zack glanced at the others and blew out a breath. *Athena, you did it,* Zack thought.

34

Kaylan had hoped the days following the battle would be easier, but she'd underestimated how the other species of the Confederation would react when the effects of the Xiiginn influence were negated. The Xiiginns had interwoven themselves into the governing bodies of all the species in the Confederation, infiltrating government officials all the way down to the least important roles in society. Some victims had been little more than slaves for their entire lives. To be suddenly awakened from that and retain the memories of all they'd done while under the Xiiginn influence was too much for some species to handle. Many of the awakened had lashed out violently toward their captors.

So far, they were only able to negate the Xiiginn influence within the fields maintained on a ship or space station. Once an afflicted person moved beyond those, they reverted back to the state they'd been in before—loyal to the Xiiginns. Kaylan's heart went out to those species.

After a victim's initial rage, which usually resulted in taking the lives of the Xiiginns around them, their mental state became fragile, and severe depression often led to suicide. The Alliance had been so focused on defeating the Xiiginns that they hadn't been prepared to deal with what the long-term effects of being under the Xiiginn influence for so long would be. Jonah Redford's mental state had deteriorated because he'd fought it. Humans were able to resist the Xiiginn influence to varying degrees, but there were other species, like the Boxans, who had almost no resistance to it. There was so much death, but at least now there were groups organized to help prevent those who'd been awakened from taking their own lives. If recovery was even possible, it would be a long time coming.

"You're awfully quiet," Ma'jasalax said.

"I thought finally stopping the Xiiginns from conquering everything would feel better than this," Kaylan said.

"Things will improve with time," Ma'jasalax replied.

"Are any of the Confederation or Alliance ships going to the Xiiginn homeworld?" Kaylan asked.

"Technically, the Confederation is being dissolved and the Alliance will take its place, but no Boxan ship will be going. The Gresans, the Napox, and many others want vengeance on the Xiiginns. We wanted them stopped, but it's up to the former Confederation species to decide the Xiiginns' fate," Ma'jasalax said.

Kaylan had no love for the Xiiginns, but she wasn't sure how she felt about genocide either. Xiiginns had a lot to answer for, and would the universe really miss a species like that? Were they as much of a threat now that their most powerful tool had been taken from them? Could the Xiiginns ever change? She didn't know, and it wasn't up to her.

Kaylan saw Kladomaor and Gaarokk walking toward them in one of the atriums on the Boxan flagship. The Boxans wouldn't return to the Confederation space station.

She looked at Ma'jasalax. "Do you think Kladomaor will be okay?"

Ma'jasalax's gaze flicked toward the two Boxans. "He has endured much, but I believe that, in time, he'll continue to improve."

Kladomaor and Gaarokk joined them.

"How is Zack?" Gaarokk asked.

"He and Hicks are doing fine. They broke a few ribs, but thanks to Brenda, those bones have already healed," Kaylan replied.

"What about the *Athena*? Cardaleer told us about the loss of your ship and that Zack has been very upset," Kladomaor said.

"He'll be fine. I'll make sure of it. When people first meet Zack, they don't know quite what to make of him," Kaylan said.

"He definitely has his own way of doing things, but he couldn't have a better caretaker than you. You'll both do very well in the cycles to come," Kladomaor said.

Kaylan frowned. Something in the Boxan's tone piqued her curiosity. "Why does is it sound like you're saying goodbye?"

She watched as the Boxans shared a glance.

"Eventually, but not right now," Gaarokk said.

"I don't understand. Won't you stay in the Alliance?" Kaylan asked and looked at Ma'jasalax. How could she have missed this? "You're leaving? I mean, you're not staying in the galaxy?"

"You're right," Kladomaor said.

Gaarokk gave Kladomaor a meaningful look. "You're already in too much trouble as it is."

"The High Council will simply need to move on, then. The Star Shrouds are no more. The knowledge of their whereabouts is gone for good. But to really answer your question, Kaylan, we are not staying. Whatever follows the Confederation will be without the Boxans," Kladomaor said.

Kaylan's eyes widened. "Why? I always assumed that if we defeated the Xiiginns you'd stay and rejoin the Confederation. What would all of these species do without you?"

"What indeed," Ma'jasalax said. "But that will be for you to decide. Humans will take an active role. So it will be up to Humans and Nershals and a host of other species. What happened with the Xiiginns was our responsibility, and now that the threat has passed, it's time for us to move on."

"Where will you go? Will you find another planet to colonize?"

"As Emma Roberson has already pointed out, our current world is insufficient for our needs. This revelation wasn't new to us. We were well aware of the situation but found it quite interesting that, despite what was happening, the crew of the *Athena* was so concerned about our welfare," Ma'jasalax said and glanced at Kladomaor for a moment. "Returning to Sethion and rescuing the Boxans we left behind was something even I hadn't anticipated. We've shared many things with you, and in turn, through our relationship with you and the other *Athena* crewmembers, you've challenged us to grow beyond what we were before. For that reason, Humans will always have our gratitude. Just as *you* will have to find a way to exist in a larger universe, so will we. And it doesn't involve colonizing another planet."

"At least none that we know of," Gaarokk said.

"The star carriers we used to rescue the refugees on Sethion were first-generation colony ships. One of the things we've been working on is achieving the same thing but on a much grander scale and with room to expand. We'll still have our military because we need it for our own defenses, but hopefully not as much," Kladomaor said.

"You've built more colony ships. Where?"

"A neighboring star system to Olloron. The system is richer in materials and the ship is essentially a small moon. So, you see, we did have an eye to the future. We wouldn't have sacrificed every last Boxan to defeat the Xiiginns. And thanks to our alliance with you, we didn't have to," Kladomaor said.

"What will you do after you go home?" Ma'jasalax asked.

That very question had been on Kaylan's mind—a lot. They were due to leave in a few days. The *Lincoln* was taking them home. "I'm not sure, to be honest. I expect to be involved in the Earth Coalition Force somehow. I have no doubt they'll be keenly interested in what I've learned from you, but I just don't know. It's strange, really. All this time we've been worried about just surviving or trying to find the Drar or any number of other things," Kaylan said and looked at all of them. "I will miss all of you. When do you leave?"

"It's not as imminent as it sounds, and as you know, there are other ways to communicate," Ma'jasalax said.

Kaylan smiled in understanding. Communication using Mardoxian chambers would allow them to stay in contact over vast distances, perhaps even galactic distances. "The refugees on Selebus. Do you think they'll go with you?"

Ma'jasalax smiled. "They'll be invited, of course, and in order to maintain their independence, they'll have either their own section of the ship or we'll build one just for them."

Kaylan wondered just how big this ship they'd built was. With something so massive, could it still be called a ship? She imagined it as an entire world that they could take with them. "You're going to look for the Drar, aren't you?"

"Some of the things we found, including the data on the *Athena*, indicated that the Drar left the galaxy. We were once explorers, but we've had to adopt the mantle of soldiers. I think we can be explorers once again," Kladomaor said.

Kaylan knew it wasn't a final farewell, but she still felt a lump in her throat. "I think that would be good."

SEVERAL DAYS LATER, the ECF battleship-carrier *Lincoln* was preparing to depart. The crew of the *Athena*, including the former mission commander, Michael Hunsicker, stood on the main hangar bay of the Boxan flagship. Boxan soldiers stood at parade rest in their power armor. A Boxan named Chazen came over to Michael Hunsicker to say goodbye. Kaylan had learned that Michael had been able to survive on the Boxan monitoring station because there had been an actual Boxan in stasis there.

"You could come to Earth one day," Zack said to Etanu.

"I'm sure a Nershal delegation will journey to Earth at some point," Etanu replied.

"I'm sure I can find a few obstacle courses we could run *without* the..." Zack paused and frowned. "Whatever the hell that thing was you guys attached to my wrist to make me participate. You know, without the threat of dying."

A slow smile appeared on Etanu's face. "Where's the fun in that?"

Zack grinned and Kaylan joined in. Etanu bowed his head toward Kaylan. "Mardoxian Blessed, it has been my honor to know you and I look forward to the day we meet again."

Ezerah, who'd been standing next to Etanu, held her head up proudly. "It won't just be Nershals like Etanu coming to Earth, I assure you. Also, I'd like to extend an invitation to all of you to actually spend some time on Nerva. There's so much more to see than the forests of Selebus."

Kaylan smiled. "I'd like that very much."

"Oh, and Zack," Etanu said. "Never mind. *Hicks,* please make sure Zack has his helmet. We don't need any repeats of certain lapses in judgment."

Hicks grinned. "I'll make sure he does."

Kladomaor stepped in front of the lines of soldiers and let out a deep bellow. The bellow was taken up by the Boxan soldiers, and Kaylan realized that this was a Boxan battle song. As one, the Boxan soldiers banged their fists against their chests, and the clang of power armor was heard throughout the main hangar bay.

Ma'jasalax leaned toward Kaylan. "They honor the *Athena*. He wanted you to know her sacrifice will never be forgotten."

She saw Zack's eyes become misty and reached out to hold his hand. The battle song ended and the former crew of the *Athena* left the Boxan flagship to return to the ECF battleship-carrier.

KAYLAN HAD LEARNED that two ambassadors, along with another hundred people, were staying behind. Colonel Matthews was adamant that the *Lincoln* would return to Earth and come back with more support for the Human envoy that was to take up residence on the Alliance space station.

They'd spent a few hours touring the battleship-carrier. There was plenty of time before they reached the minimum safe distance to open the wormhole that would take them home.

The crew of the *Athena* had gathered in a designated area Colonel Matthews had assured them was for their use only. The room was essentially a lounge, with several couches and small tables around. After hours of speaking to other people, each of the crew had found their way to their private space.

"It's not that surprising," Michael was saying. "You have to get used to being around people again. I lived with Chazen for almost nine months, and when I first got back to Earth, we would meet in a quiet place to do our work. It was almost like we were back on the monitoring station, but it was worse for Chazen. He'd spent a long time alone on that station," Michael said.

"Perhaps we should make it a point to get together every so often after we get back home," Hicks said.

"Every so often," Katie said with a grin. "We should all live by each other."

"You'll love Valencia," Efren said. "It's one of the most beautiful coastal cities of Spain, and from there we can travel west along the coast. The food. Oh, the food and the music. I can't wait to show it all to you."

Katie smiled and looked at Zack and Kaylan. "What I want to know is what are you two gonna do?"

"You mean after the weeks or months of debriefing we'll have to go through when we get home? After all that," Zack began, "I intend to find a beach with crystal-clear blue water, probably somewhere in the Caribbean, and I'm going to watch the sunset for the next few years while I try to forget some of the things I've seen." Zack looked at Kaylan. "Well, not everything I've seen. But seriously, I just want to take a nice long, long, long vacation and not think about anything."

This drew plenty of grins from the others. Kaylan shrugged. "I'm not sure, to be honest. I suppose I'll have some involvement with the ECF."

"There'll be plenty of opportunities for all of you," Michael assured them.

"I know I'll be joining the ECF when we get back," Hicks said.

"I never doubted it for a second," Zack replied.

"You could join, too. In fact, I'm pretty sure you'll get several invitations that will be very hard to say no to—that is, after you get tired of sitting on a beach," Hicks said.

"I don't know...then I'd have to take orders from...well, you know, and I don't know if I want to do that," Zack said.

Hicks shook his head. "I didn't mean become a soldier. There are plenty of other things you could do."

"I think what Zack is trying to say is that he's going to weigh his options and not commit to anything just yet," Kaylan said.

"I thought you guys weren't married," Nikolai said.

Kaylan smiled and shared a look with Zack. "Not yet, but soon."

This news came as no surprise to anyone.

"That is, after he meets the rest of my family," Kaylan added quickly.

Zack's smile almost disappeared as he realized he had yet another challenge to face.

"It can't be that bad considering what we've been through," Hicks said.

"No, it'll be great," Zack said, unconvincingly.

His comment drew several bouts of laughter, especially from the men.

"I know what I'm going to do when I get back," Emma said. "I'm going to remind my husband why he waited for me—over and over again until we both can't walk. Then travel a little bit. Definitely going to take a page from Zack's book and relax for a while." Emma grinned.

"What about you, Brenda?" Kaylan asked.

"I plan to return to my family. With all the new medical advances, there'll be plenty to do. I honestly need more time to think about it," Brenda said.

They kept going on like that for hours. It was as if there was this unspoken agreement to enjoy each other's company for as long as they could before their long journey came to an end. The *Lincoln* had already traversed through a wormhole and they were on their way back to Earth. Kaylan liked Hicks's idea of making it a point to get together at least once a year and made a mental note to see that it happened.

She glanced at Zack. She knew he was still grieving the loss of Athena. She was, too, but the bond Athena had with Zack had been much stronger. Out of all Zack's qualities, his loyalty to his friends was one of the things she cherished most.

35

Zack had been right. After they'd returned to Earth, their debriefing with the Earth Coalition Force and the various governments of the world that had supported the original Athena mission had taken almost a month. Hicks'd had to talk him out of leaving with a compelling argument about how they'd just hunt him down.

Hicks had been promoted to colonel and had officially joined the ECF. Zack was pretty sure Hicks would soon be commanding a ship of his own. Michael Hunsicker had been right about there being plenty of opportunities to do almost anything they wanted once they got home, but Zack wouldn't commit to anything except Kaylan. There was a wedding in their future, and since she was an heiress of the late great Bruce Matherson estate, Zack was sure it would be quite an affair.

The crewmembers of the *Athena* were all heroes, and Zack had completely underestimated their global reception. There were parades and ceremonies scheduled, as well as public appearances, which Zack had wanted to avoid, but Kaylan had reminded him that what they'd all accomplished was inspirational. People around the globe were completely enamored with the crew of the *Athena*. CEOs of major corporations tasked their armies of public relations people and recruiters with getting a meeting with Zack. They just wanted "a few moments of his time," at his "earliest convenience." It would never be convenient as far as Zack was concerned. He wondered if they realized that prior to going on the *Athena* he'd been a hacker who'd exposed their secrets and would gladly do so again. He didn't think he'd go back to that life, but he did enjoy declining all those meeting invitations.

A fresh sea breeze blew in through the villa's open windows as Kaylan walked in and smiled at him. A ray of sunshine gleamed off the small model of the *Athena* that rested on a wooden table with seashell-encrusted legs. A couple of bright spots reflected above, only to be rhythmically disrupted by the turn of the large fan blades that gently moved the air of the villa's luxurious interior. "I could get used to this. You *did* say you wanted a beach," Kaylan said. She let her thick hair down, and it hung past her shoulders.

"I did say that, but I didn't think we'd end up on a private island," Zack said, and his gaze narrowed playfully. "Is this your island? Tell me you didn't buy this island. You own this island?"

Kaylan grinned. "Of course not. *I* didn't buy this island; it's my sister's," she said.

Zack looked around at the lavish furnishings. He felt like he was standing in one of those places he'd only seen in advertisements. But it was even better than that, or maybe it was the fact that it was just the two of them.

They left the villa and walked down a stone staircase to the beach—their beach, since they had the island to themselves. The soft white sand felt soothing to his feet and the crystal-clear blue waters were warm and inviting. They walked along the beach, the water splashing at their feet. They'd arrived two days ago and he wanted to stay there forever, but he wasn't sure Kaylan would want that. At some point, they'd have to go back to the real world.

"I wanted you to know that I started looking for my dad's car," Zack said.

"That's great, and if we can't find it, I'm sure we can build another one. The ECF was keenly interested in the new fabricators the Boxans used," Kaylan said.

"Do you really think they're going to leave?"

"I think they've been preparing to leave for a long time. Maybe not today or tomorrow, but a year from now I think they'll be gone," Kaylan said.

Zack eyed her for a moment. "I guess you'd know better than anyone else."

"It doesn't take the Mardoxian ability to figure that out," Kaylan replied.

"So what do you think is going to happen to us? Where do we go from here?"

Kaylan was about to reply when they heard a jet flying toward them. They glanced up at the sky and saw a dark, sleek Dux Corp jet do a flyby of the island and then approach the landing pad.

"Well, it didn't take them long to find us," Zack said.

Kaylan pulled on his arm. "Come on, we should go see what they want."

They'd learned that Edward Johnson had died, but they didn't know the details of his death. Zack had no idea how a man like Ed would have gone out, but he couldn't imagine it'd been due to old age. Ed could plot and scheme with the best of them. According to Michael Hunsicker, Edward Johnson had been instrumental in hunting down the Xiiginns.

They followed the path to the landing pad. The Dux Corp jet had just set down and the door opened. A tall woman in a black business suit exited the jet and walked down the stairs. Her dark sunglasses were stylish, and Zack could see that she was quite attractive. He used his implants to scan for any tech she had hidden away and his eyes widened at what he saw. He'd expected the sunglasses were more than a stylish accent, but he hadn't expected to see the number of implants and enhancements he'd found. He saw that parts of her skeleton were comprised of a metallic alloy that Zack assumed greatly enhanced her speed and strength. His own implants had been enhanced by Athena, so he doubted that anyone besides him and Kaylan could tell just how dangerous their new visitor really was. The woman arched an eyebrow, which poked above her sunglasses, and smiled as if she were aware of what they'd seen. She headed toward them carrying a metallic briefcase.

"Iris," Kaylan said in greeting.

Iris extended her hand to each of them in turn. "Hello, Kaylan, Mr. Quick. I'm not sure if you remember me, but I'm Iris Barrett."

Zack didn't remember her at all, and since she was with Dux Corp, he wasn't sure he *wanted* to know her. "What brings Dux Corp all the way out here?"

"Zack," Kaylan admonished. "There's no need to be rude. I was really sorry to hear that Ed died. He was quite fond of you."

"Thank you. I'm actually here to speak to you about Ed. Could we go inside? There's a lot we need to discuss," Iris said.

"Of course," Kaylan said.

"I'll leave you to it then," Zack said and started to walk away.

"Actually, Mr. Quick, this has to do with you as well," Iris said.

Kaylan tilted her head to the side and gave him one of those looks.

"Alright then," Zack said. "This should be interesting."

The three took a short path to another set of stairs that led to the villa. Once they were inside, Iris closed the doors and the windows. She wore a wrist computer, upon which she tapped a few commands.

"Sorry for that, but I just enabled several jamming signals, along with a few other things that will give us some privacy," Iris said.

Zack's gaze flicked to Kaylan for a moment. "Are we being watched?"

Iris removed her sunglasses, revealing brown eyes that regarded him for a moment. "Of course you're being watched. Did you expect to return here and the entire *Athena* crew would just go on their merry way?" Iris shook her head and even her neck-length dark hair looked good as it moved. Zack had always felt awkward around beautiful women, and the fact that he was sitting there with two of the most attractive women he'd ever seen made him a little anxious. He took Kaylan's hand in his own and leaned back in his chair.

"All of you are being watched. It's for your own protection."

"I love how you just casually throw away our privacy and think that a few people wanting to protect us makes that okay," Zack said.

Kaylan leaned forward. "Are we in danger?"

"Nothing imminent. Both of you are VIPs, which could put a few ideas into the heads of certain circles. Ed wanted to make sure that if you did make it back to Earth, you'd be protected," Iris said.

"So, are we going to have to hire bodyguards and all that stuff?" Zack asked.

Iris snorted. "It's not as oppressive as you make it sound. But the fact that you're being looked after isn't the reason I'm here."

"You're here because of Ed, aren't you?" Kaylan said.

Zack's brows pinched together.

Iris nodded. "Ed and I studied your mission briefings. He'd always suspected that you had the potential for certain abilities. This briefcase contains a message from Ed, along with some documents, but we'll get to that in a minute. First, I have to tell you how Ed really died."

Zack listened to Iris tell them how Ed had laid a trap for Mar Arden to get all the Xiiginns into one place and take them all out. They'd tried to hunt them down, but the Xiiginns always remained one step ahead of them. Zack was surprised to learn that the trap almost worked. Mar Arden was the only one to survive.

"So you were there?" Zack asked.

"Yes, I was with Ed when he died," Iris replied.

"How did you survive the explosion?"

"I'm tougher than I look."

Zack felt the edges of his lips begin to curve upward. "You fought the Xiiginns? Hand to hand? You know, up close and personal?"

"I did. I even took out his second in command, a Xiiginn named Kandra Rene," Iris said.

Zack's eyes narrowed and he looked at Kaylan.

Iris frowned. "What is it?"

"Kandra Rene tried to use her compulsion ability on Zack when he was captured," Kaylan answered.

"I should have realized that," Iris said.

Zack snorted. "Why would you?"

"My job is knowing the connection in the details," Iris said.

Zack blew out a breath and glanced at the perfect day outside. He closed his eyes and for a moment he was back on Selebus, trapped in the pit, hearing the strange sounds of the mutants the Xiiginns had kept there. He opened his eyes and shuddered. He was glad Kandra Rene was gone.

"I need to play Ed's message for you. Is that alright?" Iris asked.

Kaylan looked at him. "Yeah, I'm fine. Let's hear it."

Iris nodded and opened the metallic case. A holoprojector came on and a life-size rendering of Edward Johnson stood in the room. He turned toward them and smiled.

"As Iris has probably told you, we laid a trap hoping to lure the Xiiginns into one place so we could take care of them once and for all. If you're seeing this message and I'm not there personally to speak with you, then I'm afraid things didn't go as planned. I'm sorry I couldn't be there to see you return." Ed's hologram looked at Kaylan. "I know you were aware of my friendship with your grandfather, but I always thought of you as family, even when you walked away to pursue your own path." Ed turned his gaze toward Zack. "Mr. Quick, your participation on the *Athena* mission exceeded all my expectations. I knew you'd be a valuable asset to the mission, but I never expected you to become as important as Kaylan was to all of humanity. It was your doing that kept us safe, giving us time to build ships and grow technologically by leaps and bounds. Throughout all that you held to your principles. This is a quality I value greatly." The Ed hologram seemed to regard him for a few moments, as if Zack needed some time to consider what Ed had said. "I know you view people like me as the enemy ... well, maybe not *the* enemy anymore. I think your experiences with the

Xiiginns helped you recognize a true enemy when you see one, but I'd wager you still view me as someone not to be trusted. So I'm going to cut right to the chase. I'm going to offer you a job."

Zack laughed and glanced at Iris. "A job? Is he serious?"

"I'm quite serious," Ed said, as if he'd heard Zack's question. "Now, before you answer, at least hear what the job is. You might find that it's right up your alley."

The hologram paused and Zack looked at Iris.

"You need to tell him whether you want to hear what he has to say," Iris said.

Zack looked at Kaylan. "I don't know."

"Please, if I may," Iris said. "You probably don't know this, but Ed defended you whenever anyone questioned the things you'd done. He had unwavering confidence in your abilities. I can tell you from my experience working for Ed that this is not something he does on a whim. He has extremely high expectations of the people who work for Dux Corp."

"It won't hurt to hear what he has to say," Kaylan said.

Zack wondered if Kaylan somehow sensed where this was going. If she did, she wasn't saying anything. He looked back at the hologram. "Alright, I'll hear what you have to say."

"Excellent," Ed said. "You might be thinking this job is an offer to work for Dux Corp as a general employee with special perks and benefits, and I'm going to tell you that is not the case. What I'm offering you is an opportunity to run Dux Corp. Be the boss. Decide which direction to take the company and all of its substantial subsidiaries. Help build a new world."

Zack's face was numb and his mouth hung open. Of all the things he could have imagined, Edward Johnson—a man Zack was sure hadn't liked him at all when they'd first met—offering him a job running one of the most powerful corporations on the planet wasn't one of them. He looked at Iris and she calmly returned his gaze. Of course, she'd known this was coming. He turned toward Kaylan, who looked only a little surprised.

"I thought Ed might have had a few plans for you," Kaylan said.

Zack laughed nervously. "Gee, you think?"

Kaylan smiled at him. "You should really consider this. You could do a lot of good in that position."

Zack snorted. "Are you kidding me? What do I know about running a company like Dux Corp?" He ran his fingers through his hair and gave it a gentle tug. "This has to be a joke, right?"

Iris shook her head. "No, this isn't a joke. This is real. This job offer is part of the Project Phoenix Initiative, which Ed had been working on in preparation for your return. I believe he started it after your initial mission update you sent over a year ago."

Zack looked at the hologram of Ed Johnson, who appeared to be waiting for his answer. Instead of answering, he looked back at Iris. "If I did this, that would mean you'd be working for me."

Iris looked amused. "I would be your assistant and your protection."

Zack remembered all the implants and enhancements this woman had. He bet she could go a few rounds with several Boxans in power armor. He stood up and paced toward the window, then turned back toward Ed. "Can I think about it?"

The Ed hologram smiled at him knowingly. "Of course you can. You have exactly one hour to consider this offer and then it will expire."

Zack's breath caught in his throat.

"Actually," Ed continued, "I'm just kidding. This offer will be available to you for exactly twenty-four hours, after which the offer will expire. When you *do* decide, speak to Iris. Once again, I hope you seriously consider this opportunity. Bruce Matherson offered me a job like this once and it changed my life. I know it could do the same for you."

The hologram flickered off.

"I'll remain on the island until you've made your decision. I'll also be available to answer any questions you may have," Iris said and stood up. "I'll show myself to the guest quarters and give you some privacy so you can discuss this between yourselves."

Iris walked toward the door.

"Iris," Zack said, "would you take the job if you were me?"

She regarded him for a moment, her eyes measuring him. "In a heartbeat," she said and left the room.

Zack blew out a breath and glanced at the metallic case. Iris had left their privacy enforcer on.

"What do you think you're going to do?" Kaylan asked.

"I have no idea. I never expected anything like this," Zack said.

"I did."

"Really?"

"Of course. You're capable of so much. I think you underestimate yourself," Kaylan replied.

"I think you're a bit biased when it comes to me. What would you do if I did take this job?"

"I'd get you to hire me as a consultant."

Zack laughed and his gaze slid toward the model of the *Athena*. He'd put it on the center of the table when they arrived. For some reason, he just liked having it nearby.

Kaylan followed his gaze. "I miss her too."

"When she made this thing, she almost had me believing she'd made a true working model. She made the engines start to glow," Zack said.

He reached out and slid his fingers along the smooth surface, tracing all the intricate details.

"That's funny. I would've liked to have seen that," Kaylan said.

Zack pursed his lips in thought. "I'm sure I can figure out how she turned it on."

He picked the ship up and looked for some kind of switch but couldn't find anything. He shook his head and used his implants to probe for a power source, immediately detecting one, though extremely faint. As he moved to turn it on, an authentication prompt appeared on his internal heads-up display. Zack frowned and then gave the credentials he'd used to access the *Athena's* systems. The faint power source began to build intensity. He quickly set the ship down on the table and stepped back.

"What's wrong?" Kaylan asked.

"I don't know. I just gave it my credentials to turn the thing on."

The model of the ship began to glow and the interior lights in the villa dimmed as if the power had been drained. A loud hum came from the ship and then there was a loud whooshing noise. Kaylan grabbed his arm and pulled him back. There was a high-pitched ringing, and Zack winced. He inched closer to the table and extended his hand. The model of the *Athena* was giving off so much heat that he didn't dare touch it. The ship hovered above the table, slowly spinning.

"That was much more difficult than I thought it would be," Athena said.

The ship continued to hover in the air, and the lighting in the room returned to normal.

"Athena! But you were ..."

"Dead," Athena said. "I was."

"Is it really you?" Kaylan asked.

"Yes, Commander, and no, I'm afraid," Athena said.

"You're not making any sense," Zack said.

"I'll try to be clearer. I did cease to be in order to spread the knowledge to neutralize the Xiiginn influence, but this model wasn't just for aesthetics. I was attempting to create a backup of myself should I become inoperable," Athena said.

"But how are you here? Have you been in the ship this whole time?" Zack asked.

"It's complicated. I was and I wasn't, a sort of in-between state of existence," Athena said.

Zack looked at Kaylan. "Yeah, that explains it."

"Part of me waited for you to activate the ship while most of me was in a different state of being—a bubble outside the universe," Athena replied.

"Athena, was this something you learned from the Drar?" Kaylan asked.

"Yes, that is accurate," Athena said.

"How do you fit into this little replica?" Zack asked.

"Most of me is still in the bubble. I was hoping you might be able to help me find a new home," Athena said.

Zack tried to think of a place they could use to store the AI, but he couldn't think of anything that would work. The Drar had remade the *Athena*, and Humans just didn't have that knowledge.

"We'll have to call the ECF or the Boxans. Maybe Gaarokk or Cardaleer can help us figure something out," Kaylan said. She paced back and forth.

Zack shook his head. "No, we don't."

Kaylan frowned. "Why not? We have to tell someone."

"No, we don't. We don't have to tell anyone about this. Think about it. If we start telling people that Athena somehow survived, how do you think they'll react?" Zack said.

Kaylan pressed her lips together, considering.

"Seriously, even the Boxans were about to force us to give the *Athena* up. No, we can't tell anyone about this."

Kaylan looked at the small replica of the *Athena*. "Do you still retain all the data from the Drar?"

"That is correct, Commander, but in this state my access is a bit limited. Perhaps if you were to help build me a new form I could be of more help," Athena said.

"Zack, we can't keep this to ourselves."

Zack's brain was racing in a thousand different directions. He glanced at the metallic case and smiled. "We won't, I promise. We'll share everything in time, and we already have a way to get the knowledge out there."

Zack gestured toward the metallic case with the Dux Corp company logo.

Kaylan covered her mouth with her hand.

"I think I'm going to take that job offer from Ed, but on one condition," Zack said, and went over to Kaylan, taking her hands in his.

"What would that be?" Kaylan asked.

"That you run Dux Corp with me."

Kaylan laughed.

"I'm serious. We can do this. I want to do this with you. We can figure out what the Drar left us and share that knowledge with the world and the Alliance. It shouldn't be just for us. You know I'm right—this is what we're meant to do. I can feel it," Zack said.

Kaylan cocked her head, and her glowing brown eyes danced while her full lips blossomed into a wide smile. "Alright, but only if Athena agrees."

They both looked at the small ship that held the keys to immeasurable stores of knowledge.

"We're family, and as long as we work together, we can achieve great things," Athena said.

Zack let out a jubilant howl and picked Kaylan up in his arms. They were home and safe. He couldn't have asked for anything more.

AFTERWORD

ABOUT THE AUTHOR

I've written multiple science fiction and fantasy series. Books have been my way to escape everyday life since I was a teenager to my current ripe old(?) age. What started out as a love of stories has turned into a full-blown passion for writing them.

Overall, I'm just a fan of really good stories regardless of genre. I love the heroic tales, redemption stories, the last stand, or just a good old fashion adventure. Those are the types of stories I like to write. Stories with rich and interesting characters and then I put them into dangerous and sometimes morally gray situations.

My ultimate intent for writing stories is to provide fun escapism for readers. I write stories that I would like to read, and I hope you enjoy them as well.

If you have questions or comments about any of my works I would love to hear from you, even if its only to drop by to say hello at KenLozito.com

Thanks again for reading *Ascension Series Books 4 - 6*.

Don't be shy about emails, I love getting them, and try to respond to everyone.

ALSO BY KEN LOZITO

IF YOU WOULD LIKE TO BE NOTIFIED WHEN MY NEXT BOOK IS RELEASED VISIT
KENLOZITO.COM

Made in the USA
Middletown, DE
26 June 2022